About the Authors

Ever since **Lisa Childs** read her first romance novel (a Mills & Boon of course) at age eleven, all she ever wanted to be was a romance writer. Now an award winning, best-selling author of over seventy novels for Mills & Boon, Lisa is living the dream. She loves to hear from readers who can contact her on Facebook or through her website www.lisachilds.com

Carol Ericson lives in southern California, home of state-of–the-art cosmetic surgery, wild motorway chases, and a million amazing stories. These stories, along with hordes of virile men and feisty women clamour for release from Carol's head until she sets them free to fulfil their destinies and her readers' fantasies. To find out more about Carol and her current books, please visit her website at www.carolericson. com, 'where romance flirts with danger.'

USA Today bestselling author **Julie Miller** writes breath-taking romantic suspense. She has sold millions of copies of her books worldwide, and has earned a National Readers Choice Award, two Daphne du Maurier prizes and an RT BookReviews Career Achievement Award. She is a multiple finalist for the prestigious *RITA®* Award. For a complete list of her books and more, go to www.juliemiller.org

Covert Christmas

LISA CHILDS

CAROL ERICSON

JULIE MILLER

MILLS & BOON

First Published in Great Britain 2021
by Mills & Boon, an imprint of HarperCollins*Publishers* Ltd,
1 London Bridge Street, London, SE1 9GF

www.harpercollins.co.uk

HarperCollins*Publishers*
1st Floor, Watermarque Building,
Ringsend Road, Dublin 4, Ireland

COVERT CHRISTMAS © 2021 Harlequin Books S.A.

His Christmas Assignment © 2015 Lisa Childs
Secret Agent Santa © 2015 Carol Ericson
Military Grade Mistletoe © 2017 Julie Miller

ISBN: 978-0-263-30255-4

MIX
Paper from
responsible sources
FSC™ C007454

This book is produced from independently certified FSC™ paper to ensure responsible forest management.

For more information visit: www.harpercollins.co.uk/green

Printed and bound in Spain
by CPI, Barcelona

HIS CHRISTMAS
ASSIGNMENT

LISA CHILDS

Special thanks to Patience Bloom for bringing the bodyguards of the Payne Protection Agency to Harlequin Romantic Suspense!

Chapter 1

Voices rose in anger, penetrating the thin walls of Logan Payne's office. Garek Kozminski closed the outside door so softly that it made no sound. He probably could have slammed it and they wouldn't have heard him enter. But he was used to moving silently. In the past, his freedom and even his life had depended upon it.

Not much had changed...

He crossed the reception area and approached Logan's office—not to eavesdrop. Due to the volume of their argument, he could have heard them from the parking lot. Usually Logan didn't yell; as the CEO of Payne Protection, he didn't need to yell to be heard. The other voice was female and easily recognizable to Garek even though Candace Baker didn't usually deign to speak to him.

Apparently she had no problem talking *about* him.

"I can't believe you would consider offering this assignment to Garek Kozminski!"

He had figured Logan had called this meeting about a job. In the year that he'd been working for his brother-in-law he'd had many assignments. Had Candace protested every one?

"He's proven himself over and over again," Logan defended him. "He's a damn good bodyguard!"

"Garek Kozminski is a thief and a killer!" she yelled. "I can't believe you would trust him. I never will!"

Garek felt a twinge in his chest—one he refused to acknowledge as pain. Candace's low opinion wasn't exactly a surprise or unwarranted. And of course he had done nothing to change it; he'd actually done more to provoke it and her.

Logan's voice wasn't just loud but it had gone chillingly cold when he said, "He helped save my life and my brother's life—"

"Because of his criminal connections," she interrupted.

"That's enough," Logan told her. He didn't shout now; he sounded too weary to fight anymore. "Garek and Milek Kozminski are essential members of this team."

"They're your brothers-in-law..."

And maybe that was her real problem: Logan had married Stacy instead of her. She had obviously been in love with her boss for a long time; she'd left the River City Police Department when Logan did in order to join the fledging bodyguard business he'd started a few years before.

"Candace," Logan said, "if you can't work with them, maybe you can't work—"

"Hey!" Garek said as he pushed open the office door

before Logan could finish his ultimatum. He didn't want Candace fired. Sure, she hated Garek. But he didn't hate her.

He wanted her.

He had wanted her since the very first time he'd seen her. She was all long legs and sharp curves and sass. It sparkled in her blue eyes every time she looked at him. But she wouldn't look at him now. Instead she'd tilted her head down so that her jaw-length black hair skimmed across her face, hiding her eyes.

"I'm sorry I'm late," Garek said, although he'd had a good excuse. Someone else had called him about a job, an assignment he might not be able to refuse no matter how much he wanted to…

"It's probably a good thing you were," Logan remarked. "In fact you might want to give us a few more minutes…"

Candace lifted her chin and shook her head. "There's no need. I'm doing what I should have done a year ago…"

A year ago was when Garek had started at the Payne Protection Agency—after his sister had married Logan Payne. He doubted Candace's timing was a coincidence. She had probably wanted to resign then, but no doubt her pride had forced her to stay.

"I'm quitting," she finished.

Logan jumped up from the chair behind his desk and cursed. "Damn it—"

"You were just about to fire me," Candace pointed out. "This is for the best, and we both know it." She turned then and finally faced Garek. Her blue eyes had never been so cold as she stared at him.

Conversely, heat rushed through Garek as his temper ignited. But before he could say anything, Candace pushed past him. He reached out and grasped her arm.

She stared down at his hand. Her voice as cold as her gaze, she said, "Don't touch me. Don't *ever* touch me."

He would have teased her, as he had incessantly for the past year. But he sensed that her coldness was just a thin veneer for deeper emotions.

Candace Baker was strong. She was nearly as tall as he was, and she was all lean muscle. But there was also a vulnerability about her that she desperately tried to hide beneath a tough attitude. Just like the coldness, neither was who she really was.

"I didn't figure you for a quitter," he goaded her.

"You don't know me," she said as she jerked her arm free of his grasp. "And you never will…"

Before he could challenge her claim, she was gone. And he couldn't have that. He just couldn't have that…

"I'm a fool," Candace berated herself as she tossed clothes into the open suitcase on her bed. "I am such a fool…"

Not for quitting. Hell, she should have done that a year ago. She was a fool because she'd waited too long. And mostly because she had let *him* get to her.

How?

She knew what Garek Kozminski was. And unlike everyone else, she wasn't going to forget—because she couldn't let herself forget. In addition to being a killer and a criminal, he was also a flirt. Just a flirt…

That was why he kept teasing her. And looking at her…

She shivered even now thinking about how that silvery-gray gaze was always on her, touching her like a physical caress. He was just teasing her. He couldn't really want to touch her. He couldn't really want *her.*

She was always the *buddy*, the *gal-pal*—never the woman a man actually desired. So he was just messing with her for his own amusement. She was *not* amused. She was furious. And the more he flirted with her, the most frustrated she got. That was why she had lost her temper with her boss.

The doorbell rang, echoing throughout her bedroom from the wooden box on the dark blue painted wall. She doubted it was Logan paying her a visit. He had obviously been about to fire her before Garek had interrupted him.

After what he must have overheard her saying about him, why had Garek tried to stop Logan? Instead of insisting his brother-in-law terminate her on the spot, Garek had actually tried to talk her out of quitting.

But he didn't know her. And around him, she wasn't certain that she knew herself anymore.

The doorbell rang again, or rather incessantly, as if someone were pressing hard on the button. With a sigh she turned away from her bed and headed down the hall. But before she could even reach the front door, it opened. She knew that it had been locked; she always locked her door. And nobody else had a key to her place.

She reached for her holster only to realize she had left it—and her weapon—on her bed with the half-packed suitcase. But why would someone break into her place?

She had nothing of value. And while she had once brought a Payne Protection client to her apartment in order to guard the woman, she was alone now.

But then she was no longer alone as the intruder boldly sauntered into her apartment. He was incredibly tall with lean muscles and blond hair that nearly touched his shoulders. Her breath caught, but she shouldn't have been surprised. Who else would have so easily picked her high-tech lock but Garek Kozminski?

"What the hell do you think you're doing?" she demanded to know.

"I need to talk to you," he replied. But he was looking at her that way he always looked at her—like she was an ice cream cone he wanted to lick.

"So you picked my lock and let yourself inside?"

He shrugged as if breaking and entering was inconsequential. But surely he knew there were consequences for crimes; he had spent time in prison for at least one of the probably many offenses he had committed. "You didn't answer the doorbell."

"There are reasons people don't answer their doorbells," she pointed out. "I could have been gone." If she'd packed faster, she would have been gone. That urge she'd had to run intensified—probably because she had come face-to-face with the reason she wanted to run. That she *needed* to run…

His lips curving into a smug grin, he said, "But you're here."

"Not for long," she said as she spun around and headed back down the hall toward her bedroom. It wasn't too late. She could still escape.

But he followed her. "You're packing? Where the hell are you going?"

She paused as she was about to toss a sweater into the suitcase and realized that she had no idea. She had no plan. She'd only known she needed to leave—to get away for a while. Then she could decide if she wanted to come back. Ever.

"You don't know," he surmised.

"Anywhere you're not," she replied.

He clasped a hand to his heart. "Oh, that hurts—like a knife through the heart." Despite his playful tone, there was something in his gray gaze—something almost like real pain and regret. Did he actually care that she wanted to get away from him?

"Do you have a heart?" she wondered.

"Yes," he replied. "So much so that I convinced Logan you're a better man for this job than I am."

"Man?" Now she knew what he meant about the knife through the heart; a sharp pang in her chest felt as if he'd driven his blade deep.

"Yeah, that assignment you wanted—it's all yours," he magnanimously offered.

She shook her head. "I quit."

"Because you wanted that assignment," he said.

"No, I didn't." She hadn't wanted that assignment; playing bodyguard to some reality star turned B-movie actress held no appeal for her.

His gray eyes narrowed as he stared at her. "You just didn't want me to have it?"

"No, I didn't."

"Why not?" he asked. "What would I *steal* or who would I *kill* if I took this assignment?"

He had definitely overheard her argument with their boss. Her face heated with embarrassment—not over what he'd heard as much as having to explain why she hadn't wanted him guarding a woman who rarely wore clothes on camera, or according to the tabloids, off camera either. She wasn't certain she understood why herself.

She wasn't certain about anything anymore.

She shrugged. "It's a high-profile assignment—one that will raise the awareness of Payne Protection to the national level."

"Last year—all the attempts on Cooper's and Logan's and Parker's lives—raised the awareness of Payne Protection," he pointed out. "That's why an LA actress wants to employ one of our bodyguards. We're the best."

She wanted to argue the "we," but Logan had been right earlier. He and Parker probably wouldn't have survived if not for Garek's help.

"That assignment doesn't require the best," she said—since she suspected the entire need for a bodyguard was just the actress desperately trying to get some more minutes of fame.

"Then why didn't you want me to take it?" he asked.

She shrugged. She wasn't about to admit it had bothered her a *lot* to think of him with a scantily clad reality star. "It doesn't matter now."

"It mattered enough to you," he said, his voice deepening with confusion and concern, "that you quit the job you loved."

"*Loved* is right," she agreed. "Past tense. I don't love it anymore." But that was a lie; she knew it even as she said it. It wasn't that she didn't love her job anymore. It was that she was afraid she might fall in love with something—with *somebody*—else.

"Is that my fault?" he asked. "Or Logan's?"

That was why she couldn't risk falling again—because she had already made enough of a fool of herself over love before. "If this had anything to do with Logan, I would have quit when he married your sister."

"Maybe you were just waiting around for them to

fail," he said. "It's not like anyone really thought they'd last." He chuckled. "Least of all me."

"They have a child together," she said.

"Little Penny," he murmured, his grin widening with obvious love for his two-month-old niece.

Candace's breath caught in her lungs. Garek was so damn handsome it wasn't fair. "You shouldn't be here," she said. "You need to leave."

He glanced around as if just realizing where they were. "I've been wanting to get into your bedroom for a year now..." He stepped closer to the bed and ran his fingertips across the sheets. "Silk..."

She flinched with anger and embarrassment and lashed out, "Of course you'd be surprised a *man* like me would have silk sheets."

"Man?" he repeated, his brow furrowing with confusion. "What the hell are you talking about?"

"You just said I was the best man for the job—"

"I didn't mean it like that," he said.

"Why not?" she asked. "Everybody else thinks of me as just one of the guys."

He shook his head. "I have never thought of you that way." He stepped closer now and jerked her into his arms so quickly that she didn't have time to react. If she'd had time, she would have stopped him—she would have hurt him. Instead she just slammed up tightly against his chest, so that she felt his every breath, his every heartbeat...

"And I have thought of you," he said with an intensity in his gray gaze that had her heart racing with excitement, "every moment since I've met you..."

He lowered his mouth to hers but when their lips were

just a breath apart, he paused and murmured. "And I have thought of doing this…of kissing you…"

And then he did—he kissed her with that intensity she'd seen in his eyes. He kissed her with such passion that she had no doubt he didn't think of her as one of the guys. He thought of her the way she'd been thinking of him.

And she realized something else—it was too late to escape.

It was too late. No matter how hard he tried, Garek was unable to escape his old life. It just kept dragging him back in…

Back into a life lived on the edge, back into a life of danger…

Maybe it was a good thing that Candace had taken off the way she had, because at least he wasn't dragging her in with him. He didn't even know where she had gone— just that she'd finished packing her suitcases sometime that night and she'd left.

Her leaving had hurt more than the fist that slammed hard into his stomach. He coughed and doubled over in pain, but strong arms held him up so the fist could strike him again. Harder.

A curse slipped through his lips along with a slight trickle of blood. He didn't have any internal injuries; he'd just bitten his tongue. Purposely. He'd been beaten harder than this before; hell, his brother had beaten him harder than this before. Of course that had been years ago when they'd been just kids. But he groaned as if he were in agony. The truth was the old man didn't pack the wallop he had once had. But as the godfather of

River City, Michigan, Viktor Chekov commanded respect and fear.

And with good reason. The guy was a killer. And maybe it could finally be proven...

With a jerk of his silver-haired head, Viktor called off his goons so that they released Garek. He dropped to the ground with a groan and complained, "What the hell kind of greeting was that...?"

"How do you expect me to greet you?" Viktor asked. "You just walked away—"

"I didn't just walk away," Garek said. "I was taken off in handcuffs to prison."

A muscle twitched in Viktor's slightly sagging cheek. "That wasn't because of the work you did for me."

"No, it wasn't," Garek agreed. "But I might have avoided jail time if I'd given up what I did for you, or if I'd set you up..." Like he was setting him up now...

Viktor swung again—this time right at Garek's jaw. He could have ducked. But he took it on the chin. And this time he didn't bite his tongue on purpose. He spit out a trickle of blood and wiped his mouth.

"If you'd done that, you would already be dead," Viktor told him.

And this was why he hadn't given up or entrapped Chekov. The sentence he'd served out had been for something that hadn't actually been a crime.

"I never would have betrayed you." Then. But he was a different man now. He was actually a man now whereas when he'd worked for Viktor he'd been a desperate kid, living on the streets.

"You've been out of prison a long time, Garek," Viktor reminded him. "But until tonight you have never come back to the *family*."

Viktor and his organization had never been family. They had preyed on his desperation and utilized the skills he'd learned from his jewelry-thief father before Patek Kozminski had gone to prison.

"I made my sister a promise," he said. And while it had been a struggle at times, he had kept that promise— to never leave her again for either a jail cell or a grave. They had already lost their father—first to prison and then to death. "I vowed to her that I would stay on the straight and narrow."

"You've been working for her husband, that former detective, Logan Payne." Viktor had obviously been keeping track of him over the years.

"Still am," Garek said. Unlike Candace, he wasn't about to quit a job he loved—even for another job that had to be done.

"So why are you here?"

Garek wiped the blood that continued to trickle from the corner of his mouth. Maybe Viktor had hit him harder than he'd thought. "To offer my services."

Viktor glanced at his gargantuan goons and chuckled. "You think I need another bodyguard?"

"I think you need a good one," he said.

The two muscular guys glared at him.

Viktor shook his head. "I am perfectly safe."

"But the people close to you aren't," Garek said. "I heard you recently lost a member of your *family*." Not a blood relative but a very close associate.

That muscle twitched again in Viktor's sagging jaw. "It is too late for Alexander."

Polinsky had been murdered just days ago—shot in the head execution-style. The feds believed that Chekov had been the executioner.

"What about Tori?" Garek asked. "Aren't you concerned for her safety?"

Viktor's face flushed with color at the mention of his daughter's name, so Garek braced himself for another blow. But Viktor didn't swing his fist. Instead his shoulders slumped. "Tori is safe. Safer without you near her."

Garek nodded. "I thought that once, too." Actually he'd thought the opposite. *He* was safer if he was nowhere near her. Viktor loved his little princess so much that he would probably kill anyone who made her unhappy. And Garek hadn't ever seen the young woman happy.

"Why are you *really* here?" Viktor asked. He stared at him again, as if trying to see through him.

"You already checked me for a wire," Garek reminded him. He needed more than a recording with Viktor's admission of guilt. He needed evidence. And he had to get close in order to get his hands on it. "I want to make sure Tori is really safe," he said. "For old times' sake."

"What about that promise to your sister?" Viktor asked, his dark eyes still narrowed with suspicion.

Garek shrugged. "I haven't been happy with my sister for a while now."

"Then why work for her husband?"

"Logan didn't lie to me and Milek," he said. "Stacy's the one who kept secrets." That secret had affected and devastated Milek. While Garek had already forgiven her, he wasn't sure that their brother ever would.

Viktor nodded with understanding. He had obviously kept very apprised of not just Garek's life but Milek's and Stacy's, too. A shiver of unease chilled Garek's skin. He didn't care about himself but he cared that his past association might have put his siblings in danger.

"I think Tori would like it if I hire you," Viktor admitted. "Despite all the years that have passed, I don't think she ever quite got over you." He stepped closer, his hand reached out as if to shake, but he slapped Garek instead. "And if you hurt her again, I will hurt not just you," Viktor threatened, "but everyone close to you."

The unease turned into a shiver of dread and foreboding. It was good that Candace had left town; she would be out of danger. It was just everyone else that Garek had to worry about when he took down the godfather of River City.

Chapter 2

The lock rattled—just a couple of quick clicks—before the doorknob began to turn. Candace reached for her weapon, grasping it tightly in her hand as she approached the door to the condo she'd rented at a ski resort in northern Michigan.

Nobody knew where she was. And nobody here knew her at all. So who the hell was breaking into her unit?

Had Garek tracked her down—like he had that night at her apartment? Her heart rate accelerated, and her hand trembled slightly as memories of that night rushed through with a wave of heat.

Embarrassment—she called the heat. She was embarrassed for being such a fool. She couldn't be feeling desire. Not for Garek Kozminski.

Not again...

She lifted her weapon and pointed the barrel at the

person stepping through the door. Disappointment rushed through her now. Her intruder wasn't Garek.

She recognized the dark curls and eyes of the petite young woman who stepped through the door, her hands raised. "Don't shoot," Nikki Payne said, but her smile belied any fear.

"What the hell are you doing here?" Candace asked. "And why are you breaking in? Did Garek Kozminski teach you how to do that?"

"No, I picked the lock," another voice replied as the door opened farther to Stacy Kozminski-Payne. The woman dropped a packet of lock-picking tools into her purse.

"Doesn't anyone in your family wait for a person to open their door?" Candace asked.

Stacy shrugged. With tawny-colored hair and dark gray eyes, she didn't look that much like her brother Garek but for the quick, sly smile that crossed her face. "Why put you through the trouble of answering the door?"

Since the two women had already stepped inside, Candace closed the door. "See, look, no trouble."

But it was trouble that they were here. Neither of these women was her friend. Nikki had resented that her brothers had chained her to a desk at Payne Protection while they routinely assigned Candace dangerous field work. And Stacy...

Maybe that was more Candace's fault than Stacy's. She had disliked the female Kozminski even more than the males—because Stacy had posed such a threat. Candace had thought the woman had been a threat to Logan Payne's life, but she'd been a threat to his heart instead. Not that Candace had ever had a chance of winning his heart. He'd never been attracted to her the way he'd been to Stacy. The way he still was...

Candace couldn't blame him. Even though Stacy had given birth just a few months ago, she'd regained her petite figure with little effort. Candace wanted to hate her. But Stacy couldn't help that she was beautiful and lovable.

Candace turned away from her and focused on the youngest Payne. "You went to an awful lot of trouble to track me down." Since her brothers had strapped her to a desk, Nikki had become a computer expert.

Nikki shrugged her thin shoulders. "It was no trouble."

"I haven't been using my credit cards." When she'd taken off, she'd taken out enough cash to cover her expenses for months. She'd only been gone a couple of weeks.

"You ran a red light," Nikki reminded her.

Candace's face heated with embarrassment over her transgression. She'd been distracted—thanks to Garek Kozminski.

"I was driving a rental..." She had been so careful to cover her tracks, so that no one would find her. Or at least so she could convince herself that no one could find her. Then she wouldn't have been disappointed if no one had shown up.

Nikki snorted. "Ticket goes on your driving record but the registration is also listed for the vehicle you were driving at the time of the violation. And the rental has a GPS locator. So you were easy to find."

Despite her best efforts...

"Why?"

"The ticket," Nikki said. "The first one you've ever gotten, by the way."

Like Candace didn't know that. "I meant *why* did you track me down?" She was pretty sure it hadn't been her idea. "Who asked you to?"

Garek? But then why hadn't he come himself?

"I did," Stacy replied.

"You asked her to track me down?" she asked. "Why? To make sure I stay gone?"

Stacy laughed. "I can understand why you might think that…"

Candace wouldn't have blamed Stacy if she had asked Logan to fire her. She—and everyone else—knew that Candace had been in love with her boss. What wife would be okay with a woman working with her husband when the woman was in love with him? A woman who was very secure in his love.

Stacy confirmed this when she continued, "But I actually wanted to find you to bring you back."

Panic, at the thought of facing everyone again, pressed on Candace's chest. And she shook her head. "No, I should have quit a year ago."

"But you didn't," Stacy said.

"I should have," she repeated. Not because of the embarrassment over everyone knowing how she'd felt about Logan. She'd endured worse things than embarrassment.

Before joining the River City PD, she'd been an army reservist who'd done a tour in Iraq. And in the River City PD, she'd done a stint in vice—dressing up like a prostitute. That hadn't lasted long, though, because few johns had tried picking her up. It had been quite the joke in the department. She had been the joke. But she hadn't left the River City Police Department until Logan had.

No, there were worse things than embarrassment—like heartbreak.

She should have left because of Garek.

But if she had left…

Her face heated again and this time it wasn't with embarrassment. Her entire body flushed as she remembered that kiss and what had followed…

She shook her head, as much to dislodge those memories as in refusal of Stacy's invitation to return. "I can't go back," she told her. "Logan must have told you…" She doubted he kept anything from the woman he loved. "If I hadn't quit, he was going to fire me."

"You don't have to work for Logan," Nikki said.

Candace laughed. "He's the boss." And not just because he was the oldest Payne sibling but also because it had been his idea to start the protection agency. It was his business.

"He's the CEO but he's franchising the business," Stacy explained. "After all the publicity last year, Logan felt as if he needed to expand to keep up with the demand for Payne Protection."

"Cooper and Parker will each have their own franchise now," Nikki said. "I'm going to work for Cooper. You could, too. He's bringing in his own team of former marines."

Candace hadn't been a marine. But she had served.

"Or with Parker," Nikki continued, her voice lilting with enthusiasm. "He's recruiting former cops. You'd fit in there, too."

"Logan would like you to come back to work for him," Stacy said.

Candace shook her head again. If that were true, he would have come himself; he wouldn't have sent his wife and sister to find her. He might not even know that they'd been looking for her. So it was just curiosity that had her asking, "What's his team going to be?"

"Family," Stacy replied.

"I'm not family," she said. "And that was made very clear to me."

"Is that why you left?" Nikki asked. "Because you thought there was too much nepotism—with me and Parker and Cooper?"

"It wasn't the Paynes that were the problem," Stacy said, answering for her before Candace had had the chance. "It was the Kozminskis. *We* were why she quit."

Candace flinched at how petty she sounded. She wished that had been the reason she'd quit: pettiness. But fear was what had compelled her to quit. She hadn't realized it at the time—because she had never acknowledged fear before. She wouldn't have become a soldier or a cop if she had. So because she'd never acknowledged it before, she hadn't recognized it.

"Not all of you," Candace said. "I have no problem with Milek. I actually feel sorry for him."

Stacy flinched now and quietly admitted, "I made a mistake."

Nikki glanced at her sister-in-law, and while there was affection, there was also disapproval in her dark eyes. "You kept a *secret*—a really *big* secret—from him." The youngest Payne hated secrets and didn't understand that there were reasons to keep them. To Nikki, there was only black and white.

Candace understood gray. She had kept more than her share of other people's secrets; that was another reason that she was always the buddy—the friend. She knew too much but she kept her mouth shut. "It wasn't Stacy's secret to tell."

A soft gasp of surprise slipped through Stacy's lips. "I'm glad Nikki tracked you down."

Candace shrugged. "It doesn't matter that you did. I'm not going back." Not to Payne Protection. Maybe not even to River City.

"Why not?" Nikki asked the question.

Candace suspected Stacy knew. The woman's dark gray gaze was focused on her as she studied her intensely. What had Garek told her?

She fought the urge to blush. Surely, he wouldn't have told his sister...

But what if he'd told anyone else or everyone else? Despite her best efforts, her face flushed again. So she turned away from them to gaze out the window. Snow drifted softly to the ground but melted as soon as it hit the grass. The weather was unseasonably warm for December—which had caused the ski resort to be unusually quiet. "I like it here."

It was quiet. It was safe. Due to the weather leaving the slopes more green than white, it was nearly deserted. So it was boring as hell.

"Why?" Nikki asked the question again, her voice full of confusion. She wanted excitement—had been fighting Logan for years to put her in the field. She didn't understand that sometimes boredom was good.

"It's pretty here," Stacy answered for her as she stepped closer to the window and Candace and watched the big fluffy flakes fall onto the grass. "And it's peaceful. I can see its appeal."

Candace turned back toward them. Even if she ignored them, they weren't going away. She might as well hear them out.

Unconvinced, Nikki shook her head. "I can't. You need to come back, Candace. The agency is taking off right now. We're busy as hell. We need you."

Stacy said nothing—to Candace. Instead she turned to her sister-in-law and asked, "Will you give us a few minutes alone?"

Nikki nodded and headed toward the door. "Hope your pitch works better than mine did."

Candace waited until the door closed behind Nikki then asked, "Why would you give me a pitch? Why would you care whether or not I came back?"

"Because I care about my brother."

Candace had never had a problem recognizing fear in others. She heard it now in Stacy's voice. "What are you talking about?"

And what had Garek told her?

"I'm losing him."

"Milek?" That was who they were talking about? Candace had never had a problem with the younger Kozminski brother, but she'd never had a relationship with him either. Not that she had a relationship with Garek either. She'd had just that one, unforgettable night…

Stacy's breath escaped in a shaky little sigh. "I think I already lost Milek. And now I'm losing Garek, too."

"Have they quit, too?"

Stacy shook her head. "No. They both get along with Logan."

Candace couldn't suppress a smile. Men were so simple. They could go from being archenemies one minute to best friends the next. Maybe that was why she'd always gotten along better with them than women. "Then

I don't understand what you want me to do. If Logan can't help you mend fences with your brothers, I certainly can't."

"I don't want you to help me mend fences," Stacy said.

Her patience worn thin, she asked, "Then what *do* you want?"

Stacy's dark gray eyes glistened as tears welled in them. "I want you to help me stop Garek from getting himself killed."

While she hated to admit it, she found herself leaping to his defense. "He's handled himself well in a lot of dangerous situations. He'll be fine."

"Not this time," Stacy insisted. "Not with *these* people."

"Did he take that assignment with the starlet?" That was another reason she'd gone off the grid and rented a place with no TV and no internet. She hadn't wanted anyone or anything to find her—to disturb her peace. If only she'd really found peace…

Stacy shook her head. "No. Logan sent Milek. Garek had already taken another assignment—one he sought out on his own. He's going back to his old life, Candace. He's working for Viktor Chekov."

Candace should have felt vindicated. It was what she'd been saying about him all along—that he hadn't changed. But over the past year she had watched him closely, nearly as closely as he'd watched her, and she'd never seen any evidence that he was still a thief. He'd worked hard—nearly as hard as he'd teased and flirted with her.

Had she actually been right about him?

Her legs weakened, and she felt the need to sit down. So she dropped onto the edge of the rental's lumpy couch. Of course he'd always had that effect on her—that ability to make her knees weak—no matter how much she had fought her attraction to him. She should have kept fighting.

"What does any of that have to do with me?" she wondered.

"He didn't take that assignment until you left," Stacy said, and now there was anger and resentment along with tears in her eyes. "You drove him back to his old life."

She laughed at his sister's outrageous claim. "That's ridiculous." Garek would have actually had to care about her for her leaving to affect him. And it just wasn't possible that he did.

"I know my brother," Stacy said. "I know he really liked you. But you never gave him a chance."

He definitely hadn't told his sister anything about that night.

"So he's gone back to his old life," Stacy continued. "To Viktor Chekov. Those people are dangerous, Candace."

She didn't need to tell her. As a former cop, Candace knew exactly how dangerous Chekov was. While he'd never been convicted, he had committed every crime on the books. The last news she'd heard as she'd driven out of the city had been a report that Chekov's right-hand man had been executed. While the reporter hadn't dared to speculate, it was clear that everyone thought Chekov was the killer.

"They're really dangerous," Stacy said, her voice shaking with fear. "Garek's in trouble."

Garek was in trouble—more trouble than he could have even imagined. He couldn't get Candace out of his mind. And he couldn't afford the distraction right now—not with the dangerous game he was playing.

What if he'd been followed to this meeting? He'd watched the rearview mirror and hadn't noticed anyone tailing him. But instead of the road behind him, he'd kept seeing Candace: her blue eyes wide with shock as she'd stared up at him, her lips red and slightly swollen from his kiss.

What if he'd missed a tail? He reached beneath his jacket and closed his hand around his weapon as he stepped out of the SUV. Nobody was going to get the jump on him. But he still could have been followed. And if someone saw him with the person he was meeting…

From an alley between two buildings, beams of light flashed. On and off. On and off.

Garek glanced around the deserted industrial area. Had anyone else seen the signal?

He could detect no movement but the December wind tossing snowflakes around the night sky. Maybe he hadn't been followed. But he still had that uneasy feeling, that tingling between his shoulder blades that made him feel as if he was being watched.

The lights flashed again. Of course he was being watched by the person who waited for him inside the other SUV. Garek glanced around once more before heading toward the alley. He moved, as he always did, quickly and silently—keeping to the shadows.

Slipping between the SUV and the building beside it, he pulled open the passenger's door. No dome light flashed; the person he was meeting knew all the tricks of maintaining his anonymity. In his line of work, he wouldn't have lived long if he hadn't.

FBI agent Nicholas Rus had done a lot of undercover work in his career with the Bureau. Before Garek had agreed to work with the man, he'd checked out his background. He didn't care that Rus was related to the Paynes—that with his black hair and blue eyes, he looked eerily like the twins Logan and Parker. The FBI agent hadn't been raised with them, by Penny Payne, so Garek questioned his integrity. He didn't know too many people who were beyond corruption—besides the Paynes.

"Why you acting so nervous?" Rus asked as Garek slid into the passenger's seat. "I didn't notice any tail coming in behind you. Did you see a suspicious vehicle?"

"No." But that didn't mean that he hadn't been followed. He peered through the tinted windshield, trying to see beyond the alley.

The snow had thickened, now, from flurries to sheets of white. The mild winter was over; the cold and snow coming in earnest now. He couldn't see anything out there anymore. But whoever was watching him wouldn't be able to see either.

Rus sighed and murmured, "Guess you'd be an idiot if you weren't nervous…"

"I was an idiot to let you talk me into this," Garek said.

"You're the only one who could do this," Rus said. "Viktor Chekov wouldn't have let anyone else inside, and there's no time. We have to recover the murder weapon before he ditches it."

"If he hasn't already," Garek said. "He'd be a fool if he hasn't." And Viktor Chekov was nobody's fool.

Rus shrugged. "The witness says he hasn't."

"The witness could be lying." Especially if the witness was who Garek suspected it was. Viktor would not have killed in front of her.

Rus shrugged again. "That's why we need the murder weapon."

"We need more," Garek said. "We need an admission of guilt." Because that witness would never testify—for a few reasons.

Rus laughed. "If you think Viktor Chekov is going to confess, you actually might be an idiot."

"He won't confess to authorities," Garek agreed.

"You think you can get him to confess to you?"

"Confess?" Garek shook his head. "Threaten? Brag?" He nodded. "Yeah, I can get him to do one of those."

A muscle twitched along Rus's jaw he clenched it so tightly. He hadn't been raised with his half brothers but yet he shared some of their tells when it came to stress.

The special agent asked, "Is he still having his guys check you for a wire every time you show up for a protection duty shift?"

Garek nodded. As he'd said, the man was nobody's fool; he knew not to trust Garek.

Rus's irritation escaped in a ragged sigh. "He'll kill you if he catches you wearing one."

Garek nodded again. But *his* life was the least of his concerns. He was more concerned about his family.

At least Candace was gone. He didn't have to worry about her. He only had to worry about getting her off his mind so that he wouldn't get so careless that he'd wind up dead.

Rus gripped the SUV steering wheel so tightly that his knuckles turned white. "I want this guy. I *really* want this guy. But if your family knew that you were risking your life to help me…"

"They're your family, too," Garek reminded him. Actually they were more Rus's family since he was a blood relative albeit not a legitimate one. Garek was only related through marriage, and his sister's at that.

Rus shook his head. "They don't feel that way—at least not all of them."

Garek knew the Paynes well enough to know who had welcomed Rus and who hadn't. Nikki hadn't. But of all of the Paynes, Penny had welcomed him the most—despite his being the evidence of her late husband's betrayal.

But that was the kind of woman Penny was—the kind who'd taken an interest in the kids of the man who'd confessed to killing her husband. She had welcomed the Kozminskis as warmly as she had Nicholas Rus.

"Give them time," he said. While Penny had accepted Garek and his siblings, it had taken the other Paynes more time.

"If something happens to you while you're carrying out this assignment for me…" Rus shook his head.

Garek wanted to assure the FBI agent that nothing would happen to him, but he knew Viktor Chekov too well to make any promises. "I'll let you know when I get the evidence you need…"

If I'm alive…

Rus must have had the same thought because he reached out and squeezed Garek's shoulder. "I appreciate your doing this."

Garek shrugged off his gratitude and his hand. "It's like you said. Nobody else could do it."

"But that doesn't mean you had to agree. You could have refused."

He could have. He might have…if Candace hadn't

taken off on him the way she had. But she was gone and with her any excuse he might have had to not finally do the right thing—what he should have done fifteen years ago. Take down Viktor Chekov.

He pushed open the passenger door and stepped out into the snow and the cold. "I have nothing to lose."

"Just your life…"

He softly shut the door and hurried away from the alley. He moved quickly now, not so he wasn't noticed, but so that he didn't freeze off his ass. Christmas was only a few weeks away. Hopefully he would wrap up this assignment before then, so that he could spend an honest holiday with his family.

And Candace?

Where was she?

Other than on his mind? She was always on his mind, staring up at him with such confusion and desire. Her pupils had dilated so only a thin rim of blue circled them. She'd wanted him, too. But then why had she left?

Dimly he heard the SUV pull out of the alley and drive away. But he didn't glance back as he hurried toward his vehicle. He didn't look back until it was too late—until he'd finally heard the footsteps rushing across the asphalt behind him.

He had been followed. He had been watched—just like he'd feared.

Before he could turn around, a body connected with his and slammed him into the side of his SUV. His head struck metal, and like the snowflakes, spots danced across his field of vision—momentarily blinding him. He had no idea who had attacked him and no idea if he would survive the attack.

Chapter 3

Candace was home. In River City again, at least. Raised an army brat, she'd never had a real home. But she had lived in this city longer than any others. So it was probably as close to home as she had ever come.

She had already done what she'd had to do. Not what she'd wanted to do. She wasn't sure what she actually wanted anymore.

Her hand trembled as she slid the key in the lock and turned the knob. But Candace hesitated before pushing open her apartment door.

He was gone.

She knew that. After all, two weeks had passed and she knew what he'd been doing during that time. Sort of. As much as anyone ever knew what Garek Kozminski was doing. He wasn't still in her apartment. But he'd been there the last time she had been.

So she stepped carefully inside, but she didn't stop in the living room. She carried her suitcase directly down the hall to the bedroom.

Some of the clothes she hadn't packed had fallen to the floor around the bed. And on the bed the silk sheets were as tangled and twisted as she—as *they*—had left them. Her face heated with embarrassment. What had she done? And why the hell had she come back here? To the scene of the crime. The scene of her stupidity.

The scene of the most exciting night of her life. And Candace, as a soldier and a police officer, had lived an exciting life.

Her breath shuddered out in a ragged sigh—like it had that night he'd kissed her. She should have stopped him then. She'd pulled back. But then he'd looked at her—like no one else had ever looked at her—with such hunger and desire. And instead of shoving him away, she had looped her arms around his neck and pulled his head down for another kiss.

She had been a fool that night. And she'd been an even bigger fool to come back. Garek Kozminski had gotten what he'd wanted from her. He wanted nothing else—or he would have been the one who'd tracked her down. Not his sister.

She shouldn't have let Stacy get to her. She should have just stayed away. Not that she doubted what his sister had told her. She believed that Garek had gone back to his life. What was the saying—once a thief always a thief?

But she had found no evidence that he'd been stealing anything since he'd been a teenager. Was he just so good that he had never gotten caught?

Or that lucky?

If he was working for Chekov again, his luck would probably run out. Like Stacy had said, he was in danger. Candace just didn't believe there was anything she could do to stop him. Or to protect him.

By coming back, she had only put herself in danger— her heart and maybe even her life.

"What the hell are you doing?" Garek asked when his vision cleared and he recognized his brother as the one who'd knocked him into the side of his SUV.

"What the hell are *you* doing?" Milek asked, his voice raised and sharp with anger.

Garek blinked again—making sure he was really seeing his brother. Milek didn't get angry; he didn't lose his temper anymore—not even when he had every right. "What's wrong with you?"

Milek shoved him back, knocking him against the SUV again. "What's wrong with you?"

"I don't know what you're talking about," Garek answered honestly. His brother wasn't making a whole lot of sense. "And how the hell did you find me here? Did you follow me?"

He had suspected someone might have, but he hadn't seen anyone behind him. He'd been distracted, though. But...

"Did you follow me?" he asked again.

Milek snorted. "How else would I have found you? Of course I followed you. You're not as good as you think are."

His brother must have been right—about Garek's not detecting a tail. But maybe that wasn't the only thing Garek wasn't as good at as he'd thought he was. Candace had left that night—after they'd finally given in to the attraction that had burned between them for a year.

At least he'd felt it.

"*I* taught you everything you know about following someone," Garek reminded him. That was why Milek was so good. "And I may have noticed you were behind me, if I'd known you were back already."

Milek had taken the assignment Candace hadn't wanted him to take—protecting the reality star. Why hadn't she wanted him to take it?

She had never explained her real reason. Jealousy?

But if she'd cared, she wouldn't have run away—like she had sometime in the night. She wouldn't have left him if she'd really wanted him.

"The girl wasn't in any danger," Milek said. "It was just a publicity ploy."

Which was what Candace had suspected. The woman was so astute. How had she never realized how he'd felt about her—how he'd felt about her for nearly a year?

"It took you two weeks to figure out it was all a publicity stunt?" Garek teased.

Milek shook his head. "It only took me two minutes."

"So you milked the assignment to enjoy the weather in California?" Garek gestured at the snow. "I don't blame you." He would have razzed him about staying for the starlet. But it was too soon to tease Milek about women.

"I might have stayed longer," Milek admitted, "if Stacy hadn't called me."

Garek shook his head, both frustrated with and sympathetic to his sister. "I told her to back off and give you time."

"She didn't call me about *that*," Milek said.

That was the single most devastating thing that had ever happened to his brother. So it was no wonder he didn't want to talk about it; he probably couldn't.

Garek had tried a couple of times to get him to talk, and Milek had asked him to move out of the warehouse apartment they'd once shared. He'd moved into an apartment while he'd looked for something more permanent.

Milek continued, "She called me to talk about you."

Garek chuckled. "Sounds like she was just looking for any excuse to reach out to you." And he couldn't blame Stacy for trying. He wanted to try again, but he was worried his brother would cut him completely out of his life then.

Milek shook his head. "It wasn't an excuse to talk to me. She didn't want to call me. So she hesitated—maybe too long. How deep are you in?"

Garek sucked in a breath and then choked on the cold air. "I—I don't know what you're talking about."

Milek shoved him again. But Garek was already backed up as far as he could go against the SUV. "You're working for Viktor Chekov again."

"Not like I used to," Garek assured him. And he felt a flash of pain that his sister and brother had assumed he had. Didn't they know him better than that? He could understand other people thinking the worst of him; he'd done nothing to correct misconceptions of him. In fact with Candace, he had enjoyed playing the bad boy with her—to tease her and irritate her. But he hadn't been a boy for a long while—if ever. "It's an assignment—a protection job."

Milek cursed him. "You brought Viktor to Payne Protection as a client. You sought out this assignment. I'm going to ask you again—what the hell are you up to?"

Garek opened his mouth, ready to spin the situation the way he had to Logan, so the CEO of Payne Protection had agreed to take on the Chekov family as a client. But Milek knew Garek hadn't been in love with Tori—like he had professed to Logan. His brother would immediately know he was lying.

So he admitted, "I'm not supposed to tell anyone what I'm really up to."

"Is that what whoever you just met in the alley has been telling you?"

Milek hadn't seen Rus. To keep the FBI agent out of it, Garek could lie about whom he'd just met. He hesitated as he considered it.

And Milek asked, "Don't you think I've had enough secrets kept from me?"

That question struck Garek harder than Milek had when he'd knocked him into his vehicle. He nodded in agreement. "But it's hard to be totally open and honest when you're working undercover."

The tension eased from Milek's shoulders and he breathed a sigh of relief. "That was Special Agent Nicholas Rus who you met in the SUV in the alley."

"Nobody can know."

Milek tensed again. "You're trying to take down Viktor Chekov?" The anger was back in his voice as he asked, "Are you crazy?"

"Maybe…"

But a man had been murdered. Recently. Before that there had been others. Lives Garek could have saved had he taken Chekov down fifteen years ago. He hadn't been brave enough then; he'd been a scared kid who'd given in to threats. But now he was a man, and he knew if Chekov wasn't stopped, there would be more lives lost.

"But it needs to be done," Garek said. "He has to be stopped, or he's just going to keep killing. He should have been stopped a long time ago."

"Killing…" Milek murmured.

Garek wanted to bite his tongue again—that he'd brought up a subject too close to his brother's wounded heart. "I'm sorry…"

Milek raised his voice again, which shook with anger. "Garek, this is too dangerous."

In the spirit of being honest, he had to admit, "And it's not dangerous just for me. He threatened if my assignment is more about betraying him than protecting Tori, he won't just hurt me. He'll hurt my family, too. He'll hurt everyone I care about."

Garek shuddered but not because of the cold; he shuddered because he remembered the coldness with which Viktor had so casually uttered that threat. But he knew it hadn't been idle.

"If you want to do this or you feel you have to, don't worry about me," Milek said. "I can take care of myself."

His brother always had.

"And Logan will protect Stacy just like he did before," Garek said. He was trying to assure himself that he hadn't put everyone he loved in danger. "You'll all be fine…"

But then Milek warned him, "I'm not the only one Stacy reached out to…"

Garek raised his brows. "Who else is there?"

Since their father had gone to prison, it had been just the three of them. Their mother didn't count; she had never been there for them and then she'd turned on them. He wouldn't have gone to prison and Milek juvenile detention if she hadn't testified against them. They had an aunt and uncle, too, but they had only wanted to exploit them—like Viktor Chekov had.

"Candace," Milek said. "Stacy was going to track her down and bring her back to River City."

"Damn her." He loved Stacy, but she had interfered in their lives too much. Her interference had cost Milek everything that mattered to him. What would it cost Garek?

Candace?

Logan couldn't stop staring at his wife—with his usual awe at her beauty. But he was also in awe of her powers of persuasion.

"How did you do it?" he asked.

She paused with her fingertips on buttons at the front of her blouse. "You did this," she said. "You threw me down on your desk the minute I stepped inside your office."

He grinned unabashedly. "That is true," he admitted. Then he leaned down and gently skimmed his mouth across hers; her lips were slightly swollen from his previous kisses. "But that's because you're irresistible. And beautiful and amazing…"

Beneath his, her lips curved into a smile. "I love you."

"And I love you," he said. He pulled back and leaned his forehead against hers. "I missed you."

"I guess." She gestured at the papers and pens strewn across his floor. He'd swept them off when he'd pulled her down onto the mahogany surface with him. "Nikki and I were only gone a couple of days."

"That's a couple too many," he said.

She nodded in agreement. "It was." Disappointment darkened her already dark gray eyes. She stepped back from him and uttered a heavy sigh. "And it was for nothing. I couldn't convince Candace to come home."

He skimmed his fingers along her bottom lip and tilted it back up. "You were so successful she actually beat you home."

"Really?" Stacy's eyes brightened, and her whole face lit up with a smile. He hoped their daughter took after her beautiful mother. "She must have packed right up and headed back. Nikki and I only stopped at an outlet mall for some early Christmas shopping."

"Nikki, of course…"

Stacy arched a brow. "You wondered how I found Candace on my own?"

"I don't doubt you could have done it," he said. His wife was as brilliant as she was beautiful.

"I didn't have any time to lose, though, so I asked for Nikki's help."

His sister was as brilliant as his wife. If only she could be happy doing what she did best—instead of nagging for dangerous field work.

Then Stacy's words sank in and he asked, "What's the urgency in bringing Candace back? I know I've been griping about not having her on my team, but…"

She smiled and kissed his cheek. "You think I did this for you. That's sweet."

He grinned at her teasing. "And obviously off base. Then why did you want Candace back so desperately that you and Nikki tracked her down and convinced her to come ask for her job back?"

Stacy cupped his cheek now in her soft palm and gave him a pitying smile. "Men are so oblivious."

He was used to his wife giving him a hard time; they'd been going at each other since they'd been teenagers. If only he'd realized sooner most of that resentment and anger had been attraction and passion...

"What am I missing?" he asked.

"Candace didn't come back for her job."

He tilted his head. "Then why did she ask me for it?" Even though he had been able to tell that it had been really difficult for her to bury her pride and ask...

Stacy shrugged. "I guess she needs the job. But it's not what she really wants."

Logan tensed with dread. He had been oblivious once before, totally unaware the woman he had considered a friend and only a friend had had a crush on him. "What are you up to?"

Stacy patted his cheek and laughed. "Sweetheart, once again—not about you. Candace has been over you for a long time. Not that I think her feelings even ran that deep or she wouldn't have been able to continue working for you after you fell for me. Nobody's that much of a masochist."

That was what he'd thought, too. That everyone had exaggerated what might have been Candace having a small crush on the boss.

"No, Candace came back for Garek."

He cursed as his dread rushed back.

Stacy's smile faltered, and she insisted, "That's a good thing."

Logan shook his head. "No, no, it's not."

Now hurt flashed in her dark gray eyes. "Do you think she's too good for my brother?"

He cursed. "That's not it at all. You know I love your brothers." Which hadn't always been the case. But they'd helped save his and his brothers' lives.

Then he'd gotten to know them and had learned how

hard they'd worked to build new lives for themselves. They'd also brought him a ton of business—better business than Chekov. But because Garek had brought him so many clients, he hadn't been able to refuse to take on Chekov when his brother-in-law had asked—especially once he'd explained to him why—which was also why Logan hoped that Candace hadn't come back for Garek.

"She's the only one who will be able to get through to him," Stacy insisted, "to get him away from Viktor Chekov." She shuddered—with revulsion and fear—as she uttered the mobster's name.

"What makes you think that?"

"Because she's the reason he went back to that life," Stacy said. "When she quit Payne Protection and left town, he was devastated."

Logan snorted. "He's Garek. Nothing devastates Garek." He'd never known a more resilient human being. The guy had been through hell and back and never lost his sense of humor.

"She did."

He shook his head. "You're wrong."

"He was crazy about her," Stacy insisted.

"Garek flirts with every female," Logan said. "He's even flirted with my mom."

"Penny's a hottie," Stacy said with a giggle. "But Candace was different. He tried to be a better man for her. For the past year he hadn't even dated another woman. That's why, when she took off, he was devastated—so devastated he went back to his former life."

Logan needed to find a way for her to make up with her brothers. She was so estranged from them that she didn't even know them anymore.

"No," he told her. "That's not why he went back to his old life."

"It's not?" She furrowed her brow and studied him as if he had been holding out on her. "What do you know?"

"Only what Garek told me," he said. "He had a reason for asking for this assignment with the Chekovs." One that had convinced Logan to take on a mobster as a client. "He wanted this assignment so he could protect Tori Chekov."

Stacy shrugged. "Why?"

"Because he's in love with her."

He heard a gasp, but it hadn't slipped through his wife's lips. He turned to the open door of his office. Had they forgotten to shut it? He'd wanted his wife so badly he hadn't even noticed. His desire for her only seemed to intensify the longer they were together.

Candace Baker stood in the doorway, and all the color drained from her face, leaving it stark with shock. And he realized his wife had been at least half right. Candace had come back for Garek.

Now, having overheard what she had, would she quit again? The news had obviously affected her.

While he didn't want to lose her as a team member again, he didn't want to lose her as a friend either. They had been friends for years. So he was worried about her—worried about her safety if she were to stay. It would probably be the wisest and the safest thing for her to leave again.

If Tori Chekov thought Candace could potentially be a threat to her relationship with Garek, she might have her father take care of the female bodyguard.

Permanently…

Chapter 4

At that ski cabin in Northern Michigan, Candace had gotten her quota of quiet. She might have needed it then—the boring to outweigh the excitement she'd had and left. Now she needed noise, and it had to be loud enough to drown out the voice in her head that kept calling her an idiot.

She had found it at the downtown club. The music was so loud that it wasn't heard; it was felt. It throbbed low in her body, beating as hard as her heart. But her heart hadn't started beating that hard—that frantically—until she'd seen *him*.

On some level, she'd probably known Garek would be here—since Viktor Chekov owned the club. It was probably why she'd gone home and changed after she'd awkwardly stumbled into the middle of that conversation at the Payne Protection Agency. She'd told herself that she'd just wanted to look her best to make herself feel better.

But she'd wanted to make him feel bad.

As if Garek would care...

He hadn't sought her out. And now she knew why. He'd reunited with the girl he'd loved since they'd been teenagers. Or so Logan thought. Stacy had denied her husband's claim even though it was apparently what Garek had confided in him.

Logan had broken that confidence because he hadn't wanted her wasting her time or her heart again—like she'd wasted it on him.

Yet here she was, wasting her time some more—coming down to a club to torture herself with the sight of Garek and his girlfriend. At least her martini was good. Over the rim of the glass, Candace studied them. They were a distance away since they sat at some raised-up, roped-off table near the dance floor and she sat at the crowded bar.

She'd been lucky someone had given up his seat to her. He'd even bought her martini. He stood near her now, his mouth near her ear as he tried talking to her. She couldn't hear anything, and it had nothing to do with the music. It had everything to do with that voice in her head—the one that continued calling her names.

Tori Chekov was as beautiful as Candace had suspected she'd be. Petite. Curvy. With long curly blond hair. No one would treat this woman like one of the guys—or a buddy.

But Garek...

He wasn't flirting and joking as he usually did. Instead he seemed tense, on edge—more cognizant of his surroundings than of the woman who sat beside him. He acted as if he was on a job—not a date.

But he looked like he could be dressed for a date. In a black shirt and pants, he looked dangerously sexy. His blond hair gleamed like gold under the strobe lights from the dance floor.

In Candace's mind flashed the image of how she'd seen him last, lying naked in her bed, moonlight gleaming off his bare skin. He was almost too beautiful to be a man, but he was masculine, too—all toned muscle and chiseled edges.

How had she left him lying there alone? How had she just walked away?

But she hadn't just walked. She'd grabbed her half-packed suitcase, and she'd run.

Garek continued his visual surveillance of the club—his attention on everything but the woman beside him. She knew he was assessing the entire building for possible threats like the vigilant bodyguard he was. In that assessment, he turned and his gaze met hers.

The air between them vibrated like the bass of the music. There was an electricity—a connection so overwhelming that she had that urge to run again.

And this time she needed to keep running.

"Damn it!" the words slipped involuntarily through Garek's lips as he leaped to his feet.

One of Chekov's goons reached beneath his jacket for his weapon. "Is there a problem? A threat?"

Tori reached out and grasped his arm. "What's wrong, Garek?"

He shook his head and lied, "No problem…"

But he had a problem. She sat at the bar, her legs endlessly long and sexy beneath the short hem of her strapless dress. It was red and tight and so damn sexy that it was drawing every man in the club to her.

One of those men placed his hand on her bare shoulder, and Garek ground his teeth together as jealousy and rage coursed through him. He wanted to break every finger in that man's hand for having the audacity to touch *his* woman.

Candace was *his*.

But he couldn't stake his claim—not without risking her life when Garek put Viktor Chekov behind bars. Because even from behind bars Viktor would be dangerous—maybe even more dangerous because he would be out for vengeance.

And if he wanted to hurt Garek…

He was already hurting, every muscle tense with desire and fear for Candace. He had never wanted any woman the way he wanted her. And making love with her once had only increased the intensity of that desire to madness. His body throbbed with the need to be with her again—to be inside her—because now he knew how amazing it was. How amazing they were together.

"You want me to get rid of her?" a voice in his ear asked.

He touched his fingers, which shook slightly, to his earpiece.

"What?" he asked, fear gripping his heart in a tight fist.

"I can get rid of her," the man offered.

Because the danger was real, he thought immediately she would be gotten rid of for good—forever. But then he remembered the man talking to him wasn't one of Chekov's hired goons. It was his brother's voice in his ear, offering to help—not hurt.

Not that Candace wouldn't get hurt. Hell, knowing Candace, Milek might get hurt, too, if he tried to get rid of her. The woman wouldn't go anywhere unless she wanted to. She was stubborn and strong.

So why had she left him that night?

He wanted to know. Had to know...

"I'll handle her," Garek said, although he doubted he was any more capable than Milek of getting Candace to go anywhere she didn't want to. As a former soldier and cop, the woman had skills. "I need you to watch Tori."

Her hand tightened on his arm. "Nobody needs to watch me," she said, her tone as waspish as it had been since he'd taken over as her bodyguard.

She hadn't welcomed him back into her life. In fact he wasn't sure from whom he had more to fear: her or her father. Viktor had accepted his explanation for why he'd stayed away after he'd been paroled. Tori wouldn't even let him explain. She had barely spoken to him over the past two weeks—which was probably fortunate for him, given how nasty she sounded when she did speak to him.

"It's for your protection," Garek reminded her.

She pulled her hand away from his arm and sat back in her chair. He didn't know why she'd wanted to come here. She didn't dance. She didn't drink. She didn't even seem to enjoy the music. Hell, she didn't seem to enjoy anything anymore. But then, had she ever?

He wasn't sure if he ever remembered Tori Chekov being happy—even when they'd been younger. He hadn't had the chance to be a kid; his father and uncle had recruited him into the family business at a young age. And then when his father had gone to prison, he'd gone to work for Tori's father. She hadn't had to work, though. Ever.

Her father made sure she had everything she wanted. So why wasn't she happy?

But then Milek—finally—approached the table, and she actually smiled. "It's great to see you. Come sit with me," she implored him.

Milek slid past Garek to take the chair he'd vacated, and his brow was furrowed in bewilderment. Maybe Tori's warm greeting had confused him since she'd never been that friendly to him before. Or maybe he was worried that Garek intended to speak to Candace.

He wanted to do more than speak to her. He wanted to do everything he'd done to her that night—over and over again. But she'd run from him.

She wasn't running now—which was good, since it had taken Milek too long to take over for him on protection duty. And the club was crowded, so crowded he had to push his way through a crush of bodies to reach the bar.

For a moment he thought she'd slipped away, but then a man moved and he saw her sitting on that stool, her long legs crossed. She had painted her lips as red as her dress, and they were curved into a smile as she looked up at the man standing over her.

Garek's blood heated with jealousy and anger. He'd arrogantly thought she had come to the club to see him. But what if she'd actually come here for a date?

He wouldn't have brought her to a place like this. It was too loud. He would have taken her someplace quiet and intimate—like her bedroom.

He wanted to take her there now. He pushed forward and wedged the other man aside with his shoulder. His maneuver brought his thigh flush against hers. His body tightened with desire.

"Hey!" the guy protested.

Garek turned to him and for once he dropped the mask of humor and let his true feelings show. He also lifted his arm just enough to reveal the holster strapped beneath it.

The guy lifted his hands and backed up. "I had no idea she was yours. Sorry, man."

"I am not his," Candace called after the man.

But either he didn't hear her or he didn't believe her because he hurriedly disappeared into the crowd. Before turning toward her, Garek summoned the grin and the cocky attitude he had always shown her. "I just found out a few hours ago you were back," he said casually, as if his heart wasn't pounding erratically with each breath he took.

He stood so close to her that he could feel it when she breathed in; her breast swelled and pressed against his arm. "I wouldn't have figured this for your first place to hit."

She turned back to her drink, running her fingertip around the rim of the martini glass. "You don't know me," she said. "So how would you know what kind of places I frequent? Maybe I'm a regular here."

In her sexy red dress, with her black hair fluffed up and her lips painted—she looked like the other female club patrons. But she wasn't any more comfortable than he was in his undercover assignment. She visibly fought the discomfort though, lifting her chin as if she was ready to take a blow, and her brilliant blue eyes glared at him.

"I could be a regular," she insisted.

He laughed. He couldn't help it. He loved her prickliness. That was probably why he'd spent the past year provoking her—trying to get a reaction from her. Trying to get her attention. He had missed her. He'd missed her so damn bad.

"I know you," he said. He'd made a point of learning everything about her—while being careful to reveal very little of himself to her.

She shook her head in denial. "No, you don't. But I know you."

She had to talk loud—because of the music. But there was still the danger that someone else might overhear her. It was better if no one knew how close they were. Or had been…

Nobody could know what she really meant to him. Not even her. So he lost the grin, and he drew on another mask—one of coldness. "If you actually knew me," he said, "you would have known better than to show up here."

"I didn't show up here for you," she said, her tone so disparaging he almost believed her.

He glanced toward the crowd into which the guy had disappeared. "That loser wasn't your date, was he?"

She lifted her martini glass. "He bought me this."

"So you're just here to pick up guys?"

She shrugged her naked shoulders. "Why not?"

Because she belonged with him.

"So that's why you came back to River City?" he asked. "To pick up strange men in bars?"

She glared at him again, her eyes narrowed. "You say that like you doubt I can."

He hadn't meant to challenge her. He knew she could pick up any man she wanted. Even him…

And he had no business letting her affect him. But his

body ached with wanting hers. "I say that like I wonder why you'd want to," he clarified.

"I think it's safer picking up strangers than taking a chance on a man I know." She sighed. "The men I know always disappoint me."

He opened his mouth to argue, to point out she hadn't given him a chance. For a year she had ignored him or fought with him. When he had finally gotten close to her, she had run from him.

"Maybe you didn't really know them," he said.

She met his gaze and held it for a long moment before nodding in agreement. "Maybe not…" She wriggled down from the stool, and her body pushed against his.

He remembered that night—remembered how close they'd been, nothing between them as skin had slid over skin. His breath caught in his lungs. He couldn't breathe, couldn't speak. But he could hear the warning Milek uttered in his earpiece. "You have a problem."

He'd already known that. But he glanced up and noticed Viktor had stepped from his back office into the heart of the club. If he saw Candace…

She leaned closer, her lips brushing his ear and murmured, "Or maybe I've known them too well…"

He shook his head. "If that were true, you wouldn't have come back. You would have kept running."

Anger flashed in her blue eyes. She didn't deny, though, she had run.

He stepped aside, so that she could get past him. And he advised her, "Run, Candace, run…"

She called him a name no lady should even know. But she was Candace. She'd fought in a foreign country. She'd fought in her own country. She was the toughest woman he knew. But when she walked past him, he noticed the faint sheen in her eyes. He had hurt her, and he hated himself for hurting her. But instead of reaching for her, he curled his fingers into his hands and resisted the urge.

He had to let her go.

And go she did. Her head held high, her chin up, Candace walked past him as if she didn't know him. As if she didn't care...

Had she cared? Had whatever Stacy had said to her compelled her to come back? To try to help save him from himself, or from Chekov?

And had he just thrown away whatever chance he might have had with her?

Like he'd resisted reaching for her, he resisted watching her walk away. Instead he lifted his head and met Viktor Chekov's gaze. The man had avoided prison for so many years because he didn't miss anything. He knew how to find and exploit the weaknesses of his enemies.

Had he just discovered Garek's greatest weakness?

Candace's eyes stung. But it wasn't with tears. It was the cold that was getting to her. While she'd retrieved her long jacket and winter boots from coat check, she still wasn't warm enough. The winter breeze penetrated her jacket and chilled her to the bone.

She should have used the valet parking. But she'd wanted easy access to her vehicle in case she'd needed it. Two blocks and an alley away wasn't easy access, though. She shivered and blinked. But it wasn't against tears. She was blinking away snowflakes.

They fell heavily, wetting her hair and dampening her jacket—chilling her even more. But maybe it was Garek's words and his attitude that had chilled her most.

He hadn't wanted her to come back.

She'd tried to pretend that night had never happened. She hadn't realized that he would want to pretend the same thing—until she'd looked into his face and seen no memory of their encounter in his eyes. He had looked at her as if he'd never seen her naked.

As if that night had never really happened…

Had it?

Or had she dreamed it all?

Garek Kozminski had her doubting herself all over again. She'd thought she'd known him so well. But maybe she did. Maybe that was why he'd pushed her away like he had. He didn't want her too close.

Not because of Tori Chekov. Just like she hadn't seen any memory of their night on his face, she hadn't seen any love for that woman on his face. He had lied to Logan about his reason for working for Viktor Chekov again.

Why? What was he really doing for the gangster?

For the past year she'd been claiming he hadn't changed—that he was still the criminal he'd once been. Of course she'd had no evidence to back up her suspicion. She wasn't even sure why she'd been so desperate to believe the worst of him. Because he'd irritated and frustrated her? Because she hadn't wanted to acknowledge or give in to the attraction she'd felt for him?

But maybe she had been right about him after all. Had he gone back to his old life in every way?

She stepped off the sidewalk to pass through the alley to where her car was parked on the other side—on another street. The snow was deeper between the buildings as were the shadows. Her boots slipped on the snow-covered asphalt, but she regained her balance, catching herself before she fell.

She uttered a little gasp of surprise and relief, grateful she hadn't fallen. Despite her jacket and boots, she wasn't dressed warmly enough to take a tumble in the snow. So she slowed her steps, moving more carefully as she continued into the alley.

Maybe the person behind her was moving just as carefully or maybe the snow had cushioned his footsteps—because she didn't hear him until his shadow fell across her. She barely had a moment to reach for her purse, to fumble for her gun, before he attacked.

Her purse fell from her shoulder, dropping—with the gun still inside—into the snow. She couldn't use it to protect herself. And with her limbs numb from the cold, she wasn't certain she could move quickly enough to fight off her attacker. He was big, his hands strong— as they wrapped around her neck. She couldn't see his face, though. He wore a ski mask, but it wasn't in deference to the cold. It was as a disguise. So she couldn't identify him.

Why had he bothered? It was apparent he had no intention of letting her live.

Chapter 5

Fear clutched his heart in a tight vice, making the pressure on his chest unbearable. That pressure had begun to build the minute Garek had seen that sheen of tears in Candace's eyes. She acted so tough and was so strong physically, but emotionally she was vulnerable. And he'd hurt her.

He hated himself for hurting her and just letting her walk away. But then another feeling had come over him, chilling his skin and his blood even in the crowded, heated club. Fear.

He wasn't worried about just her emotional state anymore. He was worried about her physical state, too. So he'd ignored Viktor gesturing him over to his private table. And he'd pushed through the throng of club patrons to the exit.

He asked the valets in the club foyer, "Did you bring a car around for a beautiful woman—"

"Lots of beautiful women come and go from Mr. Chekov's club," one of the valets sarcastically remarked.

"This one is really beautiful," Garek said. "She's tall with black hair and—"

The cocky kid clicked his fingers together. "Oh, yeah, that one…"

The other kid uttered a lustful sigh. "She has legs that went on forever…"

His buddy bumped his arm with his fist. "You'd know, you lucky bastard. She leaned against you to change from her heels to her boots."

At least she'd put on boots. "So did you bring her car around for her?"

The kid shook his head. "No, she didn't check it with us. She walked."

That fear clenched his heart harder. "Which way did she go?"

One of the kids pointed toward the left.

"Are you sure?" he asked. "There aren't any parking lots that way."

The valet shrugged thin shoulders. "She must've parked along the street."

She couldn't have parked close to the club then. Those spots were always already taken—no matter what time of day. Even when the club was closed, Viktor did *business* here. It may have been where his right-hand man had been killed.

That crime scene hadn't been discovered—just the man's body in a Dumpster. A Dumpster that had been near the club…

Garek pushed through the doors and rushed out of the foyer. "Mr. Koz," one of the kids called after him. "You don't have a coat."

He didn't care about the cold. He cared only about finding Candace before she wound up in a Dumpster, too. Footprints led away from the front of the club—going off in different directions. More than one set led off the way the valets had indicated she'd gone.

Had she been walking with someone? Or had someone followed her?

He tracked those footprints. None of them stopped at the curb but continued down the street and around the block. But the wind picked up with a mighty gust that obliterated the rest of the footprints—the rest of the trail.

Where the hell had she gone? Had her car been parked near here and she'd left already?

That chill had gone deeper than his skin, though—to his blood and bone, and it wasn't from the cold. It was from that odd premonition he'd had about her safety. The worry and unease hadn't left him yet.

She wasn't safe.

Then he heard it. Something striking metal—like a Dumpster. The noise ricocheted off the brick walls, as if coming from an alley.

He saw it a little farther down the block, the opening between two tall buildings. Uncaring if he stepped in front of traffic or not, he jumped off the curb, squeezed between two cars and ran across the street to the alley.

"Candace?" he called out as he ran. His shoes slipped on the snow, and he nearly fell. But he caught the wall, brick stinging his palm as he hurried around the corner into the alley. With his other hand, he drew his weapon.

Between the tall buildings, the alley was dark. He could see nothing until his eyes adjusted—too slowly. Somebody ran out the other end of the alley, but all

Garek saw was a huge shadow—a bulk of muscle and height.

That wasn't Candace.

He had to find her—had to make sure she was all right. Maybe she hadn't even been in the alley. But then his eyes adjusted, and he noticed the body lying in the snow—beside the Dumpster.

"Candace!"

He dropped to his knees beside her. Snowflakes fell on her face, melting against her silky skin and running down her cheeks like tears. "Candace!"

Her long lashes, thick with snowflakes, too, fluttered and opened. While he felt a moment of relief, she obviously didn't—her eyes widened with fear.

"It *was* you!" she said, her tone full of accusation.

"What was me?" he asked, as he leaned closer to her.

She shrank back in the snow. "You attacked me."

A pang struck his heart. Obviously her opinion of him hadn't changed any. No wonder she'd left that night. "No, I didn't. I just found you."

She stared up at him through narrowed eyes, her suspicions not appeased yet.

He studied her face, checking for blood—for injuries. "Are you okay?" She'd been out for at least a moment. Had she hit her head? He reached for her, but she flinched and lifted her hands to fend him off.

There was blood on her fingers. He caught her wrist. "You're bleeding."

"That's not my blood." She sat up and now she studied him as intently as he had been studying her. "Where are you bleeding?"

"I'm not."

She touched his neck, and her fingers were like ice against his skin. "You're not…"

"Where are your gloves?" he asked. But then he noticed them lying in the snow beside her. She must have taken them off to fight her attacker.

Her fingers stroked along his throat now, and concern replaced the suspicion in her beautiful blue eyes. "Where is your coat?" she asked.

"I didn't take the time to grab it." And while snow was falling, he barely noticed the cold. Her touch heated his blood. He lifted her from the snow, wrapping her tightly in his arms. "You must be freezing."

She shook her head, but her teeth clicked together with a slight chatter. Snow covered her, clinging to her coat and her skin. "I'm fine…"

"You're not," he said, calling her on her obvious bluff. Candace hated admitting to any vulnerability—either emotional or physical. "You've been attacked. Are you sure you're not hurt?"

She shook her head again, but then her head lulled back against his shoulder—as if she'd nearly passed out.

"I'm taking you to the emergency room," he decided. He couldn't risk that she wasn't seriously injured.

She struggled in his arms, but her struggle was far weaker than what she was usually capable of. He easily held her.

"Where's your car?" he asked. She must have been walking toward it when she'd been attacked, so he suspected it was closer than his.

She gestured toward the other end of the alley. So she'd only been cutting through on her way to her vehicle. But that was also the way her attacker had gone. Was he waiting for them at her vehicle?

"Who the hell was it?" he asked. "Who assaulted you?"

Viktor had just stepped out of his office. He wouldn't have had time to send someone after her…unless he'd noticed her on the security cameras in his office. But he wouldn't know who she was—or what she meant to Garek that quickly.

"I thought it was you," she murmured.

Her admission struck him like a blow. Pain clenched his heart over the fact she could think so little of him yet—that she could think he could hurt her. But then he remembered her tears and acknowledged he had hurt her.

But then a physical blow struck him, catching him off guard. It hadn't come from the direction her attacker had gone. It had come from behind him. Had the man circled back?

With Candace clasped tightly in his arms, he couldn't reach for his weapon. He couldn't draw his gun in time to protect her. All he could do was use his body to shield her the best he could from another attack.

Candace's hand shook so badly that she couldn't get the key into her lock. A hand covered hers, steered the key inside and turned the knob for her. The hand was strong, the man to whom it belonged tall, blond and handsome.

But her skin didn't tingle. Her heart didn't race. How could two men look so alike and affect her so differently?

As Milek escorted her inside her apartment, he murmured, "Garek is going to kill me…"

He would have—in the alley—if he hadn't turned around to discover the man who'd struck him in the back was his brother. She shivered as she recalled that intense look in his silvery eyes. He'd been so…

Protective. She shivered again. Nobody had ever been protective of Candace. They hadn't had to be; she took care of herself. Would she have been able to fight off her attacker, though, without Garek arriving when he had?

She'd clawed at the man's throat and kneed him in the groin. And when he'd been doubled over in pain, she had shoved his head against the Dumpster. But it hadn't fazed him in the least. And the look in his eyes, which were all she'd been able to see through that mask, had been more intense than Garek's. It had been murderous.

He would have killed her.

She shivered again.

"Garek was right," Milek said. "I should have taken you to the emergency room."

"I'm fine," she assured him. Or she would be. She stripped off her wet coat and grabbed up a thick, fake fur blanket from the couch and wrapped it around herself. Before she'd left that night, she'd turned up the thermostat. Heat blew from the registers, but it didn't dissipate her chill yet.

"You were attacked," Milek said.

She turned to him now and studied him with suspicion. How had he known she'd been attacked? Garek could have been carrying her because she'd fallen in the snow. Milek was tall and broad-shouldered like his brother and like the man who had attacked her. With his coat collar raised and a scarf wrapped around his neck, she couldn't tell if he had any scratches.

"How did you know that?" she asked.

He tensed and asked, "Know what?"

"That I was attacked." It was warm in her apartment,

but realizing she was alone with Milek, she shivered again. And she had always considered him the nicest of the Kozminski siblings.

He shrugged. "I just assumed…"

"Why?"

"That's a rough neighborhood." That was no lie. A lot of River City was rough, though. "A woman walking alone in that area is always at risk of being attacked."

An average woman. But Candace wasn't an average woman. As a bodyguard she protected others. And she always protected herself.

Well, usually…

But the memory of that night with Garek flashed through her mind, and heat flashed through her body— finally warming her cold skin. She had definitely not protected herself *that* night. She'd left herself vulnerable to all kinds of pain and humiliation.

"I'm not sure it was a random attack," she said.

Milek sighed. "Maybe it wasn't…"

She remembered how he'd struck his brother from behind. "You thought Garek had attacked me. You suspected your own brother."

He shook his head. "No…"

"I did, too," she admitted. "It was obvious from the way he acted in the club that he wanted to get rid of me."

Instead of arguing with her, Milek admonished her, "You shouldn't have gone there."

She couldn't really argue with him either, but she tried. "I can have a drink wherever I want."

"You knew Garek would be there," he said, as if that knowledge was an accusation.

She could be as evasive as he had been. "How would I know that?"

"Stacy told you," he said.

She shook her head. "Stacy didn't tell me to go to the club."

"Maybe not," he agreed, but his voice was gruff with doubt. She suspected it was more his sister he didn't trust than her. "She convinced you to come home because she's worried Garek has gone back to his old life."

"Has he?" she asked. If anyone knew, it'd be Milek—because he probably would have gone along with him. Until tonight—until he'd struck Garek—she'd thought he'd idolized his older brother. "Have *you*?"

He only addressed her first question when he asked a question of his own. "What exactly do you think Garek has gone back to?"

"Tori Chekov?" That was what he'd obviously wanted Logan to believe. But she agreed with Stacy. Garek hadn't looked like a man in love at the club. He'd looked like a bodyguard on an assignment.

Milek tilted his head as if about to nod.

And she snorted. "I don't believe that any more than you do."

"You don't know what I believe," he said.

Which was true. Despite or maybe because of his usual mild manner, Milek was hard to read.

"No," she admitted. "But I can tell he's not in love with her."

He arched a brow. "That sounds like what *you* want to believe."

Garek hadn't told Stacy about the night they'd shared. Had he told his brother?

"Are you going to try to convince me that he does love her?" she asked, nearly choking on the words as the thought struck her harder than she'd hit the asphalt in the alley. At least the snow had broken her fall there. "I thought you'd be the last person to lie to me. You know what it feels like to be lied to."

"My situation is a little different," he pointed out.

And shame gave her heart a twinge of regret that she'd presumed to compare their situations. He had been denied so much because of secrets.

"You're right," she agreed. "Maybe he does love her…" Again the words choked her. She struggled to swallow before adding, "But I don't believe that's why he's back working for Viktor Chekov."

"Garek works for Logan," Milek said, and for once his voice was hard with defensiveness. "He works for Payne Protection."

She snorted again. "He's working for Chekov. And I want to know why. Has he returned to his old life? Is he stealing again? Or…"

"Or what?" Milek asked.

"He went to jail for murder," she reminded him and herself. How had she forgotten for a moment who Garek Kozminski was? She'd kept bringing up his past to remind herself. But then that night had happened…

And she'd hoped he really had changed like everyone else had claimed. Of course he hadn't made any such assurances. He'd let her believe whatever she wanted while everyone else had sung his praises, saying what a good man he was. What a loyal brother. What a hard worker. She wished he really was reformed.

A grimace crossed Milek's face.

And she regretted bringing up bad memories for him. He and his family had been through a lot. But there had been different versions of exactly what had gone down. Most people said Garek had deserved a medal for killing his stepfather instead of a five-year sentence for manslaughter. He had only served six months, though—due to good behavior and probably Mrs. Payne's influence on one of the judges she'd known.

"Should he have gone to jail?" she asked.

Milek shook his head.

Maybe it was a reply. Maybe it was a refusal to answer.

"Why do you care?" he asked. "You've made it clear what you think about Garek. The worst."

She couldn't deny she had once thought the worst of him. Now she wanted to prove herself wrong. She wanted to be wrong so badly.

Milek was torn. He hesitated with his hand on the door of Candace's apartment building lobby. Outside snow fell heavily, lightening the night sky. But it wasn't the cold weather causing him to hesitate.

Should he have told Candace the truth? Garek had sworn him to keep quiet. But Garek didn't always know what was best for him.

Candace was best for him.

And that was why Milek had needed to hold his silence. But it wasn't just Garek's undercover assignment that Milek was keeping quiet about. He'd been holding his silence for years—too many years.

But it probably was better Candace continued to think the worst of Garek. Then maybe she would stay away from him and stay safe.

Milek tightened his scarf around his neck before pushing open the door and stepping out into the cold. The wind took away his breath for a moment, burning in his lungs.

What a god-awful night…

The street was so deserted there weren't even tracks in the snow. His and Candace's had already blown over on the sidewalk. And the street was snow covered, as well.

He'd parked at the curb just outside her apartment building. He'd been grateful then to find a spot so close—because he'd been concerned about Candace. Now he was happy for himself.

He hadn't been inside her apartment long, but an inch or so covered his vehicle. He clicked the lock and pulled his snow brush from the backseat. As he cleared off the SUV, he noticed movement across the street. A man stood in the shadows of the dark building.

Milek narrowed his eyes and peered through the snow. The guy was dressed too nicely to be homeless. Even huddled over inside his jacket, the guy was big— like Chekov's hired goons.

Could this be who had attacked Candace?

Had he followed them back to her place?

Milek cursed beneath his breath. His brother had pounded it into his head to always check his rearview and side mirrors, so much so it was a natural instinct for Milek. He wouldn't have missed a tail.

Or had he?

Clasping the brush tightly in one hand, he headed across the street. In addition to the brush, he always had his gun—holstered beneath his jacket. He'd use them both if necessary. But the man noticed him, turned and ran.

He was bigger than Milek, though, and slower— maybe because he'd been standing in the cold. Milek caught up to him and reached out, grasping his shoulder.

The guy swung around and smashed his fist into Milek's face. His vision wavered, blurring the man's face. He noticed nothing of his features. The only thing he registered was the claw marks on the man's throat. Then he dropped to his knees in the snow as oblivion threatened to claim him.

If this man was Candace's attacker, how the hell had she survived? And if this was the man, then he must have followed her to finish the job he'd failed earlier.

Milek had to protect her. Or Garek would kill him. If this guy didn't beat him to it…

Chapter 6

He shouldn't have trusted Milek. Hell, he shouldn't have trusted *anyone else* with Candace's safety.

If he hadn't followed her out...

Garek shuddered as he considered what might have happened to her. He might have lost her longer than two weeks. He might have lost her forever.

"Who is she?"

He glanced up from the fire burning in the hearth in Viktor's den. Tori was the one who asked the question. When he'd seen Viktor a little while earlier, the man hadn't asked him about Candace.

Because he already knew?

He actually hadn't asked him anything. He'd only glared at Garek when he'd arrived at the house.

"I'm sorry," Garek had said. That was why Milek had tracked him down in the alley—because Viktor had been leaving with Tori and his entourage. And Garek was supposed to be part of that entourage.

Viktor's glare had become even fiercer. "Some bodyguard," he'd muttered before leaving Garek alone in the study.

He could have defended himself. He could have justified his disappearance because he'd been checking out a threat. But he didn't want Viktor thinking Candace posed a threat to his daughter. No, Candace was the one who'd been threatened.

Who had been attacked...

Was she really okay? Had Milek taken her to the emergency room as Garek had ordered him?

He didn't doubt that Milek would have obeyed him— had Candace allowed him. Had she agreed to get checked out?

"Who is she?" Tori asked again as she stepped closer to the fire and him.

Garek had been standing there for a while, but the chill hadn't left his body yet. It had gone far deeper than his skin. "I don't know who you're talking about..."

"The woman at the bar," Tori said, "the one with the dark hair..."

He shrugged.

"C'mon, Garek, you noticed her the moment she walked in," Tori said. "Don't try to bluff me. I know you too well. I also saw how jealous you looked when that man talked to her. I've never seen you look like that. She obviously means something to you."

Everything...

The realization staggered him. But he shook off the romantic notion. He didn't believe in happily-ever-after. He only believed in taking his happiness where he could find it.

With Candace…

He had been very happy that night in her bed—until he'd awakened alone.

He forced a laugh. "C'mon, Tori, you know me. When has anyone or anything ever meant anything to me?"

"Your family."

He couldn't—and *wouldn't*—deny that. "She's not family." At least not blood. But Payne Protection had become an extension of his family—an extension of him.

"Who is she then?" Tori asked, her voice going sharp as it rose on a whine. "And don't try to tell me that you don't know her."

"I know her," Garek admitted. There was no use trying to deny what must have been written on his face the moment Candace had walked into the club. "But you don't need to know who she is."

Tori's face twisted into the usual petulant frown she wore. "You're not very good at this."

"This?" Relationships? He'd never had one—not with Tori anyway. They'd hung out as teenagers, but that was a lifetime ago.

She nodded. "This undercover thing."

He tensed and glanced around the den. He wouldn't put it past Viktor to have it wired. He looked more closely, but microphones were tiny now and could be hidden anywhere. If it was wired and Viktor kept the recordings…

Maybe that would be the extra evidence Agent Rus needed to finally put Viktor Chekov away. Where would Chekov keep the tapes? With the gun—if he'd kept it. In a safe? Garek would be able to crack it; he'd never met one he hadn't. He just had to find where Viktor had hidden it. In his home? Or the office in his club?

"I'm a bodyguard," he reminded her. "Just a bodyguard…"

She flashed him a snide smile. "Yeah, right…"

He laughed. "I'm an ex-con," he said.

He had never had to remind Candace of that. She'd never let him forget—his former career as a thief or the stint he'd done in prison for manslaughter. He had been crazy to think he would ever get her to change her mind about him. But then he'd never tried explaining what had really happened either. Maybe he should have…

Maybe he would have if he'd awakened with her beside him, in his arms…

That night…he'd caught her at a vulnerable moment, her usual prickly defenses down for once. But she must have been so horrified over what she'd done, since she'd run off in the middle of the night.

Why had she come back? And why had she come to the club?

He wanted to ask her. Most of all he wanted to make certain she was all right.

He also had to make certain she stayed safe from now on, and the only way he could do that was to make sure nobody in the Chekov family gave her another thought.

"How does an ex-con become an undercover agent?" he asked sarcastically. "Like that would ever happen…"

"Surely you've heard of police informants," she said. "They're usually criminals."

He narrowed his eyes and studied her. "Usually," he agreed. "But sometimes they're just someone close, someone who's seen something…"

She shivered and stepped closer to the fire. "Something they wish they could *unsee*…"

He sucked in a breath. He'd suspected she was Rus's eyewitness. Now he knew for certain. "Tori…"

She shrugged. "It's not like I didn't know what he was."

"Was?" Did she not even consider Chekov her father anymore—after what she'd seen him do? She must have been so disillusioned to discover the man she'd always idolized was really the monster everybody said he was.

"Is," she corrected herself.

"You did the right thing," he assured her. But he doubted she would follow through and testify. She adored her father and was too much of a daddy's girl to ever cross him.

"What about you?" she asked. "Are you going to do the right thing?"

He sighed. "I'm trying…"

If only he could find that damn gun…

But Viktor had had plenty of time to dispose of it. Without the gun, it wouldn't matter if Tori testified— not if she had no evidence to support that testimony.

"Then you need to let that woman—*whoever she is*—go."

He had let her go. But then he'd been compelled to follow her.

"I don't know what you're talking about," Garek said. "She doesn't mean anything to me." The lie nearly stuck in his throat.

"That's good," Tori said. "Maybe she'll be okay then."

Did Tori know something about the attack on Candace? He opened his mouth to ask.

But then she continued, "Because you and I are too much alike, Garek."

She wasn't proposing they rekindle a teenage romance? He'd worried about that—when he'd taken the position as her bodyguard—she might misconstrue his reasons. Apparently she knew them better than he'd realized—since she'd suspected he was working undercover as an informant on her father.

"When we care about someone," she continued, "they wind up getting hurt."

That was why she'd gone to the police—why she'd been willing to testify. The man that had died had meant something to her—maybe everything.

He couldn't imagine what she must have gone through—watching that man die. And he never wanted to go through that with Candace. He had to keep her safe.

Stacy gripped the top rail of the crib as she leaned over it and watched her baby sleep. Little Penny was all Payne with her dark curls; they lay damply against her head. Despite the cold outside, the baby was warm. Her blue eyes—so like her father's and her uncles'—were closed as she slept peacefully.

Stacy could find no peace tonight. She had only been gone two days to track down Candace, but as Logan had already said, it had felt longer. She had missed him and their baby. She'd missed her family.

But even though she was back home—back in Logan's arms and had had her baby back in her arms, she still missed her family.

Milek and Garek were gone yet.

She had lost them.

"Why are you awake?" a gruff voice asked.

She turned to where her husband leaned against the doorjamb, his chest bare but for a dusting of dark hair. He was so damn good-looking…

And she was so lucky he had fallen in love with her. He had saved her life—literally and figuratively. Because if she didn't have him and little Penny now…

He uttered a sympathetic sigh and stepped forward to wrap his arms around her. She leaned into his embrace, accepting his comfort—even though she didn't deserve it. She didn't deserve him. She didn't deserve this happiness.

"You have to give Milek time," Logan advised her.

Since her brother had listened to her about Garek, she'd gotten her hopes up. He'd come home to help, too. But he obviously only intended to help Garek. Not her. Because now he was ignoring her calls again, sending them straight to voice mail.

"He's not the only one not answering my calls now," she admitted. And that bothered her even more. Milek had a reason to be angry with her. But Garek…

She'd only been trying to help him.

"Da…" Logan caught himself midcuss and amended it to, "Darn it…"

She smiled, amused he was already correcting himself in front of their baby even though she was too young to talk. And she wasn't even awake.

"But you had to know he wasn't going to be happy you interfered with his life."

She leaned fully against him, confident he could support her weight. That he would support her. She wanted the same for her brothers. She wanted them to find someone strong enough to love them no matter what.

Candace was that woman for Garek. Couldn't he see

it? Hopefully he would realize it before it was too late. Before he lost Candace or his freedom or his life...

Because if he didn't get away from Viktor Chekov, he was in danger of losing all three.

After two weeks away, Candace should have been eager to sleep in her own bed again. But she had avoided it and the memories it held. Even though it was unlikely after all this time, she'd worried the sheets might have smelled like Garek—like that curiously spicy, musky male scent she could smell even now. On her.

Of course he had picked her up in the alley; he'd held her easily, effortlessly. And Candace wasn't petite and delicate like the mobster's daughter. She was tall and firmly muscled. But he hadn't dropped her, not even when Milek had struck him from behind.

Milek. He'd left a while ago. And he'd left her unsettled with his evasiveness. Had both he and Garek returned to their old lives?

What were they doing for Viktor Chekov? Were they stealing again? They had been little more than toddlers when their father had taught them how to break and enter—homes, safes, museums...

Was there some particular target Chekov wanted hit? Was that why Garek had gone back to work for him?

Or was it because of what Stacy had said? Because he'd tried to be good for her—for Candace—and she'd never given him a chance?

She had that one night—for a few hours. Muscles tightened low inside her belly as desire for him returned. It didn't matter that she'd avoided the bed; she couldn't avoid the memories. She'd curled up instead on her couch, with that heavy blanket wrapped around her, but she couldn't sleep. Maybe that was because of residual adrenaline from fighting off her attacker.

She preferred to blame that than desire for a man like Garek, a man she couldn't trust. While he hadn't been the one who'd attacked her in the alley, he could have had something to do with it. He hadn't wanted her anywhere near that club. But if he knew her at all, he would know an attack wouldn't frighten her away.

She had never feared physical pain. It was the fear of emotional pain that had had her running away that night…

And she had been right to run. She had been right about Garek all along. Hadn't she been?

Despite the blanket and the heat blasting out of the registers, she shivered. No. It wasn't desire keeping her awake. And it wasn't fear.

It was anger. Anger over the attack. And anger over the fact that her attacker had gotten away. She needed to track him down, needed to find out who he was and why he'd meant her harm—or worse.

But if it hadn't been a random attack and he'd really wanted to hurt her, then she wouldn't have to track him down. He would try for her again.

The thought had no more crossed her mind than she noticed, in the faint light streaming in from the street, the doorknob turn.

She had locked it—after she'd shown Milek out. She'd made certain of that. But the door hadn't rattled as if someone had been picking the lock. The knob turned easily, as if it hadn't been locked. Or as if somebody had a key.

She reached beneath the pillow on which her head lay. And she closed her hand around the Glock she'd put there before she'd settled onto the couch.

She had never given out a key to her apartment. She'd never been close enough to anyone—not even Logan—to give them a key to her place.

The knob didn't even click before the door began to open, spilling light from the hall into the living room. Candace shut her eyes just as it illuminated her face. But then the door closed, plunging the room into darkness again.

She opened her eyes, which gradually adjusted to that faint light coming through the window. She could make out the shadow of her intruder. He was tall and broad-shouldered—like the masked man in the alley.

He hesitated for a moment before stepping away from the door and starting—slowly—toward her. She tightened her grasp on her weapon, ready to draw it. She had no compulsion against using it.

She had fired her weapon before. But she waited—wanting to identify her intruder before she shot him. She had no doubt he meant her harm, though, or he wouldn't have broken in during the night.

Or the wee hours of the morning. She had no idea how long she'd been lying there...not sleeping. Thinking about Garek...

She couldn't remember a time when he hadn't been on her mind. Even now...

She could still smell him, but not like she had earlier. His scent was stronger now. The spice, the musk...

Her skin tingled and finally heat chased away the last of her chill.

The shadow loomed larger, as the man neared the

couch. He chased away the light and cast her in total darkness. But she instinctively knew when he reached for her.

And she was ready.

Chapter 7

He was ready for her. So when she grabbed his arm and tried to flip him over the back of the couch, he caught himself, so he didn't land on the floor. He landed on top of her. Her breath whooshed out, warmly caressing his throat. She wriggled beneath him, but her arms were pinned between their bodies. When she lifted her knee, he caught it with his thighs—before she did any damage.

"It's me," he said. "It's Garek…"

"I know." But she continued to struggle, bucking beneath him. Her breasts pushed against his chest, and her hips against his.

He groaned as his body reacted. "Candace…"

And finally she went still beneath him except for the frantic beat of her heart. He could feel it beating in her breast—feel it beating in sync with his—like it had that night when they'd made love.

"Why are you fighting me?" he asked.

She began to wriggle again. "You broke in!"

He chuckled. "I didn't break in."

She stilled again and said, "No, you didn't. How did you get in?"

"I took a key," he admitted. "When I let myself out the morning after…"

That night. That incredible night.

His body tensed, every muscle taut with desire for her. He had been attracted to her since the first moment he'd seen her—looking so strong and beautiful and irritated. But he hadn't realized the depth of the desire he could feel for her or the pleasure he could feel *with* her.

Until that night…

"You had no right to take a key," Candace said. She was tense, too, but probably with anger.

"Maybe you should have stuck around then," he said, "instead of running off the minute I fell asleep." He regretted that—regretted closing his eyes for a moment that night. But it had felt so right making love with her, being with her; he had achieved a level of peace he'd never known before. Until that night there had been very little peace in Garek's chaotic life.

"That night never should have happened," she said. And even in the dim light coming through the window, he could tell how deeply her face flushed with embarrassment. "It was a mistake."

He wanted to argue with her. But she was right. It would have been easier for him had they never made love. Then he wouldn't know how incredible they were together. He wouldn't think about her constantly. He wouldn't want her as much as he wanted her again.

"Ah hell," he murmured as he lowered his head to

hers. This was no tentative kiss. No brushing of lips over lips. He took her mouth, like he'd taken her body that night. He kissed her passionately, parting her lips, so he could taste her. He slid his tongue over hers, deepening the kiss.

She nipped at his lower lip, catching it between her teeth. She could have bitten him hard—could have stopped the kiss. But she kissed him back instead. And her hands moved between them, touching his chest and his stomach.

He wished his clothes were gone, wished hers gone. He wanted nothing between them. Like that night, he wanted skin to skin. But when he reached for the blanket covering her, she shivered.

And he remembered what she'd been through and why he'd come to her place. To check on her...

To make sure she wasn't hurt or in danger.

He dragged his mouth from hers. Panting for breath, he leaned his forehead against hers. Staring into her eyes—her beautiful eyes—he asked, "Are you all right?"

Her forehead moved against his as she shook her head. Then she moved again. Catching him by surprise, she flipped him onto the floor.

His back struck the hardwood, his head just missing the coffee table. Like hers had earlier, his breath whooshed out. "You seem just fine to me."

"I am fine," she said.

"Is that what the ER doctor said?"

"I didn't go to the ER," she replied.

Concern and irritation struck him harder than he'd struck the floor, and he sat up. "I told Milek to take you to the emergency room."

She sat up, too, on the couch. But she kept the blanket wrapped around her. The chill must not have left her body. "And I didn't want to go to the ER."

So why hadn't Milek been answering his phone? Garek had thought that his brother must have shut off his cell while he'd been in the hospital and he'd just forgotten to turn it back on.

"Where's Milek?" he asked.

She shrugged. "I don't know. He left a while ago."

Milek shouldn't have left her—unprotected after someone had attacked her. What the hell had he been thinking?

"He should have stayed," Garek murmured.

"Why?" Candace asked.

"You were attacked," he reminded her. "You're in danger."

"You don't think it was just some random attack?" she asked.

He bit his lip—harder than she had and wished he could take back the words. He didn't need to rouse her suspicions any more than Stacy already had. He shrugged. "I don't know what it was."

"I intend to find out," she said.

Panic clutched his heart. "No, Candace, you need to let this go."

"Someone attacked me, and I'm supposed to forget about it?" she asked.

Hell, no. He wouldn't forget either. He wanted that person to pay. Painfully.

"I didn't need to go to the ER," she repeated. "I needed to go to the police department and report the attack."

"No," he instinctively replied. If the police started snooping around the club, asking questions, asking for security footage to see who might have followed Candace out, then Viktor would dispose of that gun for certain.

"Why not?" she asked. Her hand slid beneath the pillow on the couch.

And Garek caught the glint of metal. She'd been sleeping with a gun beneath her head.

He was lucky she hadn't used that on him. But she shouldn't have had to be armed. Milek should have been standing guard—if not inside her apartment, then outside—to protect her.

"Why shouldn't I go to the police?" she asked again, her eyes narrowed as she stared down at him. It was times like this he could see the former cop in her; she had probably been a fearsome interrogator.

He hesitated, uncertain what to tell her.

"Who are you protecting?" she asked.

"You," he replied. "I want to protect you." That was why he'd wanted her to leave the club. That was why he should have stayed away from her.

But when Milek hadn't answered his phone, he'd worried she'd been hurt worse than he'd thought. And he'd needed to check on her. However, even if Milek had answered his phone, Garek might have needed to see for himself that she was all right.

She tilted her head. "Then shouldn't you want me to find out who attacked me?"

"I'll find out," he said. And he would make sure that person never hurt her again.

She shook her head. "I think you already know…"

"If I knew, I wouldn't be here," he said.

"You shouldn't be here." She held out her hand. "Give me back my key."

He pulled it from his pocket and, rising up on his knees, leaned over the couch and dropped it into her palm. Then he moved even closer, so his mouth nearly touched hers and asked, "Do you think it matters I don't have a key? Do you think you can keep me out?"

She pulled the gun from beneath the pillow and pointed it at him. "Yes, I do."

He laughed. "Why didn't you pull that gun on me when I first walked in here?"

She must have known it was him. And even though she obviously didn't trust him, she had kissed him back. The attraction wasn't all one-sided anymore. She wanted him, too, and if he hadn't remembered what she'd been through earlier that night, they might have made love again.

But like the first time, that would have been a mistake—it would only strengthen the connection between them. And if he intended to keep her safe, he had to break that connection. He had to keep her away from him.

"I wasn't sure who you were when you first came in," she said. But he saw the lie in her eyes—in her inability to meet his gaze.

He eased back—not because of the gun—but because the temptation to kiss her again overwhelmed him. "Next time," he advised her, "pull the gun."

"There won't be a next time," she said as she closed her hand around the key.

They both knew not having a key wouldn't keep him out. But he wouldn't break in again. He had to stay away.

He was worried that wouldn't be enough to keep her safe, though—she was still in danger. And where the hell was Milek? Why hadn't he stayed close to protect her?

He intended to find out. But he was reluctant to leave

her. Then another thought occurred to him. Maybe something had happened to Milek.

Maybe Garek had put his brother in danger, too. No, it was best he leave Candace and stay far, far away from her. Because maybe Tori Chekov was right, the people they cared about always got hurt.

The noise of the police department washed over Candace. The beeping phones, the drone of voices…

Then FBI Special Agent Nicholas Rus closed the door to his office and muted the noise. A year ago he had been assigned to investigate corruption in the River City Police Department. It had been far more extensive than anyone had realized—which was probably why he was still here.

At least career-wise. But he had another reason to stay in River City. His family.

With his chiseled features and dark hair, his resemblance to Logan and Parker was uncanny. It was as if they were triplets instead of twins. But his mother wasn't Penny Payne, which was his loss on more than one count. Penny was amazing. And her children resented Nicholas for being evidence of their late father's betrayal of their mother's love and loyalty.

While Candace had once wanted to be part of the Payne family herself, she didn't envy Nicholas Rus. And it didn't matter to Penny that Candace didn't have any Payne blood; she'd included her as family. Like she had the Kozminskis…

Special Agent Rus settled into the chair behind the desk while gesturing for her to take one in front of it. "Why didn't you report this last night?"

"I don't know…" She'd been cold and dazed and

Garek had rushed her off with Milek. "Everything happened so quickly. And the Kozminskis were there."

"Did you think they'd called?"

She nearly laughed at the thought. "That's unlikely..."

"Why?"

"You know their history."

"It's history," Rus repeated.

She knew that. But for some reason she hadn't been able to let it go. She could believe Milek had changed. But she hadn't been willing to believe Garek had. And apparently with good reason; he hadn't.

"You're in law enforcement," Candace said. "You know how often offenders repeat."

"So you're saying the Kozminskis attacked you?" he asked, and he picked up a pen as if ready to take down notes. He hadn't taken any earlier—when she'd given him the time and location of her attack.

It was almost as if he'd already known when and where it had happened. Maybe Garek or Milek had called it in. But then why had no one contacted her? She'd been the victim. Not that she'd seen enough of her attacker to make a positive identification.

She shook her head. "No, the Kozminskis didn't attack me. But Garek's working for Viktor Chekov again. Even his sister's convinced he's gone back to his old life."

His brow furrowed with obvious confusion. "What does any of that have to do with you?"

Candace wasn't certain either. But Stacy had thought it had everything to do with her. That he'd returned to his criminal ways because Candace hadn't given him a chance. But that was ridiculous...

"Really," Rus persisted. "Why would any of them— the Kozminskis or Viktor Chekov—want to hurt you?"

She considered the question for a moment before she answered honestly, "I don't know."

She was certain Garek didn't want her around, though. Or she'd been certain at the club. Then he had shown up—with her key—at her apartment the night before. Or early this morning. And he'd kissed her, like he'd kissed her that night two weeks ago. So she wasn't sure what he wanted with her.

But he'd definitely *wanted* her for a moment. She'd felt his erection against her belly. Her pulse quickened remembering his body lying heavily on hers and then his mouth on hers. She'd wanted him, too.

If he hadn't pulled away...

Rus was speaking again. "Isn't it more likely someone saw you in the club—someone you arrested while you were with River City PD—and that person followed you to attack you out of vengeance?"

That did make more sense. But the way Garek had treated her in the club—as if he wanted her nowhere near it—had roused her suspicions. He didn't want her around because he didn't want her discovering whatever he was up to. What crime had he committed or was about to commit for Viktor Chekov?

"Did you recognize anyone in the club?" he asked.

She shrugged. "Sure, faces looked familiar. That kind of place attracts criminals. More drugs and sex are sold there than alcohol."

"Allegedly," Rus said.

Alleged because no one had ever been able to arrest Viktor Chekov for any of his numerous crimes.

"But nobody was looking at me like they recognized me." Hell, she'd had someone hitting on her. That wouldn't have happened, had he or anyone else known she'd once been a cop. "And I don't remember arresting any of them either."

"Do you remember everyone you've ever arrested?" Rus asked. "Because I don't. But I'm pretty damn sure they all remember me."

"Sure," she admitted. "I've had my share of threats while I was on the force. But I haven't been with River City PD for years."

Rus nodded. "Exactly. So it's more likely some of the perps you arrested would be out on parole now."

Her head had begun to pound, maybe from lack of sleep, maybe from frustration. "You sound convinced that this attack was about me." Or he was trying really hard to convince her of that.

"It could have been random," he acknowledged. "That's a rough neighborhood."

"That's what Milek said," she admitted.

"I'll work both those angles," he assured her.

Goose bumps lifted on her skin with a shiver of unease. Was Nicholas Rus the right agent to investigate corruption in River City? "But not Viktor Chekov?"

His brow furrowed as if the question confused him. "Why?" he asked. "Has he threatened you?"

"I've never met him."

"Then why would he send someone after you?"

He probably wouldn't have. So who had? Garek? Had he been trying to scare her away? A physical threat wouldn't do that—only an emotional threat would. He should already know that, though.

"Forget it," Candace said. "You don't need to look into this at all. I'll investigate on my own."

"You're not on the force anymore," he reminded her. "You're a bodyguard."

She nodded. "Yes, I am." And the body she was protecting now was her own. But it wasn't really her body she needed to protect; it was her heart. "And you're an FBI agent. This little assault is beneath your pay grade. I shouldn't have bothered you with it."

"I'm glad you did," he said. "But why did you?"

She could have reported it to someone else. She still knew some officers on the force—the ones that had survived Rus's corruption arrests.

"If the Kozminskis are involved with Chekov, it'll reflect badly on Payne Protection just as Logan is getting ready to franchise," she said. "So it needs to be handled with discretion."

"What does?" Rus asked. "It sounds to me like Garek saved you and Milek helped you home. How would that reflect badly on Payne Protection?"

From that perspective she should have thanked Garek and his brother. But even their sister thought Garek had gone back to his criminal ways. Since Agent Rus wouldn't investigate, she would.

As if he'd read her mind, Rus said, "I'll handle the investigation. I'll check into recent paroles, other assaults in that area—see what we can turn up on security cameras."

For some reason, she doubted he would turn up any suspects. But she stood up and said, "Thank you." Then she headed toward the door.

He was there, opening it for her. Penny Payne may not have raised him, but he had the manners she'd ingrained in her children. But then he gave her a strange look, and in a deep and ominous tone advised, "Be careful, Candace."

Instead of sounding like concern, his comment

sounded like a threat. The chill rushed back over her, lifting those goose bumps on her skin again. Was there anyone she could trust?

"I trusted you to protect her," Garek said as he slammed the door to Milek's place. It was a converted warehouse space with high metal ceilings, and bare concrete floors so every sound was magnified.

Milek groaned as the crash reverberated in his already pounding head. He reached for the pharmacy bag on his kitchen counter, grateful now he'd filled the prescription he'd considered refusing. He was already in so much pain he hadn't thought his injuries would bother him at all—once he'd had his broken ribs wrapped.

"What the hell happened to you?" Garek asked.

"Protecting Candace," he murmured through his swollen lips. "You're welcome."

"Why didn't you call me?" Garek asked.

He pulled his phone from his pocket and held up the smashed screen. "It took a beating, too."

Garek uttered a stream of curses followed by a heart-felt apology. "I'm sorry. I'm so damn sorry for dragging you into all of this."

"Nicholas Rus dragged you first," Milek said. "But even then I'm surprised you'd go back—surprised you'd risk it."

Garek shrugged. "I need to do this. I could have taken Chekov out years ago—could have given him up to the authorities and gotten myself out of jail time."

"And he would have killed us all."

His brother lightly touched his swollen face, but Milek flinched at even slight pressure on his bruises. Yeah, he was glad he'd filled that prescription.

Garek warned him, "He still might kill us."

"We're not scared kids anymore," Milek reminded him. "We can handle Chekov. We can protect ourselves."

Garek raised a brow. "Really?"

"Hey, you should see the other guy."

Garek breathed a sigh of relief. "You got him? You took care of him."

"Not me," Milek admitted. "You should see what Candace did to him, though. She clawed the hell out of his neck. We'll be able to track him down easily enough if he's one of Chekov's men."

Garek shook his head. "Damn that woman. If the guy hadn't wanted to kill her before, he's going to want to now for sure."

"Candace can take care of herself." Milek tore open the pharmacy bag. "Hell, she can take care of herself better than I can. You don't need to worry about her."

"That man is still out there," Garek said. "I'm going to worry about her until we find him."

Milek shrugged. "It doesn't matter if we find him. If Chekov's behind it, he'll just send someone else." He hadn't agreed to help Garek just because he was his brother. He knew Chekov had gotten away with his crimes for too long. "We have to stop him."

Garek nodded. "I just hope we can stop him before Candace gets hurt again."

Or worse…

Chapter 8

While Garek loved his brother, it was Candace that he didn't want taking a beating because of him—like she nearly had in the alley.

He had to keep her safe. He had to stay the hell away from her—which wouldn't be easy since he was pretty damn sure she was following him. He peered into his rearview mirror but couldn't catch another glimpse of her car.

She was good. But he knew she was back there. He'd noticed her as he was leaving Milek's place for the second time that day. Of course she would have tracked him down there; she'd known he was worried about his brother.

He picked up his cell and punched in the number for the phone he'd brought back to Milek's after tracking him down the first time. He'd returned the second time to bring him the replacement phone and some food.

"That was quick," Milek answered. His voice was clear.

"You didn't take the drugs yet?" he asked.

Milek sighed. "I thought I should eat first. Thanks for the soup."

"How bad you hurting?" He wished back the question the minute he uttered it. He knew Milek was hurting badly. The man had lost everything before he'd even realized it was his.

All stubborn pride, Milek stoically replied, "I'm fine."

"Fine enough to take my bodyguard shift with Tori?"

Milek sighed. "The girl isn't in danger of anything but breaking a nail texting."

"No, she isn't in any danger," Garek agreed. "But her protection duty is what's getting me close to Viktor. And I need to get close to him if he's ever going to get caught."

But he didn't want Candace close to the mobster. He didn't want Candace anywhere near Viktor Chekov. So he couldn't lead her back there.

"Since you need to be close to Viktor, shouldn't you work your own shift?" Milek asked—speaking slowly as if Garek were the one who'd taken the beating and was confused.

"Candace is following me."

"And you figured out she was tailing you?" Milek asked. Then he uttered what sounded like a victory cry. Or maybe given his injuries it was just a cry. "You didn't realize I was tailing you that night I caught you meeting with Rus."

Garek smiled. Since they were kids, Milek had been trying to get one over on him. He definitely had that night, so Garek expected to hear about it often.

"No, I didn't make you," he admitted. That had been Candace's fault, however. She continued to distract him.

"I'll take your shift," Milek agreed. "What are you going to do about her?"

"Lead her as far from Chekov as I can…"

He wanted to lead her back to his place—not to his apartment but to the home he'd bought before Rus had pulled him into the undercover assignment. He hadn't moved into it yet because he couldn't risk Chekov finding out Garek had bought a house in the 'burbs. The mobster would know for certain there was nothing left of the corruptible kid Garek had once been. And he would never let down his guard enough to reveal anything incriminating. Hell, he'd probably fire him—at the least. Kill him at the most.

So he kept driving and acting as if he had no idea she was back there. While he didn't see her again, he knew he hadn't lost her.

"Where the hell is he going?" Candace murmured to herself. Fortunately she had a full tank of gas because he had led her all over the city for most of the afternoon. Night was nearly about to fall now.

What was he doing? Casing places for Chekov? He never went inside any building, never did more than pull his SUV to the curb outside of a building.

Did he know she was following him?

She shook her head. There was no way. She was too good. But he was good, too. She remembered how he'd easily followed Logan and Parker. And they were the ones who'd taught her how to spot and lose a tail.

But Garek wasn't following her. And he was too arrogant to consider she might be able to follow him. No, he hadn't spotted her. She was sure of it.

Each time he stopped, she picked up her phone and took a photo of the building. If something got robbed in it, she would have dated and time-stamped proof he'd been there. That had to be what he was doing for Chekov—something involving his breaking and entering and safecracking skills. He certainly wasn't protecting the man's daughter.

And despite what he'd told Logan, he wasn't in love with Tori Chekov either. If he was, he wouldn't have kissed Candace like he had the night before. His body wouldn't have reacted so physically and passionately to the closeness of hers.

Her body reacted now, flushing with heat, as she could almost feel the weight of him on top of her. But the image that flashed through her mind was from weeks ago—his naked body moving over hers, moving inside hers.

A soft moan slipped through her lips. She had never felt what he'd made her feel. So much...

Passion.

Desperation.

So much pleasure.

It had overwhelmed her. *He* had overwhelmed her.

The slamming of a car door jerked her from those intimate memories. He'd actually gotten out of his vehicle this time. She glanced around, trying to determine where they were. It was an industrial area of the city.

No jewelry stores or museums here. But maybe someone warehoused their art collection in one of these buildings. Maybe that was Chekov's target. She needed to investigate; she needed evidence to prove Garek had returned to his old life.

She wasn't certain she would share that evidence with Special Agent Rus. But she needed the evidence for herself—so she would stop wanting Garek.

She opened her door and stepped onto the street. Snow had begun to fall. But the flakes were huge and sparse. They floated softly from the sky with no breeze to blow them about, and it was warm enough again that the snow which had fallen the night before had melted from the asphalt and the concrete sidewalks. This wasn't the revitalized part of the city, but someone had decorated a few of the straggly trees along the sidewalk, stringing twinkle lights over the bare branches.

So she couldn't use his footprints to track him; she had to keep him in her sight. But he moved quickly, as if concerned someone might have followed him.

Had he noticed her tailing him? But Garek always moved with the speed and silence of a thief—either because it was in his genetics or he'd learned it so young from his father.

So she hastened her step, too. But he turned a corner and disappeared from her sight.

"Damn it…"

Had he gone inside one of those buildings? She needed to determine which one and why. She hustled up to where he'd turned. But he hadn't gone inside a building. He'd gone into an alley.

Night had already fallen between the buildings, casting the alley in darkness. She couldn't see inside—couldn't see if he'd slipped into some back entrance of a building. Or if he'd simply walked through it on his way to another street.

She drew in a deep breath and stepped into the shadows. But she'd only gone a few steps when strong arms wrapped tightly around her. She lifted her elbow, intending to drive it into his ribs.

But those arms spun her around, as if they were doing some kind of strange, fast-paced dance. She didn't need to figure out any steps, though, because he lifted her from her feet and propelled her back.

Pressed against the wall, she couldn't back away from him. And she couldn't move forward, either, because his body was there. His chest pressed against hers, his hips pushed against hers—like when he'd fallen on top of her on her couch.

"Didn't you learn your lesson last night?" Garek asked.

She'd learned the closeness of his body ignited a fire inside her. Desire overwhelmed her, claiming her common sense. She knew he wasn't good for her—he would only break her heart. She couldn't fall for him.

"You could have been attacked again," he continued. His body was tense against hers. Maybe with anger. It was in his silvery eyes as he stared down at her. But then his pupils dilated, leaving just a thin rim of silver outlining the black. And he wasn't angry anymore.

"You're not going to attack me," she murmured.

He leaned closer, pushing her more firmly against the brick wall. It might have been cold and hard against her back, but she noticed nothing of that. She felt only the heat burning between them, felt his body as it hardened and pushed against hers.

He groaned. "I wouldn't be so sure about that…"

"Why?" she asked.

"I think you know…" He leaned in, pressing his erection more firmly against her belly. And a moan slipped involuntarily through her lips.

She'd never wanted anyone the way she wanted him. If only she thought they could have a future…

"Why did you go to work for Chekov?" she asked. "Why would you back to that life?" Was it her fault— like Stacy believed? Had he really been trying to be a better man for her?

"It's just an assignment," he said.

At least he hadn't claimed to her what he had to Logan—that he loved Chekov's daughter. But which of them was he lying to?

Logan.

Or her?

Maybe she was fooling herself—or making a fool of herself again. But she didn't believe he could love one woman and want another woman like he obviously wanted her.

But then she'd always known he was a playboy, that he flirted with every woman he encountered. Even Penny Payne…

But in the year he'd been working for Payne Protection, she'd only seen him flirt. She'd never heard about him hooking up with anyone else. She'd never even heard about his dating.

"What am I?" she asked him. And she moved against him, arching her hips to rub against his erection.

He groaned again. "Trouble…"

"I'm trouble?" She smiled. No one had ever called her *that* before. She was the buddy. The friend. The person a man could rely on—not one who caused him trouble. To her it was a compliment.

But then she lost her smile because he kissed it away,

his lips moving over hers. He must have released her arms because she was able to lift them, to lock them around his neck, as she kissed him back. She parted her lips, inviting him to deepen the kiss.

He accepted her invitation. He nipped at her bottom lip, then slid his tongue over it and inside her mouth. She sucked on it before sliding her tongue over it.

Her heart pounded frantically, in rhythm with his. Even through their coats and clothes, she could feel the beat of his heart. Could feel the heat of his body…

He groaned and drove his tongue deeper inside her mouth. And she shuddered as desire overwhelmed her.

How could just his kiss drive her so crazy she didn't care they were in an alley? She wanted him like she'd had him that night of their first kiss. They hadn't been able to stop at a kiss then either. The attraction between them was too much—too explosive.

He pulled back, panting for breath. "I know trouble," he said. "And you're trouble, Candace, more trouble than I've ever gotten into before…"

That night she hadn't believed she'd affected him like he had her. She'd thought she was falling alone. That he'd only gotten what he'd been after—one night. That she'd been a challenge he'd won, a conquest.

Now she wasn't so certain. He clearly wanted her again. She arched into him, desperate to feel him inside her—as she had that night. She'd missed him—missed what she'd never imagined she would have. Passion. Crazy, desperate passion…

"You're the one who's trouble," she said. "I knew it the first moment I met you."

Unlike her, he didn't smile. He obviously didn't consider it the compliment she had. "I wasn't trouble *then*," he murmured. "But I am now…"

Because of what he'd done—or was doing—for Chekov.

"Quit the assignment," she urged him. "Let Logan give it to someone else. Or, better yet, have him drop Viktor Chekov as a client."

He stared down at her, his gray eyes going stormy with conflict. His jaw went taut as tension filled him. He wanted to—she knew it.

Or maybe she only wished it.

"Please," she implored him. And she rose up the scant inches that separated them and pressed her lips to his. "Please…"

She had never begged before. Not even Logan when she'd wanted him to fall in love with her instead of Stacy Kozminski. But then she had never wanted Logan the way she did Garek. What she'd felt for Logan had been just a silly schoolgirl crush. What she felt for Garek was…

Madness.

She kissed him again, sliding her lips over his.

A groan rumbled in his throat before his lips parted. She deepened the kiss, sliding her tongue inside his mouth. The passion ignited between them.

She wanted him so much, but she wanted all of him. She wanted his body and his soul. She didn't want him selling it out to someone like Chekov.

But most of all she wanted his heart.

"Garek…"

He leaned his forehead against hers, panting for breath, and shook his head. "I can't quit this job. I'm in too deep, Candace. I have to see this through."

"What do you have to see through?" she asked. "What are you doing for Viktor Chekov?"

But he wouldn't answer her. He only shook his head again.

Before she could press him for more information, she heard the rev of a car engine—which was odd. She hadn't noticed any other traffic passing the alley.

But then she'd been distracted, overwhelmed with her desire for Garek Kozminski.

"What the hell…" Garek murmured, as he heard it, too.

Then the car was there, roaring into the alley. With them both standing against the brick wall, they had no place to go—no way to escape.

The vehicle was certain to crush them…

Chapter 9

Logan hadn't been this angry in a while—probably not since he'd nearly fired Candace. He stared across his desk at her and his brother-in-law and threatened, "I should fire you both."

"For nearly getting killed?" Candace asked.

"Exactly."

Garek snorted. "That makes no sense."

So Logan pointed out what should have been obvious to the two of them. "Who the hell is going to trust a bodyguard to protect them that someone else is already trying to kill?"

"No one's trying to kill me," Garek replied.

But Candace shot him a glance that could have done the job. There was more than anger in her gaze, though. Stacy had obviously been right about the female bodyguard's feelings for her oldest brother.

"I wasn't the only one that car nearly ran over," she reminded him. "You were there, too."

"Lucky for you," Garek said.

Color flushed Candace's face, which was good since she'd been so pale when he had first summoned them to his office. They had had a close call. Even though he hadn't been there, Logan knew—because nothing usually fazed Candace.

She was tough.

Now she was embarrassed. But she ruefully admitted, "You did save my life."

Garek shrugged off her gratitude and turned away from her. But Logan caught his grimace of guilt.

Garek may have claimed the driver hadn't been trying to run him down, but he felt responsible for the attempt. Why? What the hell was really going on?

Apparently Stacy had also been right to worry about her brother. Logan made a mental note to never again doubt his wife. "Lucky for me that you both survived," Logan said. "With franchising the agency, I can't afford to lose any of my team. We're busy as hell right now."

"And don't need the bad publicity," Candace said with a resentful glance at Garek—her gratitude gone.

"There were no reporters there," Garek said. "And it's unlikely any would care about a car that could have just had a stuck gas pedal or something…"

"Or something…" Candace murmured.

Logan sighed. Had he and Stacy acted like that? Bickered like children? They had certainly fought a lot before they'd given in to their feelings for each other.

"We need to get back to work," Logan said. He had meetings with his brothers about the franchise. He had to focus on Payne Protection, but without his bodyguards, there would be no Payne Protection.

But these two weren't just bodyguards; they were family, too.

"You're right," Candace agreed. "You hired me back, but you haven't given me a job yet."

He nodded. "I'll find you something."

But first he wanted to talk to his half brother and learn what Nicholas knew about the attempts on Candace's life. Had they been random? Or was she really in danger?

"You don't have to look for anything," she told me. "I already know what job I'm perfect for."

Garek tensed and began to shake his head—as if he already knew what she was going to say.

Candace leaned forward and implored Logan, "Give *me* the assignment protecting Chekov's daughter…"

Logan rubbed his jaw as he considered her request.

Logan was actually considering it. Garek's heart rate had finally slowed back to normal—or at least as normal as it ever was around Candace—but now it started racing again. Like that car had raced toward them.

He didn't know if it had been instinct or his late father acting as his guardian angel that had had him diving out of the way with Candace wrapped up tightly in his arms. He had saved her that time, but if she took away his assignment, he wouldn't be there to protect her next time.

And he was pretty damn certain there would be a next time. Why?

Had Viktor figured out what Garek was up to? Had Tori warned him? She never stayed angry with her father; she idolized him too much. So was Viktor going after Candace as a warning to Garek?

"Don't even think about it," Garek advised his boss. "I brought you this client. This is my assignment."

"Why?" Candace asked. "We all know it's better if a female bodyguard protects a female subject. This should be my assignment."

Garek shook his head. "Viktor would never agree to an outsider protecting his daughter. He doesn't trust easily."

And Garek needed the mobster to trust him again if he was ever going to find wherever he'd hidden the murder weapon. His safe?

But if Tori had ratted him out, he would have disposed of the gun already. So Garek would have to find other evidence, or somehow compel Chekov to confess.

"I can understand why it's hard to trust some people," Candace said, and she turned and glared at him. All her desire for him was gone now. Maybe almost getting killed had brought her to her senses again—like it had brought him.

He had nearly told her everything in that alley. He'd nearly confessed his assignment wasn't for Viktor Chekov or Payne Protection. His assignment was for the FBI. But if he'd told her the truth, she would insist on sticking beside him. And being too close to him had nearly gotten her killed more than once. He couldn't risk her life—even if it cost him his chance of ever earning her love.

He wasn't above doing whatever necessary to keep her safe. So he asked, "And really—should she be protecting anyone if someone's after her?"

Candace gasped. "Nobody was after me until I went

to Chekov's club. Those attempts have everything to do with him and you."

He couldn't disagree with her. Chekov had to be responsible. "All the more reason you can't have anything to do with this assignment."

Logan had his thumb pressed to his temple. "Okay, enough arguing. You two are giving me a headache."

Better a headache than the heart attack Garek nearly had when that car had come rushing toward them in the alley. He still wasn't certain how they had survived. He must have a guardian angel, which was kind of fitting during the Christmas season. He would have doubted it would be his father, though—except Stacy had claimed the man had been repentant before he'd died. Maybe, in the afterlife, he was trying to make amends for being a lousy father.

"She never even got checked out after that first assault," Garek persisted. "She refused to let Milek take her to the ER. She could have a concussion."

"*I* don't have a headache," she said.

Logan sighed. "He's right. You should have gotten checked out." He pressed the intercom button on his phone. "Nikki, I need you to do something."

"You have an assignment for me?" his sister hopefully asked.

Garek wasn't worried Nikki was getting the job with Chekov. Her brother would never risk *her* safety.

"I need you to take Candace to the ER to get checked out."

"Of course I will," she said. But Garek heard the disappointment in her voice.

"But I'm fine," Candace argued.

Logan pointed at her. "If you want an assignment, you need to be cleared medically first. Go."

Candace jumped up from her chair, glared at Garek again, and then walked out of the office. She slammed the door behind her with such force Logan flinched and Garek jumped. He was on edge now and had been since she had walked into Chekov's club.

"Nikki won't be in danger taking her to the ER?" Logan asked, as if reconsidering the assignment he'd given his sister. "You think someone's really after Candace?"

"Two random attacks?" Garek asked. He shrugged. "Hell, anything's possible in River City." Rus had a long way to go before he cleaned up all the corruption and crime. That was why he needed Garek's help.

"So it is possible someone's after her?" Logan asked. He narrowed his eyes and glared at Garek now. "Is it your fault?"

He sighed. "I honestly don't know. I don't see how…"

How the hell could Chekov have figured out his feelings for Candace when he wasn't even certain of them himself? Sure, he wanted her. He wanted her more than he'd ever wanted any other woman. That desire bordered on desperation. If that car hadn't sped into the alley, he might have taken her there—against the brick wall in the cold.

"I can't give her an assignment if she's in danger," Logan said.

"You have to," Garek said, as it presented the perfect solution. "You have to give her an assignment that's far away from River City." And far away from him.

Logan nodded in agreement. "The only problem will

be getting her to take the assignment without quitting again."

"You have to convince her," Garek said. It was the only way to keep her safe.

"I'm supposed to bring you to the ER," Nikki protested as she pulled her Payne Protection Agency SUV to the curb beside the string of Christmas lights strewn over those bare branches. The lights twinkled even brighter since night had fallen completely now. "Not here."

"I don't need to go to the ER," Candace said. "I'm fine. All I need is my car." And she'd left it here because Garek had insisted on her riding with him back to the Payne Protection office. As if he'd been worried someone might try running her off the road.

She could handle herself. Sure, she hadn't reacted as quickly as he had in the alley. But she would have reacted. She was a bodyguard. She was trained to protect others and herself. She hadn't needed Garek to save her.

But she *had* needed Garek. Physically. Passionately. What the hell was the matter with her? She'd never been one of those silly women who went for the bad boy. She'd always thought those women were ridiculous. Who wanted that kind of trouble in her life? That potential for pain?

Bad boys didn't change. They didn't grow into good men. She never should have been tempted by Garek Kozminski, let alone have given in to that temptation.

"Are you sure you're okay?" Nikki asked, her brown eyes full of concern. She looked like her mother, whereas Candace actually looked more like Nikki's brothers—at least in coloring. Maybe that was why they coddled Nikki and treated Candace like one of the guys.

Garek didn't treat her like that, though. He treated her like she was a woman—a desirable woman. She shook her head, trying to get him out of her mind.

Nikki reached for the SUV shifter. "I'll take you to the emergency room."

"No," Candace said. "Physically, I'm fine."

Nikki turned to her, studying her across the console. "So someone's trying to kill you—that affects even someone like you?"

Candace smiled. "Someone like me?"

"You're like Wonder Woman or something," Nikki replied. "You're tough."

The younger woman's admiration warmed Candace's heart. But it was unwarranted.

"Physically, I'm tough," Candace clarified. Then she sighed and added, "It's not the attempts on my life that have shaken me up."

Nikki wiggled a dark brow and asked, "Garek Kozminski?"

She wasn't too proud to admit it. "Yeah…"

"You agree with Stacy then?" Nikki asked. "He's gone back to his old life?"

He had all but admitted it to her when he'd said he was in too deep with Chekov. Did he gamble? How was he in too deep? And should she even try to help him out?

Yet her lips tingled from their passionate kisses. And she knew she would try. But first she had to find out exactly how he was in too deep.

"I don't know for certain," she said. But she intended to find out.

"But you're worried he has?"

She nodded.

Nikki sighed. "I don't think any man is worth the potential heartache. How can you ever trust one?"

Especially a man like Garek, who'd had a colorful past and was keeping secrets again. Candace would be crazy to trust him.

But then she saw where Nikki's attention had gone. FBI Special Agent Nicholas Rus had pulled in front of them and alighted from his Bureau SUV.

Nikki blinked. "Even my father…"

Poor Nikki. She would never get over her father's betrayal even though her mother had made peace with it long ago—before Nikki had been conceived.

Candace had no words of wisdom to offer Nikki. She was hardly an expert where trust was concerned. She opened the passenger's door and stepped onto the sidewalk. "Thanks for bringing me back to my car."

Nikki nodded and then drove off once Candace closed the door. She had rarely said more than a couple of words to the brother she hadn't known she had.

"Hope she didn't rush off my account," Rus said as he watched the SUV drive away.

"I'm sorry," Candace said. It wasn't his fault he was too painful a reminder to his half sister.

He shrugged. "She'll get over it…" He sighed and added, "Never."

"Yeah, probably not," she agreed. "I'm surprised you showed up here. An attempted hit-and-run isn't much of a crime for an FBI special agent to investigate."

"You brought your complaint to me earlier today," he reminded her.

"I shouldn't have wasted your time with it either," she said.

He gestured toward the crime scene tape across the

alley. "There was another attempt, so it obviously wasn't a waste of time. Did you see the driver?"

She shook her head. "He was wearing a mask—like the guy was wearing the night before."

"So you're pretty sure it's the same guy?"

She shook her head. "Not at all. It could have been a similar mask and a different guy."

Chekov had a lot of muscle working for him. So why had he needed Garek as a bodyguard? He wouldn't have needed him for protection. Nobody had ever been able to touch Chekov—physically or legally.

Agent Rus drew a folder out of the inside of his overcoat and flipped it open to some mug shots. "Could it have been any of these guys?"

All guys with big heads and no necks. "It could have been all of them. Who are they?"

"Guys you arrested who've been recently let out on parole. They all potentially have an ax to grind with you."

She laughed at his hypocrisy. "You don't think they were reformed in jail like everyone—including you— believes Garek Kozminski was?"

"This has nothing to do with Garek Kozminski."

"This has everything to do with Garek Kozminski," she said. Until she'd gotten involved with him, nobody had ever tried to kill her—at least not outside of a war zone or in order to get to the subject she was protecting.

"Here's a whole gallery of suspects," Rus said. "Why is it so hard for you to believe one of them would come after you?"

"This has nothing to do with me," she insisted. Or someone would have tried to kill her before. "This has everything to do with Viktor Chekov."

Rus glanced around—almost as if he was afraid someone might have overheard her accusation. "You have to be careful, Candace," he warned her again. "Chekov isn't someone you want to go after without evidence…"

She would find the evidence—even if she had to do it alone.

Then he added, "Or an army."

She'd been part of an army before. But most of the time it had taken only one soldier to take out the enemy. She was no sniper but she was smart. Viktor Chekov would not take her out before she was able to take him down.

Chapter 10

Garek clicked off his cell phone and sighed. He hadn't needed Agent Rus's warning to know Candace wasn't about to give up and stop interfering. After having her life threatened—not once but twice—someone else might have taken the warning and backed off.

But not Candace.

Didn't she have any idea how much danger she was in? That car could have killed them both and probably would have had he not been able to move as quickly as he had. And if he hadn't gone after her when she'd left the club the night before…

He shuddered to think what might have happened to her. Sure, she was tough. But anyone could be taken by surprise—as she had been that night.

He drew in a steadying breath before pushing open the door to Viktor's office at the club. But that breath whooshed out when a fist slammed into his stomach. He doubled over in pain. "What the hell…"

When the big man swung again, Garek was ready—catapulting himself at him and knocking him to the floor. The first thing he looked for were the marks Candace had put on her attacker. But this man's neck bore no scratches—just stubble. The guy bucked him off just as two other men grabbed him. Another fist slugged him—this one belonged to Viktor.

It didn't hurt as badly as the first blow had. But he doubled over again and tugged free of the men who held him. Neither of those two had marks on their necks either. These were Viktor's usual guys—the closest of his *family* since the man killed Tori's boyfriend. If Viktor had sent someone after Candace, it would have been one of them.

Or himself…

"What the hell's wrong with you?" Garek asked. "You already put me through this gang beat down weeks ago." He must have discovered Garek was working for Rus. But if Chekov had, he probably would have done more than beat him.

Viktor laughed. "Gang? You call my *family* a gang?"

It was certainly no family Garek would want to be part of. He shrugged off his comment. "I was just trying to be funny."

"Oh, yeah, you're a funny guy," Viktor agreed. "You ask me for this job—to hire your brother-in-law's business to protect my daughter. You promise me that you're the only one who can protect her—then you pawn her protection off on your brother. What the hell's wrong with *you*?"

Garek cursed. "I trust my brother. I can't say the same for you or any of your *men*."

"What do you mean?"

"Your right-hand man was killed," Garek said—as if Chekov would have needed the reminder. "That's why I worried about Tori. Anyone gets close to you, they wind up dead."

Probably at Viktor's hand—because he'd seen something they'd done—maybe an involvement with his daughter—as a betrayal.

"Then I get close to you," he continued, "and suddenly someone's trying to kill *me*."

Viktor laughed. "This was hardly a beating. You've gotten soft, Garek."

"Someone tried running me down earlier today," he said. Of course he probably hadn't been the target—unless Viktor already believed he'd betrayed him. "And did you see my brother today? Someone really roughed him up last night."

"You and your brother both?" The color left Viktor's face. Was he shocked the attacks had happened or shocked they had survived them?

"Yeah." And Candace. But he didn't want to bring her to Viktor's attention—if she already wasn't. Could Rus be right? Could that attack in the alley have been some guy she arrested years ago?

Maybe even today—the car—that could have been someone else, too. What the hell was really going on?

And if Candace was in danger on her own—he needed to be with her, not putting her in even more danger with his involvement with Chekov. His heart wrenched as if torn in two. He didn't want to be the one who'd put her in danger; he wanted to be the one to protect her.

"Why would someone go after you and your brother?" Viktor asked. "Are the two of you into something—have you crossed someone?"

They had crossed a lot of someones when they'd helped protect the Paynes a year ago. But most of those someones hadn't survived the firefights. Or they were in such high-security prisons they wouldn't be able to get so much as a postcard to the outside.

"I don't think it's about us," Garek replied. "I think it's about you."

"Why?" Viktor scoffed. "You're not close to me."

"We're close to Tori—we've been protecting her," he pointed out. "Someone could be trying to get me and Milek out of the way, so they can get to Tori."

Now color flushed Viktor's face a mottled red, and rage burned in his dark eyes. "Nobody better hurt her," he threatened. "Or I'll tear them apart."

Garek didn't doubt him.

Then Viktor swung his arm around, encompassing all the men in the room. "And I'll tear apart anyone who lets her get hurt."

Garek restrained an involuntary shudder. He didn't believe Tori was in danger—probably even if Viktor discovered she was the one who'd gone to the FBI about his killing Alexander Polinsky. But Garek still intended to make damn certain she stayed safe. He didn't want to incur Viktor's wrath.

But what about Viktor? How could he be so worried about someone else hurting her after he already had? He was the man who'd hurt her most when he'd killed her lover. Shouldn't he at least confess to killing Polinsky in order to make amends to her? Or explain why he'd done it?

He'd heard that Alexander had been a bit of a playboy. Maybe he'd cheated on Tori, and Victor had killed him because of that betrayal.

Garek had an opening now to get Viktor to talk. And while they'd beat the hell out of him when he'd walked into the office, for the first time they hadn't checked him for a wire. There was the risk they might next time— when he was actually wearing one. But even if he found the murder weapon, it didn't put the gun in Viktor's hand that night.

Only Viktor could do that.

He had to get him to talk and soon—before anyone else got hurt.

Candace hadn't intended to return to the club. But it was where it had begun; it was from here someone had followed and attacked her.

Why?

She walked in with the intention of talking to Viktor Chekov himself—of asking him for his security footage from the night before. But, even this near closing time, the club was crowded. Nobody at the bar would ask for more than her drink order. When she demanded to speak to the owner, they walked away from her.

So she moved instead toward the roped-off table where Tori Chekov sat. She didn't watch the crowd or move with the music. Her only interest appeared to be in her phone until she glanced up and saw Candace. Recognition flashed in her dark eyes.

Milek stood up. His face was swollen and bruised. Concern filled her. "What happened to you?"

"I got involved in something that was none of my business," he told her, and his voice was colder than she'd ever heard it—than she'd thought Milek capable of being. "You need to leave, Candace."

"I want to talk to Chekov," she said.

"That's not possible," another man answered. He was big—bigger than Milek—and obviously armed, his gun too big for his holster.

She glanced at his neck, but he had no scratches. This wasn't the man who'd attacked her. What about Chekov's other men? It could have been any of them, and she suspected he had several in his employ.

"Where's Garek?" she asked.

The woman snorted—something Candace wouldn't have thought such a princess type capable of doing.

She turned toward her. "What?"

"Chasing after him like you are is very unattractive," the woman told her.

No one had ever called Candace beautiful—except Garek. He had kept saying it that night—as he'd undressed her, as he'd made love to her. And after as he'd held her...until he'd fallen asleep. Then she'd slipped away from him—because she hadn't been able to believe him. To believe in what had happened between them.

But then she'd been right to leave—since he had proved to still be the man she'd been afraid he was.

But what if she hadn't left that night? Would he be working for Chekov? Was this all her fault?

Candace shrugged. She could have told the woman Garek was the one who'd been chasing after her—that he had chased her for a year before finally catching her. That even last night he'd let himself into her apartment...

But she suspected while Garek wasn't in love with

Chekov's daughter, the same might not be true of Tori. Being around him again might have rekindled her teenage crush on him. Because she was acting almost proprietary.

Candace recognized the woman's attitude because she felt that way herself—possessive of Garek Kozminski. It was crazy. Garek Kozminski wasn't the kind of man that any woman would ever possess. He would belong to no one. The most a woman would get from him was a night like Candace had had—a magical, wondrous night of unsurpassed pleasure.

That was another reason she had slipped out that night—so she wouldn't expect more from him than he was willing or able to give. No. Nothing would have changed if she'd stayed.

"I need to talk to him," Candace persisted. If anyone could get Chekov to turn over the security footage, he could. She needed to see it—to see if any of his men had followed her out. Or maybe Rus was right and one of those mug shots he'd shown her had followed her.

As if thoroughly disgusted with her, Tori snorted again. Then she said, "You're embarrassing yourself."

"Probably," Candace acknowledged. "But it won't be the first time. Fortunately no one's ever died of humiliation."

"Maybe not but plenty of them have died of stupidity," a deep voice murmured.

Her skin tingled in reaction to Garek's closeness. But then he was grasping her arm and tugging her through the crowd.

"What are you doing?" she asked, as she tried to wriggle free of him.

"What the hell are you doing?" he asked. "Are you *trying* to get yourself killed?"

She tried to dig her heels into the floor. But it was concrete, so she caught no traction. She wasn't able to slow him down as he effortlessly pulled her along behind him.

"No," she replied. "I'm trying to find out who's trying to kill me. I need the security footage from last night."

"Do you have a search warrant?" he asked. "Oh, that's right. You're not a cop anymore. Seems like you've forgotten."

"I haven't forgotten how to investigate a crime," she said, "which is what I intend to do."

"This isn't your case," Garek said. "It's Rus's. Let him handle the investigation."

So he knew she'd gone to the FBI agent. How? Had Rus questioned him or colluded with him?

"Do you think he'll be able to get a search warrant for the security footage?" she asked.

She was surprised when he answered honestly, "No."

"Then let me see it," she said. "If Chekov has nothing to hide…"

He let out a bitter chuckle and flinched. His hand skimmed over his stomach, and she realized he'd been hit. Milek wasn't the only one who'd been roughed up. What the hell were the Kozminskis involved in?

"Chekov doesn't have anything to hide about *you*," he said. "He doesn't even know you exist."

She doubted that—since his daughter seemed to know and pity her. And since she was pretty sure the man who'd followed her from the club and attacked her in the alley probably worked for Chekov. But then most of the criminals in River City worked for him.

"And we're going to keep it that way," Garek said as he continued tugging her through the crowd toward the exit.

"You can't throw me out of here," she said. "I haven't done anything wrong."

"We reserve the right to refuse anyone's business," he said, and he pointed to the sign in the lobby proclaiming exactly that.

She tugged free of his grasp before he could toss her onto the street. The two valets in the lobby stared at them—until Garek glared back. Then they quickly stepped outside into the cold.

"We," she repeated what he'd said. "You are working for Chekov."

"I'm on assignment," he said.

"You admitted to me that you're in too deep," she reminded him.

He shrugged. "And that surprises you? You're the one who kept warning Logan that I hadn't changed—that I was a criminal and a killer." He flinched again, but she suspected it had nothing to do with whatever injuries he had and everything to do with what she used to say about him.

She reached out to him instinctively, wanting to soothe his pain—his physical ones and whatever emotional ones she might have inflicted. It had been wrong and out of character for her to act like she had with him. She was never judgmental and unforgiving—until him.

But he caught the hand she reached toward him before she could touch him. "You were right about me," he said. "Doesn't that make you happy?"

It made her sick with disappointment. And it confused her—because if he truly was the man she'd worried he was, she doubted he would have admitted it. Was he lying to her like he'd lied to Logan about loving Tori Chekov?

Why?

"But that night…" That night had changed everything, had made her want to believe in him, to trust him.

"It was a mistake," he said. "We both know that."

Tears stung her eyes, but she blinked them back and lifted her chin. She could take a hit, too. She certainly had over the years.

He continued, "And your coming here was a mistake. You need to leave and never come back."

"But I need to find out who attacked me."

"Leave that investigation to Rus," he said. "And leave me alone." He released her hand then and opened the door.

A blast of cold air slapped her in the face and brought her to her senses. She had made a fool of herself— letting herself believe Stacy was right, that he had cared about her.

"I'll leave you alone," she promised. "But you need to stay the hell away from me, too."

"I will," he said.

As she passed by him to step out the door, she heard him murmur, "I have to…"

She stopped in front of him and met his gaze. His gray eyes were dark with emotions, but she could read none of them. She couldn't read him. She could only feel her own attraction to him, in her quickening pulse, in the tingling in her body. Her breath escaped in a gasp, but all she said was, "Goodbye." Then she walked away.

This time she was ready when she left, though—her

hand on her gun. If anyone tried to attack her again, she would protect herself. Physically.

She hadn't been able to protect herself emotionally though. Garek Kozminski had gotten to her—had broken her heart before she'd even realized he had stolen it. She had been right about him; he was a thief.

Milek swallowed hard as he stared down the barrel of the gun. Last night he'd been beaten nearly to death. Tonight he nearly got shot.

"What the hell are you doing following me?" Candace asked. Even though she'd identified him, she hadn't put away her weapon. She held it on him as they stood near where she'd parked her car.

It was a couple blocks down the street from the club but nowhere near the alley where she'd been attacked. She'd been fortunate enough to find a space near the more populated area of the city, where Christmas lights and wreaths decorated the lampposts.

He knew she had never trusted Garek, but she hadn't given him the hard time she'd given his brother. "What do you think I'm doing?" he asked.

"I don't know," she said. "Do you work for Chekov, too?"

Milek wanted nothing to do with the mobster. But he wasn't going to let his brother get himself killed either.

"I'm helping Garek," he said. "He asked me to protect you." He'd also yelled at him for letting her talk to Tori. But Milek had pointed out how hard it was to stop Candace from doing what she wanted.

"By following me?"

"By making sure nobody hurts you again."

Her lashes fluttered as she blinked. She wasn't flirting, though. She wouldn't even look at him now. And he realized he was too late. Somebody had already hurt her. Garek.

"What is he doing?" she asked. "Why would he get involved with Chekov again?"

Even though he knew, Milek only shrugged. But the sight of her—so close to tears—got to him, and he added, "Everything isn't always what it seems."

Especially when it came to his brother. Garek acted as if nothing bothered him and as if he cared about nobody and nothing. But he had and would sacrifice everything for those he loved. Milek suspected Garek loved Candace, or he wouldn't be so worried about her. But he was worried because of Viktor's threat. If the mobster figured out Garek was trying to get evidence against him, he would go after everyone Garek loved. Maybe he was already going after Candace as a warning for Garek to not betray him.

But if he really wanted to make sure Garek wouldn't betray him, he might just eliminate the threat. He might kill Garek before he ever got the chance to discover the evidence he needed to put Chekov away.

"You're worried," Candace said, and finally she holstered her weapon.

Milek nodded. "He's playing a dangerous game with dangerous people."

She blinked again, but the hint of tears she fought wasn't for herself. These were for his brother. "Protect *him*," she said. "I can protect myself."

He would have argued Garek could protect himself, too. But with this assignment, he wasn't so certain. It was just too dangerous…

Chapter 11

Anger coursed through Garek. That damn woman was so stubborn—she was going to get herself killed for certain. He was furious she'd shown up at the club again. And he was even more furious she'd caught Milek following her and sent him away.

She needed protection. She needed *him*.

But Garek had vowed to stay away from her. So after seeing Tori back to her father's heavily protected estate, he'd headed right home—to the apartment he'd begun to resent. It was all white trim and beige walls—colorless and impersonal. He wanted to move into the house he'd bought with its richly painted walls and ornate trim. He wanted to move on with his life.

But he couldn't do that until he wrapped up this assignment—until he put Chekov away. Even after that was done, he doubted he would get another chance with

Candace. He never should have told her that night had been a mistake. He'd hurt her. Then he'd convinced her that she'd been right about him, so she would never trust him now. She would certainly never love him.

Distracted, as always, by thoughts of her, he nearly missed it when he slid the key in the lock. Usually he would have noticed the gouges right away—the telltale sign someone had picked his lock. He shook his head and murmured, "Amateur..."

Before he'd turned double digits, Garek had been able to pick a lock without leaving a single mark on it. What the hell had this person used? An ax? Patek Kozminski would have been horrified. But then his father hadn't tolerated incompetence—at least not in his sons. He had treated Stacy like a princess while Milek and Garek had been his lackeys—thieves in training.

No wonder Candace hadn't believed he could change— not when he'd been raised a thief. After his release from jail, he'd kept his skills honed breaking into museums and businesses. But that had been at their request—for him to test their security systems.

That was another reason Logan had hired him and Milek; they had brought in clients of their own. But Garek had made Logan keep that information from Candace. He'd wanted her to discover for herself the man he'd become—not have someone else tell her.

He had ruined any chance of that now. When he'd told her he was in too deep, he had made her think the worst of him again. But that was for the best—for her. For her safety...

He needed to keep her out of danger—because danger was all around him. As he unlocked and pushed open his apartment door, he heard the creak of floorboards moving beneath a person's weight. Whoever had broken into his apartment was still there.

He drew his weapon from his holster and stepped inside with his gun drawn and ready to fire.

Candace had found the evidence she'd needed to prove to herself and everyone else Garek Kozminski was still a thief. He hadn't stolen only her heart.

He must have stolen plenty of other things because he'd had the opportunity. She'd found tubes of plans— building plans, security plans—for museums and art galleries not just in River City or even America but all around the world.

She hadn't found what he might have stolen from those places. Those things had probably already been fenced. Or maybe he'd been hired to steal them for someone else. Was that what Chekov had really hired Garek to do?

Steal something?

She turned back to the plans—trying to figure out which place might be his next target. Most of the plans looked old, though; some dated from years ago. In addition to the dates, there were notes on them—pointing out the weaknesses in the security system. That must have been how he'd figured out where to break in. But then she noticed along with the weaknesses, there were recommendations on how to eliminate them.

And she remembered that strange comment Milek had made about his brother; everything wasn't always what it seemed. Garek Kozminski certainly wasn't.

"So which place do you think I'm hitting for Chekov?" a deep voice asked.

She shouldn't have been surprised he'd caught her. He

always moved so silently that, of course, she hadn't heard him come in. She turned to find him leaning against his bedroom doorjamb, his gun in his hand. He had heard her or maybe he'd seen the signs of her sloppy lock picking. But the barrel of his weapon was pointed down, at the hardwood floor, instead of at her.

"These plans are old," she said as she reached for them. The gun was still pointed at the floor, but her hands shook as she rolled up the papers. Maybe that was because of where she was, though.

In his bedroom…

It had just dawned on her that was where he'd caught her—after he'd told her to leave him alone. He probably thought she was stalking him.

And maybe she was.

"Doesn't mean I still couldn't use them," he said.

"After you recommended how they could improve their security systems, I doubt you could break in again."

He chuckled. "Oh, *I* could…" He chuckled again. "*You*, however, could not."

"I got in here," she said and waited for him to yell at her about it.

He shrugged. "I don't have anything I want to protect. A child could break in here." He snorted. "From the looks of the lock, I thought a child had."

She wasn't too proud to admit, "I don't have your skills for breaking and entering."

He sighed. "Fortunately for you, you weren't raised to be a thief."

And for the first time she realized how hard it must have been for him being born a Kozminski. He'd been expected to become a thief; he hadn't been given the choice to be what he'd wanted.

"No, I wasn't."

"What did your parents want you to be?" he asked.

She shrugged. "Whatever I wanted." They hadn't had any expectations for her.

"I don't really know anything about your family," he said.

Whereas everyone knew everything about his family. The Kozminskis were River City legend.

She shrugged. "Nothing much to tell. My dad is an army man. My mom a former beauty queen and housewife. She follows him to every base he gets assigned."

"So did you," he said. "That must have been hard for you—moving all the time."

She'd felt sorry for herself a time or two, but she shook her head now, disgusted with herself. She'd had no idea how hard a childhood could really be. Garek hadn't even had one.

"The moving wasn't that hard," she said. "It was my mom putting me in pageants that was hard."

She waited for him to laugh—like every other man she'd told that to had laughed at the ridiculous idea of her being in beauty contests. Garek must have been too pissed at her for breaking in—especially after he'd told her to leave him alone—to find any humor in her admission.

"I didn't see any trophies in your place," he said instead.

She laughed now. "That's because I never won."

"I find that hard to believe," he said. And finally he holstered his weapon and stepped away from the doorway.

Even though the gun had been put away, she was still shaking. Actually, she was shaking more because of the way he was looking at her—like he had looked at her that night, as if she was beautiful.

"I guess I haven't been the only one who has struggled to see the truth about the other," she said. While she'd thought he was a criminal, he thought she had been pretty enough to win a beauty contest.

"What do you think the truth is?" Garek asked.

She quoted his brother. "That everything isn't always what it seems."

"Why are you here?" He stepped even closer, so close she felt the heat of his body. "Why were you so desperate to get inside that you picked the lock?"

Heat rushed to her face. He must have thought she was stalking him. "I know you told me to leave you alone…"

He nodded and acknowledged, "I did say that…"

"And you said you'd leave me alone."

"I said that, too." He reached for her, his hands closing around her shoulders. "And I meant it…"

She swallowed, trying to force down her embarrassment. "So I should leave you alone…" She hadn't found what she'd thought she would find. But maybe she'd found what she had needed to find.

He shook his head. "I told you to leave me alone and said I would leave you alone," he reiterated. "But even as I was saying it, I knew it wasn't possible."

Her heart began to pound heavily and quickly in her chest. "Why not?"

"Because of this…" His hands moved from her shoulders to her face, which he held while he lowered his head and kissed her deeply. Passionately.

His lips moved over hers, his teeth nipping gently until she opened her mouth. Then he slid his tongue deep; it moved sensually over hers. He pulled back, panting for breath. "Because I want you…"

She wanted him, too. It was crazy. She still couldn't trust him. Even if he had been legit in the past, he was working for a mobster now and by his own admission was in deep. She needed to leave him alone like she'd promised she would.

But she couldn't leave. *She* was in too deep.

She wanted to know if she'd romanticized her memories of that night—if she was remembering it—and them—as more than they'd been. So she reached for him. Her hands cupping his jaw, she pulled his mouth down to hers. And she kissed him with all the passion burning inside her. She nipped at his lips and slipped her tongue inside his mouth.

He groaned. Then he was lifting her—as easily as he had that night in the alley—as easily as if she were one of those petite, girly girls she'd always secretly wished she'd been. With him, she felt like that; she felt feminine.

He laid her on the mattress, atop the plans she hadn't rolled up yet. Then he pulled off his coat and his holster and gun. He dropped them beside the bed. But he wasn't moving quickly enough for Candace.

She reached out and grabbed his belt, tugging it loose. But he caught her hand when her fingers touched the zipper tab. Had he changed his mind? Didn't he want her?

But then he turned his attention to undressing her. He removed her holster, then pulled her sweater up and over her head. A gasp of breath slipped through his lips, and he murmured, "Red satin…"

"It's Christmastime," she explained. And she liked red. She also liked silky things against her skin.

She liked his fingertips, too, as they glided along her

collarbone then over the swells of her breasts. He pushed the cups down to tease her nipples.

She shifted on the bed and moaned as tension built inside her body. She needed him. Now.

But he continued to tease her, with his lips and his tongue stroking over her nipples. He unsnapped, unzipped and pushed down her jeans. And again he murmured, "Red satin…"

She reached for the clasp on his pants again. This time he let her lower the zipper and release his pulsing erection. He groaned as her fingers skimmed over him.

He tugged off his shirt, revealing his muscular chest and washboard abs and bruises. She gasped and intended to ask about those bruises.

But when she opened her mouth, he leaned down and kissed her like he always kissed her—with such passion—that she couldn't think. She could only feel. She stroked her tongue along his. Her questions would keep for later; she needed him now.

He must have needed her, too. He kicked off his pants and joined her on top of those rustling plans. His body covered hers, like it had that night on the couch in her apartment. She loved the weight of him on top of her. But she really wanted him inside her.

She nipped at his shoulder and then the side of his neck. She felt his pulse leap beneath her lips. Then his mouth covered hers, and he kissed her like she wanted him to make love to her—his tongue thrusting inside her mouth. He kissed her deeply. And as he kissed her, he removed her bra and her panties. Her legs tangled with his, and she thrust up and pushed against his erection.

But he was in no hurry—not like she was. He took his time with her, with her mouth, and then he moved his lips down her body. He kissed her shoulders and then her breasts.

She writhed beneath him as the tension in her body drove her to madness. She wanted to drive him crazy, too. So she kissed him everywhere she could reach—his shoulder, his arm, his chest...

And she reached between their bodies, sliding her hand up and down his shaft. As if to reciprocate he slid his finger inside her, in and out, while his thumb teased her most sensitive spot. She screamed his name as she came apart.

Then he was inside her, filling her. She locked her legs around his waist and bucked up, knocking him to his side. They rolled across the plans until she was on top. And with the madness driving her, she rode him as he stroked her breasts. An orgasm rippled through her, overwhelming her with pleasure—with ecstasy. She screamed his name.

He grasped her hips, moving her faster as he thrust deeper. She came again. Then he joined her, his body tensing before filling hers.

She hadn't imagined that night, nor had her memories of it exaggerated what had happened. It had been as wild and wonderful as she remembered.

Maybe even more so...

He pulled her down on top of him, clasping her naked body against his as he stayed inside her. He clasped his arms around her, holding tightly, as if he didn't intend to let her get away again.

Or as if he intended to protect her. He could protect her from danger; he had saved her life twice. But could he protect himself from danger?

Her heart pounded as frantically as it had when they'd made love—as fear for his safety overwhelmed her.

Garek would need to protect himself because he was undoubtedly in danger. Viktor Chekov's right-hand man had been murdered just weeks ago. If Garek got any closer to the mobster, he might be next.

Nicholas Rus stared down at the body lying atop the steel table in the morgue. The guy's throat bore deep scratches. But those wounds hadn't killed him. The hole in his chest had done that.

The bullet had already been removed and rushed to the FBI lab. Nicholas had to know who'd killed him and with what weapon. He had to know if the man who'd attacked Candace Baker had anything to do with Viktor Chekov.

This was the man who'd grabbed Candace in the alley. Had he intended to kill her or only hurt her? And on whose orders?

His cell rang, startling Nick. He hadn't realized he'd have reception in the morgue. He clicked the talk button. "Agent Rus."

"Nicholas?"

"Chief Lynch." While Nick was on assignment in River City, the Chicago Bureau chief was still his boss. He'd had to approve the rush order for ballistics.

"I got the results."

The chief must have rushed them even more than Nicholas had thought possible.

"It's the same gun," Lynch continued, "the one that killed the man your witness says Chekov shot."

Nick didn't know if he should curse or celebrate. The gun was still in play—not disposed of as he'd feared.

But Chekov had used it to kill the man who'd tried to kill Candace. What did that mean?

Was he tying up loose ends? He had no looser ends than Garek and even his own daughter.

"This is big, Nicholas. How are you handling the investigation without more agents?" Lynch asked. "I'll send Dalton Reyes up to help."

Reyes was the Bureau's expert on organized crime. A former gang member, the guy could handle himself undercover. But there had been no time to bring him in.

"Chekov wouldn't have trusted some guy off the street," Nick explained, "no matter what background we established for Reyes."

"So you don't have an agent on the inside?"

"I have someone undercover on the inside," Nick admitted. But he wasn't an agent.

"How'd you get someone inside so quickly?"

"It's someone who used to work for Chekov, someone who once dated his daughter."

Lynch whistled. "Sounds like he might be Chekov's next victim."

Nicholas was already worried that might be the case.

"Let me know if you need Dalton," Lynch said. "I'll send him up to help."

Nick thanked his boss before hanging up. He appreciated the offer. But as he stared down at the man on the slab, he worried he'd already waited too long to accept help. And he might have cost Garek Kozminski his life.

Chapter 12

Cold penetrated Garek's coat and flesh, chilling him to the bone. Just a short while ago, he'd been warm. Hell, he'd been hot—driving deep inside Candace's body. He had made love to her again and again. Then he'd held her, tightly, so she wouldn't slip away from him like she had that first night.

He wouldn't lose her like he'd worried he had. But then he had wound up having to leave her. She hadn't awakened when his cell rang or when he loosened his hold on her and slipped from the bed.

"Why'd you summon me here?" Garek asked as he glanced around the morgue and shuddered. He'd rather have met him in an alley again. But nobody was likely to witness them together here.

And it had been a summons—not a request. He had been given no opportunity to refuse. But Rus had promised there was a police detail watching his place, watching Candace to make sure she stayed safe even after he'd left her. Without that promise, Garek would have refused to leave her—no matter how pissed Rus might have been.

"I need you to identify a body," the FBI agent replied. He pointed to the one lying on the morgue slab.

Garek stared at the body. The guy was big, his skin winter pale but for a profusion of tattoos. He shrugged. "I don't know." He looked like a lot of hired muscle.

"Could he be the guy you saw running out of the alley that night? Or the one who tried running you over?"

Garek peered more closely at the body. And he noticed the scratches. Milek had said Candace had left her mark on the guy. He cursed. Not that he was sad the guy was dead. But now that he was dead, he wouldn't be able to explain why he'd tried killing Candace.

Had it been personal, like Rus had thought? Someone she'd arrested when she'd been a cop. Or had someone hired him to hurt Candace?

"How'd he die?" he asked. In addition to the tattoos, there were bruises. There was also a hole in his chest, which could have been caused by a bullet or a knife. Due to the autopsy incisions, Garek couldn't tell which.

"Shot…"

Garek shivered. "I know it's too soon to tell but could it have been the same gun…"

"It was," Rus replied. "I rushed the ballistics."

Garek cursed.

"This is good news," Rus said, although he didn't sound all that thrilled either. "The gun is still out there. It killed Candace's attacker."

"But who is this guy?" Garek asked. "I don't recognize him."

"So you don't think he works for Chekov?"

Garek shrugged. "I don't know everyone who works for Chekov. He could have worked for him. But why would Chekov kill him?"

"You know if Viktor Chekov is unsatisfied with your work, you don't get a pink slip," Rus said. "You get a toe tag."

Garek suspected there was more to Tori's boyfriend's death than Viktor's dissatisfaction with Alexander Polinsky's work. He must have done something else to piss off his boss. Or someone else...

Garek must have pissed him off, too. But instead of going after him, Chekov had sent this goon after Candace. Then he'd killed him. Because the man had failed? Or because Viktor had personally decided to go after her?

"You have to be extra careful," Rus said. He narrowed his eyes and studied Garek as if trying to see inside his mind. "You can't afford any distractions."

Garek sighed; maybe the man had seen inside his mind. There was usually only one thing on it. "Like Candace?"

"She can't afford for you to be distracted either," Rus said.

No, she couldn't. Because if Viktor had decided to go after Candace, it would be hard to save her. Making love with her—while wonderful—had been a mistake. He needed to be totally focused now—for her sake as much as his. Or they would both wind up, like her attacker, in the morgue.

Candace had been summoned to the office, Logan's office. When her cell rang, she'd hurriedly answered it—afraid it might wake Garek. She need not have worried. He was already gone.

When had he left? And where had he gone?

He'd left no note. No explanation.

Had he done it out of vengeance? Getting her back for her leaving while he'd been sleeping that first night they'd spent together?

She hadn't thought there would be another night. Apparently there shouldn't have been. She'd just made a fool of herself again—falling for a man who had no respect for her.

But he had had desire. He'd made love to her greedily but also generously. He'd given her even more pleasure than he'd taken. So he cared about her—he had to.

Logan snapped his fingers. "What's the matter? Didn't you get any sleep last night?"

Sleep had been the problem. If she'd stayed awake, she would have known why Garek had left and where he'd gone. To Chekov?

What the hell did Chekov want Garek to do for him? Break into one of those museums or art galleries? Was he doing that now?

"I'm fine," she said.

"You didn't go to the ER like I told you to," he said.

Since HIPAA laws prevented him from looking at her medical records, Nikki must have given her up. Candace couldn't blame her, though; she knew how much the girl hated secrets and lies.

"I'm fine," she repeated.

"No more attempts on your life?"

She shook her head. Not her life. Just her heart…

For a year Garek had flirted with her and propositioned her. She didn't know if he'd begun to steal her heart then or if it had happened that first night she'd given in to her attraction to him.

She sighed.

"That disappoints you?" he asked.

She was disappointed in herself—because she'd let her attraction to Garek distract her. Someone had tried to kill her; she needed to find out who and why and how it was related to Garek and Viktor Chekov.

"It disappoints me that I haven't found out who attacked me."

He slid a photo across his desk. She picked it up and stared at it. The man's face had been covered with the mask when he'd attacked her, so she didn't recognize the meaty features. She recognized the scratches on his neck, though; she had done that. Fortunately, she'd let her nails grow the two weeks she'd been off work. She'd even treated herself to a manicure.

"That's him," she said. "Who is he and what happened to him?"

Was that where Garek had gone? To take care of this man?

"Donald Doornbos."

She shrugged. The name meant nothing to her. "Known associates?"

Logan chuckled. "You'd have to ask Agent Rus. He just sent this over to see if you could identify the man."

"He's my attacker," she said. "But I've never seen him before that night."

"You didn't arrest him when you were a cop?"

"Rus already knows I didn't." Or he would have called her down to River City PD.

Logan took the photo back from her. "Yeah..."

"So does he work for Viktor Chekov?"

"I don't know," Logan said. "Rus didn't say."

"What did he say?"

"Not much," Logan replied. And a muscle twitched along his jaw, indicating his irritation. He didn't like it any more than she did that he didn't know what was going on.

"Cause of death?"

"Gunshot wound."

"Who shot him?" Garek? Had it been in self-defense? Or revenge? This was probably the same man who'd tried to run them down in the alley.

"His body was found in a parking lot."

"Of Chekov's club?"

Logan shook his head. "No."

"He could have been killed there or at Chekov's estate and his body dumped elsewhere." Everyone assumed that was what had happened with Chekov's previous employee—Alexander Polinsky. Or at least that was what the officers she still knew on the force had told her.

"This is Rus's investigation," Logan said. "Not yours."

She opened her mouth to argue. But he held up his hand and continued, "You're a bodyguard now. Not a cop."

She'd been hearing this a lot lately. She liked protecting people and hadn't missed being a cop—until now.

"And I have an assignment for you."

"I thought you wanted to make sure I was cleared medically before you gave me an assignment?"

That muscle twitched again with irritation. This time she had no doubt it was with her. "You've been telling me that you're fine," he said, tossing her words back at her. "So you're fine to take an assignment."

"You're going to put me on Chekov's daughter's protection duty," she said. It was the only assignment she wanted, so she could find out what the hell was going on with Garek and Viktor Chekov.

"No," he replied. "You've only been off a couple of weeks, so you can't have forgotten I'm the boss. I give out the assignments."

She arched a brow in skepticism. "Really? Didn't Garek bring you Chekov as a client?"

Logan nodded. "He's brought in other clients, as well."

The museums and art galleries.

"Why didn't you tell me that before?" When she'd criticized his hiring the Kozminskis.

"Garek didn't want me to," Logan said.

He had wanted her to think the worst of him. Why? Just for his amusement?

"And the clients *Garek* brings Payne Protection want to work with *Garek*," Logan said. "I have an assignment for you. It's in Chicago—"

She shook her head. "No."

"You didn't even let me finish."

"You don't need to," she said. "This isn't a legit assignment. You just want me out of town." Probably at Garek's request.

He sighed and rubbed his forehead. Apparently his headache had returned. "You're making me regret hiring you back."

"Your wife asked me to come back," she reminded him.

"She shouldn't have," he said.

"So you don't want me working for you?"

"You're not working for me," he said. "I have a legit assignment—a female lawyer who has requested a female bodyguard for protection—in Chicago."

"Send Nikki," she suggested.

"No," he said. "I need one of my best bodyguards on this assignment."

"Nikki could be—if you'd give her a chance."

Beyond just irritated, he glared at her now. She waited for him to fire her. But he just shook his head.

"When someone was trying to kill you, did you leave the state to protect someone else?" she asked.

"They weren't trying to kill me," he said. "They were trying to kill Parker."

"You didn't know that at the time," she said.

He shrugged. "It doesn't matter now."

"No," she agreed. "Because you're no longer in danger."

"And the guy who was trying to kill you is dead," he said. "So you're free to go to Chicago."

"I'm not free to go anywhere until I know who he was working for," she said. But she stood up to leave. "And I have my suspicions."

"All you have are suspicions," Logan said.

She nodded. "Yes, until I get evidence."

"Stay away from Chekov," Logan warned her as she headed for the door. "And stay away from Garek, too."

She didn't think that was going to be a problem since she had no idea where he'd gone. So she just nodded again as she walked out of his office. She closed the door with a soft click, turned and nearly collided with Nikki.

Nikki threw her arms around her neck and hugged her. "Thank you!"

"For what?"

"For what you told him—I would be one of the best bodyguards he has if he gave me a chance."

Candace laughed. "You have his office bugged?"

Nikki pulled back and pressed a finger to her lips then whispered, "Of course."

"He has no idea how good you are," Candace said.

Nikki shrugged. "It doesn't matter. I'll work for Cooper as soon as he starts his franchise. Maybe you should, too."

She wouldn't be working for anyone unless she found out who'd hired that man to attack her—because someone must have hired him. And if they'd hired him, they had probably already hired someone else to complete the job. She couldn't worry about protecting anyone else right now; she had to worry about protecting herself.

Stacy touched the twitching muscle along her husband's jaw first with her fingertips and then with her lips. His hands caught her waist and pressed her against him. He lowered his head and kissed her lips. While her passion ignited, he hadn't distracted her from her concern.

"What's wrong?" she asked him.

He shook his head and glanced around the room at the rest of his family. They'd all gathered at Penny's to decorate her Christmas tree. Christmas was still a couple of weeks away, but the wedding planner liked to decorate early so she could enjoy her tree.

But Penny, being Penny, had fed them all first. Now she handed an ax to Nicholas Rus.

The FBI agent looked horrified. He had been uncomfortable all through dinner, too—as if he hadn't expected to be included in a family tradition. He didn't know how welcoming and loving Penny Payne was.

"Now it's time to cut down the tree," Penny told him. "The best ones are in back of the house."

Rus handed the ax to Cooper, the former marine. "I've never cut down a tree before."

"You can't swing an ax?" Parker teased him.

Parker was like Garek in that he always teased. With Parker, it was just a natural part of his personality. With her brother Garek, it was a coping mechanism—not for himself but for her and Milek. Since they'd been kids, he'd joked with them to make them feel better and worry less.

"Maybe he just doesn't want to," Nikki said as she pulled on her hat and headed toward the door. She took the ax from Cooper.

And Logan dropped his hands from Stacy and hurried after his sister. There was no way he would let Nikki swing the ax; he worried she might hurt herself—which was the same reason he wouldn't give her a protection assignment. He needed to let up or he risked losing her—like Stacy felt she had lost her brothers.

Cooper and Parker hurried out after Logan. Their wives—Tanya and Sharon—had chosen cleanup duty in the kitchen over trudging out in the snow. Like Stacy, they also wanted to stay inside the house with their babies who slept in the nursery Penny had decorated for her new grandbabies. Tanya and Cooper's son was just a month older than baby Penny. Parker and Sharon had two children; his two-year-old son who'd fallen asleep despite his protests he wasn't tired and their month-old daughter.

Penny touched Nicholas Rus's shoulder. "Go ahead," she urged. "Help them pick out a tree."

He looked as horrified as he had when she'd handed him the ax. "I don't want to intrude," he said. "It seems like Nikki is already upset."

"That's my husband's fault," Stacy said. "Not yours."

He turned to her with a skeptical look. Nikki had made her opinion of him clear.

Penny sighed. She knew it, too. She grabbed a coat from the hook by the door. "I'm going to make sure they pick one with full enough branches." She turned back to Rus. "You are welcome to join us."

He nodded, but he didn't move toward the door. She sighed again and headed out.

"She means it," Stacy said. "She welcomed me and my brothers into her family, too." Penny was warm and inviting and forgiving.

Her brightly decorated Victorian farmhouse was a reflection of her warmth. A fire burned in the hearth.

"Your brothers aren't here."

"No," she said and a pang struck her heart. Would they forgive her before Christmas? "And that's my fault."

He shook his head. "Don't blame yourself."

There was something in his tone—something that caught her attention. She studied his face, and she saw the guilt flicker in eyes that were the same brilliant blue of her husband's. "You know that Garek's involved with Viktor Chekov. You even know what it's about, don't you?" Another pang struck her heart. "Oh, God, Milek's involved, too."

She'd reached out to him to help Garek. Instead she'd put him in danger, too.

Rus didn't deny it. He refused to say anything at all. But she saw the worry on his face. And she knew she wasn't the only one concerned that she might lose her brothers. Forever.

Chapter 13

The door swung back and forth in a broken jamb. Someone hadn't just picked his lock this time. They'd broken down his door. His heart hammered with fear. Had Candace been inside when it had happened?

Rus had promised he would call Garek if the agents following Candace saw any threat. This was damn sure a threat. He drew his weapon from his holster. But this threat was meant for him.

Gun drawn, he stepped inside his apartment. Viktor Chekov sat in the middle of his couch, his feet propped up on the coffee table. At either end of the couch stood a man with a gun—the barrels pointed at Garek.

He could shoot one of them but not both. He couldn't win this gunfight. So he holstered his weapon. "If I'd known you were coming to visit, I would have left the door unlocked and some appetizers out."

Why the hell was Viktor visiting? Garek had made certain no one had followed him down to the River City morgue. If anyone caught him meeting with Special Agent Rus, he was a dead man for sure. That was why so few people could know about his assignment for Rus—because the more people who knew, the more likely it was Chekov might find out.

"We haven't been here long," Viktor said.

"Why are you here?" he asked. "Milek is with Tori right now." Garek had been with Rus for a while—pouring through Donald Doornbos's past to find a connection between him and Chekov. Garek had even stayed after Rus had left for dinner at Penny Payne's. He could have gone to dinner, too. He'd been invited.

But Candace had probably been invited, too. And he hadn't been ready to see her yet. Of course every time he closed his eyes he saw her, lying naked in his bed—her silky skin all flushed with passion, her lips wet and swollen from his kisses…

"Maybe I should have had your boss at Payne Protection assign your brother to protect my daughter," Viktor said. "It seems like he is the more focused one of the two of you. But then he has no distractions like you have."

Garek tensed. "Distractions?"

A snide grin twisted Viktor's face. "The woman bodyguard, the former cop."

Fear clutched Garek's heart.

Viktor knew about Candace. For how long?

"Maybe I should have her assigned for Tori's protection," Viktor said. "I find I may be down a bodyguard."

The dead guy had worked for him then.

"Somebody quit?" Garek asked.

Viktor cocked his head. "Quit? More likely he will be fired."

Oh, he was talking about him—which brought back Rus's warning. Viktor Chekov didn't give out pink slips; he gave out toe tags.

"I don't have any distractions," Garek claimed.

Chekov stood up and reached for Garek. He patted his face with just enough force it stung. "Don't lie to me."

"I wouldn't," Garek assured him.

"Then maybe you're lying to yourself," Chekov said. "I saw you chase after that woman."

Had he sent someone after her before Garek had followed her out?

"I didn't follow her right out," Garek protested. But someone else had. "But as you pointed out, I work with her. I wanted to make sure she made it safely to her vehicle." Which she hadn't…

Viktor laughed. "So now you're a gentleman?"

Maybe he would have been—had a woman like Penny Payne raised him. But his own mother hadn't been anything like Penny; she hadn't cared about her children at all. Even after her husband had tried to assault her daughter, she'd blamed Stacy and them; she'd even testified against them rather than admit she'd been married to a monster.

"And a woman like Candace Baker doesn't need anyone else to protect her," Viktor said with grudging respect.

And that vice of fear tightened around Garek's heart. Viktor had to be behind the attacks on her or how else would he know how well she could take care of herself?

Garek shrugged. "You're right. That's why she's not a distraction. She's nothing."

Viktor snorted.

"She's a former cop," Garek reminded him. "Do you really think a former cop would ever get involved with a Kozminski? Or a Kozminski with a former cop?"

Viktor laughed. "Your sister married a former cop."

"My sister never went to prison," he said. "She never committed a crime." He could not say the same—no matter how much he wished he could.

He wanted to be a man Candace could admire and respect. Maybe that was why he had accepted Rus's undercover assignment—because if he was successful, Candace would learn what he had done. His effort to impress her might cost them both their lives, though. He had to convince Chekov that Candace meant nothing to him.

He laughed now. "And do you seriously think I would ever go for a woman like her? She's tougher than I am. She's not my type at all."

"I thought every woman was your type," one of the other men remarked.

"Like Polinsky," the other man murmured.

Garek caught the comment and filed it away to consider later. It must have been why Chekov had killed him. Garek nodded at the first guy. "Exactly. Every woman is my type—never just one woman."

Viktor slapped him again—harder. "Then you better be careful around Tori. She seems to be getting attached to you again."

Garek didn't know how since she was still mourning another man—the lover her own father had murdered. But maybe Tori was acting interested in Garek so Viktor didn't fire him—or kill him.

But maybe her acting was why Chekov had gone after Candace. To eliminate his daughter's competition.

"*I* would never hurt Tori," he said. Not like Viktor had.

Chekov narrowed his dark eyes and nodded. "Good, Garek, then I won't fire you…" He patted his cheek with less sting this time. "Today…"

He headed toward the door, his lackeys rushing after him. "But there's always tomorrow…"

He needed to find that damn gun before Chekov used it again. On him…

Hearing the creak of the broken door, Candace released the breath she'd been holding. But it didn't ease the tightness in her chest—the pain in her heart. *She's nothing.*

Just another conquest.

She waited for the anger—for the pain—to rush over her. But she couldn't shake the fear; she trembled with it. When they'd broken in the door, she'd been in the bedroom—going through those plans again. So she'd drawn her weapon and she'd waited for them to come for her.

But they'd settled in the living room. And they'd waited for Garek. She hadn't known what they were going to do to him. Beat him—like she suspected they had before. Kill him…

She knew Chekov wasn't above that. Everyone suspected he'd killed his own right-hand man a couple of weeks ago. So why would Garek seek out an assignment working for such a madman?

She stepped from the bedroom and asked, "Why?"

He whirled toward her, his eyes wide and his handsome face pale with shock. "You were here?"

She nodded.

"They didn't see you?"

"They didn't look."

He released a shaky breath. "That's good. That's good…"

"Nothing's good about this," she said. Gesturing toward the door, she continued, "Look what they've done to your place. Why would you want to work for someone like that? Someone that dangerous?"

He clenched his jaw and shook his head. "I don't want to. I have to…"

There it was again—another cryptic comment. "What's really going on?" she asked.

"Nothing that concerns you," he replied.

She uttered a bitter laugh. "I'm nothing. I know that…" She'd suspected it herself but she'd hoped she was wrong—about him, about them…

She had hoped they could have a future. But with the way Chekov was treating Garek, she worried he wouldn't have a future with *anyone*.

"Candace…" He murmured her name, his voice gruff with emotion. It was in his eyes, too—the silver going dark gray with regret and frustration and something else…

Something she was probably just imagining.

He reached for her, dragging her up against his body. His was shaking slightly. He'd probably thought Chekov was going to kill him. But then he murmured, "They might have killed you if they'd known you were here…"

He cared. It was in his voice—in his eyes—in the desperate way he clutched her against him.

Candace's breath shuddered out, and she wrapped

her arms around him, clinging to him. "You need to get away from Chekov," she said. "You need to quit."

"You don't quit Chekov," he said.

"You did before."

"I went to jail," he reminded her.

She shuddered as she remembered why he'd gone to jail. Murder. But she accepted now there was more to that story, too. The man he'd killed had been a threat to his sister. He'd done it to protect Stacy. She wondered who he was protecting now.

"You could go to jail again," she warned him, "if you don't get away from him."

His lips curved into a slight smile. "I'd be lucky if I just went to jail."

She shivered again. "Garek, please, get away from him!"

"Like you did me?" he asked. "Like you ran away that first night we spent together?"

She couldn't deny she'd run. "You took off this morning," she reminded him. "You didn't wake me. You left me no note, no explanation."

"Is that why you came back?" he asked. "For an explanation?"

It wasn't exactly why she'd come back but she nodded.

"You want to know where I was this morning?" he asked. "The morgue."

"You identified the man who tried to kill me," she said. "Did he work for Chekov?"

He shrugged. "I don't know. All I know is you need to stay away from me. You need to leave River City again. And this time you need to make sure nobody can track you down—not even Nikki."

She doubted anyone could hide from Nikki. But she shook her head. "I'm not running."

"Then you're a fool," he said. "You need to stay away from me. I'm just going to hurt you." He touched her face then, his fingertips sliding along her jaw. His thumb brushed across her bottom lip. He stared hungrily at her mouth, as if he was dying for a taste of it. But he didn't lower his head. "And I don't want you to get hurt…"

"It's too late for that," she said. The things he'd said, the way he'd pushed her away—that had hurt her. But what hurt her more was he was still keeping things from her—things he would want her to know if he ever intended to let her get close to him—as close as she had let him get to her. She'd let him close enough to steal her heart.

"I'm sorry," he murmured.

"Me, too," she said. "I'm sorry you're a coward."

He stepped back as if she'd struck him. "What?"

"You're a coward," she accused him. "You're the one who's running."

He laughed now. "How's that?"

"You're running from me," she said. "You're pushing me away."

"For your own good!"

"Really?" she challenged him. "My own good? I can take care of myself. I don't need you to protect me. I've been protecting myself for thirty years."

"Really," he shot the word back at her. "You could have been killed—twice."

She laughed. "Twice? You think those are the only times I've ever been in danger? That's nothing. Those weren't even close calls compared to what I've been through. I've almost been *blown up* in Afghanistan and here. I've been shot. Stabbed. Hit over the head."

He flinched as if he could feel the pain she'd felt.

"You're using danger as an excuse to push me away," she said. "To stop me from getting any closer to you!" She stabbed him in the chest with the tip of her finger. "You pursued me for a year. You chased me and wore me down but now that you have me—you're scared."

His throat moved as he swallowed hard. But he didn't deny what she was saying.

"What are you scared of?" she asked. "Are you scared I'm going to hurt you?"

He laughed again, but it sounded forced and nervous. "I have never been scared of getting hurt."

He probably believed that, but she doubted him and raised a brow in skepticism.

"The only thing I'm scared of," he said, "is you're going to get hurt."

She sighed. "And I already told you it's too late…" And maybe it was. She'd spent too many years wishing Logan would love her. She wasn't going to waste any more time just wishing for a man's love—even Garek's. She nodded. "Yeah, it's too late…" She headed for the door.

He reached out again, but she jerked away before he could touch her. "Candace, Chekov could have men out there—waiting to see who leaves here. They could follow you."

She chuckled. "Like I can't lose a tail…"

"Candace…"

"You wanted me to leave," she reminded him. "I'm leaving. And this time I will stay away." She didn't want to wish or even to fight for a man's love anymore; she wanted it given freely to her.

As she walked out Garek's broken door, she accepted they had no chance for a life together. Chekov would probably kill Garek before he ever got a chance to overcome his fear of letting her close. And because he wouldn't let her close, she wouldn't be there to protect him—to protect what they could have had, had he given them a chance.

Nick stared at the Christmas tree glowing brightly in Mrs. Payne's living room. Lights of every size had been strung around it, and ornaments covered it. Most of them handmade and with a story.

He wasn't part of that story, of this family. But she kept trying to pull him into it. Shouldn't she hate him like her kids hated him? He was living proof her dead husband had cheated on her.

But instead of pushing him away, she pulled him closer. Even now she squeezed his hand as she passed him a mug of hot chocolate. "Thank you for staying," she said.

He wasn't sure why she'd asked him to stay as everyone else had been leaving. Maybe she thought he was mad. She had tricked him into dinner. He'd thought it was just one of her usual offers for a home-cooked dinner. He hadn't realized she'd dragged him into a family tradition.

He probably wouldn't have refused her request even if he'd known. He was unable to refuse her anything. He wasn't the one who'd betrayed her, but he was the only one still alive to carry the burden of guilt for that betrayal.

"Thank you for dinner," he said.

She touched his face. He wasn't used to maternal affection. He wasn't used to maternal. "You barely ate," she said.

He had been uncomfortable over more than just his younger half sister's glares. Stacy Kozminski-Payne's obvious concern for her brothers had bothered him and increased his usual burden of guilt.

"I'm sorry I ambushed you with the family dinner," Penny said.

He chuckled. "I am glad you're on the right side of the law. You'd be dangerous if you weren't."

She murmured, "Speaking of dangerous…"

He tensed. This woman had some kind of psychic sixth sense. She always knew what was going on with her family—with every member, biological or whom she had emotionally adopted like she had the Kozminskis, like she was trying with him.

"What is going on with Garek Kozminski?" she asked.

"Why do you think I would know?" he wondered. It was supposed to be an undercover operation.

She smiled. "Because you're like me, Nicholas."

He could have pointed out that wasn't possible. He had none of her DNA or her nurturing. They were nothing alike. But he didn't argue with her.

"You know what's going on with everyone," she said. "You know before *they* know."

He laughed. "You might be psychic," he said. "I'm just good at my job."

She nodded. "That's what Chief Lynch said about you."

She had met his Bureau boss at the weddings of two

of his agent friends. He hadn't realized they'd exchanged more than pleasantries, though.

"He said it's all you have," she added. "That it's all you care about."

He shrugged. "I enjoy my work."

"You need more in your life."

A face—a *beautiful* face—flashed through his mind, but he blinked the image away.

"Work is all I need," he assured her and himself.

She sighed. "You know you need more. You're so close to getting it, Nicholas. You're so close to becoming part of a real family."

He hated the pang that hit his chest and reminded him how that was all he'd ever wanted. He forced a laugh. "Nikki will never accept me."

"She will," Penny said. "Your brothers already have. But the Kozminskis are family, too."

They had once been enemies of the Paynes—at least of Logan and Parker. But now they all acted like brothers. Maybe there was hope for him and Nikki to overcome their differences someday.

"And if you've put Garek and Milek in danger," she continued, "and something happens to them…"

She was just fishing. That was all. But he couldn't lie to her, so he said nothing.

"This is where you're supposed to assure me nothing will happen to them," she said, her warm brown eyes full of concern.

But he couldn't lie to her, so he said nothing.

Chapter 14

Fury gripped Garek, clutching his stomach. He reached out and tore the broken door from the bent hinges. It dropped onto the floor. He didn't care there was no door. There was nothing in that apartment he cared about—now Candace had left.

"Damn her," he said. "Damn her…"

She was right. Even though he wasn't the one who'd left that night, even though he hadn't gone anywhere, he was running, too. He was running from her and using her safety as an excuse to do it.

Hell, she was Candace Baker. She was stronger, smarter and braver than he was. There was nothing she hadn't handled or couldn't handle. Even Viktor Chekov…

Disgusted with himself—with his cowardice as she'd called it—he kicked the door. But he got no satisfaction. The tight knot in his gut didn't ease. He had to find her—had to be with her. Had to admit she was right.

He was scared. And not just for her. He was scared *of* her. Because she could hurt him far worse than Viktor Chekov could. As he started out the door, his cell phone rang. That cell phone—the one only Nick Rus called.

He grabbed it from his pocket. "Did you find another body you want me to identify?" He hoped like hell not.

Rus sighed. "No. I just got a call Candace shook the tail I had on her."

Garek chuckled. "Of course she did."

"My guy said he wasn't the only one watching her," Rus added.

Garek cursed now. "Chekov." It was how he knew so much about her. Hell, he'd probably even known she'd been in the apartment when he'd had his guys knock down the door. "Did she shake him, too?"

Rus drew in an audible breath now, as if bracing himself for an admission. "My guy doesn't know."

Garek kicked the damn door again. "I'll find her." He had intended to look for her anyway. But now there was even more urgency. He clicked off the cell and dialed her number.

Or he'd thought he'd dialed it. It didn't ring or go to voice mail. Had he punched in the right number? He didn't have it programmed in the phone Agent Rus had given him. But he'd memorized it long ago. He used to call her often—mostly just to tease her.

And because he loved the sound of her voice in his ear. Even when it was sharp with irritation, it sounded sexy to him. Everything about her was sexy to him—even her stubbornness. He punched in the number again. But again it didn't ring. It didn't even go to voice mail. What the hell did that mean?

He punched in another number.

And a woman answered immediately. "Hello?"

"Niks, I need you to run a trace on Candace's phone."

"What's going on with you two?" she asked.

Not enough—because he'd been stubborn. Because he'd been scared. He should have told her everything. He shouldn't have kept any secrets from her.

"She's pissed at me," he admitted. Was that why she'd shut off her phone?

"Tell me something I don't know," Nikki said with a laugh.

He couldn't—not until he told Candace first—how he felt and what he was keeping from her. "Tell me where she is."

Through the phone, he heard keys clicking. Then a curse. "Sorry, Garek, her phone's dead. No way to tap into her GPS and get a location on her."

"Damn her," he said again.

"You think she deliberately disabled it?" Nikki asked, her voice a little lighter with hope.

And Garek cursed himself now. He shouldn't have automatically assumed she'd done it. But it was better than the alternative—that someone had abducted her and destroyed her phone so she couldn't be found.

"I'll find her," Garek said.

"She's not easy to find if she doesn't want to be," Nikki warned him.

But Garek was worried now she hadn't chosen to hide—maybe someone was hiding her instead. Chekov?

If he'd hurt her, Rus wouldn't need the gun or Tori's testimony anymore. There wouldn't be any trial. Garek would take care of him. But first he had to take care of Candace—had to make sure she was okay...

* * *

Because Candace hadn't been certain who was following her—Rus's men or Viktor Chekov's—she had made certain to lose her tail. She wouldn't have risked anyone following her here; she wouldn't have risked this woman's safety for any reason.

She walked up the steps of Mrs. Payne's wraparound porch and right into the arms that the woman held open for her, like she held open the front door. Candace wouldn't have risked Mrs. Payne's safety, but she'd needed her. She'd needed this.

Mrs. Payne ushered her inside the warmth of her house, closing the door behind her. Candace glanced uneasily out the window into the darkness. She had lost the tails, hadn't she? There was no one out there.

"Sorry to bother you so late," she said with a flash of guilt as she noticed the clock.

"It's not late," Penny said. "And you are always welcome. You were welcome earlier for dinner."

Candace noticed the tree glowing brightly in the front room. Mrs. Payne was a wedding planner who owned a wedding chapel with a reception hall in its basement. Probably because she did it so often, she was an awesome decorator.

"The tree is beautiful," she said. "But it always is."

Candace had always been too busy—too focused—to worry about decorating. But now she felt a longing for a tree of her own—for someone to help her decorate it. For someone to cuddle with in front of the tree.

And she imagined Garek as that someone. But the image quickly faded—replaced by the picture Logan had shown her from the morgue. But in her mind, the man in the photo was Garek—not the stranger who had attacked her.

She shivered.

"Let me get you some hot chocolate," Mrs. Payne said.

"No, please don't go to any trouble," Candace said. "I shouldn't have come here." And risked someone following her.

Penny patted her hand. "I'm glad you came. I can see you need to talk."

Candace shook her head, but then frustration overwhelmed her and the words spilled out. "I already talked too much," she said. "What I needed was for *him* to listen. But he didn't."

Penny smiled. "Garek?"

Candace nodded.

"Men don't always hear us right away," Penny said. "But eventually the words get through to them."

Tears stung Candace's eyes. But she furiously blinked them away. She wasn't sure she wanted Mrs. Payne to give her hope. Then the disappointment would only hurt more. "Garek is more stubborn than most men."

Penny laughed. "Garek? Stubborn?" Then her smile faded and she tilted her head as she considered it. "He acts so laid-back and happy-go-lucky I hadn't realized how stubborn he actually is."

"He is stubborn," Candace insisted.

"He is," Penny agreed. "He hung in there a year— trying to get you to see him for the man he is. He kept trying to get you to give him a chance."

"I was just a challenge to him," Candace said. "Because now that I see him, he's scared."

Penny laughed. "Of course he is. Who wants to be completely vulnerable to someone else?"

Candace shivered again. She didn't want that either. But she was vulnerable with Garek. He'd always seen in her what no other man had: beauty, desirability.

"Was I too hard on him?"

"Always," Penny said. "You were determined to think the worst of him."

"That was my way of running," Candace admitted.

"So you're both runners," Penny said with a smile. "He chased you first, so now it's your turn to chase him."

Candace shook her head. "I don't want to chase a guy ever again. I don't want to force someone to love me."

"You can't force someone to love you," Penny said.

"I know that." Candace sighed. "I know that…" Or she would have been Penny's daughter-in-law instead of Stacy Kozminski.

"The right person will love you," Penny said. "But he may be too stubborn to admit it."

"Damn him," Candace murmured.

"You're stubborn, too," Penny reminded her.

She was. If only she'd given him a chance earlier—before he'd gotten involved with Chekov again.

"You were determined to think the worst of him," Penny continued. "And you're still thinking the worst of him."

"I'm not wrong about his being stubborn." But she could have been wrong about Chekov. There could be another reason he was working for Chekov…

Realization dawned. He'd known about her reporting the assault in the alley. He'd been called down to the morgue to identify the attacker. Who'd called him both times? It had to have been Special Agent Rus. Was he working for Rus?

Mrs. Payne touched the end of her nose. "I think you might have it this time."

Of course Mrs. Payne would know. Nothing escaped her attention. And she had sources everywhere.

"Is he—"

Mrs. Payne pressed a finger over her lips now. "Just trust your heart, Candace. It won't lie to you."

She hugged the petite woman. "Thank you!" She always made Candace feel better. No matter how many times she'd made a fool of herself.

She would probably be making a fool of herself again when she ran back to Garek after telling him that she was really going to leave him alone this time. But she needed to know if she was right—if he was working for Rus.

With another hug, she hurried back to her car. Snow was falling more heavily now—enough that it had blanketed her car. She quickly brushed it off and slid behind the wheel. Her cell lay in pieces on the passenger's seat. She'd taken it apart as a precaution. Chekov was powerful; he might have bugged her phone—especially if he had any suspicion Garek might have been trying to entrap him.

That was why he'd roughed him up, why he'd broken into his apartment to threaten him. If she and Mrs. Payne had figured out Garek was working for the FBI, Chekov had probably figured it out, too—which put Garek's life in extreme danger.

She shouldn't have left him earlier—no matter how hard he'd been pushing her away. She tried to accelerate, but her wheels skidded in the snow. She eased off the gas and grasped the wheel tightly as she turned out of the driveway and onto the street.

She sped up on the straight stretches of road. But they were snow covered and slick. So, for the curves, she needed to slow down. But headlights suddenly appeared behind her, burning brightly and quickly coming closer.

"Slow down," she murmured. The guy was going to lose control more than she momentarily had.

But he couldn't hear her. Or apparently see her, since he continued to bear down on her. Then she realized he did see her, and he intended to plow right into her vehicle.

She accelerated again, trying to speed up and get some distance between them. But her tires spun before gaining traction. The other vehicle didn't slow; instead it smashed into her rear bumper.

Her car flew forward, propelled by the other vehicle and the snow. It spun, then rolled. Lights and darkness flashed as her car somersaulted into the ditch. Like those flashes of light, stars danced around her vision. She blinked to clear it and reached for her weapon.

Because she knew this was no accident. She had been purposely forced off the road. Whoever was attacking her this time would not dare to fail—because with Viktor Chekov, failure meant death.

Penny flinched with each shot fired as it echoed throughout the river valley she called home—where she'd raised her children. She hadn't raised Candace, but she'd known her long enough that she felt like one of hers.

Had she lost her?

Candace had left just moments ago. She would not have been far away yet—especially with the snow falling so hard. So she was definitely within range of those gunshots—even if the sound of them was carrying on the cold night air. Before the gunshots, Penny had heard what had sounded like a crash—tires squealing, metal crunching...

That sound had carried, too.

But just like she instinctively knew those shots were being fired at Candace, she knew the crash had involved her, too. Due to the late hour and the snowstorm, there wouldn't have been many other cars on the road to crash right around the time Candace had left.

It wasn't a coincidence. The accident and the gunshots involved her.

And if Candace was hurt—or worse—Penny knew Garek would never forgive himself. And he would never get over losing her.

Chapter 15

Garek slid down the snowy embankment as he rushed toward the car that had gone off the road and into the deep ditch. It was Candace's car. If not for Mrs. Payne's call, he might not have found her. And he wouldn't have found the car if the lights hadn't been left on, burning holes in the snow in front of its smashed bumper.

Snow kept falling while a gusty wind blew the flakes that had already fallen around the ground—covering the road and the tracks of the vehicle as it had gone off the road. But her car hadn't gone off alone: parts of two vehicles had lain in the snow above the bank. Bits of black plastic and chrome and glass. And bits of Candace's blue car.

Penny had been right about hearing a crash and about it being Candace's vehicle. But when he hunched over to peer inside the wrecked car, he found it empty, but for the pieces of her phone strewn about the passenger side. It looked as if it had been run over by a car, too.

No wonder Nikki hadn't been able to track down its GPS signal.

But Candace wasn't inside the vehicle. She was gone.

Where the hell had she gone? Had *they*—whoever had crashed into her—taken her?

He shook his head, refusing to believe it. They couldn't have just taken Candace. Not *his* Candace. Not without one hell of a fight. She would have left behind more than a broken phone. She would have broken someone's body, too.

"Candace!" he called out to her.

Of course she might have been too mad still to answer him. No. If she was mad at him, she would yell or fight him. She wouldn't stay quiet.

She had only been silent when Chekov and his men had broken into his apartment. That must have been who had run her off the road. Chekov must not have believed him when Garek had claimed she meant nothing to him.

Fortunately she hadn't believed him either. She'd known he'd been lying to Chekov. But he hadn't told her what she actually meant to him: everything.

Was that why Chekov kept going after her? Did he know what Garek was up to—that he was working for Special Agent Rus? Then why not just fire him?

Of course Chekov didn't fire unsatisfactory employees. He terminated them—permanently. The man in the morgue must have worked for him.

Candace wasn't in the morgue, though. No rescue crews or police had arrived on the scene. Garek had beaten them all there.

The slick roads hadn't slowed him down. After Penny's

call—and the fear in her voice—nothing would have kept Garek from getting to Candace.

But she wasn't here. Where was she? He had grabbed a flashlight from his vehicle, but he didn't need it.

Now that the snow wasn't falling as hard as it had earlier, the moon was full and bright; its light illuminated the night and gleamed and glittered on the snow. Then he realized it wasn't the snow glittering. It was glass on the snow—glass from the driver's side window. Had Candace smashed it out or had someone else?

Then he noticed there was more than glass in the snow. There were bright crimson drops of blood. She was hurt. She was out there somewhere—injured or worse.

Mrs. Payne had warned him the crash wasn't all she'd heard. There had been gunshots, too.

Was the blood because someone had been cut on the broken glass of the vehicle? Injured in the accident? Or was the blood from a gunshot wound?

"Candace!" he yelled her name. But he wasn't certain she could hear him. He wasn't certain she could hear anything anymore. "Candace!"

Why had he been such a fool—such a coward like she'd called him? If he hadn't pushed her away, they would have been together. They could have protected each other.

Instead she had gone off alone. And while Candace was tough and smart, she was probably outnumbered. Because the wind wasn't as brisk in the ditch, it hadn't obliterated the tracks down here like it had on the road above. So he could see footprints in the snow. There was more than one set—more than two.

There was more than one person after her now. But

she wasn't alone anymore. And he wanted them to know that—wanted them to know help had arrived.

He didn't care if that put him at risk, too. He would rather they came after him than her. He would gladly give up his life for hers.

"Candace!" he yelled again. His voice cracked while panic clutched his heart, cracking it, too. If something had happened to her…

He wouldn't—he *couldn't*—consider it. She had to be okay. He had to find her. If he had a guardian angel— like he'd thought when the car hadn't struck them in the alley—then he needed that angel's help now to find the woman he loved.

"I love her," he murmured to himself. And maybe to that angel. He needed all the help he could get to find her. And fast.

He wasn't running from her anymore. He was running to her.

Milek's gut tightened with the fear that cracked his brother's voice. "I can't find her. She's bleeding. She's h-hurt!"

"We'll find her," he promised. "I'm on my way."

"Hurry!" Garek urged before clicking off his cell.

Milek had never heard his brother sound like that. Garek had always seemed so strong. But maybe he'd just acted that way because he'd been the oldest, and he'd wanted to be the one on whom he and Stacy could depend.

They hadn't had anyone else to depend on. Their mother had had little to do with their upbringing; she'd cared only about money and men.

And their father's first love had been stealing. It had meant more to him than his children. Eventually it had taken him from them completely—leaving them alone with only each other to turn to.

And both he and Stacy had turned to Garek. They had always depended on Garek. Now he needed to depend on them.

Milek punched another number into his phone. Despite the late hour, his call was answered immediately.

"Yes?" Stacy asked. And despite the time, she sounded wide-awake.

"He needs us," Milek said. "All of us. Candace has been run off the road."

Stacy gasped. "Is she all right?"

"He doesn't know. He found the wreckage of her car, but he can't find her," Milek said. "He needs everyone's help to find her."

Milek was already walking out of his apartment. He sucked in a breath at the cold. If she was out there, they didn't have a moment to lose to find her. If she wasn't already hurt—like Garek obviously feared—then she was still at risk of freezing to death.

"Of course," Stacy said. "I'll let Logan know."

"Garek needs *you*, too," Milek admitted. In case they didn't find her…

Garek would need his family. All of his family. Milek knew that—he knew the loss Garek would feel—because he lived with that loss, with that gaping hole where his heart had once been.

He began to pray they found Candace alive, so his brother didn't have to live in the hell of regrets where Milek lived.

Candace's teeth chattered uncontrollably, snapping her jaw together. Afraid the noise might reveal her location, she tried to clench her jaw. But it was numb, her face chafed from the wind and the cold despite her having wrapped her scarf around her face. She had dressed for the elements—or so she'd thought—in her heavy coat, gloves and boots.

She had lost the feeling in her feet a while ago, though. But she trudged on through the snow, leading whoever was pursuing her farther and farther away from Mrs. Payne's home. She had been close enough she could have run back to her—could have used her phone to call for help. But help wouldn't have arrived before the men would have found her. She would have led whoever was after her right back to Mrs. Payne.

And she knew someone was following her. At first she had managed to run—to stay ahead of them. But she had slowed down as she'd grown colder—the chill penetrating deeply into her bones.

She had thought they had slowed down, too. Maybe she'd hit at least one of them with all the shots she had fired. She'd been lucky they hadn't hit her when they'd returned fire.

So many shots had been fired—driving into the snow near her, whistling past her head and shoulders as she'd crouched beside her vehicle. When the gunfire had ceased for a moment—probably while they'd reloaded—she had turned and begun to run.

There had been at least two of them, and maybe another behind the wheel in the big black truck that had driven her off the road. Maybe that was who was coming after her now—because he moved faster than the other men. Those men had been big—like the guy in the alley. They had lumbered down the bank—their footsteps slow and heavy.

This man moved differently. She could hear his foot-steps—his quick footsteps—crunching in the snow as he rushed forward. He could probably see her easily since the moonlight reflected off the snow, making the night as bright as day.

She couldn't outrun someone moving that fast. She was too cold. Too exhausted—both physically and emo-tionally. Because even while she ran, all she could think of was Garek. Was he okay?

Had Chekov already gone after him?

Was he dead—before she'd had a chance to talk to him? Before she'd had a chance to tell him that she'd been wrong about him? And she'd been wrong to resist him for a year. If only she'd given him a chance earlier...

Now they might not have a chance at all. But Candace was a fighter. She wouldn't easily give up.

So she hurried toward cover—toward the shadows of a stand of pine trees, their boughs heavy with snow. She ducked under those branches, knocking snow from them. It rained down onto her head, sliding beneath her scarf and down the back of her neck.

She gasped at the shock of it and shivered again. That gasp carried on the cold.

Those footsteps paused for a moment. He must have heard her. He knew he was close.

And now since the wind had stopped blowing, he could easily follow her tracks. He would come for her.

She glanced down at the glint of the gun she clutched in one of her gloved hands. Her fingers were so numb she hadn't realized she still held her weapon. Unless she could find the strength to swing it at her pursuer's head, it was useless.

She had emptied the magazine earlier—as the men

had come down the embankment toward her, their guns drawn. And she hadn't had time to grab another magazine from her purse—which had been wedged somewhere under the passenger's seat. If she'd been able to grab that, she would have had her pepper spray, TASER and knife to use as weapons, too.

Now she had nothing but her wits and physical strength. And paralyzed with cold, she wasn't sure how she could fight. But she wouldn't go down without one.

The sound of the crunching snow grew softer but only because the footsteps had slowed. But the sound grew closer as the person neared the stand of pines. He had found her.

So she drew in a breath and shifted her grasp on her weapon. She clutched it in both hands and prepared to swing it like a hammer.

The element of surprise was her only defense. If she could hit him hard enough to knock him out, or at least daze him long enough so she could get his weapon from him...

It was her only chance of survival.

Chapter 16

His heart pounded as quickly and heavily as when he'd been running—as when he'd been anxiously searching for her. And it had nothing to do with the fact that she had almost killed him. Or would have, if she had any strength left...

If the men had found her before he had...

He shuddered at the thought of what they would have done to her—how they might have hurt her. It wouldn't have just been a job to them to get rid of Candace. It would have been vengeance—because he was pretty sure she'd hit at least one of them with a bullet. That was why their tracks had eventually turned back toward the road—why their vehicle hadn't been parked there.

At least one of them had obviously needed medical attention. He worried Candace needed medical attention, too. For hypothermia for certain. Maybe for other injuries, as well. She could have been shot, too, or hurt in the crash.

"I'm lucky your gun was empty," Garek said as he carried Candace back toward the road. He held her carefully—hoping not to exacerbate any injuries she might have. But he needed to get her out of the cold—back to warmth.

Her lips, blue in her pale face, barely moved as she murmured, "I wouldn't have shot *you*..."

She'd swung her empty gun at him, though. Fortunately her blow had struck his shoulder and glanced off—instead of hitting his head. If she had knocked him out in the cold, they both might have died out there—wherever the hell they were. She'd walked—or run—more than a mile from the crash site.

He focused on their tracks, but the road—and help—seemed too far away. "Where are you hurt?" he asked. "There's blood on the snow."

She shook her head, and her hair—cold and wet with snow—brushed against his face. "It isn't mine."

"But I used it to track you down."

"I must've hit one of them," she said.

He had already figured as much. Candace was an excellent shot. She wouldn't have emptied her gun and not hit at least one of them. The men had to have left to seek medical attention. Or else they wouldn't have stopped until they'd found her.

He could call Agent Rus to send agents or officers to the local emergency rooms. They would be able to track down these guys—if they weren't already dead. Or if they had really left...

He heard the crunch of snow—of footsteps carrying

on the cold. Candace must have heard it, too, because she tensed in his arms. They were no longer alone.

And from the noise, it sounded as if there was more than one man. More than two.

Maybe the men had left for help but not medical help. Maybe they'd gone to get backup. They'd obviously needed it against Candace.

Her voice a hoarse whisper, she asked, "Do you have bullets in your gun?"

He nodded. But before he could reach for his weapon, she'd drawn it from his holster. And as a shadow stepped into their path, she pointed the gun—at his brother.

Milek held up his hands. "Don't shoot!"

Her breath shuddered out against Garek's throat. "I couldn't have pulled the trigger," she murmured, as she slumped in Garek's arms.

She wasn't unconscious; Candace was no fainter. But she was struggling for strength.

"How much farther is the road?" Garek asked his brother.

Milek sighed. "It's a ways yet. Logan and Parker are right behind me."

But Milek would have rushed ahead. He didn't care about getting shot—probably wouldn't have minded even if Candace had been able to pull the trigger. He'd lost what had mattered most to him.

Until now—until Garek had worried he'd lost Candace—he hadn't understood the depths of his brother's grief and despair. But Candace wasn't out of the woods yet—figuratively or literally. He rushed forward and nearly stumbled and slipped in the snow.

Milek reached for her and offered, "Let me help."

But Garek's arms instinctively tightened around her. "No. I have her." And now he never intended to let her go.

"Is she okay?" Logan asked as he and his twin joined them. "We saw the blood."

"We called 911," Parker said. "There's an ambulance on its way."

Candace shook her head. "I'm fine…"

But her skin was as pale as the snow except for her lips. They were nearly as blue as her eyes. Her lids drooped over her eyes, though, as she fought for consciousness. If he hadn't found her, she might have just lain down in the snow and fallen asleep.

It was often what happened when people died of hypothermia. They just went to sleep and never woke up. He tightened his arms around her, trying to warm her. And he tilted his head, listening for the telltale sound of sirens. With as cold as it was, the sharp noise would carry. They would hear the ambulance long before it neared. But he heard nothing yet.

Still he hurried toward the road, with his brother and brothers-in-law helping him through the snow. No one tried taking Candace from him. They must have known he wasn't letting her go without a fight.

Not again…

Never again…

The ambulance doors swung shut, closing on Candace and Garek, before the emergency vehicle raced away. Candace hadn't gone without a fight; she had insisted she didn't need medical attention. But Garek had insisted she get checked out. And he'd refused to leave her side.

A sigh slipped through Stacy's lips. She was torn. Had she done the right thing in tracking down Candace for her brother? She glanced down at the wreckage of the female bodyguard's car and shuddered. Or had she put the woman—her brother obviously loved—in danger?

He had barely acknowledged her presence—when he'd come up the bank with Candace clutched so tightly in his arms. The look on his face—the worry and the love—had struck her heart with a painful pang.

"I'll bring his car to the hospital," Milek murmured as he tried to slip past her.

Stacy reached out and clutched his arm. "Thank you…"

He shrugged off her hand and her gratitude. "I did it for Garek."

He was making it clear he didn't need her. But he needed her more than Garek did. Garek had found Candace; he'd saved her.

Milek had never been given the chance to save the woman he loved.

"I should have told you," she admitted. "I shouldn't have kept Amber's secret." She'd grown up with the woman. Amber had been more than a friend. She'd been a sister to Stacy—a lifeline to sanity in her crazy Kozminski world. She missed her, too.

He nodded in silent agreement.

She wished he would yell at her. Scream. Throw things. But Milek never lost his temper. He just withdrew—completely. He'd even withdrawn from Garek until she'd asked him to help. Now, seeing the bruises on his face, she realized she shouldn't have done that either. Instead of helping her family, she'd put them in danger.

As Milek walked away, she shivered—not at the coldness outside but the coldness that was all he ever offered her. Then strong arms wrapped around her, holding her close.

"You should have stayed at the house with Mom and baby Penny," Logan said.

"I thought Garek might need me," she said.

Logan sighed. "He found Candace. She's tough. She'll be all right."

This time. But until whoever was after her was caught, there would be a next time.

"I really screwed up," she said. "I shouldn't have had Nikki find her."

"Did you see them?" Logan asked. "See how they were together?"

She sighed. "I could hear them arguing even after they closed the ambulance doors."

Logan chuckled. "Who does that remind you of?"

She tilted her head back to stare up at the man she loved more than she had ever thought possible to love anyone. And she smiled.

"I didn't see it," he said with a head shake of disgust. "But you were right about them." His gaze left hers as he glanced down at the man examining the car wreckage.

"Special Agent Nicholas Rus investigating an accident scene?" she asked skeptically.

"And you were right that there's more to this assignment of Garek's…"

She had been right about Candace's and Garek's feelings for each other. But she hadn't been right about everything. She'd misjudged her brother. Milek wasn't the only one to whom she owed an apology.

But an apology would never be enough for Milek— not with all he'd lost. Hopefully Garek would forgive her interference—if he had the chance.

"He's in danger, too," she said.

Logan nodded. "We'll protect them," he promised. "Nothing will happen to them."

She wanted to believe her husband. She knew he always worked hard to keep his promises. But some things were beyond even his control.

"Where did you bring me?" Candace asked.

She should have been grateful he hadn't made her stay in the hospital. The emergency room doctor had wanted to admit her and keep her overnight. But she hadn't wanted to risk the safety of the other patients—in case those men dared to track her down there.

There was no way they could have followed Garek from the hospital. He'd driven like a maniac—but with such skill and control she hadn't worried. She also didn't question he had lost whoever might have been trying to tail them. Chekov's men or Nicholas Rus's.

She did question where they were, though, and not just because she wasn't certain to which area of the city he'd taken her. It wasn't as remote as Penny Payne's home. But it was suburban. The house sat off the road on a big lot. Pine boughs and lights had been strung from a low picket fence in front of the home. The first light of day glinted off the sparkling windows of the traditional brick home, making it look as if it was winking at her—like Garek had winked at her the past year when he'd mercilessly flirted with her.

"This doesn't look like a safe house," she mused as he pulled his SUV into the attached garage and quickly lowered the door behind them. She appreciated his precaution, but she doubted anyone would have looked for them here.

"It's not."

Before he could walk around to open her door, she pushed it open. They'd warmed her at the hospital with some special blankets and IVs. Her strength had returned, as well. But she shut the door softly and followed him to where he punched in a code on the keyless lock for the house.

He probably could have cracked the lock easily enough, but he seemed to know the code. He held open the door to the house for her.

She walked into a mudroom area and kicked off her boots. But she kept walking, fascinated with the home. While it was a completely different style, something about it reminded her of Penny Payne's house with its bright colors and rich trim. Maybe because it felt like a home...

There was even a Christmas tree standing naked in the front window, waiting for someone to decorate it. Bags of new decorations lay on the floor beneath it. Someone wouldn't have willingly offered this place as even a temporary safe house. They wouldn't want it damaged in case they were tracked down here.

"Who owns this home?" she asked.

"Me."

The admission shocked her more than anything else she'd learned about Garek Kozminski. She shook her head in disbelief. "But you have your apartment."

He shrugged. "I bought the house right before..."

"You took the assignment working for Viktor." He obviously hadn't had plans to go back to work for the mobster.

"I'm not working for Viktor."

He'd said it before. But she'd thought then it was just

semantics—because he actually worked for Payne Protection.

"You're not working for Logan either," she said, because it was obvious their boss had had no clue what was really going on with Garek.

He shook his head. "I'm working for the FBI."

She was right. Or rather Penny Payne had been right. If Candace hadn't talked to the matriarch, she might not have figured it out. And if she hadn't been attacked again, would he have told her?

She'd been attacked twice before, and he hadn't told her what was really going on. Since he'd told her now, he hadn't kept his secret before because Agent Rus had sworn him to silence, or he wouldn't have just revealed the truth.

"Why didn't you tell me?" she asked.

"It's an undercover assignment."

Milek's comment about things not always being what they seemed suddenly resonated with her. "Your brother knows."

"I needed his help," Garek said.

Anger coursed through her and she slammed her hands into his chest. "What about me?"

He hadn't turned to her for help. Had he thought she wasn't capable of keeping a secret?

She had worked undercover with the River City Police Department. Sure, most of those assignments had been as a prostitute, but she knew how to maintain a cover.

He could have confided in her—if he'd wanted. But he hadn't wanted her to know the truth. He'd wanted her to think the worst of him.

He hadn't just been running from her; he'd wanted

her to run from him, too. He hadn't wanted to give them a chance.

Pain joined her anger. "I want to go home," she said.

He shook his head. "It's not safe."

It wasn't safe for her with him, either, because he kept hurting her worse than even the men who'd driven her off the road. "I'm not staying with you!"

He reached for her, trying to pull her into his arms. And she felt the panic she'd felt when her car had tumbled over the embankment. So she shoved him again.

Garek stumbled back, but her fury staggered him more than her physically shoving at him. "I thought you would be happy."

"Happy you didn't trust me enough to tell me the truth?"

"I trust you," he said. Candace was probably the most trustworthy person he'd ever met. It was one of the things he had always found most attractive about her. "I didn't tell you because I didn't want to put you in danger—which I obviously did."

She shoved him again.

But he refused to budge this time; instead he wrapped his arms around her and held her tightly against him. "You've been in danger ever since you came back to River City—because of me."

"I'm in danger every time I take an assignment with Payne Protection," she said. "I've been in danger with every job I've ever had. I've survived war. And being a cop and a bodyguard. You weren't worried about putting me in danger. You preferred my thinking the worst of you. You didn't want me getting too close to you."

He was close to her now, so close his body reacted,

tensing as desire rushed through him. The heat of that desire chased the chill away. He had never wanted anyone the way he wanted—the way he *needed*—Candace Baker. And it had scared the crap out of him.

"That's what this has been about," Candace said, "you running from me—from what we might have if either of us was brave enough to give it a chance."

He leaned down and brushed his lips across hers. "It doesn't feel like either of us is running now."

Her breath caught, and she stared at him, her blue eyes dilating with desire. She wanted him, too—as desperately as he wanted her.

But he forced himself to release her and step back.

She cursed. "I thought you weren't running anymore."

"I'm not," he said. "That's why I'm going to tell you everything."

"There's more?" she asked, and she wrapped her arms around herself as if cold. Or scared...

He sighed. "I guess I liked people thinking the worst of me..."

"So you could keep them from getting too close to you," she surmised.

He shrugged, but his shoulders were tense. And he realized why. "Anybody who got close to me let me down—my dad, my uncle, my mom..."

"Your mom," she repeated. She must have heard the bitterness in his voice. "She testified against you in the death of her husband."

He nodded. "Yeah, she was trying to put all her children away." He wanted to throw something or break something. But he contained his anger. Now. He hadn't that night. "Her creep of a husband attacks and nearly rapes her daughter, and she blames her. She blames Stacy."

"And you and Milek," she said. "You went to prison for manslaughter."

He curved his lips into a slight smile. "You've liked calling me a killer."

"It's not true." She didn't ask a question; it was as if she already knew.

And she did know him—better than anyone else ever had. He wanted her to know the rest of it. But she finished the story for him, as if she'd been there. "You took the blame for your brother and sister."

"Stacy was unconscious," he said. "She didn't do anything. Neither did I…" Frustration and regret ate at him now. "Son of a bitch got the jump on me—knocked me out cold. When I woke up, he was already dead."

"Milek did it?"

He nodded. "It's not like he lied about it. He told everyone he'd done it."

"But no one believed him," she said.

"The judge sure didn't," he said. "But then he wanted *me* to turn on Chekov. I could have gotten out of jail time if I'd worn a wire and tricked Chekov into implicating himself in one of his many crimes."

She gasped. "You were a kid. He wanted you to put your life at risk?"

"I would have," Garek admitted. "If it had been just me, but Chekov would have gone after Milek and Stacy, too. And they had been even younger than me. I couldn't leave them unprotected."

"So you went to jail for something you hadn't done. You took the blame for Milek."

"He went to juvenile detention," he said. "And he had

done nothing wrong. He saved Stacy and me from that bastard." He should have been the one who'd done it; he should have protected his siblings.

"Poor Milek," she said with a sigh.

She seemed to understand what his brother had gone through—the guilt he had felt all these years. Did she understand why Garek had done what he had?

He couldn't read her feelings for him. For the first time in his life, he'd told someone the truth—the whole truth—about himself. Was it too much? Was he too much?

Or not enough?

Milek stared at the worn-out newspaper clipping. He didn't need to look at the words; he knew what it said by heart. Or heartbreak…

He stared instead at the picture of Amber and their son. The picture accompanied their obituaries. That was the article he'd clipped; the words he knew by rote.

They had been dead for nearly a year now. Everyone thought that was how he'd finally learned of his son's existence. They all thought he hadn't known—Amber had kept that secret from him. Instead she'd kept a secret for him—even from her best friend.

A man like him couldn't be a father. He had lost control and killed a man. While that had been fifteen years ago, he hadn't changed. That capacity was still in him; the anger and rage could erupt at any time.

He hadn't deserved Amber or their son. But now he could never earn the right to love them. He had lost them forever.

The door rattled, so he shoved the picture back in his

pocket just before Nicholas Rus stepped back into his office at River City Police Department.

"Did you get any sleep at all last night?" Rus asked him as he dropped into the chair behind his desk.

Milek shook his head. "No. But neither did you."

"Garek lost the tail I had on him."

Milek laughed. "Of course he did." He was the only one who'd followed his brother without his knowing. "He'll keep Candace safe."

"They'll keep each other safe," Rus said.

Milek wasn't as convinced as the FBI agent. "Pull Garek out and put me in instead."

Rus shook his head. "That would be too dangerous."

Milek shrugged. He didn't care how dangerous it was. He had nothing to lose.

Garek had everything to lose—and he nearly had. Again and again.

If Candace hadn't survived tonight, Milek wasn't sure his brother would have either. For certain he would have gone after Chekov and it wouldn't have been to put him behind bars. It would have been to put him in the grave.

"Are you mad at me again?" Garek asked, his deep voice tentative.

Candace shook her head as tears choked her throat. She blinked furiously. But a tear fell, sliding down her cheek. She turned away, more embarrassed by her weakness than any humiliation she had ever endured.

But Garek's arms closed around her and he turned her toward him. His thumb brushed away the tear and dried the trail. "What's wrong?" he asked. "What did I do now?"

She shook her head. "It's not what you did. It's what I did."

His brow furrowed. "You didn't do anything wrong."

"I misjudged you," she said. "And I wouldn't let it go. I kept bringing up your past. And I had it all wrong." She had called him a thief and a killer.

"I didn't correct you," Garek said. "I didn't let anyone else correct you either. I wanted you to think the worst."

Pain clutched her heart. "You wanted to keep me away."

His arms slid around her. "I don't want to keep you away any longer."

She understood why he had though—how he had worried she would disappoint him as everyone else in his life had. His father had used him. His mother had betrayed him. Nobody but his siblings had loved him.

Until now...

She opened her mouth to declare her feelings, but his lips covered hers. He kissed her deeply, desperately.

And her desire ignited. She clutched at his shoulders and the nape of his neck, holding his head down. And she kissed him back. Her lips nibbled at his, and she slid her tongue into his mouth.

He groaned. But then he took over—tilting his head to deepen the kiss even more. He thrust his tongue in and out of her mouth.

She gasped as passion flooded her. Just his kiss had brought her pleasure. But it wasn't enough. The tension began to wind up inside her body again.

His hands were there—stroking her body. He must have unbuttoned buttons and unsnapped snaps because her clothes fell away. His followed, dropping next to those bags of decorations onto the floor.

Then he pulled her down with him—onto the plush rug in the center of the hardwood floor.

"There's a bed upstairs," he murmured.

"Later," she murmured back—between kisses. She couldn't wait for a bed. She had to have him now.

He pulled her down on top of him, arched his hips and thrust inside her. She clutched at his shoulders, then his chest as she moved on him. The tension wound more tightly inside her, threatening to snap her in two.

His hands stroked over her—from her hips, up her sides to her breasts. He teased her nipples with his thumbs, winding that pressure more tightly inside her. She whimpered and moaned at the delicious tension.

But he kept thrusting, driving her up and out of her mind. Then the tension broke as pleasure overwhelmed her. She screamed his name.

Then he cried out hers as he filled her.

She collapsed onto his chest, panting for breath. Once she could speak, she would tell him—she would profess her love. But if she told him that she loved him...

Would he let her help him with Chekov? Or would he be determined to protect her again?

He lay back, his heart racing beneath her breasts. And he struggled for breath, too. But he stroked circles on her back. Finally when he could speak again, he said, "We have a job to do."

"You'll let me help you with Chekov?" She hadn't even had to ask.

His hand trembled slightly against her back. "I was talking about the tree. We have a tree to decorate."

She had wanted to decorate a tree like Mrs. Payne's. She'd wanted a house that was a home—like Mrs.

Payne's. But this place wouldn't be home if they didn't live long enough to live there together.

Not that he wanted to live with her. He had been honest with her. He'd let her get close to him. But he hadn't professed his feelings either.

He rolled her off him. Then he pulled on his pants and handed her his shirt. "If you don't put something on…"

They would make love again. Her body hummed with pleasure, but it—and she—was greedy for more. He picked up one of the bags and handed it to her.

"We'll never get this tree decorated."

Shirtless, he strung the lights; she'd never seen any sexier man than he was. She paid less attention to where she was hanging the bulbs than to the way his muscles bulged in his arms and his back. When she rose on tiptoe to reach the higher branches, he ran his fingertips along her bare thigh. She wanted to do more than decorate the tree.

But before she made love with him again—and she wanted—she needed—to make love to him, she wanted to talk about something else.

"Let me help you with Chekov," she said.

His fingers skimmed down and then off her thigh. She tensed, waiting for his objection.

All he said was, "It's not your fight. It has nothing to do with you."

It had everything to do with her because she loved him and that made his fight hers. But more than that…

"Chekov made it my fight when he kept trying to kill me," she said.

He sighed. "That's why you shouldn't be involved."

"It's too late. I am involved."

He stared at her, his silvery eyes dark gray with turbulent emotions. He shook his head. But she didn't think he was rejecting her offer.

She thought he was giving in...

But then metal creaked as the back door opened on squeaky hinges. He pressed a finger to his lips and handed over his gun to her while he shoved a magazine in hers. Now frustration and regret flashed in his eyes.

But there was no way anyone could have followed him—not the way he'd driven here. So whoever had found them must have known where they were some other way. Maybe they'd searched property records and discovered he'd recently bought this house.

How many men were coming through that door? Two had shot at her while one had stayed in the truck on the road. So there might be three of them. They could be outnumbered.

Garek held her gaze for a moment, as if he was trying to tell her something. Then he gave the signal—a quick nod of his head.

Even if they were outnumbered, they wouldn't go out without a fight. She just wished she had told him she loved him...because now she might never have the chance.

Chapter 17

Nicholas Rus flinched at the sound of guns cocking, the barrels too near his face for him to react. He didn't dare to move even enough to draw his own weapon. But he hadn't thought he would need to draw his weapon here.

"You two sure are trigger-happy," he said. Not that they'd fired. Yet. He wasn't sure they wouldn't, even after having identified him as their intruder.

"We have reason to be a little edgy," Garek sarcastically pointed out as he pulled his gun away from Nick's head.

Nick released the breath that had caught in his lungs when he'd heard the gun cock. "Yeah, you have reason. Are you both all right?" he asked. "You didn't stick around at the crash site to give your report."

"Candace had been out in the cold for hours. We needed to get her to the hospital to make sure she didn't have frostbite or hypothermia," Garek said.

"You didn't stay in the hospital," Nick said. Because he had gone by there to see them—to make sure they were all right.

"It would have been too dangerous for other patients and staff," Candace said, "if Chekov's men tracked me down there."

It would have been, had he not had agents posted in the hospital, too. "You don't know Chekov had anything to do with you getting run off the road."

"And shot at," she said. Candace hadn't uncocked the gun she held; it wasn't pointed at his face anymore. But it was close—close enough for her to shoot him quickly if she wanted.

"You don't know that was Chekov's men," he repeated. "We haven't linked the other man to Chekov yet."

"Yet," she said. "But you will. And you'll link these men, too."

"That's why you should have stuck around the hospital," he said. "To give me an incident report and their descriptions. You're the only one who saw the men."

She uttered a ragged sigh of frustration. "I'll need to think about it—to try to remember more details. It all happened so quickly."

"She's exhausted," Garek said. "That's why I brought her home. So she'd be safe and warm."

Nick took in their state of undress, but he just raised a brow and refrained from comment. He wasn't sure how far he could trust Garek Kozminski—especially if he made any disrespectful comments in front of the woman the man obviously loved.

But Candace was the one still holding the gun.

"You are safe here," Nick assured her. "Nobody knows where you are. You don't need the gun."

She glared at him, but despite her obvious anger with him, she finally uncocked the gun.

"Why are you mad at me?" he wondered.

"How dare you…" she murmured. "How dare you drag him back into that life!"

Nick groaned. "You told her! God, man, don't you know anything about going undercover? You're not supposed to tell anyone but your handler anything."

"Some handler you are," Candace said. "You're going to get him killed."

"No," Nick said. "You are."

Candace flinched.

And he instantly regretted his remark. He hadn't meant to hurt her. But he knew that a woman could distract a man—take his mind off his job and put him in danger. He knew because a woman kept distracting him.

What had happened between them had been a mistake, though. And it wouldn't happen again. She wasn't even in River City, so she wouldn't tempt him again.

It was clear Candace mattered to Garek, though.

"You're out of line," Garek told him, his silver eyes metal sharp with anger.

But Rus ignored him to explain, "He's so worried about your safety he's not watching out for himself. He's distracted, and he's going to wind up dead."

Garek closed the door behind Agent Rus and headed upstairs to Candace. Maybe she'd just been cold—like she'd claimed when she'd gone up to find the bedroom. But he'd been surprised she hadn't stayed for his meeting with the FBI agent—she hadn't insisted on planning her part of the undercover operation.

"Are you all right?" he asked.

He had expected—and maybe hoped—to find her in the antique four-poster bed he'd bought with the house and hadn't yet slept in himself.

But she had grabbed her clothes from the living room floor before going upstairs, and now she was fully dressed. She didn't answer him; she didn't even look at him. Instead she stared out the window, probably watching Rus drive away.

"Maybe you should have stayed in the hospital like the doctor wanted."

"I'm fine," she said but then shook her head. "No, I'm not."

"Then let me take you back to the hospital." He shouldn't have agreed to her leaving against doctor's orders. She had been in a vehicle crash and then out in the snow and cold much too long.

"Physically I'm fine," she assured him.

"Then Rus did upset you." He sighed with frustration that he hadn't hit the special agent.

"He's right," she said, her voice soft with regret and worry. "I am going to get you killed."

Here was his out. He could use her fear for his safety to send her away. But it wouldn't matter. He would still be distracted because he would be missing her. He would be worried that someone might have followed wherever she'd gone.

"No." He shook his head now. "From now on, we work together."

Her eyes brightened with surprise and hope. "You're not going to listen to Agent Rus?"

He sighed. "I probably shouldn't have listened to him in the first place. I shouldn't have let him talk me into taking this assignment."

"But you did," she said. "You wanted to do this."

He grinned. She knew him well now. She knew he wouldn't have done something he hadn't wanted to do. "I felt like I needed to," he admitted.

"You regretted not taking Chekov down all those years ago—when the judge offered you that deal."

He sighed. "I was a scared kid back then."

And when it came to Candace, he was a scared man. For the past year he had deliberately misled her about his character in order to keep her from getting too close. Now he worried she wouldn't stay close to him since she knew him better than anyone else ever had—even his family. He'd always acted strong and fearless for them. Only Candace knew his fears and weaknesses.

She was his biggest weakness.

"You were just a kid," she said with sympathy instead of condemnation, "and you were all alone."

"I had Stacy and Milek."

"They were younger than you, and probably even more scared."

Remembering how scared they'd been brought back a rush of emotion. He couldn't speak, could only nod.

She reached out then, wrapping her arms around him—holding him like he'd never been held. And another kind of emotion rushed over him. He wanted to express his feelings, but he didn't want to distract her either—not when they both needed to be focused to take down Chekov.

"We end this now," he said.

It was past time for Viktor Chekov's reign of terror in River City to be done.

Candace nodded. "The sooner the better. What do we need to do?"

"We have to find that damn gun—" he'd looked everywhere for it, though "—before he disposes of it."

"Or uses it to kill again."

Candace had faced down some dangerous men over the course of her career. But she had never been as uneasy as she was taking this meeting with Viktor Chekov. She had to stay true to the character she'd already shown him, though—or the character he had probably witnessed, if not in person, then on security footage. So she'd bullied her way past his usual sidekicks and into his back office at the club.

He should have been furious with her. Instead he'd looked up from his desk and laughed. "I've been expecting you, Ms. Baker. You're quite determined."

He had no idea how determined. She needed this man behind bars, so she could tell Garek how she felt about him—how much she loved him.

She shrugged off the compliment and acknowledged, "I am determined—when I'm right."

He stood and walked around the front of his massive desk. The office was big, too, and dimly lit.

So Candace couldn't determine his age. He could have gone prematurely gray, and that was why his hair was so thoroughly silver now. His face had few wrinkles—just lines of ruthlessness, which were reflected in his dark eyes. He reached out and grabbed her shoulder.

She tensed, but she didn't react. "And I'm right about

who is the better bodyguard for your daughter. I would be a much better bodyguard than Garek Kozminski."

"I cannot figure out what it is between you and Garek," he said, and those dark eyes narrowed as he studied her face. "Is it love or hate?"

For a long while she hadn't known either. So she just shrugged.

And he laughed again. "I feel the same way about that damn boy."

Garek hadn't been a boy for a long time—if ever. He'd had too much responsibility—too much disappointment in his life and too much tragedy. This man had been part of all of that.

"Sit," he told her. But he didn't give her time to comply; he pushed her down into one of the chairs in front of his desk while he sat on the edge of the desk nearest her.

She knew exactly what she felt for *him*. Revulsion. Mistrust. Anger. She wouldn't acknowledge fear. She had survived her deployment and her assignments—undercover and protection—because she hadn't admitted to feeling any fear.

"Then you must agree I'm the better person to protect your daughter," she said.

He arched a gray brow. "Why is that?"

"You can't trust Garek Kozminski," she said, "especially not around any female."

A glint twinkled in the older man's dark eyes. "Garek has always been a heartbreaker. Did he break your heart? Is that why you're trying to steal his job?"

"Revenge?" she asked. "You think that's what this is?" She didn't care what he thought if it would make him trust her enough to hire her, too.

He chuckled. "Hell hath no fury like a woman scorned..."

She uttered a heavy sigh. "I have felt scorned..."

But she'd been wrong. Garek had only been lying to protect her. He hadn't wanted to hurt her any more than he'd wanted to risk her hurting him.

"But this isn't about Garek Kozminski," she said. "He only got hired because his sister married our boss." She had thought that a year ago.

But she hadn't known then how many clients Garek had brought to the agency. He hadn't had to join Payne Protection; he'd had an active security business of his own. But he would do anything for family—for his brother and sister and the Payne family, which had become his. He was the most loyal and generous man she had ever known.

"He has no business being a bodyguard," she said. Knowing what a lie it was, she could barely utter the next line. "He has no experience protecting people." Except he had been doing it pretty much his whole life.

"I have a lot of experience," she continued. "I could show you my résumé." She had brought it along in a folder, but one of his men had taken it from her before letting her inside the club.

The business wasn't open yet, so it was only her and Viktor and his men. It could have been a suicide mission. Garek was with Tori at the Chekov estate. Hopefully he would find the safe and the gun while she occupied Chekov.

Garek wasn't certain how much he dared to look with Tori along, though. He didn't completely trust the young woman; neither did Candace. So even if he found the safe, he was going to wait for another time to crack it—

for an opportunity to be alone in the house. He already had an idea of what night would present the best opportunity—the night Viktor Chekov hosted his company Christmas party at the club.

But that plan would only work if Garek had someone else to protect Tori in his place. Viktor had already beaten him up and threatened him for letting Milek take too many of his shifts. So someone else had to take over his protection duty. That was why Candace had made her move to replace him.

The older man chuckled. "I am quite aware of your résumé, Ms. Baker," he said. "Ex-soldier, ex-cop."

"That's why I should be protecting your daughter," she said, "not Garek."

Chekov nodded as if in agreement. But then he moved quickly, pulling something from behind his back. Light glinted off the metal of his gun as he pressed the barrel against her temple.

She drew in a breath and held it, afraid to move because he might cock the gun.

If he hadn't already…

With eyes dark with hatred and maybe madness, he ruthlessly told her, "I have no use for cops—ex or otherwise."

Chapter 18

"Daddy!" Tori shrieked as she rushed into the room ahead of Garek.

She had stopped him from drawing his gun—from shooting Viktor dead. But he held his hand close to his holster, ready to draw and shoot. He wouldn't be fast enough, though. With the gun pressed against her head, Candace would be dead before Garek could put a bullet in Viktor's brain.

"Don't hurt her," Tori implored her father.

"Why not?" he asked. "I thought you'd want me to get rid of your competition."

Tori stiffened—all concern gone. She snorted derisively. "She's no competition for me."

Garek caught Candace's flinch. She was such a strong, beautiful woman, but she had a vulnerability, an insecurity...

He wanted to tell her that he loved her. But it would

seal her death warrant for certain. He hadn't liked this part of the plan—the part where she forced a meeting with Viktor alone while he picked up Tori at her father's house. He'd intended to search it for the safe, but the place had been crawling with guards and other staff. Ostensibly there had been so many people there getting ready for the holidays—decorating the house and grounds.

But the Christmas party was being held at the club the following evening. And maybe it was the club Garek should have searched first for the gun.

Had it been here all along—in Viktor's office—and now in his hand? Was the weapon pointed at Candace's head the one that had already taken the lives of two men?

"He's just testing me," Candace spoke to Tori carefully and casually, acting as though she had taken no offense at what the spoiled girl had said.

She shouldn't have taken any offense; she was the woman Garek wanted—the one he loved. She didn't know, though. He hadn't told her; now he wished he had.

Candace continued, "He's seeing if I'm strong enough to protect you..." She caught Viktor's wrist and snapped the gun from his hand. Then she checked the cartridge. "It's not even loaded."

She exchanged a glance with Garek. A significant glance. It wasn't the gun. And now that it was away from her head and he could focus on the weapon; it was the wrong caliber.

So she handed it back to Chekov.

Garek tensed, waiting for Viktor's short temper to ignite—waiting for him to strike out at her as he had at him so many times. But the masochistic mobster surprised him as he leaned his head back and barked out the loudest laugh Garek had ever heard him utter.

"You need to teach her that move," Viktor said with a dismissive gesture at his daughter. "So I don't have to hire guards to protect her. She needs to know how to protect herself."

Tori sucked in an audible breath. She was the one who was offended now.

"I can teach her all the self-defense maneuvers I know," Candace offered.

Viktor nodded as he walked back around his desk and dropped into his chair. "You're right," he acknowledged.

Had the older man just been testing her? Garek wondered. Or was he simply trying to salvage his ego now and he'd really intended to scare her away?

He could have told Viktor that Candace didn't scare easily. At least she wasn't afraid of physical threats, just emotional ones. It was another thing they had in common.

"She does need a female bodyguard." Viktor pointed at Candace. "You have the job."

Garek tensed, waiting for his pink slip. Would it be a bullet? Fortunately the gun wasn't loaded.

Viktor turned his finger toward Garek. But then he pulled his thumb back as if cocking a gun. "You—I have other uses for you…"

Candace shot him a glance of concern. Was Viktor going to coerce him into a crime? Or kill him?

"She's in," Special Agent Rus said as he snapped off his cell phone. He and Milek were sitting in a Bureau SUV, in an alley, near the club.

But they wouldn't have been effective as Candace's

backup. They wouldn't have made it inside the club before Viktor hurt her—or worse.

Rus sighed. "But Garek doesn't sound very happy about it."

Milek nodded; he hadn't had to hear his brother to know he wouldn't have been thrilled. He knew Garek well. Or at least he'd always thought he'd known him well. But he had never realized Garek could fall so hard for someone like he had fallen for Candace.

Of course Garek hadn't admitted it—probably not even to himself, let alone to her. But his brother needed to share his feelings before it was too late. Before he didn't get the chance...

"I still think you should have sent me in," Milek persisted. "I could have gotten closer to Tori than Garek had and certainly closer than Candace will." While Tori had once loved Garek, she had been flirting with Milek when he'd filled in for his brother as her bodyguard. "I could have made sure she follows through with testifying against her father."

A muscle twitched along Rus's jaw. Her recanting her eyewitness story of Viktor murdering his right-hand man was obviously a concern for Rus and rightfully so. Garek was convinced the young woman would never testify against her father.

Rus shook his head. "She wouldn't have fallen for you. Everybody knows about you and Amber."

"Amber's gone." Murdered along with their son. She had died thinking Milek hadn't cared about her or about the child they'd created together. He should have explained why he'd stayed away—for her and for their son. They had deserved a better man than he was. "She's dead, and there's nothing I can do about that."

If only he'd known she was in danger…

If only he'd been talking to her…

But he'd forced himself to stay away from her—from them. He'd considered himself the threat to her safety and her happiness.

Rus sighed and pushed a hand through his hair. That hand shook slightly, and he wouldn't quite meet Milek's gaze. He was clearly uncomfortable.

Then Milek recognized the FBI agent's emotion because it was one he'd been struggling with for years: guilt. Why was Nicholas Rus guilt stricken, though?

Suspicion niggled within Milek and he mused, "You know something…"

"I know a lot," Rus vaguely admitted. Then he quoted Milek to himself, "I know everything's not always what it seems…"

Milek's heart lifted for a moment, but he refused to hope. It just wasn't possible…

But then he hadn't thought it possible his big brother would actually fall in love. Now that he had, hopefully he and Candace would survive this assignment.

"He's playing with us," Candace said as both anger and fear coursed through her. She had never met anyone as diabolical as Viktor Chekov. "He must know we're looking for that murder weapon. That's why he pulled the gun on me."

"He pulled the gun because he's a sick bastard," Garek said. As he drove, he gripped the steering wheel so tightly his knuckles had turned white. He was obviously every bit as angry as she was—maybe more.

"But why else would he have sent those men after

me?" she asked. "He must somehow know your real assignment is for the FBI."

Garek shrugged. "I don't know what he knows or if he's just a sadist. He murdered the man his daughter loved."

Candace gasped. She'd known Alexander Polinsky had worked for Chekov, but she hadn't realized he had also been involved with Tori.

"I feel bad," she said. "I thought she was just a spoiled bitch. I hadn't realized she was hurting."

"Oh, she's definitely a spoiled bitch," Garek said. "But she is pretty devastated—devastated enough to go to the FBI and report what she'd witnessed."

"She saw her father kill the man she loved?" Candace's heart ached for the other woman's loss. "He knows she could have gone to the police or be worried she might. She really could be in danger."

"That's why I've been watching her, too," Garek said. "Or having Milek watch her when I—"

"Have been rescuing me," she said. Now guilt flashed through her. Maybe Agent Rus was right and she would be the one who'd wind up getting him killed. "I should have stayed out of it."

Bitterness deepened his voice when he said, "You would have if Stacy hadn't tracked you down and talked you into coming back."

She didn't want him blaming his sister for the danger Candace had willingly put herself in. Even when she'd considered the Kozminskis dangerous criminals, she had envied their family's closeness and loyalty. They had been like the Paynes in that respect. But now they were estranged, and she didn't want to be responsible for any part of that.

She chuckled. "You think Stacy could have talked me into something I didn't want to do?"

"How did she?" he asked, and he spared a glance from the road and the rearview mirror for her. His silver eyes held curiosity and something else. Hope?

Did he want her to admit her feelings?

She hadn't yet admitted to her feelings—even to herself—when she'd come back. She'd had other motives.

"I took what she'd told me about you going to work for Chekov as an opportunity to prove I was right about you," she said. "She handed me the means to prove you were the criminal I'd been saying you were."

He chuckled now. "So you wanted to say I told you so to Logan and whoever else had defended me to you?"

She sighed. "I didn't have to prove to other people I was right about you. I had to prove it to me," she explained. "So I had an excuse for running from you…"

He took one hand from the wheel and reached across the console. His palm skimmed over her thigh. Her skin heated and tingled from even the brief touch over her jeans. "I don't blame you for running. In my own way, I was doing the same thing."

Frustration clenched her heart over the year they had wasted—a year they could have been together—without someone trying to kill them. "I should have trusted you."

"Why?" he asked with a laugh. "I gave you no reason to trust me. I wanted you to believe the worst of me."

"I was wrong to not look into you further, to not find out what kind of man you really are…" An amazing man. A loving brother. A fearless protector.

He squeezed her leg, making her tingle inside, before releasing her. He drew the SUV to the curb outside her apartment building and shifted it into Park.

"You didn't need to bring me home," she said. "I could have driven myself."

"You're not staying here," he informed her. And that was probably why he had refused to let her drive herself. "You're picking up whatever clothes you need for that party tomorrow night…"

Every year Viktor Chekov threw a Christmas party for all his employees and associates at the club. Candace had been ordered to attend as Tori's bodyguard, but he'd wanted her to dress like a guest—not a bodyguard.

He had looked at her then as if imagining what she looked like beneath her clothes. She had barely resisted the urge to shudder in revulsion. Not that she actually thought the man found her attractive; he had probably only done it for Garek's reaction, which he'd carefully guarded.

But she'd seen the flash of annoyance on his handsome face. And something else…

Jealousy?

He reached across the console and squeezed her leg again. "After you get what you need here, we're going back to my house."

Not his apartment.

His house.

She wanted it to be theirs—to be their *home* someday. But first they had to survive this assignment. Then they would be able to find out if they could survive each other. His fingers trailed around her thigh, between her legs.

Her breath caught as desire overwhelmed her. She wasn't sure she could wait until they got back to his house.

"We could stay here tonight," she offered—because she wanted him now.

He chuckled but reached for the door. Cold air blasted her as he opened it. Then she opened her door and stepped into the snow that the wintry wind whipped around them. The icy flakes stung her face and trapped her breath in her lungs.

He wrapped his arm around her for warmth and possibly protection as they hurried toward her lobby. "Maybe we should stay here," he murmured, his breath coming out in white clouds. "It's miserable out…"

The lobby was only marginally warmer. She reached for the button of the elevator, but he shook his head and led her toward the stairway. She had been a bodyguard longer than he had, but he was better at the job—better at protecting people. Stairwells were easier to escape than elevators—in case someone was after them.

"Why would he have hired me if he is the one trying to kill me?" she wondered aloud.

Garek glanced at her. "You were totally convinced Viktor was behind the attempts. What's changed? Has Rus gotten to you with his paroled felon theory?"

"If Chekov really wanted me dead, he could have killed me today," she said, "in his office."

Garek shuddered. "Maybe he knew Rus and Milek were close." That was the only reason he'd stopped protesting her going alone to meet his former boss and current client. "They would have come in had you'd been in there any longer."

He had come to her rescue instead. And he continued to protect her, placing his body between hers and every door that opened onto the stairwell. When they reached her floor, he stepped out in front of her, his weapon drawn.

She could have been offended he was trying to take

care of her—as if she didn't know how to take care of herself. Instead she felt something she had never felt before—cared for. His protectiveness and concern touched her heart almost as deeply as his honesty had. She was the one who always took care of and protected others. He was the only person in her life who wanted to protect and take care of her.

As they neared her door, he gasped. And she drew her own weapon. But there was no one else in the hallway. "What is it?" she asked.

He gestured toward her door. And she saw it had been treated like his apartment door had been. It hung from a broken jamb. He pointed for her to step back. But she was no longer touched or flattered. She was pissed. So she followed him through the broken door.

And she gasped now—at the chaos inside. Her apartment had been totally tossed—furniture overturned. Even her dishes had been knocked out of the open cupboards and lay in shards on the floor. Her gun drawn, she headed down the hall to her bedroom. Her clothes lay in a pile on the floor—the fabrics torn into pieces.

Garek shook his head in disbelief. "This is crazy," he murmured, "even for Viktor."

"It must be a warning," she said. Maybe that was what everything else had been—just a warning to not go after him, to not try to find evidence for his conviction. It was probably the only reason she wasn't dead. He hadn't wanted to kill her—either when he sent the men after her or put that gun against her head himself. "He's warning you to not betray him."

Garek shook his head again—not totally convinced. "We should call Rus."

"And what will he do?" she asked. "It's not as if we don't already know who's responsible."

"This isn't like Viktor, though," Garek said.

She turned toward him. "Really? I was there when he had his guys break into your apartment this same way—smashing the door down."

"But they didn't touch anything inside," he reminded her. "They didn't even search the place."

Which was fortunate for her since they would have found her hiding in the bedroom. Unless they'd already known she was there...

"Maybe he sent the men I shot the other night," she said. Because this *assault* on her apartment was definitely personal and vengeful.

Garek shuddered. "You're right. There's no reason to call Rus right now. Let's get out of here."

She glanced around at the chaos that had once been her home. Growing up as a military brat, she had never gotten attached to any place before, and she wasn't attached to this apartment either. But her things...

She sighed.

"There's nothing to salvage here," Garek said. "You're going to need all new stuff."

She had never gotten attached to things either. Every move had been a purge for her family. Out with the old. In with the new. She didn't have keepsakes like Penny Payne's Christmas tree of sentimental ornaments.

She wanted that, though.

"Yeah," she agreed. "There's nothing here for me." But him...

He caught her hand and led her back out of the apartment, back down the stairwell to the lobby. Before they stepped onto the street, he squeezed her hand and regretfully murmured, "I'm sorry…"

"Why?" she asked. "You didn't do it."

"It was because of me, though."

"Maybe not," she said. "Maybe Agent Rus has been right after all."

And even Garek had thought that level of destruction out of character for Viktor Chekov.

"Maybe this has nothing to do with you and everything to do with me," she said.

But he stared at her doubtfully. "I would consider it a possibility if not for how the door was broken down."

It was too weird a coincidence. It must have been Chekov—playing with them some more.

"Let's go…" she said and wanted to add *home*.

But she held the word inside just like she had held in the other words when they'd made love. She was more scared of expressing her feelings than she was of whatever game Chekov was playing with them.

But then they stepped onto the street and gunfire erupted. And as Garek went down, she wished she'd said all the words. She wished she had told him how much she loved him. But all she could do now was scream.

Chapter 19

"The bullet in your leg matches the one that killed Donald Doornbos and Alexander Polinsky," Nicholas said. It was the only good thing that had come of the shooting outside Candace's apartment building. They knew the gun was still in play.

So maybe Nicholas's special assignment could be salvaged yet. Maybe Viktor Chekov could finally be arrested and actually convicted. If he could trust the man Nick had enlisted to carry out the assignment didn't kill the mobster first...

Garek shook with fury, or maybe it was standing on his injured leg that had him wobbly. He glanced down at his bandaged thigh. "The bullet's not in my leg anymore."

"You shouldn't be checking yourself out yet, though," Nicholas said. While he was lying low so nobody spotted the two of them together, he'd heard the doctor warning Garek to take it easy while he'd lingered in the hall outside the private room. He had waited until the doctor had left to slip inside and close the door.

Not that Garek's cover hadn't already been blown. Why else would someone have tried to kill him or Candace? And it had been more than once. If not for that bullet matching the gun's ballistics, he would have cancelled Garek's assignment and pulled him out.

"We have to end this now," Garek said. "Eventually Chekov's common sense will overtake his arrogance and he'll get rid of that weapon."

Nicholas was surprised the notorious mobster hadn't. But then everything about this assignment had surprised him.

"I didn't think it would go like this," he admitted. With an eyewitness willing to testify, he had thought he would have a slam dunk open murder case for a grand jury and then a jury—once he recovered the murder weapon. And he'd thought a man like Garek Kozminski—a former thief and former associate of Chekov's—would easily recover that murder weapon. "I didn't think you'd get hurt."

Garek snorted. "I'm not hurt."

"You took a bullet in your leg," Nick reminded him. But maybe he shouldn't have. He didn't want Garek backing out of the assignment now—not when they were so close. But Chekov was close, too. "Three gunmen ambushed you and Candace when you left her building. You could have both been killed."

"We're not the ones in the morgue," Garek said.

Two of the gunmen were while the third had gotten away; he must have been the one who'd had the gun.

The weapons recovered at the scene had been tested and hadn't matched—like the bullet from Garek's leg had.

"We'll find the other guy," Nick vowed.

They had to in order to recover the weapon—unless he'd brought it back to Chekov already. Hopefully he had because Nick needed that gun discovered in Chekov's possession.

"We've already identified the dead men," he told Garek, "and we'll track down their known associates."

"Was Donald Doornbos one of them?" Garek asked. Nick nodded.

"Any connection to Chekov?"

Nick sighed. "Who in River City doesn't have a connection to Chekov?"

"Thanks to your assignment—nobody anymore," Garek said. "Payne Protection has him as a client."

Regret had Nick flinching. Penny was right. The family would never forgive him if something happened to one of them. Fortunately nobody knew about the shooting last night outside Candace's apartment. At least he didn't think they knew because he had received no outraged phone calls.

And Garek was alone at the hospital.

"Where's Candace?" he asked. The two had seemed to be inseparable until now.

In order to protect whatever was left of Garek's cover, Nicholas hadn't gone to the scene last night, but he'd been told she hadn't been hurt. Garek had probably taken the bullet meant for her. Or maybe the bullet had been meant for him. Maybe Chekov was already aware Garek was really working for the Bureau.

Should he call off the investigation?

Garek glanced at his watch and sighed. "Candace is Christmas shopping with Tori Chekov."

"Alone?"

"Milek is nearby," Garek said.

It was an FBI investigation; there should have been some agents on protection duty. But Nicholas could understand Garek not trusting any of them—because it certainly appeared Viktor Chekov was somehow aware of the investigation.

Why else had he gone after the man trying to take him down? Actually what Chekov had done was even more diabolical, he'd gone after the person who mattered most to Garek Kozminski: Candace.

"Should we call this off?" he asked.

Garek tensed, then laughed. "Why would you ask that *now*?"

"Because it's gotten dangerous as hell," Nick replied. "And it's clear your cover was probably compromised."

Garek shrugged. "It may have been. Or it may be Chekov is just a sick bastard. We still have a chance of putting him behind bars. We need to take that chance."

"You're the one taking chances," Nick said, "with your lives." And he was afraid the risk might be too great—Garek and Candace might not live till Christmas.

Candace hadn't wanted to leave him—wounded and alone at the hospital. But she was also so mad Garek had been shot she didn't want the man responsible to get away with it. He had already killed and hurt enough people.

Even his own daughter...

"Garek told you," Tori said as she pushed hangers back on a rack of dresses.

"What?"

"You know about Alexander," she said. "I can see the sympathy on your face."

She hadn't realized she was showing any sympathy. Worry, anger, exhaustion…those were all the things she was feeling now. It hadn't helped that Tori had dragged her through every store in the entire mall either. At least the woman had let Candace teach her some self-defense maneuvers before the shopping trip.

"Don't pity me," Tori said defensively.

After last night—after Garek had taken a bullet right in front of her—probably for her—Candace could sympathize even more with what Tori had gone through when her lover had been shot in front of her.

Fortunately for Candace, she hadn't lost him. Garek had managed to get back up, and he had returned fire with her. And before she'd left the hospital, the doctor had assured her that he would be fine. The bullet had done no real damage to his leg.

"I don't pity you," Candace assured her. "I'm sorry…"

"Sorry he told you?" Tori asked. "Now you can't hate me?"

"I don't hate you," Candace said.

"You didn't like me, though."

She didn't like her any more now. She just understood her better. And she also respected how quickly the woman had caught on to the self-defense maneuvers. Tori Chekov was smarter and stronger than Candace had initially thought.

"If I were you, I wouldn't like me either," Tori said. "What woman would actually like the old girlfriend of the man she loves?"

Candace didn't deny her feelings for Garek but she

didn't admit to them either. She needed to declare her love directly to Garek before she confessed it to anyone else.

Tori took one of the dresses from the rack and held it against Candace. "This is it," she said. "And blue is Garek's favorite color."

Candace didn't know Garek's favorite anything. While she had learned a lot about him recently, Tori Chekov had known him longer. And she was making it clear to Candace.

She shook her head. "I'm not shopping for me."

Tori Chekov was supposed to be Christmas shopping, but all she had done was shop for herself. Until now—until she'd taken this sudden and unsettling interest in Candace's wardrobe.

"You need a dress for the Christmas party," Tori said.

Candace cocked her head. "How do you know I don't have one?"

She would have worn the red one she'd worn to the club that night—and to last year's Payne Protection Agency's Christmas party—but it lay in tatters on her bedroom floor.

Tori shrugged. "You don't seem like a cocktail dress kind of person."

"I was wearing one the first night I came to the club," Candace reminded her.

"But you can't wear that anymore." Tori bit her lip to stop herself as her face flushed with color.

"You know about my apartment," Candace said. "You know it was broken into and my things destroyed."

Tori grimaced. "I'm sorry…"

"Did you hear your father order someone to do that?" she asked. "You could testify to it, too."

"Too?" Tori asked. Anger flashed in her dark eyes. "Garek did tell you everything…"

And Candace agreed with his conviction that Tori wasn't likely to testify against her father—even after he had killed the man she loved. They needed to find that gun. They needed to see their plan through.

She took the deep blue velvet dress from Tori. "It is a pretty color."

"It'll look beautiful on you," Tori said as she grabbed a gold dress and held it up against herself.

"And you'll look beautiful in anything," Candace said—because Tori Chekov was one of those women who probably would have looked stunning even in army fatigues.

But she couldn't hate her. All she could do was promise her, "We'll make sure there's justice for Alexander."

Tears filled Tori's dark eyes, and she nodded. "Thank you…"

Last night she had been tempted to call off the assignment—to let Chekov scare them off. But then she'd gotten angry and determined to put him away for the rest of his life. She was even more determined now to follow through on the assignment. She just hoped no more lives were lost—especially not hers or Garek's.

Wincing against the twinge of pain in his leg, Garek hobbled across his living room. He leaned over and plugged in the extension cord for the lights, setting the tree to twinkling and glowing. Then he took a present from his pocket and slid it under the tree.

Candace wasn't the only one who had gone Christmas shopping. He had made a stop on his way home—at his sister's store. He only hoped he had a chance to give the gift to Candace—that they survived the assignment.

Stacy had apologized for involving Candace and for doubting him. His gut tightened even now as he remembered her tears and her concern when she'd seen his leg. He'd been concerned, too—that she knew the truth. That everyone knew about his *undercover* assignment. If Chekov didn't already know, he was bound to find out soon. Garek hoped it was after he found the murder weapon, though.

Boards creaked overhead, and he reached for his weapon. Who had found his house? He had been so careful to make sure no one had followed them last time they'd come here or had followed him tonight.

But Rus knew about it. Someone else could have found out however the FBI agent had. Or maybe even from the FBI agent. Had Garek been a fool to trust him?

Biologically Nicholas Rus was a Payne, but Penny hadn't raised him. So he didn't necessarily possess the integrity and honor of the other Paynes. Maybe he could be bought; maybe Chekov had paid him off.

Grasping his gun, Garek headed to the stairs. Each step was an exercise in torture, making him flinch as pain shot through the wound in his leg. Maybe he had already overdone it—as the doctor had warned him. Maybe he should have stayed another night. But he hadn't had that luxury. With the Christmas party tonight at the club, he'd never have a better time to search Chekov's home.

If only the weapon had been returned to Chekov...

If only Garek could find it...

But to find it, he had to escape whoever had broken

into his home. But he hadn't noticed the lock had been picked. There had been no telltale gouges.

Whoever had broken in was good. Finally upstairs, he moved toward where he'd heard the noise—in the master bedroom. And he found his intruder standing before the antique oval mirror, which was one of the antiques he'd bought with the house—like the four-poster bed.

His intruder wasn't just good. She was beautiful. His breath escaped in a gasp of awe.

She whirled toward him. Then she rushed over to him, throwing her arms around his neck. "Are you all right?" Candace asked.

He nodded. "Yeah..." But since he had promised to be honest with her from now on, he admitted, "My leg hurts like hell, though."

"How did you make it up the stairs?"

"Painfully," he murmured. "I didn't know you were coming here."

"I made sure I wasn't followed," she assured him. "And I remembered the code for the door."

He nodded. "That's why there were no marks on it."

She smiled. "You'll have to teach me how to pick a lock better."

He wouldn't deny her the knowledge; the skill had proven useful even after he had quit his family business. He just hoped he had time to teach her. "You're already dressed for the party."

The dress was a deep blue that matched her eyes, and in a warm velvet that hugged her curves and even covered her arms. But then she turned again and showed him where the fabric dipped low in the back, showing off the sexy ridge of her long spine. He couldn't help himself, or maybe had to help himself, so he leaned forward and brushed his lips across the bare skin of her back.

She shivered.

"Maybe you should find another dress," he suggested.

"You don't like this one?" she asked, and disappointment lowered her voice.

"I like this dress too much," he said. "And so will every other man in the club."

He wouldn't be there, though. He would be at Chekov's estate—breaking in and then finding the damn safe—if Chekov or his men didn't catch him first.

And if they caught him, he wanted to make sure he didn't have this regret—that he hadn't taken the dress off her. So he pushed the sleeves and the dress from her shoulders until it dropped to the floor.

She wore only a thin strip of lace beneath it. Not even a bra. He groaned as his body hardened and began to pulse, demanding release. Demanding her…

He quickly dropped his coat and shirt onto the floor next to hers. But to take off his pants, he had to sit on the bed—had to wriggle to get them off.

"Garek," she murmured, joining him on the bed. But she reached out and skimmed her fingers along the edge of his bloodstained bandage. "We can't do this. You're hurt."

He was hurting; his body aching with tension, with wanting her. Just her fingers on his thigh had his heart pounding faster and harder.

He pushed her back onto the bed and said, "I'd have to be dead to not want you."

Her eyes widened with fear. She was afraid he might wind up dead. Tonight.

He didn't want her afraid. He wanted her—wanted

her wild with desire for him, like he was for her. So he touched her, running his fingers and his lips over every silky inch of her skin.

She moaned and writhed as he kissed her breasts and then moved his mouth lower, to make love to her body. She screamed his name as pleasure claimed her. But then she pushed him back. And she took over, making love to him with her mouth and then her body.

She carefully lowered herself onto him—moving slowly as if to not jar his leg. He was beyond feeling pain—he could only feel her heat and her passion. Out of his mind with need, he thrust up and grasped her hips. She met his frantic rhythm and screamed again as another orgasm shuddered through her. Then finally the tension broke inside his body, and he came—filling her.

She moved to separate their bodies, but he clutched at her hips, holding her. Joined as they were, he felt as if he were part of her, and she was part of him. He didn't want to lose their closeness. He didn't want to lose her. He stroked his fingers down her naked back, over the sexy ridge of her spine.

She shivered and murmured his name, "Garek…"

There was regret in her voice; she had to leave. They both knew it. But he still held her, reluctant to separate. What if this was the last time they were together? Should he tell her what he felt for her?

Should he give her the present he'd put under the tree?

But then she might be distracted. And he would never forgive himself if he was the reason something happened to her. Even if she wasn't distracted—and something happened—he would still be the one to blame. Despite Stacy's guilt over tracking her down, he was the one who'd gotten her mixed up in his dangerous assignment—in his dangerous past. Not that she hadn't faced her share of danger on her own. She was strong. He had to trust she could take care of herself—as she always had. But he wanted to take care of her, too.

"I'm going to be late," she said. "We shouldn't have done this…"

"Then maybe it's a good thing I got shot," he said.

Her lips curved into a smile. "What do you think this was? Sympathy sex?"

"Wasn't it?" he asked. "I feel very sympathized with…"

She laughed—like he had wanted her to. And finally he released her. She sprang up from him and from the bed. Grabbing her dress up from the floor, she headed toward the bathroom but left the door open.

Like him, she must have been reluctant to be apart from him. To leave him…

He needed to get up, too. But he moved slowly, as pain shot through his leg. He flinched, but he had no regrets.

"While you're at the club with Tori and Viktor, I'll search the house," he said.

She was already aware of the plan. They had *all* gone through it before she had confronted Chekov and stolen his job the other morning.

But he needed to repeat it, needed to remind himself it would all be over soon. "I'll find the safe tonight for certain."

She stepped out of the bathroom, fully dressed again. She looked so beautiful but there was also sadness in her blue eyes now. A fear—not for herself, of course. Her fear was for him.

"You're hurt," she said again. "Milek could search the house instead."

He shook his head. "He's not as good as I am," he

said it with no arrogance. It was just a statement of fact. When they were learning the family *business*, he had made certain he was better than his younger brother, so their father had taken him on jobs instead of Milek. And that was why Viktor had wanted him—instead of his brother—after their father had gone to prison.

"You didn't get better because you were competitive," she said. "You got better because you were protective."

She had gotten close to him—closer than he had even feared she would. It was as if she could see into his mind, his soul, his heart…

"Milek might be able to find the safe," Garek continued, "but he wouldn't be able to crack it. *I* have to do this. I am the best man for the job."

She nodded. "It's going to end tonight…" She didn't say the rest of it. But he was close to her, also—so much so he could read her mind, too.

One way or another it would end. Tonight was the night they might both die.

She kissed him—skimming her lips over his. Then she headed for the door, her heels clipping across the hardwood. But at the bedroom doorway, she paused and whispered, "I love you…"

Or maybe he'd only seen into her heart and imagined or wished she'd said the words. Before he could say anything back, she was gone.

And with his leg, he wouldn't be able to make it down the stairs before she left. He could only hope she had seen into his heart, and she knew he loved her, too.

And he hoped they both lived to say the words to each other again.

Chapter 20

Milek stared through the windshield at the snow falling on the hood of his SUV. Each flake melted the minute it hit the warm metal and slid off like teardrops.

"Where do you need me?" he asked, speaking into the microphone with which Special Agent Rus had wired him. Tonight everyone was wired but Candace.

Chekov may have hired the ex-cop to protect his daughter. But he wouldn't have trusted her enough to confess to her. And he would have searched her for a wire anyway. He had when she'd picked up his daughter to go shopping earlier.

Milek, through his binoculars, had watched the exchange in the driveway. With the way Chekov's hands had lingered, it was good Garek hadn't witnessed the pat down. Not that the gangster wasn't already fully aware of how Garek felt about the female bodyguard. No one could miss his feelings; he wore them all over his face. Even the ever-oblivious Tori had noticed right away the first night Candace had shown up at the club.

"I need you out near the estate," Rus replied. "In case Garek needs you to help him. His leg is still a mess. He shouldn't be out there alone."

"He shouldn't be out there at all," Milek said. But he couldn't argue his brother was the better safecracker.

"Garek can get past the security system," Rus said. "He can get past the skeleton crew of human security Chekov left out there, too. But he can't get out of there in a hurry if he needs to—not with that leg. That's where you'll be best. You know the estate."

"*Garek* wanted me at the club," Milek reminded the FBI agent.

Rus might have been the one in charge of the investigation, but during their meeting the other morning, Garek had made it clear he was in charge of this plan. And it was clear why.

Milek said, "He's more concerned about Candace's safety than his own."

"I brought in a team from Chicago," Rus said. "Guys I know I can trust."

Uneasiness lifted goose bumps on Milek's skin. "You have guys here you can't trust?"

"I don't know," Rus admitted. "I don't understand why anyone's going after Candace."

"To get to Garek."

"But why would anyone want to get to Garek?" Rus asked. "Unless they knew what he was really doing working for Chekov. And how would they know?"

Milek sucked in a breath. "You think someone betrayed the investigation?"

"I don't," Rus said. "I thought I had a team in place I could trust—that I'd gotten rid of most of the corruption in the department."

"But you never know who you can really trust…" After that day—that horrible day—when he'd killed a man, Milek had been unable to even trust himself.

Rus's sigh rattled the cell phone. "I'm sorry," he said. "About the other night…"

"Are you sorry about what you said?" Milek asked.

He hadn't really said anything, though. His cryptic comment about everything not always being what it appeared to be could have been alluding to anything. It was something Milek said all the time himself.

It was like this assignment Garek had agreed to take. Stacy and Candace had thought he had gone back to his old life. But that hadn't been case at all. Garek had been trying to correct the mistakes of his old life—trying to take down a man he could have taken down fifteen years ago and would have if he hadn't been protecting him and Stacy.

And maybe there was something else that really wasn't what it appeared to be regarding this assignment. Maybe Viktor Chekov was not the only danger in this case.

After a long pause, Rus sighed again. "I don't know if I should have said something now. Or a year ago…"

Now Milek had no doubt about what Special Agent Rus was alluding to. But he couldn't consider all the implications of the man's admission. Not now. He had to give all his attention to tonight—for Garek's and Candace's sake—for their lives.

And Milek had just drawn another conclusion about this case equally unsettling—they had been focused on the wrong person this entire time. There was another threat out there, and they had to determine who before it was too late.

Red and green strobe lights flashed across the crowded dance floor. The whole club vibrated with the beat of the bass. Candace's head lightened as she twirled away and then back into her dance partner's arms.

Viktor Chekov had to be younger than he looked, or he moved very well for an older man. He held her closely against him as he continued to move them around the dance floor.

She was supposed to be working this shift of protection duty for Tori, but Chekov was monopolizing her time, at least her dance card. That worked with the plan, though, so Candace could make sure Chekov didn't leave the party early to head home. Garek was there, searching the estate for that weapon. Hopefully he'd already found it and left because she wasn't certain how much longer she could keep up—or put up—with Chekov on the dance floor.

Fortunately—or unfortunately—she'd had his full attention since she had walked into the club.

"I can't get over how beautiful you look," he murmured again, his mouth close to her ear. His hand trailed down her bare back.

She barely resisted the urge to shudder with revulsion. She had an even stronger urge to grab his hand and break it. Garek was the only one she wanted touching her. Hopefully he was touching the safe now, cracking it open and finding the damn gun.

But even then would it be enough? If Tori backed out of testifying against her father, would they have enough to convict him? Or would he remain as unscathed as he always had?

"Tori picked out the dress for me," she said.

"That's right," he said. "The two of you went *shopping* today." His voice held patronization and disparagement—as if he thought all women just liked to shop.

She leaned back and stared up into his face to gauge his reaction as she said, "Well, I had no choice. After my apartment was ransacked, I will have to buy all new clothes, not just this dress."

His dark eyes widened with shock. "What happened to your apartment?" he asked, as if he hadn't heard her correctly.

Why was he so surprised if he'd ordered the destruction? Maybe he hadn't thought his guys would carry the threat so far, though.

"The door was broken down," she said. "Kind of like Garek's had been."

The gangster's dark eyes narrowed. "There was a break-in at Garek's," he acknowledged. "But that's the only break-in I am aware of."

He had just admitted the truth about Garek's; of course he might have known she'd been there—hiding in the bedroom when his men had broken down the door. But still, he'd told the truth. So why would he lie about her place? He had no reason to lie to her. But if Viktor hadn't known about the break-in, how had Tori known?

She'd claimed she'd heard it from him.

Viktor spun her again but instead of reeling her back into his arms, he led her off the floor—to that roped-off table where Tori sat with some of his other men. Milek must have been with Garek.

But Special Agent Rus had assured she would have

other backup in the club. She hadn't met them, though, so she wasn't sure who they were—or if they were really even there. And she had no way of signaling for help; she wasn't wired with a microphone.

It would have been too dangerous. With as close as she'd been dancing with Chekov, he would have noticed if she'd been wearing a wire. Maybe that was why he'd been so handsy—because he didn't seem interested now. He held out the chair next to his daughter for Candace. But he didn't take one at the table himself.

"Enjoy the rest of your evening," Viktor said. He gestured at his men who stood and hurried to his side.

"Where—where are you going?" Candace asked.

He tilted his head, and his dark eyes flashed a warning at her imprudence. "You are protecting Tori," he reminded her. "No one else…"

She wanted to protect Garek. And if Chekov caught him at the estate, he would need protection—especially if Chekov was bringing all those guys with him.

"Of course," Candace quickly agreed with him. "I just thought this was your party…"

"It is," he said. "And I've put in an appearance. Now it's time for me to leave."

Before she could say anything else—come up with any other excuse to stall him—he walked away—in the middle of his entourage. Would Rus's backup even realize he was leaving? Would they warn Garek in time?

She reached for her purse and the cell phone she'd left inside. But it was no longer hanging over the back of her chair. Where had it gone?

"Daddy stayed longer than he usually does at this party," Tori informed her. "Probably because he was busy dancing with *you*…"

Dancing in the hot and crowded club had made Candace thirsty—so thirsty she picked up her water from the table and took a quick gulp.

"He couldn't take his eyes off you," Tori continued. "I can't imagine Garek would have been too thrilled with the way you two were behaving."

It sounded as if Tori was the one who wasn't too thrilled. Candace turned toward the other woman. "We were just talking…"

And she remembered what Viktor had said. "…about the break-in at my apartment."

Tori tensed. "What about the break-in?"

"He didn't know anything about it."

"Of course he wouldn't admit to it," she said with a disparaging snort. "He knows you're an ex-cop. He probably knows you and Garek are working together to get evidence against him."

How did she know? How did Tori know everything?

Candace narrowed her eyes and tried to focus on the woman. But it was as if the strobe lights had started flashing faster—blinding her. She could see only red and green—no images. And her head began to pound.

She had been drugged.

And there was only one person who could have done it and only one reason why: Tori; she was the one who wanted Candace dead. And now that she'd been drugged, Candace had no way of protecting herself.

Viktor's safe wasn't in his den. Of course that would have been too obvious. The safe was in his master suite—in the floor of the walk-in closet. It was more than a safe, really. It was a vault. And like a vault, it hadn't been easy to open. Garek could have used dynamite. Or backup.

But he'd had to sneak in—slowly, thanks to his wounded leg—and alone. He'd bypassed the security system with no problem. Hell, he knew the code. Even if Tori hadn't told him, he'd watched Viktor enter it enough times to figure it out. Her birthday…

How could a man who seemed to love his daughter as much as Viktor loved Tori have killed the man she loved right in front of her? It made no sense. But could a man like Viktor—a man as ruthless and violent—really love anyone—even his own daughter?

Agent Rus would have to convince the woman that her father didn't love her, if he had any hope of getting her to testify against him. Garek doubted she would. No matter how much he had hurt her, she wouldn't betray her father.

Any more than Garek thought Viktor would have betrayed her…

What had Alexander Polinsky done? He'd heard the man was a player. Maybe Viktor had found out the guy had cheated on Tori. But then why would she have been upset about his killing him?

Garek shook his head and returned his attention to the vault. He didn't have much time. Chekov never stayed long at his own parties. It was why he held them at the club instead of the estate—so he could go home whenever he wanted.

There were guards outside, though. And Milek. He'd heard his voice earlier. But since he'd stepped inside that closet, he hadn't heard any of the voices through his earpiece. Either things were awfully quiet outside. Or the closet was soundproof and signal proof.

That probably meant they couldn't hear Garek either—if he needed to call for help. Despite the warmth of the house, Garek shivered.

This was not good.

Maybe he needed to step out of the closet and make contact—at least let them know where he was inside the massive house. But then the lock clicked and the door popped open. The vault was deep and filled nearly to the top. Heavy plastic bags displayed contents of money and drugs. And there were guns...

Long guns. Automatic rifles. Handguns. He needed to call in the others to help him catalogue the contents. As far as he could see there were no tapes. Viktor was probably too smart to have his office wired, to risk recording his meetings and have those recordings fall into the wrong hands. Into hands like Garek's.

"Hey, can anyone hear me?" he asked.

Not even static emanated from his earpiece, nor the echo of his own voice. He doubted anyone could hear him.

He leaned into the vault and drew out a couple of the handguns. They were the same caliber of the bullet that had been pulled from his leg. But somehow he knew they weren't the weapon for which he searched.

There were a lot of guns in that vault, but he suspected not one of them was the murder weapon he needed for evidence. But would Viktor have the weapon if he wasn't the murderer?

Oh, the man was a killer. He'd killed before, and he would kill again if he wasn't stopped. But had he killed Alexander Polinsky?

Maybe someone had heard him, because he heard a

door open—the only door he would be able to hear in the soundproof room—the door to the closet itself.

"Milek?" he called out hopefully.

"Your brother won't be able to help you anymore," Viktor said.

His deadly tone chilled Garek's blood. Had he found Milek outside? Had he killed him?

He shouldn't have gotten his brother involved. But like always, Milek had given him no choice. He still followed him around like he had when they were kids.

But his brother wasn't his only concern. Viktor had been with Candace. What had he done to her?

Garek looked up from the vault to confront the killer. And he stared directly into the barrel of a gun. If he'd ever actually had a guardian angel, the celestial being must have deserted him, or he would have had some warning that Chekov was coming.

Now it was too late. Whatever had been done to his brother and the woman he loved—Garek was about to suffer the same ill fate.

Chapter 21

"What do you mean—you lost contact with both of them?" Nicholas demanded to know.

His heart began to hammer in his chest. His whole investigation was falling apart. And if that fell apart, so would his chance of ever really being part of the Payne family. They would never forgive him if Garek or Candace were harmed. Hell, he'd never forgive himself. Those people had come to mean a lot to him, too.

"What about Milek Kozminski?" he asked.

"We found his SUV running, the door open and blood on the seat and on the snow beside it."

"Oh, God…" It didn't look good for Milek either.

"Yeah," Agent Dalton Reyes said. "You should have brought me in from the beginning, instead of using bodyguards to carry out an investigation like this. Organized crime is my specialty."

"It was theirs, too," Nick said, "before they became bodyguards. They worked for Chekov years ago."

Dalton breathed a sigh of respect. He had once been a gang member himself. He understood the education and skill gained through a life lived even momentarily on the wrong side of the law.

"I'm surprised they've lived this long," Reyes said. "You don't leave an organization like Chekov's alive."

Just like you didn't leave a gang and live. Dalton knew the danger well.

"We have to find them," Nicholas said.

"You want us to go inside the estate?" Reyes asked. "We don't have a warrant."

"Milek's blood is your warrant," Nick said. "He's in imminent danger. You have cause to go in."

"But whatever we find inside could be inadmissible in court," the other agent pointed out. He knew what it took to make a case.

Nicholas cursed his opinion of a warrant. A conviction didn't matter as much to him as saving lives—especially *these* lives.

"We have to find them," he repeated and added, "Alive."

"That may not be an option," Reyes warned him.

There was no other option. If they hadn't survived this investigation, Nicholas would never forgive himself and neither would the Paynes. He would have no reason to stay in River City. It didn't matter that his career would be over; he would lose much more than that.

He could only hope the Kozminskis and Candace had not already lost everything as well—including their lives.

Pain throbbed dully in Candace's head—not as if she had taken a blow to her skull but as if she had a hangover. She dragged her lids open and peered around. No lights flashed—red and green—like they had at the club. In fact it was black—wherever she was. She tried to reach out, to test her boundaries, but her arms couldn't move. Hard plastic bit into her wrists so sharply it nearly broke the skin. She stilled her movements and assessed her situation.

She had obviously been drugged. The water...

She had also been tied up, apparently with zip ties. They were harder to break than handcuffs. She might have been able to pick the lock on the handcuffs. But she needed a knife to cut the plastic and free herself.

She'd had a knife—in her purse. But that was already lost at the club. She didn't feel the gun she'd had holstered to her thigh either. It was gone. She was completely defenseless. And she hated the feeling.

Hell, she didn't even know where she was. Then a light flashed, blinding her. She squinted against it until her eyes adjusted to the sudden brightness of the fluorescent lights hanging down from the open rafters above her. She was lying on a cold concrete floor in a basement—probably of the club. And a woman stood over her.

Tori still wore the gold dress they had picked out on their shopping trip. She looked beautiful—or she would have—had jealousy and madness not twisted her face into a grotesque mask of hatred.

"Daddy thought you would teach me how to protect myself?" She laughed. "You can't even protect *yourself*."

Candace had no defense for that comment. The woman spoke the truth, so there was no point in arguing with her. There was probably no point in yelling either. If Tori had thought anyone could hear her, she would have gagged her. She had just tied her up instead.

"He has no idea I don't need any protection," Tori said. "I take care of myself."

But a man stood behind her—a heavily muscled man who looked vaguely familiar to Candace. He wasn't one of Chekov's men whom she'd met earlier. But this man had either run her off the road, or taken shots at her and Garek outside her apartment. Or both…

He was no doubt the person who'd carried her down the stairs, too. While Tori was stronger than Candace had initially thought, she wasn't strong enough to have carried her.

The woman bitterly continued, "I also take care of anyone who messes with me."

Yet it was probably this man who had tied her up—after carrying her. The zip ties had been pulled tightly—too tightly for Candace to easily free herself.

"*I* didn't mess with you," she told the crazy woman. She had done nothing to her but momentarily feel sorry for her.

Tori snorted. "You showed up here at the club—distracting Garek."

"You wanted his attention?"

Tori sighed. "A lifetime ago Garek was all I wanted."

She had loved him then. Stacy was lucky Candace hadn't acted like this when Logan had fallen for the female Kozminski instead of her. She'd been bitter, but she hadn't gone all *Fatal Attraction* like this.

"But I loved what Garek had more than who he was," Tori continued.

Candace tensed with confusion. "I don't understand…"

"He had Daddy's respect," she said. "My father adores Garek."

Remembering his bruises and the way Viktor had broken into his apartment, Candace had concerns about how Chekov showed his affection. No wonder Tori was so messed up.

"You're jealous of Garek?"

"I wanted Daddy to see him for the man he is," she said. "Weak…"

Candace laughed now. She had thought the wrong things about Garek most of the time she'd known him, but even she had never considered him weak. "Garek Kozminski?" she asked. "How is he weak?"

Tori pointed to her—with the barrel of the gun she grasped so tightly. Even if Candace could work her zip ties loose, she wasn't certain she could get that gun from the smaller woman without taking a bullet.

"You're his weakness," Tori said with disgust. "The minute you showed up, he lost all focus."

"On you…" This was all about jealousy. But Candace wasn't certain of whom the woman was jealous: her or Garek. Maybe both?

"So you were behind the attempts on my life?" Candace asked.

Tori just shrugged. But the man standing behind her looked at the female Chekov; clearly she was his boss. Not her father…

She had ordered him to go after Candace—like she had probably ordered that first man to follow her from the club. They'd all thought the spoiled Chekov princess had just been texting friends on her phone. They should have realized the woman had no friends. She must have been texting her own team of goons.

"Daddy noticed how easily Garek got distracted," she said and a brief, smug smile crossed her face. "He realized Garek wasn't as great and wonderful as he'd thought."

"Garek saved my life every time," Candace reminded her. And she hoped he would once again. But he was already hurt and completely across town. Would he figure out in time who was really responsible—would he know where to find her? "I think he's pretty great and wonderful."

Tori snorted. And as if she'd read Candace's mind, she said, "He won't save you this time. He won't even be able to save himself."

Candace held in a gasp as fear stabbed her heart. The woman was too smug; she knew something—something Candace wouldn't like to learn. "What's happened to Garek?"

Tori glanced at her watch as if she'd had everything timed. Of course she had been playing them all for weeks—even Special Agent Rus. "By now Daddy has caught Garek breaking into his safe."

Garek had been wearing a wire; that was the plan. He should have had a warning when Chekov returned to his estate. But then he'd been wounded. He wouldn't have been able to move fast enough to escape getting caught.

Tori clicked her tongue against her teeth in a *tsk*ing noise. "All that trouble and he didn't find what he was looking for."

Of course she would have known what Garek was looking for; Tori had put everything in motion when she'd gone to FBI agent Rus. Had that been on purpose, too? Had she known he would enlist Garek to help find the weapon? She may have even suggested it to him.

Tori wiggled the gun she held on Candace. "Because I have it. I had it all along. Garek gave his life for something he was never going to find."

Fear and panic clutched Candace's heart. If Chekov had caught him, would he kill Garek? The man was ruthless; of course he would. But she refused to give in to panic and despair. She had doubted Garek before. She wouldn't doubt him again. She would trust if anyone could survive—Garek could.

"What the hell's going on?" Chekov asked. "You had your brother out front—as a lookout—"

"What did you do to him?" Garek demanded to know. Milek couldn't be dead; he had already lost too much to lose his life, as well.

Chekov laughed. "Always so protective of your younger siblings—that protectiveness is what landed you in prison."

Garek played on it—reminding Chekov of his loyalty. "I landed in prison because I wouldn't give you up."

"You landed in prison because you killed a man," Chekov said. Clearly he believed Garek's mother's twisted testimony. "You did it to protect your siblings. And you didn't turn on me to protect them."

He hadn't done as good a job protecting Milek now. Or Candace…

"I need to know what happened to my brother," he persisted. "I need to know if he needs medical help."

Viktor chuckled. "I doubt it. From what I've seen he's as hardheaded as you are."

So he'd been hit over the head…

Depending on how hard he'd been struck, he could have survived. Garek drew in a breath and held on to hope, like he held on to the gun he'd taken from the vault.

"What the hell are you doing—breaking into my vault?" Viktor asked.

All his life Garek had handled stress with humor, so he strove for levity now. "Once a thief, always a thief…"

"Problem with you, Garek, is you weren't really a thief," Viktor said with great disappointment.

"I'm a Kozminski," Garek reminded him. And by virtue of his very heritage, he'd had no choice.

"Oh, you have the skills, obviously," Viktor said as he gestured at the open vault. "But you never had the heart of a true thief. You never really *wanted* to steal."

Garek couldn't deny that. "I was a disappointment to my father."

"He had to force you to do what he loved," Viktor said. "And after he went to jail, I had to force you to continue what he loved." Chekov gestured at the open vault again. "Is that what this is about? Revenge?"

"Maybe," Garek admitted. It was probably part of the reason why he had agreed to the assignment Rus had offered him—to get back at Viktor for his coercion and threats—for terrorizing him as a kid. The other part was just the man eluding justice for too long.

"You can't shoot me with the gun," Chekov said. "It's not loaded. None of them are." He cocked the one he held, though. "But this one…"

"You're going to shoot me like you shot Alexander Polinsky?" Garek asked.

Viktor tensed then repeated, "Like I shot Alexander?" He laughed but with sadness rather than humor. "Alexander was like a son to me. I would not have hurt him."

Garek could not doubt the sincerity and pain in Viktor's voice. He had obviously cared about the murdered man. Not that he still couldn't have killed him. Rumor had it he'd killed his own brother years ago—in order to get ahead in their *family*.

"Why would you accuse me of such a horrible thing?" Viktor asked, and he was clearly appalled.

Garek shook his head and hastened to clarify, "*I* didn't accuse you of anything."

"Who did?" Viktor demanded to know.

He would not give up Tori, so he just shrugged. "People are always saying things about you. Horrible things."

"But to say I killed a man I loved and respected?" Anger burned in Viktor's dark eyes. "Why would anyone say that?"

Why indeed? Garek could think of several reasons, but the main one was to deflect guilt. His stomach lurched as he briefly considered the implications of the realization. It couldn't be…

"Why would anyone have killed Alexander?" Garek asked.

Viktor shook his head. "I don't know. I figured it was about me—someone was trying to hurt me."

Garek had suspected the same reason for why someone had gone after Candace—to get to him. He'd suspected that person had been Viktor. Now he wondered.

"That's why I hired you—or Payne Protection—to protect Tori," Chekov continued. "I figured someone was after me and would use everyone close to me to get to me."

"So no one had any reason to want to kill Alexander Polinsky?"

"There was no reason," Viktor maintained, "no reason for him to die."

And now Garek had no doubts—not even a niggling one. Viktor Chekov had not killed his right-hand man. Fear clenched his heart as he realized who had. He hadn't wanted to consider it, but it was the only thing—*she* was the only person who made sense.

"Where's Candace?" he asked.

The man stared at him—as if he'd lost his mind. "Candace?"

"The female bodyguard you hired to protect Tori," he reminded him.

"She's protecting Tori," Viktor said—his voice full of condescension and then confusion.

She was protecting Tori. But who was protecting her?

Had she realized yet who the real killer was? Because Garek had just figured it out, and he hoped it wasn't too late to stop Tori Chekov from killing again. From killing the woman he loved...

Chapter 22

Logan pressed a quick kiss to her lips before he hurried out of their home. He wasn't going alone into the danger; he never did. He would meet his brothers. Parker and Cooper would back him up.

Would they be too late to save the others, though?

Stacy shivered.

"Close the door," Milek told her. But he didn't leave with the others. Instead of waiting for her to do it, he pulled it shut himself—with him inside with her. "It's freezing out there."

But it wasn't the cold that had chilled her. It was why he had come to their home—what he had told them.

She had expected him to leave with the others—even though he was hurt. Blood had crusted in his hair, turning the light blond strands dark and rusty colored. She lifted her hand to reach out to him but then she pulled it back—certain he would reject her, he would leave if she tried to get too close. He was like an injured animal—too hurt and mistrustful to let anyone close enough to help him.

"I can have Penny watch the baby," she said, "and I can bring you to the hospital." But she was already certain he wouldn't accept her help. "Or Penny can take you…"

"One of the FBI agents checked me out at Chekov's… once they found me."

Before Milek had shown up, Logan had taken a call from his half brother. From his end of the conversation and the worry in his voice, she'd thought she had lost her immediate family. That both her brothers had died. Then the doorbell had rung, and Logan had opened it to a pale and wounded Milek.

According to what Nicholas Rus had told Logan, some FBI agents had found Milek in the snow quite a distance from his vehicle—as if he'd been crawling toward the gates of the estate—determined to help his older brother. But he'd given up on Garek and had come to her.

And he hadn't left yet.

"Do you think he's dead?" she asked. Not that Stacy expected him to tell her the truth. She had kept the truth from him for years. He didn't owe her any honesty; he didn't owe her anything.

He shook his head and grimaced, the movement no doubt causing him pain. "I'm not as worried about Garek as I am Candace."

"She disappeared?"

He nodded and grimaced again. "Right under the noses of Rus's backup agents." His voice was gruff with disgust and frustration. "They never even saw her leave the party."

"Then she'll be close to the club," Stacy said. "They'll find her." They had to find her.

But Milek said nothing now. He offered no false assurances—because they would be false. When he finally spoke again, it was with brutal honesty. "I think they'll find her too late."

Too late to save her...

She shivered again—with concern and dread and regret. Just that afternoon Garek had come to see her at the jewelry store she owned, and he had bought one of her favorite pieces—something he had long admired. She'd wanted to just give it to him, but he had insisted on buying it. He hadn't confirmed anything, but she had guessed why he'd wanted it.

"I shouldn't have dragged her into this," she said. "I shouldn't have talked to her about Garek." Especially since she had been wrong. "I shouldn't have doubted him..." She had told Garek all that, and he'd acted as though he'd forgiven her—but it had been before tonight.

Before Candace had gone missing...

"I doubted him, too," Milek admitted, and now his grimace was of guilt instead of pain. "I wondered if he'd gone back to that life."

He had, but not for the reasons she had thought. He'd gone back to bring a man to justice. She had apologized to him earlier, but it wasn't enough. It would never be enough if Candace didn't survive—like Milek obviously feared.

Pain squeezed her heart, and she murmured, "He's going to hate me." She glanced at Milek. "Like you hate me..."

She turned away to spare him her tears. But strong arms wrapped around her. Logan was gone; it was Milek, holding her. Offering comfort…

"I don't hate you," he assured her. "I could never hate you. And neither could Garek."

But Stacy hated herself—for interfering in their lives, for costing Milek his happiness and maybe costing Garek his. Candace had to survive. At least one of her brothers needed to be able to spend the rest of his life with the love of his life.

Blood trickled over Candace's skin, trailing down to drip onto the floor behind her. The plastic cut deep into her wrists, but she ignored the pain and continued to work at freeing herself.

It was her only chance to escape. But she couldn't just free herself. She had to distract Tori, so the woman would lower the weapon she'd trained on her—because one twitch of her finger and she would blow a hole through Candace.

She already had a hole in her heart—an aching fear Garek had been hurt. How would Chekov react if he'd caught Garek in his safe?

Would he kill him?

Tori thought so and appeared to relish the horrible thought.

"Did you ever really love him?" Candace asked.

"Alexander?" Tori tilted her head as if considering the question. Then she emitted a lustful sigh. "He was so handsome and sexy. Maybe even more so than Garek."

Candace snorted now.

And Tori laughed. "You really love him." She pursed her lips with mock pity and added, "*Loved* him…"

Pain stabbed Candace's heart, and she gasped. Then she shook her head. "I refuse to believe he's dead." And that was why she fought with the zip ties, and finally the plastic gave a little. She could almost free herself. "Your father has a soft spot for Garek…"

Probably the only soft spot Viktor Chekov had—beyond his daughter.

"He won't kill him," Candace said, but she was assuring herself.

Tori shrugged. "It doesn't matter either way. You're not going to be together—because you will be dead." Her finger moved near the trigger, and she pointed the gun toward Candace's heart.

"Why kill me?" Candace asked. "What do I have to do with anything?"

Tori sighed but it was ragged with frustration. "You're smart. You must know why."

Candace shrugged, which helped her work the zip tie over her palms. A little farther was all she needed to free herself.

"You're jealous of Garek's feelings for me?" she asked. "You want me out of your way?"

Tori laughed. "Oh, please… I want Garek out of my way. I thought using you to distract him would get Daddy to fire him, at least…"

"I don't understand," Candace said. "Why did you go to Special Agent Rus? Why did you claim your father killed a man you killed?"

Tori uttered a patronizing chuckle. "I thought it was obvious. I want my father out of the way."

Candace had seen her love for him. "It's not obvious at all. If you wanted that, you would have tried to kill him instead of me."

"I don't want him dead," she said. "I just want him in prison."

"Are you afraid of him? Has he hurt you?"

"He's been holding me back," Tori said, "assuming because I'm a girl all I can do is play on my phone and shop." She snorted. "I wanted to be his right-hand man. But he chose Alexander over me."

"That's why you killed him." She was almost free.

Tori nodded. "Of course. He was in my way."

"Garek wasn't in your way."

"I didn't think he would be," Tori said. "I thought he'd changed. That he would help me bring Daddy down. But nothing was happening—except him and Daddy getting closer. And my father was still running everything."

Realization dawned. "And you want to…"

Tori smiled. "I will. If Daddy went to prison, I would be his go-between—or so everyone would think. I would be the one visiting him and carrying out his orders…"

"You think he would trust you—after you testified against him?"

"I won't need to testify now," Tori said. "I will only need to plant this weapon on Daddy. It will have killed so many people by then—including you. It will be easy to convict him. He'll never get out of prison."

"Garek won't believe it," Candace said.

Tori smirked. "If he survives Daddy…"

"You said yourself that your father has a soft spot for Garek," she said. "He won't hurt him. And Garek will figure out what you've done—you're responsible for all the killings."

Tori smiled and acknowledged, "If you hadn't distracted him like you have, he probably would have already figured out the truth."

She was right. Candace knew Garek would have—had he not been worried about her. He knew all these people and he would have put together the pieces of Tori Chekov's twisted jigsaw puzzle of deception and greed. But she'd gotten in his way.

"And after you die, he's going to be too distraught to figure out anything." Tori sighed. "And he's going to need me to console him."

He would be upset. And he would blame himself.

She raised the gun. "Don't worry, Candace, I'll take care of him for you."

Outrage coursed through Candace. She didn't want this woman touching Garek, trying to get close to him. She wanted this woman nowhere near him. So she ignored the pain as she forced the zip tie over her palms and down her fingers. But before she could move, shots rang out—reverberating off the walls of the basement.

She tensed, waiting for the pain as bullets tore through her.

Garek's heart hammered frantically inside his chest. The big man, who had been standing beside Tori like a trained ape, dropped his gun as he fell to the floor. But Tori held hers as she stood over Candace's prone body. Ignoring the pain in his leg, he hurried down the steps.

"And this is why my father shouldn't be in charge anymore," Tori murmured. "I can't believe, after catching you in his vault, he would let you live." She made the annoying *tsk*ing sound. "He's gotten too soft. Too soft to lead the *family* any longer."

"All this…" Garek gestured around at the basement, hoping to distract her—to draw her attention and her gun barrel—away from Candace.

He couldn't tell if she had been hit, if she was lying there bleeding. He wouldn't let himself look at her for fear he would bring Tori's focus back to her.

"You've done all this," he continued, "because you want to take over the *family*?"

"It's my birthright," Tori said bitterly. "Not yours. Not Alexander's."

"That's why you killed him?"

"Daddy was grooming him to take over," she said. "Alexander is not family. I am Daddy's only *real* family." Her mother had died during childbirth, so it had always been just her and her father. But Viktor had always called the men who worked for him *family*.

Garek nodded in agreement. "That's true. You are."

She swung her gun barrel toward him now. "You're not family either," she said. "But Daddy always treated you like you were."

"He used me to steal for him," Garek said. "That's not how you treat family."

"He let you work for him," Tori said with bitter resentment.

"He let me go to prison for him," he said. "That's the risk, when you do what we do. I had no choice, Tori—not with the way I was raised. I had to steal. That's all your father knows, too. But he wanted a better life for you. He didn't want you to have to do what he and I have done."

She shook her head, and now there wasn't just greed and resentment in her dark eyes—there was madness. "He didn't think I could handle it. He thinks I'm some weak female." She swung her gun back toward Candace.

He should have shot her when he'd had the chance— when she had been pointing that gun at him. He wouldn't have cared if she'd shot him. He didn't want her shooting Candace. Again?

The woman he loved lay unmoving on the concrete floor. And there was blood—behind her. Had she been shot in the back? How else would Tori have gotten the jump on her, though?

Or had he done it? Had one of the bullets he'd fired at Tori's cohort ricocheted off the concrete walls and struck the woman he loved?

Fear and panic threatened to overwhelm him, but he fought those feelings back. He had to focus.

"He didn't think *she* was a weak female, though," Tori said. "He respected her. He should see her now." She snorted disparagingly. Then she turned back to Garek, peering at him over her shoulder while her gun remained trained on Candace. "You should have seen him earlier—he was all over her on the dance floor."

She wanted him to react—to act like a jealous fool. All he could manage was a gasp, but that wasn't over what she'd said. It was over Candace's sudden movement.

She leaped up from the floor and grabbed for the gun. Her hands locked around the barrel, but Tori's finger was too close to the trigger. She fired.

Again and again. The sound and shots reverberated off the walls.

The agents above had to hear the gunfire. But Garek had convinced them to stay away. He'd promised he could handle Tori.

And he'd thought he could. But he had never known the woman at all. Not like he knew Candace…

She was strong. But not strong enough to fight off

an armed Tori. He jumped into the fray, wrapping his arms around Tori from behind—lifting her off her feet.

The gun clicked as the cartridge emptied. And Tori dropped it to the floor. Her body shook as sobs racked her.

"Are you okay?" he asked Candace—all his concern and fear for her.

She panted for breath but nodded. "I'm fine. I didn't get hit."

He wanted to reach for her, wanted to pull her into his arms and make sure she was really all right.

The same longing was in Candace's brilliant blue eyes. "And you?" she asked. "Chekov didn't hurt you?"

Garek shook his head. "No. He even told me where she had probably taken you."

If Chekov hadn't revealed the club had a basement, Garek doubted they would have found her—at least not in time. After Candace's murder, Tori would have had her goon dump the body somewhere it would have been found without a search warrant having to be obtained. And she would have wanted Candace's body to be found. She would have wanted Garek to suffer. And she would have wanted to implicate her father as the killer—like she'd been framing him all along.

Tori's body stilled as the tears abruptly stopped. "Daddy knows?"

"Yeah," Garek said. "He knows."

"Where is he?" she asked, and her voice cracked with madness.

How had Garek never noticed it? He'd always thought she was spoiled and unhappy. He hadn't realized her problems were so much deeper than that. But he suspected her father had known.

"Isn't he proud of me?" she asked. "Doesn't he know now he was wrong about me—that he's always been wrong about me?"

Garek didn't know what to say—didn't know what she wanted to hear, or if she would hear him at all in her current state. But before he could think of any words, she moved—striking out at him with her elbow and her foot. She followed the maneuver Candace had perfected and apparently taught her. She stomped on his foot and jammed her elbow into his ribs and the back of her head into his chin.

He lost his grip—for just a moment. But before he or Candace could reach for her again, she had dropped onto the ground. She didn't pick up the gun she'd dropped; she picked up the gun her sidekick had dropped.

Garek couldn't remember if the gun was empty or not. Had the man fired all his shots at him when he'd come through the door at the top of the stairs?

Candace shook her head, as if silently answering his unspoken question. They were so connected she must have read his mind. And the fear on her face answered his question.

There were bullets left. They both dove for Tori and the gun just as she began to fire it.

Chapter 23

The hospital waiting room overflowed with people and voices. Paynes. FBI special agents. Kozminskis. It was loud and crowded; it was chaos.

And usually it would have made Nicholas Rus very uncomfortable. He wasn't used to chaos—to family. But he realized now he'd always had one. He'd had a family in the Bureau with the fellow agents who had become good friends. Now he had another family: the Paynes.

He had expected them to be furious with him—for what he'd done, for the lives he'd risked when he'd gotten Garek involved in his investigation of Viktor Chekov. But Penny had hugged him. Stacy Kozminski-Payne had hugged him, too, and murmured, "Thank you."

"For what?" he'd asked.

She hadn't replied. She'd only rejoined her brother Milek, who'd slid his arm around her.

Had Milek told her what Nicholas had had no business revealing? He cursed himself for his admission. But he had come to care about his family—about all of his family, which included the Kozminskis. And Milek's pain over his loss had affected Nicholas the most.

But Milek wasn't the only one who'd experienced loss. The room went suddenly and completely silent. And the crowd parted as a silver-haired man walked through it—heading straight for Nicholas.

He had seen surveillance photos of Viktor Chekov. He had even seen him through a lens himself when he'd personally staked out the man. But Chekov looked different in person. Less ruthless. More haggard.

He had aged in the past few hours.

"Special Agent Rus," the man said. It wasn't a question or even much of a greeting. He was just acknowledging he knew who Nick was. "You're the one in charge."

Again an acknowledgment. Not a question. Was this where he swore vengeance on Rus and his entire family?

Garek had warned him that would happen. Viktor Chekov was vengeful and ruthless. He wouldn't forgive a betrayal—any betrayal.

Nicholas spared a glance to his family. He had only begun to admit what they meant to him. Would he have to leave them now—before he'd even really gotten to know them—to be part of them?

For their safety, he would. He would do what was best for them rather than himself.

He nodded. "Yeah, I'm in charge. The whole operation— the assignment—was *my* idea. Not Garek Kozminski's. I forced him to take part in it."

Viktor laughed, but without humor. "What—did you

threaten his family? That's the only way to force Garek Kozminski to do anything."

"I talked him into it," Nicholas insisted. Maybe he could convince Chekov that Garek had done it to find out what Nick had known about the murder of Milek's ex-girlfriend and son. The gangster might buy that…

But Garek didn't know what he knew. Rus had only admitted vague things to Milek.

"You didn't talk him into saving my daughter's life," Viktor said. "He could have shot her like he shot the man working for her—the men. But he spared her life. And then when she tried to take her own, he stopped her."

The bullet had only grazed Tori's forehead instead of killing her—like she'd wanted. Garek had saved her life.

"I want you to spare her, too," Chekov urged him.

Stunned the man could even ask such a thing—or rather demand—Nicholas shook his head. Was he going to threaten or offer him a bribe here? In a crowded waiting room of witnesses? Maybe the daughter wasn't the only crazy one in the Chekov family.

"She killed a man," Nick said. "She admitted it. She also killed the guy she hired to go after Candace. And she ordered those hits on her."

Maybe Chekov would go after Candace, too. He turned his attention to her as she stepped into the waiting room. Her wrists were bandaged from where she'd torn them up getting untied. The woman was fearless. Viktor wouldn't be able to scare her out of testifying against his daughter.

Garek stepped into the room behind her, his hand on her waist. Maybe it was for his own support since he limped. But Nicholas suspected it was because he couldn't *not* touch the woman he loved.

Chekov tapped his shoulder, drawing Nick's attention back to him. "You can arrest and convict Tori," he agreed. "But she's not the person you really wanted."

Nicholas focused on the older man again. "What are you saying?"

"Hers is not the arrest and conviction that will make your career." He tapped his chest. "I'm the one you want."

Nick shook his head—not in denial, though, just amazement. "Yeah, I want you," he admitted, "but not like this. I won't let you take the fall for someone else's crimes."

"I'm not suggesting that," Chekov said. "Pick a crime— any crime you want me to confess to, and I'll do it."

"What?" His mind reeled with the offer. "I still can't let her off."

Chekov sighed and nodded in reluctant agreement. "Work a deal for her," he suggested. "As tough as she thinks she is, she wouldn't survive in prison. It's not the place for her. She belongs in a psychiatric hospital."

"He's right," Candace chimed in.

Nick had seen them enter the room, but he hadn't heard her and Garek make their way through the crowd to join them. Even with a limp, the former thief moved silently. And Candace must have lost her shoes during her ordeal that night because she wore hospital slippers instead of heels.

"You would agree to that?" Nicholas asked the female bodyguard. "She tried to kill you—several times."

Candace sighed. "She's messed up. She needs help."

Garek looked less convinced, clenching his jaw as he stood closely by Candace's side.

Chekov must have recognized Garek's resistance because he beseeched him, "Let her get help."

No one had helped Garek years ago—when he had gone to jail. Nicholas would understand if he refused to help the man who had threatened him and his family.

But Garek sighed. "She needs to stay there," he said. "She's a danger to others and herself. This can't be some short stint in a country club."

"It won't be," Nicholas assured Garek while also warning Chekov. "She's going to serve a long sentence."

"As long as she gets help," Chekov said and nodded his agreement. "Can I see her?" he asked. "Before I go with you to your office? Can I say goodbye to her?"

Nick nodded. There were guards with the woman; she wouldn't escape with her father. But he believed it wasn't what Chekov wanted. He really wanted her to get help—to heal—so much so he would give up his own freedom for her.

"She was wrong," Candace murmured. "Her father really does love her."

Garek heartily slapped Nick's back. "You did the freaking impossible. You got Chekov to serve himself up on a silver platter."

"You did it," Nick said. He couldn't claim any of the credit. "If you hadn't saved her…"

Garek shrugged off his accolades.

"If you hadn't taken this assignment…" Unlike Chekov, Nick hadn't threatened him to do it; he had only asked and the man had readily agreed.

Garek shook his head now, refusing any credit. "It's all you, Rus. You wanted him. You got him. Enjoy your victory." Garek entwined his fingers with Candace and tugged her toward the door. "I'm going to enjoy mine."

"I'm a victory?" Candace asked. But she was smiling, her eyes shining with love for Garek.

"We're alive," Garek said. "That's a victory and a cause for celebration." But he stopped only to hug his family. He didn't stay to celebrate with them. Like a man on a mission, he led Candace through the crowd.

Another hand slapped Nicholas's back. "You did it," Milek said. "You must be thrilled."

But Nicholas felt no great thrill over what was the coup of his career. He felt only envy as he watched Garek and Candace leave the waiting room—hand in hand.

They were going home—to the house Garek had bought in the suburbs right before Nick had enlisted him in his investigation. He'd wondered then why a man everyone had considered a playboy had bought a traditional house like that; now he knew.

He had already fallen in love with Candace.

He had already begun to envision a future with her.

Milek probably couldn't imagine the future anymore. But then he turned to Nick, and the knowledge was in his silver eyes.

While Nicholas hadn't dared to say too much, he had apparently said enough. Milek finally knew the whole truth now.

Happiness warmed Candace. She felt none of the cold outside as they rushed—as fast as they could with Garek's limp—into the house. He must have left the lights on because the Christmas tree twinkled.

Overwhelmed with the beauty of it and her happiness, Candace stopped in front of the tree and sighed. "It's so…"

"What?" Garek asked, and his arms wrapped around her from behind, looping around her waist. He pulled her tightly back against his chest.

"Perfect."

"I didn't know you were so into Christmas," he mused.

Candace laughed. "Neither did I." She had always been such a no-nonsense girl. Not into frilly dresses or decorations or holidays. But she had changed. Love—real love—had changed her. "But now I have reason to celebrate…"

Or did she? She had professed her love, but he hadn't professed his. Had he even heard her, though? She had just whispered the words as she'd left.

She needed to gather her courage and repeat them.

"We don't have reason to celebrate yet," he said.

"We don't?" she asked, and she turned in his arms to face him. Desire ignited, heating her skin—making it tingle. She wanted him so much—loved him so much. "You heard Chekov—it's over. He won't go after us or any of our family."

Garek chuckled. "No, he's too appreciative she's alive. That was some kind of Christmas miracle."

"Yes…" She reached up to link her arms around Garek's neck. "Thanks to you…"

But he slipped away from her, as he dropped to his knees. A grimace of pain twisted his chiseled features.

"Are you okay?" she asked, as concern and alarm and guilt filled her. She had only been thinking about desire earlier—about how much she wanted him. She'd forgotten he'd been hurt.

"I'm fine," he said—despite the grimace. "I'm just looking for something…" He dropped even lower to the floor as he reached beneath the tree.

She knelt down beside him. "What are you looking for?" she asked. "Let me get it for you."

"No," he said. "I have it." And he pulled out a small,

brightly wrapped package. The silver metallic paper glittered under the lights of the tree.

"What is that?" she asked.

He held it out to her. "Open it and find out."

She shook her head. "It's not Christmas yet."

"It will be soon," he said.

She sighed as she realized he was right. They had been so busy—trying to stay alive—time had flown. "I know I went shopping with Tori the other day, but I didn't start my Christmas shopping yet."

He reached out and brushed his fingers across the bodice of her velvet dress. "You got this."

"It was for me—not you."

Desire glowed in his silver eyes. "Oh, no, it's definitely for me…"

She smiled. He was always so charming. She had doubted his charm before, but she had no doubts about him anymore. She had nothing but love.

"Open the present," he urged her.

Her fingers trembled against the bow. She couldn't remember a man ever giving her such a beautifully wrapped gift—and ever showing such anticipation and excitement over her opening it. But she wasn't used to being the receiver; she would rather be the giver—especially with Garek. She felt as if nobody had ever really appreciated him for the wonderful man he was.

"I can wait," she said. "I can wait to open it when you open your present."

She wasn't certain what to get him, though.

As if he'd read her mind, he warned her, "You can't buy me what I want for Christmas."

"I can't?"

"It's nothing you can wrap up and put under the tree either."

"What do you want?" she asked.

"For you to open that damn present," he impatiently replied.

She laughed. But she pulled the red bow loose and lifted off the top of the small box. There was another box inside that box—this one was velvet like her dress. She recognized the logo etched into the velvet. "This is from Stacy's store…"

She'd always thought it so ironic the daughter of a convicted jewel thief designed jewelry and owned her own store. But she had also secretly admired and coveted Stacy's beautiful pieces.

"You shouldn't have," she murmured.

He tensed, and the color drained from his face. "I shouldn't have? Why not?"

"Stacy's designs are beautiful…"

He smacked his own forehead. "But they're Stacy's and the two of you don't have the greatest relationship after…"

Logan. She had never felt about her boss the way she felt about Garek, though. But before she could correct him, he continued, "Of course you wouldn't want something she had designed."

She laughed. "Of course I would. She's brilliant and everything she makes is beautiful. I just meant you shouldn't have gone to the expense or the trouble."

He stared at her now, and his eyes widened in disbelief. "How can you not believe you're worth every expense and all the trouble in the world?"

She shivered at the look in his eyes—at the intensity of that look—and what she saw in the silvery depths.

He hadn't said the words, hadn't returned her feelings when she'd confessed to them, but the love was there. In his eyes. Nobody had ever looked at her like he was looking at her.

"You have gone to a lot of trouble over me," she admitted. "You pursued me for a year, and then you nearly got killed coming to my rescue again and again."

"And you were worth it," he said. "Worth every minute I chased you, worth every hit and bullet I took for you."

She laughed. But he didn't. He didn't even smile. He was actually being serious.

Her fingers shaking, she reached out and pulled the velvet box from the gift box. And she popped open the lid. She'd known she would be impressed by whatever was inside, but she had expected earrings. Or maybe a pendant. Perhaps a bracelet...

She hadn't expected a ring. A brilliant round diamond sparkled from inside a ring of sapphires—all set in a shiny platinum setting. Her breath caught at the beauty and the implication. "This...this is a ring..."

Maybe it wasn't what she thought it was—what she hoped it was.

"It's a ring," Garek said. He took it from the jewelry box and held it out to her. "You told me you loved me."

She swallowed as emotion choked her. But she nodded in acknowledgment of the feelings she'd professed.

"Did you say it because you thought we weren't going to make it?" he asked. "I didn't say it, because I knew we would. And I wanted the first time I told you I loved you to be like this..."

"What is this?" she asked. Confusion and hope overwhelmed her. It could have just been a ring...

But as she'd learned, nothing was ever as simple as it seemed with Garek Kozminski.

"It's a proposal," he replied.

He was already on his knees. But he took her hand and slid the ring onto her finger. Somehow it fit perfectly—as if he'd known her size. Or maybe Stacy had.

"I'm telling you I love you and I'm asking you to marry me. Will you marry me, Candace Baker? Will you be my partner in crime, my protector, my heroine, my soul mate?"

Her breath shuddered out at the shock. She had just noticed the love in his eyes when he looked at her; she hadn't realized he loved her this much.

"Are you sure?" she asked. Because no man had ever professed his love to her, let alone proposed.

Anger flashed in his eyes, darkening the silver.

"I'm not rejecting you," she assured him. "I just don't—"

"You don't know how beautiful you are," he said, and now the anger was in his voice. "You have no idea how amazing you are."

Tears stung her eyes—because she actually believed him. He said it with such sincerity and certainty and irritation. But then the anger and irritation was gone.

His fingers caressed her cheek. "You awe me," he said. "With your beauty and your strength and intelligence." Then his fingertips trailed from her face, down her neck to her breast. "And you have such heart—so much loyalty and devotion and love."

The tears spilled, falling from her eyes to follow the path his fingers had taken down her face and throat.

"You said you loved me—"

"I do love you," she said. "I love you so much. I love your heart—your loyalty and devotion to your family. You are the amazing one. The strong one."

"Then marry me," he said. "Say yes."

She couldn't say anything—as the tears choked her. She could only nod and throw her arms around his neck.

Over the past year Garek had seen Candace in many states: embarrassed, angry, hurt, angry—he'd seen angry a lot. But he had never seen her as emotional as she was now.

"I'm sorry," he said. "I didn't mean to upset you." Maybe he shouldn't have yelled at her, but it frustrated the hell out of him that she thought so little of herself—she was so unaware of her beauty.

She was even beautiful when she cried. But he hated seeing her like this—hated even more that he'd caused her tears.

He clutched her closely, pulling her trembling body into his arms. "I should have known I'd screw this up," he berated himself. "That I'd get it all wrong—because it means too much. You mean too much…"

She pulled back, and her hands cupped his face now. "Your proposal was perfect," she assured him. "You're perfect."

He laughed at her outrageous claim. He was as far from perfect as a man could be. But maybe he shouldn't draw it to her attention.

As if she'd read his mind, she smiled and amended, "You're perfect for me."

"We're perfect for each other." He leaned in and covered her mouth with his. She tasted as sweet and exciting as she always tasted, her tongue darting between his lips. He groaned but forced himself to pull back.

"So you will?" he asked. "You'll actually marry me?"

She giggled—a sound he had never heard her make. And she nodded again.

But he caught her chin in his hand and held her gaze. "I need the words…"

"Yes, I will marry you," she said. "I love you." She glanced down at her hand. "And I love my ring."

"And I love that dress," he said—even as he tugged it off her. "I want to make love to my fiancée."

Her breath escaped on a gasp. "You're my fiancé."

"Don't get used to it," he warned her.

She tensed for a moment—until he pushed her onto the floor and lowered his mouth to her breast. Then she melted into the floor with a shaky sigh of pleasure.

"Don't get used to being my fiancée," he said. "Because you're going to be my wife as soon as Penny Payne can plan our wedding and make it happen." Penny didn't have the connection in the courthouse that she'd once had—the judge who'd waived the waiting period for marriage licenses. But knowing her, she had other means to get him and Candace married quickly.

Candace smiled. Then she reached for him. His clothes fell as quickly as her dress had. Their naked bodies entwined so completely he couldn't tell where one of them ended and the other began. He could feel her heart beating against his—just as fast and frantically—as he slid inside her.

She was hot and wet and ready for him. Her body tightened around his, pulling him deeply inside her—joining them completely, irrevocably. They made love as one—came as one. And they lay, panting for breath, beneath the tree, wrapped in each other's arms. He had never been so happy and couldn't imagine ever being happier than he was at this moment.

Epilogue

Candace saw it—finally—as she stared into the mirror of the bride's dressing room. She saw the beauty Garek saw when he looked at her—the way he always looked at her. Her breath caught in surprise and pleasure. Her skin was pale and flawless, her eyes such an enormous and brilliant blue.

"You are stunning," Stacy told her.

The woman stepped up behind her and adjusted her veil. It was just a short little veil coming out of the hat atop her shiny black hair. Her dress was short, too, but with long sleeves and a lot of antique lace. She couldn't believe how quickly Penny, Stacy and Nikki had helped her find the perfect dress. She couldn't believe how quickly they had put together the perfect wedding.

"Thank you," she said.

Stacy shrugged off her gratitude. "I'm just stating a fact."

Candace shook her head. "I'm thanking you for so much more than the compliment. I'm thanking you for being my matron of honor."

"Thank you for asking me," Stacy said, and there was still the hint of surprise in her voice she'd had when Candace had asked her. Their history wasn't pretty, but they'd overcome their differences. And Candace had replaced her resentment of the female Kozminski with appreciation and respect.

"I wouldn't be here if not for you," she said. "You found me—"

"Nikki found you," Stacy said.

Nikki was a bridesmaid—dressed in the same blue velvet gown that Stacy wore. Candace hadn't left her out. But her bond with Stacy was stronger.

"You're the one who convinced me to come home," she said. "To Garek." More than the house he had bought, *he* was home to her. "You knew he had real feelings for me, and you helped me realize it was possible he could actually care about me."

"He adores you," Stacy assured her.

But Candace didn't need the assurance. She knew how much he loved her. And as her father walked her down the aisle to her groom, she saw it—as she always did now—when he looked at her. She barely noticed how pretty the church looked—aglow with Christmas lights and fragrant pine boughs. She saw only her groom, standing tall and straight, in a black tuxedo. He was so handsome, so sexy. And so in love...with her, as she was him.

This was his real Christmas assignment—his Christmas day wedding to the woman he loved more than his life itself. He had been wrong—so wrong—the day he had proposed. He'd thought then it wasn't possible for him to be any happier than he had been at that moment.

But he was happier now. So happy. And so in love. He took Candace from her father. The man wore his military uniform and a smile of reluctant approval. Garek, with his checkered past, probably wasn't the man he would have wanted for a son-in-law. But there was no denying he made Candace happy. And he would spend the rest of their lives making her as happy as she had made him.

Garek held her hands in his. And he stared deeply into the eyes of the woman he loved. The love she felt for him reflected back as they repeated their vows.

He was so happy he felt a twinge of guilt when his brother handed him Candace's ring. It wasn't fair he should be so happy and Milek so miserable. But his brother had been acting differently lately—almost as if he had some hope again. Maybe he would recover from his loss.

"I now pronounce you man and wife," the minister proclaimed.

Garek knew what came next, so he didn't wait until he was given permission. He stole the first kiss from his bride—just like she had stolen his heart. It was hers now and so was he—for the rest of their lives.

* * * * *

SECRET AGENT
SANTA

CAROL ERICSON

To Margery, hope this Christmas brings you
fond memories

Chapter One

Password Failed.

The message mocked her, and Claire almost punched the computer monitor. She didn't think it would be easy figuring out her stepfather's password, but she didn't think it would take her almost fifty tries over the course of three weeks, either. How did those hackers do it?

Placing her fingers on the keyboard, she closed her eyes, racking her brain for the next possible password. The voices in the hallway stopped her cold, sending a ripple of fear across her flesh.

She had no reason to be in this office, especially with a lavish party going on downstairs—*her* lavish party. She whipped her head around, the action loosening her carefully coiffed chignon, and lunged for the French doors. She parted the drapes, grabbed one handle and slipped through the opening onto the balcony.

She clicked the glass door shut just as she saw the door to the office crack open. Placing her palms against the rough brick, she sidled along the wall until she reached the edge of the balcony farthest from the doors.

Feathers of snow drifted from the night sky, leaving a dusting of white on the Georgetown streets. DC rarely saw snow in December. Just her luck.

She crossed her arms, digging her fingers into the cold

skin exposed by her sleeveless gown. She couldn't stay here long or her stepfather's security detail would find her and would have to chip her stiff body from the brick façade of the town house.

The French doors next to her swung open and Claire flattened herself against the wall. Her stepfather, Senator Spencer Correll, must've noticed the parted drapes or the chill in the room and had decided to investigate. What possible excuse could she offer for being out on the balcony in the snow in an evening gown in the middle of a party?

"I love it when it snows in DC." Her stepfather's hearty tone reassured her that he had no idea anyone was lurking out here—it also sounded forced. He must be putting on an act for someone—but then, when didn't he put on an act?

"We're not going to have a white Christmas in South Carolina, so maybe I'll stay here for a week or two and soak up the atmosphere."

The other man's Southern drawl marked him as a constituent from her stepfather's home state. She just hoped the snow didn't enthrall him enough to step onto the balcony.

"I suggest you do. Nothing like Christmas in DC."

Spencer's voice sounded so close, she was surprised he couldn't see her breath in the cold air. She held it.

"It'll be an especially merry Christmas for you, Senator Correll, if you vote for that…uh…subsidy."

"It's a done deal. I'll introduce you to my assistant tonight. Trey will take care of all the details. After tonight, your boss should be reassured."

"Looking forward to it." The toe of a polished dress shoe tapped the pavers on the balcony, and Claire clenched her teeth to keep them from chattering.

"There's quite a crowd here tonight, Senator. I understand your stepdaughter, Claire, is an amazing fund-raiser."

"If by fund-raiser you mean relentless harridan, that's Claire." Spencer chuckled. "Just like her mother."

Claire's blood ran like ice through her veins, and it had nothing to do with her rapidly dropping body temperature. The chill in Spencer's voice when he mentioned her mother buoyed her suspicions that he'd had something to do with Mom's death. Maybe by discovering what he was up to with his vast amount of fund-raising and secretive meetings with suspected terrorists she would finally uncover evidence tying him to Mom's so-called accident.

She still had the video—the video that had sent her reeling and tumbling down a rabbit hole.

"A great lady, your wife." The shoe retreated, and Claire never heard Spencer's response to the compliment to his dead wife as the doors closed on the two men.

She let out a long breath and a new round of chills claimed her body. Even though they'd closed the door, her stepfather and his crony were still in the office.

She turned toward the low wall around the balcony and peered over the edge. She could hike up her dress and climb over and then try to reach the trellis that was positioned on the side of the building. She was just one story up.

"Are you going to jump?"

She gasped and jerked her head toward the sound of the voice from below. A man stood just outside the circle of light emanating from the side of the house. What was he doing out here? More important, why was he yelling? She put her finger to her lips and shook her head.

He caught on quickly. He shrugged a pair of broad shoulders draped in a black overcoat and turned the corner back to the front of the house, his red scarf billowing behind him.

Could this night get any worse? She rubbed her freezing hands together, and couldn't feel her fingertips.

Then the shadows from the office stopped their dance

across the balcony and she knew the two men had left the room. Biting her lip, she tried the door and heaved a sigh of relief. At least Spencer hadn't locked it. He didn't need to with the sensors, cameras and security guards monitoring this place—her place.

She tripped back into the room, her feet blocks of ice in her strappy silver sandals. She made a beeline for the door, throwing a backward glance at the computer. She'd finish checking passwords another time.

She crept down the hallway toward the stairs, but instead of heading down to her party, she climbed the steps to the third level of the expansive townhome her mother used to share with Spencer Correll, Mom's third husband.

She needed to warm up before mingling with her guests, anyway, and a visit to her son was a surefire way to warm both her heart and body.

Pushing open the door next to her bedroom, she tiptoed into the darkened room, the night-light shaped like a train her beacon. She knelt beside Ethan's bed and burrowed her hands beneath the covers, resting her head next to his on the pillow.

His warm mint-scented breath bathed her cheek, and she traced the curve of his earlobe with her lips.

She whispered, "Love you, beautiful boy."

His long lashes fluttered and he mumbled in his sleep. She had to get him out of here, out of this viper's nest. His grandparents had been clamoring to take him snowboarding in Colorado over the holidays, and even though this would be her first Christmas without him, she was making the sacrifice to protect him. He'd be leaving her in two days.

"Claire?" The shaft of light from the hallway widened across the floor.

Her stepfather's voice always made her skin crawl.

"I'm in here, Spencer."

"You have a surprise guest downstairs."

"I hope this guest came with his or her checkbook."

"Oh, I think he came with a lot more than that." Spencer stepped into the room. "Where have you been all night? I haven't seen you since the festivities kicked off with the tree lighting."

"I had a headache, and then I stopped in to see Ethan. I'm getting in some extra time with him before sending him off to his grandparents."

"I still can't believe you're parting with your son over Christmas."

"The Chadwicks haven't had him for the holidays—ever. They deserve that."

"They should've told that son of theirs to stay home once he had a baby on the way. If he couldn't keep out of harm's way for you, he owed that to his child."

"That's enough." She straightened up and pulled back her shoulders. "Shane was doing what he loved. His work was important to him. I don't want you ever to say anything like that in front of Ethan."

Spencer held up his hands. "I wouldn't do that. Now, come downstairs. They're getting ready to serve dinner, and you'll want to see this guest. Trust me."

She wouldn't trust her stepfather if he told her it was snowing outside after she'd just been standing in the stuff. She smoothed her hands across the skirt of her dress, flicking a tiny crystal of ice onto the floor, and joined him at the entrance to Ethan's room.

He closed the door and placed a hand on her bare back. "You're cold."

"I feel like I'm coming down with something." She shrugged off his clammy hand and headed for the curving staircase with Spencer close on her heels.

Did he suspect something?

With her fingertips trailing along the carved bannister, she descended into the warmth and chatter below. She scanned the room, her gaze skimming over glittering jewels and black bow ties. She didn't see any special guest— just a bunch of strangers with checkbooks.

Looking back at Spencer, she asked, "Where's this special guest?"

"You don't have to pretend anymore, Claire." He drummed his fingers along her shoulder. "He told us everything."

A knot twisted in her stomach. What kind of game was her stepfather playing this time?

From the step above her, Spencer leveled a finger toward the foyer. "There he is."

Claire's eyes darted among the faces of the strange men gathered in the foyer shedding coats, and then her breath hitched in her throat when she caught sight of a tall, dark-haired man unwinding a red scarf from his neck.

Had he seen enough of her on the balcony to identify her?

He must've felt her stare burning into him because at that moment, he glanced up, his eyes meeting hers and his mouth twisting into a half smile.

Spencer nudged her from behind. "Don't be shy now that the cat's out of the bag. Go greet your fiancé."

CLAIRE CHADWICK LOOKED like a ghost at the bottom of the staircase, her pale skin, blond hair and long, sparkling silver dress blending together to form a glittering cloud. Only her eyes, big, round and dark, stood out in relief.

Lola hadn't exaggerated her friend's beauty, but Claire didn't have the look of a woman greeting her fiancé for the holidays. Of course, what did he expect of a novice? He'd have to take the reins here.

He dropped his scarf on top of his overcoat, resting in

a maid's arms, and took the ticket from her fingers. Nudging his bag on the floor with the toe of his dress shoe, he asked, "Could you please check this, too?"

Straightening his cuffs, he descended the two steps from the foyer into the great room, decorated with twinkling lights and crystal stars hanging from the ceiling. An enormous Christmas tree dominated one corner of the room, coated with silver flocking and sporting gold ornaments amid its colored lights.

He made a beeline for Claire, taking tentative steps in his direction, her stepfather, Senator Spencer Correll, almost prodding her forward.

This scenario wasn't going as planned.

As the distance between them shortened to two feet, he held out one hand. "Sweetheart, I hope you don't mind that I surprised you like this. My conference ended early." He took her cold, stiff fingers in his hand and squeezed. "Lola sends her love."

He pulled Claire toward him and kissed her smooth cheek. At the mention of Lola's name, her hand relaxed in his. He didn't know where the communication had failed, but at least Claire had some expectation of his presence here.

Her arms twined around his neck and she pressed her soft lips against his. "Babe, I'm thrilled to see you here, even though you spoiled my surprise."

His arm curled around her slender waist, and they turned to face Spencer Correll together. Correll's assistant had joined them.

Mike stuck out his hand to introduce himself to the assistant, just to make sure Claire knew his name...or at least the name and identity he'd devised for this assignment. "Mitchell Brown, nice to meet you."

Correll clapped his hand on his assistant's shoulder.

"Trey Jensen, this is Claire's fiancé, Mitchell Brown. Mitchell, my assistant, Trey Jensen."

He shook the other man's hand, already knowing his name, bank account balance and sexual predilections. "Good to meet you, Trey. Now, if you gentlemen don't mind, I'm going to steal my fiancée away from her own party for a few minutes."

Claire pinched his side. "I thought you'd never ask, babe."

Spencer chuckled. "You two go ahead. I'll hold down the fort for you, Claire. It's not like you've spent much time with your guests anyway."

Claire responded to this zinger by pulling Mike toward the staircase with a firm grip. "We won't be too long."

They held hands up the stairs and across the landing until she dragged him into a library, its shelves lined with books and the floor covered by a thick carpet that muted their steps.

She shut and locked the door and then turned toward him, her unusual violet eyes alight with fire. "Fiancé? You're my fiancé?"

"I thought it was the best cover to keep me close to your side and privy to Correll's comings and goings. That way I can stay in this house. I even brought a bag. This is still your house, isn't it?"

"Yes." She narrowed her extraordinary eyes. "Did Lola send me someone I can actually work with, or a bodyguard?"

"Can't I be a little of both?" He spread out his hands. He liked it better when she had her arms curled around his neck, kissing him, instead of skewering him with a frosty gaze. He needed to get on her good side if he wanted her to give Lola a good report—not that it mattered at this point.

"Just so you know, Mitchell Brown is not my real name. It's Mike. Mike Becker."

"Suits you better." Crossing her arms, she tapped the toe

of her glittering sandal. "When did this fiancé stuff all go down, Mike Becker?"

He put a hand in the pocket of his dress slacks and toyed with his coat-check ticket. "From the look on your face when I walked in, I figured you hadn't received Lola's final text."

"She told me she was sending someone from her husband's agency, but I didn't know the details. I certainly didn't know I was acquiring a fiancé."

"I didn't even give Lola all the details."

"I have a five-year-old son. To him, you'll be nothing but a friend, got it?"

The mama-bear attitude surprised him coming from this glittering goddess, but it figured she'd be protective of her son. He knew all about the boy and the tragic demise of her husband, Shane Chadwick.

"I know about…your son, and I have no intention of playing the doting fiancé or future stepdad in front of him."

She blinked and brushed a wisp of blond hair from her eyes. "Ethan's going out to his grandparents' place in a few days, anyway. I'm glad Lola gave you some background, although I'm sure you did some checking on your own."

"Of course." Didn't she realize that every covert-ops agent at home and abroad knew the story about her husband? Hell, didn't the entire world know? Mike cleared his throat. "Jack Coburn isn't too pleased you contacted his wife directly, but when you mentioned a connection between Correll and a terrorist group, we thought it best to investigate. You have some video proof?"

"I do. I'm sure it proves…something. You'll see." She'd hooked her finger around a diamond necklace encircling her neck, and the large pendant glinted in the low light of the library.

"When can I see it?" Jack wasn't all that convinced

Claire had any proof of anything, but he didn't want to leave any stone unturned—especially when that stone involved his wife's friend.

"I have it in a secure location. I'll show it to you tomorrow."

"Your stepfather would be playing with fire if it's true. He has access to the highest levels of government."

"That's the scary part. My stepfather is a member of the Senate Intelligence Committee and was on the short list for director a few years ago. He still may be on that list."

"We'll get to the bottom of your suspicions one way or another."

Claire tapped her chin with two fingers, and a diamond bracelet matching the necklace slipped to her elbow. "I have more than suspicions. I'm almost positive Spencer is involved in terrorist activity."

"You'll have to give me more of the details, including that video, and I'll start digging around, but let's play the loving couple to establish my cover first—just not in front of your son." He straightened his bow tie as she wandered toward the window to gaze at the winter wonderland. "You weren't going to jump from that balcony, were you?"

"So you did know that was me." She met his eyes in the glass of the window.

"Not when I first saw you outside, but I figured it out when I saw your dress. It's rather—" his gaze meandered from the hem of her full skirt to the top of the dress that had a deep V slashed almost to her waist "—distinctive."

"Well, I would hope so. I paid enough money for it." She tapped a manicured fingernail on the windowpane. "I was hiding from Spencer. I had been in his office trying out passwords to unlock his computer when he and some smarmy donor decided to have a meeting."

Whistling through his teeth, Mike joined her at the window. "Claire, why are you really after your stepfather? Most people don't see a few odd signs, a meeting on video with someone suspicious and immediately think 'terrorist plot.'"

"Just wait until you hear the whole story and see the videos before jumping to conclusions about me and my motives."

"Deal." He held out his hand and they shook on it. Still keeping her hand in his, he said, "Now, let's go downstairs and pretend to be a newly engaged couple."

Pointing out the window, she pressed her forehead against the glass. "Speaking of terrorism, there's the director down there. Isn't he technically your boss?"

"Technically, although I've never met him and most of what we do at Prospero is under the CIA radar." He glanced into the street, where a balding man was exiting a town car as a valet held open his door. "I'm surprised to see him at your party. Didn't you have some beef with him a few years ago?"

Another valet hurried to the front of the vehicle, stooped over and then continued up the street at a jog.

The hair on the back of Mike's neck quivered at about the same time one of the director's security detail lunged across the car toward his charge.

Mike instinctively grabbed Claire around the waist and yanked her away from the window just as the explosion shattered the glass and rocked the town house.

Chapter Two

Claire landed on the floor with Mike's body on top of hers. Acrid smoke billowed into the room from the shattered window and her nostrils twitched.

Mike's face loomed above hers, his mouth forming words she couldn't hear over the ringing in her ears. Sprinkles of glass quivered in his salt-and-pepper hair like ice crystals, and she reached out to catch them on the tips of her fingers.

The crystals bit into her flesh and she frowned at the spot of blood beading on her fingertip.

Mike rose to his knees over her and dragged her across the carpet, away from the jagged window. She couldn't breathe. Cold fear began to seep into her blood.

Rolling to her stomach, she began to crawl toward the door.

Mike's voice pierced her panic. "Claire. Are you all right?"

Cranking her head over her shoulder, she had enough breath left in her lungs to squeeze out one word. "Ethan."

Mike jumped to his feet and hooked her beneath her arms, pulling her up next to him. "Where is he?"

She pointed to the ceiling with a trembling finger, and then launched herself at the door of the library, her knees wobbling like pudding.

Mike followed her upstairs, keeping a steadying hand on the small of her back. Through her fog, Claire heard shrieks and commotion from downstairs. The noise shot adrenaline through her system, and she ran up the rest of the stairs to Ethan's room.

She shoved open the door and rushed to her son's bed, where he sat up rubbing tears from his eyes.

"Mommy?"

She dived onto the bed and enveloped him in a hug, blocking the cold air breezing through one shattered window. "Are you hurt?"

Shaking his head, he wiped his nose across her bare arm. "That was loud."

"That *was* loud." She kissed the top of his head, her gaze taking in Mike hovering at the door of the bedroom. "Don't worry. It was just an accident outside. Are you sure you're okay?"

Ethan disentangled himself from her arms and fell back against his pillow. "Uh-huh. Can I look out the window to see the accident?"

"Absolutely not. There's glass all over the floor. I'm going to move you to another bedroom across the hall, as long as there are no broken windows on that side."

Ethan squinted and pointed at Mike. "Who are you?"

"Pointing is rude." She grabbed his finger and kissed it. "That's my friend Mr. Brown."

Ethan waved. "Hi, Mr. Brown. Did you see the accident?"

Mike took two steps into the room accompanied by the sound of sirens wailing outside. "No, but I heard it. You're right. It was loud."

Ethan's nanny stumbled into the room, her hands covering her mouth. "Ethan? Oh, Claire, you're here. What was that?"

Claire held a finger to her lips. "Just an accident outside, Lori. Did the windows shatter in your room on the other side?"

"No. Do you want me to take Ethan to the room next to mine?"

"I'll come with you, and then I'd better see what's going on downstairs." Claire pulled Ethan from his bed and stood up with his legs wrapped around her waist. "Lori, this is Mitchell Brown, a friend of mine."

Lori's eyes widened. "Oh, I heard…"

Claire gave a jerk of her head, sending her chignon tumbling from its pins, and Lori sealed her lips.

"Yes, I heard you were here, Mr. Brown." Lori spun around and led them down the hall and around the corner to the other side of the town house.

She opened the door to the room next to her own.

Mike stayed outside in the hallway while Claire tucked Ethan into the queen-size bed and patted the covers. "Don't go back to sleep, Lori. I have no idea how extensive the damage is. The fire department may not even let us stay here tonight."

Lori gripped her arms and shivered. "As if I could go to sleep." She glanced at Ethan snuggling against the pillows and whispered, "Was that a bomb?"

Claire nodded.

Lori slumped in a chair across from the bed. "I'll stay here until you get back."

"I appreciate it, Lori." Claire closed the door with a snap and leaned against it, closing her eyes.

A rough fingertip touched her cheek, and her eyes flew open.

Mike raised his dark eyebrows over a pair of chocolate-brown eyes. "Are you ready?"

"He's dead, isn't he?" She grabbed the lapel of his dinner

jacket. "The director is dead, along with his security detail and probably that valet."

"Most likely." He took her hand. "Let's go see if anyone else is."

He kept hold of her hand down the two flights of stairs and into the chaos that reigned in the great room. Even though she'd just met him, the pressure of his fingers kept her panic in check.

They reached the great room, and the glass that littered the floor crunched beneath their shoes. All the windows had been blown out, and snow swirled into the room.

Claire staggered, but Mike caught her and tucked her against his side. She cranked her head back and forth, but she could barely make sense of the scene before her.

Mike grabbed the arm of a passing fireman. "Are there any serious injuries?"

"Nothing too bad, no fatalities." He grimaced. "At least not on the inside."

She didn't even have to ask him if the director of the CIA had survived the blast—nobody in his position could have survived.

"Claire!" Spencer, his shirtfront bloodied, shouldered his way through the crowd. "Claire, are you and Ethan okay?"

All she could think about when she looked into his cold, blue eyes was that he was at the top of the list to replace the director. "We're fine. How about you?"

"Me? I'm indestructible."

"What happened?"

Mike squeezed her waist. They hadn't even discussed whether or not they'd reveal what they'd seen out the window, but instinct screamed *no* and Mike seemed to approve of her discretion. She didn't want to be questioned as a potential witness, and Mike's real identity would have to be revealed if he stepped forward.

Dipping his head, Spencer pinched the bridge of his nose. "Oh, my God, Claire. It was a car bomb. Jerry..."

"Jerry Haywood? It was his car? Is he all right?" She dug her fingers into her stepfather's arm—as hard as she could.

He laid his hand on hers. "I'm afraid not, Claire. Jerry's dead, one of his security guys is dead and a valet."

"One of his security guys? Doesn't he usually travel with two? And is the other one okay?"

"He'd already stepped away from the car. He's injured but hanging on." He patted her hand again and then pulled away from her death grip.

"What about the other valet?" Mike stepped aside to let an EMT get by. "I noticed two tonight when I arrived."

"You know, I'm not sure about him. I'm going to make some inquiries. And stay tuned. The fire marshal may kick us all out of here tonight even though it's just broken windows." Spencer chucked Claire beneath the chin and made a half turn. His gaze lit on Mike's hair, still sprinkled with glass. "Where were you two?"

"In the library." Claire kicked a shard of glass to the edge of the floor.

"That's at the front of the town house. Were you standing at the window by any chance? Did you see the explosion?"

Mike slipped his arm around her shoulder and kissed the side of her head. "We were too wrapped up in each to see anything."

Spencer's eyes narrowed briefly before he launched back into the crowd of people, shouting orders.

Claire blew out a breath. "There goes the new director of the CIA."

MIKE CUPPED THE cell phone against his ear. "If Senator Spencer Correll becomes the next director and he is involved somehow with a terrorist organization, we're going to have a major problem on our hands."

"That's an understatement," Jack Coburn's voice growled over the line. "How valid are Claire's concerns? Has she shown you her so-called evidence yet? I sent you out there to appease my wife and calm the fears of one of her best friends. I didn't believe she had anything—until this car bombing tonight."

Mike winced. Why *would* Jack send him on one last important mission after how badly he'd flubbed his previous assignment? Looking after Jack's wife's friend was just about his speed now.

He coughed. "I agree. After tonight's bombing, I'd say Claire might be onto something."

"Unless..." Jack sucked in a breath.

Mike's grip tightened on the phone. "Are you implying Claire set something up to bolster her story? That's crazy."

"After the murder of Claire's husband, she had it in for Jerry Haywood when he was deputy director."

"I know that, but it's a huge leap to think she'd plan his assassination."

Jack grunted. "Why would Correll be involved in an assassination at his own party?"

"Technically, it was Claire's party, and that's what I'm here to figure out, right? That's why you sent me." Mike sat on the edge of the bed in the room next to the one where Claire and her son were sleeping.

Since the bomb hadn't done any outward damage to the town house except for the broken windows, the fire department had allowed the family to stay the night. Workers had been busy boarding up the windows, and the DC Metro Police, the FBI, the CIA and a swarm of reporters were still milling around at the site of the car bomb.

Jack cleared his throat. "Just a warning about Claire

Chadwick. She's had it pretty rough the past five years with the gruesome death of her husband and then her mother's accident. She blames her stepfather for her mother's death. You know that, right?"

"Lola mentioned something about it. Do you think that makes Claire's suspicions about Correll's current activity invalid?"

"Not invalid, but she does have another agenda, a definite ax to grind. Her troubles have led to some…instability. Just be careful, and don't get sucked in by her beauty. From what I remember, Claire Chadwick's a real looker."

He'd remembered right. "Duly noted, boss."

"You sure you still want to retire, old-timer?"

A soft knock at Mike's door saved him from reciting all his reasons for retirement again to Jack. "Someone's here. Gotta go."

He pushed off the bed and padded on bare feet to the door. He cracked it open.

Claire, her disheveled hair tumbling over one shoulder, crossed her arms over her animal-print pajamas and hunched her shoulders. "Can I come in?"

"Of course." He swung the door open and stepped to the side.

"You weren't sleeping." Her gaze swept over his slacks and unbuttoned white shirt.

"I was on the phone." He closed the door behind her. "How's your son?"

"He's fine—sleeping. All he knows is that there was an accident that broke a bunch of windows in the house." She sat on the foot of the bed and then fell back, staring at the ceiling, her blond hair fanning out around her head. "Spencer did it. He's responsible."

As much as he wanted to join her on the bed, he parked himself on the arm of a chair across from her, resting his ankle on one knee. "You have one video of him meeting with a suspicious person and all of a sudden he's guilty of killing the CIA director?"

"It's more. It's a feeling." She hoisted herself up on her elbows.

"Whether Correll is responsible or not, this attack is bold, hits right at the heart of our security. If they can kill the director of the CIA in the middle of Georgetown, what else do they have planned?"

Her eyebrows shot up. "Something more? Do you think other attacks are planned?"

"There has to be some endgame here, and if your stepfather is involved somehow and can lead us to—"

"Shh." She put a finger to her puckered lips.

He cocked his head, holding his breath, and heard the wood creak on the other side of the door.

Claire bolted from the bed, launching herself at the door, but Mike caught her around the waist before she reached it. He swung her into his arms and sealed his lips over hers.

He groaned, a low guttural sound that was only half pretense as he felt her soft breasts beneath her silk pajama top press against the thin cotton of the T-shirt covering his chest.

He moaned her name against her luscious lips. "Claire. Claire."

She sighed and answered him in a breathy tone. "Mmm. Mitchell."

The board outside the room squeaked again, but he tightened his hold on Claire as she made a move toward the door.

Would he have to kiss her again to keep her from bursting into that hallway? It was better to err on the side of caution, so he backed her up against the door and took possession of her lips once more.

She placed her hands against his chest as if to push him

away, but her fingers curled against the material of his T-shirt instead.

He kissed her long enough for whoever was outside that door to walk away—and then some. He raised his head, and she blinked her violet eyes.

Reaching around her, he opened the door. In a loud voice, he said, "Go back to Ethan. I'll be right next door all night."

"I'm so glad you're here, Mitchell." She peered down the hallway and shook her head. "I'm just sorry it couldn't have been a happier reunion."

He clicked the door behind her and fell across the bed, inhaling the sweet musky scent she'd left behind.

His first meeting with Claire Chadwick couldn't have been any happier.

Chapter Three

Claire fluffed Ethan's hair as she sat on the edge of the bed where she'd spent a sleepless night next to her squirmy son. If Mike had let her fling open the door, she might've caught Spencer in the act of eavesdropping.

And then what? He'd be alerted to her suspicions. Right now he suspected her only of nosing around his finances, and she wanted to keep it that way. Mike had been right to stop her.

But did he have to stop her by kissing her silly? She traced her mouth with her fingertips. Not that she'd minded.

Her son fluttered his long lashes and yawned.

Typically, Ethan woke up with the early birds, but last night's commotion had him sleeping late. Commotion? Was that what you called the murder of a CIA director by the man who would replace him? She had no doubt that was what had gone down. Now she just had to convince Mike Becker.

She hadn't trusted Spencer Correll since the fourth or fifth year of his marriage to her mother. She'd been in college at Stanford when her mother married Spencer. Claire hadn't given him much thought. He was the type of man her mother had dated since Dad's death—charming, a few years younger, in need of some financing.

Despite her wariness, nothing set off any alarm bells until that phone call and then her mother's accident.

"Mommy?"

"Good morning, sleepyhead." She skimmed her fingers through Ethan's curly brown hair. "It's late."

His eyes grew round. "Can I look at the accident now?"

"I think that's been all cleaned up." At least she hoped to God it had been. "Let's have some breakfast. Are you hungry?"

"Uh-huh." He smacked his lips. "Is Mr. Brown eating breakfast, too?"

"You remember Mr. Brown from last night?" She tilted her head, wrinkling her nose. Mike must've made quite an impression on Ethan, which meant she couldn't get her son out of here and with his grandparents fast enough. She didn't want to confuse him or get his hopes up.

"Mr. Brown was giant, like Hercules." Ethan raised his hand over his head as far as he could.

"Yeah, he's tall." She grabbed him under the arms and tickled. "Now let's go eat."

The smells of bacon and coffee coming from the kitchen lent an air of normalcy to the house after Claire had made her way through the cleaning crews in the great room. The giant Christmas tree she'd lit up with a thousand bulbs last night had shed its gold ornaments in the blast and now stood in the corner, a forlorn reminder of the Christmas spirit.

Ethan had shoved through the dining room doors first and came to a halt in front of Mike, his plate piled high with eggs, bacon and Jerome's flaky biscuits.

Mike eyed Ethan over the rim of his coffee cup. "Who are you, the cook?"

Crossing his arms, Ethan stamped his foot. "I'm Ethan. I saw you last night."

"Oh." Mike snapped his fingers. "You looked a lot

smaller in bed. I thought you were a little boy, but you're not. You're a big boy."

Claire pulled out a chair with a smile on her face. Mike must have kids of his own, and if he wasn't divorced, he should be after the way he'd kissed her last night. No happily married man would be kissing a woman he'd just met like that—assignment or no assignment.

Ethan climbed into the chair next to Mike's, studied his plate and proceeded to ask Liz, the maid, for the same food Mike had.

Claire tilted her head at her son. "Are you sure you can eat that much?"

"I'm hungry." Ethan patted his tummy.

"How's your nose? Any sniffles or coughing?"

"Nope."

She turned to Mike. "Ethan's been having some problems with allergies, and the doctor is thinking it might be asthma."

"He looks good to me." Mike winked at Ethan.

"Ms. Chadwick, do you want anything besides coffee this morning?" Liz poured a stream of brown liquid into her cup.

"Just some orange juice." When Liz finished pouring the coffee, Claire tipped some cream into her cup and dipped a spoon into the white swirl.

"Did you get a good night's sleep despite everything?" Mike broke open a biscuit, and steam rose from the center.

Did he mean despite the murder of the director, or the kiss? She watched his strong hands as he buttered one half of the biscuit, then tore off a piece and popped it into his mouth.

Swallowing hard, she shook her head. "I didn't get much sleep at all. You?"

"Slept like a baby." He winked at Ethan again, who giggled.

"You're not a baby." Her son jabbed a fork in Mike's direction.

Claire drew her brows together as she glanced at Ethan's eyes, shining with clear hero worship. Since he'd started kindergarten a few months ago, Ethan had been asking more questions about his father and had become more aware of the absence of a father in his own life. She didn't want him getting too attached to Mike, especially since he'd seemed to form an immediate liking for him.

Like mother, like son.

"I don't even know why anyone would say they slept like a baby when they slept well." She pinched Ethan's nose. "Because you certainly didn't sleep all through the night when you were a baby."

Ethan giggled again and Mike added his loud guffaw just as Spencer walked into the dining room.

He raised his brows. "What a nice family scene, especially on a morning like this."

Claire jerked her head around, her finger to her lips. "Shh. Not now."

Spencer shrugged and refilled the coffee cup in his hand. He took a seat across from her. "When do you plan on telling him?"

"In our own time, Spencer." She sent Mike a look from beneath her lashes. "Did you learn anything more about what happened last night?"

"The Security Council had an emergency meeting this morning, and the FBI gave us an initial report."

She folded her hands around her cup, trying hard not to break it. "Anything you can pass along? Has anyone claimed credit?"

"Not yet." Spencer slurped at his coffee. "Too bad this had to spoil your visit, Mitch."

Mike reached across the table and curled his fingers around Claire's. "I don't plan on letting it ruin my visit. Of course, it's a tragedy, and I'm sorry it happened in front of your house, at Claire's event, but nothing can get in the way of our happiness."

She sent Mike a weak smile. He was really laying it on thick.

"My house?" Spencer folded his arms on the table. "Is Claire hiding assets from you already?"

"Sir?" Mike's fingers dug into her hand.

"This house belongs to Claire." Spencer spread his arms. "This house and everything in it."

"Mitchell and I haven't gotten around to detailing our assets yet." Heat crept up her chest and she took a gulp of chilled orange juice to keep it in check. She and Mike should've been covering this ground last night. Nothing much got past Spencer.

"Our—" Mike slid a glance at Ethan, busy marching his dinosaurs over a mound of scrambled eggs on his plate "—courtship was fast."

"I have to admit, when you showed up last night, it was the first I'd heard of you, but then, Claire plays it close to the vest. So your announcement didn't surprise me in the least, and it was quite welcome."

"I'm glad you approve." Mike gave her fingers one last squeeze before releasing her hand. "Are we still on for sightseeing today, or did the…accident change our plans?"

"I don't see any reason why your plans should change." Spencer pushed back from the table. "You might find a few monuments closed for security reasons, and you might have to drive through a few security checkpoints."

"Maybe we'll take a drive down to Virginia, Mount Vernon." She tugged on Ethan's ear. "You're going to Mallory's birthday party today."

Ethan dropped his dinosaurs. "She's gonna have cupcakes. She told me at school."

"And pony rides." She handed Ethan a napkin. "Wipe your face and I'll help you get ready to go."

Mike placed his own napkin by the side of his plate and smiled at Ethan. "Will you bring me a cupcake?"

"Yes. What color?"

"Surprise me."

Spencer hunched forward and whispered, "I think we should send some security with Ethan and Lori to that party. Just to be on the safe side."

She nodded. One more reason to get Ethan out of this town—and away from Spencer; not that her stepfather would ever hurt her son, but his connections might not be so sensitive.

FORTY-FIVE MINUTES LATER, Claire was staring out the car window at a gray sky threatening another dusting of snow. She shivered and wound her blue scarf around her neck.

"Are you cold?" Mike's fingers hovered at the dial of the car heater. "I can turn it up."

"I'm fine." She crossed her arms. "I'm just thinking about my stepfather sitting at that security meeting this morning, blood on his hands."

"How can you be so sure he's responsible, Claire? A few overheard conversations and a few suspicious emails don't prove anything concrete, and we need concrete."

"Be patient. You're here, aren't you? What I told Lola must've been convincing enough for her husband to send you out here to investigate."

His gaze narrowed. "Do you want the truth?"

"Considering you're my fiancé, that would be nice." She batted her eyelashes at him.

"Funny." He turned down the heat. "The truth is, you're Lola's friend. She's worried about you."

She clenched her teeth to keep her jaw from dropping.

After a few deep breaths, she smoothed her hands over the pressed denim covering her thighs and then clasped her knees. "Are you telling me that none of you believe my stepfather is up to his neck in something nefarious? The CIA director was just murdered—in front of my house on his way to our party."

"Which may or may not have anything to do with Spencer Correll."

A sharp pain stabbed her between the eyes, and she pinched the bridge of her nose. "Are you here to help find evidence against my stepfather, or to play fiancé and protector to the poor, addled widow?"

"A little of both." He held up his hand when she took a breath, clenching her fists in front of her. "Nobody thinks you're poor and addled—especially not poor."

"You're insulting." She blew out a breath and flicked her fingers in the air. "Turn around. The engagement is over, and you can leave."

He raised his eyebrows. "That was insulting? I admit I'm brusque, comes from living in a world of subterfuge and secrets. When I have the opportunity to tell the truth, I take it. You want the truth, don't you?"

"Lola doesn't believe me?" Her nose stung. Lola Coburn was one of her oldest and best friends. She knew Lola had been concerned about her after Shane's…death, but Lola had sounded so sincere on the phone.

"Lola believes you have every right to suspect Spencer of complicity in your mother's death."

"But not that he's involved with a bunch of terrorists?"

"Nobody is dismissing that out of hand, Claire, and yes, the director's murder is convenient for Senator Correll."

"But…"

"No buts. I'm here to look into everything."

"Including my mental health." She scooted forward in

her seat and tilted her head at him. "Why did Jack Coburn send one of his agents on what could very well be a wild-goose chase?"

"The truth again?"

"Why not? We seem to be on a roll."

"I'm retiring. I've been in this business too long, and I'm on my way out."

She scanned the touch of gray in the black hair at his temples and the lines in his rugged face. "So Jack asked if you'd mind checking in on the poor, addled widow on your way out?"

He reached out as quickly as a cat and chucked her beneath the chin. "Would you stop calling yourself that? You're not poor or addled."

"I know, I know, especially poor."

Tapping the car's GPS, he said, "Are we still going to Mount Vernon?"

"Why not? I just want to get out of DC, and Mount Vernon's as good as anyplace. Besides, I'm supposed to be showing you the sights."

"It's going to be a madhouse in DC for the next several weeks. Director Haywood's death is going to affect us, too."

"I think his assassination serves many purposes. I have no doubt that it was to put Spencer in position, but there must've been another reason. Maybe the director knew something." She squeezed her eyes closed trying to remember the last time her stepfather and Haywood had met.

"This is a lot bigger than you now, Claire. You're not going to discover anything the CIA or FBI isn't going to discover."

"Is that your way of telling me to back off?" She gripped her knees, her fingers curling into the denim of her jeans. "If the CIA and the FBI had anything on Spencer, they would've made a move by now. I know things those agencies don't know."

He glanced at her as he veered off the highway, following the sign pointing toward Mount Vernon. "That's why I'm here."

They rode in silence as he maneuvered the car to the parking area. He swung into a slot, leaving a few spaces between her car and the next one over. "Not very crowded today."

"Too cold, and maybe people don't want to be hanging around tourist areas after last night."

"Do you want to head inside the mansion or get a cup of coffee at the Mount Vernon Inn so we can talk?"

"Since I dragged you out here so we could talk away from prying eyes and pricked ears, let's get some coffee."

Claire opened her door and stepped onto the parking lot, the heels of her knee-high boots clicking dully against the asphalt. The bare trees bordering the lot gave them a clear view of the mansion and the shops and restaurant next to it. "I don't think I've ever seen it so empty here."

"That's a good thing. The last time I visited, I couldn't get a table at the restaurant."

"I don't think we're going to have that problem now." She shoved her gloved hands into the pockets of her coat and hunched her shoulders. "Shall we?"

Mike locked the car and joined her, his own hands concealed in his pockets. They passed just two other parties making their way to the mansion.

Mike opened the door of the restaurant and ushered her into the half-empty room with its Colonial decor. A hostess in Colonial dress, a little white mob cap perched on her curls, smiled. "Do you have reservations?"

Raising his brows, Mike's gaze scanned the room. "No. Do we need one? We just want some coffee."

"Just checking. You don't need a reservation today." She

swept her arm across the room. "We've had several cancellations. I think it's because of that awful business last night."

"You might be right." Mike nodded. "Can we grab that table by the window?"

"Of course."

They sat down and ordered their coffees, which their waitress delivered in record time.

Mike dumped a packet of sugar into the steaming liquid and stirred. Then he braced his forearms on the table, cupping his hands around the mug of coffee. "Start from the beginning."

"The beginning." Claire swirled a ribbon of cream in her coffee and placed the spoon on the saucer with a click. "It all started when Spencer Correll came out of nowhere, married my mother and then killed her."

"Your mother fell down the stairs."

She took a sip of her coffee and stared at Mike over the rim of her cup. "He murdered her."

"You think he pushed her down the stairs? That's hardly a surefire method for murder. People can and do survive falls like that."

"He pushed her and then finished the job by smothering her with a pillow." Her eyes watered, and she dabbed the corners with her napkin.

"And you know this how?"

"I saw the pillow." She dashed a tear from her cheek.

"Lying next to your mother's body? What did the police think about it?"

"No, no." She took a deep breath. "That's just it. There was no pillow there. I noticed my mother's pillow on her bed later—with her lipstick on it."

"What is that supposed to mean?" Mike cocked his head, his nostrils flaring.

"My mother was meticulous about her beauty regimen." As Mike shifted in his seat, she held up her index finger. "Just wait. She never, and I mean never, went to bed with makeup on. She'd remove it, cleanse, moisturize. I mean, this routine took her about thirty minutes every night. There is no way there would be lipstick on her pillow, no reason for it."

"Let me get this straight." Sitting back in his chair, Mike folded his arms over his chest. "Your mother loses her life falling down some stairs, you see lipstick on her pillow and immediately believe your stepfather murdered her?"

"It wasn't just the pillow." She glanced both ways and the cupped her mouth with her hand. "It was the phone call."

"You just lost me." He drew his brows over his nose. "What phone call?"

"A few years before Mom's so-called accident, a woman called me with a warning about Spencer Correll. She said he was dangerous and that he'd killed before and would do so again to get what he wanted."

"Who was the woman?"

"She wouldn't give me her name."

"Did you inform the police?"

"At the time of the call?" She widened her eyes. "I thought it was a prank, but I told them about it when Mom died."

"They dismissed it."

"Yes, even after I showed them the pillow."

He rubbed his knuckles across the black stubble on his chin. "Did the cops tell Correll about your suspicions?"

"No."

"Did you ever hear from this woman again? After your mother's death?"

"No."

He dropped his spikey, dark lashes over his eyes, but not before she saw a glimpse of pity gleaming from their depths.

She clenched her jaw. She didn't expect him to believe her, but she didn't want to be pitied. People generally reserved their pity for the crazy or delusional. Neither applied to her—anymore.

He huffed out a breath and took a sip of coffee. "So, you believe your stepfather killed your mother, but how in the world does that link him to terrorists?"

Pursing her lips, she studied his lean face, his dark eyes bright with interest. At least he hadn't called for the little men in the white coats yet. "I didn't say the murder had anything to do with terrorism, but it prompted me to start nosing around his personal effects."

"What did you discover?" He gripped the edge of the table as if bracing for the next onslaught of crazy.

She reached into her bag and pulled out the envelope containing the picture, the picture she'd taken from the video she rescued from the trash can on Spencer's computer. She pinched it between two fingers and removed it from the envelope. Then she dropped it on the table and positioned it toward Mike with her fingertip.

Picking it up, he squinted at the photo. "It's your stepfather talking to another man. Who is he?"

"He's the terrorist who killed my husband."

Chapter Four

Mike's gaze jumped to Claire's flushed face, her violet eyes glittering with a challenge, her lips parted.

She'd really gone off the deep end. Nothing she had to say about Correll could be of any importance now. A hollowness formed in the pit of his stomach, threatening to engulf him.

How could he possibly save this bright, beautiful, damaged woman?

He toyed with the corner of the picture, a piece of paper really, with the image printed on it. "How do you know this man is the one who killed your husband? On the video, your husband's executioner was masked."

"Do you know how many times I watched that video? It's seared into my brain."

Swallowing, he grabbed her hand. "Why? Why torture yourself?"

"My torture paled in comparison to the torture Shane endured." She blinked her eyes, but no tears formed or spilled onto her flawless skin. "I watched that video frame by frame. I memorized every detail about that man, mask or no mask."

"You really believe this man—" he flicked the edge of the paper "—is the same man in the video with your husband."

"I'm sure of it."

Her voice never wavered, her eyes never lost their clarity.

"Why?" He loosened his grip on her hand and smoothed the pad of his thumb over her knuckles. "Explain it to me."

"This—" she tapped her finger on the picture "—is a still from a video I found on Spencer's laptop. It's the video I was telling you about before. I have the entire thing. I can see the way the man moves, the tilt of his head…his eye."

"His eye, singular?"

She drew a circle in the air over her own eye. "He has a misshapen iris. I researched it, and the defect is called a coloboma. I had blowups made of my husband's execution video and I had this picture blown up. The man's eye is the same in both. This is the guy."

Mike buried his fingers into his hair, digging them into his scalp. What had this woman put herself through for the past five years? What was she willing to put herself through now?

"I can prove it to you. Let me prove it to you. I have the videos and the stills in a safe deposit box."

He owed her that much, didn't he? He owed Lola Coburn's friend an audience for her manic obsession.

"What is the video you retrieved from Correll's laptop? Who took it? Where was he meeting this man?"

Claire's shoulders dropped as she licked her lips. "It's not DC. Florida, maybe—warm weather, palm trees. I don't know who took the video or why. I don't know why Spencer had it, but I can guess why he trashed it."

"Because it's evidence tying him to this man, whoever he is."

"Exactly."

She wiggled forward in her seat, and a shaft of guilt lanced his chest. He didn't want to give her false hope that he was going along with this insanity, but he had to investigate. He had one last job to do for Prospero, for Jack, and he'd go out doing the best damned job he could, considering his previous assignment was such an abject failure.

"Why would Correll be so careless about the video? Why would he leave it in his trash can?"

She lifted one shoulder. "Maybe he doesn't realize you have to empty your trash can on the computer."

He snorted.

"Don't laugh. Like my mom, Spencer didn't grow up using computers. I'm sure his assistants do a lot of his work on the computer for him. You don't think he actually posts those messages to reach the youth vote on social media platforms himself, do you?"

"How'd you get into his laptop? You told me earlier that you were trying to access his computer last night before the bomb blast."

"That was his desktop at the house. He has a laptop that he keeps with him. I know the password to the laptop and I was able to get to it one night when he was…otherwise engaged."

"Does he keep confidential information on this laptop?" He waved off Betsy Ross as she hovered with the coffeepot.

"No. Personal emails and games mostly, nothing work-related. I don't know how that video got on there, but the minute I saw it, I knew Spencer was up to his eyeballs in something."

He swirled the coffee in his cup, eyeing the mini whirlpool that mimicked his thoughts.

"You don't believe me."

He raised his eyes to hers. "It's a fantastic set of circumstances."

"I know that."

"Does anyone else know about your…suspicions?"

"No." She twirled a lock of blond hair around her finger.

"You don't think I realize how crazy this all sounds? That's why I called Lola."

"Lola's an old friend of yours from when you and your mother lived in Florida, right?"

"Yes. We lived there after my father died, with Mom's second husband."

"Correll sits on the Security Council. He must at least know about Jack Coburn even if he's never met him. Does he realize that you're friends with Coburn's wife?" He steepled his fingers and peered at her over the tips.

"No. Like I mentioned before, he and my mother married when I was in my late teens. Lola and I didn't see each other for a while. She was busy with medical school on the East Coast, and I had gone to college at Stanford on the West Coast."

"How do you know he hasn't done some kind of background on you?"

She spread her hands on the table, the three rings on her fingers sparkling in the light from the window. "I don't know, but he has no clue I suspect him of being in bed with terrorists. He realized I was suspicious about Mom's death—that's it, and he thinks I've dropped that train of thought."

Her jaw hardened, and he almost felt a twinge of pity for Senator Spencer Correll. Claire Chadwick would never relinquish her vendetta against her stepfather.

Clasping the back of his neck, he massaged the tight muscles on either side. "Can you show me the videos today?"

"They're at a bank in Maryland."

"Why didn't you take me there right away?"

"I wanted to feel you out first. I wanted to see if I could trust you."

"Why wouldn't you be able to trust me? Lola's husband sent me out here."

She lodged the tip of her tongue in the corner of her mouth and studied his face, her violet gaze meandering from the top of his head to his chin. "I was waiting for you to jump up and down and call me crazy, or worse, talk to me like a child and humor me."

"And?" Her inventory of his face had kindled a slow-burning heat in his belly. If she brought this same level of intensity to bed, she might be the best lay he ever had.

Lola had teased him that her friend's attractiveness would make it difficult for him to concentrate on the job, but he'd shrugged off the warning since a pretty face had never posed a threat to his professionalism before.

Until now. The combined effect of Claire's beauty, sympathetic story, passion and those eyes created a combustible mix that had hit him like a thunderbolt.

He cleared his throat and repeated his question. "And?"

"And you didn't do either one of those things. You don't believe me and you do feel pity for me, but you're a man of honor and you're here to do a job." She leveled a finger at him. "I respect that."

He ran a hand across his stubble, wishing he'd shaved this morning and wondering where he'd misplaced his poker face. Did she just nail that, or what?

"I want to see those videos." He dug his hand into his pocket and pulled out a five-dollar bill, dropping it on the table. "How long is the drive?"

"Less than forty-five minutes."

"Do we have a way to watch the videos?" He stood up and flicked two more dollars on the table.

"I have a laptop in the back of the car."

He ushered her outside and flipped up the collar of his jacket against the cold air. He welcomed its bite, which seemed to wake him up from a dream state. He threw a sideways glance at Claire in the hopes that the chilly slap had made her come to her senses.

She charged across the parking lot with more purpose to her gait than when they'd arrived.

He opened the passenger door of the car. "Unless you want to get your laptop out of the trunk."

"I'll wait." She shrugged out of her coat and tossed it in the back before sliding onto the seat.

He settled behind the wheel. "Can you enter the bank's address in the GPS?"

"I'll give you directions verbally. I'm very careful about what I enter into my GPS."

He raised his eyebrows before starting the car. "You said you weren't on Correll's radar."

"For his terrorist ties, but he knows I've been snooping around his finances."

Rolling his eyes, he said, "There are so many threads here, I can't keep track."

She laughed and then snapped her fingers in front of his face. "Stay with me here, Mike."

"You can laugh?" He pulled away from the parking lot.

"If you can't laugh, you don't stand a chance in life. I still have a son to raise who doesn't have a father."

"You're definitely putting him on a plane to Colorado tomorrow?"

"He needs to see his grandparents. Shane had brothers and sisters and nieces and nephews, so Ethan will have a big family around him. Besides, I need to get him away from you."

"Ouch." He flexed his fingers. "I don't have kids myself, but I always thought I was pretty good with them. I even coach some youth basketball."

She touched his arm. "I'm sorry. That didn't come out

right. It's *because* you're so good with Ethan that I want to get him away. Does that make sense?"

"You don't want him getting attached or overhearing the gossip about us." He rolled his shoulders.

"Exactly. I could tell he thought you were something special." She turned her head to look out the window. "You don't have kids?"

"No."

"Ever been married?"

"No."

She jerked her head toward him. "How did that happen?"

He shrugged, all the old familiar excuses curled on his tongue.

Tucking her hair behind her ear, she said, "I suppose your job makes it hard to have a relationship, but even Jack Coburn is happily married with three children."

"Jack has a desk job now, and that desk is at his home."

"You'll be retiring soon. Are you thinking of settling down?"

"With a dog."

"A dog?"

"That's all I can handle."

Her warm laugh had a smile tugging at his lips. Let her think he was joking.

"What kind of dog? Not a little froofy one?"

"Probably a Lab—basic, uncomplicated."

"I didn't know dogs could be complicated." She tapped on the windshield. "You're going to want to take the next exit."

Glancing in his mirror and over his shoulder, he moved to the right. As he took the exit, Claire folded her hands in her lap, revealing two sets of white knuckles.

Her mission always lurked beneath the surface, despite her chatter, smiles and laughter.

Her husband, a journalist kidnapped in Somalia, had died five years ago and her mother had taken a tumble down the stairs a year later. Maybe Claire needed this fiction about her stepfather to keep her from focusing on the primary tragedies. Correll gave her a target for her grief and anger.

He could understand that. He'd had a lot of different targets over the years for his.

They rode in silence for several more miles until they entered the city of Brooktown.

"Are we getting close to the bank?"

"Turn left at the next signal in under a half a mile. It's the Central City Bank. You'll see it on the left after you make the turn."

He turned at the signal and pulled along the curb just past the bank. "Do you want me to go in with you?"

"I don't want anything to seem unusual. I'll just go to my safe deposit box and take the thumb drives."

"You got it." He turned off the ignition and Claire slipped out of the car before the engine stopped.

He'd nabbed a space not too far from the entrance to the bank, and she didn't bother to put on her coat. He watched her tall frame disappear through the glass door, a striking figure in her skin-tight jeans and high boots that came up over the top of her knees.

If he called Jack now, his boss would probably tell him to start his retirement early. Claire's story was too fantastic. It had to be just a coincidence that the CIA director was hit last night—didn't it?

He fiddled with the radio and turned up the classic rock song while drumming his thumbs on the steering wheel. He was about ready to break out his air guitar on the third song in a row when the tap at his window made him grab the steering wheel with both hands.

He glanced out at Claire jerking her thumb toward the rear of the car. He popped the trunk and unlocked the doors.

The car shook as she slammed the trunk of her Lexus. Then she dropped onto the passenger seat, clutching a laptop under one arm. "Got 'em."

"Where are we going to watch? You can't bring them back to the house even if Correll is still in meetings on The Hill."

"Of course not. Hang on a minute." She dipped into her giant bag and pulled out her phone. She tapped the display and started speaking. "How's the party? Is Ethan having fun?"

She cocked her head as she listened, a soft smile playing about her lips. "Don't let him eat too much junk. I'm still packing both of you on a plane tomorrow, stomachache or not."

Mike jabbed her in the ribs. "Tell him not to forget my cupcake."

"Yeah, and Mitchell wants his cupcake." She nodded at him. "Thanks, Lori. See you later."

"Is Ethan bringing me a cupcake?"

"He is." She patted the computer on her lap. "Drive up two blocks to the public library."

Claire had an amazing ability to compartmentalize. It was either a sign of insanity or supreme mental health. "We're going to watch the videos in a public library?"

"The library has small meeting rooms. The schoolkids use them for tutoring but school's out for winter break, so I think they'll be free."

"You seem to know this area well."

"I've used that library for research."

He didn't bother asking her what kind. The woman had tons of money at her disposal and could spend her days playing tennis, going to the spa and lunching with other pampered ladies. Instead she wiled away the hours studying gruesome videos and stalking her stepfather, a US senator.

"Here, here, here."

He slammed on the brakes and jerked the steering wheel to the side to pull up at the curb. "Check that sign. Is it okay to park here?"

"I don't even have to look. Street cleaning tomorrow. We're good."

She hadn't been kidding that she knew the area. He followed her into the library, the large bag hitched over her shoulder with the laptop stashed inside. The musty smell of library books insinuated itself into his consciousness and infused him with a sense of calm. The public library had been one of his refuges, the library and the basketball court.

Claire tugged on the sleeve of his jacket. "This way."

They walked through the stacks, and he trailed his fingers along the spines of the books as if reconnecting with old friends. He read all his books on an electronic device these days, but he missed the feel of a book in his hand.

They passed one glassed-in room where two teenagers hunched over a laptop, giggling.

"Not much work getting done there."

Claire skipped over the next room and then yanked open the door of the following one. "There's free Wi-Fi, too."

"Not that we need it. We're going to be watching the videos from the thumb drives, not posting them on the internet."

"Shane's execution was posted on the internet."

"Still?" Sympathy washed over him as he pulled out a chair for her.

She sank into it with a sigh. "I'm not sure. I haven't searched for it lately."

"Lately?"

Leaning forward, she plugged the laptop into the socket.

"I wanted to know where it was so I could keep Ethan away from those websites, block them from our computers."

"Makes sense, but he's a little young."

"I know. That was years ago—when I was obsessed."

He searched her face for any sign of irony, but he saw only concentration as she shoved the first thumb drive into the USB port on the side of the laptop.

She double-clicked on the device and then dragged the lone file to the desktop. "I can bring up the videos side by side. The similarities are more apparent that way."

She pulled out the drive and inserted the second one. She repeated the drag-and-drop action.

As she opened the first video, he held his breath. Before she clicked Play, she double-clicked on the other video.

"Are you ready?"

His heart pounded in his chest and he didn't know why. He'd seen the Shane Chadwick video before, and he'd seen a lot worse. But if he saw nothing in the videos, no likeness between the terrorist who murdered Shane and the man meeting with Correll, he'd have to leave. He'd have to leave Claire Chadwick to her delusions and fantasies.

He didn't want to leave her.

"Mike? Are you ready?"

He scooted his chair closer to the table. "I'm ready. Let's see what you've got here."

She played the first video for a few minutes, stopped it and then played the second. Back and forth she went, freezing the action, pointing out the tilt of the man's head, a hand gesture, the slope of his shoulders, the shape of his face.

She brought up several frames where she'd zoomed in on his eyes, where it looked like the pupil was bleeding into the iris.

It was as if she'd prepared and delivered this presentation many times before. She probably had—in her head.

At the end of the show, she placed her hands on either side of the laptop and drew back her shoulders. "What do you think?"

Had she cast a spell on him with her violet eyes? Had his desire to stay with her, to protect her, colored his perception?

He drew in a deep breath. "I think you're onto something."

She closed her eyes and slumped in her seat. "Thank God. You do see it, don't you?"

"I do. Both men definitely have the same condition with their right eye."

She grabbed his arm. "I'm not crazy, am I? I'm not imagining this?"

He took her slender hand between both of his. "You're not crazy, Claire. He may not be the same man. I mean, it would be quite a coincidence, but there's enough of a similarity between them, especially that coloboma in his eye, to warrant further investigation."

She disentangled her hand from his and, leaning forward, threw her arms around his neck. "You don't know how much that means to me to hear you say that."

Her soft hair brushed the side of his face, a few strands clinging to his lips, and the smell of her musky perfume engulfed him. He dropped one hand to her waist to steady her so she wouldn't topple out of her chair.

A tremble rolled through her body and she pulled away, wiping a tear from her cheek.

"I'm sorry." She sniffled. "I usually don't get emotional like this, but it's been a long time since I could confide in someone."

"I understand, but—" he clicked the mouse twice and closed both videos "—I'm just looking into it at this point. It may lead to nothing."

She dabbed her nose with a tissue and squared her shoulders. "Of course. I didn't mean to put any pressure on you."

He bit the inside of his cheek, drawing blood for his punishment. He should've comforted her, held her, wiped her tears instead of bringing her back to cold, hard reality.

"What's the first step?" She snapped the laptop closed and swept it from the desk.

"I'm going to send those stills and close-ups I copied to your thumb drive to our team at Prospero. I need to get to my secure computer, which I left in the hotel safe."

"We should go back to your hotel anyway, so you can bring the rest of your stuff over to the house." She stuffed the laptop back into her bag.

"Exactly, but I'm keeping the hotel room and I'm leaving a few of my things there."

"Like your secure laptop?"

"Yeah. Speaking of security, I think you should put both thumb drives back in the bank once I complete my transmission."

"Don't worry. I've been guarding those little storage devices with my life." She waved the other thumb drive and zipped it into an inner pocket of the coat she'd flung across the table.

"So," he said as he held up one hand and ticked off his index finger, "we head to my hotel back in DC, I send the images and then we return here to stash everything back in your safe deposit box."

She glanced at her expensive-looking watch. "If we can get back here in time. It's already late."

"Then we'll put both thumb drives in my hotel safe this afternoon, and come back here tomorrow after you drop off Ethan and Lori at the airport." He stood up and stretched, glancing out the window at the rows of stacks. They'd had the laptop with its gruesome images facing away from the window—just another couple of coworkers poring over a project together.

"Sounds like a plan." She shoved out her hand and then laughed when he took it lightly in his own. "Don't worry, Mike. I'm not going to fall apart again."

He squeezed her hand and pulled her in until they were almost nose to nose. He was close enough to see the flecks in her deep blue eyes that gave them their purple hue. "You have every right and reason to fall apart."

She lifted her shoulders. "Doesn't mean I should."

She broke away from his grasp and spun around to sweep her coat from the table and sling her bag over her shoulder. "Let's get down to business."

He stuffed his arms into his jacket and opened the door for her. The giggling teens had finished whatever it was they were doing, a homeless guy slouched in a chair in the corner and the stacks were empty.

Mike stepped outside behind Claire, and an insistent car alarm assaulted his ears, an unwelcome jolt after the peace and quiet of the library. He stuck his fingers in his ears. "That's so annoying."

"Mike." Claire quickened her pace down the library steps, clamping her bag against her side.

"What? Is that your car?"

"I think it is." She plunged her hand into her coat pocket and aimed the key fob in front of her, pointing it at her car at the curb.

The alarm went silent, but the alarm bells in his head replaced it. "That *was* your car."

"I hope nobody bumped it. I haven't even had it a year."

While Claire inspected her front bumper, Mike trailed around the perimeter of the car. He ran his hand along the driver's side door, skimming his fingers along the windows. "Claire?"

"Yeah?" Her boots clicked as she walked toward him. "Everything looks okay in the front."

"Did you have these scratches on your window like this before?"

She bent forward rubbing her fingers over the grooves in the glass. "No."

"Feel the edge of the door here. Rough, isn't it?"

Her eyebrows collided over her nose as she bent forward and traced a finger along the seam where the window met the door. "It does feel rough. How would that happen?"

His eyes met hers, wide in her pale face. "Someone was trying to use a slim jim to break into your car."

She gasped and shot up to her full height. "Do you think the alarm scared them off? Who would do that in broad daylight on the street?"

"Someone who thought he could make it look like he was just opening the door with a key." His lips formed a thin line and a muscle jumped in his jaw.

"You don't think…?" She flung out one arm. "How would anyone even know we were here? I don't have any business in Brooktown."

He headed toward the trunk, crouched down and poked his head beneath the chassis of her car.

"Mike, what are you doing?"

A few minutes later, his fingers greasy from his exploration, he straightened up and stalked to the front of the car. He dropped to his knees and trailed his fingers along the inside of the wheel well. They tripped over a hard, square object.

"Bingo."

"Bingo? Bingo what?" The slightly hysterical edge to Claire's voice told him she knew what was coming.

He yanked the tracking device from her car and held it up. "Someone's been following you."

Chapter Five

She swayed and braced her hand against the hood of the car. Spencer knew. She'd given herself away somehow. She'd been naive to think a man like Spencer would allow himself to be investigated without turning the tables.

"I—I don't understand. I've been so careful. Why would he have me followed?"

Mike squinted at the tracker and then tossed it in the air. "He doesn't trust you. He probably never forgot that you suspected him of murdering your mother."

"That was almost three years ago. Do you mean to tell me he's been tracking my movements for three years?"

"Maybe. Have you been anywhere, done anything in those three years that would tip him off to anything?"

"Just coming here, where I have no reason to be. I just got the safe deposit box about a year ago."

"So he knows you have a bank account in Maryland. That's not much." He circled to the front of the car and crouched before it, reaching beneath the body.

"What are you doing? You're not putting it back?"

"If you take it off and throw it in the trash, he's going to know you found it. You shouldn't do anything different." He popped back up and wedged his hip against the hood. "Are you sure it's Correll? Do you have any other enemies?"

"None that I'm aware of." She plucked some tissues

from her bag and waved them at him. "Wipe your hands on these."

"No ex-boyfriends stalking you?"

"Are you kidding? I haven't had any boyfriends since..." She shoved the tissues into his hand.

"Then we'll assume it's your stepfather, and all he knows is that you come out to a bank and library in Brooktown a few times a month."

"If you leave that thing on there, he's going to know we went to your hotel in DC."

"So what? I already told him I'd taken a room at the Capitol Plaza and left most of my stuff there." He'd shredded the tissues wiping his hands and then crumpled them into a ball. "Let me get rid of this and we'll satisfy Correll's curiosity by going to my hotel."

She held up her key as he walked back from the trash can near the steps of the library. "Do you still want to drive?"

"Sure." He snatched the dangling keys from her fingers and caught her wrist. "Don't worry. That tracker told him nothing."

She let out the breath trapped in her lungs and nodded. His touch made her feel secure, but she had to be careful. She'd made him uncomfortable with her previous display of emotion. For all his outer friendliness and charm, he had an aloof quality—except when he'd been kissing her last night. He hadn't seemed to mind her touch then.

Of course, the drive for sex came from a completely different place than the trigger for empathy. She'd rather have him desire her than pity her, anyway.

His lashes fell over his dark eyes and he pressed a kiss against the inside of her wrist. Then he dropped her hand. "Let's get going."

She had no idea what emotions had played across her

face for him to do that, but she'd have to try to duplicate them sometime soon.

She slipped into the passenger seat of the car, glancing at the scratches on the driver's-side window as Mike opened the door.

When he settled behind the wheel, she turned to him. "If Spencer's lackey had managed to get into my car, then what? What exactly had he been looking for?"

"Your laptop? That video?"

"Spencer couldn't possibly know about the video. I left it in his trash can after I discovered it."

He cranked on the ignition and pulled away from the curb. "He's grasping at straws, just like you. How did you manage to get into Correll's laptop?"

"I bribed his admin assistant, Fiona."

"How do you know she didn't tell him?"

"She wouldn't. She let me have access to his laptop and gave me his password. If she had told him that, he would've gotten get rid of her for sure and changed his password."

"How do you know that wasn't his plan all along? Why'd she do it? Money?"

"I'm not going to lie. Money did exchange hands, but I played on the emotions of a woman scorned."

"Fiona? Scorned?"

She plucked an imaginary piece of fuzz from the arm of her sweater. "Spencer had been having an affair with Fiona. I overheard him making plans with another woman for an afternoon tryst. I figured it was a good time to hightail it to his office and do some snooping, and while I was there I let Spencer's plans for a little afternoon delight drop into Fiona's lap. She was more than happy to cough up his password and let me into his office."

He whistled. "You're pretty good at this cloak-and-dagger stuff. Does Correll have a weakness for the ladies?"

"Oh yeah. I can almost guarantee you that he cheated on my mom."

"That's good."

She jerked her head to the side and he held up one hand. "Not that he cheated on your mother, but that he has a wandering eye. It's a weakness that can be exploited, as you discovered."

"I like how you think, Becker." She shoved her hair behind one ear. "I know you have to continue to analyze the videos before committing yourself or the Prospero resources to investigating any further. I'm not getting ahead of the game here, just so you know."

"I got it."

She lifted her phone from a pocket in her purse. "Excuse me a minute while I check on Ethan. The party should be wrapping up soon, and after finding that device on my car, I honestly can't wait to get my son out of this town."

She got Lori on the phone, but Ethan was too busy with the pony rides to talk. Lori filled her in on all the details, which soothed the twinges of guilt she felt for missing out on spending time with her son.

When he'd received this party invitation earlier in the month, Claire had arranged for Lori to take him, since Lola had told her an agent would be heading her way before Christmas. As much as she loved seeing all the kids having a blast and chatting with the other moms, this day with Mike had proven to be fruitful.

She ended the call and sighed as she cupped the phone in her hand while Lori sent her a picture of Ethan on the back of a dapple-gray.

"Missing the fun? Sounds like a pretty extravagant party if it includes pony rides."

"Yeah."

She held the phone in front of his face as he idled at a signal.

"Wow. I never went to birthday parties like that."

She traced her finger around Ethan's smiling face. "Every party he's been to at this school, it seems like the parents are trying to one-up each other. I'm not sure that's a very healthy environment for kids. What were your birthday parties like?"

"I only had one birthday party—for my seventh birthday—and there were definitely no ponies there." His mouth twisted. "It ended early when my old man showed up unexpectedly, drunk as a skunk, and started popping all the balloons with a lit cigarette."

"I'm sorry. That doesn't sound like much fun."

"That was my old man—life of his own party." He dropped his shoulders, which he'd raised stiffly to his ears.

He pointed to the phone in her lap. "You must've had parties like that."

"I did."

"And you turned out okay."

"Did I?"

"Well, we've established you're not crazy."

"Did we?"

"Even if the guys in the videos aren't the same person, you have several good reasons to believe they are."

Leaning her head against the cold glass of the window, she stared at the landscape whizzing by. "It's good to have someone on my side."

"I tend to be a loner, but having backup is always good."

Claire thumbed through a few text messages on her phone, her mind on the man next to her. He reminded her of a chameleon. He could be the charming fiancé, the kid-friendly visitor, the no-nonsense spy. Would she ever get to truly know him?

She stole a glance at him sideways through her lashes, taking in the strong hands that gripped the steering wheel and the hard line of his jaw. Without a wife, without children, what did he plan to do in his retirement years? He was too young to sit on some pier fishing or to stroll along some golf course.

"My hotel is coming up. We'll retrieve my computer from the safe, send the video stills and lock it back up along with your thumb drives."

"Then when we get back to the house, we act as if everything's normal and that we never found a tracker on the car."

"And we don't lie about our whereabouts."

She covered her mouth with her hand. "Depending on how long that tracker's been attached to my car, it's already too late for that. I've never admitted going to Brooktown, but he's going to know I've been there."

"So what? He doesn't know what you're doing there and it's really none of his business, is it?"

"None at all." She tilted her chin toward a glittering high-rise hotel. "Isn't that it?"

"Yeah, I'm hoping to find a spot in the short-term parking out front so I don't have to leave the car with a valet."

He pulled into the circular drive in front of the hotel and slid into the last available parking space in the small lot to the right of the main building.

He guided her up to his room and ushered her in first.

"Nice." She took a turn around the suite.

"Only the best for Mitchell Brown. He's supposed to be a successful businessman. Do you think Correll will be checking me out?"

"Two hours ago, I would've said no. He doesn't care who I marry since my marriage isn't going to take anything out of his pocket." She perched on the edge of a chair by the window. "After finding the tracking device? My bet is he's going to look up Mitchell Brown to make sure he's no threat. Will he be?"

"Mitch? Nah. He works for an international conglomerate that makes plastic coffee-cup lids, stir sticks and sleeves. Grew up in Chicago, went right to work in sales." He yanked open the closet doors and dropped to his knees in front of the safe.

"Where did we meet, sweetheart?"

He cranked his head over his shoulder and she fluttered her eyelashes at him.

"We should've had this discussion last night. In fact, I was planning on it until that car bomb exploded." He turned back to the safe and punched in some numbers.

"It's a good thing Spencer didn't ask this morning. I think Ethan's presence at the breakfast table saved us." She crossed one leg over the other and tapped her toe. "So, where did we? Meet, I mean."

"Don't you remember? It was that fund-raiser for the girls' school in Yemen. My company committed a million bucks to the cause."

"Was it love at first sight?"

"For me, it was." He held up his laptop and crossed the room to place it on the table next to her. "That's why I fell so fast."

"And you were so different from anyone else I'd ever known—politically obtuse, culturally challenged, a breath of fresh air."

He chuckled as he fired up the laptop. "Don't get too carried away."

He turned the computer away from her as he tapped on the keys, probably entering passwords. Then he inserted the thumb drive, waited and continued clicking away.

Blowing out a breath, he powered down the laptop. "All done. Let's see if Prospero can get a line on this guy. It's not like agencies besides ours haven't tried to discover the identity of your husband's executioner. The English accent alone has puzzled us for years, and I'm sure others have noticed the eye, but they've never gotten another possible look at him—until now."

"So, we wait?"

"The least exciting aspect of my job." He held out his hand. "The other drive? I'll put everything in this safe since it's too late to return to Brooktown, and I'm sure you want to see Ethan when he gets home from the party…and I want my cupcake."

"Don't hold your breath." She dropped the thumb drive into his cupped palm. "He's five. He tends to forget anything that doesn't relate to his immediate happiness."

"Ah, to be five again." He placed the items in the safe and locked it. "Do you want to watch the news for a while before we go back? I haven't seen any coverage on the director's murder since I tuned in to the morning news shows."

"Are you going to tell Jack what we saw last night? The valet placing the device beneath the car and running off?"

"I already told him, but that story is out anyway. There were a couple of other witnesses who got a better look at the man than we did."

"I'm sure he's a low-level guy who'll never talk even if they find him. He's not going to be implicating Spencer or anyone else."

"Maybe." He aimed the remote at the TV. "It remains to be seen how much Prospero will be involved in the investigation. We come into play once the person has been identified, except…"

"Except what?" She averted her gaze from the images shifting across the TV screen—Jerry Haywood's life in review.

"We've been tracking a…situation for the past four

months, one that involves the assassination of high-level officials, but these hits have all been on foreigners so far."

"This might be related." She rose from the chair and took a turn around the room.

"Anything is possible."

"That means Spencer was involved with those other murders, because there is no doubt in my mind he's responsible for what happened last night."

"Slow down." He turned up the volume on the TV. "We wait."

While Mike soaked up the news of the day, she retreated to the bathroom, washed her hands and splashed some water on her face. She returned to the room to find Mike sprawled across the sofa, his long legs hanging off the edge.

"Anything new?"

"The talking heads have nothing, but while I was listening to my stomach growl it occurred to me that you haven't eaten anything today. I, at least, had a big breakfast." He shook a finger at her. "You can't run with the big boys on a couple cups of coffee."

She placed a hand on her stomach. "I forgot all about food."

His gaze raked her from head to toe. "That happen a lot?"

"Are you implying I'm skinny?"

"You look like one of those high-fashion models who wear the weird clothes—not that you're wearing weird clothes—and eat two olives a day."

"My mom was a model. I inherited her build."

"Yeah, yeah, well, you're not a model, so you can actually eat more than two olives a day." He turned off the TV. "The restaurant downstairs isn't bad. Do you want to grab a sandwich before we return to the scene of the crime?"

"We're about fifteen minutes away from my house. There's plenty to eat there." Narrowing her eyes, she wedged a hand on her hip. "Are you putting off going back there for some reason?"

"For some reason? Let's see, I have to pretend I'm engaged, have to pretend I'm someone else, my boss's boss was just murdered there." He stood up and stretched. "Seems to me I have a lot of reasons."

"Sounds like a whole bunch of whining to me. Besides, what is all that compared to a cupcake?"

"You have a point there."

When they arrived back at the house, everything looked normal—except for the yellow tape that still fluttered in the crisp breeze, the men and women in dark suits and dark glasses milling around, and the press hovering like a bunch of vultures across the street. Completely normal.

The security detail in front of the house waved them through, and they ducked into the house. Claire tilted her head back to take in the towering Christmas tree at the end of the foyer, which had been restored to last night's glory.

Mike whistled. "The Christmas tree is redecorated and all of the windows have already been replaced. Your stepfather must've had an army out here."

"It took an army." Spencer jogged down the staircase. "I hope you two had a good day and were able to set this all aside."

"We did." Claire hooked her arm through Mike's. "Any leads? Did the FBI find the valet yet?"

"Nothing yet, although they're splashing a composite of him all over the news. You haven't seen it yet?" Spencer placed a well-manicured hand on the curved balustrade at the bottom of the staircase. "Where did you go today?"

Mike pressed his shoulder against hers. "We drove

down to Mount Vernon and then to a very special place in Maryland."

She stiffened, but plastered a smile on her face and nodded.

"What's so special about Maryland?" Spencer cocked his head, but the smile on his lips didn't reach his eyes.

"Oh, Mitch." She tapped his arm. "I thought that was supposed to be our secret."

"Now I'm really intrigued." Spencer leaned against the banister as if he had all day to listen, and panic flared in her chest.

Mike ran a hand through his dark hair. "Claire and I communicated a lot face-to-face through our laptops, and I proposed to her while she was in Maryland. I wanted to visit the exact spot in person."

"Modern technology. I'm glad I'm not dating these days." Spencer winked.

Claire gritted her teeth behind her smile. He didn't have to date. He just bedded half the women who worked for him.

"Are Lori and Ethan home from the party yet?"

Spencer raised his eyes to the ceiling. "I was just upstairs getting a detailed account. Lori's getting him all packed up for tomorrow—that is, if you still want him going out to the Chadwicks'."

"Don't you think it's even more important now after what happened last night?"

"I don't think anyone here is in danger. Some terrorist organization targeted the director and was successful. We're not expecting any more hits."

Because you got what you wanted?

"You sound so confident." Claire hugged herself. "I'm not so sure about that. Has anyone taken credit yet? Director Haywood's assassination was a huge coup. I can't imagine the people responsible won't want to crow about it."

Spencer reached out and patted her shoulder, and she tried hard not to recoil. "Don't concern yourself with it, Claire. You don't want to go down that road again, do you?"

Her nostrils flared and her palm tingled with the urge to slap his smug face.

As if sensing her urge, Mike took her hand and circled his thumb on her palm. "Claire's just asking normal questions. I think we all wait for the other shoe to drop when something like this happens."

"Since you two are engaged, I'm sure Claire told you about her...troubles." Spencer touched her cheek with the smooth tip of his middle finger. "She's worked hard to come back from those dark days, but she's still a little shaky."

Claire reared back from him, hot rage thumping through her veins. "I am not...shaky."

Mike put his arm around her shoulders and brushed past Spencer still perched on the bottom step. "Claire's fine. We're going to check on Ethan."

She preceded Mike up the staircase, her body trembling with anger. When they got to the second-floor landing, she grabbed his hand and pulled him into the library.

She shut the door behind them and leaned against it, her eyes closed, her breath coming out in short spurts. "Bastard!"

Mike took her by the shoulders. "Don't let him get to you."

Her eyes flew open at the same time they flooded with tears. "You know what he's talking about, don't you? You, Prospero, would've checked me out thoroughly before taking this assignment."

Pulling her close, he whispered in her ear, "Anyone would've had a breakdown, Claire. He's a jerk for bringing it up, especially when you're asking honest questions, but we already know that."

"Y-you know he had me committed? They took Ethan away from me."

His arms tightened around her and she melted against his solid chest, allowing herself a moment of weakness. He rested his cheek against the top of her head. "It must've been tough, but I don't think anyone who knew your situation would think you're crazy. What you discovered on those two videos has real merit."

She pressed her nose against his shirt and sniffled. "I'm sorry. That's twice today I got weepy and used you as a tissue."

Smiling a crooked smile, he looked down into her eyes. "I don't mind. I've been used in worse ways."

She quirked an eyebrow at him and he laughed. "Wait. That didn't come out right."

"Okay, let's go see Ethan." She took a long, shuddering breath.

They hesitated outside Ethan's door, which had been left open a crack, and Claire practiced her brightest smile.

Mike nodded and gave her a thumbs-up.

She scooped in a breath before pushing open the door. If she did have another breakdown, at least she had the right man on hand to catch her.

Chapter Six

The following morning Mike jogged downstairs, leaving Claire in Ethan's bedroom. Mother and son should have some alone time before the boy left for the holidays. Claire hoped to be able to join Ethan in Colorado for Christmas, and maybe that was where she belonged, away from this craziness.

If Prospero came back with any kind of match between the two men in the video, the agents could handle it from there. Claire needed a break from all this, and maybe once he retired he could do a little skiing in Colorado. That wouldn't be too obvious, would it? He'd already kind of bonded with Ethan last night over that cupcake.

He pushed through the dining room doors and Correll popped up from where he'd been…hovering over Lori Seaver, Ethan's nanny.

"Good morning." He pulled out a chair across from the two of them as a quick blush stained Lori's cheeks. Had Correll been putting moves on the nanny?

"Just giving Lori some skiing tips. Do you ski, Mitch?"

"I do, took it up as an adult." In fact, skiing and snowboarding had been part of his training with Prospero. His family could've never afforded a sport like skiing. Hell, his family couldn't have afforded sending him downhill in an inner tube.

"So did I." Correll pushed off the table where he'd been parked next to Lori and tapped his nose. "I think you and I are alike in a lot of ways, Mitch."

Mitch swallowed a mouthful of coffee too fast and burned the roof of his mouth, but he kept a straight face. "Poor boy making it good?"

"Something like that." Correll narrowed his dark eyes as he studied Mike.

God, the man thought he was marrying Claire for her money. Maybe that wasn't such a bad cover story.

Liz, the maid from yesterday, came in from the kitchen bearing a plate of food. Couldn't these people get their own damned food? He and Correll were nothing alike since it seemed the senator had adapted easily to being waited on by the minions that kept his life running like a well-oiled machine.

"I remember what you liked from yesterday, Mr. Brown."

"Thanks, Liz. After that dinner Jerome made last night, I'm not sure I'm up for a full breakfast."

She put the plate down in front of him, overflowing with eggs, bacon and home fries. A basket of Jerome's biscuits were already steaming on the table. "Give it a try."

When Liz disappeared back into the kitchen, Correll chuckled. "You'll get used to it, Mitch."

"Sir?"

"Getting waited on." He winked. "You might even learn to enjoy it."

Had the man been reading his mind?

The doorbell chimed deep within the house and Lori jerked her head up.

Correll patted her hand. "You still nervous, too? You and my stepdaughter need to learn to relax."

Mike concentrated on his plate and stabbed a blob of

scrambled egg. Correll had a very odd attitude toward an obvious terrorist attack in front of his own place of residence.

He seemed to be expecting the visitor as he excused himself and left the room.

Mike swallowed and took a sip of coffee. "Are you looking forward to the trip? That must be a nice perk working for a family like this."

"It is, but Claire isn't one to take her son all over the world. I think she'd planned to raise him in Florida…before she decided to get involved in the investigation of her husband's murder. Then when she…well, had some problems, she ended up staying here."

"Were you here when Claire had her problems?" Lori's brown eyes rounded, taking up half of her heart-shaped face.

"Oh, no. When Claire got better, she wouldn't have that woman—Andrea—anywhere near Ethan."

Any more probing came to an end when Correll entered the dining room again with two men in suits following him.

Not that Mike wanted to go behind Claire's back and question Lori about her breakdown. If he had questions, he'd ask Claire straight-up.

Correll gestured to the suits. "These men are from the FBI, and they'd like to talk to Claire before she takes Ethan to the airport. Do you want to get her?"

"Sure." He glanced at the older man. "I'm assuming this is about what happened the other night."

The older agent adjusted his glasses while the younger one answered. "It is, and you are?"

Mike thrust out his hand. "Mitchell Brown, Ms. Chadwick's fiancé."

He shook hands with both agents, confident that his cover would stick even with the FBI. "I'll get Claire."

Lori got up from the table. "I'll come with you to stay with Ethan."

Mike took the stairs two at a time, leaving Lori in his dust. He tapped on Ethan's door as he pushed it open.

Two faces looked up from the bed where Claire had Ethan in her lap with a book in front of them.

"Hate to interrupt your story, but a couple of men are downstairs and want to talk to you."

"Really?" Claire tossed her blond hair over one shoulder. "What kind of men?"

"I'll tell you on the way downstairs."

As Claire slid off the bed, Lori joined them. "I'll keep an eye on Ethan, Claire. Is he ready to go?"

"Yes, are you?"

"All packed."

Claire handed her a book with a bull sitting in a field of flowers on the cover. "We're right in the middle."

"I'll finish reading the story for you, Ethan." Lori took Claire's place on the bed.

When they were in the hallway, Mike shut Ethan's door. "They're two FBI agents."

"About the car bomb?"

"That's what they said."

She put her hand on his arm and lowered her voice. "Are we not admitting we were witnesses?"

"Nothing to be gained by it at this point, and I don't want to draw attention to myself."

"Got it." She squared her shoulders and walked downstairs, graceful on a pair of high-heeled boots, her slim hips swaying hypnotically.

He blinked and shook his head. *Snap out of it, Becker.*

When they reached the bottom of the staircase, the agents were waiting for them.

They introduced themselves to Claire as Agents Finnegan and Glotz.

Glotz, the younger agent, asked, "Is there someplace we can talk privately, Mrs. Chadwick? Senator Correll suggested the small office off the foyer."

"Since that's my office, that'll work. You don't mind if my fiancé joins us, do you?"

The agents exchanged a glance that made the hair on the back of his neck quiver.

"No."

Claire swung open the door and ushered them all inside the small, feminine office. The seat in the bay window sported rose-colored cushions, and Mike sat in a chair with such spindly legs, he had a feeling that it would collapse beneath him at any moment.

The agents in the chairs facing Claire's ornate desk must've felt the same way, as they perched on the edges of their seats.

Claire folded her hands in front of her, the rings on her fingers sparkling beneath the desk lamp. "What can I help you with?"

Glotz placed a folder on the desk, flipped it open and positioned a photograph in front of Claire. "Do you recognize this man, Mrs. Chadwick?"

Mike craned his neck over the shoulders of the agents but only got a glimpse of a young, dark-skinned man.

"It's Ms. Chadwick, and yes, I do recognize him. And you know I recognize him or you wouldn't be uncomfortably shifting in those Louis Quinze chairs staring at me."

Mike gulped, his stomach twisting into a knot. Had Claire been keeping secrets from him?

Glotz tapped the picture. "Can you tell us who he is, Ms. Chadwick?"

She snorted. "You know who he is. The question is, why are you asking me about him?"

Agent Finnegan hunched forward in his chair, his face red up to the line of his gray hair. "Tell us his name, Ms. Chadwick."

Mike cleared his throat. "Claire?"

She held up a hand. "It's okay, Mitch. This man is Hamid Khan."

"And you've been in contact with him?" Glotz's calm tone contrasted with his partner's aggressive one.

Good cop, bad cop, but why were they playing this game with Claire?

"Lately? Have I been in contact with him lately? No."

"You've contacted him before." Finnegan jabbed a stubby finger in Claire's direction.

"Agent Finnegan…" Mike half rose from his chair, his hands curling into fists.

Glotz cast an apologetic half smile in his direction. "We don't have a problem with your presence, Mr. Brown, but please don't interfere with our questioning."

Mike spluttered. He could be a protective fiancé, but not someone overly knowledgeable about FBI procedures. "Does Claire need a lawyer? I don't like this questioning."

"I'm fine, babe." She picked up the picture with both hands. "I contacted Hamid when I was looking into my husband's execution at the hands of terrorists. Why are you asking me about him now?"

"Hamid Khan was the man posing as a valet parking attendant at your party the other night. We have a composite sketch from witnesses."

Claire dropped the picture, and Mike sat up in his chair to try to get a look at the man again. He didn't know any Hamid Khan, but why in the hell had Claire been in contact with terrorists?

She recovered herself and folded her hands on top of the photo. "That's impossible. I had been in touch with Hamid because of his uncle, but Hamid was no extremist. He was studying to be an engineer and wanted no part of his uncle's radicalism. I was able to get him into the US on a student visa, but that's as far as it went."

Finnegan pinched the picture between the tips of his blunt fingers and slid it from beneath Claire's hands. "Maybe then, but this is now."

"I don't believe it for a minute. I would've..." She stopped and huffed out a breath. "I would've known if he was someone capable of this—he wasn't."

Mike's muscles tensed. She was going to spill the beans about seeing the valet from the library window. These guys would've been even more suspicious than they were now if they discovered she'd lied about seeing anything from that window.

Glotz slid the photo from his partner's possession and put it back in the folder. "You're not going anywhere in the near future, are you, Ms. Chadwick?"

"No."

"If we—" Glotz steepled his fingers "—came back with a search warrant for any computers you own, that wouldn't be a problem, would it?"

The color on her cheeks heightened and her long lashes fluttered for a second. "No."

"Very good." Glotz placed his hands on the desk and pushed up from the chair, still mindful that his ass had been planted on a chair that cost more than he'd see in one year's salary.

Finnegan stood up with much less grace and hunched over the desk. "Thanks for your cooperation, Mrs. Chadwick. If we need anything else, we'll let you know."

With the questioning over, Finnegan had reverted back to his gruff but civil self.

Mike hurried to the office door and swung it open. The tail end of Correll's suit jacket disappeared around the corner of the foyer. Had he been listening at the keyhole?

"Gentlemen, if there's nothing else, we'll see you out. Claire and I need to take her son to the airport."

A maid appeared on silent feet with the agents' coats.

"Just don't hop on any planes yourself, Mrs. Chadwick." Finnegan hunched into his overcoat and saluted.

When the front door closed behind them, Claire sighed. "What they're saying isn't true."

Mike shook his head as Correll came into view from the corner behind her.

"What the hell was that all about, Claire?"

"The FBI thinks they have the valet. It's someone I was in contact with after Shane's murder." She flicked her fingers in the air. "It's all garbage anyway. We need to get Lori and Ethan to the airport. Mitch and I will probably be out the rest of the day."

"Be careful out there, Claire. Those two agents seemed pretty serious. I knew the time you spent looking into Shane's death would come back to haunt you."

She started up the stairs and glanced over her shoulder. "It's not haunting me."

Correll shrugged his shoulders and gave Mike a pitying look. "She's your problem now."

ONE HOUR AND one tear-filled goodbye later, Mike accelerated out of the airport with Claire sniffling beside him.

"He looked so grown-up with his little backpack." She clutched his arm. "He didn't look scared, did he?"

"I haven't known your son that long, and I'm no expert on little kids, but I don't think a smile from ear to ear and hopping from one foot to the other on the escalator signals fear for a five-year-old boy."

She dabbed her eyes and then waved the tissue in the air. "I don't want him to feel sad, exactly, but a little longer hug would've been nice."

"It probably won't hit him until he's at his grandparents' in the middle of the night and realizes he can't run into your bed whenever he wants."

Her hand returned to his arm. "I hope he's not going to be scared."

"You said he had lots of cousins out there for the holidays?"

"Yes, tons."

"He'll be fine. Everything's always better when you have kids your own age around."

"Did you?"

He fumbled for his sunglasses in the cup holder. "Only child here. I almost had a younger sibling once, but my mother lost the baby after a particularly bad beating at the hands of my father. She never tried again."

Claire pressed a hand to her mouth. "I'm so sorry, Mike. Did your mother ever leave your father?"

"Not until the day she died in a car accident—his fault. He was driving drunk and they were fighting. He crossed the median and wrapped his car around a lamppost. The wrong person died in that accident."

"H-how old were you when that happened?"

"Seventeen." He ran a hand over his mouth. "I almost killed the bastard, but my basketball coach got to me first. My dad went to prison, and I lived the rest of my senior year of high school at Coach's house and enlisted in the marines the day I graduated."

The gentle pressure of her hand on his thigh brought

him back to the present. "I'm sorry. That sure as hell falls into the too-much-information category."

She didn't answer except to give his leg a gentle squeeze.

Why had he spilled his guts like that? If he didn't watch it, he'd be blabbing about his worry that witnessing all that violence as a child had ruined him for any kind of relationship. She was already worried about her own mental health; she didn't need to start worrying about his.

"So, what's the plan? My hotel first to pick up the drives, check on a response from Prospero and then head to the bank to secure the drives in your safe deposit box?"

"Sounds good."

He rolled his shoulders to relieve the tightness that had bunched his muscles when he'd revealed his sob story to Claire. He needed to get this ball back into her court.

"Do you have anything else to tell me about this Hamid Khan? I don't think he's on Prospero's radar at all."

"Why would he be? Except for the connection to his uncle, he's not an extremist."

"Who's his uncle?"

"Tamar Aziz. Are you familiar with him?"

"Yeah, low-level guy, a driver, bodyguard type."

"That's right, but he's in the thick of things, and that's not Hamid."

"How'd you get in contact with Hamid?"

"Through some different channels. I got some leads from Shane's interpreter. He'd been kidnapped along with Shane, but he was released."

"You play dangerous games, Claire—then and now."

"Maybe so, but Hamid was never a danger, and as you may have gathered, I almost blurted out that the valet I saw near the director's car was most definitely not Hamid." She swept the hair back from her face. "They're getting bad information from someone."

"I wonder how the FBI came up with his name. They must've been looking into his activities thoroughly to come across your connection to him."

"If they are, they're allowing the real perpetrators to escape."

"The real perpetrators who are somehow connected to your stepfather?"

"Exactly."

"So your stepfather must've been thrilled to see the FBI show up on his doorstep and question you about Hamid Khan." He reached out and dialed down the heat. He was starting to sweat under his layers of clothes—or maybe it was the subject matter.

She tapped the edge of her phone against her chin. "Are you implying that Spencer himself somehow implicated Hamid?"

"He knew you'd been contacting players. It's no stretch to believe he knew their names."

Hunching her shoulders, she crossed her arms. "He's probably been spying on me ever since he couldn't have me committed for life."

"And you've been spying on him. What a game of cat and mouse."

"He's going to think we're a couple of sentimental fools coming back out to Brooktown." She turned to face him, a smile playing about her lips. "How did you come up with that story, anyway? You proposed to me online? That's romantic."

"Hey." He smacked the steering wheel before pulling into the hotel's circular drive. "I wanted to see the very spot where you were sitting when I popped the question. That's romantic."

"If you say so." She rolled her eyes.

He pulled up behind a car and stuck his head out the

window, yelling at the valet. "Is it okay if I leave my car here for about fifteen minutes?"

"Sure. Do you mind leaving the keys in case we have to move it?"

He killed the engine and dangled the keys out the window in exchange for a red ticket, which he dropped into the pocket of his shirt.

The valet opened Claire's door and she paused. "Do you think it might take longer than fifteen minutes if you've gotten a response?"

"I don't expect any feedback this soon. Besides, they have your car keys if they have to move the car."

With no response from Prospero, it took them less than fifteen minutes to gather his laptop and Claire's thumb drives from the safe.

He hauled a small carry-on bag onto the bed. "I might as well stuff the rest of my clothes in here and take them back to your place."

She pointed as his computer. "And the laptop? Do you think it'll be safe at my house with Spencer there?"

"Why would Correll want to poke around my laptop?"

"You never know."

"Don't worry. It's as secure as Fort Knox, and I want to have it with me in case Prospero comes through with something today."

He slipped his laptop into a separate case and then wedged the case on top of his wheeled bag. "You all set?"

"Yes. It's not like I don't trust the hotel safe, but I'll feel a lot better when these are back in my safe deposit box." She patted her bag where she'd stashed the drives.

"Onward to Maryland, then."

On the drive east, they kept the conversation light—no abusive fathers, no nervous breakdowns, no terrorists. This was what he looked forward to in retirement. He'd never pictured a woman by his side before, but Claire's presence felt right, felt good.

By the time they reached the bank, he felt as if they were on a date—the small talk, the mutual discovery of the petty likes and dislikes that comprised a person, the palpable sexual tension that buzzed between them.

In fact, he hadn't had such a successful first date in a long time—or maybe ever.

WHEN THE BANK came into view, Claire's stomach sank. For a short time with Mike in the car, she'd felt almost normal.

She liked him, everything about him. Why did she ever think he was standoffish? He'd revealed quite a bit about himself today. The story about his abusive father had her heart hurting for the pain Mike must've endured as a child.

Ethan would grow up without a father, but she'd make damned sure she'd surround him with love. Who knew? Maybe one day she'd meet a man good enough to be Ethan's dad.

Mike parked her car at the curb about half a block down from the bank. "I'll wait in the car."

"I won't be long—in and out." She grabbed her coat from the backseat and put it on while standing on the sidewalk. Then she waved to Mike and slammed the car door.

Entering the bank, she veered toward the end of the teller windows and stopped in front of Dorothy's desk. Dorothy looked up from a computer screen, where she was helping a teller. "Be right there, Claire."

Two minutes later, Dorothy's heels clicked on the floor as she approached her desk. She opened her drawer and withdrew a key chain, and then buzzed the security door for Claire.

Claire joined Dorothy on the other side of the door and followed her down a short hallway to the safe deposit area.

Dorothy used her key along with a code to open the main door of the safe. They both stepped through the door, and rows and rows of metal boxes stretched out on either side of Claire.

"Twenty-two sixty-one, right?" Dorothy moved to the left and bent forward to insert her key into Claire's box.

"You have a good memory, Dorothy."

"Well, I did just open it earlier today."

Claire nodded and smiled as Dorothy backed out of the room. Maybe Dorothy's memory wasn't that great. Claire had been here yesterday, not this morning. She inserted her own key into the second lock on the box and slid it out of its cavity.

She turned and placed it on the table that ran the length of the small room. She reached into her purse, her fingers searching for the two drives. Curling her hand around both at once, she pulled them out.

She lifted the lid on the box and froze. Licking her lips, she tilted her head to check the number on the box and then glanced to her left to squint at the number on the empty slot.

With her heart pounding, she plucked the first stack of bills, neatly bound, from her box and ran her thumb along the edge.

Where had this come from? Even though she knew she was alone in the room, she looked around as if expecting to find an answer from the tight-lipped safe deposit boxes guarding their own secrets.

She dropped the packet of money on the table and picked up the second stack of bills, again neatly bound. Four more bundles nestled in the safe deposit box, giving her a total of six.

How could the bank make a mistake like this? She was the only person with the other key. She didn't want to leave the bills in her box. She'd better bring them out to Dorothy.

She dumped the money onto the table and scanned the room for a bag. Of course, the bank didn't just leave those lying around, and she couldn't walk into the main area clutching the cash in her hands.

Her big bag gaped open on the table, and she started stuffing the stacks inside. She left her box open on the table and hugged her purse to her chest as she walked out of the safe deposit box room. The door slammed behind her as it was designed to do.

She exited the door to the main area of the bank and turned toward Dorothy's desk. That was when she saw them.

A man and a woman in dark suits were talking to Dorothy, whose eyes were bugging out of her face. They bugged out even farther when she caught sight of Claire. Dorothy pointed at her and the man and woman turned in unison.

A chill zipped down her spine and her step faltered.

The two feds pivoted toward her, the female reaching inside her jacket.

A flood of adrenaline surged through her. She clasped the purse tighter, wrapping her arms around the money and the two thumb drives still inside. Her long stride got longer. She put her head down and made a beeline for the door.

"Ms. Chadwick," the woman called behind her.

Claire shoved through the glass doors and took off down the sidewalk toward the car. Mike must've seen her in the rearview mirror because the engine growled to life at her approach.

"Ms. Chadwick, stop." This time it was the male who yelled after her, but she had no intention of stopping for him, either.

Despite her high-heeled boots, she took off in a run, extending her hand in readiness for the door handle. When her fingers tucked around the cold metal of the handle, she could hear the flurry of someone sprinting behind her.

She tugged open the door and scrambled inside the car. The man had caught up with her and made a grab for her coat as it flew out behind her.

"Claire?" Mike's voice gave her strength and purpose.

"Go, Mike! Just go!"

That was all he needed from her. No questions, no answers.

He floored the gas pedal and the car lurched away from the curb, flinging the door open and shedding the government man hanging on to it.

Chapter Seven

The familiar streets of Brooktown passed by in a blur. Mike had slowed the car down a few blocks past the bank to give Claire a chance to close the door and loosen her death grip on the seat.

Now only their heavy breathing filled the silence between them as Mike maneuvered through the streets at high speed. His gaze darted between his rearview and side mirrors, and then he suddenly screeched to a stop before the bridge.

He charged out of the car, disappeared in the front and then popped up holding the tracking device.

He stepped away from the car and chucked the device into the water. Then they sped across the bridge.

After another five miles or so, he balanced his palms on top of the steering wheel and flexed his fingers. "What happened back there?"

"I opened my safe deposit box to put the drives back and found this." She unzipped her bag, plunged her hand inside and withdrew the packets of neatly stacked bills. "Money."

Mike swore. "How much is it?"

"I didn't stop to count it, but there are six stacks of varying denominations."

"So, your natural response was to stuff the cash in your bag and run from the FBI?"

She jerked her head around. "I was scared. How do I know those two aren't working for Spencer?"

"We don't know anything at this point. I saw them enter the bank, and it gave me pause. In fact, it set off low-level alarm bells in my head."

"Exactly." She formed her fingers into a gun and pointed at him. "When I discovered the money, I freaked out. How could a bank make a mistake like that? I didn't want to leave the stacks in there for one minute and there were no bags in the room, so I put the bundles in my bag, and I was going to bring them to Dorothy."

"Who's Dorothy?"

"She's the bank employee who has the safe deposit box keys." She dropped the money in her lap as Dorothy's words flashed across her mind. "Mike?"

"What is it? Do you think Dorothy put it there?"

"No, but she made a comment that didn't make sense to me at the time. She mentioned something about how she remembered my box number because she'd just opened it earlier this morning. I thought she was confused, since I'd been in yesterday, not this morning."

He picked up on her thought. "Unless she opened your box for someone else this morning."

"She can't do that, can she?"

"If that someone has a key, she can. Anyone can get into a safe deposit box with the right key and the box number."

Her nervous fingers creased the corner of a thousand-dollar bill, one of many. "Why would someone put all this cash in my safe deposit box?"

"Why would the FBI be questioning you about a man you contacted five years ago?"

"Do you think they're linked?" She sucked in her bottom lip to stop it from trembling.

"If you hadn't had the same suspicion, you never would've run out of that bank."

"As soon as I found the money, I knew something was off—not just that the bank had made a mistake, but that the money represented something sinister. When I walked out into the bank and saw those two talking to Dorothy, I panicked."

"That's understandable." Mike checked the rearview mirror for the hundredth time. "They didn't show up to help you count your money."

Shoveling the bundles back into her purse, she said, "They came to arrest me, didn't they?"

"I don't want to scare you, Claire," he said as he brushed the back of his hand against her arm, "but I think so."

Her mouth felt dry even though Mike wasn't telling her anything she hadn't suspected already. Maybe she'd suspected it from the moment Agents Finnegan and Glotz showed up at her house this morning, flashing pictures of Hamid.

She bolted forward in her seat. "Mike."

"Don't worry, Claire. We'll figure this out."

"It's not that. What about Hamid?"

"What about him?"

"If they're setting me up, they're setting up Hamid, too."

"He's their fall guy."

"But he didn't do anything. Hamid is a good kid, a university student. He tried to help me."

"He must live in the States if they're fingering him as the valet. Is he visiting, or does he reside here?"

"H-he lives here...now. Remember, I told the FBI agents that I'd helped him with a student visa." She stuffed her hands beneath her thighs.

"And he's still here? How long has he been here?"

"Mike, I sponsored him. I facilitated his relocation to the US from Pakistan. He's a student at MIT."

"I heard you tell the FBI agents that you'd helped him, but not that much." Mike groaned and pressed the heel of his hand against his forehead. "That's not gonna look good."

"Let's face it. Nothing's going to look good at this point. They managed to turn even something as harmless as a safe deposit box into poison for me."

"Correll must know you have something on him—something other than suspicions about your mother's accident, unless he's using the car bomb as an excuse to get rid of your petty meddling and direct the suspicion away from him." He snapped his fingers. "He kills two birds with one stone."

"I really don't care what his motivation is at this point. The question is, what are we going to do now?"

He pointed to the road ahead. "Disappear and regroup."

"Where are we going?"

"Vermont."

"That's so far. What's in Vermont?"

"A safe house, seclusion." He patted the dashboard. "We're going to have to get rid of this sweet ride first."

"Get rid of, as in *get rid of*?"

"I'm not going to send it to a dismantler, if that's what you're thinking. We'll leave it at the airport in Newark and take a very long bus ride to Vermont."

"I want to get to Ethan."

He squeezed her hand. "I know you do, but he's safe where he is, and if you try to see him, they could be waiting for you."

"How did this get so crazy so fast?" She massaged her temples with her fingertips. "Once Prospero identifies the man meeting with Spencer as the same one who executed my husband, will this all end?"

"It's not as simple as that, Claire. We'd have to get more on Correll than just the meeting."

"And I'm supposed to hang out in Vermont—without my son—until you do?"

"It's a start." He tugged on a lock of her hair. "Trust me, Claire. Can you do that?"

"I don't think I have a choice, Mike. You're all I've got."

And she could do a lot worse than Mike Becker.

THE SWITCH AT the Newark airport went smoothly. He parked Claire's Lexus in the long-term parking, buried it among rows and rows of cars so it wouldn't be lonely.

It had been a stroke of luck that he'd taken his laptop and another bag from his hotel room before going to the bank. The FBI probably would've staked out his hotel, and he never would've gotten to his computer.

If that man and woman at the bank were even FBI. He didn't want to worry Claire with his suspicions—yet.

He had cash and documents in his bag and more waiting for him at the cabin in Vermont.

And Claire wasn't hurting for cash. Guaranteed those bills in her safe deposit box weren't marked and traceable. Whoever put them there hadn't expected Claire to make a run for it with cash in hand.

That was one thing he'd learned about his pretend fiancée in the past few days—expect the unexpected. Her stepfather hadn't been paying attention all those years.

The bus slowed to a crawl as it rumbled over the railroad tracks, and Claire turned from the window, her beautiful face pinched with worry.

He knew her furrowed brow and pursed lips owed more to her concern about Ethan and Hamid than for herself. She could worry about them, and he'd worry about her. Someone had to.

"Are you doing okay? We can get something to eat at the next stop. We're not going to be in Vermont until almost ten o'clock tonight."

"Food is the last thing on my mind." She nudged her toe against the bag between his feet. "Are you going to contact Prospero when we get settled in the safe house?"

"Uh-huh."

"Can you bring up the news on your phone and see if we've made the Most Wanted list yet?"

He pulled his phone from his pocket and dropped it into her cupped hand. "Knock yourself out."

He extended his legs into the aisle between the seats and slumped down, crossing his arms over his chest and closing his eyes.

If Prospero found no link between the men in the two videos, he'd have a problem on his hands. He didn't believe for one minute that Claire had anything to do with the assassination of the CIA director, who'd been the deputy director when Shane Chadwick had been murdered, but evidence pointed to her involvement, and others might not see it the same way he did.

Claire nudged his shoulder, and he opened one eye. "I was planning on getting some shut-eye until we hit Philly."

She held up the phone in front of his one eye and said, "Look. They have Hamid's picture out there as a suspect in the car bombing."

He opened his other eye and studied the earnest face of a young man captured in a black-and-white photo. "Did the FBI pick him up?"

"No." She skimmed the tip of her finger along his phone's display. "They can't locate him."

"Didn't you tell me he was at MIT? Does he stay in Boston during the winter break?"

"I have no idea. I wasn't lying to the agents. I haven't been in touch with Hamid for a while."

"Did the article mention your name?"

"No." She held out his cell to him. "Not yet, anyway."

He dropped the phone into his pocket and closed his eyes. "Maybe we'll be in Vermont by the time your name is out there. It's going to be a long night. Let's try to get some rest."

What must've been a few hours later, the low rumble of the bus startled him awake, and his eyes flew open. Claire's head rested against his shoulder, her blond hair cascading down the length of his arm.

He inhaled her scent, which held a hint of dusky rose petals. Her proximity gave him crazy ideas, and he couldn't tell if these ideas were based in reality or had bubbled up as a result of his overriding need to protect a woman in jeopardy, any woman in jeopardy, just like he'd tried to protect his mom all those years.

"Claire?"

"Mmm?" She shifted her head and then jerked it up. "Sorry."

"That's okay." More than okay. "The rhythm of a bus ride always puts me to sleep, too. Looks like we're stopping outside Philly, and I'm starving." He hoisted his bag from the floor to his lap. "Do you want a sandwich or whatever they have at the station?"

"I'll take a sandwich and a diet soda. I'd offer to stay on the bus and watch your bag, but I have to use the restroom."

"I've got it." He hitched the strap of his bag over his shoulder and stood up, swaying slightly as the bus came to a halt.

Mike ducked to look out the window past Claire, and his gut rolled as he took in the multitude of people crisscrossing in front of the station. Anybody could be out there, but the FBI hadn't gone public with Claire's picture yet. Maybe they were hoping to shield a sitting senator's stepdaughter, not that the sitting senator would mind at all.

He knew a little about the perks enjoyed by politicians and their families. Jase Bennett, one of his Prospero team members, was the son of Senator Carl Bennett and used to talk about the privileges his family enjoyed.

He followed Claire down the steps of the bus and took her arm. "I'll get some food, you hit the restroom and we'll meet back on the bus. Fifteen minutes—don't be late."

He watched her head toward the ladies' room, and then he turned the corner in the direction of the food concession. He shuffled along in line, and when he got to the counter, he ordered two sandwiches and grabbed a bottle of water, Claire's soda and a bag of chips.

He stashed the food in his bag and lingered in the hallway outside the restrooms. He hadn't noticed Claire going back out to the bus, but then he hadn't been paying attention. His eye twitched, and he rubbed it. No way had anyone followed them to the airport or followed the bus. He'd double-checked and triple-checked.

Claire must've gotten back on the bus.

He strode outside where the bus spewed exhaust as it idled. He hopped on, and his step faltered. Their seats were still empty.

He scanned the rest of the bus and the passengers that didn't even fill half the seats.

He cranked his head toward the driver. "Do we still have a few minutes? My wife isn't back yet."

"Yeah, I'll wait for you, but not too long." The driver tapped a clock above the windshield. "We're on a schedule."

"Understood." Mike hopped off the bus, his heart slamming against his chest.

He entered the station again, swiveling his head from

left to right. He jogged toward the restrooms, his bag banging against his hip.

This time he didn't wait, he shoved open the door to the ladies' room. A woman looked up, her brows colliding over her nose.

"This is the women's restroom."

He bent forward, looking under the doors of all the empty stalls. No Claire.

"Doesn't anyone have any boundaries anymore?"

"I'm sorry. I'm looking for someone."

"That's what the other guy said."

Chapter Eight

Claire stared at the barrel of the gun. She never should've left the ladies' room with him. He wouldn't have shot her with that woman in the other stall.

Would he shoot her now?

She swallowed as she glanced down the alley with the car parked at the end. He just might.

"Just keep walking, Claire, all the way to the end of the alley. It's going to be okay. We don't really believe you had anything to do with the assassination of the director. We want to talk, to protect you."

Her gaze shifted from the gun to the man aiming it, dressed in faded jeans and a dark jacket zipped over a hoodie. Had the FBI changed its dress code recently?

She shook her head. "I'm not going with you. You're going to have to shoot me here."

A slight movement behind the man caught her attention. Mike's face appeared in the opening of the door leading to the bus station. She quickly directed her focus back to her assailant's face.

"Nobody wants to shoot you, Claire. Just get in the car at the end of the alley, and we'll discuss this whole misunderstanding."

"There's no misunderstanding on my part. Someone,

my stepfather, is setting up me and Hamid Kahn for the car bombing. Who are you? You're not FBI."

Mike had pushed open the door without a sound, but something must've alerted the man.

He spun around, but Mike had anticipated the move. He dropped into a crouch and then flew at the man, his long leg extended in front of him.

"Get down, Claire!"

She dropped to the cold ground just as Mike's foot hit the man midchest. They both fell over with Mike on top.

The gun skittered to the side of the struggling men and with one fluid movement, Mike grabbed it and drove the butt against the side of the man's head with a sickening thud.

Claire sprang to her feet. "Let's go!"

Mike had his hands buried in the man's pockets. "The money, Claire. Leave the money."

Her movements shifted to autopilot and she dumped the bundles of cash on the ground next to the inert form of her attacker.

Mike grabbed her arm and they barreled back through the door and ran toward the front of the bus station.

The bus had just closed its doors and Mike banged on the glass. The driver opened the doors. "I almost left you."

Mike panted out his thanks and they stumbled down the aisle to their row.

Claire dropped to her seat, pressing her hands to her still-thundering heart. "H-how did that happen? How did he find us?"

"The money. There must've been a tracking device in the money. I was stupid not to check it."

"He wasn't FBI, no way."

"The FBI didn't bug the cash, either. They still think that

money belongs to you, that it's Hamid's payoff. That must be why someone put it in your safe deposit box."

"That guy in the alley? He was Spencer's guy." She brushed some dirt from the knees of her pants. "Are you sure that's how he tracked us down, the money?"

"It must be. I made sure we weren't followed, Claire. Now that you dumped the cash, we should be safe." He put his arm around her shoulders. "Are you okay?"

"I'm fine, shaken up, but fine." She threaded her fingers through his and brought his hand to her cheek. "Are you okay? I thought for sure he was going to shoot you when he spun around."

"I had the element of surprise, thanks to you. Good job not giving away my presence."

"I saw you searching his pockets. Did you find anything?"

"I found a phone, which I didn't take in case it could be tracked, and a couple of other items, which I'll take a look at later—no ID, no wallet, nothing like that."

"Do you think whoever sent him gave him orders to kidnap me or kill me?" Her muscles tensed. Either way, if she hadn't had Mike by her side, she'd be dead meat by now.

He disentangled his fingers from hers and squeezed the back of her neck. "I'm not sure, but this is looking better and better for your story about Correll. The fact that someone other than the FBI was tailing you proves that this is some kind of setup."

"No call to your boss yet?"

"I'll wait until we get to our destination. By now, he's probably heard that you took off. He'll have plenty of questions."

She sighed. "Unfortunately, we don't have many answers for him. If the ID of the man in the two videos comes through, will Prospero have enough information to go after

Spencer, along with what just happened in the alley back there?"

"It might be enough to start looking at Senator Spencer Correll more closely." He reached down for his bag and unzipped it. "In the meantime, let's eat."

She peeled back the plastic wrap on the sandwich he'd handed her and spread a paper napkin on her lap. She took a bite and raised her eyes to the ceiling of the bus. "I never thought cold turkey on white bread would taste so good."

"Sorry, that was the only kind of bread available." He unwrapped his own sandwich and took a huge bite.

"I'm being serious. It tastes great."

He popped open a bag of potato chips and shook the bag in front of her. "Want one?"

"No, thanks, but do you have my soda in there?"

"Be careful." He pulled it from his bag. "It's been through the ringer."

She twisted the cap and the bottle hissed at her, so she settled for another bite of her sandwich while the bubbles fizzed out. "I can't wait until this is all behind me. I've been living with it for so long—my husband's death, my mother's death, my suspicions, walking on eggshells around Spencer. I just want a normal life, a safe space to raise my son."

"You'll get there, Claire, if I have anything to say about it." He crunched another chip and she laughed.

"Somehow you don't inspire a lot of confidence with potato chips all over your face." She reached out to touch a crumb on his bottom lip at the same time his tongue darted from his mouth to catch it. When his tongue touched her fingertip, their eyes met for a split second, and she jerked her hand back as if scorched.

"Sorry." The fire continued in her belly and she made a fuss of opening her tamed soda. "I should keep my hands to myself. You're not a five-year-old."

"No, I just had food on my face like a five-year-old." He sucked the salt from the tips of his fingers, which did nothing to quell the warmth that was infusing her entire body.

He balled up the chip bag and cracked open his bottle of water. "You don't happen to have any hand sanitizer in that huge bag you call a purse, do you?"

"Would I be the mom of a five-year-old if I didn't?" She pawed through her bag, happy for the diversion. "Got it."

He held out a cupped palm. "Hit me."

She squeezed the clear gel into his palm and he rubbed his hands together.

"Tell me about Ethan."

"Really?" She dropped the sanitizer into her purse. "You're just trying to get my mind off of things, aren't you?"

"Partly, and partly I want to hear about Ethan. Maybe I'm trying to get *my* mind off of things. I had switched gears into retirement mode, and now I'm on the run to another safe house in a long line of safe houses."

She huddled into her coat. "I'm sorry. You're so good at your job, I forgot this was a second-thought, last-minute assignment for you before retirement. Now you're in it."

He shrugged. "I've learned not to take any job for Prospero lightly, but I do want to hear about Ethan."

"You don't have to twist my arm to talk about my son."

As the bus rumbled north into the night, she slid low in her seat and spoke softly about Ethan. And Mike was right, just as he was right about so many other things—the day's fears and anxieties receded, replaced by warm memories of her son.

Several hours later, as they reached the end of the line, she jabbed Mike in the arm. This time she'd woken up first, which gave her the chance to raise her head from his shoulder. She was pretty sure she'd tipped her head toward the window as she began to doze off, but Mike just had that kind of shoulder—the kind a girl could lean on.

She owed Lola Coburn big-time for sending him her way.

Mike was alert in an instant. "We're here?"

"Yes." She twisted her head around. "And we're among the last few passengers. What next?"

"We pick up our next mode of transportation and then get a good night's sleep."

"We just slept."

He rubbed the back of his neck. "I said a *good* night's sleep, and we still have some work ahead of us before we reach that point."

Mike hadn't been kidding. Once they got off the bus, they picked up what looked like an abandoned car at a junkyard. The keys had been stashed on top of the visor, and Mike had retrieved a black bag from the trunk.

The car didn't have chains, but the snow tires had enough traction to get them safely to a cabin tucked in the woods at the end of a harrowing journey on a two-lane road, just beyond a small town.

Mike pulled the car around to the back of the dark cabin.

"I'm hoping this place has heat and light." She dragged her purse, much lighter without the cash, into her lap.

"It has everything we need for at least a month's stay. Our support team is top-notch."

"A month?" She grabbed her coat from the backseat of the junker. "I hope we're not going to be holed up here for a month."

"It's like the end of the earth up here, isn't it?" He opened the door a crack and the cold air seeped into the car. "Ready?"

"Ready as I'll ever be." She swung her legs out of the car, her high-heeled boots, ridiculously unsuited for a cabin in the middle of the Vermont woods, in the snow.

She slogged through the white stuff in Mike's wake as he trod a path to the back door of the cabin.

He jingled the key chain that he'd picked up from the car. "Our key to paradise."

Tipping her head back to take in the log cabin, she twisted her lips. "You've got a funny notion of paradise, Becker."

"Let's put it this way." He inserted the key in the dead bolt at the same time he punched a code in the keypad she hadn't noticed before. "We have food, water, heat and a bed. Sounds like heaven to me."

He must've heard the breath hiss from her lips because he jerked his head around.

"I mean two beds, of course—clean sheets and everything."

Shoving open the door, he stomped his boots on the porch mat and then reached for a switch on the wall. "Welcome to paradise."

Yellow light flooded the small room decked out like a snug getaway—a trio of love seats hugged an oval braided rug in front of a stone fireplace. End tables carved from logs stood sentry on either side of the love seat facing the fireplace, and a huge set of antlers graced the space above the mantel.

She swept her arm across the room. "Nice setup…except those antlers. I can't help thinking about the poor buck who lost them."

"Not my thing, either, but I didn't decorate the place." He dropped his bags by the door, closed it and reset the alarm. "Are you hungry? Tired? There's a kitchen, and I'm almost positive there are toiletries in the hall closet—stuff like toothbrushes and combs. Probably none of the high-end stuff you use."

"Hey, beggars can't be choosers, but I'm not all that tired."

"Hungry?"

She eyed the kitchen on the other side of the room. "What's in there, astronaut food?"

"I'm sure we're low on the fresh fruits and vegetables and the free-range chicken."

She shrugged the strap of her purse from her shoulder and placed it on one of the log tables. "I'll check it out. You want something?"

"I'm starving."

"When aren't you starving?" She moved into the kitchen and started throwing open the cupboard doors.

"I'm six-four. That's a lot of space to fill. Check the freezer."

She opened the freezer door and the stack of colorful boxes almost made her dizzy. "What do you want? We have lasagna, French-bread pizza, chicken wings, taquitos and a bunch of other stuff. This truly would be heaven for Ethan."

"Make an executive decision."

She peeked around the freezer door at Mike setting up his laptop.

"Are you going to call Jack now?" She grabbed two French-bread pizzas from the middle of the stack and steadied the leaning tower of frozen goodies with her other hand.

"That's exactly what I'm going to do."

"Are you sure there's internet and cell reception out here?"

"Unless the weather has interfered, we'll have reception. We make sure of that before we set up shop in any area. Even going as far as installing our own tower."

"I'm sure the neighbors are thrilled to have you." She placed the two pizzas in the microwave and set the time.

"If we had neighbors. That bus stop was in the nearest town."

While she'd been in the kitchen, Mike had cranked on the furnace and started a fire for good measure.

She sauntered out from the kitchen and sat on the arm of the love seat where he'd set up his computer.

He tapped in a number on his phone, followed by a series of other taps.

"It's Mike." He tapped his display once more. "Jack, I just put you on speaker, and Claire's in the room with me."

Jack's low voice reached out from the phone. "Claire, are you okay?"

"I'm fine. D-do you know what's going on?"

"I know that the FBI suspects Hamid Khan of placing the car bomb that killed the director of the CIA."

"No way, Jack. Hamid is innocent, according to Claire."

"The Fibbies are citing communications between Claire and Hamid, but they haven't named Claire as a suspect yet." He cleared his throat. "And then there's the small matter of the escape from the two agents sent to pick up Claire at the bank."

"Is that what the FBI is reporting?"

"I haven't seen anything official about that from the FBI."

"I'm still working that one out. In the meantime, some guy pulled a gun on Claire at a bus station outside Philly. That means the money in Claire's box had a tracking device hidden in it. You know the FBI doesn't work like that."

Jack whistled. "This has gone beyond informing on Claire to the FBI."

Claire leaned forward. "I knew it was a setup, Jack, and my stepfather's fingerprints are all over it."

"We're working on that, Claire. Where are you, Mike?"

Claire poked Mike in the arm and drew her finger across her throat. Jack Coburn might be married to one of her oldest friends, but he still worked for the US government, the same government that just might be trying to set her up.

Mike scowled at her. "We're at a safe house, Jack. I'm assuming we can't come in yet."

"No. It's one thing for you to be on the run with Claire, since everyone still thinks you're the hapless fiancé, the cover, but we can't let the intelligence community believe we have any part in this. We can't offer Claire any official protection."

Claire couldn't wait any longer, so she ducked her head and whispered in Mike's ear, "Ask him about the videos."

"Any news on those videos I sent you?"

"Nothing yet, although the evidence is compelling."

Claire sighed, her shoulders sagging. "Finally."

"I thought so, too." Mike squeezed her knee. "No ID yet on the man with Senator Correll?"

"Not yet. If the guy spent most of his career as a terrorist covered up, we might have a hard time linking him to any cells or groups."

"But his eye. That means something."

"Means a lot, Mike. Like I said before—compelling."

Mike picked up the phone as if by speaking into it directly, he had a better chance of convincing Jack. "If we can tie Spencer Correll to terrorist activity, the Agency and the FBI are going to have to look into him for this hit on the director. He's going to step into Haywood's shoes any day now."

"He'll need confirmation first, and that's not gonna happen before the holidays. The deputy director will run things for now."

"We need to make that connection, Jack. Isn't there still a heightened alert at the White House for Christmas Day?"

Claire sucked in a breath. This was the first she'd heard of that.

"There is, or there was until McCabe discovered all of Tempest's plans."

Claire folded her arms and tapped her fingers against her biceps. They'd just lost her. She didn't know a McCabe and had no ideas what a Tempest was, except that she was in one.

"The assassination of Haywood could be part and parcel of the same attack." Mike rubbed his knuckles across the scruff on his chin.

"We considered Tempest as soon as we heard about the car bomb. All I can tell you is we're on it, Mike. We have your back."

"And Claire's?" Mike shifted his gaze to her and watched her beneath half-mast lids.

"As long as you're with Claire, we have her back, too."

"I'm with Claire, Jack. I'm staying with her. That's why you sent me on this assignment."

"That's before she became a suspect in a terrorist attack."

"I'm still on the phone, Jack." She clenched her jaw.

"I know, Claire. I'm sorry, but we have relationships to maintain. We gave you Mike, and that's all we can do right now."

Her tight lips curved into a smile and she dropped her hand to Mike's back. "And I thank you for that."

The two men ended the call and Mike collapsed against the back of the love seat. "Life would be so much easier right now if they could ID the man who murdered your husband and link him to the man meeting with Correll."

"I've been saying that for five years." The sadness tugged at the corner of her lower lip.

Mike dabbed the rough tip of his finger on her cheek. "I'm going to make this right for you, Claire."

The gesture and the sentiment made her lip turn up

again. "You don't have to fix anything, Mike. The fact that you're here, on my side, means everything."

She covered her mouth and jumped from the arm of the love seat. "The buzzer for our French-bread pizza went off a while ago. I hope they're not ruined."

He called after her as she scooted into the kitchen. "They're French-bread pizzas in the microwave. What could possibly be ruined?"

She punched the button that released the door on the microwave and the cheesy smell of the pizzas wafted out. She removed their cardboard cooking containers and slid each one onto its own plate. "Water?"

"Are there bottles in the fridge?"

"Yeah, no beer, though." She tucked the water bottles under her arm and carried the plates out to the living room. "Since the FBI hasn't outed me as a suspect yet, is it okay if I use your phone to check in on Ethan?"

He handed her his cell. "Sure, but don't give anything away."

She placed the call and chatted briefly with Ethan's grandmother since Ethan was already sleeping. Nancy Chadwick assured her that Ethan and Lori had arrived safely and mentioned that they'd be out snowboarding all day tomorrow.

Claire ended the call, followed by a long exhaled breath. "Here's your phone, thanks."

"Everything okay in Colorado? Nobody sounded suspicious?" He looked up from digging in his bag, his hands full.

"Everything's fine. I put your water on the table."

"Yeah, I could use a beer. The safe houses don't contain any alcohol, but there's nothing stopping us from picking up a six-pack in town tomorrow."

"Yeah, nothing but that *America's Most Wanted* poster

with my face plastered on it that could go up any day now."
She settled on a cushion at right angles to Mike, her knee
bumping one of his long legs.

She pointed to the items in his hands as he put them on
the love seat next to him. "What's all that?"

"The stuff from your phony FBI agent's pockets." He
picked up his pizza and crunched into it.

"He's not *my* phony FBI agent." She placed a paper towel
on his thigh. "High-class all the way."

Mike devoured his pizza with a few more bites and
wiped his hands and mouth. "No ID, but let's see what
this guy deemed important enough to carry with him on
an abduction."

She shivered and picked a triangle of pepperoni off her
pizza.

Mike held up a red-and-white hard pack of cigarettes.
"Smokes, a key, some change, a little cash—not as much
as he has now."

"Maybe he should take the money and run. I can't imagine Spencer or his cronies being very forgiving of his failure."

Mike held up a card, running his finger over the em-
bossed lettering on the front. "Interesting. A plumber's
business card. I think I'm going to have some questions
about my pipes."

He had placed each item on the table at the corner of
their two love seats, and Claire picked up the key. "I wonder if this is the key to my safe deposit box. He could've
been the one to deposit the money."

"The bank has to have cameras on that room. You'd
think the FBI would've looked at that tape by now to determine if you really did deposit that money."

"The fact that they probably did and it didn't prove

my innocence is slightly troubling." She toyed with the cigarette carton. "This feels empty."

Mike shrugged and chugged some water from his bottle. "Open it."

She flicked the lid open with her thumb and peeked inside the box at the crumpled silver packaging. "It is empty."

Mike's dark brows formed a V over his nose. "Why would he carry an empty cigarette box in his pocket?"

"There's this." She plucked the foil wrapping, which had been rolled into a ball, from the box and bounced it in her palm.

"He's gotta have something in there. Drugs?"

She pinched the edges of the wrapper with her fingers and pulled it apart. "Maybe drugs or medication."

"What's in there?"

She held out her hand to Mike, where five little blue pills lolled in the foil.

Mike's features sharpened and two spots of color formed high on his cheekbones.

"Mike, what's wrong?" She could barely form the words in her suddenly dry mouth.

He closed his hand over hers and the blue pills. "If Correll really is behind this action against you, then he's involved with a terrorist organization—the worst—and the danger to the White House is back on the table."

Chapter Nine

Claire's eyes widened and something in their violet depths flickered. Did she understand that bad news for the country meant good news for her?

Of course she did. There wasn't much Claire Chadwick didn't understand except maybe that her obsession with getting justice for her husband and then her mother had put her life on hold and, even worse, in danger.

He could detect the movement of her Adam's apple in her slender throat as she swallowed. "These blue pills mean something to you?"

He squeezed her hand before releasing it and them. "You heard me mention Tempest on the phone just now, didn't you?"

"Yes." She crumpled the foil in her fist and stuffed it back into the cigarette box with the tips of her fingers. "It didn't mean anything to me then and it doesn't mean anything to me now."

"It's a covert ops organization, like Prospero, deep undercover. In the past few months we've become aware that they've been using their power to destabilize the world."

"What have they been doing?" She trapped her hands between her knees and hunched forward.

"Assassinations."

"Just like Director Haywood." Tilting her head to one

side, she gathered her hair in her hand and twisted it into a knot. "What do the blue pills mean?"

"Tempest has agents, just like we do. But unlike Prospero, Tempest has been experimenting with its agents—drugging them, brainwashing them."

She ran a thumb between her eyebrows. "That man at the bus station in Philly was one of these agents?"

"Looks like it." He flicked the cigarette box with his long fingers. "I'll send these in for analysis, but the coincidence is too great."

"So, since Spencer sent this man after me, this superagent, that proves he's in league with Tempest, doesn't it?"

"*If* your stepfather is behind the death of the director and ordered that man to abduct you."

"We're back to that."

"We have no proof Spencer Correll is involved in anything—including your mother's accident."

"Unless we get a match on those videos."

"And this latest discovery just might light a fire under that investigation." Mike grabbed his phone again and called Jack, pressing the speaker button.

"Nothing's changed, Mike."

"It has here, and you're still on speaker."

"What's up?" Jack's voice lost its bored edge, and Mike nodded to Claire.

"I emptied the pockets of the man who tried to abduct Claire from the Philly bus station, and I just made a crucial discovery." He reached for the cigarette pack as if he needed concrete verification. "He had some blue pills on him, and they look exactly like the T-101 pills Max Duvall showed us."

Jack whistled through the phone. "If Tempest is in DC and was responsible for the director's murder, they might still be plotting something bigger for the White House, just like McCabe said."

"And Correll just might be the guy on the inside of it all."

"If we can tie him to Tempest and this setup of Claire."

"The videos, Jack." Mike tossed the cigarette pack back on the table. "ID the guy in the videos."

"We're on it. In the meantime, send us those pills for analysis."

Mike ended the call and cupped the phone between his hands. "If there's anything else you can think of, Claire, now's the time."

"Maybe Hamid knows something."

"You can't just give him a call on his cell phone. If he's off the grid, he probably dumped his phone already."

She slumped back in the love seat and stretched her long legs in front of her, tapping her boots together. "I've been thinking about that."

"Don't look at me." He threw up his hands. "Believe it or not, Prospero doesn't have a line on every suspected terrorist in the US."

"Hamid is not a suspected terrorist." Her eyes glittered at him like jewels through the slits of her eyes.

"He is now." He tapped the display of his phone, where she'd read the news about Hamid on the bus.

"In the beginning of our association, Hamid and I communicated via a blog, more like an online discussion group."

"The FBI already tracked your communication with Hamid. That's why they dropped in on you in DC."

She shook her head and her blond locks caught the low light from the lamp on the table next to her, giving a glow to her face, already animated with this new idea. "Once Hamid got to London, we stopped that form of communication. There was no more need for it. He was no terrorist and I was helping him gain entry to the US on a student visa. The kid is seriously a genius."

"Your communications with him from that point on were out in the open?"

"For all the world, and the FBI, to see. There's no way the Feds know about our back-and-forth on this website prior to Hamid's arrival in London."

"How can you be so sure?"

"Because I communicated with others in this discussion group, as well. They picked out, or my stepfather led them to, Hamid because he's the only one they knew about. That's the stuff they traced."

He rubbed his chin. Prospero would want to talk to Hamid, anyway. Claire could do the work for them to bring him in. "So, you'd try to make contact with Hamid through this blog? How do you know he'll check it?"

"I don't, but there's a good chance." She drew her knees up to her chest and wrapped her arms around her legs. "If Hamid is in trouble, he's going to try to reach me. He knows I'll try to reach him, too. He knows I have connections, political connections. What he doesn't know at this point is that it's those connections that got us both into trouble."

"Give it a try." He twisted to the side, grabbing his laptop. He logged in, entered a few passwords and launched a web browser. Holding the computer in front of him, he rose from his seat and positioned the laptop on Claire's thighs. "Do you remember the URL?"

"Absolutely." She tapped his keyboard while he circled around behind her on the love seat.

He hunched over the back, peering over her shoulder as the page filled the window, populated with pop-up ads for clothing and instruments and music lessons. "What kind of discussion group is this?"

"On the surface?" She clicked several links on the page

in rapid succession. "It's a blog and discussion for people looking for musical hookups, but in reality it's a message board for people who want to hide their communications."

"Really?" He squinted at a variety of messages on the page. "Whatever happened to using the drafts folder of a shared email account?"

"I haven't heard about that method. Have you ever had to use it?"

She jerked her head around so suddenly, her nose almost collided with his chin. He reared back. "Sorry. Didn't mean to get into your personal space. My damned eyes are getting worse and worse since I hit forty."

She snorted. "Yeah, you're a pathetic physical specimen."

Her gaze swept across his shoulders and down his arms, still wedged against the back of the love seat. His nearness gave her butterflies in her belly—just like a high school crush. He could get into her personal space as much as he wanted.

She patted the cushion next to hers. "Sit here. You can see better, even though all I'm going to do is post a message. Right now I don't see anything that could be from him."

Her side of the cushion sank when he sat next to her, causing her shoulder to bump against his. She left it there.

"Would he use his real name?" He ran one finger down the list of posts on the screen.

"He's Einstein—for obvious reasons."

"And you're...?"

She wrinkled her nose as her cheeks warmed. "Paris."

"How'd you come up with that?"

"Hamid actually came up with it himself." She shrugged. "He's a fan of American pop culture, and I'm the only blond heiress he knows."

"Makes perfect sense to me. What are you posting?"

Her fingers hovered over the laptop. "I just want to let him know we can help."

She chewed her lip and started typing.

Mike read her words aloud as she entered them. "'Everything okay with the band? I think we're in the same boat. Let me know if you need a backup singer.'"

She clicked the button to post her message under the username Paris. "If he sees that, he'll know what I mean."

"Why so cryptic if the message board is a safe zone?" He took the computer from her lap and logged off.

"You can never be too careful." She raised her arms, stretching them toward the ceiling and yawning.

"It's past midnight. You gotta be tired even after all that so-called sleep on the bus."

She jerked her thumb over her shoulder. "I haven't even looked past the bathroom in here. Are there two bedrooms?"

"Yes. Do you want to check them out first and call dibs?"

She wanted to call dibs on him.

She stuffed the thought back down into her tired brain. She wanted Mike Becker because he believed in her and it had been a long time since anyone had believed in her. It couldn't be real attraction. She didn't have time for that.

He crouched before the fire to douse it, and her gaze traveled from his broad shoulders, down the length of his strong back and settled on his tight backside encased in worn denim.

He believed in her *and* he was as hot as that fire he was smothering. The sensations pummeling her brain and body emanated from overwrought emotions and pure lust—nothing more.

She forced her languorous muscles to move and pushed off the love seat. "Do you know if the beds are made?"

"Should be."

She clicked on the hall light and poked her head into the first bedroom—standard-issue bed, including sheets and a turned-down bedspread, a dresser, and a small nightstand sporting a lamp and a clock radio.

She crossed the hall to the other bedroom, where a king-size bed dominated the room and a dark chest of drawers stood in the corner.

"You can have this room."

He appeared behind her, and she jumped.

"You okay?" He placed his hands on her shoulders from behind and the warm breath caressing her ear made her heart beat a little faster.

"On edge."

"I can't imagine why." He pinched her shoulders. "I found some toiletries in the closet and left them for you in the bathroom—toothbrush, toothpaste, soap. What were you just saying?"

"You can have this room." She flung out her arm into the space. "You need the bigger bed."

"Are you sure?"

"Besides, the other room has a mirror. I'm going to need to spend long hours in front of that mirror tomorrow morning to fix myself up after the day I had today."

"You did have a rough day, and yet—" he shifted to her side and cupped her face with one hand "—you still look beautiful."

A pulse thrummed in her throat and she parted her lips to protest, to assure him she hadn't been fishing for a compliment. She never got the chance.

He swept his lips across hers, and when she didn't make a move, not even a blink of an eyelash, he pressed a hard kiss against her mouth that felt like a stamp. He pulled away just as abruptly.

"Get some sleep, Claire."

"G-good night." She sidled past him out the door and practically flung herself into the bathroom across the hall.

She slammed the door behind her and hunched over the small vanity, almost touching her nose to the mirror. She couldn't.

She hadn't been with a man since she lost Shane. Her attraction to Mike felt like such a betrayal to her dead husband.

A sob welled up from her chest and she cranked on the water in the sink, letting her tears drip down her chin and swirl down the drain with the water.

She'd kept telling herself that she'd let go once she found justice for Shane, but maybe she'd been fooling herself. Once Shane's killer was brought down, would she have another excuse?

Maybe Mike Becker had been sent not to save her from Spencer, but to save her from herself.

THE NEXT MORNING she shuffled into the living room in the same jeans and sweater from yesterday and wedged her hands on her hips as she watched Mike make coffee in the kitchen. "No fair."

He looked up, a lock of dark hair falling in his eyes. "What's not fair? I said you could have the bigger bed. Do you regret your generosity now?"

"I'm not talking about that." She perched on one of the stools at the kitchen island that doubled as a table. "You're wearing different clothes."

"From the bag I took from the hotel." He pinched the gray material of the waffle-knit, long-sleeved shirt away from his chest. "Luckily I had some casual clothes in there."

She folded up the sleeves of her blue cashmere. "This used to be one of my favorite sweaters, but I'm pretty sure I'm going to be sick of it by the end of the week."

"We can get you some clothes—not those designer duds you favor, but there are a few stores in town."

"Do you think I need to wear a disguise?" She fluffed her hair. "I can color my hair, but I refuse to cut it."

He cocked his head to the side. "You'd look good as a redhead, but those eyes…"

She blinked. "What about them?"

"They're violet."

"Only sometimes, and so what?"

"I can't imagine anyone looking into those eyes once and being able to forget them."

"You're waxing very poetic this morning." She jumped from the stool and pulled open the freezer door, inhaling the iciness from its depths in the hopes it could cool down her heated blood. "Anything for breakfast in here?"

He clinked some cups behind her. "I'm not exactly sure what 'waxing poetic' means, but I'm sure I've never done that before in my life. Coffee?"

"Do you like playing the poor, rough boy from the streets?" She yanked a box of breakfast sandwiches from the inside door. "Does that usually work for you with the ladies?"

She clutched the cold box to her chest, afraid to turn around. But Mike laughed, and she spun around to face him.

His lopsided grin had her warming up again despite the frozen breakfast pressed against her body.

"The poor, rough boy from the streets *does* work with the ladies, but I never once thought you'd be susceptible to the act. Are you?"

She smacked the box on the counter. "Nope."

"Hey, watch that. You're breaking my…breakfast."

"No news from any quarter yet?" She needed to get this conversation and relationship back on the business track. They didn't have to play engaged couple anymore.

"I don't know about your discussion board, but I haven't heard anything from Prospero." The coffee dripped to a stop and he poured two cups. "The news media are still flashing Hamid's picture, but you haven't even been mentioned as a person of interest yet."

She raised her eyes to meet his. "That's not good, is it? I mean, if a legitimate agency like the FBI is after me, at least I know they're not going to shoot me on sight."

"But we don't want your picture and name splashed all over the media, either."

"At least the Chadwicks have no idea what's going on. Should I call them again to find out if they've heard anything?"

"Don't invite trouble. If you act suspiciously, you're putting them on the spot if the FBI goes out there to talk to them."

Her hand trembled slightly as she picked up her coffee cup. "I don't want that. They've been through enough."

"Ethan's safe with them and Lori." He wrapped his hands around his own cup. "Lori's reliable?"

"She's wonderful. Ethan adores her." She narrowed her eyes. "Why do you ask?"

"At breakfast yesterday morning I caught the tail end of something between her and Correll."

"Ugh, yes. He's propositioned her a time or two, but she came right to me." She blew on the surface of her coffee, wishing for some half-and-half. "Lori can handle herself. She's tougher than she looks. She's actually a former army nurse."

"Impressive." Folding his arms, he leaned against the kitchen counter. "Correll had a thing going on with his admin assistant, too, right? Fiona? That's how you got into his laptop in his office."

"That's right." She tapped her head. "The eyes may be going, but you're not senile yet."

"Thank God."

"Why did you bring that up?"

"Would Fiona be willing to do more snooping for you? For a price, I mean."

"She might be, although I think she's still sleeping with him."

"After he cheated on her?" He reached for his cup and took a sip of coffee. "Some women don't know when to quit."

Was he talking about Lori, her or his mother?

She turned away and slid her thumb beneath the seam of the box. "A little jewelry can go a long way. Do you want me to contact her?"

"We'll keep her in our toolbox."

"We have a toolbox?" She pulled two plastic-wrapped frozen sandwiches from the box and held one up. "Looks like egg and sausage on an English muffin."

"Sounds good to me."

She ripped open the plastic with her teeth and placed the sandwiches on a plate. "Is this town safe for us?"

"The FBI hasn't released any info about you yet. I'm positive we weren't followed, once we got rid of that money." He tugged on the end of her hair. "And you need some fresh clothes."

"I just might risk getting nabbed by the FBI for a change of clothes at this point."

"We'll be fine, and I need to go to the post office and send off these pills."

With visions of new clothes before her eyes, Claire wolfed down her breakfast almost as quickly as Mike did.

As she rinsed their cups in the sink, she asked, "Can you log in to your laptop so I can check the message board?"

"Sure." He wiped the crumbs from the counter and swept their trash into a paper bag.

"Ah, a self-sufficient bachelor."

He was beside her in an instant with a dish towel. "I've had years and years of practice. Now hand me that mug so I can dry it and put it away."

He put the dishes in the cupboard and leaned over the counter where his laptop was charging. He powered it on and entered his thousands of passwords before spinning the computer toward her. "Go for it. I'm going to brush my teeth before we head into town."

With a little hitch in her breath she accessed the discussion board and scanned the messages. She blew out a breath. Nothing much new and nothing from Hamid. Her message waited for an answer.

"Anything?" Mike came up behind her smelling like mint.

"Not yet, but I'm confident he'll check this board."

"If you say so." He logged off and slipped the computer into the bag. "I'm taking it with me, so we can check again while we're out. Let's get ready to go."

"I'm going to brush my teeth and pull my hair back."

When she returned to the living room, she joined Mike, standing in front of the mirror by the front door.

He pulled a fur-lined cap with earflaps low on his forehead. "How's this? Do I fit in?"

She turned the flaps down over his ears, brushing his hair back. "You look like any other Northeasterner in the winter."

"I'd still be more comfortable with a bit of a disguise." She wound a dark scarf around her neck, covering the lower half of her face. "What do you think?"

"It's a start." He threw open the closet door next to them and pawed through the coats. He yanked one off its hanger and held it up. "You'd look less like you with this cover-up than with that long, black coat that screams well-heeled city girl."

She glanced at her coat draped over one of the love seats and stepped forward to take the dark green down coat from Mike. But he held it open and said, "Turn around."

She did so, and he draped it on her shoulders, his fingers skimming the sides of her neck. She shivered as she stuffed her arms into the sleeves. Why did his touch always feel like an electric current dancing across her skin?

The down coat fell right above her knees, leaving a gap of denim between the hem and the top of her black boot.

She finished the look by twisting her ponytail into a knot on top of her head and pulling a red cap over it. She arranged the scarf around her neck and face.

"Nobody's going to recognize me out and about, but as soon as I take all this stuff off there goes my disguise."

"Like I said, after what happened in Philly, I don't think Correll is anxious for the authorities to pick you up. I think he'd rather use his own methods."

Despite Mike's implication and the frisson of fear tingling down her spine, her lips stretched into a smug smile. "You did it again. You mentioned my stepfather, so you do believe he's behind this."

"I always believed you, Claire. We just need to prove it."

"We'll prove it, and Hamid is going to help me."

"If he ever gets that message."

"He'll get it." She pointed to her boots. "I suppose there are no snow boots here, are there? Walking in the snow in these heels is hell, and walking on ice is going to be even worse."

"There might be some boots in the mudroom in the back. What size?"

"Eight."

He disappeared down the hallway and came back with a pair of snow boots. "These are a men's nine. Do you think you can manage until you buy something in town?"

"Walking in boots that are too big for me can't be any worse than four-inch heels." She changed shoes and then followed Mike into the winter wonderland. She huffed out a breath and watched it freeze in the air. "If there's snow in DC, I guess this is what you get in Vermont."

Mike started the engine of the car and cranked on the heat and defrosters. Then they both got to work on the front and back windshields, clearing the ice from the glass.

They hopped into the car and made the slow, winding drive back to the small town of Maplewood.

Her knees bounced as they drew closer to civilization. Had the FBI plastered her picture all over the place like Hamid's, or did Spencer have his own private hell planned for her that didn't involve the authorities?

What would the good people of Maplewood do if they recognized her? Make a citizens' arrest? Would the Maplewood PD try to take down a terror suspect?

Her eye twitched. How could anyone believe she'd throw her lot in with terrorists when she'd spent the better part of the past five years in her own private war against them?

Spencer had used her former instability and irrational threats against Deputy Director Haywood to set her up, and she'd walked right into his trap.

But he didn't know she'd have Mike Becker in that trap with her. Did her stepfather still believe her fiancé was a politically naive salesman from Chicago?

Let him. Spencer had unwittingly walked into a trap called Prospero, and he'd pay the price.

"Are you nervous?" His gloved hand ran down her arm, making the slick material of her coat whisper.

"Nobody followed us up here, right?"

"That's right."

"Of course, we thought that before when we dumped the tracker, my phone and then my car, and they still caught up with us."

"My fault." He returned his hand to the steering wheel. "The money was a foreign object introduced into our environment. I should've checked it out before allowing you to bring it into the car."

"As I recall, we were in a hurry when I brought that money into the car. An FBI agent was literally hanging on to my coattails, or what I thought was an FBI agent."

"Then after." He raised his shoulders. "I should've examined it later. Total fail on my part."

"You redeemed yourself by saving me in the alley."

"I'll redeem myself when this is over and you're safe."

"Mike?"

"Yeah?"

Her lip trembled and she clasped her mittened hands together in her lap. "I won't know what to do when it's over. I won't know who I am."

He wheeled the car into a parking space in front of the local post office and cut the engine. "You'll be one tough chick who never gave up and who will be able to face anything—even if that anything is the monthly PTA meeting."

Her nose stung and she sniffed. "I think I can handle a PTA meeting."

As they walked into the post office, Claire kept bundled up in the chilly interior of the building. Her gaze darted among the items on display, half expecting to find her mug on a wanted poster.

Mike selected a priority mail pouch and shoved the cigarette box inside, the blue pills nestled in the box.

He paid the clerk with cash and asked, "Is there a

women's clothing store nearby? My wife needs to pick up a few more warm items."

"Down about two blocks there are a couple of stores." She tossed the package into the wheeled cart behind her and gave Mike his change. "It sure is an early winter this year. Maybe it'll be a short one."

"We can only hope." Mike rapped his knuckles on the counter. "Thanks, and happy holidays."

When they got outside, he asked, "Can you walk a few blocks?"

"Absolutely not." She kicked up one foot. "These boots are practically falling off my feet."

They got back in the car and crawled down the street until a few clothing stores came into view.

"Ready to shop till you drop?"

"Sure. I'm not picky."

He dropped his jaw in mock astonishment. "I don't know much about clothes, but I'm pretty sure yours cost an arm and a leg."

"I mean," she said, punching his arm, "I'm not picky when faced with wearing the same thing day after day. I'm really not high maintenance. You should've seen me when I was with the Peace Corps in Guatemala. Not a designer thread in sight."

"You were a Peace Corps volunteer?"

She nodded as she grabbed the car door handle. "It's where I met Shane."

On the sidewalk, Mike stopped in front of a newspaper dispenser. "I need some reading material while you try on clothes."

"I won't be that long, but you can check out the news on me and Hamid, if there is any."

She scurried into the store while Mike fed some coins into the dispenser.

A clerk looked up from folding sweaters. "Good morning. Can I help you find something?"

"Just some casual clothes. I didn't pack enough for this cold."

"I hear you. It's crazy for December, even for us." She plopped a sweater on the pile and turned toward rows of cubbies on the wall. "We have jeans on this side, and even snow pants if you need them."

"I just might need them." Claire fingered the slick material of a pair of black snow pants hanging on a rack.

The little bell above the door rang as Mike pushed his way into the store, the newspaper tucked under his arm.

"Can I help you?"

He waved the paper at Claire. "I'm with her."

"Well, you're in luck. We have a few chairs outside the dressing room just for the gentlemen."

"Perfect." He collapsed in one of the chairs and said, "Knock yourself out, sweetheart."

Claire rolled her eyes and stationed herself in front of the array of jeans, scanning the labels for her size.

After she selected a few pairs of pants, she browsed the long-sleeved T-shirts and sweaters. With her arms piled high with clothes, she approached the clerk. "I'm ready to try these on."

She flicked Mike's newspaper as she walked by. "Do you want me to model anything, *sweetheart*?"

"You look good in everything, babe."

The clerk smiled as she unlocked the dressing room for Claire. "You have a keeper there."

"Don't I know it?" *He even takes out bad guys with a flying leap and roundhouse kick to the midsection.*

She shimmied in and out of several pairs of jeans, dropping more in the keep pile than not. She pulled on sweaters and shirts and held on to anything halfway decent.

She called out, "Do you want me to leave the clothes I'm not buying in here, or do you want them?"

"I'll take care of them."

Claire loaded up her arms and squeezed out of the dressing room. She brushed past Mike. "That wasn't too bad, was it?"

"No."

The curt response had her twisting her head over her shoulder, and she nearly dropped her clothes in a heap.

The relaxed, loose-limbed man in the chair had been replaced by a tense one, vibrating with alertness, every muscle in his body primed for action.

Her gaze dropped from his face to the newspaper open in his lap. He must've read something about her, something bad.

"Oh, you're taking all those?" The clerk held out her arms for Claire's finds.

"Y-yes. These'll do. I also need some underwear."

"Long underwear?"

"Yes, and panties, bras."

"In the back."

Mike had folded the paper and joined the clerk at the counter.

Claire rushed to the back of the shop and scooped up several pairs of underwear and a couple of bras in her size—they'd have to do. She couldn't spend one more minute in this store.

The clerk bagged her purchases while Mike pulled out a wad of bills. They clearly hadn't needed the money from the safe deposit box, since Mike carried oodles of what he called untraceable cash.

He couldn't get rid of it fast enough as he paid for Claire's clothes.

If the friendly clerk had noticed a change in Mike's demeanor, she was too polite to react to it. "You two have a great day, and stay warm."

Mike nodded and Claire said, "You, too."

When they hit the sidewalk, burdened with bags, she spun toward him. "What happened? What did you read in that newspaper?"

"In the car." He popped the trunk and they tossed the bags inside.

When they got inside, Mike dropped the folded-back paper in her lap and jabbed his finger at an article, poking her thigh in the process. "Look at this."

She glanced at the black print in her lap, heaving a sigh. At least her face wasn't plastered there.

She held up the paper to the light coming through the window and read. "'Gathering to honor fallen CIA director. The White House announced plans to pay tribute to Gerald Haywood, the director of the CIA, who was killed in a car bomb on Tuesday in Georgetown, with a gathering of his friends and colleagues, both domestic and international, on Christmas Day.'"

She trailed off. "So? Isn't that to be expected?"

"Don't you get it?" He grabbed the paper from her hand, crumpling it in his fist. "The attack on the White House is back on—and this is the venue."

Chapter Ten

Mike paced the living room of the small cabin. He'd already contacted Jack, and Prospero was formulating a plan to infiltrate the gathering.

Even though Tempest knew Prospero's agent, Liam McCabe, had uncovered its plans for an attack at the White House, it hadn't deterred Tempest. They were going forward with the attack—Mike was sure of it.

When he passed by Claire for the hundredth time, she grabbed his arm. "Sit down and relax, Mike. You're going to wear a hole in the floor."

He raked his fingers through his hair. "I can't believe they're going through with it. They have to know Prospero is going to pull out all the stops to foil them."

"That's good, then. They're so single-mindedly crazy, they're not thinking straight." She squeezed his biceps. "Have one of those beers we picked up."

His eyebrows collided over his nose. "It's lunchtime."

"You know what they say—it's five o'clock somewhere."

He narrowed his dark eyes. "You're calm about this whole thing."

She stepped back from him. "I'm not happy about it, if that's what you're implying."

His eyebrows jumped to his hairline and then he took her in his arms, wrapping her in a warm embrace. "I didn't think that for a minute. Nobody could blame you for feeling satisfied on some level that your gut instincts were right."

"I don't care about that right now." She grabbed handfuls of his shirt and tugged. "I'm going to get you that beer."

"Okay, you win."

He dropped his arms, and a chill flashed across her body. She shouldn't have been so eager to break that clinch. Whenever Mike held her, or even touched her, he gave her a sense of safety and security.

If she was honest with herself, Shane had never given that to her. He'd been all about the thrill first and safety— his and hers—second.

She shook her head to dislodge the disloyal thoughts then went into the kitchen and grabbed two bottles of beer from the fridge.

She rummaged through the utensil drawer until she found a bottle opener. "Do you want yours in a glass?"

Instead of an answer, she heard tapping. She leaned back to see into the living room. Mike was on his laptop, clicking away. "I thought you were going to relax?"

"We haven't checked your message board in a while… and no glass."

She opened both bottles and returned to the living room, where she stood in front of him, holding out his beer. "It's happy hour."

Glancing up, he said, "I'm all logged in. Whenever you're ready."

Her fingers were itching to attack that keyboard and check for a message from Hamid, but they both needed ten minutes to breathe.

When he'd explained the significance of that White House gathering, she'd been as freaked out as he was, but for once she wanted to be the one with the calm exterior.

Mike had been keeping it together for her through it all, and she wanted to prove she could keep it together, too.

She hadn't quite figured out yet whether she wanted to prove she could be calm and collected to Mike or herself, but both had value.

"Skol." She lifted the bottle and then tilted it to her lips and took a swig of the malty brew.

He reached up to take the other bottle from her hand. *"Skol."*

He shoved the laptop from his legs. "Have a seat."

"That's better." She settled on the love seat next to him and touched the neck of her bottle to his with a clink. "Tell me about your last assignment with Prospero."

"This is my last assignment with Prospero."

"I mean your second-to-last. What were you doing before Jack asked you to check in on his wife's crazy friend?"

"It's top secret." He put his finger to his lips, but his frame had stiffened and the lines on his face deepened.

"Are you serious?" She dragged her gaze away from his delicious mouth. "You've already told me plenty of—what I can only guess is—classified information. Hell, you've let me use your secure phone and laptop."

"Because you're involved in this case." He took a sip of his beer. "I'd be breaking a code if I told you about anything else."

She toyed with the opening of her bottle. "That must get lonely."

"Lonely?"

"Keeping everything to yourself all the time."

"There are other things to talk about besides work."

"The weather?" She laced her fingers around the bottle of beer. "You're not exactly forthcoming about your personal life."

He was in midsip and he choked on his beer. "Really?

Given the amount of time we've had to talk about anything but our current situation, I think I've revealed a lot."

"You know what?" On an impulse, she reached out and brushed a lock of dark hair from his forehead and then studied his face. "I think you have. You've parsed it out between car bombs, fleeing from the FBI and an attempted kidnapping, but I actually know quite a bit about you."

His eyes widened and his nostrils flared as if he was getting ready to take flight. "Have I been going on and on about my pathetic childhood?"

She laughed and took another chug of her beer. "I'd hardly say you over-shared. It's good. I'm glad I got to take a little peek behind the curtain."

"I'll have to watch that curtain thing, but you know I had it better than some and worse than others. That's the way it goes. At least I had Coach to guide me through a lot of stuff, or I probably would've ended up on the wrong side of the law."

"I'm grateful you didn't, but I apologize."

"For what?"

"This was supposed to be a relaxing interlude between stops in Crazytown, and I had to dredge up stuff you're clearly not comfortable discussing."

"You know what?" He took the bottle from her hand and rose from the cushion. "It wasn't so bad telling you about it."

"Anytime. God knows my life could fill a couple of volumes." She wiped her damp fingers on her new jeans and pulled the computer into her lap. "Time to check on Hamid. Was there anything in that paper about him?"

"Just that they had no leads on his whereabouts."

"That makes all of us." The screen displayed a prompt for a password. "You need to reenter your password. I guess happy hour lasted too long."

He returned from the kitchen, wiping his hands on a dish towel. He bent his long frame over at the waist and entered his password while covering her eyes with one hand.

He was serious about his security.

"While you do that, I'll put together some lunch. I'm glad you insisted on stopping at a grocery store to pick up some fresh food."

"I couldn't handle any more of that frozen stuff." She entered the address for the message board and held her breath as she scanned the page. She squealed.

"He responded?"

"Yes, I got a message from Einstein. He wrote that he is in the same boat and he needs backup." She looked up. "We've got to help him, Mike."

"We can bring him in."

"By bring him in, you mean what? Not take him into custody?"

"Protective custody, not an arrest. Prospero can protect him on an unofficial basis, but we'll want some intel from him." He ducked into the fridge, so she couldn't see his face.

Hopefully, he was telling the truth. "I honestly don't think Hamid has any intel."

"He was set up somehow and he may have noticed something leading up to it, talked to someone, had an encounter. We'll want to know all that."

"So, should I suggest a meeting? He's not going to agree to meet with anyone but me."

"He's not going to have a choice. You're not meeting him alone." He reappeared hugging an armload of veggies. "Is he still online?"

"I don't think so, but I'm sure he'll be monitoring this board."

"Set it up."

"I don't even know where he is."

"Find out, Claire."

She drummed her fingers on the computer. "He's not going to want to meet in Boston, too close for comfort."

"DC's out."

"Would we be safe in New York? We could drive down in about five hours, park and take a subway into the city."

"Crowds aren't necessarily a bad thing. It should be a public place for everyone's safety."

"A club with noise and music."

"Sounds like a plan." Mike waved his knife in the air. "Do it."

She followed the rules of their cryptic communication, suggesting they meet at a jazz club in Chelsea, a place she'd told him about before.

She posted the message. "That's it. Now we wait. If he can't get to Manhattan, we'll move to plan B."

"It's always good to have multiple plans." He began chopping on a cutting board.

She carried the laptop with her to the kitchen counter and set it down. "Do you want some help?"

"When the water boils, dump in the pasta." He jumped back as the oil sizzled in the pan on the stove top. "Where are we meeting him?"

"We? I still think I should meet him alone. He might not agree to see me if I'm with someone, and if I don't tell him, he might bolt when he sees you."

"Like I said before, he doesn't have a choice." He shoved the contents of his cutting board into the olive oil in the pan and stirred, the aromatic scent of garlic filling the kitchen. "You just happened to know of a club in Manhattan where we could meet?"

She dumped the fettuccine into the roiling water and added a pinch of salt. "The kid likes jazz, of all things. He was visiting the city on a break and asked me for a few recommendations. He went to the 629 Club in Chelsea, so I thought he'd feel comfortable in a place he'd been to before."

"You like jazz?" He tapped the pot of boiling pasta with his knife. "Stir that so it doesn't clump."

"Who are you, Emeril Lagasse?" But she dutifully dipped the long plastic fork into the bubbling pot. "Yeah, I like jazz. You?"

"Jazz? Most of it sounds like weird, disjointed noises to me."

She rolled her eyes to the ceiling as she stirred. "Let's see…tough guy from the streets…my guess is rock and roll."

"Easy guess."

"I like that, too. I like all kinds of music." She held up the fork with a few strands of pasta dangling from it. "What do you think? Al dente?"

"Hasn't been long enough." He pinched the steaming pasta between his fingers anyway and dropped it into his mouth. "Too chewy. You can rip up that lettuce and dump the rest of these vegetables in there, though."

She made the salad while he hovered over the stove. "I suppose longtime bachelors learn how to cook, learn how to use the microwave or go out to eat a lot."

"My mom taught me how to cook a few things, but I definitely know my way around a microwave and I have every take-out menu from every restaurant within a five-mile radius of my apartment."

"Your apartment." She plunged a pair of tongs into the salad. "My God, I don't even know where you live. Where do you hang your hat when you're not gallivanting around the world pretending to be someone's fiancé?"

"Chicago." He bumped her hip with his in the small space of the kitchen to get to the pasta.

"But that's where you grew up, right?"

"Is that a surprise? Wouldn't you have stayed in Florida where you grew up if your mother hadn't married Correll?" He grabbed the handles of the pot and lifted the boiling pasta from the stove. "Watch out."

She scooted over and he dumped the water into a colander in the sink. "Yeah, but my childhood wasn't..." She put two fingers to her lips.

"A nightmare?" He shrugged. "The one person who made it a nightmare is in prison...again, so Chicago isn't so bad. I'm not sure about retiring there, but I'll go back once this is over."

Once this is over. Maybe once this was over, she'd return to Florida with Ethan. Maybe Mike would want to flee to a warm climate to escape the Chicago winters once in a while.

Reaching around him, she opened the fridge and took out the Italian salad dressing they'd bought earlier.

Mike put the finishing touches on the pasta, adding a couple of sprigs of fresh basil, and they sat side by side at the counter to eat their lunch.

"Mmm." She twirled her fork in the fettuccine. "This smells good and it looks almost too pretty to eat."

"Maybe I'll open a restaurant when I retire."

She stabbed a tomato. "You're too young to retire completely. Would you want to work as a security contractor?"

"I'm done, Claire."

"You thought you were done when you took this job, didn't you? You figured you'd be reassuring some woman with an overactive imagination and then you'd be going home to Chicago."

"That about sums it up, but now that I'm here, now that I'm in this with you, I'm in it all the way."

They finished their meal and both reached for the plates at the same time. "I'll do this. Check the message board."

She poured herself a glass of water and sat back down on the stool, pulling the laptop toward her. "It went to sleep. I need you to log in again."

He leaned over and punched several keys. "It's all yours."

She sucked in a breath when she saw a response from Einstein. "It's here. He's good with it. He's already in Queens and he remembers where the 629 Club is. Ten o'clock okay?"

"That'll give us plenty of time to drive down and then catch a subway into the city. He knows enough to watch for a tail, doesn't he?"

Raising one eyebrow, she said, "His uncle is Tamar Aziz. He's been watching his back his whole life."

Mike turned from the sink, the dish towel wrapped around his hands. "And you know for sure Hamid has nothing to do with his uncle's activities."

"I'm positive. I told you, Hamid is the one who told me to look closely at the right eye of the man who murdered Shane."

"Wait. You never told me that before. How'd he know about the coloboma?"

"He wouldn't say directly, but I'm pretty sure he got that particular bit of information from his uncle."

"All right, then." He smacked the towel against the counter. "Looks like we have a date to listen to some jazz."

MIKE DIDN'T LIKE IT—not at all.

Their journey south through the snowy landscape couldn't have gone any better. The white flakes coating the fields and decorating the trees had plunged them into their own personal and interactive Christmas card. With the heat blasting and music playing on an oldies station, Mike felt like he was exactly where he should be in retirement.

Except he wasn't retired. He had one more job to do, and because this job had gotten personal, it was proving to be more stressful than all the assignments he'd had over the life of his career. Even more stressful than the previous one that he'd bungled.

Coming into the city, dressed in its holiday finest, had made it worse. The closer they got to the club, the more resentment he'd felt toward the Christmas shoppers with their normal lives and their normal families.

He used to feel that resentment because that normalcy was something he feared he'd never have. Now the resentment burned even brighter because he felt as if he were closer to it than he'd ever been in his life.

He'd found a woman, in Claire, who gave him hope that he could have a family without the expectations of perfection. He couldn't do perfection, but he knew he'd never hurt Claire the way his father had hurt his mother.

The dissonant sounds of a saxophone in distress assaulted his ears, and he peered into the bowels of the dark club. "That sounds like an elephant in distress...or in love. I haven't decided yet."

Claire jabbed him in the ribs. "Have a little respect."

"Do you see him yet?"

A pretty African-American girl with a hippie vibe approached them, the beads braided in her hair clicking. "Are you looking for a seat? There are a couple of tables near the bar."

Mike shouted over the noise from the stage, "We're meeting someone."

Claire tugged on his sleeve. "I see him. Thanks."

The hostess bowed her head and slipped through the

black curtain that separated the front door from the interior of the club.

"This way." Claire grabbed his hand and led him through the small tables where all the patrons sat facing the stage.

As they neared a table in the corner by a hallway, a young man half stood up, the whites of his wide eyes glowing in the darkness.

"Claire?" Hamid's gaze darted toward Mike's face.

"He's helping us." She pulled out her own chair and hunched over the table toward Hamid. "This is Mike. Mike, Hamid."

Mike shook Hamid's hand, damp with sweat or the beads of moisture from the drink he was nursing.

"You look good, Hamid. How's school?"

"Are you serious?" Hamid glanced to his left and then his right, looking exactly like a fugitive on the run. "It was fine until a friend told me the FBI was looking for me."

A waitress, balancing a tray of drinks on her hand, dipped next to the table. "What can I get you?"

The club had a two-drink minimum, but Mike had already discussed the importance of sobriety with Claire. His gaze dropped to Hamid's glass, empty except for a few half-melted ice cubes. Obviously, the kid hadn't gotten the memo.

"We'll have a couple of beers, whatever you have on draft."

She slapped down two cocktail napkins and melted back into the gloom.

Mike rapped his knuckles on the table in front of Hamid. "Someone gave you a heads-up about the FBI?"

"A couple of friends in Boston. I was already on my way to visit another friend in Queens."

"Why'd you immediately take off, think the worst?" Mike folded over a corner of the napkin.

"I'm at MIT, not living under a rock. When that car bomb went off and killed the director of the CIA and then two FBI agents came looking for me, it gave me a bad feeling."

"Had anyone been following you?"

"Following me?" He swallowed. "Why would they follow me? Wouldn't they just arrest me?"

"Not sure." Mike smoothed out the napkin. "Not if they wanted to see if you were meeting with anyone."

The waitress returned and put two beers on the table, along with another cocktail for Hamid.

He folded both hands around the short glass and took a long drink.

When he put the glass down, Claire reached over and squeezed his hand. "Take it easy, Hamid. We're going to help you. Mike's…agency can bring you in."

"Oh, no." Hamid held up his hands. "I'm not going with anyone, not the CIA."

"Mike's not CIA, and you can't be out here on your own." She grabbed Mike's hand so that she was forming a human chain with the two of them. "I'm not."

With his other hand, Hamid snatched up his cocktail napkin and wiped his forehead. "When I saw that message from you, I really got spooked, Claire." He licked his lips. "What's going on?"

"We're being set up. That's all I can tell you."

Mike broke Claire's grip on his hand. Kumbaya time was over. He asked him in Punjabi, "What can you tell us, Hamid?"

Hamid's eye twitched, and he spoke to him in English. "Are you CIA? Claire, is he CIA?"

Claire glared at him, her eyes pools of liquid violets. "He's not. Why would I be with a CIA agent when I'm under suspicion myself?"

Hamid licked his lips. "Are you? Are you really? Because I haven't seen your name and picture in the papers like mine."

"Tell us what you know, Hamid. Did anyone contact you before the bombing? Did you hear anything from your uncle? Why did you tell Claire to zero in on that assassin's eye? What do you know about him?"

A bead of sweat rolled down Hamid's face and he rubbed his glassy eyes. Either the kid couldn't handle his booze or he was coming down with something.

"That man," he said, then coughed and continued, "they called that man the Oxford Don."

Claire gasped. "Why didn't you tell me that before, Hamid? You told me nobody knew who he was."

Hamid took another gulp of his drink. "C-couldn't tell you. They used him for propaganda, for high-profile executions."

"Where is he?" Claire had curled her fingers around the edge of the table. "Where is he now?"

Hamid choked and a trace of saliva trickled from the corner of his mouth.

Mike started from his seat. "Do you need some water?"

Claire leaned in close to Hamid and whispered, "Where is he?"

Hamid pitched forward on the table and murmured something Mike couldn't hear above the din coming from the stage, and then his hand jerked and his breath rattled.

"Hamid." Claire nudged him and then turned to Mike. "Is he okay?"

Mike reached over and felt the young man's pulse. "He's dead."

Chapter Eleven

Claire shook Hamid's lifeless arm. "Hamid, wake up."

Every fiber in Mike's body quivered on high alert as his gaze darted around the dim, crowded club. She obviously hadn't processed what he'd just said. "He's not asleep, Claire. He's dead."

"What?" The face she turned to him was drained of all color, and the perfect oval stood out in stark relief against the murky backdrop. "How?"

"Poison would be my first guess."

"What?" She patted Hamid's black hair. "Who?"

"Claire, we need to get out of here—right now."

Her head jerked up and her hair fell over one eye. "Here? Someone here killed him?"

"Shh." He shifted his body in front of Hamid's slack form as he glanced toward the hallway leading to the bathrooms. "I'm hoping there's an exit that way."

"W-we can't leave him here."

"Do you suggest we carry him out? Call 9-1-1?" He took a breath and trailed his fingers down her arm. "I'm sorry, Claire. We have to leave him here, and we have to leave now."

As if on cue, the drummer launched into a solo. Mike stood up and slipped his hand beneath Claire's arm. "Let's go."

She followed his order as if sleepwalking, throwing one backward glance at Hamid's inert form.

Mike led her toward the hallway in the back of the club with his heart pounding. His step quickened when he spied the green exit sign above a metal door.

Nobody had followed them down the hallway, but Claire's body was now trembling more and more with each step. He whispered in her ear, "It's okay. We're almost there."

When they reached the door, he pushed on the horizontal release bar. He held his breath, waiting for the alarm. If there was one, he couldn't hear it above the drummer.

The cold air blasted his face, and he ducked his head against it, pulling Claire close to his body. She matched him stride for stride down the alley, although he could tell she was on autopilot.

They burst out onto the street and merged into the foot traffic, still heavy at almost eleven o'clock at night. People rushing home with their packages, filled with Christmas spirit, leaving no dead bodies behind in clubs. A curbside Santa rang his bell and they both jumped. Mike took a deep breath.

"You're doing great, Claire. Just keep on moving." He steered her toward the subway entrance and down the stairs, cranking his head over his shoulder.

He hadn't noticed anyone following them, either from the bar or picking them up on the street, but there must've been someone in the bar. Someone had spiked Hamid's drink. Maybe their own beers had been drugged. Someone had either followed Hamid to that location or they'd picked up on his communication with Claire.

Grabbing Claire's hand, he kept her close as he jogged down the stairs. He fed money into the machine to buy two single-ride tickets, the blood pounding in his ears, lending urgency to his actions.

A man rounded the corner behind them, clutching something beneath his long black coat. Mike curled his hand around his own weapon in his pocket while yanking Claire in his wake. "We need to hurry, Claire."

He nudged her through the turnstile and the clattering sound seemed to rouse her from her petrified state.

Her stride lengthened until it turned into a jog, and they ran together toward the train squealing to a stop. The doors flew open and they jumped on as one.

Mike continued moving, dragging Claire along with him, making a beeline for the next car as he kept one eye on the other passengers boarding. The man with the coat was not among them.

The train swayed into motion, and Claire grabbed on to the bar above her. She swung into a seat and closed her eyes.

Mike took the seat next to her, still assessing the other passengers.

He finally let out the breath trapped in his lungs and took Claire's cold, stiff hand in both of his. She must've left her gloves in her pocket. He rubbed some warmth back into her flesh.

"I'm sorry, Claire."

Her eyes clicked open like a doll's and shifted sideways to his face. "We got him killed."

"We don't know that." He tucked a strand of hair behind her ear. "They'd made Hamid. They knew just where to find him."

She shook her head, dislodging the lock of hair again. "They couldn't have known about that message board. No way."

"If they tapped into his computer, they'd know his every keystroke, or maybe they put a tracker on his phone. I have a hunch they didn't realize he'd be meeting you."

"Why do you say that?" She finally turned her head and met his eyes.

"I could be wrong, but my guess is that his first drink was already drugged. They wouldn't want him dead before we even got there."

"Maybe our drinks were drugged, too. I didn't even have a sip of mine, did you?"

"No, thank God." He slipped an arm around her. "I just can't believe they'd let us get away that easily if they'd still been there."

"They drugged all our drinks and left."

"There's no way of knowing at this point."

A tear rolled down her cheek and she made no move to catch it, so he brushed it away with the pad of his thumb.

"Don't blame yourself, Claire. It's the fault of those who dragged him into this, set him up and then murdered him. I'm not sure he would've come with us, anyway. He was too spooked."

"H-he betrayed me. He'd been lying to me all this time."

"You mean about the man who executed Shane?"

"He knew. He knew who he was all along, or he at least knew more than he was telling." She pressed her fingertips against her temples. "I was so naive. Hamid was using me, probably to get into the US."

"Don't be so hard on yourself, Claire, or on Hamid." He caressed her shoulder. "You two helped each other at the time. Maybe he protected you by keeping you away from the truth. He understands that world better than you do."

"Did you hear what he said? He called him the Oxford Don."

"We knew he was English from his accent. That's not a surprise, and I've never heard that name before, so it must've been just among the locals."

"But at the end. He whispered something to me before he…died."

His pulse quickened. "He actually whispered something that you understood?"

"I leaned forward to catch what happened to be his last words."

"I didn't realize he'd said anything to you. What was it?" The corner of his eye twitched and he rubbed it.

"I'd asked him about the Oxford Don. I asked him where he was now."

"Did he answer you?" The air between them stilled.

"It doesn't matter." She lifted her shoulder. "He said something that made no sense at all."

"What did he say?"

"Caliban. He said the Oxford Don was with Caliban."

CLAIRE JERKED BACK from the expression on Mike's face. His jaw hardened and his dark eyes glittered with an emotion she couldn't fathom…but it scared her.

"What? What is it?"

The train lurched into the next station, and her gaze bounced from the sign outside to the map of the line inside the car to make sure they weren't missing their stop.

Mike's body had tensed up beside her, and she bumped her shoulder against his. "Mike? Does Caliban mean something to you?"

"Claire, I can't believe this." He dragged his long fingers through his hair until it stood on end. "This is all linked somehow—Shane's execution, the car bombing the other night, Tempest."

"Wait." Icy fear gripped the back of her neck. "What are you talking about? How is Shane's death linked to Tempest? What is Caliban?"

The train screeched to a stop, and Mike took her arm. "Let's get back to the cabin. Are you up for driving all night?"

"Maybe it'll take that long drive for you to explain everything to me."

They linked arms, huddling together against the cold night and the dark forces that seemed to be closing in on them.

When they got back in the car, their first stop was a drive-through coffee place, where Mike ordered a large black coffee and she got a decaf hot tea.

She had a feeling that Mike's story would be enough to keep her awake on the long drive back to their cabin in Vermont. She also had a feeling that after hearing the story, she'd want to stay in that cabin forever, keeping both Mike and Ethan close to her side.

When they got back on the road, Mike slurped at his hot coffee and turned down the radio. "Caliban is the head of that agency I told you about—Tempest."

She drew in a quick breath. "And the man who killed Shane is now connected to Caliban, to Tempest?"

"It would seem so if that's the name Hamid gave you, and it doesn't mean that Tempest was responsible for Shane's kidnapping and murder. Caliban could've recruited this Oxford Don later. Tempest wasn't active five years ago."

"Who is this Caliban? Does anyone know? Does Jack know?"

"We think he's former US military."

"Spencer knows him."

Mike jerked his head toward her. "How do you know that for sure?"

"I'm just guessing, but it makes sense. He probably knew him before Caliban became the evil mastermind behind Tempest."

"There has to be some way to tie Correll to Tempest and stop this attack against the White House."

Claire stretched her cold hands out to the vent on the

dashboard blasting warm air. "And to clear me, right? I mean, that's still a priority for you, or is it all about stopping the attack on the White House?"

His hands tightened on the steering wheel and his knuckles turned as white as the snow outside the car window. "Of course it is. That's still my number one objective."

Or it was until he found out he was poised to foil one of the most significant terrorist attacks in the world. She didn't want to delve too deeply into Mike's priorities right now.

Reaching for his cell phone in the cup holder, she asked, "Is it okay if I check your phone for some news?"

"I don't think you're going to find anything about Hamid in the breaking news right now—too soon—but hold up the phone and I'll punch in my code."

She complied and said, "I'm just wondering if I'm in the news yet. If I'm not, you know Tempest plans to take me out just like Hamid."

He finished his code and she swept her finger across the display to wake up the phone.

"Claire, we can't even link Correll to Tempest or Tempest to Hamid."

"But all the puzzle pieces are there, aren't they?"

She tapped the screen and scrolled through various news sources as Mike drove on through the night and the falling snow. On the way in to the city, even though they'd been coming in to meet Hamid, the mood in the car had been almost festive. The music, the conversation, the scenery had all contributed to a sense of normalcy, but all that had changed with Hamid's death and his dying words.

The name of Caliban had dropped between them like a curtain. It had propelled Mike back into his covert world, where he kept secrets from her.

She stumbled upon an article about the White House

gathering to honor the director and as she skimmed it, she let out a snort.

"This is interesting."

"What's that?" Mike smacked his cheek and took another gulp of coffee.

"Are you okay to drive? Do you want to switch?"

"A Florida girl driving in the snow? I can handle it." He jerked a thumb at the phone. "What's interesting?"

"I'm reading a short news brief about the ceremony honoring the director. It's more of a name-dropping puff piece, but it looks like Spencer is taking Julie Patrick."

"Who's Julie Patrick? The name sounds familiar."

"She's English, the widow of Benedict Patrick, and a major shareholder in Brit-Saud Oil. She's a big political donor and philanthropist."

"Sounds about right to me. If she's a mover and shaker in political circles, it doesn't surprise me that Correll knows her."

"Oh, he not only knows her—" she dropped the phone back in the cup holder "—he dated her. It looks like my stepfather is zeroing in on another rich widow."

Mike snapped his fingers. "The secretary."

"Huh?" She yawned and rubbed her eyes. "What secretary?"

"Correll's secretary—Fiona, the one who got you into his computer before, allowing you to copy that trashed video, the video that started it all."

She blinked. Maybe she should've gotten some coffee. "What about her?"

"Claire." He tapped his temple. "She gave you that info before when she'd believed Correll had moved on. If that's the case again, maybe you can use that to tap into more information. Would she help you again if she felt Correll had used her and was moving on to greener and richer pastures?"

She scooted forward in her seat, her fingertips tingling with excitement. "She might. Fiona is all about Fiona."

"If you contacted her, would she tell anyone?"

"Not if we sweetened the pot with some money. If she can make money on the deal *and* stick it to Spencer, she'll be all in."

"We can do that, offer her money."

"I'll contact her tomorrow and see what she can do for us." She slumped down in the seat, bunching the coat into a pillow and stuffing it between her shoulder and the window. "I'm going to make myself comfortable for the rest of the trip. Let me know if you need a break from driving."

"Relax, Claire. I'm good."

She drifted in and out to the monotone of talk radio and Mike's hushed call to Jack, the slick material of the coat whispering under her cheek every time she shifted position.

She wanted to be Mike's priority. She wanted to be someone's priority for a change. She squeezed her eyes shut against the self-pity. She usually didn't indulge…must have been the exhaustion.

Just as she found a good spot, Mike brushed her cheek with his knuckle. "We're almost at the cabin. Did you sleep?"

"In fits and starts. You must be exhausted."

"I had my thoughts to keep my mind busy—and the caffeine to keep me awake."

He pulled around to the back of the cabin, and Claire pressed her palm against the car window. "We just left here this afternoon, and I feel like it was a lifetime ago."

"Hamid's lifetime."

The cloud layer had cleared and the sun was poised to

make its full ascent. The snow sprinkled on the tree tops sparkled under the early morning rays.

She crunched up the pathway to the back door behind Mike. What now? It was too early to contact anyone. Mike had already called Jack to fill him in on Hamid and Hamid's last words, and the gulf had widened between her and Mike.

All she wanted to do right now was curl up and get warm, on the inside as well as the outside.

Mike ushered her inside the cabin and turned up the furnace. "Let's warm this place up."

"Exactly what I was thinking."

"Are you hungry?"

"I can't even…" She covered her eyes with one hand. "No."

"What happened to Hamid—not your fault, Claire."

"I—I…" Was that what he thought, that she still blamed herself? That had been her immediate response when Hamid collapsed on the table in front of her, but she'd long ago given up feeling guilt for the horror that seemed to dog her steps.

But the concern in Mike's eyes? Addictive.

"I just can't help feeling that if we'd never contacted him, he'd be alive right now."

"I don't think so." Mike took her by the shoulders. "They had him pegged for the fall guy long before you posted that message on the board. I don't think they even knew he was meeting us last night."

"That makes sense, but it still hurts." She drove a fist against her chest. "It hurts here."

And she meant every word. Hamid had been her protégé. In a way, he'd been her lifeline after Shane lost his life in the most brutal way. Even now that she knew Hamid had been holding out on her, she mourned his death.

Mike's grip on her shoulders softened. "You have dark circles under your eyes. You need some sleep."

She needed him, but her seduction skills were rusty, and dark circles beneath her eyes wouldn't cut it.

"I'd like to take a warm bath first. I'm just so chilled." Again, no lie.

"Good idea." He pointed at the kitchen. "Do you want me to make you some hot tea while you run the bathwater?"

"That would be perfect."

They brushed past each other, her on her way to the bathroom and he on his way to the kitchen.

Once inside the claustrophobic bathroom, she spun the faucets on the tub. Unfortunately, the keepers of the safe houses hadn't thought to stock bubble bath or scented candles.

She shed her clothing and almost felt as if she was casting off the past five years of her life, a celibate life paying homage to the memory of a dead husband, a husband who'd never put her first.

The steam from the tub curled up in welcome invitation. She cracked open the bathroom door and then stepped into the bathtub, sinking into its warm embrace.

Stretching her legs out, she braced her toes against the porcelain at the end of the tub, bending her knees slightly. She shimmied her shoulders beneath the lapping water and cupped handfuls of it, splashing her thighs.

The tap on the door set the butterfly wings to fluttering in her belly. It had been a long time since she'd seduced a man.

"I'm in the tub."

"Are you warming up? I have your tea."

"I feel like I'm melting." She turned off the water by gripping the faucets with her toes. "You can come in with the tea."

He pushed open the door and froze as his gaze collided with hers. "Sorry. I thought you'd have the shower curtain drawn."

"It was a little too claustrophobic for me."

"Okay." Keeping his gaze trained at the ceiling, Mike shuffled into the bathroom, holding the cup of tea in front of him. "Just warn me if I'm going to trip over the toilet or something."

"You're good, just a few more steps. It's not like the bathroom is cavernous." She sat up in the tub, the water sluicing off her body, and held out both hands to accept the tea.

The toe of Mike's bare foot hit the side of the tub and he went into a crouch, extending the cup. "Got it?"

She curled her fingers around the cup, brushing the tips along Mike's knuckles. "Thanks. Can I ask you two more favors?"

"Sure." He backed up, still averting his gaze from the tub.

"Can you bring me that T-shirt of yours I wore to bed last night, and can you get a fire going?"

"Absolutely." He smacked the doorjamb on his way out and called back, "That T-shirt looks a lot better on you than me, anyway."

Claire placed the cup on the edge of the tub and slid down until the water lapped at her chin. She blew out a breath, creating a flotilla of bubbles.

She'd set the stage even though Mike had been too much of a gentleman to take a peek at her bare breasts. She cast her eyes downward. Yep, she still had 'em.

Mike tapped on the door again. "Here's the T-shirt. I'll hang it on the doorknob inside and work on that fire."

The white T-shirt swung on the handle as Mike snapped the door shut. Claire's mouth twisted into a frown. Seemed as if *she* needed to work on that fire.

She flicked up the stopper with her big toe and yanked

the towel from the rack. She shivered as she patted herself dry. It was time to warm up—for real.

She pulled Mike's T-shirt over her head and released her hair from its knot, the tendrils at her neck damp. Fluffing her mane, she leaned in close to the mirror and touched up the drugstore makeup on her face leftover from yesterday.

A full-on makeup job would look a little ridiculous, but she was no twentysomething who could get by on good bone structure alone, especially after the night they'd just had.

Tugging on the hem of the T-shirt, she made her grand entrance.

Mike looked up from his phone, and something flickered in his dark eyes, something almost predatory. Her long cat-like stride faltered as those butterflies took up flight again in her stomach.

She was supposed to be the aggressor here, so she pinned back her shoulders and continued her saunter toward the love seat facing the fireplace. When she reached it, she fingered the edge of a blue blanket.

"I thought since you were wearing a T-shirt, you could use the extra warmth."

"Thanks, but this fire feels great." She dropped to the edge of the love seat and held up her hands, palms out, to the flames dancing in the fireplace. Being bundled up in a blanket would hardly add to her sex appeal.

"I can get you closer." He came up behind her on the love seat and pushed it and her a few feet closer to the fireplace.

Reaching around, she squeezed his biceps. "You've got some muscles there, big boy."

"What are you doing, Claire?" He straightened up and folded his arms over his chest.

Her cheeks blazed as hot as the fire. She'd been such an idiot. Just because the man had never been married, it didn't mean he didn't have experience with women and wouldn't catch on to what she was trying to do. With his looks and manner, he probably had women across the globe trying to seduce him on a regular basis—women a lot more adept than she.

"I thought…" She bit her bottom lip to stop the lie. Tears puddled in her eyes at her pathetic behavior. "I just didn't want to take a backseat to Tempest, even though I know that's where I belong."

The tight look on Mike's face dissolved and he clambered over the back of the love seat, as if he couldn't wait to be next to her. "What are you talking about? You are my priority right now. You're not in the backseat and you don't deserve to be in the backseat."

She laced her fingers together and dropped her head to study her nails. "The minute I told you about Caliban, you got this look in your eye—a gleam of excitement and anticipation—like you'd finally found a purpose in this whole tangled web."

"Am I really that transparent?" His big hand covered both of hers. "That pathetic?"

"Pathetic? You? I'm the one who plotted a seduction to make you like me again."

"Really? You were seducing me?"

She snorted. "Now, *that's* pathetic. You didn't even realize that was a seduction."

"It never occurred to me that a beautiful widow, obviously hung up on her dead husband, would be seducing me."

"Is that how you see me?" She tilted her head to look into his face. "Hung up on Shane?"

"You've spent the better part of five years skating on the edge of danger trying to identify his assassin. How would you describe it?"

"I want justice for him."

"And justice for your mother."

She jerked back. "Of course."

"What about you?" He rubbed a circle on her back. "What about Claire?"

"I—I don't need justice."

"Maybe not justice, but you need a break from all this. You need to put yourself first, Claire."

"I put Ethan first." Her tense muscles were screaming at her. She didn't want to have this conversation with Mike. He saw too much.

"I know you do." He hand crept up to the base of her neck, where his fingers kneaded her taut muscle. "Outside of your child, you need to start putting yourself first—because nobody else ever has."

The truth, voiced aloud by someone else, punched her in the gut, and she doubled over. "Sh-Shane."

"Shane left you for a story opportunity in a dangerous part of the world, knowing full well the US government does not negotiate with terrorists. He walked into a trap, blinded by visions of a Pulitzer."

"Why are you saying this? You sound just like my stepfather."

"God help me, but Correll was right about that."

She bolted up from the love seat, but Mike was beside her in a second, grabbing her around the waist. "Give yourself a chance, Claire. Give yourself a chance at life…at love."

Her body stiffened as she tried to hold her world together, and then Mike crushed her against his chest. He bent his head to hers and pressed a hard kiss against her lips, which parted under his assault. Then he thrust his tongue inside her mouth.

She wanted to repudiate him, reject everything he'd said about her and Shane—reject the truth. Digging her fingers into his back, she squirmed in his viselike hold.

He broke off the kiss that had seared her lips and then released her, catching her arm as she staggered back. His dark eyes kindled with that predatory look again and he growled deep in his throat. "Say the word, woman. Just tell me no—once."

Her chest heaved with each ragged breath she took, the thin cotton of Mike's T-shirt abrading her erect nipples adding pain to the pleasure that surged between her legs. Never breaking eye contact, she twisted out of his grasp and knocked his arm away.

A pulse throbbed in his throat, and the line at the side of his mouth deepened. Holding up his hands, he took a step back.

She licked her bottom lip, wedging the tip of her tongue in the corner of her mouth. Then she pinched the hem of her T-shirt and pulled it up one inch at a time, watching the fire reignite in his eyes.

She hadn't bothered with underwear after her bath, and when the T-shirt hit her waist, Mike's gaze dropped, scorching her, weakening her knees. She rolled the shirt over her breasts, heavy with desire and aching with need.

Yanking the T-shirt over her head, she tossed it behind her, standing in front of Mike totally naked, bared to his scrutiny and judgment.

He reached out and cupped the back of her head, entangling his fingers in her hair. He took possession of her lips again, walking her backward until the backs of her calves brushed against the cushion of the love seat.

The fire crackled and spit behind him, the glow highlighting the silver in his hair. He tugged gently on her hair, lowering her to the love seat. As she sat down, he hovered above her, her lips still captured by his.

By the time he broke the seal of their kiss, molten lava coursed through her veins, pooling in her belly—and below.

He traced a finger from the indentation of her throat to her mound, and she quaked at his touch. He knelt in front of her and opened her legs by placing his palms on the insides of her thighs.

His dark head moved toward her and she curled her fingers in his thick hair. The touch of his tongue made her gasp and throw her head back.

His lips against her swollen folds teased her to dizzying heights and she had to force herself to take a breath before she passed out.

The minute she took a sip of air, her world shattered. She raised her hips and Mike slipped his hands beneath her bottom and rode out her orgasm with her, his tongue still probing her depths as she shuddered and sighed.

She felt boneless and breathless as Mike hunched forward and cinched his hands around her waist.

He kissed the corner of her mouth and whispered, "That wasn't a no, was it?"

"I don't even remember the question."

He draped the blanket around her shoulders and lifted her in his arms.

"I'm too tall to be carried around."

He hoisted her higher. "I'm taller."

He took her into his bedroom and yanked back the covers on the bed, then placed her on the cool sheet. "You can take a nap in here."

She pulled on his T-shirt. "Is that what they're calling it these days?

"I meant, you can take a nap after I ravish you. Unless…" He pulled off his shirt and dropped it onto the floor.

Sitting up on her knees, she ran her palms across his well-defined chest. "Unless what?"

"Unless you want to kick me out after what I said about Shane."

Her hands stilled. "You were right. I never felt that Shane valued me, or at least he didn't value me as much as he did his career."

She hooked her fingers in his waistband. "I don't want to talk anymore."

She didn't want to put Mike on the spot, didn't want to force him to choose between her and his career. She always lost that battle.

Running her hand up his thigh, she pressed a kiss against his collarbone. "I don't want to talk."

As she unbuttoned his fly, he buried his hands in her hair and kissed her mouth. She slipped her hands inside his boxers and caressed his erection.

"Mmm, I don't think you've forgotten anything." He nuzzled her neck. "Your touch feels so good."

She helped him peel his jeans from his hips, and then she fell back on the bed, beckoning with her hands.

He kicked off his pants and straddled her, his knees on either side of her hips. She took him in her hands again, reveling in the feel of his smooth, hard flesh.

"I want you, Claire. I've wanted you from the minute I saw you on that balcony looking like the snow queen." He eased into her. "Do you believe me?"

Did it matter if she believed him? From the way that he kissed her and the way his body shuddered when she ran her nails along the bare skin of his back, she knew she was his priority—right now. And all she had was right now.

He filled her completely and asked again, "Do you believe me, snow queen?"

Closing her eyes, she whispered, "Yes. Yes, I do."

HER EYES FLUTTERED open and the gray light in the room mimicked the gray fog in her head. She had no idea what time it was or even what day it was. Hell, she could barely remember her name after the thorough lovemaking last night…this morning.

Mike's breath warmed the nape of her neck and she wriggled against him, feeling his erection come to life against her backside. She could wake up to *that* for the rest of her life.

Mike kissed the curve of her ear. "Did you get enough sleep?"

"I think so." She yawned. "What time is it?"

He'd obviously already looked at his watch or his phone because he answered promptly, "It's four forty-five."

"P.m.?"

"Of course, unless you think we slept for twenty-four hours."

"I really have no concept of time right now." She shifted onto her back. "Do you think there's any news about Hamid?"

She might as well be the one to bring them back to cold, hard reality. She didn't want him to think she actually believed she'd remain his priority in the face of this developing plot.

"Not sure." He reached for his phone, and his eyebrows collided over his nose. "I got about ten texts and voice mails in the past thirty minutes."

"What?" The sensuous languor that had seeped into her body evaporated, and she bolted upright. "Who are the texts from?"

Before Mike could answer, the room exploded around them.

Chapter Twelve

The blast rocked the floor and slammed Mike into the wall. His eyes watered as he blinked against the acrid smoke filling the room.

"Claire!"

"I'm on the floor. What happened?"

"Put your clothes on, but stay close to the floor. I have to get my bags from the other room."

"Wait! There's fire, and my clothes aren't in this room."

"Stay on the floor and cover your face with the sheet. I'll be right back."

"Mike! No!"

Crouching low, he put his T-shirt over his head and charged out of the bedroom. He collected a few of Claire's things from the room across the hall and ventured into the living room to get his bag of money and weapons and his computer.

Hot spots of fire dotted the room and flames engulfed the ceiling above the front door. He clasped his bags to his chest and loped back to the bedroom where he'd left Claire. The room where they'd just spent a morning exploring each other's bodies and an afternoon wrapped around each other in satiated sleep had suffered the least damage—but he knew there was more to come.

He burst into the room and tossed Claire's clothes in her direction. "Get dressed."

"C-can we get out that way? Through the front door?"

"We're not exiting this cabin through the front door."

"What? Is it so bad? The back? Can we get out through the back?"

"Enough questions, Claire. Put your clothes and shoes on. Take whatever you can in those plastic bags."

He hurried into his own clothes and whipped back the carpet on the wood floor. He ran his hands across the planks until he felt an edge.

He slipped his knife from his jeans pocket and jimmied it into the space between two boards. Then he slid them apart and lifted them, exposing an open space.

Hovering over him, Claire gasped. "We're going down there?"

"It's the escape route. Every one of our safe houses has one."

"Why do we need an escape route?" She glanced over her shoulder, her wide eyes taking on the color of the gray smoke billowing around them.

"They're waiting for us."

Her face blanched but she didn't hesitate when he nudged her toward the gaping space in the floor.

"Once through, there should be some steps but then you're going to have to crouch down and probably army crawl." He kissed her forehead. "Can you do that, Claire?"

She nodded and dropped into the hole, the plastic bags crinkling against her chest.

Mike lowered himself after her, dragging his bags with him. He dropped them into the space and then pulled the carpet back over the entrance to the escape route and then reset the planks of wood. Unless Tempest had also gotten the blueprint of the cabin, they wouldn't know where to look.

When he covered the opening, blackness descended on the space around them and Claire trembled beside him.

He flicked on a small but powerful flashlight. "We're good. It's going to be okay."

Two feet into the tunnel they had to drop to their bellies and move single file, pushing their bags in front of them.

Claire choked. "I don't think I can handle this."

"Sure you can, snow queen. Just keep crawling. They're not going to come after us down here."

"But they're waiting for us up there, outside the cabin?"

"That text I got before our world got rocked? That was Jack warning me that our safe houses along the East Coast had been compromised." He tickled her ankle above her boot. "Keep movin'."

She scrambled forward. "How did that happen?"

"It's the spy business. We get intel on them, and they get intel on us. We have to stay one step ahead of them."

Which he may have done if he hadn't succumbed to his desire for Claire. What had Jack told him? Don't get taken in by the widow's beauty? If it were just her beauty, he could resist.

He'd met a kindred spirit in Claire. Who would've figured a poor boy from the wrong side of the tracks and a society babe would have so much in common? But they'd both been starved for love and had tried to fill that void with other obsessions.

Her gasping breaths filled the tunnel, and he squeezed her foot. "Are you okay? Try not to breathe so heavily."

"Easier said than done. How much farther do we have to go, and where are we going to end up?"

"Not sure, maybe another half a mile. We should wind up right outside that little town."

"How are we going to get out of there? If Tempest agents blew up the cabin and then lay in wait for us outside, once they discover we're not there or not coming out they're going to be watching the bus station."

"You're probably right, which is why we're going to steal a car."

"Are you crazy?"

"We'll make it right—later. Stop talking, save your breath and crawl."

Several feet farther in the tunnel he missed her chatter, but they didn't have enough air in here to be carrying on a conversation, and he didn't want Claire probing his plans too thoroughly. Truth was, in situations like this, it was best not to have too many well-laid plans.

He had no idea if he could find a car to steal or even if there'd be someone waiting for them at the other end of this tunnel.

Claire didn't need to know any of his doubts.

So, they squirmed forward in silence to the beat of their panting breath.

"Mike? I think this is it."

"The end?"

"It looks like solid dirt in front of me and the space opens up a bit."

"Move to the side and I'll squeeze past you."

"This is it. There's a panel of some sort overhead."

"Okay, hang on."

Claire was able to sit up in the space, and his light flicked across her dirt-smudged face.

He clambered beside her and rubbed the dirt from her face with the side of his thumb. "You did great. Almost there."

"Mike?"

"Yeah?" Reaching up he felt along the edges of the panel.

"What if there's someone waiting for us up above?"

He didn't have to tell her his worries. She'd figured them out on her own.

He withdrew his .45 from his pocket and brandished it in the light. "That's why I have this."

He tapped the panel and found an edge. "Stay back, Claire. Get into the farthest corner until I get this thing open and get our bearings."

He pushed against the door and it shifted, allowing a sliver of weak light into their black world. The sun hadn't quite set yet. He pressed his eye to the crack and took in the clearing surrounded by small trees and shrubs. The town lay due east less than half a mile away, and nobody was pointing guns at them—yet.

Shoving the panel aside, he led with his weapon. He poked his head up and sucked in the cold air so fast, it seemed to freeze his lungs. He gulped in a few more frosty breaths.

"It's clear. We're fine."

A small sob escaped from her lips, but she turned it into a cough. "All right, then. Let's get out of this hellhole, and I never meant that statement as literally as I do now."

He climbed up the two steps and stretched out on the ground, cracking his back. Then he rolled over and extended his hands into the opening to help Claire.

She handed him the bags first and then scooted out of the tunnel and collapsed beside him on the frosty ground, breathing heavily.

He inched his hand over and entwined his fingers with hers. "We need to get moving."

"I realize that. I'm just not so sure I can stand up."

He rose to his feet and stomped his boots. "Feels good to be upright."

"Feels good to be alive." She extended her arms, and he took both of her hands and pulled her up until she stood beside him.

"All right. Let's go steal a car."

Forty minutes later, Mike gunned the engine of an old pickup truck and hit the highway heading south.

Claire knotted her fingers in her lap. "Where are we going? I thought all the safe houses had been compromised."

"Do you know Senator Bennett from Connecticut?"

"Not personally."

He steered the truck onto the highway. "I know his son, Jase, and they have a family place in Maryland. We can crash there in between…skulking."

"The senator's not there, is he?"

"The house is empty, except for staff."

Claire shuffled through the glove compartment. "I feel bad about this truck, and it's almost Christmas. What if the guy needs his truck for Christmas?"

"Think of it as a rental. We'll get the truck back to him along with a nice sum of cash. That should brighten his Christmas."

"You're a real Santa." Bending forward, she held the registration up to the little light from the glove box. "Gary Lockhart. He lives in Barnhill, Vermont."

"I'll have someone contact him when we drop the car off at the train station."

"He'll still report the truck as stolen. What if we get pulled over before we get to the station?"

"Then I guess we get booked for car theft, but we won't be in jail for long. It helps to have friends in high places, and we're still not on the FBI's radar." He tapped the radio. "Music? Or do you want to sleep?"

"I slept all day. You must think I'm a slug or something." She rubbed her finger across her teeth. "I could use a toothbrush, though."

"I don't think you're a slug, but our sleep patterns are

kind of messed up. That can make you tired no matter how much sleep you get."

She hit the volume button on the radio. "Crank it up."

Static filled the cab of the truck, so he tried a few other stations. "Nothing but classical coming in. You wanna listen to that?"

"Sure, if it doesn't drive you crazy."

He set the station and put the volume on low for background music. "How are you feeling? Any irritation of your eyes or throat from that smoke?"

"I'm okay." She brushed his forearm. "I noticed the hair on your arms got singed. Are you okay?"

Her touch gave him a thrill. He'd been ready to make love to her all over again when they woke up, but Tempest treated them to fireworks of another kind. And it had to be Tempest. No other organization would've been able to compromise a Prospero safe house. Had agents been sent to destroy all of the safe houses they'd discovered, or did they know he and Claire were in Vermont?

He flicked at the burnt hair on his arm. "I hadn't noticed. There were several fires in the living room when I went to retrieve my laptop and bag."

"Thank God you were able to get them and they weren't destroyed." She jerked her thumb over her shoulder. "Is that the money bag in the back?"

"The money and the weapon bag, so along with the laptop, I got all the essentials out of there." He captured her fingers and brought them to his lips. "And the most essential item of all—you."

Sighing, she scrunched down in her seat. "It's a good thing we did sleep in today. If we'd been in that living room, we could've been injured."

"The way that living room looked? There's no doubt."

She swept some dirt from her jeans and then brushed her

hands together. "Whoever killed the director must know who you are now and must know that I'm with you. That firebombing proves that, doesn't it?"

"I agree. I doubt that anyone is after me for any other reason."

"I led them to you."

"Or I led them to you. Does it matter?"

"What I'm wondering is if Spencer went through all the trouble to set me up in the eyes of the FBI, why is he trying to kill me now?"

"It's easier." He squeezed her knee. "Sorry, but it's easier for him to have you killed than to have the FBI bring you in for questioning and start answering all kinds of uncomfortable questions. That is, if those were really FBI agents at the bank."

Her knee bounced beneath his hand. "You mentioned that before. How long has that suspicion been swirling through your brain?"

"Since that Tempest agent tried to abduct you from the station in Philly. If someone really wanted to set you up, those would've been FBI agents waiting for us at the station, not some guy with a gun in the ladies' room. Also, your name was never mentioned in the papers, never mentioned in connection with Hamid."

"I don't know if that makes me feel better or worse. At least I don't need to fear getting recognized at the train station or walking down the street." She sat up and grabbed the edge of the dashboard. "That also means I can call Ethan again without the Chadwicks wondering what's going on, right?"

"Were they expecting your call? You said they had him out all day for snowboarding."

"No, but they won't be surprised by a call. If I call on your phone again, the call can't be traced."

"Let me think about it. First things first."

"My son *is* first."

"I know that." He stroked her hair, littered with specks of dirt, but still soft.

"Okay, so what's first for you?"

"Right now? You."

Leaning against the window of the truck, she turned to face him, her eyes glittering in the low light of the truck. "You don't have to say that."

"I know." He drew a line from her cheek to her chin. "But it's true."

"Well, you don't have to worry about me. I'm fine." She gathered her hair into a ponytail with one hand. "So, what's next?"

"We're going to pay a visit to Fiona."

"Tomorrow? In person?"

"Correll's taking that rich widow to the White House. It's the perfect time to visit Spencer's spurned lover."

"We're going to waltz right into Spencer's office after he's been presumably trying to kill me?"

"Presumably." He held up one finger. "Ever hear of a disguise?"

She planted her palms on either side of her head. "My head is spinning. We're going to Maryland first, though, right? Hiding out in Senator Bennett's house? That makes a lot of sense."

"He won't be there, and you should fit right in. The Bennetts are loaded, too, and that house is staffed with servants. In fact, I'm surprised you don't know Jase Bennett. You two must've traveled in the same circles, although you're a little older than he is."

"Watch it." She punched his shoulder. "Do you think all rich people just sort of hang out together and go to the same schools and the same parties?"

"You mean you don't?"

She stuck out her tongue at him, which gave him all kinds of ideas.

"Hey, as long as the Bennett house has hot and cold running water and a roof, I'm there."

And after several hours and three different modes of transportation, they were there.

The brick colonial house with white siding and dark green shutters gleamed behind a tall gate. Mike had already put the word out, and Jase had facilitated their arrival.

One word from Mike into the intercom and the gates opened as if by magic. A housekeeper greeted them at the front door and didn't even turn up her nose at their appearance, as grungy as they must've looked—and smelled.

"I'm Mrs. Curtis. Mr. Jason phoned ahead. None of the family is in residence, however, and the senator and his wife are in Paris for the holidays."

"We won't be any trouble." Claire hugged her plastic bags to her chest and smiled.

"Mr. Jason indicated that you were to make yourself at home. You can call me via the intercom system in the house if you need anything, or just help yourself. There's food in the kitchen, and there are two rooms at the end of the hall, upstairs to your right, ready for you."

"Thank you, Mrs. Curtis. We can manage." Mike took Claire's arm and steered her upstairs. He whispered in her ear, "Two rooms?"

"I guess you forgot to tell Mr. Jason that you crossed the line between work and pleasure."

He grabbed her hand. "Did I tell you I like the pleasure part a lot better than the work part?"

They stopped at the second-to-last room on the right, and Claire pushed open the door. "This is nice. I think the two rooms are joined by a bathroom."

"You can have the shower first. I need to make a few more phone calls."

She swung her plastic bags in front of her. "The shower will be great, but I'm afraid I wasn't able to salvage many of the clothes I bought in Vermont."

"Jase has a sister and he said you're welcome to any of her clothes in the house. I don't think she's as tall as you, but she's not short. You should be able to find something to wear."

"And where are we getting our disguises? Not from Jase's sister's closet."

"We'll figure out something." He pulled off his boots and fell across the bed. "When was the last time we ate? My stomach is growling like a hungry bear."

"We had dinner on the way to the city to meet Hamid, unless you had something when we got back to the cabin."

"That was a long time ago. I think a midnight snack is in order even if it's not quite midnight. Should we trouble the accommodating Mrs. Curtis or forage for our own meal in the kitchen?"

"The less contact we have with anyone in this house, the better."

"This is the domain of the Bennett family. Discretion is the word." He held a finger to his lips.

"Yeah, well, you'd be surprised at how much servants talk."

"You mean that loyal retainer stuff is a myth?"

"For some." She shook out some clothes and draped them over her arm. "I'm going to hit the shower. Maybe you can try the kitchen for some food."

"That'd be the first place I'd look."

She rolled her magnificent eyes at him and shut the door of the connecting bathroom behind her.

Mike managed to make it downstairs and find the

kitchen without running into another human being in the huge house. He opened the door of the stainless Sub-Zero refrigerator and poked around the containers.

He settled on slicing some cheese, grabbing a few apples and ripping off half a loaf of French bread. He piled his booty onto a big plate and then snagged a bottle of Napa Valley chardonnay from the fridge.

He opened the bottle of wine and shoved the cork back in the top. He carefully threaded his fingers through the stems of two wineglasses, stuffed some paper towels beneath the plate and carried everything back upstairs.

When he entered the room, a cloud of lilac-scented air greeted him, and Claire floated from the bathroom dressed in one of his white T-shirts, toweling her hair dry.

She widened her eyes when she saw him. "Did you clean out the kitchen?"

"Hardly. You should see the stuff they have in there. Those servants must be living it up." He held up the bottle of wine. "Nabbed some good stuff, too."

"Wine? You took a bottle of—" she strolled toward him and squinted at the label "—what appears to be some very expensive wine?"

He looked at the blue label adorned with a yellow squiggly line through it. "Really? This is expensive?"

She brushed her thumb across the year printed on the label. "I think so."

"Good." He dislodged the cork and poured a measure of the golden liquid into one of the glasses. "You deserve it, and Jase assured me that his casa was our casa, or something like that. Said to take whatever we needed—food, clothing, cars."

"Cars, too?" She took the glass from him and swirled the wine up its sides. "Generous guy, this Jase."

"You got that. He owes me anyway. I've saved his careless ass more times than I can remember."

She took a sip of the wine and closed her eyes. "This is good. That shower was even better."

He set his glass down and peeled off his shirt, crumpling it into a ball. "You eat and I'll get in the shower."

"You said you were starving. Are you sure you don't want to sit down and eat first?" Her fingertips trailed across his pecs and down to his belly, where a fire kindled. "I don't mind that you're…dirty."

He swallowed. "I have a confession to make."

"Really?" She walked her fingers back up his chest and drummed them against his collarbone.

"I already ate a banana downstairs, so I'm not starving anymore." He took her hand and kissed her fingers. "And you're so perfectly fresh and rosy from your shower, I don't want to smudge you."

She lifted her wineglass. "Hurry back…before I eat everything."

He practically ran into the bathroom, unbuttoning his fly on his way. The steam from Claire's shower still fogged the mirror.

He cranked on the water in the stall, big enough to house a family of four, and read the labels on the two bottles of shower gel. At least he didn't need to smell like a lilac.

He squeezed a puddle of fresh ocean breeze into his palm and lathered up. He washed and rinsed his hair, sluicing it back from his forehead as he faced the spray. He almost felt human.

Then he felt superhuman when he walked back into the bedroom with the towel wrapped around his waist and saw Claire sitting cross-legged on the bed biting into an apple.

She said around chews, "You clean up nicely."

"I was thinking the same about you." He ran a hand

through his wet hair. "Hard to believe you were crawling through an underground tunnel about six hours ago."

"Hard to believe we made it out alive." She wiped her hands with a paper towel and then rolled up her apple core in it.

He dug into his bag and pulled out a clean pair of boxers. He put them on beneath his towel and then dropped the towel.

Half closing her eyes, she tossed back some wine. "Damn, I was looking forward to the striptease with the towel coming off."

"How many of those glasses have you had?" He sat down next to her on the bed and curled his hand around the neck of the wine bottle, lifting it up to the light.

"Enough." She yawned and fell over on her side, dragging a pillow beneath her cheek.

He smiled and stroked a length of creamy thigh that was exposed as his T-shirt hiked up around her hips. "Can I tempt you with a toothbrush and some toothpaste?"

"Absolutely." She shot up, the thought of brushing her teeth giving her new life. She tumbled from the bed, yanking the T-shirt down around her thighs.

Mike finished off the bread and cheese and had started on another glass of wine by the time Claire stumbled back into the bedroom.

"Ah, such a simple amenity can make all the difference in the world." Running her tongue along her teeth, she fell across the bed. "Did I leave you enough food and drink?"

"Plenty. Are you ready to go back into the fray tomorrow?"

She cocked her head. "By *fray* do you mean go to Spencer's office and try to pump Fiona for information?"

"Exactly."

"It feels dangerous being back here." She folded her arms behind her head. "Back in the vicinity of the political world, close to the White House. What do you think Tempest is going to do?"

"Not sure, but I plan to be in the thick of it to stop them."

"It's important to you, isn't it? I mean, it's important to everyone, but it's personal with you. What happened on your last assignment?"

He choked on the smooth sip of wine trailing down his throat. Even slightly tipsy, she could read him. "Who says anything happened on my last assignment?"

"You don't have to tell me if you don't want to, Mike, but it's so clear that things didn't end well for you. This White House plot fell into your lap, a way to redeem yourself."

"No wonder you had Spencer Correll figured out. You're one perceptive lady."

When it didn't involve her own motives.

"I just understand that drive to prove yourself."

He tossed back the rest of the wine in one gulp. "Okay, my previous assignment didn't have the ending I wanted. We lost hostages. I'd never lost hostages before."

"It happens." She stared past him into the space over her shoulder. "Those situations are chaotic and dangerous. I'm sure it wasn't your fault."

"I was leading the charge, so to speak."

"Nobody else blamed you, did they? Jack didn't blame you."

"I blamed me." He pushed off the bed and collected the dishes. "Do you want anything else from downstairs? Water?"

"Yes, water, please." She waved her hand up and down his body. "Are you venturing out in your boxers? You might give Mrs. Curtis a fright…or the thrill of a lifetime."

His lips twisted. "I suppose I'd better pull on some sweats."

"Chicken."

He left the wine and took everything back downstairs. Again, silence greeted his presence. He stayed in the kitchen for several minutes, throwing away their trash and washing the plate and glasses.

By the time he crept upstairs with a couple of bottles of water tucked beneath his arm, Claire was curled up on the bed, her hand beneath her cheek and her damp hair fanning out on the pillow.

Any thoughts he'd had of making wild, passionate love to her ended on a sigh from her lips.

He drowned his disappointment by gulping down the rest of the wine straight from the bottle—the only way to drink the good stuff.

He then brushed his own teeth and killed the lights in the room. Tugging on the covers, he nudged Claire's body aside and then pulled the covers over her, tucking them beneath her chin.

He yanked off his sweats and crawled into the bed beside her. Crossing his arms beneath his head, he peered through the darkness at the ceiling.

They had to get something on Spencer Correll, and if he was involved with Tempest, he'd get the details of the White House Christmas Day plot out of him one way or another.

Mike let out a long, slow breath. Two days until Christmas…two days until redemption.

CLAIRE LAID A line of kisses down the length of Mike's very long back. If she thought she could slowly awaken him with her kisses, she had the wrong spy.

He turned to face her with a suddenness that had her gasping for breath, her lips against his stomach.

Plowing his fingers through her hair, he growled, "Did you think you could toy with me?"

"A girl can hope." She flicked her tongue against his bare skin and he sucked in a sharp breath.

"You fell asleep last night before I got back from the kitchen. I thought I'd lost my touch."

She rolled up the T-shirt, baring her breasts to his hungry gaze. "So, touch and let's see if you lost it."

Before the last word left her lips, Mike pounced on her and made thorough love to every inch of her body.

They showered again—together this time—and then raided Jase's sister's closet.

Claire fingered the silk Prada jacket. "Nice stuff, but if I'm going to be someone else and try to blend in, I'd better not wear flashy clothing like this."

Mike jerked open another closet door. "We have the cold weather on our side. Jackets, scarves, hats—just like you dressed up when we went into that town in Vermont. We even have the sun out today to warrant a big pair of sunglasses."

Claire dangled a pair of black leggings from her fingers. "I can wear these with the boots I bought in Vermont, pile on a long sweater with a scarf, hat and sunglasses. It's not like Spencer's going to be on the lookout for me, right?"

"Right. Maybe we can avoid the office altogether. Is there someplace you can meet Fiona outside the building?"

"There are a couple of cafés on the street, although they're frequented by a lot of politicians. I'd hate to have to hide in plain sight with someone I know looking at me."

"Most of those politicians are out of town for the recess." Mike yanked a long blue coat from a hanger and held it up. "Is there any place Fiona goes at lunchtime? Does she get her nails done?"

"I know." Claire dropped the leggings. "Fiona goes to a psychic in the area."

"Like to get her fortune told? Do people really do that?"

"I think it's tarot cards and astrological charts, and Fiona's been seeing this psychic, Madam Rosalee, for a while. She was going on and on about the psychic when she gave me Spencer's password, about how Madam Rosalee had predicted the end of her relationship."

Mike shrugged. "It takes all types. Do you think Fiona will meet you there?"

"I'll talk to Madam Rosalee first and have her get Fiona down there on her lunch hour."

"I'm assuming you'll need some money to make that happen?"

Claire rubbed her thumb across the tips of the rest of her fingers. "I'm going to need money for all of it."

"That I have." Mike tossed the coat at her. "I don't have to be there, but I'll be nearby. You know what to ask Fiona, right?"

"If she knows anything suspicious about my stepfather and if she's willing to spill."

"Let's do this."

Mike borrowed the least flashy car in the Bennett stable—a black Mercedes sedan—and drove them back to DC.

He had his own disguise, as he'd let his beard grow out and now sported a substantial scruff, liberally streaked with gray. Before they left the house that morning, he'd also cropped his longish black hair and then shaved his head down to a stubble.

Claire stole a sideways glance at him in the driver's seat of the car and clicked her tongue. She'd loved the way that long lock of hair had fallen over one of his eyes, but the shaved head and beard gave him a decidedly dangerous look.

"Why are you clicking your tongue at me?"

"I sort of liked your shaggy hair."

He ran a hand over his scalp. "Good disguise, though, right?"

"It makes you look…different for sure, kind of lethal."

She stuffed her hair beneath her hat. "Do I look different enough?"

"It's hard to tell what you look like since you're all covered up, but then so is everyone else in this cold spell we're having."

She directed him to Madam Rosalee's and he laughed every time she said the psychic's name.

"Stop." She smacked his thigh. "It's as good a name as any for a psychic."

"Do you believe in that stuff?"

"No, but that doesn't matter. Fiona does, and I know she'll jump at the chance to see Madam Rosalee, especially now that she's on the outs with Spencer."

She pointed out the psychic's small blue, clapboard house between two office buildings. The sign on the house sported a yellow hand with the words *Psychic Readings* in squiggly blue script in the middle of it.

Mike dropped her off in front and went looking for parking.

Claire cupped her hand over her eyes as she peeked in the window. She saw no one, so she opened the door and a bell tinkled her arrival.

The smell of sandalwood incense permeated the air, and a few shelves contained decks of tarot cards, more incense, candles and other psychic accoutrements.

Claire called out, "Hello? Madam Rosalee?"

A beaded curtain clicked and clacked and an enormous woman bedecked in flowing scarves and a green peasant skirt threaded with gold emerged into the room.

Claire pressed her lips together to vanquish her smile. Mike would've gotten a kick out of the cliché that was Madam Rosalee.

Madam Rosalee stopped and spread her arms, closing her eyes. "I sense an aura of danger. Are you safe?"

The smile on Claire's lips died and she crossed her arms over her chest. "Yes, I'm safe. I didn't come here for myself."

"They never do." Madam Rosalee's heavily lined eyes flew open. "What can I help you with?"

"I need to talk with one of your clients, on the sly, and I thought this might be a good place to do it."

"Why would I lure one of my clients here on a false premise?"

"I'll give you m-money." Claire faltered at the look from Madam Rosalee's dark, slitted eyes.

"You think you can come into my establishment and give me money to get one of my clients here so you can ambush him or her?"

"I'm sorry." Claire blew out a breath. Would Mike have been able to handle this any better? "It's really very important. It's crucial that I talk with her. I can't go to her office and I'm afraid to meet her in public."

Afraid? Where had that come from?

Madam Rosalee held up one pudgy finger with an extremely long red nail on the end and a ring that snaked over her first knuckle.

"You're afraid to meet her in public?"

"Yes. Yes, I am." Claire held her breath.

"Then this is related to the danger and fear that are coming off of you in waves."

"It must be. I guess it is." Who said Madam Rosalee was a fake?

"I don't want your money."

"Is that a refusal? I'm begging you, really, to contact Fiona Levesque. I need to talk to her. Sh-she may be in danger, too."

"I don't want money, but you'll give me something else."

"Anything, just ask and I'll get it for you."

Madam Rosalee approached her slowly and circled her,

waving her silky scarves around Claire's body. Claire felt as if she'd landed in the middle of someone's magic show.

"What? What do you want?"

Madame Rosalee trailed a scented scarf over Claire's head. "I want to do a reading for you."

Chapter Thirteen

Claire's shoulders sagged. She'd almost expected Rosalee to ask for her firstborn child. "Of course, if that's all you want. But can we hurry so we can get Fiona here on her lunch hour?"

"I'll take care of that right now." She picked up her cell phone and gestured to the small table covered with a black velvet cloth. "Sit."

Claire took a seat at the table, stroking the soft velvet with her fingertips, and listened to Madam Rosalee's call to Fiona.

"Yes, something very important, my dear. Your very life could depend on it." She ended the call and placed her phone on the shelf next to the small table. "Fiona will be here just after noon. Are you ready?"

"As ready as I'll ever be." Claire folded her hands on the table and gave Madam Rosalee a tight, polite smile.

"Have you ever had a tarot reading before?"

"No."

"Your name?" Madam Rosalee settled her massive girth into the winged-back chair across from her.

"Claire." She glanced over her shoulder at the window. Had Mike expected her to come outside once she'd convinced Madam Rosalee to set up the meeting with Fiona?

As if she'd summoned him with one of Madam Rosalee's

charms, Mike burst through the door of the shop, sending the little bell into a tizzy.

His arrival didn't disturb Madam Rosalee at all, maybe so she could make the claim that she'd expected him to show up all along.

She lifted an eyebrow. "Are you with Claire?"

"Yeah, what's going on?" He dropped a hand to Claire's shoulder. "I was worried about you."

Madame Rosalee nodded. "Could you please turn around the sign at the door and lock it?"

"Claire?" He put pressure on her shoulder.

"Madam Rosalee's payment for luring Fiona over here is a tarot reading for me."

"Is that okay with you?"

She patted his hand still resting on her shoulder. "It's a tarot reading, Mike. Go switch the sign at the door and lock it."

"I'm not going anywhere." He stepped back and locked the door while flipping the sign over to read Closed to the outside world.

"Nobody's asking you to, Mike, as long as you sit quietly during the reading." Madam Rosalee handled a deck of tarot cards, the heavy rings flashing on her fleshy hands.

Mike shrugged at Claire and took a seat in the corner of the room.

Madam Rosalee turned over a row of cards in the middle of the table, tapping them, changing their position, crossing one over another.

The colorful figures and symbols meant nothing to Claire, but the atmosphere in the room grew heavy with anticipation.

After several minutes Madam Rosalee finally spoke. "You are in danger, but we'd already established that."

Mike shifted forward in his seat, and Claire threw a glance his way.

Claire cleared her throat. "Is the danger imminent or vague?"

"It's imminent."

"Avoidable?"

"It's avoidable as long as you aren't alone. On your own, the black sword of death hangs over your head."

Claire rolled her shoulders. That made sense for anyone.

"Love," Madame Rosalee said as she tapped a card, "and death. The two are linked for you and have been for some time."

Claire covered her mouth with one hand. "That was true in the past. Is it true in the future?"

"Just as in the past, in the future and for all time, if love is strong enough, it can vanquish the danger."

Madam Rosalee droned on about money and family, but nothing she said could replace the uneasiness in the pit of Claire's stomach.

Love? Mike didn't love her. They'd had a connection and some great sex, but that didn't equal love—at least not a love great enough to vanquish the evil they faced.

Madame Rosalee gathered her cards and pushed up from her chair. "I'll be in the back to give you some time to talk to Fiona."

The disappearance of her large presence seemed to suck the life and the drama out of the room.

Mike got up and stretched. "Pretty generic stuff, huh?"

"Yes, yes, of course."

"Why did she want to tell your fortune?" He peered out the curtains at the front window and unlocked the door.

"I'm not sure. As soon as I walked in, she sensed the danger of my aura."

He turned and grabbed her around the waist. "As soon as

I saw you, I sensed the sexiness of your aura." He nuzzled her neck.

Leaning back in his arms, she rubbed her knuckles across the black stubble on his head. Annoyance niggled at the edges of her mind. Madam Rosalee had just been telling her how love could stave off the danger, and all Mike could think about was sex.

He blinked his dark eyes, the lusty gleam dimming. "I'm sorry. The palm reading really upset you."

"It was a tarot card reading."

"That's what I meant." He released her and returned to the window. "Fiona's coming at noon?"

She swallowed the lump in her throat. She'd better prepare herself for Mike's departure as soon as he single-handedly saved the White House. And if he couldn't single-handedly save the White House? He'd be unbearable company anyway.

"A little after, I think."

"Is Fiona a busty redhead with a little wiggle in her walk?"

She snorted. "I suppose a man would describe her that way."

"She's here in three...two...one."

The bell on the door jingled and Fiona poked her head into the room. "Madam Rosalee?"

Claire plucked the hat from her head and shook out her hair. "It's me, Fiona. It's Claire Chadwick."

"Claire?" Fiona covered her mouth. "What are you doing here? Are you okay?"

"Okay? Why wouldn't I be okay? What story is Spencer floating around town about me?"

"Spencer." Fiona spit out his name, which was all kinds of wonderful. "Is he spreading lies about you? I wouldn't doubt that for a minute."

"What's he saying, Fiona?" Mike wedged a shoulder against the wall.

"Who's this tall drink of water?" Fiona batted her lashes. "Oh, wait. Are you Mitch, the fiancé?"

"Sort of. What's Senator Correll been saying about us?"

Fiona flipped back her red hair. "Am I here to meet you? Is Madam Rosalee even here?"

"She's here." Claire tugged on Fiona's scarf. "I'm sorry, Fiona. She helped me get you here. I need your help."

"The same way I helped you before?"

"Yes."

"I don't know, Claire. I think Spencer found out about the last time."

Claire's heart skipped a beat. "How? You didn't tell him?"

"Me?" Fiona's voice squeaked. "I value my life too much. Trey figured something out. Spencer had him look at his office laptop because someone kept sending him emails with photos and videos. I think Trey figured out that Spencer was just dragging them into his trash can without doing a hard delete on them. While Trey was helping him, he figured out that someone had viewed a video from the trash."

"That's probably when he started tracking you, Claire." Mike paced the small room. "Maybe that's when he formed his plan against you, also."

He landed in front of Fiona, towering over her petite frame. "You still didn't tell us. What's Spencer saying about Claire? How's he explaining her disappearance?"

Fiona took a step back, and Claire tugged on Mike's coat. "Don't scare her. She's not the enemy."

"Enemy?" Fiona flipped up the lapels of her coat. "There's an enemy here? I thought this was some kind of dispute between you and your stepfather over money."

"It is, and other stuff."

"Well..." Fiona glanced at Mike, who had returned to

the window and stuffed his hand into his pocket. "Spencer is implying that you've had another breakdown."

Claire cursed. "That's almost worse than being wanted by the FBI."

"Wanted by the FBI?" Fiona's blue eyes got round as she shook her head. "He's not saying that. He said Director Haywood's murder in front of your house shook you up so much, you started making wild accusations and your fiancé had to take you away."

"So, I can walk back into my own house right now without fear of being taken into custody?"

Fiona lifted a shoulder. "I don't know anything about that, Claire. You know the man they suspected of putting the car bomb on the director's car is dead?"

Claire and Mike exchanged a quick glance. "Hamid Khan."

"That's right. They're calling him a lone wolf."

Mike coughed. "A lone wolf who poisoned himself?"

"I don't know all the details." Fiona waved her hands. "I just know he's dead and we're supposedly out of danger, but I can't wait to get out of this city. It's Christmas Eve tomorrow, and I'm outta here."

"Can you help us before you leave, Fiona?" Claire held out the envelope of cash she'd been ready to give Madam Rosalee. "I'll make it worth your while."

"I'll take it, but it's just icing on the cake. Do you know that SOB is taking that rich widow to the White House on Christmas Day? If he thinks he's going to squire her around in public during the day and end up in my bed at night, he's dreaming."

Claire suppressed a shiver of revulsion at the thought of Spencer Correll in bed with anyone. "He's a pig, Fiona. Do you have anything you can give us to use against him?"

"I told you, someone keeps sending him emails with

videos and pictures. It freaks him out. I don't know if it's blackmail or what."

Mike asked, "Has he gotten any lately?"

"He gets something almost every day."

Claire clasped her hands in front of her. "Can you get them out, Fiona?"

Fiona tilted her red head. "Why don't you come and get it yourself? It's the day before Christmas Eve. There's hardly anyone in the office. Spencer is busy with God knows what. He told me not to expect him in the office until after the break."

Mike shook his head. "Claire, he might be monitoring the office. He might have eyes and ears there. It's too risky."

"I don't like what I'm hearing." Fiona shoved the envelope of money into her purse. "Why would Spencer be watching for you, Claire? And what's he going to do if you show up?"

"If I give you a thumb drive, Fiona, can you copy Spencer's emails to it?"

"I can do that." Fiona skimmed her nails along the velvet cloth covering Madam Rosalee's tarot reading table. "But this is my last day in the office until after New Year's. How am I going to get it back to you?"

"Do you still get off at five?"

"Yeah."

"Mike?" Claire turned toward him.

He scratched his beard. "How do you get to work, a car or public transportation?"

"I take a bus. The stop is a block down from the office."

"We'll be waiting on the street in front of the office when you get off—black Mercedes sedan. Hand the drive to Claire through the window and have a happy holiday."

Claire pressed the thumb drive into Fiona's hand, and she dropped it into her purse.

"What if there's nothing in the emails?" Fiona clutched her bag to her chest. "Do I still get to keep the money?"

"Absolutely. I appreciate this so much. You have no idea." She gave Fiona a one-armed hug.

As Fiona opened the front door and set off the bells, Rosalee swept aside the beaded curtain and pointed at her. "Be careful. The aura of danger is strong."

WHEN THEY LEFT Madam Rosalee's, Mike headed a few miles outside the city center where he drove through a fast-food place.

They parked in the lot and Mike wolfed down a couple of burgers while Claire sipped on soda.

Between bites, he said, "I am so done with this. If I go through one fast-food place when I retire, that'll be one too many."

Claire chewed on the end of her straw. "I hope Spencer still has some of those incriminating photos in his email. Who do you think is blackmailing him?"

"It could be anyone. It could be Caliban himself. Once you start playing games like Correll, you're in bed with some very dangerous people."

His phone buzzed and Claire jumped. She'd called her son this morning and had given Ethan's grandparents this number to call in case of an emergency.

Cupping the phone in his hand, he glanced at the display and shook his head at Claire. "It's Jack."

He pushed the button to answer. "I'm still alive, in case you're wondering, oh, and you're on speaker. Claire's in the car."

"Good. You both need to hear this."

Claire bolted upright in her seat. "The videos?"

"We've identified the Oxford Don, Claire. Donald Yousef

is the one who executed your husband and he's the one in the video with Senator Correll."

A sob broke from Claire's throat and she covered her face with her hands.

Mike rubbed her back. "Do you know where he is, Jack?"

"He's somewhere in the States. He's a British citizen on a visit and has overstayed his welcome."

"So, he could be here in DC."

"He could be anywhere."

Claire sniffled. "Is this enough to move in on Correll, Jack?"

"We have no audio from the video, no way of knowing why or how he met Yousef. He could claim it was a chance meeting or that Yousef contacted him and he had no idea who he was."

Mike slammed his hands against the steering wheel. "But it's gotta be enough to bring Correll in for questioning, to start an investigation."

"It is, and we're working on it right now. Are you two safe?"

"Safe and working on a new lead on Correll. Anything on the White House plot?" Mike held his breath. He wanted in on that in the worst way.

"We've notified White House security and the CIA that there's a credible threat against the White House on Christmas Day. They're sweeping the buildings and the grounds, including the room where the memorial for Haywood is being held. They haven't come up with anything, and that room has been sealed off since the sweep—nobody in or out."

"Then it's a threat from the outside in. Correll must know about the extra security precautions."

"He does."

"I wonder if he realizes that Mike and I are behind them." Claire brushed her wet cheeks.

"He just might, Claire. That's why you two still need to keep a low profile."

Mike crumpled up the paper from his burgers. "Is sitting in a fast-food parking lot in Virginia low profile enough?"

"Figures you'd be eating, Becker. Just so you know, Bennett and Liam McCabe are heading out to DC to work this White House threat."

Mike closed his eyes briefly as a shaft of pain knifed his temple. "Sure, boss."

Jack paused. "Mike, you've been my number-one guy for a long time and you're number one on this assignment, too. You have nothing to prove."

"Got it, boss. Keep me posted."

"Same atcha."

Mike ended the call and then curled his arm around Claire, pulling her close. "You did it, snow queen. Justice for Shane. How does it feel?"

She blinked wet lashes at him. "Like some huge weight off my shoulders, like I can move forward with my life."

"You're not going to shift your focus back to your mother's accident?"

"If Prospero or the CIA can link Spencer to these terrorists, to Tempest, and put him away? That's justice for Mom, too."

He kissed the side of her head. "Maybe Fiona can give us something that'll put the nail in Correll's coffin, and then he'll give it up on the White House plot and Caliban."

"It's good that Prospero is sending backup, right?" She entwined her fingers with his. "The point is to stop the attack. You'll still be in on the action."

"Of course." He squeezed her hand, cursing his transparency in her presence. "It's almost five o'clock. Let's go meet Fiona."

They drove back to DC and through the crowded streets near the Mall with Claire directing him toward her stepfather's office building.

As they turned the corner, Mike's hands tightened on the steering wheel. An ambulance, fire truck and three Metro police cars took up the space on the curb in front of a high-rise office building.

"Is that his building, Claire?"

She had one hand at her slender throat. "Yes. It can't be... Please, God."

Mike slowed the car as he pulled up behind a fire truck parked at an angle. He rolled down the window and shouted to a guy at the edge of a crowd of people on the sidewalk. "What's going on? What happened?"

The man took a step back from the crowd. "Some woman. Someone said she was attacked in that stairwell in the parking structure."

Claire hung on the edge of the car window. "Is she okay?"

"No idea. I think they're putting her on a stretcher now."

Mike threw the car into Park. "Climb into the driver's seat in case you have to move the car. I'm going to have a look."

He jumped out of the car and shouldered his way through the crowd, peering over everyone's head. The EMTs raised the gurney and started wheeling it toward the open doors of the ambulance. A white sheet was pulled up to a woman's chin, but not over her face. Mike's gut knotted when a tumble of red curls spilled over the side of the gurney.

With his heart thudding in his chest, he made his way back to the illegally parked car with Claire in the driver's seat, her head bowed.

He slid into the car next to her and slammed the car

door. Punching his fist into his palm, he swore. "Damn. It's Fiona. She looks badly beaten, but she's not dead. Thank God, she's not dead."

Claire put the car in gear and squealed away from the curb, glancing over her shoulder.

She took the next turn hard and then gunned the sedan on the straightaway.

"Claire?" Mike drew his eyebrows over his nose. "Are you okay? It was Fiona on that stretcher."

"I know." She plunged her hand into the cup holder and swung a thumb drive from its ribbon. "But we got the goods anyway."

Chapter Fourteen

Mike snatched the drive from her fingers. "How the hell did you get this?"

"While you were on the sidewalk, Madam Rosalee came up to the car window and gave it to me."

"Madam Rosalee?" He drove the heel of his hand against his forehead. "Now I'm really confused."

"She didn't have much time to talk. You can imagine she wanted to get out of there, but she told me she'd had a bad feeling about Fiona when she left her place—that dangerous aura."

"Yeah, or maybe she just eavesdropped on our conversation."

"Whatever." Claire flicked her fingers in the air. "She went to Fiona's office on the pretense of delivering her astrological chart and told her that if she hung on to that thumb drive I gave her, she'd be in mortal danger. She assured Fiona she'd get the drive to me.

"Fiona told her to give it to us when we pulled up to the curb, that she'd wanted to leave the office early anyway since it was her last day before the holidays. Madame Rosalee stopped for coffee to wait for us when all the commotion started. Someone had discovered Fiona in the stairwell, beaten to a pulp, and called 9-1-1."

"My God. They knew. Somehow they knew Fiona had

taken that info. Maybe Trey Jensen placed a tracer on Correll's computer." He made a fist around the thumb drive. "But we got the info anyway."

Claire bit her lip. "Whoever beat up Fiona didn't find anything on her. They might believe they were mistaken."

"I doubt it, Claire. They know she took something, and they may know that we have it. I just hope to God she pulls through."

"H-how did she look?"

"Bad, had an oxygen mask over her face, but I didn't hear anything about her getting shot or knifed."

"Thank God for small favors." She huffed out a breath. "After what Fiona paid to get this out, I hope there's something on it we can use to nail Spencer for sure."

"So do I. I'm also hoping there's something about the Christmas Day attack. We need all the help we can get on that." He tapped the GPS on the car's control panel. "Do you know the way back to the Bennetts'?"

"I have a terrible sense of direction. Punch it in."

Mike entered the address into the GPS and checked his watch. "We'll check on Fiona later when they get her to the hospital."

The voice on the GPS directed her to take the next turn, and Claire turned down the volume. "Do you think she told her attacker about the thumb drive? About us?"

"Fiona is a pampered admin assistant in a senator's office." Mike traced the edges of the thumb drive. "I think she told them everything and would've given up the drive if she'd had it on her, and I don't blame her for it at all."

Claire squeezed her fingers around the steering wheel as a sick feeling seized her gut. "But she didn't tell them about Madam Rosalee, or they would've gone after her. She didn't tell them about the handoff at five o'clock or we would've seen someone—emergency vehicles or no emergency vehicles."

"My guess is she told her assailant that she already gave the drive to us. At that point, she could assume Madam Rosalee would be successful in putting the drive in our hands."

"Once Spencer goes down, I'll make sure Fiona gets another job on The Hill if she wants it." Claire ground her back teeth together. If Spencer could arrange for his former lover to get beaten, who knew what else he'd be capable of doing?

"That would be a hard sell."

"What would?"

"Finding a position for someone in government who'd sell out her boss for a few bucks."

"Ah, but she didn't sell out her boss. She was assisting in the takedown of a terrorist."

"Let's hope she survives to take advantage of your salesmanship."

They drove in silence for the next several miles, during which time Claire said a number of prayers for Fiona and even a few for Madam Rosalee.

They crossed into Maryland and Claire asked, "Is Jase going to be at his house when we get there?"

"I'm not sure. He's been with his fiancée, who's expecting a baby. She's been through a tough time, so I'm surprised Jack got him to come out here, although Jase probably jumped at the chance to take down a Tempest plot."

"He has history with Tempest, too?"

"Yeah, Liam and Jase—and now me."

Another few miles and Claire pulled the sedan up to the Bennett fortress. Mrs. Curtis had given them the code for the gate, and Claire entered it.

Mrs. Curtis met them at the front door, her eyes popping

at Mike's altered appearance. She hadn't seen him since they first arrived.

"It's me." Mike skimmed his hand over his buzz cut. "Do you mind if Claire gets some lunch from the kitchen?"

"Of course not. I'm sure Mr. Jason told you to make yourselves at home. There's cold chicken, some salad and some hummus and pita bread."

Claire plucked the hat from her head. "That sounds good, but, Mike…"

He took her by the shoulders and aimed her in the direction of the kitchen. "Eat. I'll bring my laptop into the kitchen and we can multitask."

Mrs. Curtis bustled ahead of her, but Claire put a hand on her back. "Don't go to any trouble, Mrs. Curtis. I can help myself."

"I'll just take it out for you, and then I'll leave you two alone to discuss business."

How did she know they had business to discuss? Must be all those years looking after Mr. Jason.

Mrs. Curtis puttered around the kitchen, unwrapping some chicken and popping a few rounds of pita bread into the microwave. "Would you or Mr. Becker like some coffee?"

"I wouldn't, not sure about Mr. Becker."

Mike barreled back into the kitchen, his laptop tucked beneath his arm. "Not sure about what?"

"Would you like some coffee, sir?" Mrs. Curtis held up the coffeepot.

"No, thanks."

"Then I'll leave you two." Mrs. Curtis stopped at the door. "Only Mr. Curtis and I are in residence, in the back house, and we're leaving for Mississippi later tonight to visit our grandchildren for Christmas."

Mike issued a mock salute. "Thanks for everything, Mrs.

Curtis, and enjoy your holiday. We'll be fine on our own, and Jase is due back tonight or tomorrow morning."

She smiled and wished them a merry Christmas, then headed out the side door toward the back house on the grounds.

Mike set up his laptop on the granite island in the middle of the kitchen while Claire spooned some hummus onto a plate. She removed the pita from the microwave and tore off a piece.

Mike looked up from his computer. "Jack sent me the file they have on Donald Yousef, and it's not much."

Clicking the keyboard to scroll through the file, he continued, "He's been keeping a low profile. He's not on any watch lists, hasn't attended any training camps that we know of. There's been no indication in the past that he's been involved in terrorist activity."

"But Prospero is still sure he's the man in the video with Shane?"

"They've verified it through some very sophisticated computer matching of features, body type, gestures."

"Will that hold up if they decide to pick him up and detain him for questioning?"

"The system we're using is not recognized in court, but for us it's enough to bring him in—when we locate him."

He tapped the keyboard a few more times and then frowned.

"What's wrong? You look confused."

"Who's that woman your stepfather is taking to the White House event? Brit-Saud Oil, right?"

"That's right." She licked some hummus from her fingers. "Julie Patrick. Her husband owned massive shares of Brit-Saud Oil, and now they're all hers."

"Brit-Saud Oil." Mike tapped his finger against the laptop's screen. "Don Yousef is a beneficiary of Brit-Saud Oil."

Her heart jumped. "What does that mean, *beneficiary*?"

"The company offers scholarships to promising students in the Middle East who have been adversely affected by war."

"Is that how Yousef got to Oxford?"

"Yes, and you'll never guess who's chairperson of that program."

Claire dropped her pita bread on the counter. "Julie Patrick?"

"Exactly." He hunched over the laptop. "Where did you read that puff piece about the guest list for the director's memorial?"

"The *Washington Spy*."

"That's appropriate." He brought up the website and did a search for the article. "This only mentions Correll and his guest, Julie Patrick. We need to get ahold of that guest list."

"If Prospero is monitoring security at the White House for the event, they'd have the guest list, right?"

"Yep." Mike had already lunged for his phone. "Jack, I need that guest list for the Haywood memorial. More specifically, is Julie Patrick bringing a guest?"

Jack's voice came over the phone's speaker. "Hang on. Do you want me to send it to you or just tell you over the phone?"

"I just need to know if she's bringing a guest—over the phone."

Jack paused and then came back on the line. "Julie Patrick is most definitely bringing a guest."

"Who is it, Jack?" Claire gripped the edge of her stool. "Is it Donald Yousef?"

"Donald Yousef? Of course not. After ID'ing him as your husband's executioner, you don't think we'd notice his name on the White House guest list?"

Mike held up his index finger at Claire. "Then who is it, Jack? Who's she bringing?"

"Some kid named Assad Ali-Watkins. He's one of her scholarship kids."

Claire jumped off her stool and shouted into the phone, "Jack, it's him. He's the threat."

"What's she talking about, Mike?"

"Donald Yousef was one of those Brit-Saud scholarship recipients, too. There's a good chance that Julie Patrick is working to help identify possible recruits for Tempest through this program. The kid is clean, right? He's going to pass any background and he's presumably already been vetted by Brit-Saud Oil."

"Son of a bitch. What are you thinking? Suicide vest?"

"That's exactly what I'm thinking, and if he sees White House security doing a pat-down of dignitaries before they enter the reception, he's going to know something's off and he'll detonate right there or take off."

"We'll have to head him off before he gets to that point. *You'll* have to head him off, Mike. This is yours."

Mike glanced at her, his dark eyes gleaming. "We need to be able to tie this Ali-Watkins to Senator Correll."

"Did you get any more info on him?"

Mike grabbed the thumb drive. "We did, but we haven't looked at it yet because we got sidetracked with the dossier you sent on the Oxford Don."

"Well, get on it. I have complete faith in you, Mike."

On that high note, Mike ended the call and grabbed Claire's face, kissing her on the lips. "I think this is it, snow queen."

The pulse in her throat galloped wildly. "Let's see what Fiona got for us."

Mike inserted the thumb drive and double-clicked on it

to open it. Several email files popped up, and Mike opened the first one.

Claire's shoulders sagged. "It's an airline's special deals."

"Fiona probably just copied over all his emails. That's okay. She said he'd been getting emails almost daily, so there has to be something here, unless Jensen was deleting them remotely."

Mike's cell phone vibrated on the countertop and he grabbed it, cupping it in his hand.

"Is it Jack again?"

Mike cocked his head. "It's the Chadwicks from Colorado."

Claire put her fingers to her lips. "I hope Ethan didn't have an accident snowboarding. Should I answer it?"

"Let me." He put the phone back on the counter and tapped the screen. "Hello?"

"H-hello? My daughter-in-law, Claire Chadwick, gave me this number to call."

Mike nodded at Claire.

"Nancy, this is Claire. Is Ethan okay?"

"Oh, no, Claire. Ethan is not okay. He's missing."

Chapter Fifteen

Claire's brain went numb for a moment as she shook her head. It was a joke, some kind of joke.

Claire laughed. "Missing? What does that mean?"

Nancy sobbed, "He's gone, Claire. I'm so sorry, but we thought he was safe. He was with Lori in a class and then he was gone. We've had the snow patrol looking for him, but an instructor in another class thinks Ethan walked away with a man."

Claire doubled over, clutching her stomach.

"Claire?" Barry's voice boomed over the phone. "Does this have anything to do with Shane? Tell us this doesn't have anything to do with Shane."

Mike grabbed Claire's hand. "Mr. and Mrs. Chadwick? This is Claire's friend Mike Becker. Have the kidnappers made any demands yet?"

Through her fog, Claire heard Barry respond. "Nothing. The police and the snow patrol are still searching the mountain. They're not convinced it's an abduction—yet."

"Good." Mike squeezed her hand. "Listen to me very carefully. When the kidnapper calls with his terms, he's going to demand that you leave the police out of it. Do what he says. Is Lori there with you?"

Nancy sniffed. "No, she's at the police station."

"Don't tell Lori you talked to me. Got it? Don't even mention my name."

"Why?" Barry coughed. "Who are you? Where's Claire?"

"Barry?" Claire wiped her face. "I'm right here. You can trust Mike. This is more complicated than a simple... kidnapping."

She shuddered, and Mike wrapped his arm around her. "Do what Mike says. Follow the kidnappers' instructions, and don't tell Lori about Mike."

"Mr. Chadwick, I'm going to hang up now so your line is free. My guess is you'll hear something soon, something before the police set up operations at your house and tap your phones. Play along with that."

Nancy's voice quavered. "This has to do with what happened to Shane, doesn't it, Claire? When will it ever end?"

Claire set her jaw and dashed the last tear from her face. "It ends now, Nancy."

IT TOOK HIM thirty minutes and one glass of wine to calm Claire down and to get her shaking to subside. He'd held her close and whispered in her ear while a black dread grew in his gut.

Now anger had replaced Claire's fear, and she paced the kitchen floor as he continued opening emails.

His frustration had him practically breaking the mouse on the next email he clicked. "There has to be something on here or Correll wouldn't have arranged Ethan's abduction."

Claire dug her fingers into her scalp, grabbing her hair by the roots. "I can't believe he'd actually do harm to Ethan. He played grandpa to that boy."

"He's diabolical, Claire. Tempest and Caliban must've promised him something big for his cooperation in this plan—a starring role in the new world order."

"What about Lori?" She clasped her hands behind her neck and tilted back her head. "Do you suspect Lori?"

"There's no way she let Ethan out of her sight when he was in that snowboarding class." He squinted at the next email, an invitation to play a social media game. "I told you that first day. I walked into something between the two of them. I guess she wasn't as unwilling as she pretended to be."

Claire swept up a knife and stabbed a cutting board. "I should've never let him out of my sight. I should've let this all go and taken him to Colorado myself."

"Hey, you did what you thought was right at the time. You thought you were keeping him safe."

She covered her face with her hands. "It's Christmas Eve tomorrow. He must be so scared."

"I'm sure he's okay right now."

"Right now." Her hands fisted at her sides. "I'll kill Spencer myself if any harm comes to Ethan."

"Wait a minute. This email has an attachment." He double-clicked on the image file and swore. "Bingo—Correll is trying on a suicide vest."

"What?" She tripped over her own feet getting back to him and the laptop. Hovering over his shoulder, she said, "Oh, my God. There he is. That has to be Ali-Watkins next to him, but who sent the picture and why? Who sent him the video of the meeting with Yousef?"

Mike wiped a bead of sweat from his sideburn. "Someone who wants to keep him in line. All of Correll's meetings with these people have been recorded without his knowledge. By sending the videos and pictures, Tempest is making sure he keeps up his end of the bargain—access to the White House and the highest echelons of government."

His cell phone buzzed, and Claire pounced on it. "It's the Chadwicks."

"Hold on." Mike took the phone from here. "Hello?"

Mr. Chadwick's harsh whisper came over the line. "Someone called us. The police aren't here yet and don't know about the communication, and Lori is resting in her room."

"Good. You're on speaker and Claire's listening in. What do they want?"

"It was a man, disguised voice. He told me not to contact the police about the call and to give a message to Claire."

Claire dragged in a shuddering breath. "What's the message, Barry?"

"It's a phone number, Claire. Just a phone number for you to call, and a picture."

"A picture?" Mike's heart thundered in his chest.

"It's Ethan. He's eating something from a bowl, soup or cereal, and he's sitting in front of a TV with the date and time stamped on the screen. It was taken minutes before the call. Ethan's okay. He's okay right now, Claire."

"He'll be fine, Barry. I won't let anything happen to our boy. We won't lose him."

Barry read off the telephone number while Mike entered it into a file on the computer. He told Barry to hold tight and then he ended the call.

"Are you ready?" He spun the computer around to Claire and pushed his phone toward her.

She licked her lips and tapped the number into the phone.

Spencer Correll answered on the first ring. "Yes?"

Claire growled deep in her throat. "Give me my son back, you son of a bitch."

Correll tsked. "First things first, Claire. Return my emails to me."

"You have to know it's too late for that. I can't unsee what I've already seen—you cavorting with terrorists and suicide vests."

He sighed. "Well, I was afraid of that. Why Caliban felt

he had to hold a threat over my head is beyond me, and it backfired. So, there's more to my demands."

"Spill. What do you want me to do in exchange for Ethan?"

"Forget about the Christmas Day plot."

She snorted. "Again, too late. You must know about the heightened security surrounding the event."

"I also know your so-called fiancé is a Prospero agent, and he's going to be front and center during the security check. He needs to facilitate the attack by doing nothing."

Mike pinched the bridge of his nose but kept his mouth shut.

"He's going to do his job. You have to know that."

"If the Prospero agent does his job and the Christmas Day plot doesn't go off as planned or at least close to plan, Ethan dies."

Mike's gaze jumped to Claire's pale face, her violet eyes blazing.

"You wouldn't do that. You wouldn't harm Ethan."

Correll coughed. "I admit a fondness for the boy, but I have a greater fondness for power. After the successful completion of the Christmas Day plot, we'll be in a position to take control. We've been setting up our coup for over a year now. We're ready. And now that I've gotten rid of Caliban, I'm ready for my close-up."

Mike's head jerked up.

"What do you mean you've gotten rid of Caliban? Who's Caliban? You mentioned him before."

"Stop the pretense, Claire." Correll laughed, a short bark of a laugh. "If you've been keeping company with a Prospero agent, you know all about Tempest and Caliban."

"Who is he, and if you got rid of him, how is he still sending these emails to you?"

"Hell if I know. The power of a technology I don't understand. In fact, you know Caliban very well. He was your archnemesis at one time."

As dizziness swept over her, Claire gripped the edge of the counter. "You can't mean CIA director Haywood."

"Believe it or not. I took him out, using one of his own superagents to position myself for the takeover. I didn't want to be forever looking over my shoulder. He doesn't matter anymore. Tell your Prospero agent to back off, or your son dies."

Mike reached out and pinched Claire's chin between his fingers. Her gaze locked on to his and he nodded.

"I'll try, Spencer. All I can do is try."

"You do that, Claire, because if our plot is foiled, Ethan dies, just like his father before him."

Claire squeezed her eyes shut, and a burning fury raced through Mike's veins.

"The Christmas Day plot will go off as planned. You have my word."

"I'd feel more comfortable about your assertion if I didn't already know you for a lying bitch, just like your mother."

"I think you're the one who lied to my mother."

"Oh, I admit to a few fibs, but she told me all her assets would be mine when she passed away. She even got an attorney to lie to me. Imagine that."

"Then I guess you murdered her for nothing."

"Not nothing, Claire, just not everything. Let the plot go as planned or lose your son."

He cut off the call, and Claire buried her head in her arm, her shoulders shaking. "He did it. He killed my mother, and now he's going to kill my son."

"He's not going to kill Ethan."

She rolled her head to the side and stared at him through red-rimmed eyes. "What's one boy? What's one little boy compared to a plot to destroy the White House and take over the world?"

"I'll save Ethan, Claire. We'll do both. I'll rescue your son and *then* we'll foil the suicide bombing."

"Ethan's in Colorado. How are you going to do both?"

He stood up and stretched, extending his arms to the ceiling. "I'm only going to do one—save Ethan. That's my number-one priority. You're my number-one priority."

And he'd never been surer of anything in his life.

Chapter Sixteen

The red-eye flight landed in Denver at the break of day. Jack had pulled some national security strings to get them on the flight at the last minute, and then he'd delved into Correll's claim that Jerry Haywood had been Caliban.

Mike picked up the four-wheel-drive rental and they took off for the mountain town where the Chadwicks lived. The snowy landscape flew by in a white blur. They'd exchanged one white Christmas for another.

"Are you sure this will work?" Claire trapped her fidgeting hands between her knees. "How do we even know for sure that Lori is involved?"

"Gut feeling, Claire. Something bothered me about her exchange with Correll in the dining room."

"But she doesn't have to tell you anything. They'll kill her if she does. I'm sure she knows that."

"After tomorrow, Tempest will see all its plans come to nothing. Correll won't be in a position to get back at anyone." Mike turned up the defroster and rubbed the inside of the windshield with his fist.

"Will Prospero be able to root out all the Tempest superagents? Or will another Caliban rise in the vacuum?"

"I'm not sure, but the agency will be crippled all the same, and if the CIA under Haywood had been protecting Tempest all this time, that will all come to an end."

"If Lori doesn't talk, if we can't get to Ethan—" Claire traced a pattern on the passenger window "—what happens? You won't be able to stop Jase and Liam from nabbing Ali-Watkins and thwarting the attack…even if you wanted to."

"You're right. That's not even a possibility at this point." He cupped her cold cheek with his hand. "But this will work. Trust me."

"You asked me to trust you when we set out for Vermont."

"And?" He ran his hand down the length of her hair. "How has that worked out for you?"

"Well, I'm still alive, we've been able to tie Spencer to a terrorist plot and Prospero is about to foil that plot, so I guess it was a smart move on my part." Her bottom lip trembled. "But now they have Ethan."

"I'm going to get him back for you, Claire, and when this is over, we can start fresh—both of us."

"You'll head off into the sunset of your retirement, and I'll take Ethan back to Florida and a normal life." The corner of her mouth turned down.

Was it the thought of going their separate ways that made her sad…or something else? He had to find out, not that her answer would change his current plan to rescue Ethan.

"Will that normal life for you and Ethan include that shrine to Shane?" He sucked in a breath and held it.

She jerked her head toward him, her lips forming an *o*. "I—I'm free of that now. As soon as Yousef is captured, I can put that to rest."

"And what if he's never captured? There is that possibility. We have terrorists on watch lists for years sometimes." His jaw ached with tension.

"I'm done, Mike."

"Good, because if you're my priority, I'm going to have to be yours—or at least a close second to Ethan."

"You weren't just saying that back at the Bennetts'? I was afraid…"

"Afraid of what?" He twirled a lock of her hair around his finger.

"That maybe you'd just gotten carried away with the situation."

"The only thing I'm carried away with is you. I love you, Claire. I want you in my life, whatever that life looks like after this."

Covering her mouth with one hand, she closed her eyes. "You don't know how much I wanted to hear those words from you."

"Sure I do, because I've wanted to hear the same words from you." He held up his hand. "I'm not putting you on the spot. Your focus right now is getting Ethan back, and that's my focus, too, that's my commitment to you."

"I believe you, Mike. I believe you'll get him back."

And that was what he wanted to hear even more than her pronouncements of love. He needed her confidence and faith in him that he could do this. He'd let his Prospero team members bask in the glory of disrupting the Christmas Day plot.

He wanted to rescue Ethan and bask in the glory of a pair of violet eyes.

Almost an hour later, when they turned up the mountain road that led to the Chadwicks', Mike spotted the police car parked on the side of one of the cabins.

He pointed it out to Claire. "I'm guessing that's their place."

"It is. How are we going to play this?"

"You're not going to play anything. You head straight

to the Chadwicks and the rest of the family and talk to the police. Leave the rest in my hands."

She nodded. "Got it."

He parked the rental car down the road from the cabin. No need to give Lori a head start.

Their boots crunched on the ground up to the front door and a sheriff's deputy greeted them. "Can I help you?"

A woman with a long gray braid over one shoulder peered around the officer. "This is Ethan's mother. Claire, we didn't expect you so soon."

Claire brushed past the deputy and embraced the older woman in a hug. "Where else would I be?"

The rest of a very large family crowded around Claire, and Mike looked over their heads and locked eyes with Lori.

She nodded, her face flushed, and stayed in the background.

He kept her in his peripheral vision as Claire made the introductions to about twenty family members. It didn't take long for Lori to shuffle toward the back of the cabin and a side door.

Mike broke away from the group hug and followed Lori outside into the chilly afternoon.

She already had her phone in her hand.

In two long strides, Mike was beside her, snatching the phone from her hand. "I don't think so."

She widened her eyes. "Mr. Brown, is there a problem?"

"I'd say so. Where are they holding Ethan?"

Her mouth dropped open, but fear flashed across her face. He could smell it coming off her.

"I-if I knew that, I'd tell the police. I know it's my fault for not watching him more closely. I'm torn up about it. I can't even face Claire."

"Yeah, I can imagine it would be hard for you to face

Claire after what you've done. How much did Senator Correll pay you, or is he promising something else? Marriage?" He laughed. "Get in line, sister. Correll's a man whore. He spreads around whatever he's got to all the ladies. He must own stock in Viagra."

Lori gasped. "I don't know what you're talking about."

He grabbed her arm, pinching it through the slick material of her jacket. "Let's take a walk."

"Wait." She dug her heels into the frozen ground. "I don't want to leave the house."

"I'll bet you don't." He dragged her away from the cabin. "Especially not with me."

"I don't know what you think is going on. I didn't have anything…"

He shoved the muzzle of his gun in her side. "Cut the crap."

She froze, except for one eyelid that twitched and fluttered. "You wouldn't."

"Kill you?"

"You can't kill me."

"Why? Because you can't tell me where Ethan is if you're dead?"

She parted her dry lips, but didn't answer.

He didn't like roughing up or scaring women. Given his past, it was the hardest part of the job for him when required. But sometimes it was required, and for a woman complicit in the kidnapping of a child—Claire's child—it was more than required.

"Who said anything about killing you, Lori?" He prodded her with his gun farther from the cabin and curled his lip. "Do you know who I am? What I do?"

A line of sweat broke out on her upper lip, despite the cold.

"We reserve death for those who are no longer of any

use to us." He cinched his fingers around her wrist. "I have something altogether different planned for you."

"I don't—I don't know anything. I don't know where they have him."

He loosened his grip. "But he must still be in the area if Correll plans to release him after the White House blows tomorrow."

Lori tripped. "White House? What are you talking about?"

"I guess Correll saves his truly intimate conversations for like-minded ladies such as Julie Patrick."

Lori's face twisted, giving everything away.

"He's here in the area, isn't he?"

Dropping her chin to her chest, she whispered, "Yes. Spencer told me when Claire handed over what was rightfully his from his marriage he'd release Ethan to me. I—I don't know anything about the White House."

"We'll take that into consideration. Now, you're going to call the people who have Ethan and tell them you need to see him."

Her head came up as if on a string. "How am I going to manage that? I have no reason to see Ethan until he's released."

Mike narrowed his eyes. "His medicine. He has asthma and he's going to need his medicine. If anything happens to him before Correll gets his…money, the whole plan is ruined. Now get back on the phone and put it on speaker."

She took the phone from his fingers as if his touch would burn her and placed the call.

A man answered on the first ring. "What's the problem?"

"The boy—he doesn't have his asthma medication. I need to get it to him."

"Are you crazy?"

She lashed back. "Are you? If anything happens to him before the boss gets what he wants, we're all dead."

"Are they lookin' at you? Are the cops lookin' at you?"

"No, not at all. Nobody suspects me." She raised her eyes to meet Mike's.

The man on the other end of the line sniffed. "I'm giving you these GPS numbers. You just have to put 'em in a GPS and you'll get here, but you better delete 'em after... and wait until dark."

Mike cocked his head. The guy didn't sound like an elite Tempest superagent.

When he read off the GPS coordinates, Lori scribbled them on her palm while Mike committed them to memory.

"You get your ass over here, deliver those meds and get out. I don't want the kid seeing you. He's already yapping about Christmas. I don't wanna hear any more out of him."

"I'll be there around seven o'clock."

When she ended the call, Mike took the phone away from her and tapped it against his chin. "Who are the kidnappers?"

"I don't know. I only talked to him once before."

"Him? One guy?"

"Spencer figured the fewer people involved, the better."

"He's a local? Some local scumbag?"

"He's from Denver. Spencer knew someone who knew someone."

Mike chuckled. "And he thought he could take over the reins from Caliban? Caliban would've used his agents for an assignment like this."

Lori looked at him like he was the crazy one instead of her. "Who's Caliban?"

"The good senator really did keep you in the dark, unless you're lying—but you're not that good of a liar. I sensed something between you and Correll the first morning I was there. Too bad I didn't know enough then to act on it."

She held up her hand. "I have the GPS coordinates."

"Wash your hands." He tapped his head. "I have them right here."

CLAIRE DIDN'T KNOW what Mike had said to Lori but when they returned to the house, Lori couldn't even meet her eyes. Hope surged within Claire.

She didn't have to pretend to be the frantic mother for the police. She *was* that mother, but she had something other frantic kidnap victims' mothers didn't have—six feet four inches of solid man, willing to do anything to get her son back for her, even give up his chance to make himself whole by foiling the biggest plot of his career.

She and Mike couldn't get any time alone together, until the end of the day.

Mike had been sticking to Lori all day like a burr, and while the others gathered in the kitchen to order some pizza, Mike brought Lori over to Claire and one of the police officers.

"Lori agreed to take me out to the mountain where she last saw Ethan. I'd just like to get a visual, and Lori could use some air."

Did Mike really think she'd let him do this on his own?

"I think that's a great idea."

The deputy scratched his chin. "It's going to be dark soon."

"Night skiing on Christmas Eve, right? We're not going to be searching for clues, Officer. I just want to see the area." He pinched Claire's shoulder. "It might be too up-setting for you, Claire."

"I'm going stir-crazy in here. Maybe Ethan just needs to hear my voice. If someone does have him, maybe he's not far from that spot."

"I—I agree with Claire." Lori took Claire's coat from

the hook by the door and pressed it into her hands. "And I'd like an opportunity to explain what happened."

With a furrowed brow the deputy's gaze bounced between the three of them. "You're free to do what you like. Be careful, and report anything to us immediately."

"Of course, and you have Lori's phone number if anything happens here."

Mike took her arm and Lori's as he marched them toward the rental car. He stopped at the rear bumper. "You can go back inside now, Claire. Tell him you changed your mind."

"No way. You're going after Ethan now, aren't you? Do you think I'm going to stay here? He's going to need me. What if…?"

"Nothing's going to happen to Ethan. I'll bring him home safely."

"I won't go unless Claire comes along." Lori folded her arms, hunching her shoulders. "Mitch or Mike or whatever the hell his name is pulled a gun on me, threatened me with bodily harm."

Claire put mittened hands over her ears. She didn't want to know how Mike got his results. "I don't care, Lori. It serves you right. I thought you loved Ethan. I thought you cared for him."

Lori sobbed, "I do. Spencer assured me he'd come to no harm."

"No harm? He's been kidnapped by some lethal superagents."

"What?" Lori stepped back.

Mike heaved out a breath. "No, he hasn't, Claire. I guess Correll thought all he'd have to deal with was the local sheriff's department. He hired some dirtbag out of Denver to do the job."

"Oh, my God." Claire's knees weakened and she put

a hand against the car to steady herself. "I don't know if that's better or worse."

"Better, much better." Mike unlocked the doors. "Now let's get going and rescue Ethan."

Mike punched some numbers into the GPS and turned to Lori, whom he'd put in the passenger seat beside him. "Does this guy know your car?"

"No. Spencer sent him a picture of me, that's it."

They followed the directions the GPS intoned, which took them deeper into the mountains. From one ridge, Mike pointed out some lights. "That's probably it, nothing else around here."

He parked the car on an access road and said, "We walk in from here. Claire, you're not coming to the cabin with us. You wait at a distance."

She nodded. She didn't want to upset his plan. She just wanted to be there for Ethan.

"Do you know how to use a gun?" He pulled a second weapon from his coat and held the butt toward her.

"After all we've been through the past few days, I can't believe you're asking me that now." She gripped the handle. "As a matter of fact, I do."

They all exited the car and hiked down the access road with Lori leading the way.

The cabin up ahead played peekaboo with the trees, and Mike took her arm. "You stay right here, behind this tree. Don't go into that cabin. Don't go anywhere near it."

She grabbed his pockets. "Save my little boy."

"That's what I'm here for." He pressed a quick kiss on her mouth and turned, pushing Lori in front of him.

From her hiding place, she heard Lori call out, "It's me. I have the meds."

Claire leaned against the tree, her hair clinging to the

bark. Mike must've remembered that she'd told him about Ethan's asthma scare.

What happened next literally flashed before her eyes in a matter of seconds.

A rectangular patch of light appeared, and then Mike crowded the door behind Lori. There was a shout and then a flash and a bang. Another bang and a long, high scream.

Claire's feet sprouted wings and she flew through the trees to reach the cabin. She tripped over Lori, collapsed at the entrance, rocking and whimpering, blood oozing through the fingers she had clamped to her shoulder.

On her hands and knees, Claire crawled through the door and cried out when her hand met the boot of a man lying on the floor, a puddle of blood beneath his head.

Then her gaze locked on to the tall man in the center of the room, cradling her son in his arms.

Crying out, she launched to her feet and threw herself at both of them. She wrapped her arms around Mike and rested her head against Ethan's legs.

"Mommy?"

"I'm right here, Ethan. Are you okay?"

"I'm okay." He rubbed his sleepy eyes and yanked on Mike's beard. "Mommy, is this Santa?"

"Yes, baby." She pressed her lips against the back of Mike's hand. "This is our Santa."

Epilogue

"Dude, you really didn't miss that much. Ali-Watkins got out of the limo and we swarmed him, dragged him to the staging area we'd set up and disarmed him—or de-vested him."

Mike narrowed his eyes at the young agent, Liam McCabe, stuffing a shrimp puff into his mouth. "Why do people of your generation feel it necessary to call everyone *dude*?"

Claire grabbed Mike's hand. "You're becoming the crotchety old retiree already. Watch yourself."

"Just trying to make you feel better about missing the takedown, du…Mike." Liam pointed to the TV, where Ethan was sitting with Jack and Lola's older son, Eddie, and their twins. "Hey, hey, that's Katie's game."

"What do you mean?" Claire left Mike's side and sauntered up behind the kids. She tousled Ethan's hair as she took in the cartoonish images of the video game playing out across the screen. "How is this Katie's game?"

"She designed it." Liam hung his arm around the shoulders of his girlfriend and kissed the side of her head. "She's a computer whiz, and that's why I got Jack to hire her at Prospero."

"Really?" Claire smiled at Katie. "I'm impressed. Ethan loves all these games."

"Thanks." Katie ducked her head, her asymmetrically cut black hair falling across her face and the gold ring in one nostril gleaming. "I can show him some tricks to beat the game faster."

Katie pushed off the arm of the chair and sat cross-legged in front of the TV with the kids.

Jase came in from the Coburns' kitchen with a sparkling water for his fiancée, Nina, who was expecting a baby—not Jase's. Her ex-fiancé had been one of Tempest's super-agents before he'd gone off the rails and died.

Nina smiled her thanks and patted the cushion beside her. "Sit. I'm fine. I don't need anything else."

Jase perched on the edge of the sofa next to her as if he expected her to go into labor at any minute. He hunched forward toward Jack. "Do you believe Correll that Haywood was Caliban? Or do you think he was covering for himself?"

"I'm not sure. The way Correll bungled that—" he glanced at Ethan "—job in Colorado, I find it hard to believe he was the mastermind behind all the chaos Tempest created, or even second in command behind Haywood. Besides, there was definitely someone trying to ensure his co-operation by sending him those pictures and video. Whether or not that person was Haywood is going to require more research on our part."

"Is he giving up any information in prison?" Lola, Jack's wife, came up behind Claire and ran a hand down the back of her hair. "Sorry, sweetie."

Claire twisted her head over her shoulder. "Do you think I care that Spencer's in prison where he belongs? He should be there for what he did to my mother, too, but the authorities told me there's not enough evidence, even the passing reference he made implicating himself in that phone call. But that's okay. I know in my heart that I got justice for Mom, and the rest of the world now knows him for the lying psychopath he really is."

"I know you don't care about Correll. I'm sorry Jack and I doubted you at first."

Claire turned and hugged her longtime friend. "You sent Mike my way, and I'll always be grateful for that."

Jack snorted. "Yeah, Prospero has become a regular dating service, and in answer to your question *mi amor*, Senator Correll has lawyered up and is keeping mum—so far. We do know he was in contact with the man who beat up Fiona. I think that was more personal than anything else."

"And Hamid?" Claire twisted her fingers in front of her. "Can you tie him to Hamid's death?"

Jack lifted a shoulder. "I think Hamid knew more than he'd been telling you, Claire. When he agreed to meet with you, Tempest had to take him out. I'm sure Correll gave that order, too."

Jase jumped up from the sofa. "Then Caliban could still be out there, and we still haven't found the Oxford Don."

Mike glanced at Claire. "Donald Yousef is not going to be able to hide out for long, and if the real Caliban is out there, we've completely defanged him."

Jack said, "Mike's right. We've even brought in most of the Tempest superagents."

"Did I ever thank you for the use of your palatial estate?" Mike clapped Jase on the back, and Claire knew he was trying to change the subject from Don Yousef.

"Not really. And how did a poor boy from the wrong side of the tracks manage to identify the most expensive bottle of wine in the kitchen?"

Mike jerked his thumb toward Claire. "I had help from the upper-crust broad."

Jase peeked out the curtains. "Someone's coming—tall guy and a petite blonde."

"It must be Max Duvall and Ava Whitman." Lola put her glass down on the coffee table next to her husband. "I invited them. Jack's going to talk to Max about working for Prospero."

Liam popped his head up from the game controller. "Is that a good idea, Jack? The guy was one of Tempest's superagents."

"So was Simon." Nina rubbed her pregnant belly. "They were duped."

"Shh." Lola put a finger to her lips as the doorbell chimed, and she headed into the foyer to greet them.

The conversation lulled when a tall man with black hair and wary dark eyes entered the room with a woman his polar opposite—all blond sunshine and light.

She took the initiative. "Hi, all. I'm Ava. This is Max. Hope you don't mind that we crashed your Christmas party."

Lola hugged the perky blonde and shook hands with Max as the others in the group waved or got up to shake hands with the newcomers.

Ava held up a bottle of Patrón. "I brought a bottle of tequila for a peace offering just in case any of you still think our loyalties lie with Tempest."

"Tequila?" Katie hopped up from the floor. "Why didn't you say so when you walked in?"

Her lame joke broke the tension, and soon all the adults in the room were talking business.

After several minutes, Lola tapped her wineglass with a fork. "You know, you guys live with this stuff 24/7. It's Christmas, or at least five days after Christmas. Let's enjoy the holiday and each other's company without the darkness intruding."

"You heard the good doctor and lady of the house." Jack clapped his hands. "Eddie, take the kids to the playroom and weed out those violent games for the younger ones.

Liam, dude, put some football on and start pouring the shots."

Mike came up behind Claire and curled his arms around her waist. "Is this crazy enough for you?"

"Me? Aren't you going to miss it all?"

"They'll still invite me to their parties." He entwined his fingers with hers. "Come outside with me for a minute. I have a Christmas present for you."

"You've already given me the best gift of all." She kissed him but allowed him to pull her outside into the Florida sunshine.

Mike squinted in the brightness. "I guess we had our white Christmas in Colorado."

"It was the best Christmas of my life. The Chadwicks will never forget what you did for Ethan. They wouldn't have been able to endure another loss."

"You didn't let on how easy the rescue was, did you?"

"Mike." She trailed her fingers across his clean-shaven face. "It wasn't easy for you. You gave up the opportunity to foil the White House plot."

"You heard Liam. It was nothing." He took a flat package, wrapped in glittering Christmas wrap, from behind his back. "Here's your gift."

With a thrill of excitement, she ripped off the paper. She held up a poster board of a large circle with lines crisscrossing the center and moons and stars and astrological signs. "What is this?"

"It's an astrological chart from Madam Rosalee. She did one for you and one for Fiona."

She held it up. "I love it, but what does it all mean?"

"You see this line here?"

"Yes."

"That one means you'll meet a tall, dark stranger and fall in love."

"Really."

"This one means you'll have three children."

"Three? I'd better get busy, then. I've got two to go."

He waggled his eyebrows up and down. "We can get started on that right away."

She rubbed her knuckles across his dark hair, still growing in. "And the two lines that cross here? What do they mean?"

"They mean you'll live happily ever after with the man of your dreams, once you find him."

"You mean that tall, dark stranger?" She threw her arms around his neck. "I've already met him, and I'm ready. I'm ready for my happily-ever-after."

* * * * *

MILITARY GRADE MISTLETOE

JULIE MILLER

In honour of the seventy-fifth anniversary of
Camp Pendleton, home of the
1st Marine Battalion.

My dad and brother were both once stationed
there.

For the real Muffy. Yes, that dog is a he.
And yes, he's in charge. Just ask him.

Prologue

"You're not the first Marine this has happened to."

But it was the first time it had happened to *him*. Master Sergeant Harry Lockhart didn't fail. When he was given a mission, he got the job done. No matter what it cost him. But this? All the doctors, all the physical training and rehab, all the therapy—hell, he'd talked about things nobody knew about him, and it had gutted him worse than that last firefight that had sent him stateside in the first place—and they were still going to give him the boot?

Harry didn't know who he was going to be if he couldn't be part of the Corps, anymore.

His given name was Henry Lockhart Jr., but nobody called him by his daddy's name unless he or she outranked him or wanted a fist in his face. Henry Sr. was serving time in a prison in Jefferson City, Missouri for a variety of crimes, the worst of which was being a lousy excuse for a father. Between Henry's drinking, neglect and natural affinity for violence, it was a miracle Harry and his older sister, Hope, had survived to adulthood. Hope wouldn't have done that, even, if at the ripe old age of nine, Harry hadn't picked up his daddy's gun and shot one of the dogs that had attacked her when she tried to leave the house to get him food so he wouldn't starve.

A muscle ticked beside his right eye as a different memory tried to assert itself. But, with a mental fist, he shoved that particular nightmare into the tar pit of buried images from all the wars he'd fought, determined to keep it there.

"How many years have you been in the Corps?" The doctor was talking again.

If Dr. Biro hadn't also been a lieutenant colonel, Harry might have blown him off. But Biro was not only in charge of his fitness assessments, he was a decent guy who didn't deserve his disrespect. Harry met his superior's gaze across the office desk. "Seventeen, sir."

Biro nodded. "A career man."

"Yes, sir."

Hope was the only family he'd ever had, the only person he'd ever trusted, until he'd enlisted in the United States Marine Corps the day after he'd graduated from high school. The Corps had whipped his rebellious butt into shape, given him a home with regular meals on most days, introduced him to the best friends he had in the world and given him a reason to wake up every day and live his life.

Now his sister was married and had her own family. So he'd really, really like to keep the one he'd found. His physical wounds from that last deployment had left their mark on his stiff, misshapen face, but the scars were a sign that those had healed. He knew it was the mental wounds the lieutenant colonel was worried about.

Not for the first time in his life, Harry was going to have to prove himself worthy. He was going to have to earn someone else's unshakable trust in him again.

He was going to have to relearn how to trust himself.

Do this. That was Harry's motto. He couldn't lose the only home he had left. He scrubbed his fingers over the bristly cut of his regulation short hair. "You said I was improving."

"You are."

The medical brass seemed to like it when he talked, so he tried again. "I've done everything you asked of me these past four months."

Biro grinned. "I wish all my patients were as dedicated to following my orders as you. Physically, you could handle light duty, maybe even a training assignment."

"But…? Tell me the truth, Doc." Was he washed out of the Corps or not?

The lieutenant colonel leaned back in his chair. He wasn't smiling now. "You need to get your head on straight or we can't use you."

"You're not comfortable sending me out in the field?"

"I'd be doing you a disservice if I did." Biro leaned forward again, propping the elbows of his crisply pressed lab coat on the desktop. "At the risk of oversimplifying everything you've gone through—something broke inside you. I believe it's healing, but the scar is still new and I don't want you to rip it open again."

"I appreciate the honest answer." Harry did some mental calculations on how long he'd have to play this game before he could come in for his next assessment and change the doctor's prognosis. "So, peace and quiet, huh? Normalcy?"

The lieutenant colonel didn't understand how far away from *normal* civilian life was for Harry. The jarheads he served with didn't care where he'd come from or how rough his altered face looked, as long as he did his job. But on the outside, expectations were different, and he was ill-equipped to handle them.

"That's my prescription."

"And I don't need pills on the outside? I just need a shrink?"

Lt. Col. Biro opened a folder and pulled a pen from his chest pocket. "That's my recommendation. If you can't sleep, or the mood swings become unbearable, call me. Otherwise, take the time off. Relax. Give yourself a few weeks to reconnect with civilian life. Enjoy the holidays. Get yourself a Christmas tree and eat too many sweets. Kiss a pretty girl and watch football all New Year's Day. Whatever you like to do to celebrate." *Relax* and *celebrate* sounded like daunting tasks for a man who didn't have much experience with the examples on the good doctor's list. "If you still want to after that, make an appointment with my office in January and we'll reevaluate your fitness to serve. Or, if you decide the clean break is what you need, I'll have your honorable medical discharge waiting for you. It's not like you haven't earned it."

Harry stood, clasping his utility cover, the Corps' term for a canvas uniform hat, between his hands. "I'll be back, sir."

The lieutenant colonel nodded before signing off on his medical leave papers and dismissing him. "You're from Kansas City, Missouri, right?" Harry nodded. "You might have snow there this time of year."

What was Biro going to prescribe now? Building a snowman to get in touch with the inner child Harry had never had the chance to be? "Sir?"

"My best buddy from basic training was from KC. I've always enjoyed my visits. I'll have my aide give you some recommendations for therapists you can see there."

"Thank you, sir."

Harry's cover fit snugly over his head as he pulled the bill down and hiked outside into the sunny Southern California weather. He drove to the base housing he shared with two other Non-commissioned Officers, or NCOs, slammed the door on his truck and hurried inside before he cussed up a blue streak that would have all of Camp Pendleton talking by sundown.

Thankfully, his bunk mates were both on duty so he had the house to himself. But that empty echo of the door closing behind him was a curse as much as it was a blessing. Damn, he missed the way his best friend used to greet him.

The remembered thunder of deadly fireworks and images of blood and destruction seared him from the inside out, leaving him with beads of sweat on his forehead and his hands clutched into fists.

Hell. The doc was right. His head wasn't on straight.

Using some of the calming techniques Lt. Col. Biro had taught him, Harry breathed in deeply through his nose and out through his mouth. Then he grabbed the pull-up bar hanging in his bedroom doorway and did ten quick reps until he felt the burn in his biceps, triceps and shoulders, and the anger that had flared behind his eyes receded.

He took the pull-up bar off the door frame and tossed it onto the bed beside the duffel bag he'd already packed that morning, having known he was either shipping out or going home by the time the medical team was done with him today.

You need to get your head on straight or we can't use you.

The lieutenant colonel's blunt words made the tiny, impersonal bedroom swim around him. Squeezing his eyes shut against the dizzying, unsettled feeling he hadn't felt since he was a little boy wondering if he was going to eat that day, Harry sank onto the edge of the mattress. He needed to find that happy place inside him. He needed to feel the holidays and the hope they inspired. He needed to find a way to push aside the nightmares and the anger and learn how to cope again. Or else the brass wouldn't let him be a Marine anymore.

On instinct, he opened his duffel bag and pulled out a bulky, crumpled manila envelope that held the lifeline to sanity that had gotten him through that last hellish deployment and the long days in the hospital and physical therapy which had followed. He brushed his fingers over the torn envelope flap before sliding his thumb underneath and peeking inside. Now here was a little bit of sunshine. He pulled out a homemade angel ornament that had been a gift to him last Christmas. Then he studied the stack of cards and letters that were battered and smudged from travel and rereading. Words from a compassionate oracle who understood him better than he knew himself. His stiff jaw relaxed with the tremor of a smile that couldn't quite form on his lips.

Harry hadn't been this uncertain since he was that starving little boy with a black eye and clothes that didn't fit. He didn't need a shrink. He needed the Corps. But he'd need a miracle to make that happen. He needed the angel from all these cards and letters to work her magic on him again.

None of them were recent, but that didn't matter. The effect on him was always the same. He opened the very first letter and started to read.

Dear MSgt. Lockhart...

Chapter One

> *Dear Daisy,*
> *Merry Christmas from your Secret Santa.*

Daisy Gunderson stared at the gift tag, dotted with sparkles of glitzy snow, in the top right drawer of her desk and wondered who hated her enough to wage this terror campaign against her. This should be the happiest time of year for her, with the holidays and her winter break from school coming soon. Either somebody thought this sick parade of presents left on her desk or in her mailbox in the faculty work room was a clever idea for a joke, or that person intentionally wanted to ruin Christmas for her.

Typically, she made a big deal of the holidays, as evidenced by the greenery and ornaments decorating her classroom, and the hand-carved menorah and colorful Kwanzaa mat she had on display that had been gifts from former students. But the red glass candy dish filled with rat poison, the decapitated elf ornament and the X-rated card that had nothing to do with holiday greetings hidden away in her drawer were disturbing signs that not everyone shared the same reverence for celebrating this time of year.

The gifts were an eerie reminder of the tragic mistake she'd made three years ago that had cost her so dearly. But Brock was locked up in a prison cell, and would be until her roots turned gray. Daisy had already called the prison to confirm Brock Jantzen hadn't escaped or been accidentally released. These gifts couldn't be his handiwork. Men in prison who'd tried to kill their ex-girlfriends didn't get to send them cards and presents, right?

Daisy inhaled and let the long exhale flutter her lips. Of course not. These gifts had nothing to do with Brock. Or losing her father. Or even losing her mother, in a way. They had nothing to do with the scars on her chest and belly or her missing spleen.

Deciding that her thinking made it so, Daisy adjusted her purple-framed eyeglasses at her temples, spared a glance for the lone student muttering at the laptop on his desk, then looked up at the clock on the wall to wonder how much longer it was going to take Angelo to finish his essay before they could both go home for the day. Since she'd promised to give the teenager all the time he needed to complete his work, Daisy closed the drawer, picked up her pen and went back to grading papers.

But her thoughts drifted to the small stack of letters she'd locked away in a keepsake box under her bed at home. Letters from a Marine overseas. Short, stilted and impersonal at first. Then longer, angrier, sadder. Master Sergeant Harry Lockhart yearned for quiet and routine just as much as he longed to complete the job he'd been sent to the Middle East to accomplish. She could tell he loved serving his country. That he loved the military dog he worked with, Tango. That he grieved the young men and native soldiers he'd trained and lost. She'd grieved right along with him when he'd written to say that Tango had been killed. Those letters had been part of a class writing project she'd initiated last year, with help from a friend at church, Hope Taylor, who had connected Daisy to her brother and his unit. She'd give anything to hear from

Harry Lockhart again, even one of his short missives about the heat or the sand in his bunk. But sadly, those letters had stopped coming months ago. She hoped the unthinkable hadn't happened to her Marine. More likely, he'd simply tired of the friendship after the class had ended and those students had stopped writing the servicemen and women with whom they'd been pen pals.

Now the only notes she received depicted graphic sexual acts and violence. All under the guise of a friendly game of Secret Santa.

She'd reported the gifts to her principal, and he'd made a general announcement about the appropriateness of everyone's anonymous gifts at the last staff meeting. And, she'd alerted the building police officer, who promised to keep an eye on her room and try to figure out when the gifts were being left for her. But, short of canceling the faculty party and gift exchange, and ruining everyone else's Christmas fun, there was little more she could do besides staying alert, and doing a little sleuthing of her own to try and figure out who was sending them. Daisy wondered if the wretched gifts might even be coming from someone who hadn't drawn her name in the annual gift swap—a disgruntled student, perhaps. Or maybe there was someone else in her life who thought this terror campaign was a cute way to squash her determination to make the most of every holiday celebration.

If that was the case, she refused to give in and take down one tiny piece of tinsel or play her Mannheim Steamroller music any less often. She already had enough reasons to mourn and resent the holidays. The Scrooges didn't get to win. If grief, abandonment and solitude couldn't keep her from saying *Merry Christmas* every chance she got, then a few morbid trinkets from a disturbed mind weren't going to make her say, *Bah, Humbug*, either.

"Finished. Five hundred and two words." A small laptop plunked down in front of her on her desk. "Before the deadline."

Daisy smiled up at Angelo Logan, a favorite student with as much talent as he had excuses for not doing his work. She knew no one in his immediate family had gone to college. And since that was a goal of his, she didn't mind putting in some extra time and pushing him a little harder than some of her other students. She skimmed the screen from the title, *The Angel and the Devil*, down to the word count at the bottom of the page. "Wow. Two words over the minimum required. Did you break a sweat?"

"You said to be concise." A grin appeared on his dark face.

"Did you map out why you're deserving of the scholarship?"

"Yeah. I talked about my home life, about being a twin and about what I can do for my community if I get a journalism degree."

Daisy arched a skeptical eyebrow. "In five hundred and two words?"

Angelo tucked the tails of his white shirt back beneath his navy blue sweater and returned to his desk to pull on his blue school jacket. "Can I have my phone back now, Ms. G?"

"May I?" she corrected automatically, and looked up to see him roll his deep brown eyes. The standard rule in her class was "No cell phones allowed," and anytime a student entered her room, he or she had to deposit their phones in the shoe bag hanging beside the door. Getting a phone back meant the student was free to go. Daisy smiled at the seventeen-year-old who looked so put upon by grinchy teachers who held him accountable for procrastinated essays and college application deadlines, when he probably just wanted to take off with his buddies for some Thursday night R & R. "You're too good a writer to miss this opportunity." She turned the laptop around. "Email me this draft and I'll get it edited tonight. I can go over any changes that need to be made with you tomorrow. Then we can send the whole thing off before Monday's deadline."

Angelo zipped back to her desk and attached the file to an email. "I've got basketball after school tomorrow. I won't be able to come in. Coach will bench me if I miss practice two days in a row."

Ah, yes. Coach Riley and the pressure he put on his players, despite the academic focus of Central Prep. "Can you do lunch?"

"Yes, ma'am."

She pointed to the shoe storage bag hanging by the door. "Grab your phone. Have a good night and I'll see you tomorrow."

But he didn't immediately leave. He exhaled a sigh before setting his backpack on the corner of her desk and digging inside. He pulled out a squished plastic bag with a red ribbon tied around the top and shyly dropped a gift of candy on her desk. "Thank you, Ms. G."

An instinctive alarm sent a shock of electricity through her veins. But then she saw the blush darkening Angelo's cheeks and realized she couldn't be paranoid about everything with a gift tag this time of year. Plus, the smushed present didn't look anything like the carefully prepared gifts she'd received from her Secret Santa. She feigned a smile before genuinely feeling it, and picked up the gift. "Are these your grandmother's homemade caramels?"

"Yeah. She wanted to thank you for the extra hours you're putting in on me."

Daisy untied the bow and pulled open the bag to sniff the creamy brown-sugary goodies. This present was safe.

She'd seen it delivered, and there was nothing hinky about the candies wrapped in this modest bag. She could let herself enjoy it. "I love her caramels. She made a special batch without nuts for me?"

The blush faded as the grin returned. "I don't know why you want to eat them without the pecans, but she remembered that was the way you like them."

Daisy pulled out one of the individually wrapped caramels and untwisted the waxed paper. "Hey, between her and me, we're going to get you into college."

"Yes, ma'am. Um… I wanted to…"

Wondering how long Angelo was going to stand there before he said whatever was making him shift back and forth so nervously, Daisy popped the caramel in her mouth and started to fill the awkward silence. "These are the yummiest—"

She almost choked on the chewy treat when a sharp knock rapped on her door. "'Lo. You coming or what?" Although the baggy jeans and sideways ball cap were a vastly different look than the school uniform Angelo still wore, Albert Logan shared his twin brother's face. "Just because you got in trouble with the teacher doesn't mean I have to be late."

"I'm not in trouble," Angelo insisted.

"I don't care. I just know I have to drive your sorry ass home before I meet the guys."

"Granny's going to kill you if you skip dinner again."

"She ain't killed me yet." Albert jerked his head down the hallway toward the exit. "Move it."

"Hey, Albert." Daisy stood and offered a friendly greeting.

"Hey, Ms. G."

Despite looking alike, the two brothers couldn't be more different. "You know, my offer to stay after school and work with students who need extra help extends to you, too."

"I ain't in your class no more."

"You aren't anymore," she corrected. "I'm here with Angelo. I could easily tutor you, too. Get your grades back up so you can be on the basketball team again."

"Whatever." He turned down her repeated offer to help him raise his D's and F's into acceptable grades and pointed to his brother. "My car leaves in five. Be in it or walk home."

Although she was already plotting different arguments to convince Albert to get the help he needed, Daisy trained her smile on Angelo while he zipped his backpack and hurried to grab his phone. "Be sure to thank your grandmother for the caramels."

"Bye."

Once the teens had left her room, the silence of an empty school long after classes had ended closed in on her. Shaking off the instant sensation of loneliness before it could take hold of her, Daisy packed up her pink leather shoulder bag. She jotted a note to Bernie Riley, the boys' basketball coach, asking him to have a chat with his former player to encourage Albert to take her, or someone else, up on the tutoring offer. Without sports to keep him interested in school, she feared he'd wind up dropping out without a diploma. Then she grabbed her scarf and wrapped it around the neckline of her tunic sweater and pulled her coat from the closet before shutting off the lights and locking the door.

She'd make one quick stop at the faculty lounge to drop off the note, then head out. Besides hurrying home to let out her three dogs to do their business, she needed to get the place tidied up before showing the upstairs suite to the potential renter who'd answered her ad in the paper. Her friend Hope's husband was a KCPD cop, and he'd done a routine search on the guy and a couple of other tenant prospects to ensure they didn't have a criminal record or pose any obvious threat to her.

Having the dogs with her eased her concerns about living alone. But with the advent of the creepy cards and gifts, she'd decided that having a man on the premises, preferably an older one who reminded her of the security her father had once provided, would scare away whoever was threatening her. Besides, one of the hazards of living alone in the two-story 1920s Colonial her parents and grandparents had once lived in was that she was spending a small fortune renovating it. With taxes due at the end of the year and her savings already tapped out, thanks to the new HVAC system and roof she'd been forced to install, she could use the extra income of a tenant to get through the expense of the holidays.

Her steps slowed on the hallway tiles as her imagination surged ahead of her logic. Of course, the idea that her tenant might wind up being a serial killer, or even the sicko who was sending her that crap, was more than a little unsettling.

But no, Officer Pike Taylor had vetted this guy, so he couldn't be a danger to her. She sifted her fingers into the wavy layers of her hair and shook it off her shoulders. "Stop imagining the worst, Daisy Lou, and go home."

Her stop in the faculty lounge and work room revealed that she wasn't the only staff member working late this evening. "Hey, Eddie."

Daisy dropped her bag onto the chair beside one of the school's science teachers. It hit the seat with a thunk and Eddie Bosch laughed. "Taking a little work home tonight?"

"Just some papers to grade. And my laptop." Plus all the items a woman would keep in her purse, along with a few emergency snacks, a stash of dog treats and an extra pair of shoes in case the knee-high boots she wore got too wet with the snow outside and she needed to change before her feet froze. Daisy shook her head as her friend in the loose tie and pullover sweater grinned. "I guess I carry my life in there, don't I?"

"Well, you won't have to go to the gym and work out if you keep lifting that thing." He closed the laptop he'd been working on and pointed a warning finger at her. "Now about that chiropractor bill you'll be getting…"

"Ha, ha." Squeezing his shoulder at the teasing remark, she circled around him and went to the wall of cubbies that served as the staff's mailboxes and searched the alphabetized labels for Bernie Riley's name.

She was glad Eddie had gotten to the point where he could joke with her. When they'd first started at Central Prep together, he'd had a sadness about him he wore like a shroud. He'd been new to Kansas City, had moved there for a fresh start after losing his fiancée to a long illness. Daisy had made it her personal mission to cheer him up and make him feel welcome. Now, he often made it feel like she was working with the teasing big brother she, as an only child, had never had.

But the comfortable camaraderie quickly ebbed as her gaze landed on her mailbox. She backed away when she saw the corner of a red envelope lying there.

Daisy startled at the hand that settled between her shoulder blades. "Don't worry." Eddie reached around her to pull the red envelope from her box and hold it out to her. "It's the teacher appreciation gift from the school board. A gift card to your favorite coffee shop. We all got one."

Taking the envelope, she clutched it to her chest, nodding her thanks. Eddie and a few other teachers were close enough friends that she'd shared some of the weird messages she'd been receiving. They'd all agreed that none of the staff could be responsible, and were now on the lookout for any signs of a disturbed student who might be sending the gifts. She appreciated that Eddie and the others were protective of her.

He pointed to other red envelopes still sitting in the mailboxes of teachers who'd already gone home, to confirm his explanation. "It's nice that they remember us each year. Although I'd trade gourmet coffee for a bump in salary if it'd do us any good."

Daisy agreed. "I hear ya."

He nodded toward the paper in her hand. "Is Riley giving you grief about keeping Angelo out of practice again?"

During basketball season, Bernie Riley gave everyone grief. "I think we've reached a mutual understanding."

"You mean, you've agreed to do things his way."

"Bernie and I both have the students' best interests at heart. He let Angelo stay with me today, and I'll adjust my schedule tomorrow." She held up her message about Angelo's brother. "Actually, I'm hoping he'll help me with Albert."

"Albert doesn't have half the brains Angelo does."

She was surprised to hear the insult. "Maybe we just haven't found the right way to motivate him yet."

"Uh-huh." Eddie pulled away and opened his satchel to stow his laptop. "Deliver your note and I'll walk you out." He nodded to the window overlooking the parking lot and the orange glow of the street lamps creating pockets of light in the murky evening air. "I hate how early the sun goes down this time of year."

Smile, Daisy Lou. Don't let anyone bring you down.

"Me, too." Daisy stuffed the note into Coach Riley's cubby and put on her insulated coat and gloves while Eddie pulled on a stocking cap and long wool coat. "Although, I do love it when the sky is clear at night, and the moon reflects off all the snow." She pulled the hood with its faux fur trim over her head. "In the daylight, the city snow looks dirty, but at night it's beautiful."

"You're a regular Pollyanna, aren't you," he accused with a smile, holding the door open for her. "It's twenty degrees, it's dark and I'm tired of shoveling my driveway."

"Scrooge."

"Nanook." He followed her out the door and walked her across the nearly empty lot to her car. "Are you expecting a blizzard I don't know about?"

She fished her keys out of her bag and unlocked the doors. "Fourteen degrees? That's plenty cold enough for me."

Eddie swiped his gloved hand across her windshield, clearing a swath through the blowing snow that had gathered there. "Want me to scrape this off for you?"

"You're a scholar and a gent, Mr. Bosch." Daisy thanked him for his gallant offer, but shooed him back to his own car. "The windshield wipers will take care of it. Go get warm. I'll see you in the morning."

"See ya. And hey, I didn't mean to sound flippant earlier. If there's anything I can do to help you with Albert, let me know."

"I will. Thanks." With a smile that no longer felt forced, Daisy climbed inside. Once she had her car started, he waved and trudged away to his own vehicle.

Daisy locked her doors and shivered behind the wheel, waiting for the wipers and defroster to clear her windows. Allowing the engine time to warm up, she crossed her arms and leaned back against the headrest, closing her eyes. She took on a lot this time of year, and she was tired. The stress of dealing with her Secret Santa, and the mental battle not to compare his gifts to the terror campaign

Brock had waged against her three years ago, were taking their toll, as well. It was a challenge to get eight hours of uninterrupted sleep when every sound in the old house woke her. She made up for the fatigue by stealing short naps when she could. Like right now. Just a few minutes to rest before…

Daisy's eyes popped open as a sixth sense nudged her fully awake.

Someone was watching her.

She wiped the condensation off the inside of her window and peered out. Her gaze first went to Eddie's car. But he was busy brushing the thin layer of snow off the windows and top. His back was to her until he tossed the scraper into the back and climbed in behind the wheel. Then he was on his cell phone, chattering away in an animated conversation as he backed out of his parking space.

She pulled her glasses away from her nose to let the foggy lenses clear before sliding them back into place and scanning the rest of the staff parking lot. There were only four vehicles left. Coach Riley and the girls' basketball coach had both parked near the gym entrance while they finished with practice. She recognized the truck and van driven by the school custodians, as well.

The uneasy sensation of being watched crept beneath the layers she wore, making her shiver as if a cold finger was running along her spine. But a check of her rearview mirror revealed no one. Not one visible soul. Certainly no one spying on her.

Unless that person was hidden.

Behind one of the Dumpsters. Or around the corner of the building. Or peering out from the shadows of a dark room in the nearly empty school.

"Really?" Daisy smacked the steering wheel and pulled on her seat belt, irritated with the way her tired mind could play tricks on her. Those stupid gifts had spooked her more than she'd realized. "You are perfectly safe," she reminded herself, shifting the car into gear. Turning on her lights, she drove out of the parking lot. "The bad guys don't get to win." If she lived her life like a paranoid mouse, they *would* win. And she wasn't about to let that happen. She turned on a radio station playing Christmas music 24/7 and belted out rock anthems and traditional carols all the way home.

Daisy was a little hoarse from the songfest by the time she pulled into the detached garage behind her home. She pushed the remote button, closing the door behind her before unlocking her car and climbing out. Night had fallen, so she flipped the switch to turn on the Christmas lights lining the garage roof and fence, knowing they'd cast enough light to illuminate her path across the sidewalk to the deck and backyard entrance to her home. She smiled when she opened the door and looked out into the fenced-in yard. Beyond the edges of the walkway and deck she'd cleared, the red, green, orange, blue and white lights reflected off the snow like the warm glow of a sunset.

After pulling her hood up over her ears, she shut the door behind her and locked it. The damp bite of wintry air chapped her cheeks and hurried her steps past the gate and up onto the deck where the motion sensor light over the back door popped on, turning a small circle of night into day.

"Daisy? Is that you?"

Startled by the voice in the night, Daisy spun around. Once she'd identified the disembodied voice, she drifted beyond the edge of the light to bring her neighbor to the north into focus. "Good evening, Jeremiah." Although Jeremiah Finch's balding head was little more than a balloon-shaped shadow above the hedge on his side of the fence, she recognized his little Chihuahua in a pink and black sweater underneath the hedge where the snow wasn't as deep. As much as her neighbor loved his little princess, he liked to keep his yard in pristine condition, and would either immediately clean up after the dog, or hook her onto a leash and lead her to the bushes as he had tonight. "I see Suzy is bundled up against the cold. New sweater?"

"Knitted it myself. Are you coming down with a cold?" he asked, no doubt hearing the rasp in her voice.

"I'm fine. Just a little too much singing. And you?"

"I'm well. Suzy and I will be going in now. Good night."

"Good night." As formal and shallow as their conversations might be, Mr. Finch had proved himself to be a good neighbor. Besides maintaining a beautiful home, he didn't mind picking up her mail and watching over her house when she had to leave town. And she often returned the favor.

After he and Suzy had gone inside, Daisy slipped her key into the dead bolt lock.

One sharp, deep bark and the excited sound of yapping dogs told Daisy her furry family already knew she was home. She peeked through the sheers in the window beside the door and saw her beloved trio gathering in the mud room with tails wagging to welcome her before pushing open the door. "Yoo-hoo! Mama's home."

Muffy, her little tiger of a Shih Tzu led the charge out the door. A silver-and-white-haired boy cursed with a girl's name by the elderly owner who had to surrender him when she moved into a nursing facility, Muffy often made up for the insult by being the toughest and loudest guard dog he could be, if not the most ferocious-looking. Patch, her deaf Jack Russell terrier mix, took his cues from the other dogs, and followed right behind the smaller dog, no doubt barking because Muffy was. Both stopped for a friendly greeting and some petting before dashing out into the snowy yard. Patch, especially, loved being outside, leaping from snow bank to snow bank and snuzzling through the drifts as though feeling the cold against his skin made him giddy.

Her senior dog, Caliban, hobbled out the door on three legs. Daisy got the feeling that when her biggest dog stopped for a scratch around the ears, the Belgian Malinois was humoring her rather than seeking her affection. Poor guy. He'd spent a career at KCPD before the cancerous tumor that had led to the amputation of his left front leg forced him into retirement, and then he hadn't been able to live at his handler's home because the K-9 officer's child was allergic. Daisy reached inside the door to grab one of the rope toys that seemed to be the tan-and-black dog's only joy and tossed it out into the snow. As she watched him trot down the two steps into the yard, Daisy's heart squeezed in her chest. The experts who claimed that dogs didn't feel emotions didn't know Caliban. That dog was sad. He'd lost his job, lost his favorite person, lost his home and routine. When Pike Taylor had asked if she could take the dog for the last year or so he had left, Daisy had willingly opened up her home and her heart. Muffy and Patch had welcomed the older dog, although the two little spitfires made him cranky at times. Caliban had a good home here, but Daisy was still looking for the key to breaking through that reserve of his.

Smiling at the distinct personalities of each of her *children*, Daisy crossed to the railing to watch her three charges. Muffy was all business, inspecting the perimeter of the yard and trees along the back fence. Caliban was nosing around the gate and garage, avoiding the snow as much as possible. And Patch…

"Patch?" Daisy hiked her purse behind her hip and leaned over the railing. Where had he snuck off to? He wouldn't answer her summons unless he was looking right at her or following one of the other dogs. "Where did you go?"

Daisy looked down to see the clear impression of man-sized boot prints in the snow. The security light created shadows through the deck railings that had obscured them earlier. But there they were, a messy set of prints circling around the deck to the gas and water meters on the back of the house. She spotted Patch, his muzzle and jowls white with a snowy beard, following the tracks past the meters to the dormant lilac bushes at the corner of the house.

That wasn't right. Goose bumps pricked across Daisy's skin. She crossed to the side railing and squinted into the darkness beyond her porch light. Between the blowing snow and the shadows, she couldn't make out whether the tracks ended at the side of the house or if they continued into Mr. Finch's yard next door. Or maybe they'd originated from there? Maybe Jeremiah had spotted something that concerned him in the backyard. Still, she couldn't see the fastidious gentleman climbing over the chain-link fence when there was a perfectly good gate between the house and garage that granted easy access to the yard. It would be hard to tell exactly where the footprints led unless she went out in the knee-deep drifts to look with a flashlight. And as much as Daisy wanted answers, she wasn't keen on being anywhere alone in the dark.

She swallowed hard, trying to come up with a logical explanation as to why someone would be wandering around her backyard. She'd had the same utility worker from the city for years. He knew his way around her backyard, and didn't mind the dogs when they were out. Maybe he had a substitute walking his route, someone who didn't know there was only one gate. Patch spent a lot of time snuffling around in each footprint until he lifted his leg and peed in one. Why were there so many tracks? Had more than one person been in the backyard?

"Muffy? Caliban?" She put her chilled lips together and tried to whistle, but she doubted even a dog could hear the wimpy sound that came out.

Then she spotted Caliban's white muzzle as he carried his toy back up the steps to dutifully sit beside her. "Good boy." Had he sensed her fear? Did he just have impeccable timing? "Good, good boy." Daisy scratched around his ears and rewarded him by pulling on one end of the rope and letting him enjoy a gentle game of tug of war. But the game ended quickly when Caliban released the toy and spun toward the back door. A split second later, Muffy zipped past her, barking like mad. That response could mean only one thing. They'd heard the doorbell at the front of the house. She had a visitor.

Although she was hardly prepped for company, she was more than ready to go inside. She caught Patch's attention and gave the signal for him to come. He dashed through the doorway in front of her.

The doorbell chimed again while she bolted the back door. The dogs raced ahead of her, yapping and tracking snow across the long, narrow rug and refinished oak of her hallway floor. Patch leaped over the two plastic tubs of Christmas ornaments she'd stacked beside the stairs, waiting for the tree she planned to get this weekend. Daisy hurried after them, dumping her purse on the bottom step of the staircase leading up to the second floor, pulling off her hood and stuffing her gloves into her pockets.

She pushed her way through the semi-circle of barking dogs, put Caliban and Patch into a sit and picked up Muffy, her brave boy who had the most trouble following orders and greeting an unfamiliar visitor. If this was the potential tenant Pike Taylor had okayed for her, she wanted time to explain that her pack of dogs were looking for treats and tummy rubs, not the opportunity to take a bite out of a stranger. Daisy flipped on the Christmas lights over the front porch and made sure the dead bolt was engaged before peering through the window beside the door.

"Wow." She mouthed the word, fogging up the glass.

The man standing on her front porch was hot, in a rugged sort of way. He stood six feet tall, give or take an inch. He wore a black stocking cap fitted tightly to his head and a beige coat that pulled at his broad shoulders and thick arms. With his hands down at the sides of his jeans and his legs braced apart, he stood there, unmoving. If it wasn't for the puffs of his warm breath clouding around his gray eyes, she'd have thought him a statue, impervious to the cold. Daisy's throat went dry at the inverse response of heat that could be nerves, or something decidedly more… aware…that he triggered inside her.

Not the fatherly figure she'd been hoping for. His face was a little too craggy to be handsome. The scars that peeked above the collar of his sweater and crept up his neck to the edge of his mouth and cheek to circle around most of his left eye, coupled with the stern set of his square jaw, added to his harsh look. She was certain Pike wouldn't send her anyone she wouldn't be safe with. Still, *safe* was a relative term. This guy didn't project calm reassurance so much as he looked as though he could scare off anyone who glanced crosswise at him. Although he would fulfill the purpose of having a tenant, she wasn't sure she'd be comfortable having a man like him in the house.

Still, if Pike said he was okay, she'd at least interview him.

She startled when his head suddenly tilted and his gaze shifted to her silhouette in the window. He'd caught her staring at him. He didn't smile, didn't wave an acknowledgement, didn't react, period. He simply locked his gaze onto hers until she muttered, "My bad," and hurried to atone for her rudeness. Muffy whined in her arms, and Daisy unbolted the door and opened it, leaving the steel-framed storm door secured between them.

The rush of heat she'd felt dissipated with the chill that seeped through the glass. "Hi. Are you here about the room to rent? I thought we weren't meeting until after dinner."

"Master Sergeant Harry Lockhart, ma'am," he announced in a deep, clipped voice. "Are you Daisy Gunderson?"

Recognition and relief chased away her trepidation and she smiled. "Master Serg…? Harry? Pen pal Harry?" She plopped Muffy down between the other dogs, then unlatched the storm door and pushed it wide open. "Harry Lockhart! I'm so excited to finally meet you." The dogs followed her out onto the brick porch and danced around their legs. Daisy threw her arms around Harry's neck, pressed her body against his rock-hard chest and hugged him tight. "Welcome home!"

Chapter Two

Welcome home?

Harry's vision blurred as something gray and furry darted between his legs. A mix of squeals and barks blended with the deafening boom and shouting voices inside his head, and his nose was suddenly filled with the stench of burnt earth and raw skin.

One moment, the memories were there, but in the next, he blanked them out and focused on the here and now. His body was hyper-aware of the softness wrapped around him like a blanket, and the creamy chill of the woman's cheek pressed against the side of his neck.

Daisy Gunderson was on her tiptoes hugging him. Bear-hugging him. Giving him a squeeze-the-stuffing-out-of-him kind of hug. What happened to polite introductions and handshakes? This wasn't the greeting he'd expected. She wasn't the woman he'd expected.

But when a woman hugged a man like that, it was his natural instinct to wrap his arms around her and…pat her back. He could hear his men ribbing him now, giving him grief over his lousy moves with the ladies the same way he gave them grief about staying sharp and keeping their heads down. He'd been short on this kind of contact for a long time. Months. Years, maybe. The instinctive part of him wanted to tighten his grip around her. A baser part of him wanted to reach down and see if the curves on the bottom half matched the ones flattened against him up top—or whether all that luscious body he felt was just the pillows of her coat squished between them. A different part of him, the part that was still fractured and healing, wanted to bury his nose in the sugar-cookies-and-vanilla scents radiating off her clothes and hair and skin, and let it fill up his head and drive out the nightmares.

Harry did none of those things. Although her scent was as sweet as he'd imagined, nothing else about this meeting was going according to plan. Dogs were barking. She was plastered against him. He patted her back again because he wasn't sure how he was supposed to react to this welcome. After all, he'd never met Daisy in person before.

She started talking before pulling away. "This feels like a reunion between old friends. I just got home myself. A few minutes earlier and you would have missed me. What are you doing here?" She shooed the dogs into the house and grabbed his wrist, pulling him in, as well. "Sorry. I'll stop talking. Come in out of the cold."

He watched the little gray-and-white fuzz mop dart back and forth across the area rug in the foyer while the white terrier jumped over him with a yip of excitement when he got too close. Those dogs were wired. They needed a good bit of exercise to take some of that energy out of them.

After locking the thick mahogany door behind her, Daisy pointed to the little one. "Muffy, down." Muffy? The long-haired one was clearly a dude, but he had to give the little guy credit for flopping down on his belly to pant until he got permission to go nuts again. "I can put them in their kennels if you want, but they'll mind if you tell them to stay down. Make sure Patch is making eye contact with you and use your hand. He's deaf. But smart as a whip. Jack Russells usually are. He knows several commands. Patch?"

She demonstrated a universal hand signal. The terrier sat, all right, but so did the Belgian Malinois. Who looked a lot like… That muscle ticked beneath Harry's right eye as he slammed the door on that memory and focused on the dog with the graying muzzle. Poor old guy had lost a leg. But those deep brown eyes were sharp and focused squarely on him, as if awaiting a command. Maybe the dog recognized another wounded warrior. "Is he a working dog?"

"KCPD-retired," she answered. "That's Caliban. He lost his leg to cancer. I inherited him when his handler couldn't keep him. Sorry about the mess. I'm in the middle of decorating for the holidays." Daisy was moving down the hallway beside the stairs, which were draped with fake greenery and red bows tied along the railing. She swerved around a couple of plastic tubs and kicked aside little bits of melting snow with her low-heeled boots. "Stick to the runner and it won't be slippery," she advised. "Could I get you something hot to drink? Coffee? Cocoa? Are you hungry? I baked a ton of cookies last weekend."

Did the woman never stop talking? He couldn't even say hello, much less ask a question or explain the reason he was here. "That's not necessary."

"Don't be ridiculous. It's cold. I'm cold. I'd be fixing it, anyway."

Clearly, she expected him to follow her through the house, so Harry pulled the watch cap off his head and stepped out. A parade of curious dogs followed him into a cozy kitchen that opened up to a dining room that appeared to be a storage area for unwanted furniture, more plastic tubs and paint cans.

"Ignore that room. My goal is to clear that out this

weekend and finish decorating. I'm hosting my school's staff Christmas party next weekend." She shed her coat and scarf and tossed them over a ladder-back chair at an antique cherrywood table. "Have a seat."

"I wanted to talk about the letters."

"Sit." She pulled out a stool at the peninsula counter and patted the seat. "I'd love to talk about the letters you sent. Wish you'd kept writing after the school year ended." He'd stopped in June because that's when he… He hadn't written any letters from the hospital. "You're the first one of our pen pals I've met in person."

"That was nice of you to keep writing, even after I dropped the ball." Harry put his leather gloves on the counter, unzipped his coat and settled onto the stool. He didn't have the heart to tell her that some of those pen pals were never coming home. "I want you to know how much my unit appreciated all the letters you and your class sent them. Even if we, if I, didn't always respond."

She was running water now, measuring coffee. "That was one of my more inspired projects. I started it with last year's composition class. Anything to get them to write. Plus, at Central Prep—the school where I teach—we encourage our students to be involved in the community, to be citizens of the world and aware of others. It seemed like a win-win for both of us, supporting the troops while improving their communication skills. When your sister mentioned your Marine Corps unit at church, looking for Christmas cards to send them last year, I jumped right on it." She tugged at the hem of her long purple tweed sweater after reaching into the refrigerator for some flavored creamer. As she moved about, Harry noticed that her glasses were purple, too, and so were the streaks of color in her chocolate brown hair. "I always model what I ask my students to do, so I adopted you. I don't mean adopt you like that—no one would adopt…you're a grown man. We drew names out of a hat. You were the one that was left, so you lucked out and became my pen pal. It's nice—no, amazing—to finally meet you in person." She stopped to take a breath and push a plate of sugar cookies decorated like Christmas trees and reindeer in front of him. "And now I'm rambling. Thank you for your service."

Now she was rambling? Harry was still replaying all the dialogue in his head to catch everything she'd said. "You're welcome. I was just doing my job. Thank you for your letters. They meant a lot to me."

"*You're* welcome. And I was just doing *my* job." She pulled two turquoise mugs from an upper cabinet while the earthy smell of coffee brewing filled the room. "You're home on leave for the holidays, I imagine. Are you visiting Hope?"

"I'm staying with my sister and her husband for a few days."

"How's their little boy? He's about two, right?"

"Gideon is…" A little afraid of the growly uncle who was rooming with him for the time being. Or maybe the fact that Harry was a little afraid of holding his energetic nephew without breaking him was what created the awkward tension between them. Who was he kidding? Pretty much every relationship was awkward for him right now. "Yeah, he's two in a couple of months."

"And Hope is pregnant with baby number two? That's good news. Although that apartment over her bridal shop only has two bedrooms, doesn't it? She and Pike will have to be looking for a bigger place soon." Daisy filled two mugs and carried them to the counter across from him. Although that bulky knit sweater covered the interesting bits between her neck and thighs, her leggings and boots hinted at earth-mother curves. He was busy filling in with his imagination the shape he couldn't see, enjoying the mental exercise a little more than he should when she set a fragrant, steaming mug in front of him, and cradled the other between her hands, warming her fingers. "What can I do for you, Master Sergeant?"

Harry dutifully pulled his gaze up to the blue eyes behind her glasses. "Top. You don't have to call me Master Sergeant every time. Top is the nickname for an NCO of my rank."

"All right, Top. What can I do for you?"

"I wanted to meet you in person and thank you for your letters."

"You said that already." She picked up a red-nosed reindeer cookie and dipped it into her coffee before taking a bite, waiting for him to continue.

Exactly how did a guy broach a subject like *I need the woman from those letters to help me regain my sanity? The golden, ethereal one with the soft voice, gentle touch and quiet mien I imagined in my dreams? I need that angel's healing touch.* He definitely didn't need a woman who talked nonstop, owned a pack of dogs and triggered a lustful curiosity he hadn't acknowledged for longer than he cared to admit. Harry picked up his mug by the handle, then turned it in his hands, staring down into the dark brew that reminded him of one of the colors of her hair. "Writing your students gave my unit something to do during the slow times. Getting those letters could really... You know, some days were harder than others, and, um..." This wasn't right. *She* wasn't right. Time to abort this crazy ass mission and call one of the shrinks Lt. Col. Biro had recommended for him. Harry set his mug down on the counter with enough force to slosh the coffee over the edge. "Sorry." He shook the hot liquid off his skin and shot abruptly to his feet. "Now's not a good time, is it?" While she retrieved a dish cloth to clean up his mess, he grabbed his gloves and headed toward the front door. "Sorry to show up on your doorstep unannounced."

"You haven't even touched your coffee." Harry strode past the trio of dogs who hopped to their feet to follow him. He heard Daisy's boots on the floor boards behind him. "You must have stopped by for some reason. We have lots to talk about, don't we? Your dog, Tango? Your friends who were wounded in that IED explosion? Are they okay? Were you hurt? I mean, I can see the scars, so clearly you were, but—"

"That was a different skirmish."

"You were hurt more than once?" Harry had his cap on, his coat zipped and the front door open when Daisy grabbed his arm with both hands and tugged him to a halt. "Wait."

Her fingers curled into the sleeve of his coat, tightening their hold on him. Harry glanced down at her white-knuckled grip, frowning at the unexpected urgency in her touch before angling around to face her.

"Please don't leave." Her face was tipped up, her eyes searching his as if she was struggling to come up with the right words to say. Odd. Words didn't seem to be a problem for her. "If you really have to go, I understand. And if you don't want to talk, that's okay. But..." She looked back over her shoulder, past the dogs and holiday decorations before she finally let go of his sleeve and shrugged. "Totally unrelated thing, but, before you go, would you do me a favor? I'm not saying you owe me anything. I mean, you barely know me—"

"I know you better than most people." Correction. He knew the person who'd been his lifeline to normalcy and home and hope. This chatterbox with the wild hair and effusive personality felt like someone different. "After reading your letters, that is. You shared a lot. About your ex, your parents, this house…" He glanced around at the refinished wood and fresh paint of the drafty old Colonial that was far too big for one person—even if she did live with a pack of dogs. "Some of your school stories made me laugh or made me want to wring someone's neck."

She took half a step back. "You remember all that?"

He'd memorized nearly every sentence. *Laughter. Concerns. Wisdom. Compassion.* The Daisy Gunderson he knew had shared her heart.

"I know the men and women I work with," he clarified. "My sister and her husband… I mean, you're not the only person I know."

He couldn't tell if the pinch at the corners of her mouth and eyes meant she was touched by his confession, or if she felt a little sad to learn how few connections he had outside the Marine Corps. "Thank you. I feel like I know you better than someone I just met a few minutes ago, too. You wrote some touching things that, well, some of them made me cry."

He made her cry? Harry shifted uncomfortably inside his coat. "Sorry about that."

"Don't be. You shared the truth about what was on your mind, what you were feeling. I was honored." She hugged her arms around her middle. "You made me smile sometimes, too."

So why wasn't he seeing that smile? The Daisy in his dreams always smiled. This was not going well. Daisy Gunderson was supposed to have a serene smile and a calm demeanor that made all the crap he had to deal with go away. But just because the real Daisy didn't fit the ethereal angel he'd imagined, it didn't mean he should blow her off. "You were going to ask me something?"

"Right." She shrugged one shoulder. Then she pointed

at him, at herself, then back at him. "I'm here by myself and I wondered... Would you...?"

Now she couldn't come up with words? "Ma'am, I really should be going."

Her manic energy returned in a burst that faded into breathless hesitation. "One. Don't call me ma'am. My students call me ma'am, and it's after hours and I'm off duty. Besides, it makes me feel like I'm old enough to be your mother. And two... I could use a man right now." Now wasn't that a suggestive request. The parts of him south of his belt buckle stirred with interest, even as his chest squeezed with anxiety at the possibility she wanted something more than a pen pal, too. "But I don't have a big brother or a boyfriend or a dad to call and..." She gestured down the hallway toward the back of the house. "Would you check something out for me?"

His disappointment surprised him more than the relief he felt. "You've got a problem?"

"Maybe. I don't know." She tucked a stray lock of hair back into the purple and brown waves behind her ear. "I hope not, but..."

He could change a flat tire for her, or do some heavy lifting or pull something down off a high shelf. He owed the fantasy Daisy from his letters at least that much. But as Harry waited for the details, he read something more troubling than the awkwardness of this conversation in the blue eyes behind her glasses. She was scared.

Seventeen years of military training put him on instant alert.

"Show me."

Stopping only to put on her coat and order the dogs to stay inside the mudroom, Daisy walked out onto the back deck, and Harry followed. She went to the railing and pointed down into the snow. "Those footprints. Something seems off to me."

This was about something more than tracks through her backyard. Her cheeks should be turning pink with the dampness chilling the air. Unless the colored lights were playing tricks on him, her skin had gone pale. The buoyant energy that had overwhelmed him earlier had all but disappeared. Seemed he wasn't the only one keeping secrets.

With a nod, he accepted the simple mission she charged him with and went down into the yard. Stepping farther out into the snow so as not to disturb the suspicious tracks, Harry switched his phone into flashlight mode and made a quick reconnaissance. This was an awful lot of traffic through the yard of a woman who lived alone. And all of these tracks were too big to be Daisy's. His boots were digging into snow instead of sand, but the hackles at the back of Harry's neck went up just as they had overseas when he sensed an enemy lurking somewhere beyond his line of sight.

Trusting suspicions he wasn't sure he was equipped to deal with yet, he retraced his own path a second time, kneeling to inspect some of the deeper tracks. They'd frozen up inside after a bit of melting, meaning they'd been there long before the afternoon sun had reached them. He pushed to his feet and moved closer to the house to confirm that the deepest boot prints were facing the house, a good five feet beyond the gas and water meters. Harry looked up to a window with a shade drawn halfway down and curtains parted a slit to reveal the blackness of the room inside.

Harry glanced up at Daisy, who was watching his every move from the edge of the deck. She was hugging her arms around herself again. Something definitely had her spooked. "That's not just a case of a new meter reader guy thinking he could get out on that side of the yard, is it?"

"I don't think so. He'd only have to see that part of the fence once to know there's no gate over there." And yet her visitor had walked back and forth multiple times, then stopped here to look inside that window. "What room is this?"

She paused long enough that he looked up at her again. "My bedroom."

Harry walked straight to the deck, braced one foot on the bottom planks and vaulted over the railing. The snow flinging off his boots hadn't settled before he'd turned her toward the door to walk her back inside. "You need to call the police. You've got a Peeping Tom."

Chapter Three

Harry sat in the darkness of his truck watching Daisy's light blue Colonial with the dark blue shutters and dozens of Christmas lights, wondering if she was going to give the balding guy at her front door the same kind of hug she'd given him when he'd left a half hour earlier. He already wasn't a fan of the older gentleman who'd insisted she leave the barking dogs on the other side of the glass storm door and finish their conversation on the brick porch where Daisy was shivering without her coat. If she hugged the guy, then Baldy was definitely going on Harry's do-not-like list.

Not that he'd handled either her enthusiastic greeting or grateful goodbye terribly well. But something simmered low inside him at the idea that Daisy's stuffing-squishing hugs were available to anyone who came to her front door.

Finally. The would-be renter handed Daisy a business card and shuffled down the steps. Harry exhaled a deep breath that fogged his window, relieved to see the thoughtless twit depart without a hug. He approved when Daisy crumpled the card in her fist, clearly dismissing the inconsiderate anti-dog man. She huddled against one of the big white pillars at either corner of her porch to watch the rejected tenant drive away.

"Go back inside," Harry whispered, urging the woman

to show a little common sense and get out of the cold night air. But she was scanning up and down the street, searching for something or someone. Was she still worried about those snowy footprints in her backyard?

Harry hunkered down behind the wheel as her gaze swept past his truck. The brief glimpse of fear stamped in the big blue eyes behind those purple glasses when she'd asked for his help had been imprinted on his brain. And since the gray matter upstairs was already a bit of a jigsaw puzzle, he wasn't quite ready to have any worries about her safety lingering on his conscience. So he'd decided to hang out at least until Baldy left. But Daisy already had one pervert who thought looking through her bedroom window was a fun idea. She probably wouldn't be assured to know that he was still out here in the darkness, spying on her, too.

After one more scan, she went back into the house, petting the dogs and talking to them before closing the door. The colored Christmas lights winding around the pillars went out, followed by the bright light of the foyer. She must be moving toward the back of the house because a few seconds later, the lights decorating the garage went out, too. From this vantage point, Harry wouldn't know if she was fixing dinner or changing her clothes or making a path through the mess of projects in her dining room.

Not that it was any of his business how she spent her evenings. Baldy had left her house and it was time for him to go.

Harry started his truck and cranked up the heat, obliquely wondering why he'd felt compelled to sit there in silence, putting up with the cold in lieu of drawing any attention to his presence there. Probably a throwback to night patrols overseas, where stealth often meant the difference between avoiding detection and engaging in a fire fight with the enemy.

But he shouldn't be thinking like that. Not here in Kansas City. He watched Daisy's neighbor to the north open his garage and stroll out with a broom to sweep away the snow that had blown onto his front sidewalk. That was a little obsessive, considering the wind would probably blow the dusting of snow back across the walkways by morning. The neighbor waited for a moment at the end of his driveway, turning toward the same revving engine noise that drew Harry's attention. They both watched from their different vantage points as a car pulled away from the curb and made a skidding U-turn before zipping down the street. Probably a teenager with driving like that. The neighbor shook his head and started back to the garage, but paused as a couple walking in front of his house waved and they all stopped to chat. Yeah, Christmastime in suburbia was a real hotbed for terrorists.

Muttering a curse at his inability to acclimatize to civilian life, Harry pulled out, following the probable teen driver to the stop sign at the corner before they turned in opposite directions. Although this was an older neighborhood, the homes had been well maintained. The sidewalks and driveways had been cleared. Traffic and pedestrians were the norm, not suspicious activity he needed to guard against.

Bouncing over the compacted ruts of snow in the side streets, Harry made his way toward his sister's loft apartment in downtown Kansas City, avoiding the dregs of rush hour traffic as much as possible. This evening's visit to Daisy's house needed to go on his list of dumb ideas he should have reconsidered before taking action. What had he thought was going to happen when he showed up on her doorstep? That the woman who'd sent him all those letters while he'd been overseas and in the hospital, would recognize him? They'd never exchanged pictures. He'd thought that trading news and revealing souls and making him laugh meant that they knew each other. That the same feeling he got when he saw her name at mail call would happen to him again when they met in person. If he was brutally honest, he'd half expected a golden halo to be glowing around her head.

Golden-halo Daisy was supposed to be his link to reality. Seeing her was supposed to ground him. The plan had been to let go of the nightmares he held in check, and suddenly all the scars inside him would heal. He could report back to Lt. Col. Biro and never look back after a dose of Daisy.

So much for foolish miracles.

Daisy Gunderson wasn't fragile. She wasn't golden-haired. And she certainly hadn't been glowing. She was a brunette—a curvy one, if his body's humming reaction to those impromptu bear hugs were any indication. A brunette with purple streaks in her hair and matching glasses on her nose and a need to chatter that just wouldn't quit.

And the dogs. He hadn't expected the dogs. Or the mess. Everything was loud and chaotic, not at all the peaceful sort of mecca he'd envisioned.

The fact that some pervert had been peeking in her bedroom window bothered him, too. He'd foolishly gone to a woman he only knew on paper—a stranger, despite the letters they'd shared—for help. Instead, it looked as if she was the hot mess who needed help.

Harry needed the woman in the letters to help him clear his head and lose the darkness that haunted him.

He didn't need Daisy Gunderson and her troubles.

He'd done his good deed for her. He'd assuaged his conscience. It was time to move on.

To what? What was a jarhead like him supposed to do for six weeks away from the Corps?

If he was overseas, he'd be doing a perimeter walk of the camp at this time of the evening, making sure his buddies were secure. Even if he was back at Camp Pendleton in Southern California, he'd be doing PT or reading up on the latest equipment regs or putting together a training exercise for the enlisted men he intended to work with again. He was used to having a routine. A sense of purpose. What was he supposed to do here in Kansas City besides twiddle his thumbs, visit a shrink and reassure his sister that she didn't need to walk on eggshells around him?

He supposed he could find the nearest mall and do some Christmas shopping for Hope, his brother-in-law, Pike, and nephew, Gideon. But even in the late evening there'd be crowds there. Too many people. Too much noise. Too many corners where the imagined enemy inside his head could hide.

Pausing at a stop light, Harry opened the glove compartment where he'd put the list of local therapists Lt. Col. Biro had recommended and read the names and phone numbers. Even before he'd finished reading, he was folding the paper back up and stuffing it inside beside the M9 Beretta service weapon he stored there. He closed the glove compartment with a resolute click and moved on with the flow of traffic.

He'd already made an appointment for tomorrow afternoon. He wasn't ready for an emergency call to one of them yet. Maybe he should ask his brother-in-law where he could find a local gym that wouldn't require a long-term commitment. He could lift some weights, run a few miles on a treadmill. That was all he needed, a physical outlet of some kind. A way to burn himself out until he was too tired to have any more thoughts inside his head.

It was almost eight o'clock when Harry pulled into the driveway beside Fairy Tale Bridal, the wedding planner business his sister owned. He pressed the buzzer and announced himself over the intercom before Hope released the lock and he jogged up the stairs to the apartment over the shop where she and Pike lived. He heard her warning Pike's K-9 partner, Hans, to stay before opening the condominium door. His sister had a quiet beauty that seemed to have blossomed with the confidence she'd found in marriage and motherhood. He was happy to see her soft smile when she welcomed him home.

But that smile disappeared beneath a frown of concern before she shooed the German shepherd into the living area of the open layout and locked the door behind her. "That coat is too small for you. You need to get a new one that fits."

"Guess I've filled out a bit since the last time I needed my winter coat. There's not much call for them in Southern California or the Middle East."

Although he'd fully intended to put his own things away, Hope took his coat from him as soon as he'd unzipped it. "You're later than I thought. Did you get any dinner? I can heat up some meatloaf and potatoes in the microwave." Seven months pregnant and wearing fuzzy house slippers with the dress she'd worn to work, she shuffled into the kitchen, hanging his coat over the back of one of the kitchen chairs. "Would you rather have a sandwich?"

Harry followed her, feeling guilty that, even after all these years, she felt so compelled to take care of him. "I'm good."

"Did you eat?" she stopped in front of the open refrigerator and turned to face him.

Hope was only a year older than Harry, and he topped her in height, and had outweighed and outmuscled her for years. But she could still peer up at him over the rims of her glasses with those dove-gray eyes and see right into the heart of him, as though the tragic childhood they'd shared had linked them in some all-knowing, twin-like bond. Lying to Hope wasn't an option.

"No."

"I wish you'd take better care of yourself. It wasn't that long ago you were in a hospital fighting for your life. Besides getting winter clothes that fit, you need sleep and good food inside you." She nudged him into a chair, kissed his cheek and went to work putting together a meatloaf sandwich for him. "You found Daisy's house okay? What did you think of her?"

Harry pictured a set of deep blue eyes staring up at him above purple glasses, in an expression similar to the pointed look Hope had just given him. Only, he'd had a very different reaction to Daisy's silent request. Yes, he'd reacted to the fear he'd seen there and taken action like the Marine he was trained to be, but there was something else, equally disconcerting, about the way Daisy had studied him in her near-sighted squint that he couldn't quite shake.

"She's a hugger." Surprised that those were the first words that came out of his mouth, Harry scrubbed his palm across the stubble itching the undamaged skin of his jaw.

But the faint air of dismay in his tone didn't faze Hope. In fact, something about his comment seemed to amuse her. "I told you she was friendly and outgoing. She approached me that first morning in our adult Sunday School class. I'd still be sitting in the corner, just listening to the discussion if she hadn't sat down beside me and started a conversation."

Yep. The woman certainly had a talent for talking.

"There's Uncle Harry." Pike Taylor strolled into the living area, carrying their squirmy, wheaten-haired son,

Gideon, who was decked out in a fuzzy blue outfit for bed-
time. Even out of uniform, dressed in jeans and a flannel
shirt, Pike carried himself with the wary alertness of the
Kansas City cop he was. But the tall, lanky man who'd
been there to protect his sister from both their abusive
father and a serial rapist while Harry had been stationed
over in the Heat Locker reminded Harry of an overgrown
kid when he set his son down and chased him over to
his play area in the living room. Even the dog got into
the game, joining in with a loud bark and circling around
the toddler, which only made the little boy chortle with
glee. That muscle ticked in Harry's cheek as the urge to
smile warred with the images of something darker trying
to surface. Gideon lost his balance and plopped onto the
extra padding of his diaper before using the German shepherd's fur to pull himself back onto his pudgy little feet
and change directions. "Look out," Pike warned from his
wrestling position on the floor. "He's been asking for his
roommate all evening."

Gideon toddled over to Harry's knee, joyfully repeat-
ing a phrase that sounded a lot like "Yucky Hair," which
was apparently going to be his nickname for the duration
of this visit. Gideon's little fingers tugged at Harry's jeans
and reached for him, demanding to be picked up. Although
Harry was half afraid to hold the stout little tyke, he could
feel the expectation radiating off Hope not to deny her son
the innocent request. Unwilling to refuse his sister anything that would put a smile on her face, Harry picked up
his nephew and set him on his lap. He pushed aside the
salt and pepper shakers that Gideon immediately reached
for, and let him tug at the buttons of his Henley sweater,
instead. Hans lay down close by Harry's feet, keeping
an eye on the little boy as if he didn't trust Harry with
the toddler, either. Harry shifted in his seat, uncomfort-

able being the center of all this attention. Gideon batted at Harry's face and he lifted his chin, pulling away from the discomfiting contact. Hell, the dog was better with the child than he was. He needed to distract himself fast, or he was going to end up in a dark place that no one in this room wanted him to visit.

Turning his chair away from the watchful German shepherd, Harry latched onto the first thought that came to mind. "Daisy's a little scattered, isn't she?"

Pike tossed a couple of toys into Gideon's playpen before rising to his feet and crossing to the table. "Scattered? You mean her house? She's been working on it for three years. I can't imagine what it's costing her to redo it from top to bottom like that. Plus, she's doing a lot of the cosmetic work herself."

"I meant she rambled from one topic to the next. I had a hard time keeping up."

"She does live alone," Pike suggested. "Maybe she was lonesome and wanted to talk to somebody."

Hope snickered at her husband's idea. "She's been at school all day, with hundreds of students. She's had plenty of people to talk to."

"Teenagers," Pike countered. "It's not the same as talking to an adult."

Dismissing the explanation with a shake of her head, Hope opened a cabinet to pull out a bag of potato chips. "It's not exactly like you're Mr. Conversation, Harry. You're quiet like I am with new people. Maybe you made her nervous and she was chatting to fill the silence. I do that when my shy genes kick in."

Not in any universe would he describe Daisy Mega-Hugger as a shy woman. But maybe something about him *had* made her nervous. The scars that turned his ugly mug into an acquired taste? Not announcing his visit before showing up on her doorstep? Was there something more to those footprints in the snow than she'd let on? The idea of a Peeping Tom had upset her, yes, but now that he considered her reaction, she hadn't seemed surprised to discover signs of an intruder.

Hope ripped open the bag of chips and crunched one in her mouth before dumping some onto the plate beside his sandwich. "She is one of those women who seems to have a lot of irons in the fire. She's always volunteering for one thing or another. Daisy has the biggest heart in the world."

Harry pulled a toddler fist away from the tip of his nose. Was that big heart why she'd even considered giving Mr. Rude a place to live as her tenant? "I actually waited there a little while after I left. She had a guy coming in to talk about renting her upstairs."

Pike came up behind Hope and reached around her to snatch a chip and pop it into his mouth. "Mr. Friesen is the uncle of one of our receptionists at the precinct. I ran a background check on him for her."

"He showed up before I got out of there. I waited outside for half an hour to make sure he left without incident."

Hope's eyes were wide as she set the plate in front of Harry. "Without incident? That sounds ominous."

Harry ate a bite before breaking off a morsel of the soft bread for Gideon to chew on, in an effort to distract the toddler from grabbing the whole sandwich. "While I was there, she had me check out some suspicious tracks in her backyard. Looked to me like someone had been casing her house."

Pike pulled out the chair at the head of the table and sat. "Did you report it to KCPD?"

So, he thought the situation seemed troublesome, too. "I advised her to."

Hope moved a subtly protective hand to her swollen

belly. "You checked out the house for her, didn't you? Her locks and everything are secure?"

"She's got new windows on the ground floor. Dead bolts on the doors." But he hadn't checked any of them to see if they were locked. Surely, the woman had sense enough to... The second bite of his sandwich went stale in his mouth. He should have done that for her, at least.

Pike pulled Hope onto his lap, soothing her concern for their friend. "We've had a rash of burglaries across the city. Pretty standard for this time of year. Thieves looking for money or credit cards, or even wrapped presents they can pawn."

Either coveting his meal or sensing Harry's increasingly testy mood, Gideon squealed and stabbed at the plate, scattering the pile of chips across the table top. Harry shoved the plate aside and pulled the boy back, scooting the chair across the tile floor. His boot knocked against Hans, sending the dog to his feet with a startled woof.

All at once, the dark place inside his mind erupted with a fiery explosion. He felt the pain tearing through his flesh. He heard the shouts for help, the whimpers of pain.

Harry staggered to his feet. "*Platz*, Tango," he ordered, mixing the past and the present inside his head. "Hans, I mean. *Platz*." Pike's well-trained dog instantly obeyed the German command to lie down. Slamming the door on the flashback, Harry thrust Gideon into his frightened sister's arms and grabbed his coat. "I'm sorry. I need to walk around the block a couple of times. Clear my head."

"Harry?"

"Let him go, honey."

An hour later, Harry had come in from the cold, apologized to his sister, finished off the meal she'd saved for him and shut himself inside the bedroom he shared with Gideon.

The flashback had receded to the wasteland of buried images inside his head, although he was still having a hard time settling his thoughts enough to sleep. With Gideon snoring softly from his crib across the darkened room, Harry lay back on the double bed, using the flashlight from his duffel bag to read through the stack of cards and letters that normally soothed him on nights like this.

He grinned through Daisy's account of catching one of her students licking a potted plant in her classroom because the girl had been curious to find out what the sap oozing from the stalk tasted like. The girl had been perfectly fine, but the spate of dumb jokes that had followed would have given a stand-up comic plenty of material. The story had made his unit laugh to the extent that when any one of them made a boneheaded move, they'd teased the Marine by calling him or her a plant-licker.

Gideon gurgled in his sleep, reminding Harry that he was the interloper here. In another couple of months, Hope and Pike would need this space for Gideon's new little brother or sister. Although he had every intention of returning to his duties with the Corps by that time, Harry acknowledged another stab of guilt. Maybe Hope wanted to redecorate this room. She had talked about expanding their loft into the shop's second-floor storage area, but a renovation of that scale wouldn't happen until after the baby's birth. Maybe he was in the way here, and Hope was too kind-hearted to say anything. Maybe he could camp out in their condo for just a few days longer, then find himself a quiet place to rent until his penance was over and he could report back to Lt. Col. Biro.

Daisy was looking for a tenant.

Harry returned the letter to the thick manila envelope. Nah. He couldn't. He needed a quiet place to heal for a month or so. He didn't want to get locked into a long-term lease, and he didn't want the place to be chaos central, either.

Dismissing the idea, he pulled another letter out of the envelope and turned his flashlight on it.

Dear MSgt. Lockhart,

I'm so sorry to hear about your friend. I know your work is important to you, but it sounds as though you need more time to grieve. Can you take leave for a couple of days? Please talk to someone there if you need to. A chaplain? Another friend? You're probably not comfortable dropping your guard like that.

When my father died so suddenly, I was in shock. It just didn't seem right that one tragedy should lead so soon to another one. That hurt me worse than Brock's assault because it felt so random. I could fight Brock, but I couldn't fight my dad's heart attack. Fortunately, I had a counselor who reminded me of the different stages of grief. That we all grieve differently, and that there's no timeline for when you stop being angry about your loss, or you get over feeling so heartsick. I sense that you're toughing this out. Be kind to yourself. I'm thinking kind thoughts for you.

Rainbows and unicorns and apple pie. Or chocolate cake? Steak dinner? What's your favorite food to eat or thing to do when you want to have fun and spoil yourself? Let me know, and that's what I'll imagine for you.

Despite her attempt at humor, Harry's thoughts darkened as he thought about Daisy's old boyfriend breaking into her apartment and attacking her with a knife. No wonder she was leery of someone scoping out her house. Harry swung his legs off the side of the bed and sat up. A few letters earlier, Daisy had said her ex had been sent to jail. How long would a guy be locked up for a crime like that? Was she worried about him returning? Sleep was feeling more elusive than ever as Harry made a mental note to ask Pike to check into her ex's status.

His breath stuttered through his chest as he forced his concerns for her aside. There were cops for worries like that. He wasn't in a good place to take on somebody else's trouble right now.

Harry turned his gaze and the beam of his flashlight down to the rest of Daisy's letter, needing to recapture the peace and comfort of her words.

> *If I was there right now, I'd listen to whatever you wanted to say. For however long it takes to get it all out. If the feelings are too private for you to share with me, maybe you could write them down just for yourself. Get them out of your head so there's not so much you're holding inside that you have to deal with. You don't have to send the words to me, but I find journaling like that helpful.*
>
> *Believe it or not, I'm a good listener. And a good hugger, or so I'm told. If you're ever in Kansas City, I'll have a hug waiting for you.*
>
> *Take care,*
> *Daisy*

The hint of a smile eased the tension in him at the hugging part. She hadn't been kidding. But the smile never fully formed. Because Harry had taken her up on that offer to write down all his anger and grief. He'd sent her a vitriolic letter—three and a half pages of crap that no one should have to know about. And she'd still answered with another note saying that she had cried on his behalf because she understood that he'd never been able to, that Marines didn't cry.

She'd helped him through that nightmare when all had seemed lost. Forget about his own present needs for a second. He owed Daisy a lot more than a brusque brush-off and the silent blame he'd heaped upon her for not living up to the image of the all-knowing angel of his fantasies.

Steeling himself for a half-formed mission, Harry folded up the letter and returned it to the others before shutting off the flashlight and tying his boots back onto his feet.

Hope was right. He was a man of duty. His brain might have a missing chunk filled with anger and darkness, but he was trained to protect and serve.

Maybe all Daisy needed was a man on the premises to scare off lusty lookie-loos or potential burglars or a crazy ex-boyfriend. She'd be safe. He wouldn't feel this added guilt. Hope wouldn't look at him with those big worried eyes and he'd have a roof over his head for the next six weeks.

Hard to argue with logic like that.

Peace of mind and sleep weren't happening tonight until he dealt with at least one of the problems bugging him.

He picked up his phone, but realized he didn't have a number for Daisy. Just the Gunderson address.

Harry grabbed his keys and his coat and quietly shut the bedroom door behind him. Pike and Hope were in the living room, snuggling on the couch as he suited up and walked to the front door. "I'm heading out for a bit."

Hope set aside the book she'd been reading. "It's late."

Harry pulled on his watch cap. "It's not that late."

She shifted her awkward weight and turned to face him. "Are you okay? Did I say something that upset you earlier?"

Pike had muted the news show he'd been watching and risen to his feet. The taller man was watching Harry very carefully, probably to make sure he didn't say or do anything to hurt her. Good. Harry was glad that Hope had someone in her life who loved her enough to take care of her like that.

Did Daisy?

I don't have a big brother or a boyfriend or a dad to call.

Harry leaned over the back of the couch to kiss Hope's cheek. "I'm fine. I just need to run an errand."

"Take the spare keys," Pike advised. He strode into the kitchen and pulled a ring of keys from the nearest drawer before tossing them across the room to Harry. "In case you're out after we've turned in. I'll put Hans in his kennel, Remember, the down command is—"

"*Platz.* Yeah, I know." He knew a lot about working with trained dogs like his brother-in-law's K-9 partner. That had been his job overseas. Him and Tango and… *Nah. Don't go there.* Shutting down the memory he couldn't yet face, Harry stuffed the keys into his pocket. "Hans won't be a problem."

"Let us know how Daisy is doing," Hope prompted.

No sense lying about where he was headed. His sister knew him better than he knew himself. Harry paused in the open doorway before letting himself out. "I will."

Chapter Four

Sleep wasn't happening tonight.

Although the logical part of Daisy's brain told her that the scratching noise at her bedroom window was the wind blowing bits of wintry debris against the panes, she sat up for the third time, clutching her spare pillow against her chest. She stared at the gingham drapes, her vision blurred by nearsightedness and shadows, half expecting them to fly open and reveal a man standing on the other side. Fighting to form a coherent thought over the pulse thundering in her ears at that unsettling idea, she picked up her old tortoise-shell framed glasses from the bedside table and blinked the glowing red numbers of her clock into focus.

2:49 a.m.

Her breath seeped out on a weary sigh. Her six o'clock alarm was going to beep mighty early if she couldn't shut down her fearful imagination and get some sleep.

She flipped on the lamp beside her, flooding the room with a gentle light. Muffy stretched his short legs on top of the quilt, scooting closer to reclaim the warmth from the crook of her knees where he'd been sleeping. Patch sat up behind her on the far side of the bed, his posture indicating he was alert and ready to start his day.

"Not yet, you silly boy," she chided. But her smile was the only invitation Patch needed to climb into her lap to lick her chin in exchange for some petting. Daisy indulged in a few seconds of warmth and affection before looking past him to see Caliban curled into a ball at the foot of the bed. The older dog seemed annoyed to be disturbed from his slumber yet again and tucked his nose under his front leg and tried to go back to sleep.

The furnace kicked on and Daisy startled again, rattling the headboard against the wall. Damn. Who needed some creeper sending her unwanted gifts when she could spook herself with her own imagination? By the time she reminded herself that the drapes were swaying because the vent beneath the window stirred the air and not because a Peeping Tom had moved them, all three dogs were sitting up, looking at her intently, no doubt wondering if they were going to be taking another jaunt with her around the house in search of an intruder they knew wasn't there.

A floorboard creaked overhead and Daisy tilted her gaze up to the ceiling. Again, logic said the noise was the old wood of the house shifting with the changing temperature of heat ducts running through the walls and beneath the floors. But the board above her creaked a second time, and a third, and logic became a voice her fears wouldn't let her hear anymore.

That sounded like footsteps. It shouldn't be possible. The dogs would be barking. The police had taken her statement about the tracks in the snow. She'd locked all her doors and windows.

Downstairs.

She hadn't been upstairs since she'd hung the lights and greenery on the bannister earlier in the week. Not that there were any outside doors or even fire escapes on the second floor where someone could...

Something banged against an upstairs wall and she jumped inside her skin. Brock had shattered the lock on her apartment door the night he'd broken in to assault her. The locks on this house were doubled, heavier.

Didn't make any difference.

She heard another bang. Then another that was slightly muffled.

"Sorry, guys." Daisy couldn't stay there a moment longer, fighting her imagination. Pushing the dogs aside, she tugged on her sticky-bottomed slipper socks and tied her chenille robe over her flannel pajamas. "If I don't double-check what that noise is, none of us will be getting any sleep."

While the dogs jumped down from the bed and stretched, Daisy crossed to the window. She pulled aside the edge of the drape and window shade underneath, bracing for a gruesome face staring at her from the other side. Relieved to see nothing but the dim glow of moonlight reflecting off the snow in her backyard, she exhaled the breath she'd been holding. Quickly tucking the window coverings back into place, she pulled her cell phone and keychain with its pepper spray from her purse and opened the bedroom door.

Daisy had no qualms about running up her utility bill if it meant feeling safe. She flipped on the hall light and the mudroom light, along with lights in the kitchen, dining room and living room. After a quick check of her office, she flipped the switch to illuminate the second-floor landing and climbed the stairs. Muffy followed at her heels, with Patch darting up ahead of them.

"Please be a tree branch caught in the wind and knocking against the side of the house. Or snow." Snow was good. Normal. Maybe a clump had melted off the eaves and landed on a window sill. Ignoring the logic against anything melting in this single digit weather, Daisy nodded, liking that explanation for the discomforting noises. "Please be snow."

A sweep of the empty landing allowed her a moment's reprieve to look back down to the foyer. Her heart squeezed in her chest when she saw Caliban standing with his one front paw on the bottom step, anxiously looking up at them. He bravely hopped up two more steps, but his paw slipped from underneath him on the polished wood and he reversed course, returning to the area rug at the foot of the stairs and sitting at attention. "It's okay, boy. You keep an eye on things down there."

Although she suspected he'd push through his phobia and obey the command to join them if she called to him, Daisy turned her back on Caliban's big brown eyes and flipped on the switch in the first bedroom. This was the room she planned to rent out, along with the bathroom across the hall. This was where she'd heard the floorboards creak, and the thump against the side of the house. Her eyes had barely adjusted to the bright light when Caliban let out a deep warning bark. Daisy answered with a startled yelp. A split second later, someone banged loudly at her front door and she clutched her chest at the double shock to her heart. "Brock is in prison," she reminded herself out loud. "He can't hurt you."

But Secret Santa could.

All three dogs ran to the door, sounding a ferocious alarm. Her thumb hovered over the numbers on her phone. 9… 1…

"Daisy! Daisy, open up!" Did she know that voice? A man's voice. Loud enough to be heard above the barking dogs. Brock had a scary, loud voice, usually slurred by alcohol. But this voice was sharp, succinct. "It's Harry Lockhart. Open up!"

"Harry? What…?" The relief surging through her veins made her light-headed as she raced down the stairs. She pocketed her phone and pepper spray before attacking the locks.

He was a broad, imposing silhouette outside her storm

door until she thought to turn on the porch lights. Adding the glow of Christmas colors to his stern features did nothing to ease the frantic mix of urgency, confusion and relief that made her hands tremble on the latch. Her fingers lost their grip on the storm door as he pulled it right out of her hand.

"Caliban, *sitz!*" Harry ordered the dog to be quiet and sit while he clamped his hands around her shoulders and pushed her inside.

"Is that German? What are you doing here?" she asked, obliquely marveling that her Belgian Malinois obeyed commands in two languages, while Muffy managed to ignore orders in any language. "Is that a gun?"

She barely had time to recoil from the holster cinched around his thigh with a web belt before he trapped her between the thick wood door and his equally solid body and locked the dead bolt. The holster and webbing were military khaki in color, a sharp contrast against the dark denim of his jeans. The wood was cold against her back as he flattened her there, folding his shoulders around her as his chin swiveled from side to side, his gaze inspecting the crossroads of archways that met in the foyer.

"You turned on all the lights. What's wrong?" he demanded in the same clipped tone he'd used with the dogs. Without surrendering the shielding posture of what she could only describe as warrior mode, he pulled back just enough to look down into her eyes.

"What's *wrong*?" she echoed. Daisy curled her fingers into the nubby weave of his charcoal sweater exposed by the unzipped front of his coat, feeling so off-balance by his surprise visit she needed something to cling to. She wanted to push some space between them. The heat of his body was too close, his gun too hardpressed against her hip, his masculine scent too distracting for her to think straight. But all she could do right now was hold on. "Have you been watching my house?"

His gray eyes narrowed on her face. "Your glasses are different."

"What?" Oh, right. She was wearing the brown frames. That observation was as random as her own thoughts right now. Damn, the man had muscles. With his coat hanging open she could see that the burn and shrapnel scars on his face and neck ran down beneath the collar of his sweater. He had been so terribly hurt. An explosion? A fire? He'd nearly lost his eye. And that would be a shame because they were such a beautiful, deep color, like an endless, storm-tossed ocean. *Focus!* Daisy shook her head, still not comprehending why he was here. But she could answer his question. "I have different frames for different outfits. These are my knock-around-the-house pair."

He pulled away as suddenly as he'd pinned her there, and her knees nearly buckled as chilled air rushed between them. He peeled off his gloves and stuffed them into his pockets. "Caliban, *fuss.*"

Foos? Apparently, that meant *heel*, at least to Caliban. Harry spun away to inspect her living room, with the three dogs trotting behind him. Once she thought she could walk again, Daisy tightened her robe around her waist and followed them in a circle through the house, watching Harry stop at every window and door.

When they ended up back at the front door, Daisy caught the sleeve of his coat and halted his search. She could think now, at least clearly enough to know that she still didn't understand why Harry Lockhart was prowling through her house at three in the morning. "What are you doing here?"

"I didn't check your locks before I left earlier."

Was that supposed to make sense to her?

"Why did you turn on all the lights?" he went on. "Something's happened. I thought someone might have broken in."

He *was* spying on her. Daisy tucked her hair behind her ears, unsure whether to be flattered or creeped out. He couldn't know about those disturbing gifts she'd been receiving, could he? Why was this man who'd been so anxious to leave her the last time they'd met so eager to protect her now?

"Daisy?" he prompted. "Why did you turn on the lights?"

She responded to that succinct tone as readily as the dogs had. "I heard noises upstairs. Something hit the side of the house. We went to check."

And then he was off again, taking the stairs two at a time with Muffy and Patch right on his heels.

Daisy knelt on the rug beside Caliban, hugging her arm around his shoulders to stroke his chest, soothing the thrumming energy quaking through the muscular dog's body. Either she was absorbing his edgy alertness or she was just as anxious as Caliban to know what Harry was seeing up there before muttering the word "Clear" as he left each of the three bedrooms and bathroom.

She pushed to her feet as he turned off the second-floor lights and came back down the stairs. Patch's entire butt was wagging with excitement at the late-night adventure as he propped his front paws against Harry's thigh. But Harry pushed him away and signaled for the Jack Russell mix to sit. With Muffy dancing around his legs, paying no heed to either voice commands or hand signals, Harry muttered something under his breath and bent down, picking up the dog.

"Har..." For a split second, Daisy reached for the Shih Tzu, worried that Harry's limited patience couldn't tolerate another yap. Instead, he set Muffy down between Caliban and Patch, pushed the dog's rear end to the rug and ordered him to sit. He repeated the process twice more before Muffy got bored enough with the exercise that he stretched out on his tummy and batted at Harry's boot.

She arched an eyebrow in apology. "He's a hard-headed one to train."

"Yep. He needs an exercise program like fly-ball or agility training to get rid of some of that energy." Harry straightened, propping his hands at his waist, reminding her of the military issue gun strapped to his side before his chest expanded with a heavy sigh. "You got any irate neighbors?"

"What?"

"Kids who'd be out roamin' the neighborhood on a school night?"

"No." Not the questions she'd expect from a man who hadn't found anything to worry about. Daisy was suddenly aware of the icy remnants of slush left from Harry's boots on the foyer rug soaking through her socks and chilling her from the toes up. "What did you see?"

He pulled back the edges of his coat to splay his fingers at his waist. "The house is secure. No signs of forced entry."

"But?"

"It's hard to tell from inside, but it looks as though someone used the side of your house for target practice." He inclined his head toward the stairs. "You've got a snow-ball stuck in the screen of that bedroom window. I opened it up to knock it clear, but it looked like a couple more splats of snow just beside the window, too."

A few minutes ago, she'd been hoping that snow was the culprit. Not so much now. "Someone was throwing snow-balls at my house at three in the morning?"

"Whoever threw them isn't there anymore."

"Or never was." She thought of the sick gifts hidden in-side her desk at school and wondered if she was just being paranoid to think that that terror campaign had somehow followed her home. "Maybe the snow fell from the roof or blew off the branches of Mr. Finch's sweet gum tree."

"Don't discount your instincts. Being aware of danger is half the battle of protecting yourself from it."

But Daisy wasn't any kind of Marine. "Sometimes my imagination gets the better of me. I remember that night Brock broke into my old place… I told you about him, didn't I?" She interpreted his unblinking glower as a yes. "I know he's locked up in Jefferson City…" She put up her hands, blocking the mental images of her ex's bared teeth and wild eyes, and that bloody knife poised above her. "Bad guys don't get to win." Brock didn't even deserve the time and space inside her head to sour her thoughts. "A few snowballs aren't any kind of threat. I let the noises of the old house get to me."

"The ghosts caught in our heads can be—"

"Relentless." His gray eyes locked on to hers, wide with surprise before narrowing to question her response. That look was too intense for her to hold, so she shrugged, nervously catching her hair behind her ears before looking directly at him again. "You said that in one of your letters."

"I remember. Didn't think you would." Harry shifted on his feet and glanced at the front door, as though an alarm had just gone off inside him, warning him it was time to end the conversation and leave. But then that piercing gaze was on her again. "One of the parts that made you cry?"

"I suppose I wear my emotions pretty close to the surface." While he barely showed his at all, other than this urgent need to escape her company. Again. "Crying isn't a bad thing." When he nudged aside the dogs and turned toward the door, Daisy followed, stopping him before he could leave. "Do I make you nervous, Harry? Is it the dogs? Do they remind you of Tango?"

"Tango?" He glanced over the jut of his shoulder at her. "Your K-9 partner."

"I know who Tango is." A muscle ticked across his taut cheekbone and he reached for the doorknob. "Was."

"I'm so sorry you lost him. I can't imagine what that must feel—"

"Like I said, everything looks secure. I'll walk around the house to see if I can find signs of where the snowballs came from before I leave."

"You're leaving?"

Of course he was. Only the crazies wanted anything to do with her. Harry just had an overdeveloped sense of responsibility, the kind of alertness and protective instincts she'd expect from any career Marine. He might be her friend on paper. She might have fancied herself half in love with the uniformed hero from their letters. But that was her fantasy, not his.

That still didn't stop her from moving between him and the door and sliding her arms beneath his coat, hugging him around the waist. With his coat unzipped, she could get closer than she had yesterday evening. Turning her cheek against the thick wool of his sweater, she felt his body warming hers. She breathed in the rugged smells of soap and Harry. "Thank you for looking out for me."

A fraction of a second longer and she would have pulled away. But his thick arms folded around her, his hands settling between her shoulder blades to gently pat her, almost as if he was trying to burp a baby. Not the most romantic embrace. But this was just a friendly hug, right? At least he wasn't holding himself completely stiff or pulling away. Maybe the taciturn tough guy with the scarred-up face was shy? Smiling against the beat of his heart at that tender notion, Daisy snuggled beneath his chin. She knew he wasn't married, and he'd never mentioned a girlfriend—past or present—in his letters. His sister, Hope, seemed to be the only woman in his life. Could his reticence to carry on a social conversation extend to the physical expression of emotion, as well? But if he was willing to hold on right now, she was more than willing to surround herself in his strength and heat.

"It's not like I could sleep, anyway." Harry's hands stopped their awkward petting and settled against the ribs of her chenille robe long enough for her to feel their warmth seeping through the layers of cotton and flannel. His voice was a growly whisper at the crown of her head. "Thought I'd put my time to good use. Those boot tracks worried me enough that I wished I'd run a security check like this before I left. Felt guilty that I hadn't. It was so late I didn't want to wake you. I thought it'd be enough to watch from outside the house."

"So I'm not the only one with insomnia. We're a pair. I toss and turn in bed out of worry, and you sit out in the cold out of guilt."

His nose rubbed against her temple as he breathed in deeply. Was he sniffing her hair? Why not? Standing here, she'd been memorizing the scent of his clothes and skin. His fingers curled into the back of her robe, pulling it tight across her back for a moment, as if he wanted to hold on tighter but didn't dare, before he released her and backed away. Filled with static electricity, a few wisps of her hair clung to his sweater like tiny, grasping fingers. Before she could smooth them back into place, his hand was there, tucking the wayward strands behind her ear. "Will you be okay now?" he asked.

She reached up to cup the side of his face. When he tipped his head away from her touch, Daisy suspected it was vitally important that she not retreat. Maybe it wasn't just shyness, but a self-consciousness about the wounds he couldn't hide that made him so awkward around her. She brushed her fingertips along his cheek and jaw, noting the rough textures, marveling that she could still feel the warmth and rugged bone structure beneath the stiff ridges of scar tissue there. She imagined Harry had a lot of reasons why socializing and human contact might not come easily for him. "I know you went through something horrible when you were deployed. I'm sorry if bringing up Tango upset you. I know that dog meant a lot to you. You mentioned him in nearly every letter."

Harry turned away and opened the door. "I'll wait on the porch until I hear the dead bolt engage."

Clearly, they hadn't gotten off on the right foot in person. But if he wouldn't talk to her, she didn't know how to fix whatever the problem was between them. "I'm sorry if I've done anything to—"

He spun around, leaning toward her with such a hard expression that she backed away a step. "Don't apologize to me. Ever. If anything, I owe you." Owe her what? But he wasn't going to explain that cryptic remark, either. He was already on his way out the door. "Good night, Daisy."

"Good night, Harry."

She locked both doors and moved to the side window to watch him stride through the snow around the side of the house. A few minutes later, apparently satisfied with his reconnaissance mission, he returned to his truck and climbed inside. She was glad to see he had a cup of coffee waiting for him, and wondered if it was still hot. She wondered if he'd appreciate her brewing up a fresh pot and offering to refill his disposable cup. If sleep was an issue, though, he wouldn't want more caffeine. And if being with her made him so edgy, he'd probably appreciate her turning off the lights and going back to bed so he could relax his vigil. If she could do that much to thank him for both his service to their country and standing watch here on the home front, she would.

"Good night, Top," she murmured before shutting off the Christmas lights. "Come on, boys."

Daisy turned off the rest of the lights except for the lamp beside her bed. After she gave each of the dogs a crunchy treat to chew on, they settled into their respective spots on top of her quilt. She draped her robe over a chair, along with her damp slipper socks, and set her glasses aside. Sensing that sleep would remain elusive, either out of fear of the unknown crazy stalking her or curiosity about the US Marine who'd made it his mission to make her feel safe tonight, Daisy dropped to her knees and lifted the eyelet dust ruffle to pull her father's old metal tackle box from beneath the bed. She sat on the bed, pulling the quilts over her lap and tucking Muffy against her side before opening the box.

She pushed aside the keepsakes she stored there and pulled out the small stack of letters she'd tied together with a ribbon. Then she propped up the pillows behind her and leaned back to read through Harry's letters again. She held one close to her face to bring the tight, angular handwriting into focus.

Dear Daisy,
Thank you for your letter from 2 May. I hope you are well.
  Not that you asked for my opinion, but one of my jobs here is to correct disruptive behaviors. I wouldn't let a man I outranked talk back to me, and you shouldn't let that student talk to you with that kind of language, either. My first instinct would be to shove the jackass young man up against the wall and wash his mouth out with soap. But I suppose

your principal and his parents would frown upon that. Are there parents? I had a potty mouth until I got placed with my second set of foster parents. Used to shock the hell out of Hope. (Clearly, I've gotten a little lax. If my pen wasn't about to run out of ink, I'd rewrite this thing so I wasn't swearing in front of you, either.) But if he's not learning it at home, he needs to learn it from you. That student needs to respect your command. Take charge.

I recommend avoiding direct eye contact, not speaking to him unless absolutely necessary, not giving him the attention he's looking for. That works on the dogs I train when we need them to be quiet. I'm not telling you to treat your students like dogs, but I can see that regular, consistent training in expected behaviors would be beneficial to managing a classroom.

We've had a slow week here. It makes me nervous when things get too quiet. Your letter offered a nice reprieve from the tension. Tango appreciated the dog treats, and I enjoyed the cookies. And no, I didn't get the two packages mixed up. (Although Tango did actually have some of both. I think he liked the cookies better.)

Yours truly,
MSgt. H. Lockhart

Daisy was in the middle of her third letter when she drifted off to sleep, surrounded by her dogs and watched over by the mysterious Marine who had touched her heart.

Chapter Five

It was a good day to be a teacher. But then, Fridays usually were.

Daisy deposited the holiday-scented hand soap on Mary Gamblin's desk, straightening the gift bag and Secret Santa card before peeking into the hallway to ensure the coast was clear before dashing across to her own classroom to grab her bag and coat. With the gift delivered, her to-do list at school was done. She locked up her room and hurried down to the teachers' lounge. She needed to zip in, grab her mail and get out of here for a couple of hours.

She'd had a busy day, working through lunch with Angelo Logan, dressing up in toga-draped sheets with her sophomore literature class to reenact scenes from *Julius Caesar* and celebrating a stack of vocabulary quizzes that everyone in her composition class had passed. Despite having such a short night's sleep, she'd enjoyed a couple of hours of the deepest slumber she'd had in a long time. When she awakened, she'd rolled over onto a pile of letters strewn around her in the bed and on the floor. Remembering the closeness she'd felt reading Harry's letters, remembering he'd been worried enough about her to keep watch over her house all night, remembering the abundant strength of his arms folding around her, all made her smile. She woke up feeling hopeful, renewed and unafraid to face the day.

With the light of day, Harry's truck was gone. But the feelings remained. While coffee brewed and the dogs ran around the backyard, Daisy had unpacked a few more Christmas decorations and hung them around the house. She wouldn't be putting up a tree until this weekend, but little by little she was getting the rest of the house ready to go for the faculty holiday party. Although she still had no explanation for the snowballs tossed against the side of her house, there had been no more boot prints in her yard beyond Harry's that she needed to worry about, and Daisy was feeling Christmasy again. For a little while last night, she hadn't felt as horribly alone as she usually did in that old house. Harry had offered her enough of a reprieve that she could put her imagination to rest and find her fighting spirit again.

Daisy zipped up her coat and looped her bag over her shoulder, heading down the hallway with a purpose to her step, humming a holiday tune. She was going all out this Christmas, partly because of the party, but mostly because she hated that fear, paranoia and even a little depression were such easy moods to succumb to this time of year. Especially this year, when her mom was celebrating Christmas with her stepfather's family and her creepy Secret Santa gifts were making December feel like a scary Halloween movie.

She exchanged a wave with her principal, Ryan Hague, as he locked up his office and headed out. He was probably heading home for a quick bite of dinner before coming back to supervise tonight's basketball game with a cross-city rival. Daisy smiled, glad she'd taken the time to hang up the white silk ball decorated with plastic mistletoe in the archway leading into her living room. She wasn't expecting any kissing action herself over the holidays, but Mr. Hague was a newlywed who'd married his second wife over the summer. It would be a fun way to start the Christmas party when he and other staff members arrived with their spouses or dates and she ushered them inside.

The clicking of her boots on the marble floor slowed as she tried to remember the last time she'd been kissed. The memory of Brock's dark head bending toward hers while she pushed his sour breath out of her space gave way to an illusory image of Harry Lockhart's damaged face with all its interesting angles and soulful gray eyes. She didn't suppose he was a mistletoe kind of man, indulging in silly holiday traditions, but that didn't stop her from picturing his mouth sliding over hers and those massive arms gathering her up against his chest again. Daisy's breath caught in her throat and she was suddenly uncomfortably warm inside her coat.

When had her patriotic pen pal become the stuff of her fantasies? She had a feeling she hadn't made a terribly good impression on Harry. He seemed to have a hard time relaxing around her. Although he'd been kind enough to check out her backyard, and set up a guard around her house last night, she didn't have to be psychic to sense the antsy energy coming off him. Without any kind of explanation beyond his obvious injuries or perhaps being an introvert, it was far too easy to suspect that *she* was what made him so uncomfortable.

Other footsteps, heavier and moving faster than her own in the hallway behind her, dragged Daisy out of her thoughts. She peeked over her shoulder and saw Bernie Riley's familiar blue and gold jacket and light brown hair. She nodded a greeting to the tall, lanky man. "Coach."

"Gunderson." He jogged a few steps to catch up and

walk beside her. Apparently, he was en route to the teacher's lounge, too. "You coming to the game tonight?"

"I'm working the front gate." Selling tickets, checking passes from the other school's staff. "But I'll try to get into the gym to watch some of it. Are you starting Angelo?"

"That kid's my star point guard. Not as tall as his brother. But faster. Smarter on the court, too."

Speaking of brothers… She knew Bernie was focused on tonight's game, but she had to ask, "Did you get my note about Albert?"

"I did." He stuffed his hands into the pockets of his slacks and chuckled. "So he's your new pet project, huh? Always trying to rescue somebody, aren't you."

Daisy bristled at the condescension hidden behind his teasing tone. "We need to do the best we can for all our students, not just the star athletes."

His long fingers clamped around her upper arm, stopping her. "You're not implying that I only care about the students who play for me, are you?"

She had to tilt her head back, way back, for him to see the glare in her eyes as she tugged her arm from his grip. "We're an academic prep school. We shouldn't have students who are failing English. We're going to lose Albert if we don't do something." She wasn't fond of being grabbed like that, but for a man with Coach Riley's ego, perhaps she'd be smarter to make this request about him. "You know how much Albert loves basketball. He respects you. If you encouraged him to—"

"Did you ever stop to think that maybe *you* were the problem?"

"Me?" Daisy rocked back on her heels, as surprised by the accusation as she'd been to feel his hand on her arm. "What do you mean?"

Bernie shrugged, his gaze checking up and down the

hallway before landing on her. "Some of those boys—they're young men, really—aren't comfortable being in your class or working one-on-one with you because, well, they have a crush on you."

"Impossible." How could they? She was more than a decade older than the teenagers. She made them write nearly every day, and most of the novels she taught weren't on any high schooler's must-read list. "Did one of them tell you that? Miss Wadsworth is younger than I am. Prettier, too."

"Yeah, but you're friendlier, funnier. You've got that cool hair vibe going." He flicked at a strand of her hair. "Wasn't this red last year? And you were a blonde when I met you. Like my Stella. The kids like that kind of stuff."

"I have never encouraged any one of them on a personal level. When it comes to teaching I have never been anything but professional with my students." She was appalled to hear that she was any part of the school's gossip mill. "There has never been one complaint filed against me."

Bernie's hands were up in surrender and he was grinning again. "Hey, I'm not accusing you of anything. But when you're a walking hormone, it doesn't take much for a kid to think he's in love with somebody who smiles at him or gives him a good grade. You should hear some of the questions I get in health class."

"About me?"

"About women." He arched his brows in a wry expression. "And sex."

No. *Sex* and Ms. G should not be anywhere together in a sentence where students were concerned.

"You think Albert has a crush on me?" Was that why he'd dropped her class? Or was that the explanation for those sick gifts she'd been receiving? Could the beheaded elf and other disturbing mementos be Albert Logan's idea of expressing his feelings for her? Or expressing his frustration that she didn't return his feelings?

"I don't know. The boys don't usually talk about specifics."

If there were some misplaced emotions going on, she shouldn't try to help Albert personally. But that didn't mean she was giving up on helping the young man succeed. "Encourage him to talk to another teacher, then. You could help him."

Bernie took a step back, shaking his head. "Whoa. I'm not an English teacher."

"Even if he starts turning in his assignments, it'll raise his grades. You can teach him responsibility, can't you?"

Bernie considered her request for a few moments, scratching at the back of his head before replying. "I could use his height back on the team. But I'm so busy this time of year."

Daisy took half a step toward him, encouraged that he would consider her request. "Would you at least promise to talk to him?" When he nodded and turned toward the faculty lounge again, Daisy fell into step beside him. "And if you do find out that he's got the hots for me, will you please remind him that I will never be available to a student in that way. It's not just school policy, it's *my* policy."

Bernie reached over her head to open the door. "I'll sit him down and we'll have a chat."

"Thank you." She had to raise her voice to be heard over the animated conversation inside. Eddie Bosch was regaling a couple of their coworkers with a story while Mary Gamblin ran off copies of worksheets and Carol Musil sorted through the catalogues in her mailbox. They were laughing at the light-up tie Eddie had gotten from his Secret Santa, and lamenting other unfortunate fashion choices they had made over the years.

So much for making a quick exit. While Bernie joined the conversation, Daisy moved toward the bank of mailboxes, already spying the stack of reworked papers from a student who'd been serving an in-school suspension. She'd tuck those into her bag and go, knowing she couldn't linger if she wanted enough time to get home to let the dogs out, change into a pair of jeans and get back to school for tonight's game. Dinner would have to be a hot dog from the concession stand.

She was sorting through the papers, making sure they were all there, when Eddie came up beside her. "How did that interview go last night? You got a new tenant?"

Hardly. When the guy had said he'd only move in if she kenneled her dogs or left them outside 24/7, she'd been only too happy to show him the door. "No. But I'm meeting with two more prospects tomorrow."

Bernie pulled down a six-pack of sports drinks with his name and a big bow on it from on top of the mailboxes. "Nice."

Clearly, he was faring better with the gifts he'd been receiving from his Secret Santa. Daisy braced herself and stuck her hand inside her own mailbox, dreading what she might find today. She breathed an audible sigh of relief when she found no surprise packages, which made her feel good enough to elaborate on her answer to Eddie's question. "Mr. Friesen liked everything about the place except for me and my dogs. Didn't think we'd be a good fit."

Eddie laughed. "Probably not. But I think you're on to something, leasing part of that big house. Income property. That's what they call it on TV. I'm thinking about finishing my basement and renting it out. How much are you asking for rent? I'm curious to know if it'd be worth the investment."

But Daisy didn't hear the question. She couldn't hear

much of anything over the pulse thundering in her ears. She'd been a fool to think her tormentor would have forgotten her for even one day. There it was, clipped to the bottom of the stack of papers—a plain white envelope with just her name and the usual message, typed onto a Christmas label.

> *Dear Daisy,*
> *Merry Christmas from your Secret Santa.*

"Daisy?"

She ignored both Eddie's prompt and Bernie's effort to join the conversation. "You didn't fill the vacancy at your house? Are you still lookin' for someone to rent that room? I might know a guy. Strictly short term."

She hated that her fingers were shaking as she peeled open the back flap of the envelope. She hated that Eddie, Mary and Carol knew enough about the gifts she'd been receiving that Eddie placed a steadying hand on her shoulder, and the two women stopped their work to watch as she pulled out the enclosed card and opened it.

Suddenly, it hurt to breathe. If she'd been alone, she would have screamed.

The graphic sexual act, although drawn in stick figures, left nothing to the imagination. Neither did the caption beneath the picture. *You and me, bitch. When you least expect it. Merry Christmas to me.*

"You okay?" Eddie asked.

No. She wasn't. But the words wouldn't form.

"Is that from your Secret Santa?" Bernie's height made it far too easy to peer over her shoulder to inspect the defiled holiday card. Daisy crushed it in her fist and stuffed it into the pocket of her coat before he could see the disturbing missive. She didn't need anyone else knowing her fear and shame. "You don't like your gift?"

Daisy tilted her face to Bernie's, thinking for one brief second that his friendly smile was a cruel joke. It took a few seconds longer to realize he hadn't seen the sick drawing and remember that he wasn't one of those close friends who knew about the other gifts.

"What's wrong with it?" Bernie asked. "There's not a gift card in there? Is it empty?"

"I have to get out of here." Daisy shrugged off Eddie's hand and hurried to the door while she wasn't too blind with terror to see it.

Coach Riley cursed behind her. "I need to call my wife. If that bitch is playin' another game—"

"Put a sock in it," Eddie warned before hurrying after her. "Give me ten minutes, Dais. I need to finish entering these grades and then I'll walk you out."

"I don't have ten minutes." She glanced in Eddie's direction without really seeing him. "I need to go home and take care of the dogs before I come back for the game."

"Bernie." Eddie snapped at the tall man and gestured for him to follow her.

Bernie glanced up from the cell phone at his ear. "It's still daylight. But if you want me to walk you out, I guess I can."

"No." Daisy needed to get out to her car so she could scream, and maybe get a hold of her thoughts again. No one had hurt her. This was just about getting under her skin and scaring her. She needed to get away from this place and these people and remember she was strong enough to deal with the fear again. "I'm fine," she lied. "Make your call. I'll see you tonight."

HARRY WAS BEGINNING to wonder if anyone in this neighborhood spent much time looking out their windows and butting into other people's business. Although he knew a lot about staying off the radar when he needed to, he wasn't about to assume that he didn't look like some kind of suspicious figure. He glanced into the rearview mirror to study his reflection. Black cap, scarred face, perpetual scowl? Not suspicious—make that threatening. Unless you got to know him. And maybe even then, that was the impression he made on the civilian world.

But clearly, there was no neighborhood watch on this block because he'd been sitting across from Daisy's house or walking the area for most of the past twenty hours without anyone approaching his truck or calling the police to come check him out. That didn't bode well for anyone else keeping an eye out for the well-being of the purple-tinted hug-meister who lived alone in that big blue house.

He spotted her in his side-view mirror, turning the corner in a mini-SUV. Lime green. Obviously, the woman loved color and couldn't get enough of it in her life. Black and khaki suited him just fine. Maybe that opposing difference in their tastes explained a lot about why he was having such a hard time connecting with her. More than the fact she didn't look like the woman he'd imagined in those letters, her cheerful, touchy-feely, ninety-mile-a-minute personality didn't match the reserved, ladylike angel he'd hoped was going to save him from himself.

But those differences hadn't stopped him from looking out for her. He was certain the shrink he'd talked to earlier this afternoon would say he identified with her isolation. Those early years when it had just been him and Hope in a remote cabin in the Ozarks, when they'd had no idea whether their father was going to come home drunk and angry, or not come home at all, had certainly taught him to be self-sufficient. Had taught him to appreciate the comradeship he'd found in the Corps. But what that little boy wouldn't have given to have a real daddy he could truly depend on, someone who would have looked out for him and Hope. Daisy needed someone reliable in her life. For right now, at least, he was it.

Harry raised his hand to wave as she drove past him. But she didn't see him and he curled his fingers into a fist and drew it back into his lap. Like everyone else in this neighborhood, Daisy was unaware of his presence. She was singing along with the radio or talking to someone on a hands-free phone, as she turned into her driveway and shut down the engine. Why didn't she pull into the garage? Was she waiting for the song or phone call to finish? Was this just a quick stop before she went somewhere else? Should he follow her if she left again? Just how far was he going to take this new let's-spy-on-Daisy hobby of his?

After checking his watch, Harry huddled down inside his coat and waited to get a better idea of her immediate plans before he made that decision.

Maybe this need to keep an eye on her had something to do with the unexpected curiosity that made him want to understand her better. Or maybe his fractured brain needed to resign itself to the differences between imagination and reality so that he could put that ideal Daisy to rest and get on with a new plan for getting himself fit to return to active duty.

Ten minutes later, he sat up straight behind the wheel, wondering how long she was going to sit inside her car.

At fifteen minutes, he got out of his truck and jogged across the street.

Harry walked up her driveway, assuming she'd see him approaching in one of her mirrors. But when he reached the driver's side window, he saw her clutching the steering wheel, resting her head against it. There was no music playing. No phone that he could see. She was unaware of his presence. And he could see her lips moving, muttering something over and over. Was she praying? Angry? Crazy?

Already uneasy with her just sitting in the parked car, Harry rapped his knuckles against the window. "Daisy?"

She screamed in response, sliding toward the center console. Harry stepped back, but pointed to the lock on the door, asking her to open it. He retreated another step into the snow as she shoved the door open and climbed out.

"Damn it, Harry, you need to announce yourself." She slammed the door and swatted his shoulder. Now that she was standing and facing him, he could see she'd been crying. Even her glasses—blue this time, a shade lighter than her eyes—couldn't hide the puffy redness behind the lenses. With a noisy harrumph, she grabbed the front of his coat and pulled him out of the snow bank before venting her emotions with another painless swat. "This is the second time your surprise visits have nearly given me a heart attack. Why don't you call first?"

"I was worried." The suspicion that had brought him out of his truck twisted in his gut at the sight of those crystallized tears drying on her cheeks. "People don't sit in their car for fifteen minutes without going someplace unless something is wrong. Besides, I couldn't call. I don't have your number."

He wasn't going to get it, either. Her little fit of temper vanished with an unladylike curse. "Fifteen minutes? It's been that long?" She opened the door again and reached inside to drag her heavy pink bag over the console. "I have to let the dogs out and then be back at school in an hour. I'd like to eat something and change out of these clothes."

She looped the bag over her shoulder and hiked it onto her hip so she could reach back inside to pull her keys from the ignition. But the bag slipped and the door tried to close, and when she jostled between them a wadded-up card fell out of her pocket and bounced across the concrete to land beside his boot. Harry bent down to pick it up, catching a glimpse of green sparkles in the shape of a Christmas tree and… "What the hell?" He smoothed the wrinkled card stock in his palm, ignoring the pornographic artwork to read the threat typed underneath it. "First you've got some guy peeking in your bedroom window and now this crap? Is it the same guy? Have you gotten other garbage like this from him?"

Dots of pink colored her cheeks and she snatched it away. He'd take that as a yes. She stuffed the card into her pocket and hurried through the back gate.

Harry followed right behind her, demanding answers. "Daisy, where did that come from? Who sent it to you? An angry student?"

"I don't know."

"You don't know who sent you that filth?"

She spun around to face him when she reached the deck. "If I did, don't you think I'd put a stop to it?" She looked down on him from the top step. "What are you doing here, anyway? Don't you have a life?"

He didn't, actually. A wry sigh clouded the air around him. "I'm home on leave for six weeks. I don't have anything to do except hang around Hope's apartment and make her worry. The Corps gives me a job to do every day. Here in Kansas City I'm going nuts. Nothing to do but think and walk and think some more."

"I'm a project for you? A hobby to keep you busy?"

He wondered if that hurtful note of sarcasm in her tone was aimed at him or herself. "You're a friend." The women in those letters was even more important to him. "Something's going on and I can help by keeping an eye on things."

"You've been watching my house all day?"

Except for that hour he'd met with Dr. Polk. "Pretty much. I walked around the neighborhood a little bit. In the daylight, I found where the guy was standing when he used your house for target practice last night." He moved past her up the steps and pointed over to the neighbor's house. "That guy's backyard. I missed the tracks last night because of the shrubs, but once I got over the fence—"

"You trespassed in Mr. Finch's yard?" She joined him at the railing.

Could the threat be that close to home? "You got issues with your neighbor?"

"No. It's just—he's so compulsive about his yard and taking care of things. You didn't knock any leaves off his boxwood bushes, did you? Or dent the top of the fence? Patch dug under the fence last summer, tore up some of the roots—"

"You've got somebody stalking you, Daisy." He pounded his fist against the top of the railing. "I wouldn't worry about the damn shrubbery!"

His outburst shocked her. Hell, he hadn't raised his voice like that for weeks now. Watching her clutch the strap of her bag over her chest and retreat from him, he wished he'd been able to control his frustrated concerns. The dogs were barking inside the mudroom and her back was pressed against the door. Her eyes never left his. "I'm sorry. The last thing I want to do is be the person who scares you." That muscle ticked beneath his eye as he buried the useless rage inside him where it belonged. He put his hands up and stepped back, suspecting where her mind had gone and hating himself for taking her there. "I remember you said your ex was violent. I swear I would never hurt you." He shook his head as he heard the words leave his mouth. "That's probably what your ex said, too."

"Actually..." He held himself still as he waited for her

to finish that sentence, praying she didn't believe he was as messed up as the man who'd stabbed her. He prayed even harder that she'd be right. "Brock promised that he *would* hurt me if I left him." She pushed her glasses up at her temple, the action making him think she wanted to make sure she was seeing Harry clearly, evaluating him. "He was too controlling. Obsessive. I had to break it off so I could have a life. Rescue dogs. Stay after school with students. Visit my parents and friends. He was drunk that night he broke into my apartment." She dropped her hand to clutch the strap of her bag again. "He kept his promise."

Harry's hands curled into fists again. With the violence he'd seen, it was far too easy to picture how she'd been hurt. But knowing his response should be his issue, not hers, he blanked the images—both real and imagined—and drew in several breaths of the cold winter air to chill the anger simmering through his veins. "Could he have anything to do with those messages?"

"Brock is in prison."

"You know that for a fact? He doesn't have friends on the outside who might be willing to do some dirty work for him?" Daisy was wilting, like a colorful flower that he'd just sprayed with pesticide. He stuffed his hands into his coat pockets and leaned his hip against the railing, hoping the relaxed posture made him look a little less intimidating, a little more like the friend he meant to be. "Look, I know I'm short on tact and charm, and I've got issues with PTSD that I can't always control. But I protect people for a living. I know how to get a job done. I'm trained to assess the enemy. I know how to scout a perimeter and keep the people I'm guarding safe." He looked away, needing a break from those searching blue eyes. "Right now, I'm trying to protect you. I'm not bothering anybody by keeping an eye on your place. And clearly, somebody's trying to bother *you*. Let me do this." When she didn't answer, he faced her again. "You said you didn't have anybody."

"You feel you owe me this protection because of those letters?" He wouldn't deny it. But he was here for other reasons, too, ones that were too difficult to put into words right now. "I can't have somebody around me whom I can't trust."

"I'm the man in those letters, Daisy. I promise. You can trust me with your life." Maybe he couldn't promise her anything else, but that much he would guarantee. If she'd let him. "I'm here now. Use me."

She considered his vow for several moments before she nodded. She turned away to unlock the door. "It's been a long day and I'm tired, and I have no time to rest. I'm probably extra sensitive to probing questions and hot tempers." Not to mention receiving that message, which had clearly unnerved her. The dogs darted out, circling around her with wagging tails for a warm greeting. Once they'd been sufficiently petted by their mistress, they trotted over to greet him. Seeing Patch prop his front paws against his thigh and Caliban push his head into Harry's hand while Muffy tried to squeeze between the other two dogs seemed to reassure Daisy more than any words he could utter. "I'd be lying if I said I didn't appreciate you keeping an eye on things. I felt safer last night after you left."

Instincts took over the dogs' need for affection and they trotted down the steps to explore the yard. Harry followed Daisy inside the mudroom and stomped the snow off his boots while she hung her coat and bag on a hook.

But when he pulled off his gloves and watch cap and followed her into the hallway, she stopped him with a hand at the middle of his chest, straightening her arm to keep him from coming any farther into the house. He wasn't used to Daisy needing space. In the twenty-four hours since they'd met face to face, she hadn't once been this eager to put some distance between them. He should relish her backing off from all the touchy-feely stuff that bamboozled him.

But now, it only made him worry. "I thought you were okay with me being here."

She pulled her hand away. "Would you make sure the dogs do their business and get some exercise while I change my clothes?"

Harry hesitated a moment, both in leaving her and in being alone with the dogs. But he'd made a career out of doing what needed to be done. "I can do that."

"Thanks." She reached for his hand and gave it a friendly squeeze. Why hadn't he noticed sooner that she had a beautiful smile?

He reversed the grip to hold on to her when she would have pulled away. "And then you're going to tell me what's going on. I want to know how many other threats you've received and when they started. I need to know your schedule, where you'll be and when, and I need to know if there's anyone you suspect."

Smile killer.

Seemed he had a habit of doing that with this woman.

"Daisy, I…" Another verbal apology didn't seem sufficient. And he couldn't just tell her things would be okay because he knew far too well how *not* okay the world could be. Obeying an impulse that felt as right as it was unexpected, Harry tugged on Daisy's hand, pulling her up against his chest and wrapping his arms around her in one of those hugs she seemed to like so well. He turned his nose against the clinging static of her hair and breathed in that sweet scent that was hers alone.

He patted her back a few times, until he thought he heard a soft giggle. Daisy relaxed against him, slipping her arms beneath his coat and flattening them against his back.

She rubbed her palms up and down his spine in strokes that warmed his skin through his sweater and soothed the guilt and concern tensing every muscle. Harry stopped patting and started mimicking the caressing motion up and down her back. He felt pretty lame for not having much experience with comforting embraces, but he felt pretty lucky, too, that Daisy was making the effort to help him improve his skills. And he was a quick study, down to the curve of her hip, up beneath the silken weight of her brown and purple hair.

Idly, Harry wondered how the sensations of curves and gentle heat would change without the ribs of her sweater and wrinkled blouse between his hands and her skin. An interested party stirred behind the zipper of his jeans at the idea of touching Daisy's warm skin. He'd like to kiss her, too, to see if those lips were as soft and luscious as they looked—to find out if they'd respond with the same bold enthusiasm of her hugs or be more like the gentle tutelage of her hands. His whole body thrummed with anticipation as he rubbed his lips against her temple, kissing the earpiece of her glasses before adjusting his aim to press his lips against the warm beat of her pulse there. Daisy's arms tightened around him, aligning her body more perfectly against his. Her breasts pillowed against his chest and the tips beaded into pearls that poked through the layers of clothing separating them, making his palms itch to touch those, too.

"Why do I get the feeling you haven't had much of this kind of contact, Top?" she murmured against his neck. "Which is a shame because you're good at it." She added the undeserved compliment, reminding him that while he'd had sex, he'd never once been in a relationship with a woman. Not long distance and certainly not up close and personal like this.

But this was Daisy, his pen pal angel and long-distance friend, and she was scared. He might even be a big part of what scared her. This wasn't the time to give in to curiosity and crude impulses. Right now, all he needed was for her to be safe.

Reluctantly, he loosened his grip on her, turning his head to kiss the same spot on her hair. But never one to be demure or predictable, Daisy lifted her chin and caught his lips with hers. The kiss was surprising, but not so brief that he didn't have a moment to press his mouth over hers, confirming at least one of his speculations. Her lips were as soft and succulent as he'd imagined. And he wanted to kiss her again.

Daisy dropped back onto her heels and pulled away before he fully acknowledged that impulse. "You gonna be okay?" he asked.

She was smiling again when she nodded, and his chest swelled. Yeah. There was a lot to be said for trading hugs and comfort. He didn't feel quite so guilty about stealing that smile away in the first place.

He tugged his hat back over his short hair and pulled on his gloves. "I'll go take care of the dogs."

Chapter Six

"One hot dog with ketchup and extra relish."

Daisy closed the money box and stamped the hands of the three students who'd paid their fee at her table outside the Central Prep gym, encouraging them to enjoy the games before accepting the dinner Harry offered. "I'm starving. Thank you." She took a big bite, savoring the tangy flavors before nodding toward the bottles of soda in Harry's hands. "You're not hungry?"

"Already finished mine." He set one of the sodas on the table and pulled a paper napkin from the pocket of his jeans. He reached over and wiped a dribble of ketchup and pickle juice from the side of her mouth, showing her the stain on the napkin before she snatched it from his fingers. "Why doesn't it surprise me to discover you have a healthy appetite?"

Daisy turned away, feeling the heat of embarrassment creeping into her cheeks. She wiped her mouth a second time before facing him again. "I haven't eaten since lunch, and that was seven hours ago."

"I'm not criticizing." His bottle hissed as he twisted the cap and released the carbonation pressure. "Just observing. You don't do anything halfway. Decorating for Christmas. Hugs. Eating hot dogs."

"Are you sure you're not making fun of me?" Daisy took a daintier bite this time.

"No, ma'am."

She arched an eyebrow. "We talked about that, Master Sergeant."

"Ouch." For a split second, his stiff mouth crooked into a smile. But then there was a big roar from the crowd in the gym as someone on the junior varsity team made an exciting play. Harry's alert gaze darted through the doorway toward the bleachers. A muscle tightened across his angular cheekbone before he swallowed a drink of soda and brought his gaze back to hers. "No more fancy titles for you and me. In my defense, though, we are back at school. Technically, you're on duty."

Daisy wadded up her napkin and tossed it at him. He deftly caught it and tossed it into the trash can beside the table. Although this familiar camaraderie had settled between them, not unlike the conversation they'd shared in their long-distance letters, Daisy felt raw inside. Harry had insisted he drive her to school, and for a man so averse to long conversations, he'd had plenty of questions to ask about her Secret Santa. At his insistence, she'd unlocked her classroom to show him the gifts hidden inside her desk, as well as her mailbox in the teachers' lounge where most of the messages and gifts had been delivered. Seemingly immune to the curious stares at his scarred face, he'd asked her to introduce him to several coworkers, glossing over thank-yous for his service to the country and turning the conversations around to learn a little more about Principal Hague, Eddie Bosch and Mary Gamblin.

Despite security protocols that were in place to protect the school from outside threats, access to her inside the school was too easy, he'd complained. And she was too isolated at home for him to deem either place safe. Although she'd teased him about his natural talent for bringing down the mood of a room, the underlying truth to his words had left her feeling unsettled. His advice that she be hypervigilant to her surroundings, avoid being alone or even one-on-one with any of the male students or faculty in the building, and report anyone lurking near her classroom or faculty workroom to the principal made her that much more edgy and distrustful of the people she interacted with nearly every day of her life.

Two weeks ago, before the first message had been delivered, she'd been content to surround herself with students and work. She was a social creature by nature. She was proud of her school, liked her students and coworkers, reveled in the holiday season, loved being busy and doing for others.

But tonight, despite her spirited blue and gold facade, all she wanted was to go home to her dogs and lock her doors. She couldn't say whether it was Harry's reserved, imposing presence, casting suspicion in a wide net around her, or the fact this damaged yet fit, virile man was enduring his aversion to the crowd to not only protect her, but to also be kind to her, that left her feeling so off-kilter this evening.

"Daisy."

She hadn't realized how far into her troubling thoughts she'd sunk until Harry spoke her name and nodded toward the group jostling for position on the opposite side of the table.

Complete with two sets of grandparents, two elementary-aged children and a curly-haired toddler who was fussing to climb down from her mother's arms and explore, the family's arrival required Daisy to focus on her job. After calculating the discounts, she gave them the price for their tickets, even splitting the cost in half for them when both grandfathers insisted on paying.

By the time she finished counting back their change and stamping hands, Daisy realized the little girl had stopped squirming and was staring at Harry. Harry was staring right back. In that grim, clenched-jaw look that made the muscle beneath his right eye spasm. The little girl smiled and pointed at Harry. "Bomba No-man."

"Abominable Snowman?" The mother saw where her daughter was pointing, and pulled her hand away. "I'm sorry. You must remind her of a character in one of those animated Christmas shows she watches."

"Not a problem, ma'am," Harry reassured her. "I've been called worse."

But it *was* a problem. Even as the family moved into the gym to find seats on the bleachers, Harry was retreating against the cinder block wall behind him. She heard the plastic of his soda bottle cracking as he squeezed it in his hand.

However, pointing out the disfiguring scars didn't seem to bother him as much as the noise. The referees blew their whistles and the timeout buzzer sounded. The pep band struck up an enthusiastic rendition of the school fight song. That muscle ticked across Harry's cheek and he turned his head as if the cacophony hurt his ears.

"Are you okay?" She took a drink, trying to hide how much his charged, yet overtly still, posture worried her. She gestured to the metal chair beside hers. "You can sit if you want."

"I'm better standing." So he could make a quicker getaway if he had to, no doubt.

With no one waiting in line for tickets, Daisy sat on the edge of the table, facing him. "You said you suffer from PTSD. Do the loud noises bother you?

Harry's dark gray eyes scanned the lobby, from the glimpse inside the gym to the line waiting at the concession stand. "A basketball game is not going to make me freak out."

"But other things will?"

His gaze landed on her. He hesitated a moment before dropping his volume and answering. "Sometimes a loud bang will trigger memories. Your dogs charging at me last night kind of..." He twirled his fingers beside his head, indicating some kind of flashback, she supposed. "Usually it's the smells that are the worst."

"Like what?" More than once, she'd caught him sniffing her hair. And she'd already memorized his unique scent, undoctored by any aftershave or cologne. He must be particularly sensitive to certain odors. "Do you smell anything here?"

He rolled his shoulders as if his sweater was suddenly uncomfortably tight. "This isn't the place for that kind of conversation."

"Maybe when we get home. You could stay for a while." Daisy pushed to her feet, needing to touch him to comfort him somehow. She reached for his free hand and squeezed his fingers. "Do you need to talk about it? I could make us some hot chocolate and stay up as late as you need to. You mentioned things in your letters—like you needed to get them off your chest. I don't claim to understand everything you've been through, but I do know a little about how horrible the world can be."

He stared at her hard for a moment, muttering something about an angel that she couldn't quite make out over the squeaks of rubber-soled shoes on the polished gymnasium floor.

"I've got a therapist for those kinds of talks." Harry's

grip pulsed around her hand. "I'm not interested in making you cry anymore."

Daisy leaned in, matching his hushed tone. "Even if I did, it would be all right. If I can help... I want to."

"Are you asking this guy for a favor, too?"

Recognizing the smug woman's voice behind her, Daisy plopped her forehead against Harry's chest for a moment and audibly groaned. Then she released his hand and turned to the statuesque blonde in a coat most likely from a pricey boutique. "Excuse me?"

Stella Riley, resident trophy wife and all-around ego buster as far as Daisy was concerned. Stella grinned, waving off what had sounded like an accusation. "I'm just teasing. Bernie said you'd asked for his help."

"With a student."

"Is this your new gentleman friend? Bernie thought you might have met someone, but that you were keeping him a secret." The woman extended her hand across the table. "Hi. I'm Stella, Coach Riley's wife."

"Basketball coach," Daisy whispered, explaining the pronouncement. While part of her wanted to correct the assumption that Harry was her boyfriend, she also knew this conversation would end sooner if she just let Stella say what she wanted to and move on.

Daisy startled at the brush of Harry's fingers against the small of her back. Was he reassuring her? Or grounding himself? He tossed his empty bottle into the trash before shaking Stella's hand. "Harry Lockhart."

"Military, right?"

"Yes, ma'am. Marine Corps."

"I could tell by the haircut." She winked before releasing him. "It suits you. We're proud of you boys. And we're all glad that Daisy has found someone again." Stella pulled her ID card out of her wallet and flashed it at Daisy. "Not that you need this to know who I am. But I want to follow the rules."

"You're good to go, Stella." Daisy had a hard time zeroing in on Stella's name on the list of faculty and spouses who got in free because Harry's palm had slipped beneath the hem of her gold cardigan and flattened against her back. Daisy felt the brand of his touch through her blouse as surely as the stamp she inked onto Stella's hand.

Stella tipped her blond curls toward the gym. "How's it going?"

"I haven't been able to check the score yet, but there's lots of cheering, so I'm guessing pretty well."

"Great. Bernie will be in a good mood, then." Stella's wave included both Harry and Daisy. "Nice to meet you, soldier boy. Don't be a stranger. I'll see you next week, Daisy. If you need any help with the party, let me know."

"That was like a tornado blowing through," Harry muttered, absentmindedly rubbing his hand in small circles against her spine. "Is she a friend of yours?"

Whether soothing her taut nerves or assuaging his own, Daisy had to step away from his distracting touch so she could think of words to speak. "She *is* first lady of the basketball court. When the team has a winning season, I guess she deserves some of the credit, too."

"You didn't answer my question."

"I work with her husband."

"Still not an answer." Daisy busied herself straightening the items on the table. "You know, other people say bad things about people. You're too big-hearted to do that, aren't you? The fact that you won't makes me think there's some friction between you and the first lady."

Daisy stopped her busy work. "I never have understood people who think they're all that. It feels like I'm back in high school whenever I'm around her. Of course, maybe if I'd been one of the popular kids back then instead of an artsy geek, I might feel differently."

"Still avoiding the question, Ms. Geek."

"I liked you better when you wouldn't talk to me."

Harry laughed. Although far too brief, his laugh was a rich, chest-deep sound that made her smile. She adjusted her glasses to see the pliant side of his mouth smiling, too.

A hundred little wishes locked up inside her heart unfurled at the knowledge she'd put that smile there. "Maybe her snootiness stems from insecurity. I imagine she's alone a lot during basketball season with all the games and practices. Sometimes, I think she's jealous that other people get to spend more time with her husband than she does."

Harry's smile vanished as quickly as it had appeared. "How jealous?"

"Jealous enough to send me those threats?" Daisy shook her head. While she'd never felt especially comfortable around Stella Riley, she couldn't see any reason for the woman to have a personal grudge against her. "Those have to be from a guy. Right?"

Harry wasn't probing for answers anymore. He was moving to intercept the tall young black man who circled around the table.

"Now you got Coach Riley callin' my granny on me?" Albert Logan's Central Prep ball cap was cocked off to the side, giving him a deceptively juvenile look. But there was nothing childlike about the anger in his expression. "Ain't 'Lo man enough for you? You want to give me some private tutoring, too? Let's do it, Ms. G."

Daisy planted her feet, cringing at his grammar and hating the innuendo in his tone. "Not if you're going to talk to me like that. I'll report you to Mr. Hague. This isn't a punishment. We're concerned about you, Albert."

"You stay out of my business, or I'm gonna get all up in yours."

The moment Albert's pointing finger got too close, Harry palmed the teenager's shoulder and pushed him away, sliding between her and Albert.

Albert knocked the restraining hand away. "Get your hands off me, old man."

Harry squared off against the bigger, younger man. Although she couldn't see Harry's face, she could read every wary line of tension in his muscular stance. There were rules against touching students. Harry wasn't staff, but this standoff could escalate in a heartbeat if he thought he had to protect her.

"It's okay, Harry." She closed her hand over his rock-hard bicep, knowing she had to reach him with words and touch because there'd be no way she could physically restrain him. She splayed her other hand against his back, remembering how distracting his touch had been to her just a few minutes earlier. "This is Albert Logan, a former student of mine." With Harry's hands fisting at his sides, she appealed to Albert, as well. "Master Sergeant Lockhart is my pen pal from last year's writing project. He's home on leave."

"Take a step back," Harry warned. His muscles vibrated with tension beneath her fingers.

"Albert, please. I don't want to call the principal."

Albert glanced back and forth between the two of them, considering how a confrontation with Harry would play out, then wisely decided to retreat a step. Curiosity replaced the wounded pride and anger that had puffed up his posture, reminding Daisy that in many ways, these nearly grown students were still just big kids. Albert rubbed his knuckles across his cheek. "Dude, did that happen to you over there?"

The poised wariness didn't waver. "Yes."

"Was it a car bomb?"

"Albert…"

Picking up on subtle clues had never been Albert's strong suit. "You know Corporal Benny Garcia?" he asked. "That's the guy I wrote to. When I still had Ms. G for class. He drove one of those armored cars."

"I knew Garcia." *Knew?* Harry's shoulders lifted with a deep breath. "He drove an LAV—Light Armored Vehicle."

Compassion squeezed Daisy's heart. Was Albert hearing any of those past-tense references? She curled her fingers into the back of Harry's sweater, wishing they were in a less public place so she could wind her arms around his waist.

"Yeah. He used a bunch of initials I didn't understand. But it was cool when he talked about the motor and stuff." Albert's dark gaze suddenly shifted to her. "Angelo know you got a boyfriend, Ms. G?"

Why was everyone assuming that she and Harry were an item? Then she saw the way she had latched on to Harry, and the way he'd blocked her into a corner between the table and wall, defending her. Was there some unacknowledged longing she was projecting out into the universe that everyone but her could see?

"Who is Angelo?"

Albert dragged his focus back to Harry. "'Lo's my brother. He's playing tonight. He and Ms. G… He…" He glanced to her, looking for what? He knew exactly what kind of relationship she had with his brother. Was he hinting at something else? "Uh…"

"I'm helping Angelo with his scholarship applications. He's one of my best students. I think Albert could be, too."

Apparently satisfied with Albert's family history, Harry gave a curt nod and switched topics. "Where I come from, a man doesn't wear his cover inside. His hat," he explained, when Albert frowned. "And he speaks to a woman with respect. I suggest you do the same."

Albert shrugged. "Okay."

"Okay, what?"

"Okay, sir?"

Harry eyed the sideways hat until Albert pulled it off and stuffed the brim in the back pocket of his jeans. "Now we understand each other."

Instead of acting chastised, Albert grinned. "Benny said you were a tough son-of-a…" He glanced at Daisy, watched Harry's stance change, and thought better of finishing that phrase. "Benny respects you, sir."

"It was mutual."

Albert looked at Daisy and shrugged. "Sorry, Ms. G. Granny said I had to check in with you Monday before I go to work. Just don't call her no more."

"Anymore," Daisy automatically corrected.

"Yeah. She's scarier than both of you put together." The whole confrontation forgotten, Albert whistled to a couple of friends and joined them in line at the concession stand.

Harry dropped his gaze where her hand still clung to his arm. "Afraid I was going to take him out?"

She released her grip. "Were you?"

"I know I'm not surrounded by insurgents." His breathing seemed a little labored, though, when he faced her. "But you don't let them get close like that unless you know them. I didn't know that kid. The way he was coming at you…"

She wanted to ask about Corporal Garcia, find out if he'd lost his friend in an enemy attack. She desperately wanted to wind her arms around him and hold on until that tightly leashed tension quaking through his body eased.

But the buzzer sounded, marking the end of the first

basketball game. Fans cheered. The band played again, loud even to her own ears. A swarm of students and families spilled through the archway, flooding the lobby between the JV and varsity games. Harry muttered the very curse he'd kept Albert from saying and grabbed his coat from beneath the table.

"Are you okay?" Daisy moved to keep his face in sight, worried he was having some kind of meltdown. "This is too much for you, isn't it."

"I need some fresh air." He was struggling. His eyes were clear, but they locked on to hers while he zipped up, as if focusing on her, and not the people gathering in the space around them, centered him. Fine. She'd be still and let him focus. "I better call Hope and let her know where I am. She worries more than she needs to, and that's not good for the baby. Besides, I'd like to familiarize myself with the layout of the school grounds. I want to know every way somebody could get in or out."

Daisy understood his sister's need to worry. She sensed it was taking every bit of strength he had not to explode. "Will you be coming back?"

"I'm your ride home, aren't I? I just need to move. I'll probably run a couple laps around the building."

"Through the snow?"

"I like the cold." His fingers were unsteady when he threaded them into the hair at her temple and smoothed the waves down behind her ear. He cupped the side of her neck and jaw, and the trembling stilled. Daisy turned into his touch. With his heat warming her skin, her concerns ebbed to a less frantic pitch, and she hoped he was taking at least the same from her. "When you're ready to leave, go to the front door. I'll watch for you. You don't step foot outside until I'm here to walk you out, okay?"

"Okay."

His fingertips tightened against her skin. "I mean it, Dais."

She smiled. "Okay, *sir*."

His eyes widened for a split second at her sass. And then he was leaning in, kissing her. The press of his lips was firm, their movement stilted, but urgent enough to demand her response. The tip of his tongue moistened the point of contact between them with a raspy caress, but retreated before she could catch it. Harry's kiss was not quite chaste and over far too quick. Slightly breathless, she was still clinging to his bottom lip when he pulled away. His eyes had darkened like charcoal, and she wondered which of them was swaying on their feet.

Without a word, Harry released his grip and turned away. He darted through the crowd and disappeared out the double front doors into the night.

PDA might be frowned upon on school property, but Daisy wasn't complaining. The warmth of that surprising kiss stayed with her the rest of the evening. And though she kept one eye on the door, even when she stood in the archway to watch the last few minutes of the second game, Harry never came back. She hoped he'd snuck in to get some hot coffee instead of waiting for her out in the cold for an hour. But she was half afraid that the run-in with Albert, the noise and energy of the crowd, or even the kiss itself had frightened him off.

She had no doubts that he was still out there, waiting to drive her home, making sure she was safe. But she was sad for him that it was so hard to relax and enjoy himself for very long. And she was antsy to get back to him to see if they could recreate a little of that one-on-one magic where they joked with each other, and touched and cared and kissed.

That was why Daisy had the money counted down and locked up inside the office before the final buzzer sounded.

While the building cleared, she did a quick walk-through of the gymnasium bleachers with Eddie and Mary, picking up trash while the custodian swept the floor. She kept her distance from the heated conversation between Bernie and Stella Riley outside the boys' locker room, quickly diverting her attention when both their gazes landed on her. "What did I do?" she whispered to Eddie before dumping the stack of paper cups she'd collected into the trash bag he carried.

"Who knows?" Eddie shrugged. "Sometimes I think that woman's even jealous of me. And Bernie's certainly not *my* type."

Daisy wanted to laugh, but couldn't. "That's sad that she's so insecure. I know Bernie's got an ego the size of Arrowhead Stadium, but has he ever really cheated on her?"

Mary climbed down the bleachers to add her trash to the bag. "I heard that she's the one who cheated on him, in college, before they got married."

Daisy tuned out the bickering couple and headed toward the lobby. "Whatever their issues are, I wish they'd leave me out of it."

The band parents who'd been working the concession stand for their booster club fundraiser had cleaned up their area and locked the serving window partition by the time she said goodbye to Eddie and Mary. Eddie made sure Harry was still there to drive her home before escorting Mary out to her car. Mr. Hague was doing a walk-around to make sure all the doors were locked. The players and the opposing team members would leave by the locker room entrance. Daisy was alone in the lobby when she realized the chairs and table from gate duty had been left out.

It wouldn't take her five minutes to fold up the chairs and take them down to the basement storage room. The table would be a two-person project to carry down the steps, but by the time she put away the folding chairs, either the custodian would be finished or Mr. Hague would be back, and they could help. Then she'd be done with her assignment and she could get to Harry and that private conversation and maybe even another kiss.

She stuck her keys into the pocket of her jeans, then pulled out her phone. She had a split-second idea to call Harry in to have him help her, but just as quickly she realized she didn't have his number. Was it too late to call Hope and ask for it? That seemed silly when it'd be quicker to run outside and ask Harry herself. But he'd insisted that she not leave the building without him. He said he'd be watching the front doors. She could step outside and wave...

"Stop overthinking this, Daisy Lou." She stuffed her phone into another pocket. "Just finish up and go."

Tossing her coat over her bag, she picked up the chairs. Using one of her school keys, she unlocked the metal gate blocking off the stairs from the public and pushed it open. She carried the folding chairs down the concrete steps and descended half a century into the past. The long gray hallway was broken up by four heavy steel doors. Hung on runners like an old barn door, these doors simply unlatched and slid open. After the boiler room, the rest of the doors led to old classrooms from the original building before state regulations and a school improvement bond had required a new facility be built around the old one. With the original windows enclosed by new construction, the storage rooms doubled as tornado shelters now.

She pulled on the latch of the second metal door and shoved it off to the right, cringing at the grinding whine of metal on metal. The keyless latches were a throwback to the original building, too, before terrorists and school shootings made it vital that every school could be locked down to keep intruders out. After flipping on the light switch, she carried the chairs over to the closest of several racks lined up against the far wall. After setting the chairs into place, Daisy glanced around her. Metal racks with metal chairs. Gray concrete walls. In a basement. With no windows.

She shivered. This level was uninviting enough in the daytime. No natural light. No color. No warmth. At night, it felt even colder, despite the boiler room cranking out heat next door. If she ever had to teach a full day down here in this tomb, the powers that be would be carrying her out in a straitjacket. She was more than happy to pay a few extra cents on her taxes to have two whole floors of bright, well-lit rooms above her.

Metal grated against metal behind her. Daisy turned to see the last few inches of hallway disappear as the door slammed with an ominous clank. "Hey! I'm in here."

She heard a second clank as she dashed across the room.

What was going on? Daisy pushed on the latch and stumbled into the door when nothing happened. "No," she whispered, pumping the latch a half dozen times with the same result. Nothing was catching inside the locking mechanism to release the door. She pulled on the latch even though the metal clearly said *Push*. She tried sliding the door along its runner, in case the latch was the only problem. But the heavy steel wasn't budging. "This isn't funny," she yelled, slapping the flat of her hand against the door.

She was locked in.

Had the custodian or Mr. Hague not seen the light and carelessly closed the door? Was this a practical joke? Not funny. She pounded on the door, pushed the broken latch. "Let me out of here!"

Daisy drifted back a step, feeling suddenly light-headed. Could someone have locked her in on purpose?

Then she heard noises that locked her breath up in her chest and turned her blood to ice.

Scratching against the metal. Something heavy being dragged across the floor. Someone breathing harder with the exertion. Whoever had locked her in was still there.

Her Secret Santa.

"Who are you?" she demanded. A pungent odor stung her nose. "Why are you doing this to me?"

She backed away even farther when the person on the other side refused to respond. Tamping down the fear that scattered her thoughts, she remembered her cell and pulled it from her pocket. "I'm calling the police," she warned.

As soon as the screen lit up, she said a prayer of thanks for good cell service and punched in 9-1-1.

Everything went quiet on the other side of the door as the call connected. "That's right. *You* be afraid this time."

But her bravado was short-lived.

The silent person on the other side nudged a familiar piece of cardstock beneath the door at her feet. White, with a sparkly green Christmas tree, and three words staring up at her.

Ho. Ho. Ho.

The 9-1-1 dispatcher answered the call, but Daisy couldn't speak.

The sick torment of another message wasn't the only thing coming from beneath the door.

Daisy blinked away the tears burning her eyes.

Smoke.

Chapter Seven

Harry rubbed his gloved hands together, keeping them warm as the visiting team's bus left the parking lot. He was more of a football guy than a basketball fan, but he knew enough about high-school sports to know the players and their coaches were generally the last people to leave the building. He bounced on the balls of his feet as two more cars followed the bus onto the main road. That left just his truck, a van and two other vehicles in the nearly empty parking lot.

"Come on, Daisy."

The images of how some sicko wanted to hurt her made his skin crawl. The bad joke gifts, graphic pictures and Peeping Tom all said coward to him. Daisy's stalker wasn't brave enough to confront her face-to-face. But he sure seemed to be getting off on scaring her, on watching her from afar and savoring how his psychological terror campaign controlled her life. He didn't understand enough about profiling to know whether her stalker had some skewed idea of love for her, or if this obsession was some kind of punishment.

But a coward like that could become unpredictable in a heartbeat if he thought his control over her was slipping—just like Daisy's ex. She'd been brutally honest in one of her letters about the night her ex had come after her with a knife. She'd wanted Harry to know that she could deal with the things he'd shared with her, that she was a survivor and that she was stronger for it. But a woman like Daisy, with such zest for people and life, should never be punished or controlled like that. Acid churned in the pit of his stomach at the thought of someone hurting her like that again.

He'd never thought he'd be stepping up for guard duty for a chatty, compassionate free spirit. For months now, he'd focused solely on fixing himself—and that project wasn't complete yet. Did he really think he had what it took to keep Daisy safe?

Like right now, Harry had a bad feeling about the number of vehicles left in the parking lot.

But then he was the one whose head wasn't on straight. He had a bad feeling about almost everything these days, seeing an enemy where there was none. He knew the van belonged to the custodian on duty tonight because the guy had come out for a cigarette during the second game. The well-appointed Cadillac must belong to the principal. Harry had seen him at more than one door, locking up. The other car could be abandoned for all he knew. It had a yellow sticker on the windshield, so it belonged to someone who worked at or went to the school.

He stopped at the front of his truck again. Although he couldn't see any movement through the bank of glass doors at the front of the building, the lights were still on inside the lobby and gymnasium, so chances were that Daisy was just fine.

He probably shouldn't have left her alone for this long. But the crowd and cheers and drums had been too much for him. That kid, Albert, had been ticked off with Daisy. Wounded pride over some school problem. Harry's instinct was to intervene—to keep the danger at bay before he had to become a part of it. But then Albert had mentioned

Benny Garcia, and that had taken him right back to the middle of that last firefight, and he knew he was losing it.

Lt. Col. Biro was right. He wasn't much use to anybody in this condition. A wounded warrior. Damaged goods. He had a Purple Heart and a Silver Star, but he couldn't handle teenage smart-assery and a noisy basketball game.

If he was at Hope's apartment with his duffel bag, he'd be pulling out one of Daisy's letters right about now. He'd read her words and feel her caring. He'd cool his jets and come back to the normal land of the living. At least, as normal as he could get.

This time, instead of reading the words and letting his angel lift him out of his mental hellhole, Harry's thoughts drifted back to myopic blue eyes and a beautiful smile. The real Daisy Gunderson was a far cry from the woman he'd imagined. But different meant just that—not any better or worse. And *different* hadn't stopped him when the noise and the stress had gotten to be too much, and he'd anchored his senses on her luscious, irresistible mouth. He'd kissed her. Not a peck on the lips like the thank-you she'd given him at her house that afternoon. A real kiss. He hadn't been sure he could still kiss a woman. But the need had been too powerful to resist.

He hoped his damaged nerves and scar tissue hadn't completely grossed her out because Daisy had been wonderful. He'd felt her mouth soften under his. He'd tasted her. He'd felt her response through every surviving nerve ending and deeper inside in places that had nothing to do with nerves.

Selfishly saving himself by coming to Kansas City and meeting her in person had become doing a favor for a friend. And now looking out for Daisy was becoming something…selfish again. So much for putting his ideal Ms. G. up on a pedestal. For a few blissful seconds, he'd forgotten everything except his desire to kiss that beautiful mouth.

A smoother operator in a less public place would have deepened that kiss. A man who was a little less *abominable* and little more sure this unplanned attraction he felt was mutual would have pulled Daisy into his arms and pushed her up against that wall to feel every inch of those curves and grasping hands while he plundered her heavenly soft mouth. Those unexpectedly heated thoughts about all the ways he wanted to kiss Daisy had required a third hike through the snow to ease the ill-timed fantasies about the earthy, purple-haired temptress and the embarrassing hard-on they'd aroused.

He hadn't felt like that much of a man in months. He hadn't felt that kind of normal. He hadn't felt such a deep connection to another human being since opening that first letter overseas all those months ago.

And already he felt like that connection was fading.

"Come to the damn door, woman." The wintry night air was moving past being a healing remedy and was becoming a nose-numbing reminder that he'd been out here far too long without having any contact with her.

Harry pulled out his phone to call her and swore. He'd known Daisy for almost a year and a half and had been with her most of the past twenty-four hours—and he'd never once remembered to get her phone number. Not very slick. Or practical.

He was scrolling through information on his phone, looking for the Central Prep Academy number when he heard the first siren in the distance.

If an empty parking lot had given him a bad feeling, the sinuous noise of two more sirens cutting through the crisp night air was telling him to trust that feeling. "Daisy?"

A shrill, uninterrupted ringing from a much closer source jerked him around. Fire alarm. "Daisy!"

He needed her with him. Now.

Harry pulled a crowbar from the toolbox behind the seat of his truck. He ran to the front doors, tried two of them, but they were both locked. He didn't bother with the third or fourth door. He jammed the crowbar between the door and frame and forced it open. He'd probably just triggered another alarm in the office or at a nearby police station. But he knew he could use the backup the moment the door swung open and he dashed through the vestibule. A thin, gray haze hung in the air, stinging his sinuses with the distinctive smell of smoke. The memory of an explosion went off inside his head, but he clenched his jaw, forbidding the nightmare to seize hold of his thoughts. No Tango. No bomb. He was home in Kansas City. The damn school was on fire and Daisy was in it.

Harry surveyed the lobby and saw no one, just a folded-up table with Daisy's pink purse hidden behind it. He found the custodian inside the gym on his cell phone, talking to a dispatcher. Harry waved him toward the front doors, ordering him to report that there were at least two other people inside the building.

Then he followed the hazy wisps of toxic fumes to the top of a stairwell where a darker cloud of smoke was gathering beneath his feet. He inspected the open padlock and gate, heard the distinctive whoosh and pops of live flames. The smoke swirled around his ankles as he went partway down the steps. "Daisy? Daisy Gunderson, are you down here?"

His answer was a couple of loud bangs, a muffled curse and then a croaky, "Harry? I'm trapped. There's smoke. I called 9-1-1. I pulled the fire alarm in here."

Smart woman. Harry took the stairs two at a time, running straight at the sound of her voice. "I heard the sirens. The fire department is on its way." The smoke was denser down here, the breathable air more pungent. There was nothing accidental about this blaze. The fire itself was a small pyre in the middle of the hallway, piled with rags, a bag of trash and what looked like a woman's coat, all shriveling into ash and goo as they burned and melted. The concrete and metal down here would be hard to burn, but he smelled enough acetone, probably varnish or paint solvent, to make his eyes water. He shoved open the first door and discovered the boiler room. "Daisy?"

He heard her coughing again and kept moving. Metal banged against metal. "In here."

The next door. Right beside the blaze. With more accelerant splashed on the door itself so that rivulets of fire ran down the heavy steel.

"Hang on, honey, I'm coming." Harry edged around the puddle of flames dripping on the floor to get his hand on the door, but he quickly snatched it away. Even through the leather and lining of his glove, the rising temperature scorched him. "Don't touch the door," he warned. "It's hot."

"That's why I've been hitting it with this metal chair." Her brave voice stuttered with another fit of coughing. "I can't get it open."

He couldn't, either, unless he could put out some of those flames and get closer. He swung his gaze around. Through the chimeras of heat rising toward the ceiling, Harry caught a glimpse of a ghostly figure climbing the stairs at the far end of the long corridor. Was that a trick of the smoke? A flashback to tracking insurgents in that village outside Fallujah? The instinct to give chase to the potential enemy tensed through every muscle. "Hey!" he shouted. "Stop!"

"What is it?" Daisy gasped.

The apparition was gone. The reality was here. "Nothing. Never mind."

"He's jammed the door or broken the lock." Daisy's

coughing reminded Harry that his priority was to keep her safe. That meant finding a way to get her out of there.

He spotted the fire extinguisher cabinet anchored to the wall. On the other side of the fire. "Are you hurt?" Harry asked, using the crowbar to shove the center point of that fire, a heavy bucket that was melting with the heat, off to one side. The bucket tipped, and more flames shot out across the floor. But in that split second the fire was moving away from him and the door, Harry darted past.

"I burned my hand on the door, but it's not serious. It's getting harder to breathe."

He couldn't breathe. The old memories snuck around his defenses, blending with reality. *Tango had hit on something. He knew that dog's reactions the way he knew his own thoughts. Harry raised his fist, warning his patrol to stop their advance. "What is it, boy? Show me." He heard the thwap of the bullet and watched Tango fall. "Tango!" Harry's world exploded around him. IED. The dog had known. He ran toward the heat. He couldn't leave his partner behind. "Top, you got to leave him! We have to retreat!" He jerked his arm away and raised his rifle, charging toward his downed partner when the second blast hit.*

"Harry?" It was a woman's voice calling his name. Daisy's voice. "Harry, are you still there?"

Do this, Marine!

Harry swore, forcing himself into the present. He ducked his head and swung the crowbar, shattering the glass in front of the fire extinguisher.

"I'm here, honey." Harry pulled the pin and fired a stream of foam into the flames, dousing a path before aiming the extinguisher at the door itself. "I'm going to get you out."

The sting of the burning chemical was in his eyes now. The toxic air tickled his throat and filtered into his lungs.

The heat from the flames themselves had puckered every pore in his skin, making him feel like his boots and clothes were melting. The foam trickled down the door, taking the flames with it. Every new inch revealed burnt streaks and blistered paint and a single word etched into the metal itself. *Mine.*

A rage as hot as the fire itself seared through Harry's brain. How could one person be so sick in the head that he would want to hurt a woman with a heart as big as Daisy's? He turned down the smoke-filled hallway. He should have run down that SOB. He didn't need to be armed to take a man down. He could have put a stop to this insane terror campaign once and for all.

"Harry, please." She was coughing again.

Stay focused on the mission, Top. Harry tossed the extinguisher aside and picked up the crowbar. "Stand back. When I open this, it may suction the flames into the room."

"I'm ready."

The latch was busted, useless. This was going to take brute force. Finally. Something he could manage without thinking twice. Harry wedged the crowbar between the door and wall and pushed against it, then pulled back, roaring with the strain through his arms and shoulders before the warping metal finally gave way. Once he'd moved the door a couple of inches, he dropped the crowbar and muscled the hanging door across its track. He was coughing now, too. "Daisy?"

"Harry!" She launched herself against his chest, heedless of the flames licking into the room she'd just vacated. He cinched an arm around her waist and turned her away from the conflagration, carrying her several feet beyond the worst of the fire. He felt her lips press against his damaged cheek and jaw again and again. "Thank you. Thank… Oh, my God."

Harry turned her away from the hateful epithet and tried to keep moving. But she squiggled in his grasp, wanting

to see. "Did you see him? Was that who you were yelling at? Who was it? Is that my coat? Why would he—?"

"I didn't get a good look." Her body shook with another
fit of coughing and he tried to pick her up. "Keep your
head down. The smoke is getting thick."

"He slipped a card under the door. We need it for evidence."

She batted his hands away, turning sideways against him,
although he wasn't letting her get any closer to the blaze.
"No you don't. The cops will know this was intentional."

"There may be fingerprints."

"No."

"I heard the scratching. He was carving..." Her toes
touched the floor, tangling with his feet. He lost his grip as
they stumbled into the wall. She fought with him, struggling
to get a better view of the destruction. "...that. *Mine?* I belong to him? He owns something I need to stay away from?"

He grasped her shoulders. "We have to move."

"He must have been watching, waiting until I was—"

"Stop talking and get your butt moving!" Daisy flinched
away from him, her red-rimmed eyes wide behind her
glasses as she clutched at the wall instead of him. Harry
heard his voice echoing through the hallway and truly understood why Lt. Col. Biro had been so worried about his
ability to serve. "I'm sorry." He backed away to the opposite wall, his hands raised in apology. He'd just yelled
in her face as if she was a raw recruit. As if he wasn't any
better than that bastard who'd hurt her. The fumes rubbed
like grit in his eyes. "My head's not right. I didn't mean
that. Don't... Don't ever stop talking to me. Please."

And then that woman did the most remarkable thing.
She pushed away from the wall, grabbed the front of his
coat and dragged him toward the stairs. "Get me out of
here, Top," she ordered. "We both need fresh air."

When she doubled over in another coughing jag, Harry's training took over. He swung her up into his arms and carried her up the stairs and out the front door. By the time he reached the median in front of the school, his lungs were screaming for oxygen and he collapsed to his knees in the snow. Daisy tumbled from his arms. He bent over, coughing again. But suddenly, she was on her knees in front of him, rubbing a palmful of snow across his face and another along the nape of his neck, coughing right along with him as she shocked his senses. "Are you with me? Harry, are you okay?"

He raised his head to meet her worried gaze. He hoped her eyes were irritated and watering, and that she wasn't wasting any tears on him. Still, he pulled off his heat-damaged glove and reached out with the pad of his thumb to wipe away the lines of moisture cutting tracks over her soot-stained cheek. "I'm okay."

"Don't lie to me." Even red-rimmed and weepy, that look over the top of her glasses wasn't one he could ignore.

"I'm okay *now*," he amended. Her skin was cool to the touch and she was shivering. "You're freezing." From the snow soaking through her jeans or the adrenaline leaving her system, it didn't matter. Harry pushed to his feet and peeled off his coat to wrap it around her shoulders. He hugged her to his chest and guided her to the cleared asphalt of the circular drive as a third fire engine pulled up.

A team of firefighters was already grabbing gear and fanning out around the building. A tall man in a white helmet was on his radio as he stepped down from the last truck. His slight limp didn't detract from the square set of his shoulders and air of authority. He was clearly the man in charge. After a brief chat with the principal and custodian, he sent one of his men off to cut the power to the building. Daisy huddled even closer against Harry when the chief approached them. "You're the teacher who called this in?"

"Yes. Daisy Gunderson."

Harry relished the cold night air seeping through his sweater and T-shirt because it kept his head clear, but he wished he had a little more body heat to share with Daisy. If she wasn't coughing, she was shaking, but he held her upright in one of those bear hugs she was so fond of. While she detailed the events and the chief deployed his crew into the building, Harry surveyed the parking lot through the swirl of emergency vehicle lights and first responders. The car with the yellow sticker was gone. Why hadn't he written down the license plate number? He hadn't even thought to look. Of course, the arsonist could have walked out the back door or had a car waiting for him someplace else. He was still no closer to identifying the creep terrorizing Daisy than he'd been when he'd first set up camp outside her home.

Harry snapped to when the crew chief addressed him. "She said you saw someone?"

Had he? "He was running up the east stairs, away from the fire. I didn't get a good look at him. That was five minutes before we got out of there."

"So, chances are he's clear of the scene and there's no one else inside. Can you describe him in case we run into him in there?"

Harry closed his eyes and replayed that brief impression distorted by heat and smoke. "Taller than me. Slender build." Shrugging, he opened his eyes. That was almost less than nothing to go on. "I can't even give you a hair color. I saw him from behind and he was wearing a blue coat and yellow hat."

Daisy lifted her chin. "Blue and gold? Like school colors?"

"Maybe. It was a blur."

"That narrows it down to about three-hundred people," she grumbled in a wheezing voice.

But the description seemed to be enough for the fire chief. "I'll go ahead and send a team in to sweep the building. Once we have the fire contained, we'll check the basement, too."

"He'll be long gone," Daisy added. "He thrives on me not knowing who he is."

"We'll check, all the same." He nodded toward the uniformed police officer waiting a few yards away. "The police will want to ask you the same questions."

Daisy nodded, but Harry felt her fingers curling into the front of his sweater. Her spirit might be willing, but her strength was flagging. "She needs a medic first. Probable smoke inhalation and shock."

"The ambulance is pulling up now." Harry and the chief walked her over to the ambulance where two EMTs sat Daisy in the back of the truck and immediately gave her oxygen and a blanket, and started taking her vitals. Before they made room for Harry to climb up, the tall firefighter tapped him on the shoulder. "Marine?" Harry nodded. The crew chief extended his hand. "John Murdock, USMC Retired. Did a couple of tours in Afghanistan."

Harry shook his hand, appreciating the bond that was always there between Marines of any generation. "Master Sergeant Harry Lockhart. First Marine Expeditionary Force out of Pendleton. How did you know?"

"Not many men run *into* a fire except for firefighters and Devil Dogs." And maybe a crazy guy who thought he was about to lose someone he was learning to care about more and more with each passing minute. Before Harry could process exactly what that revelation meant, Murdock continued the conversation. "Lockhart. You any relation to Hope Lockhart Taylor?"

Harry nodded. "My sister."

Murdock nodded. "I thought something about you looked familiar. My boss, Meghan Taylor, is Hope's mother-in-law. I went to Hope and Pike's wedding a few years back." That had been the last time Harry had come home to Kansas City. He'd never realized how many people he was connected to beyond his sister here. "Small world, isn't it?"

"Bigger than I thought, actually."

Chief Murdock inclined his head toward the ambulance's interior. "Your friend hasn't taken her eyes off you. You'd better get in there and get checked out, too, so she stops worrying."

"Yes, sir."

Harry realized he shared another connection with John Murdock. As the older man limped away, he saw the distinctive void space of his pants catching around a steel rod above his boot. The KCFD crew chief had an artificial leg. They'd both sacrificed for their country. And apparently, John Murdock had adapted to civilian life just fine, even though all of him hadn't come home from the war, either.

Harry had never considered civilian life as an option for him. But if he did ever move on to life outside the Corps, he wanted it to be his choice—not because he was so broken that the Corps didn't want him. If he wasn't good enough for the USMC, how could he be good enough for anything, or anybody, else?

How could he be good enough for Daisy?

Forty minutes later, the fire was out and the building had been cleared. There was no sign of the man who'd set the blaze, unless his footprints were one of the hundreds tramped through the snow in the parking lot left by students and fans attending tonight's games or by the firefighters and police ensuring the entire school was secure. Harry sat on a gurney across from Daisy in the back of the ambulance as she sorted through her bag, making sure all her belongings—beyond the coat that obsessive creep had burned—were there. They reeked of smoke, and he couldn't detect that homey sweet scent that was uniquely hers anymore. He'd given his statement to the uniformed officer and a pair of detectives. He'd had his eyes rinsed, his vitals checked, and he'd held an oxygen mask over his nose and mouth for longer than he wanted, simply because Daisy took her mask down and asked him if he was all right every time he stopped the flow of purified air he wanted her to keep breathing. They were both wrapped in blankets, waiting to be cleared by the EMTs.

If he wasn't scaring her, then she was worried about him. He was raw with guilt. Hard to feel like much of a Marine—like much of a man—when the only two emotions he could evoke from a pretty woman were fear and concern. He should reassess this unofficial mission. While he wasn't about to leave her alone against the jerk who wanted to hurt her, maybe he needed to rethink his whole plan to have Angel Daisy help him heal. She didn't need his kind of mess in her life.

"Harry?" He must have been quiet for too long because Daisy was sliding across the ambulance to sit on the gurney beside him. She tucked her hands beneath his arm and leaned her head against his shoulder. "Talk to me. We've been long-distance friends for a long time, and I know I don't have any real claim on you. Still, it's crazy how fast I've gotten used to having you around. But for a few seconds down there in the basement, I thought you'd left me."

He adjusted his blanket around both of them and rested his cheek against the crown of her head. Dr. Polk had advised him that the first step in dealing with his problem was admitting the extent of it.

"For a few seconds there, I did."

Chapter Eight

Harry got up to pace the house again.

The first two times he'd come downstairs from the guest room, the dogs had trotted out from Daisy's bedroom to inspect the noise and identify his presence. The two little dogs had trotted back into her room to go back to sleep. Caliban limped around the house with him, reminding Harry of the hundreds of night patrols he and Tango had gone on together. It was a bittersweet treat to work with a well-trained dog again. Caliban was willing to answer his commands to go out ahead of him and come back, to seek, to sit and to play a game of tug-of-war with his rope toy before the older dog, too, tired and went back to his comfy spot in Daisy's bedroom.

Losing a leg hadn't stopped the retired K-9 officer from belonging somewhere and having a purpose. Just because Caliban wasn't serving KCPD anymore didn't mean he didn't have a home and companions and a reason to get up in the morning—or the middle of the night when restless house guests roamed the halls and raided the cookie supply in the kitchen.

There was a lesson to be learned there. But the hour was late and a lot of the things Harry was feeling since first ringing Daisy's doorbell were new and alien to him.

The dogs must be getting used to the sound of his tread

on the floors because none of them came out to greet him this time. Good. He hoped they stayed close to their mistress and that all of them were getting a good night's sleep. Daisy had stayed up far too late, running their clothes through the laundry twice, to rid them of the smells of smoke and acetone. Pike had brought over Harry's duffel bag with all his belongings and stayed to keep watch on the house while Harry showered the grime and nightmares off his skin. Then Daisy had soaked in the tub for nearly an hour before declaring she finally felt tired enough to sleep and had gone to bed.

Harry came down the stairs in his jeans and bare feet, with his M9 strapped to his hip. The enemy was different and the temps were colder, but this detail wasn't different from any other watch he'd served over the years. There was somebody out there who wanted to hurt the thing he'd sworn to protect. He stopped at the window beside the front door, folded his arms over his bare chest and stared out into the moonless night. Although the snow on the ground reflected the glow of the street lights, there were plenty of shadows, plus darkened vehicles and shaded windows in other homes where someone could hide. Still, the neighborhood looked secure for the moment. Unlike all the activity at Daisy's school earlier that night, this part of Kansas City seemed quiet.

Didn't make it any easier for him to fall asleep.

But he'd be damned if he'd get hooked on those sleeping pills Lt. Col. Biro said he would prescribe for him.

Harry could get by with an occasional nap and dozing on and off through the night. Maybe staring at something besides the tin-tiled ceiling in the upstairs guest room would be enough of a change of pace for him to grab some much needed rest. He'd give one of the recliners in Daisy's living room a try. At least on the ground floor, he'd be closer to any ingresses an intruder might use to break in. Surely, that was enough of an advantage to drop the alert buzzing through his veins to a level that would allow him thirty winks.

After checking the mudroom door and backyard, Harry wandered into the kitchen. He poured himself a glass of milk and downed half of it before eyeing the cookie jar again. One more reindeer cookie would take the edge off his growly stomach and give his taste buds something to savor instead of focusing every brain cell on replaying nightmares and envisioning the stalker he wanted to take down with his bare hands. He hoped the cookies weren't all for that party Daisy kept talking about, because he'd made a serious dent in her supply. He'd have to buy her some groceries or run to the bakery for her, although he had a feeling store-bought cookies wouldn't taste as good.

He was licking the icing off his fingertips when he strolled into the living room and found Daisy standing there in front of the empty fireplace, staring at him. His hands went instinctively to his shoulder and chest to cover himself, not out of modesty, but out of horror that she was getting a full-on view of the scarring he hid from the rest of the world. He couldn't hide his face, but why the hell hadn't he taken two seconds to put on a T-shirt?

He was glad that the only light in the room seeped in from the night-light in the kitchen and the glow from a street lamp filtering through the sheer curtains at the front door. "Have a nightmare?"

"I was worried about you, beating yourself up because you don't think you did a good enough job protecting me. The way I see it, the alternative is that I would have suffocated from the smoke and fumes if you hadn't been there."

Daisy crossed the room and reached for his hands, lacing their fingers together and holding on as she pulled them away from his disfigurement. He held himself still as she

studied the hard ridges, stitch marks and skin grafts that
were pinker and lighter than the rest of his chest, wishing he could spare her the horrific events that she must be
imagining. She tilted her gaze above the brown glasses—
that were far too plain for her colorful style—up to his for a
moment before she released his hands and walked straight
into his chest. She wound her arms around his waist and
turned her cheek against the very scars he thought would
repulse her. Her breasts pillowed against him, and the undamaged half of him was awkwardly aware of the tender
nipples pearling against him. When her damp hair caught
beneath his chin and her lips grazed across his collarbone,
Harry surrendered to their mutual need to be held, and
wound his arms around her back.

Daisy squeezed him in a hug, and Harry automatically
tightened his hold on her, pulling her onto her toes. "Yes,
I had a nightmare. About what happened tonight, and I
was wondering if we could talk?"

Her voice trailed away, allowing him a glimpse of the
vulnerability she worked far too hard to hide. He nuzzled
the crown of her head, unsure that comfort was the best
thing he could give her. From this angle, he could see the
damp tendrils of purple and brown clinging to the collar of
her flannel pajamas. And heaven help him, he could see and
feel the siren silhouette of her hourglass figure cinched in
at the waist by her robe. As much as he wanted to hide his
own body, he wanted to see more of hers. He imagined everything about her was soft and touchable—from that sham-
pooed hair to those sweet lips and delectable curves, right
on down to the fuzzy green socks that covered her toes.

An answering male heat licked through his veins, reminding Harry that at least one part of him hadn't been
affected by nightmares or injury. Everything about Daisy
being here, standing close enough for him to breathe her

scent, reminded him of how much time had passed since he'd been with a woman, how badly he needed a woman's gentle touch. But he reined in that feverish blast of longing that was stirring where her thighs pressed against his—this woman only wanted to talk.

"What's up?" he asked, mentally beating back his hormones and focusing on her needs, not his. He moved his grip to her shoulders and urged her warm body away from him.

Her gaze had landed on the gun he wore. "Do you sleep with that?" Before he could answer, her gaze bopped up to his. "Or don't you sleep at all?"

"I don't wear it *in* bed if that's what you mean. But I keep it close." Harry released her to unhook his belt and remove the Beretta and its holster. He set the weapon up on the mantel. "I don't want to be too far from our best protection. But I don't want to scare you more than I already do." He gestured toward the pair of recliners facing the fireplace. Separate seats would be best, considering the ill-timed lust simmering in his veins. "Shall we?"

"You don't scare me, Harry. I'm not afraid for me, at any rate." Once she settled in the first recliner, Harry sat in the other. But before he could raise the footrest, Daisy surprised him by moving over to his chair and sitting in his lap. "Is this okay? I want you to be comfortable. I have a feeling you won't like what I need to talk about."

He had a feeling he wouldn't, either. She wanted to finish that conversation they'd started during the game. For some reason he couldn't yet comprehend, Daisy was feeling the same attraction he was, but she wanted to know just how screwed up he was before anything else happened between them.

And yet, she was sitting in his lap, her hand braced at the center of his chest. Her hip and bottom warmed his thighs and...other things. "After everything that happened, you want to be with me?"

Her fingertips clenched into his skin. "Do I scare *you*?"

"A little. But I'm not saying no." Harry raised the footrest and leaned back, pulling Daisy into his arms and letting her settle into the chair, half beside and half on top of him, giving his body a taste of her curves pressed against him. He curled his right arm around her back, his hand hovering above her before settling on the swell of her hip in a grip that felt more possessive than it should. Her body was as perfect a fit as he'd imagined it would be, and that desire he'd tried to check flared to life again. But she needed to talk, and maybe he did, too. With his left hand, he sifted his fingers into her hair, smoothing damp strands off her face, stirring her sweet scent around him. "I should have stuck closer to you tonight, and not let everything get to me."

When her glasses butted against his chest, and got pushed askew, he took them off and lay them on the table beside them. She snuggled into a more comfortable position, brushing her stockinged feet against his bare toes and tucking her forehead at the juncture of his neck and shoulder. He was okay with her not being able to see him clearly. Talking about his past was going to be hard enough without Daisy seeing how ill-equipped he was to handle this kind of emotional intimacy.

"I don't blame you for what happened, Harry."

"I blame myself."

"You have post-traumatic stress. I remember when I was in the hospital after Brock's attack, I was so afraid of men that I only wanted female doctors and nurses working on me. Then Mom told me my father had died. She blamed me for bringing Brock into our lives and causing Dad so much stress. I blamed myself." Where was she going with this? When he felt her tensing against him, Harry covered her hand where it rested against his chest, silently telling her it was okay to continue. "I curled up into a ball in that hospital bed and wanted to be left completely alone. I didn't want anyone touching me, talking to me. I holed up in this house once I was released. I didn't see anyone but my lawyer. I didn't do anything but help Mom go through Dad's things and sleep."

"You? You're the most social creature I've ever met."

She switched the position of their hands, lacing her fingers with his. "PTSD. I was depressed. I got counseling. I made it through Brock's trial and Mom remarrying and moving away. And then, finally, one day I was done with it. I didn't want to be sad and paranoid anymore. I didn't want the bad guys—the bad feelings—to control my life. I got busy living again. Got a new teaching position. Got Muffy from her elderly owner who was moving into a nursing home and rescued Patch from the shelter. I started fixing up this house. I wanted to do for others and make friends and have a meaningful life."

"You've succeeded."

"But I needed that time to heal. So do you. Losing Tango must have devastated you." He tightened his grip around hers, confirming her suspicion. "I know you've lost friends. You nearly lost your own life. Be kind to yourself. Be patient. I believe you'll eventually learn to cope, too."

"I don't know. I was almost out of control tonight."

"Almost. So you yelled. To my way of thinking, you were yelling for help." She tilted her face away from his neck and cupped his damaged jaw, asking him to meet her solemn gaze. "You didn't hurt me. Trust me, I know what it's like to be hurt."

Harry touched his lips to hers for a brief kiss, sitting up enough to slide his hand behind the crook of her knees, pulling her across his lap so he could hold more of her in his arms. "I hate that you know that."

"The smells of the fire were a powerful trigger for your flashback. I imagine someone coming at me with a knife would do the same for me. In the meantime, I do the best I can every day. I try to be honest about what I'm thinking and feeling, but I try to stay positive and keep moving forward." She wiggled in his grasp, innocently planting her hip against his groin and snuggling beneath his chin again. "And I give myself a break when I don't. You should try it."

The tension in him eased at the gentle reprimand. "How do I express what I'm thinking and feeling without completely losing it?"

She traced mindless circles across his chest and shoulder as she considered her answer. "What would you say if you were writing it to me in a letter?"

He was aware of each surviving nerve ending waiting in hopeful anticipation for her fingers to brush across it again. "Dr. Polk suggested something similar—that I start journaling. Write things down and get 'em out of my head so I'm not always fighting to control everything in there. But I wouldn't know where to start."

"Sure you do. Give me the rough draft. I'm an English teacher—I can make sense of just about anything. The beginning is usually the hardest part for my students. But you know how to start a letter."

"Dear Daisy?"

"So far, so good."

"I thought I was going to lose you tonight."

The circles stopped. "That's a dramatic opening."

"I'm not very good at jokes."

But she wasn't letting him off that easily. "The point is honesty, not humor. When you flashed back tonight, where did you go?"

His hand traveled up and down her back, squeezing her bottom and coming back to hug the nip of her waist before he mustered the courage to tell her about the insurgent sniper taking out Tango before the dog could pinpoint the two IEDs planted in an ambush. He told her about the two men he'd lost that day, including Albert Logan's pen pal, Benny Garcia. He glossed over the details of shrapnel shredding his body and fire searing his face and neck. His speech was halting, his sentences disjointed. But with his senses focused on the scent of her hair and the heat of her sensuous body warming his, other defenses inside his head crumbled. He'd gotten what was left of Tango and his men out of there before blacking out. Then he didn't remember anything until waking up in the hospital in Germany.

He'd been angry. All the time. Afraid he might lose his eye or the use of his arm. He'd been wild with guilt—about the dog who'd been with him since Day One of shipping into the hot zone, and about the men he was responsible for who weren't coming home. He'd endured numerous surgeries and painful rehab. He'd been taken off active duty, told he wasn't good enough to do the job he loved anymore. He'd talked to shrinks—reawakened memories of the violence from his childhood, felt that same violence seething inside him and had been afraid he couldn't control it. He'd read Daisy's letters, over and over, clinging to the hope in her words, internalizing the wisdom and compassion she'd shared.

When he made it back to the present, Harry realized his skin was wet and that Daisy was trembling against him. He cupped her chin and tipped her face up to his, inspecting the pain he'd inflicted there. "Damn it, I'm making you cry again."

"That means I'm not just hearing, I'm feeling what you're saying." Bracing her hands on his shoulders, she closed the few inches separating them to press a kiss to his lips. When he responded, she lingered, and the quiet kiss lasted for several endless moments. Her tongue reached out to his in a tentative mating dance and Harry caught it, caressed it, before thrusting his tongue into her mouth and continuing the dance there. Harry felt the tender solace all the way down to his toes before he tasted the salt of her tears on her lips and he pulled away.

"Daisy—"

"Stop it. If you can yell, I can cry." She slid a hand behind his neck, scraping her palm over the short cut of his hair. "It's an honest expression of emotion. You should try it sometime."

Harry anchored his hands at her waist, keeping her from moving close enough to resume the kiss. "You want honest? When I lost it tonight in that fire, you were afraid of me." She squinted, keeping him in focus, listening to his words as she always had. "I never want to see that look in your eyes again. What if something happens and I scare you?"

"What if it doesn't? What if I cry again? Are you going to stop caring?"

She knew he had feelings for her? "No."

"Then why do you think *I* would?" She stroked the back of his neck, sending soothing comfort and tremors of anticipation down his spine and out to every working nerve in his body. "Crap happens to people sometimes. You get help, you work through it—you do the best you can. Sometimes you falter, but you get up and try again—and with the important people in your life, that's all that really matters."

His arms shook, the whole chair vibrating with the tension and doubt working through him. "You've never been afraid of me, have you? Even beat up and scarred like I am, you hug like it's going out of style. You kiss, you grab, you talk—"

"Sounds a little annoying when you put it that way."

He shook his head, still wrapping his mind around the

idea that Daisy wanted to be with him. "I'm taking advantage of your kindness."

"You're giving me value by trusting me with your fears, by sharing your darkest feelings, by helping me understand you." She pushed a lock of hair out of her eyes and Harry's fingers were there to capture the silky wave and tuck it behind her ear. "I was with Brock for a year and a half. Believe me, I'll take trust and honesty with a fractured brain and sexy masculinity over control and isolation any day."

His fingers feathered into her hair. "Sexy?"

"Beautiful eyes, muscles for days." He held himself still as she crawled up his body. She gently kissed the lid above each eye, then kissed his cheek, the point of his chin, the hollow of his neck, gently, seductively working her way down to his chest where she kissed both the scarred surface and the healthy skin that leaped with eagerness at her touch. "Interesting that *sexy* is the word you keyed in on."

"After everything I've told you, you still want this—us—to happen?"

She harrumphed a dramatic sigh, folded her arms over his chest and rested her chin there. "I'm lying on top of you, I can feel your arousal pressing against my hip, which is really good for my ego because it means I'm halfway irresistible, and if you don't kiss me—I mean, really kiss me like I think you want to—soon, then I'm just going to keep right on talking. And you will never be able to shut me up."

"You aren't halfway anything." Harry didn't need much encouragement to give in to what his body had been craving.

He righted the chair, spilling Daisy into his lap. His hands were there to catch her bottom and pull her back against his chest. She slipped her arms around his neck, welcoming his kiss as he laid claim to her beautiful mouth. He wasn't smooth, but he was hungry for her. Her fingers teased the nape of his neck again, skidded over his prickly hair, then boldly framed his face to keep their lips aligned as her knees parted and dropped to either side of his thighs. Her warm soft heat cupped the aching desire growing stiff inside his jeans and he moaned. He needed more. He needed everything.

Harry moved his hands to the front of her robe to free the knot, knocking into her hands as they worked the top button of his jeans. She laughed and he pressed his lips to the sound in her throat. The angle was wrong, and he was a little too ready for her to work his zipper down, so he caught her wrists and moved her hands to his chest where they happily explored each spasm of muscle that yearned for her touch.

Harry pushed her robe open and tugged at the buttons of her pajama top. Flowered flannel shouldn't be so damn sexy, but it was as he dragged the soft cotton over her shoulders and down her arms, revealing her heavy breasts to his appreciative gaze. The tips were a pretty pink, and straining to attention in the chilly air.

Her arms were trapped in the ends of the sleeves, but he let her wiggle herself free. He was too busy sliding his hands around to the soft skin of her back while he dropped his lips to the generous swell of one breast, and then the other, catching a nipple in his mouth when it bounced too close. Harry closed his lips around the tip, laving the sweet bud with his tongue until he heard a whimper against his ear.

"I'm sorry." Harry withdrew immediately, drawing in deep breaths to reclaim his equilibrium. He clasped her face between his hands and sought out any sign of pain he might have caused in her darkened blue eyes. "I can't feel everything I do to you. There's nerve damage. If I'm doing something you don't like—"

"That, sir, was the brink of ecstasy. I'll let you know when I'm not enjoying myself." Daisy freed her arms from the sleeves that bound her, cupped either side of his jaw and guided his mouth to the other breast.

She didn't say another word.

Harry scooped Daisy up in his arms and carried her to her bedroom. After scooting the dogs out and closing the door, he pulled out his wallet and tossed it onto the bedside table before shucking his jeans and shorts and climbing onto the bed beside her.

Daisy had stripped off her pajama bottoms and was reaching for him. But he pushed her back into the pillows, wanting to feast his eyes first. In the soft glow of the bedside lamp, he took in every inch of her. She was too much, too beautiful…too vulnerable. His gaze stopped on the small pucker of scar tissue on the underside of her breast. He gently touched the tip of his finger to it. He wasn't the only wounded warrior here.

Harry leaned over to kiss the permanent evidence of the brutal attack she'd survived. She flinched and tried to roll away, but he wouldn't let her. "You've seen me."

After she lay back against the pillows, baring herself completely to him, he reverently touched each scar, first with his hand and then with his lips. He kissed her chest, her belly, her breasts, until her hands were on his hair again, holding his mouth to each mark as if his touch healed her the way she was healing him.

He lingered over one mark just below her belly button, his heated breath raising goose bumps over her quivering flesh. "Are you…okay…inside? Did he…?"

"The surgeon removed my spleen and one ovary and the Fallopian tube, and he sewed up a nick in one of my lungs and my stomach. Theoretically, I can still make babies, so we need to use protection." He lifted his head to meet her squinting gaze. "Otherwise, what you see is what you get."

"I want it." Harry climbed over her the way she had

climbed up his body in the chair, and claimed her mouth for a deep, drugging kiss. "I want you."

"Please tell me you have something in that wallet."

Harry rolled off her to retrieve the foil packet from the bedside table. "It's dusty, but it should be reliable."

He felt a kiss between his shoulder blades as he sat on the edge of the bed and sheathed himself. "Dust it off, Marine. You have a job to do."

Do this.

It was the most glorious order he'd ever obeyed.

Daisy climbed onto his lap before he'd even considered a position. But he was just fine with this one. Stars exploded behind his eyes as she sank, wet and hot and ready, over his shaft. Oh, yeah, he was more than fine with this position. Already matching her rhythm and rocking inside her, he kissed her breasts, nibbled her neck, claimed her lips until the need became too great. Harry squeezed her in a tight hug, clamping every curve of her body against his as he detonated inside her.

Daisy cried out with her release and Harry held her to him until the waves of her climax faded away and her head collapsed against his neck. They fell back onto the bed together, with Daisy resting on top of him for several long minutes until their breathing returned to normal and the perspiration on their bodies began to cool.

Then Harry tucked her under the covers and made a quick trip to the bathroom to dispose of the condom. Daisy was half asleep when he returned, but she was smiling as he crawled under the quilts with her and gathered her into his arms.

She wedged one soft thigh between his and wrapped her arm around his waist, clinging to him in a very sexy version of a hug. Harry stroked his fingers up and down her back, feeling a rare, satisfied fatigue creeping into his muscles.

He couldn't believe that any man would try to control this woman's brave spirit and generous heart. She was such a gift.

Such a completely unexpected gift. This Daisy wasn't anything like the woman in his letters.

Harry's fingers came to rest beneath her soft, damp hair. "For some reason, from your letters, I pictured you as a blonde."

"I was once." That made him laugh and he felt her smile against his skin. "You have a wonderful laugh. You should practice it more often."

He'd never had much reason to. "I will if you don't change your shampoo."

Don't change anything about you.

"Strange request." She yawned and burrowed in beside him.

Harry drifted off to sleep along with her, his nose buried in the sweet scent of her hair. No stranger than Harry Lockhart falling in love with her all over again.

This time, with the real Daisy Gunderson.

DAISY WAS IN a deep, blank sleep when she startled awake to a man's hand clamped over her mouth.

Her muffled scream quickly fell silent when Harry's face hovered into focus above hers. He pressed a finger to his lips and didn't remove his hand until she nodded her understanding to remain quiet. Her clock was a blur of red light from this distance, leaving her adrift with no idea of the time or situation. The sun wasn't even up yet. But sometime in the hours since that cathartic conversation and making love, while she was replete with satisfaction and feeling more cherished than she had with any man in her life, Harry had been getting dressed and sneaking around the house.

Well, half-dressed. As far as she was concerned, the man never needed to put on a shirt again. Not that that was terribly practical, but Harry's fit, supple body moving over to the window and back to the edge of her bed certainly improved the scenery.

"Dais?" he whispered. "Honey, are you awake?"

Honey? Focus!

Something was wrong. Even in her nearsighted haze, she could see Harry was strapping on his gun again. She pulled the sheet around her and sat up as he handed her the brown glasses they'd left in the living room.

She slipped them on, hoping that bringing clarity to his grim expression would give her understanding. "What is it?" She heard one of the dogs growling from the foot of the bed, and all the beautiful aftermath of making love vanished in a clutch of fear. "Harry?

He pushed her phone into her hands. "Call 9-1-1. There's someone outside."

That's when Daisy jumped at the pop, pop, pop of tiny explosions and shattering glass out on the back deck. Muffy leaped onto the corner of the bed and barked an alarm. Patch jumped up beside him, yapping with equal fury. Harry swore at the noisy outburst.

Those pops hadn't been gunshots. But they definitely weren't anything natural. Neither was the distinct sound of running footsteps.

Harry was already moving to her bedroom door, drawing his gun. The man wasn't prepped for battle. He didn't even have shoes on. "You can't—"

There was no pretense of hushed and discreet now.

"Get dressed. Stay in this room. I'm leaving the dogs in here with you. Caliban, *Pas Auf.*" Apparently, that meant he should guard the place because the Belgian Malinois never moved from his post, even after Harry pulled the door shut.

Daisy slipped out of bed, pulled on her jeans and the first top she could find and placed the call.

Chapter Nine

At the swirl of red and white lights pulling up in front of the house, Daisy zipped up Harry's coat and ran to the mudroom door, eager to see where Harry had gone when he'd run out the back. Had he found the man who'd been terrorizing her? Or—the frightening possibility entered her head before she could stop it—had the man found Harry?

She unlocked the door and dashed onto the deck. "Harry?"

Her boot crunched with the first step, then the second, and she stopped. She was walking on glass. The security light had been shattered and she was walking across dozens of broken Christmas light bulbs. The path of so much destruction littering her deck and the sidewalk down to the gate was disturbing enough.

The little dots of blood that grew into half a bloody footprint triggered a different kind of fear. "Harry!"

Without the lights, the air was dim, but with the sun cresting the horizon in the east, the trail of bloody prints through the snow was easy to follow. There were two sets of footprints now, far apart, left by one man running after the other. "Harry?"

Daisy broke into a run. Harry was hurt. Protecting her, he'd gotten hurt.

"Harr—" She spotted his back and the legs of his quarry

when she reached the front of the house...the same time she saw the two uniformed officers duck behind the open doors of their cruiser and pull their guns, ordering Harry to stand down. Daisy ran toward the cops, her hands raised in a plea. "Officers, wait! Don't shoot!"

"Damn it, Daisy, I told you to stay inside," Harry warned. He was facing the house, his broad body blocking the man he had pinned to the siding. The tension radiating off his body was thicker than the wintry dampness hanging in the air. Tiny shards of colored glass littered the snow out here, too, and she looked up to see dangling wires and empty sockets where her Christmas decorations used to hang. There were indentations in the snow beside the porch where a scuffle must have occurred, but apparently, Harry had put an end to it. Although she couldn't see the man, she could hear him panting, almost blubbering with fear after losing a fight to Harry. "This guy busted up every one of your decorations. He's angry with you."

"I know. I saw it. One of you is bleeding," she added, hoping he might reassure her that he was in one piece and the other guy wasn't mortally wounded.

"I'm not letting him go. If he'd done that to you instead of a bunch of—"

"Gun!" one of the officers shouted.

Daisy moved closer to the police car, placing herself in the potential line of fire. The two men immediately lowered their weapons if not their guard. "I'm Daisy Gunderson. I called this in. This man is with me. There haven't been any gunshots. He caught the intruder I reported. My house has been vandalized, and he caught this guy running away. Don't hurt him."

The shorter of the two officers holstered his weapon while the other came around the hood of the cruiser to back him up. "I'm Officer Cho, KCPD. I'd feel a lot better if that weapon he's wearing was secured."

"What if I hand it over to you?" Daisy suggested.

Cho nodded. "Slow and easy."

"Harry?" Daisy announced herself before creeping up behind him. His skin was wet and ice-cold as she touched his back. "I'm going to hand your gun over to the officer so they can put their weapons away. I don't want anyone here to get hurt."

The ramrod tension she felt beneath her hand didn't waver. "Do it."

She unhooked the snap on his holster and moved in beside him to pull out the gun. Once she had the weapon safely in hand she looked up and gasped in surprise.

"Angelo?"

Harry had her prize student flattened against the house. Stunned was an understatement for the shock chilling her from the inside out. The teenager was crying, but his eyes were clear as his gaze darted to hers.

"Ms. G.," he gasped. He pawed at Harry's forearm. Although his gold Central Prep ball cap had been knocked off his head and was crushed under his feet, he didn't appear to be harmed. Frightened, yes, but not hurt. "I wasn't thinking. Tell your boyfriend how sorry I am. I didn't mean it."

There was that boyfriend word again.

"Harry. Let him go. He's half your age. He doesn't know how to fight like you do." She handed the gun off to Officer Cho and came back to gently lay her hands on Harry's arm and shoulder. "He's just a kid."

"I've seen kids do worse. Decoys, suicide bombers."

"You're not in a war zone. You're in Kansas City. With me. And I'm safe. Look at me. I'm fine. KCPD is here now. Let them handle it. Angelo won't hurt me. Please let him go."

Harry shifted his gaze to hers. His eyes were shadowed, and that taut muscle ticked beneath his right eye. Then he nodded, stepped back and Angelo was free. "Sorry, kid."

"I did it," Angelo confessed, scurrying around Harry. The young man looked relieved to be dealing with the officer asking him about weapons, feeling his pockets and handcuffing him, rather than facing Harry Lockhart. "I broke all the lights. It was me."

Daisy's heart was crushed. She needed answers for any of this to make sense. Why would Angelo want to do this to her? Why hadn't she known he was sending her those gifts? Why? There were other questions that needed answers, too. She pointed to the trail of blood in the snow. "Whose blood is that?"

"Not his." Harry lifted each foot from the snow. Her heart stuttered again when she saw several small cuts oozing blood on the pale skin of his feet.

"Why don't you go inside and finish getting dressed. There's a first-aid kit in the downstairs bathroom. Unless you need my help?"

"I don't need anybody's help." He looked down at her concerned expression and relented the argument. He scooped up Angelo's cap and placed it back on the young man's head before the officer walked him to the cruiser. "Did I hurt you, kid?"

Angelo's head shook with a jerk. "No, sir."

"You scared of me?"

"Yes, sir."

"Good. Then you know not to do anything that'll upset Ms. G. again, right?"

Angelo nodded.

Harry shifted his gaze to the two police officers, glancing down at the gun tucked into the shorter man's belt. "I'm an NCO with the US Marines, home on leave. My

ID is inside the house, but I've got a permit to carry that thing. It hasn't been fired. I'll be back out in ten to give my statement and retrieve it."

Officer Cho identified himself in a way that Harry seemed to appreciate. "Captain. Missouri Army National Guard." The shorter man okayed Harry's departure with one condition. "Officer Bulkey here is going to accompany you."

"Yes, sir." Harry gave the officer a curt nod before the two men went inside the house.

Angelo took half a step toward Daisy before Cho tugged on his cuffs and warned him to keep his distance. "Sorry, Ms. G. I was just mad that you… That he…" He looked up at the house where Harry had disappeared before inhaling a deep breath and spewing out his confession. "You haven't had a boyfriend in all the time I've known you. And now GI Joe shows up for Christmas? In a month I'm going to be eighteen. Then those stupid rules at school don't apply. You and me, we've got a thing. I was going to ask you out."

"Angelo, I can't date you. Even if you are legal age. I wouldn't jeopardize my job or your school year. And we don't have a thing." Daisy sputtered, replaying the year and a half she'd had Angelo in junior and senior English, trying to think of what she might have said or done that would have given him the slightest hint of encouragement. "I've always enjoyed having you in class. Just because I believe in your talents and abilities doesn't mean I have those kinds of feelings for you."

"But I have those feelings for you." Angelo leaned toward her, his young face lined with hurt. "Then Albert said he saw you two making out."

That peck on the lips at the game? That was all Albert could have seen. Nothing else had happened between her and Harry until they'd gotten home. How could one tentative kiss in a public place equate to so much anger and violence?

"Angelo, I could have died in that fire last night."

"What fire?"

He didn't know? She couldn't help but notice he matched the vague description of the man Harry had seen running from the blaze—blue team coat, gold hat. "In the school basement, after the game."

The teenager's brown eyes widened with concern. "Are you okay? Is the school still there? We've got a home tournament next Saturday."

More than her suspicion that he wasn't a very good liar, Angelo's sudden shift in loyalty to his true love—basketball—eased her fear that her student could be Secret Santa. The broken decorations were a temper tantrum, a child not getting his way and lashing out. Hormones. Crazy teenage hormones and a misplaced crush. Not some sick obsession that promised to hurt her. That was all this was, right? All the same, she had to ask, "Have you been sending me gifts?"

He shrugged, confused by the question. "I gave you Granny's caramels."

"No anonymous cards? Presents?"

"No, ma'am." His concern had moved away from her. "Did the school burn down?"

She almost laughed. Almost. "No. You'll still have to show up for class on Monday."

Officer Cho interrupted the conversation. "Ms. Gunderson, I'm going to read Angelo his rights and put him in the back of the cruiser. No sense us all standing out in the cold. Since you seem to know him, do you want to handle this or would you like to press charges?"

"Press charges?" Angelo gasped. "Oh, hell no. I'll get benched."

He'd probably only get probation if this incident ever made it in front of a judge, but that could cost his chance at a good scholarship. The teacher in Daisy took over for the woman who'd been so worried and afraid. She squeezed Angelo's arm, giving him her sternest teacher look. "You wait in the car with Officer Cho for now. Let me make a couple of phone calls to see if we can get this straightened out. But there will be consequences."

Officer Cho nodded, turning Angelo toward the police car.

"Don't call Granny," Angelo begged. "Please, Ms. G. She will tan my hide and I'll be hauling groceries and taking out trash for every old lady in my building for a month."

Although she wasn't a proponent of hide-tanning, the rest sounded like a fair trade-off. Daisy pulled her phone from the pocket of Harry's coat. She had another idea, a consequence that would mean something to Angelo without jeopardizing his future. "I'll see what I can do."

An hour later, the sun was shining on her front porch. The daylight sparkled off the ice crystals in the snow and warmed the air to a tolerable twenty degrees. Officers Cho and Bulkey had left to file their reports, and Angelo was sitting in the passenger seat of Bernie Riley's car, waiting for the basketball coach to drive him home. Coach Riley promised to have a heart-to-heart talk with his starting point guard about inappropriate crushes on English teachers, and how it was a bad idea to trash her Christmas decorations because he was jealous of the grown man paying attention to her.

Hopefully, Bernie would get started on that heart-to-heart soon. For now, the tall man was standing on Daisy's porch, ignoring her surly house guest leaning against the white pillar behind him, thanking her for not pressing charges against his star player. "I'll have him running extra laps and coming in early to practice his free throws. And I'll make sure he's back here this afternoon to clean up the mess he made," Bernie affirmed, as if the idea had been his and not hers. "I'll clear things with his grandmother, too. We'll make sure he knows he's done something wrong without involving the police and endangering his standing at school."

"I appreciate you coming over, Bernie."

"Not a problem. Always happy to help you out, Gunderson."

He leaned in to give her a hug that felt awkward, not just because of the faintly pungent smell clinging to his clothes that stung Daisy's nose, or the fact that she'd hugged him maybe once, at last year's Christmas party—but because she was blatantly aware of Harry's gray eyes drilling holes in the other man's back. At least he made no effort to *take him down* as he'd reported to the police when Angelo had run from him earlier.

When Bernie pulled away and started down the steps, Daisy breathed a sigh of relief. But she regretted the momentary celebration when Bernie stopped on the bottom step and turned to face her. "Hey. I heard about those gifts you've been getting from your Secret Santa. The naughty ones."

Naughty was a politically correct way to describe them, she supposed. Daisy hugged her arms around the front of Harry's coat. "After the fire, I guess word has spread all over the school."

"Pretty much." Bernie reached up under his gold stocking cap and scratched his head, frowning before he smoothed it back into place. "I think you should know that I'm your Secret Santa."

"What?" She gasped, instantly recoiling. "You're Secret Santa?"

This time, Harry pushed away from the post. When he started down the steps after Bernie, she grabbed his arm. Although Harry halted at her touch, she slid her hand down to his and waited for him to lace his fingers with hers before she trusted that he was clearly in the moment with her.

"Let's hear him out," Daisy suggested.

Harry might be willing to listen, but he wasn't about to step down from protecting her from a possible threat. Standing with his shoulder between her and Bernie, he did as she asked. "So talk."

Bernie's green eyes looked serious for a change, and his tone was surprisingly genuine. "I'm not the one giving you those things. Someone must be replacing my gifts. I put the envelopes in your mailbox and the gifts on your desk—but I told Stella to get you the things on your list. Chocolate. Gift cards for coffee. Ornaments."

Daisy slipped her other hand down to hold on to Harry's unwavering strength. "Your wife is giving me those gifts?"

"I don't have time to shop." Bernie shrugged. "I don't like to shop. So she does all that for me. Wraps them up, sticks in the fancy cards. All I do is deliver."

"Why would your wife do that?"

"I'm not saying she's sending you those things. I mean, Stella gets crazy sometimes, but I don't think she even knows what some of that stuff in the pictures is. I mean, it's porn, right? She's uh, she's a lady."

Daisy had a feeling any woman of any background would know exactly the kind of violence the images in those drawings depicted.

"How do you know what's in the pictures?" Harry asked.

"Bosch and Gamblin were talking about it at the game last night."

"Eddie and Mary told you?" Her friends had betrayed her confidence?

"I could tell there was something funky going on with the present you got yesterday. I thought Stella might be trying to make me look bad by giving you a lump of coal." She should be so lucky. "I didn't know there was something wrong with the gifts until I saw what happened in the school basement. I was down there this morning after going over game tapes in my office. You must have been terrified. This morning I asked some people what was going on."

"Some people?"

"I called Principal Hague and he explained what was going on. Now that announcement he made at the faculty meeting about appropriate gifts makes sense." Bernie scratched under his cap again.

She felt the muscles in Harry's arm tense a split second before it snaked out and he snatched the gold stocking cap off Bernie's head.

"What the hell, dude?"

"You got a bad case of dandruff? Why do you keep scratching?" Harry put the cap up to his nose and instantly averted his face. "It smells like smoke and acetone."

Bernie snatched the cap back and pulled it over his head. "I told you I was down in the basement this morning. The place still reeks. Hague said they're airing out the whole school all weekend so we can get back in there on Monday."

Daisy supposed that was a perfectly logical explanation for a man with a blue jacket and yellow hat—like the man Harry had seen running from the fire—to have clothes that smelled like the crime scene. Although logic wasn't making it any easier to tamp down her suspicions about her colleague. "Where were you last night?"

"Coaching two ball games."

Harry took a step closer. "What about afterward? When did you leave? With the players? Later than that?"

Bernie puffed up to his six and a half feet of height. "Are you accusing me of something?" He sidled closer to Daisy, and Harry shifted, keeping his shoulder and dark-eyed glare between them. "Look, I came here to help you out, not to be given the third degree by your bully boyfriend here."

"Where were you?" Harry pressed. Had the smell of the cap triggered a bad memory? Was he getting angry again?

"None of your damn business." Bernie looked straight at Daisy, ignoring Harry. "I just wanted you to know that I drew your name for Secret Santa, and that Stella has been buying the gifts. She has high-class taste. I'm sure she's only getting you nice stuff. I don't know how they're getting swapped out for those other things or who's doing it. But I didn't want you to blame me. Or her." His forehead wrinkled with a rueful expression. "She and I—we've been having some troubles lately. Heck, I even thought about taking you up on renting that spare room of yours for a few weeks instead of staying in a hotel."

"A hotel?" Daisy knew she should feel sorry for Bernie instead of thinking that a struggling marriage could be a motive for either one of them to threaten her.

"Like I said, troubles. That room wouldn't still be available, would it? I've been keeping a change of clothes on me and showering at the school locker room in the morning. It'd be nice to be in a house again."

"She has a tenant," Harry announced. He draped his arm over her shoulders and squeezed her to his side, warning Bernie that no other man was going to get close to her while he was around.

A twinge of discomfort pinged in Daisy's memories

and she quietly extricated herself from Harry's grasp. Had being protective of her just taken a step over the line into Brock Jantzen land?

Bernie got the message loud and clear, instantly backing off from the possibility of moving in with her. "Yeah. Well, if I had known the kind of stuff you were getting, I'd have said something sooner."

Daisy nodded, putting another step between her and Harry. "Thanks for letting me know."

Perhaps Bernie still didn't realize the depth of terror she'd been living with the past two weeks. "Guess that's going to ruin the party for you next Saturday. It won't be a surprise for you when we reveal who had whose name."

She'd already had plenty of surprises this week. She glanced over at the back of Harry's dark, close-cropped hair that she'd had such fun tickling her palms against last night. Only one of those surprises had been good. Harry Lockhart. The surprise of this relationship—if that was what it even was—was awkward. Difficult and uncertain. But a good surprise, nonetheless.

Cognizant of their audience here and in the car, Daisy tabled her analysis over what, exactly, Harry meant to her, and whether the reality of a relationship with a man struggling with PTSD was something she wanted to take on. She waved to Angelo and offered Bernie a smile. "Thanks for helping with Angelo. And I'm sorry to hear about you and Stella."

"Thanks."

"Talk to her," Daisy suggested. "Listen, too. If you can communicate, you can solve just about anything." She wondered if Harry was hearing any of that advice. "And—maybe you shouldn't give me any more presents. Not even the big one for the party. Return it. Donate it to charity. Give it to someone else. If this guy doesn't have that anonymous way to send me gifts, maybe he'll stop."

"If you say so." Bernie strode around the clear path of the sidewalk and climbed into his car, doffing her a salute before driving away.

Harry watched the car all the way to the stop sign at the corner before looking up at her. "He won't stop."

Although she was the one wearing the coat, Daisy shivered and turned to the front door. "Thank you for those fine words of comfort."

He caught her hand and stopped her. "This isn't a joke. Perverts like that, they'll find a way to get to you if that's what they want. If you cut him off, if he thinks you're on to him, he might escalate."

"Someone locked me in a room and started a fire that could have killed me." So much for subtle hints. Daisy tugged her hand free, regretting that she'd forgotten the soldier sorely lacking verbal communication skills after being with the passionate, bravely vulnerable man last night. "Things have already escalated."

"Damn it, Daisy, I'm not making light of what happened." When she snatched her hand from his, he fell back to the top step. "Don't be a fool. What if Riley confessed to being your Secret Santa just to throw you off track so you wouldn't suspect him? Why do his clothes smell like that fire? What if Angelo isn't as innocent as you seem to think?"

"What if Stella Riley is so jealous of something she thinks I've done that she wants to torment me?" Daisy crossed the porch to look him straight in the eye. "I'm not stupid. You don't think I've thought of any of that? All I have are suspects and threats. What I don't have are answers. I don't know who to trust anymore. This isn't over.

Not until I know who is doing this to me, and that creep is in jail. But I am—"

"—going to stay positive?" That was sarcasm, deriding her for the very trait he'd praised the night before.

"I was going to say I'm keeping my guard up."

"You didn't with me." He threw his hands up. "You worry too much about everybody else. You're too forgiving. You're going to get hurt."

"You're being a jerk right now, you know that?" The differences between them had finally erupted into an argument that neither one of them could win. His heart might be in the right place, believing he was protecting her, but she couldn't live her life being judged and criticized and ordered around. "Where's my Harry? Where's the man from those letters?"

He jolted back, as if she'd slapped him across the face. When he spoke again, it was a quiet, unemotional tone. "I warned you I wasn't any good at this. I was a different man then."

Daisy touched his chest, splaying her fingers until she could feel the strong beat of his heart beneath her hand. Her tone was hushed, too. "No. You're the same man. That's the man who was with me last night. But you went through something awful, more than a good man should have to bear. You just have to find him again."

That muscle ticked beneath his eye again as he evaluated her words. "You don't have to welcome me into your bedroom anymore, but I'm not leaving you unprotected. My gear's already upstairs. I'll sleep up there and start paying you rent."

He was serious about becoming her tenant, about taking a relationship that had heated to incendiary in the span of forty-eight hours back to let's-just-be-friends. Her life was safer this way, right? Her heart most certainly was.

She should be glad that one of them could think sensibly here. Instead, she felt hollow inside, as though she'd lost something that was more important than she realized. "If that's how you want it."

"That's how it needs to be."

The man needed his distance. He didn't trust himself not to hurt her. But how was she ever going to accept that the man she'd fallen in love with didn't want to be in a relationship? He didn't believe he could be. "Harry—"

The dogs started barking inside the house, ending the conversation. All three of her fur-babies were at the storm door, telling her she had company. She recognized the bark. It was the I-spy-another-dog alert. Her neighbor, Jeremiah Finch, was strolling by with his Chihuahua, Suzy, on a long black leash. "Good morning, Daisy."

"Good morning, Mr. Finch." Harry didn't turn, didn't offer any polite greeting to the older man in his trim wool coat and neatly tied scarf. Harry snapped his fingers and used a hand signal to calm Caliban and Patch into a tail-wagging sit, leaving Muffy as the only noisemaker announcing their visitor. When Jeremiah stopped to let Suzy sniff out the new smells of all the visitors Daisy had had that morning, she moved off the porch to continue the conversation. "It's shaping up to be the nicest day we've had in weeks. I'm glad you and Suzy are getting out."

"I'm not sure I want to, even in the daylight."

"What do you mean?"

He clucked his tongue behind his teeth. "We have a crime wave in our neighborhood."

"A crime wave? You mean the police car that was here earlier?" She summoned a smile to reassure him that whatever was happening was only happening to her. "The situation has been taken care of."

"Has it?" He came halfway up her front walk, as if

she couldn't hear him tsk-tsking over the short distance already. "Some punk vandalized your house. I have trespassers in my backyard—one of my boxwood bushes was trampled on." He peeked around her, eyeing the gun strapped to Harry's thigh. "Men with guns are roaming at will—"

"Harry is not roaming the neighborhood."

Suddenly, Harry was interested in joining the conversation. He trotted down the steps to join her, holding up his phone. "Mr. Finch, do you mind if I take pictures of the footprints in your backyard?"

Jeremiah seemed taken aback to be addressed directly by the bigger man. "As long as that's all you do."

With a nod, Harry jogged through the snow and disappeared around the corner of the house.

Once Harry was gone, Jeremiah tugged on Suzy's leash so he could lean in toward Daisy. "Don't think I didn't see your thug sitting outside your house the night before last. He was probably casing the joint. He's casing mine now. But I could hardly stop him. And you've invited him into your home. After what happened with your last boyfriend, I would think you'd be more careful about who you associate with. I try to keep an eye on you and protect you—"

"First of all, Master Sergeant Harry Lockhart is no thug. He's a decorated Marine. Second, my student may be a misguided young man, but he is not a punk and he is no threat to you. If he damaged one of your bushes, I'll make sure he pays to replace it. And third, what happened to me is my business, not yours. How I protect myself is none of your concern."

"I can see you're upset." Jeremiah's face had turned red all the way up to his hairline. "So, this person—is a bodyguard? What kind of threat are we talking about?" He clutched at his chest. "Am I in danger?"

"No." Daisy reached down to pet Suzy when the tiny dog put her paws on Daisy's knee. Dogs had always been a stress reducer for her. She couldn't imagine losing any one of hers the way Harry had lost Tango. "I'm sorry I lost my temper. I've been receiving threats. Harry is a…friend… who's helping me keep an eye on things."

"I see." Jeremiah tugged the Chihuahua back to his side. "I still don't like seeing guns in my neighborhood. And your friend is so…rough-looking. Are you certain you're safe with him?"

Wasn't that the question of the hour?

"I know you were friends with Mom and Dad, and you have been friends with me—but to come over to my home and lecture me about my choices…" Even if they were bad ones, he had no right to make her feel stupid for trusting her heart or wanting to help a good man. Mr. Finch didn't have that right. Harry didn't. No one did.

Jeremiah glanced over to the side yard where Harry had gone. "Well, if something happens and you do need me, you have my number. Come along, Suzy."

As Mr. Finch and Suzy moved on down the street to continue their walk, Daisy pressed her hands over her mouth, fighting back the urge to cry or cuss up a blue streak. She wouldn't apologize for defending the people she cared about, but there had to be a better way to cope with the fear and uncertainty and raging need to have control over her own life again. Maybe this was what Harry felt like when he lost it. But she was years past her trauma while his was still fresh. The stress was getting to be too much. She was tired of being afraid, of suspecting everyone she knew. She needed this to be done.

"Daisy?" She started at the clipped voice behind her, and quickly swiped at the tears in her eyes before they could fall. "Are you all right?"

She turned to face Harry, wishing she had the right to walk into his arms and be held. But there was a tension between them now that hadn't been there before, an underlying sizzle of attraction that was complicated in a big way by far too many issues that neither of them could control.

When she didn't answer, he pulled out his phone. "I found something important. Something that should exonerate Angelo."

"I never believed he was sending me those gifts."

"But would it make you feel better to know for sure? To have one less person around you who could be a suspect?"

He was trying to make her feel better? That earned him the shadow of a smile. He wasn't offering comforting words or a hug. But it would be nice to be able to look over her classroom on Monday and not have to be afraid of anyone there. "What did you find?"

"The footprints were made by two different kinds of shoes. Angelo's has a tread, like a running shoe. The prints in Finch's yard, like the ones by your window the other night, were made by boots."

She wasn't comforted yet. "Maybe Angelo wore boots the other night to peek in my window. He's not so poor that he can't afford more than one pair of shoes."

"Only if he figured out a way to shrink his feet." Harry pulled up the pictures on his phone and showed her the images. "It's not scientific, but it's enough to make me suspicious." Harry had photographed all three sets of prints frozen in the snow, using his own boot as a marker beside each one to compare the size. Angelo's running shoes were a good two to three sizes bigger, while the others were smaller and skinnier than Harry's foot. "I'm going to send the pictures to Pike. He's not a detective, but he'll know who to show them to."

"Thank you." Daisy appreciated the effort he was making to ease some of her fear. Maybe it was the only way he thought he could help.

"I'm sorry I thought the worst of that kid. But it does prove that this guy isn't just targeting you at school. He knows where you live. He's been here. Watching you."

"And the gloom and doom is back." Daisy marched up the stairs into the house. She shooed the dogs ahead of her while Harry locked the door behind her. "You think I don't know that he's watching? That I don't feel him around me all the time?" Harry followed her into the kitchen where she poured herself a cup of coffee and held the steaming mug between her hands. "This is where you're supposed to say something to make me feel better."

When he didn't say anything, she shrugged out of his coat and tossed it at him. He dropped the coat onto a chair and followed her to the refrigerator. "I heard you defending me against Finch. You didn't have to do that. I was losing it with that kid. I got territorial with Coach Riley. I was making decisions without asking you. I'm fighting to keep you safe. But the way I talked to you—the words, the tone? I could tell I hurt you. Last night was…amazing. A perfect moment out of time between all the nightmares." Just as she closed her eyes to let the raw poetry of his words warm her battered heart, he added, "But I'm not good for you, Daisy. Maybe I am a thug."

She refused to believe that.

"Normal people have arguments just like we did. Normal people lose it every now and then. You're not going to be cured after one late-night conversation and…" *a perfect moment out of time.* Hugging the creamer to her chest, she closed the fridge and turned to find Harry standing right there. He was close enough to touch, close enough to stretch on tiptoe to kiss that handsome, awkward mouth that had loved her so thoroughly. But she did neither. The mixture of pain and longing stamped on his chiseled features tore at her heart. "You've taken a big first step toward healing. But there are bound to be relapses. Fight through them. Accept that sometimes you're going to fail, then move on. You don't think I get depressed sometimes? That I don't get angry? Look at me yelling at poor Mr. Finch. You have to give it time."

"Time is one thing I don't have. If I don't get my head on right before I return to the Corps in six weeks, they won't take me." He captured a strand of hair that had fallen over her cheek and rubbed it between his thumb and fingers before smoothing it behind her ear and backing away. "Maybe no one should." He grabbed his coat and headed to the front door. "Lock yourself in with the dogs. I need to clear my head."

Daisy hurried after him. "You can't go for a walk with your foot cut up like that."

"Then I'll drive." He opened the front door and pointed to the lock behind him. "I'll be back by lunch. Anything happens, you call me or the cops."

"What if something happens to *you*?" That stopped him.

Then he tunneled his fingers into the hair at her nape, cupped the back of her neck and pulled her onto her toes for a hard, potent kiss. He kissed her a second time. And a third. "I'll think about that. And how much I want...to be fixed. For you."

Chapter Ten

Harry returned two and a half hours later with several new strings of outdoor Christmas lights and an eight-foot Scotch pine tree for Daisy's living room. He'd also purchased a properly sized winter coat for himself in basic beige and a lavender parka with a bow on the belt he guessed would be about Daisy's size. The thank you hugs were a nice bonus, but he hadn't let her smile or welcoming arms sway him from his mission. He had something to prove, not only to Daisy, but to himself.

This time, he hadn't hiked through the snow or spent a couple of hours breathing fresh air. Sure, he'd driven around the neighborhood for about ten minutes, thinking he needed to clear his head. But then he realized he didn't need to clear anything—he needed to accept everything that was jumbled up inside him and attack it with a plan. He needed to think like a Marine.

Protect the base. Get intel. Know your enemy. Trust your allies.

He'd called Pike to drive over and keep an eye on Daisy's house while he was gone. Then he'd asked his brother-in-law about the photos he'd taken, and ended up talking to one of his friends, a Detective Nick Fensom, who was familiar with Daisy's assault case. The detective confirmed to Harry's own peace of mind that Daisy's ex was still incarcerated, and that the people around her, Bernie and Stella Riley, Angelo and Albert Logan, didn't have criminal records. Nick reminded Harry that just because a person didn't have a record, it didn't mean he or she didn't have it in for Daisy. She might be the stalker's first target, or he simply hadn't been reported or caught for this kind of behavior previously.

Detective Fensom also wanted to know more about the threats she'd been receiving, and promised to contact both the Central Prep principal, Ryan Hague, and John Murdock at the KCFD to get details on the events that had happened at the school. Fensom also wanted to document the messages and gifts Daisy had received, along with a timeline so he could put together a case against her stalker once he was caught. And he would be caught, if Harry had anything to do with it.

When he got back to the house, Pike and his son, Gideon, were building a snowman in the front yard, away from where the shards of broken bulbs still littered the snow. Hope was in the kitchen helping Daisy fix them all some lunch. By the time Gideon and Hope lay down for afternoon naps, he and Pike had put up the Christmas tree, swept off the deck and put all the dogs through their paces in the backyard. Caliban was an old pro, slow but responsive to each command. Patch picked up on the training quickly, even learning a couple of new tricks. And Muffy was, well, what the dog lacked in attention span he made up for in personality. The misnamed Shih Tzu was never going to make it in the K-9 Corps, but he sure knew how to sound an alarm. Whether he was letting them know that Albert and Angelo had arrived to help clean up the yard, or he was chasing a bird off the fence, Muffy had something to say about it.

After they ordered pizza and finished dinner, Hope and

her family and the two teenagers left. Trying to remember that he was the tenant/bodyguard and not the crazy boyfriend who wanted to peel the bright red Chiefs sweatshirt and matching glasses off Daisy and see if the miracle of last night had been a fluke, he put the dogs out, checked the locks, then resolutely ignored Daisy's blue-eyed disappointment and went upstairs to shower and get whatever sleep he could.

After his shopping trip that morning, he'd also come back with personal supplies he needed to put away, and a wood train set for his nephew that he hid on the top shelf of his closet until he could get it wrapped. All in all, it was a productive day. A healthy, normal, "worn out by work instead of an ongoing mental battle" kind of day. He hadn't wigged out and he hadn't hurt anyone.

Now if he could do this again tomorrow. And the day after that.

Harry toweled off and pulled on a clean pair of shorts and the faded USMC sweatpants he slept in. The lights were off downstairs and Daisy and the dogs had gone to bed. Alone in the soothing quiet, he stowed his service Beretta in the nightstand and dumped out his recent purchases on the bed. He packed the fresh bar of soap, disposable razors and condoms in his toiletry bag, set the pack of gum on the dresser beside his wallet, and opened the box of bandages and antibiotic salve before sitting down to redress the cuts on his feet. None of them were bad enough to need stitches, but an infection was the last thing he needed right now. When he'd finished medic duty, he folded down the quilt, piled the pillows against the headboard and picked up the package of ink pens and the spiral notebook he'd bought.

This was going to be the hard part.

Harry flipped open the notebook and stared at the blank

piece of paper. He breathed deeply, steeling himself for the task at hand. He might not be a natural talent for this relationship stuff, or understand the intricate workings of the human brain, but he knew how to follow orders.

He started writing.

Day one. Mission accomplished.

A list was easier than coming up with sentences and paragraphs. He stated his objectives, and how well he'd met them.

Lt. Col. Biro had ordered him to get a Christmas tree and eat too many sweets. Check and check.

The lieutenant colonel had also ordered him to kiss a pretty girl. Definitely a check. Multiple checks. If he succeeded with this plan of action, he hoped to fill up this entire notebook with check marks on that assignment.

But for now, he'd sustain himself on the memory of Daisy's patience with him, her acceptance of his scars, her passionate abandon to touch and be touched that forced him to tip his head back and breathe deeply to cool his body's desire to march down those stairs to be with her again. She'd probably welcome him to her bed because she was Daisy—the woman who cared too much and forgave too easily. But Harry had every intention of proving he was worthy of that compassion and forgiveness before indulging his physical needs. He didn't want to be another rescue mission for her. He wanted to be a whole man—one who never left her second-guessing her willingness to trust him. He wanted to be a man she could love without any regrets.

The objective was clear. Follow orders. Complete the mission.

Back to the notebook.

Dr. Polk had advised him to get plenty of exercise, journal his thoughts and keep his appointments. Check. Check. Check.

Daisy said to write her letters.

Harry hesitated. What exactly was he supposed to say to her that wouldn't sound pitiful or controlling or downright scary?

He clipped the pen onto the paper and rolled out of bed to do twenty reps on the pull-up bar he'd hung over the door. When he focused on the burning muscles, the memories in his head sorted themselves.

Daisy liked to talk. And if he was a smart man, he would listen.

You're giving me value by trusting me with your fears, by sharing your darkest feelings, by helping me understand you.

He went back to the bed, turned to a new page in the notebook and started writing.

Dear Daisy…

HARRY LED A normal life for the next four days.

He drove Daisy to school and picked her up afterward. He restocked her groceries and took out her trash. He spent a long two hours babysitting Gideon so that Hope could take a break and have lunch with a friend. He and Daisy met with Nick Fensom in her classroom, handing over the evidence from her desk and briefing the detective on anyone she suspected.

Since his feet were too sore to do a daily run, Harry put the dogs in the truck and hauled them to a dog park for a good workout. He discovered Patch had an affinity for catching flying discs and Albert Logan had an interest in learning more about training dogs. He'd picked up Albert after a tutoring session with Daisy and brought him to the house to teach the young man some of the skills he'd learned as a handler. He took Daisy out to dinner one night on a real date, even kissing her good-night at the front door before heading upstairs to his room as if they were getting newly acquainted. Daisy was frustrated with the distance he was keeping. The frustrated desire was wearing on him, too. "I'm trying to get your Harry back," he promised her. Ultimately, she seemed to understand that he needed to do this and gave him the space he asked for.

There were no more messages from Secret Santa, no odious gifts delivered. Bernie Riley kept his promise and stopped leaving items for her at school. The quiet spell seemed to back up Riley's claim that someone had been swapping out the innocent gifts his wife had picked out with the cruel taunts and graphic images. Daisy wanted to believe that, with no outlet, the threats had stopped for good. But neither she nor Harry really did. This was simply the calm before the storm. Harry suspected that, like an enemy whose line of propaganda had been cut off, the pervert's frustration was building like a volcano about to erupt. Without a daily avenue to get his message across to Daisy, he was probably planning something even bigger and more terrifying to grab her attention. Harry intended to be ready to protect her from whatever that threat might be.

Harry might be broken inside, but he'd been trained to adapt and overcome to get the job done. If his job was proving to Daisy, and more importantly to himself, that he was healthy relationship material, then he was going to do whatever it took to make that happen.

Including writing in that spiral notebook every night.

Some of the entries were horrible, angry scratches that cut through five sheets of paper. Some were just a report of his day—his successes and his failures. The fresh batches of cookies he'd volunteered to sample. The training sessions with the dogs. Working with Angelo and Albert to move some furniture and crates into the garage and finish a couple of painting projects before the Christmas party, when the house would be invaded by thirty-seven teachers and staff, along with their significant others.

His chest got tight just thinking about a crowd of noisy revelers invading Daisy's home. If Secret Santa was one of her coworkers, would he try something that night? Or would he wait until he had a private time and place to finish whatever he had in mind for Daisy?

Tonight, those troubling thoughts about where all this was headed had morphed into a nightmare. Sitting bolt upright in a cold sweat, Harry kicked back the covers that had twisted around his legs and cursed the darkness. He flipped on the lamp beside him and focused on it, inhaling several cooling breaths. He didn't know how long he'd been thrashing in the bed, or if he'd been swearing out loud in his sleep, but he'd been caught up in a dream long enough to have knocked a pillow, his cell phone and the notebook to the floor. He straightened the mess and picked up his pen.

14 December 3:17 a.m.
Dear Daisy,
Thought I was having a good day today. But you were right. Relapses happen and suddenly I'm in the middle of a nightmare. I know it's just in my head. But the fear felt pretty damn real.

You were in that fire again. Only, I couldn't get to you. I don't know what's wrong with my brain that it can only picture the worst. Why aren't I dreaming about the way your blue eyes squint me into focus when you want something from me? Or the way they darkened like midnight when you flew apart all around me? Any other guy would be dreaming about the sex. And don't think I haven't imagined being with you again.

But no, my brain took you with me when I went back to that firefight with the IEDs going off. I had Tango in my arms that day, and I guess a lot of the blood I saw on him was my own. But it all got jumbled up and I was holding you and there was nothing but blood and fire. I couldn't see your smile. I couldn't hear your laugh. I couldn't stop screaming.

The smell of burning skin is an awful, awful...

A soft metallic clinking noise turned Harry's attention to the door. Any mild sense of alarm that he hadn't detected the noise sooner ebbed when he identified the familiar sound of jangling dog tags and the click, click, click of paws slowly coming up the stairs. Who was making the rounds tonight? "Patch? Fur ball?"

He slept with the door open so that he'd be able to hear anything happening on the ground floor he needed to investigate. But he was unprepared for the furry gray muzzle peeking around the door frame or the Belgian Malinois panting for breath as he stared at Harry from the doorway.

"Caliban?" The dog's dark ears pricked up with recognition. For a brief moment, Tango's dark muzzle superimposed itself over the old dog's face. Harry blinked and Caliban returned. But the same heart and spirit remained in those dark brown eyes. "You worried about me, buddy?" The dog cocked his head to one side as if they were having a conversation and Harry chuckled. "I would be, too." He tossed the notebook aside. "Come here, boy. *Hier.*" Caliban trotted over in his rolling gait and Harry patted the top of the mattress, inviting him up beside him. *"Hopp."*

When Caliban jumped up onto the quilt, Harry rewarded him with a little bit of wrestling that ended with a tummy rub and him smiling. "Good boy. I guess those sharp old ears heard me." Caliban thrust his front paw into the air so that Harry could scratch the leg pit there. "You're used to looking out for a partner. And now you're looking out for me."

The nightmare faded and some good memories of his time with Tango made his eyes gritty with tears. "Tango used to wake me up when I got to tossing and turning too much, too. You lost your partner and I lost mine. We'll look out for each other, okay?"

Caliban rolled onto his belly, sitting up like a Sphinx and eyeing the door.

Harry swung his legs off the edge of the bed. "I hear it, too."

A parade of dog paws rushing up the stairs, followed by the noise of creaking wood as someone slightly heavier hurried behind them. Muffy and Patch dashed in and jumped right up on the bed, jockeying for petting position beside him. "Hello, you two."

At the last second, he remembered to shove his notebook out of sight under his pillow before rising to meet Daisy when she appeared in the doorway.

"Hello." Her hair was tousled and sexy, she had a wrinkle on her cheek from her pillow, and she was wearing those shapeless flannel pajamas that were almost as soft as her skin. The hungry sweep of her gaze over his bare chest intensified the gut-kick of desire already rushing through his blood and threatened to undo every well-planned good intention of his recovery mission. He pushed the excited dogs away and took a step closer. "Did I wake you?" Dumb question. Clearly, she was worried about him.

"You mean the headboard banging against the wall up here?" She held up her thumb and forefinger pinched together. "Little bit."

"Sorry." He nodded over his shoulder. "Caliban came up to…"

"Are you all right?"

Her question topped his statement and they both fell silent.

Daisy hugged her arms beneath her breasts and nodded toward the three-legged dog. "When I woke up, I realized he was missing. This is the last place I would have looked if I hadn't heard you. He's never come up the stairs before. He must really like you."

"He probably recognizes a kindred spirit."

She wasn't wearing her robe or those fuzzy slipper socks. As she drew invisible circles on the hardwood with her big toe, he noticed something he hadn't before. She painted her toenails. Purple, like the highlights in her hair. It was hard to remember the way he'd first pictured Daisy—the golden angel dressed in white and bathed in sunshine. The real Daisy was meant for moonlight and bold color and ill-timed fantasies in the middle of the night.

"Do you need to talk about it? The nightmare?"

"I'm not dumping on you."

The circles stopped. "It's not dumping. It's one friend listening to another."

"No."

"What about your therapist? Or your sister?" Her shoulders puffed up with a sigh and she kept talking. "I know you're on some kind of healing journey. You're afraid that you're going to scare me or hurt me or make me worry too much. Well, I'm always going to worry about you. That's what people who care about each other do, so you're not doing me any favors by isolating yourself."

"I am not dumping on you." When her blue eyes peeked above the rims of her glasses, he put up his hands and tried to reassure her. "But I'm not bottling it all up inside, either. I'm following doctor's orders. And Lieutenant Colonel Biro's orders. And...your orders."

"Mine?"

"Something you said the other night. I've been writing letters."

"To me?"

"In a journal of sorts." Muffy knocked aside his pillow to claim a spot on the bed, and revealed his secret. "Thanks for ratting me out, fur ball." Harry picked up the pillow and set the spiral notebook on the bedside table. "I don't know if anyone is ever going to read it. But it helps to get it out."

"I'm proud of you, Harry. I know it can't be easy."

"It's important to me that I'm in control of myself—how I react to people, how I treat you—before I let you and me go any further." He'd already given her his heart—there wasn't much further he could go. But he didn't want to ruin the best thing that had ever happened to him before it had even gotten started. "The dream tonight kind of rattled me. Made me think that I wasn't the right man to protect you."

"Harry, I don't want—"

He pressed a finger against her lips to silence her argument. "I make no claims to be a hundred percent yet. But I'm not trusting anyone else with the job of keeping you safe."

"Okay," she murmured beneath his finger. "May I talk now?"

He lingered a little longer where he shouldn't before curling his fingers into his palm and pulling away. "I needed you to understand that."

"There's no one I trust more to protect me. I just wish you'd let me do something for you in return."

Maybe there was something. "Could I hold you for a while? After what I saw, I won't be able to sleep unless I know you're safe. And the only way I can know that when I'm dozing off is to—"

She walked straight into his chest and wrapped her arms around his waist. Her forehead found that familiar spot against his neck and she softened against him, fitting all her curves to his harder planes. "I can stay."

Feeling the tension of his nightmare leaving his body already, Harry wound his arms around her to complete the hug and nestled his nose against her hair. "Just to sleep, honey." He was reminding his own body's eager response to her touch, as much as clarifying the request for her. "You've got school tomorrow morning."

"I am happy to hold and be held by you anytime, Harry Lockhart." She pressed her lips to the scar beneath his collarbone. "Do you think I've been getting good sleep downstairs by myself? I need you close by so I know you're safe, too."

They stood like that until Harry's body began to respond in a way he hadn't intended. Forcing himself to pull away, he led her to the bed and tucked her under the covers. After setting her glasses aside, he claimed the spot Muffy wanted, lay down on top of the quilt and pulled Daisy into his arms. As the three dogs settled in behind her and at the foot of the bed, Harry reached over and turned off the lamp.

"This is better," she whispered, resting her head on his shoulder.

"Much better."

Daisy and the dogs were all asleep when Harry heard a car door slamming outside. He gently extricated himself from the arm around his waist and went to the front and side windows to peek through the curtains. He scanned up and down the block, looking for the exhaust from a running car or any signs of movement. But there was nothing suspicious—no one in her yard or walking the street. He went across the hall and looked out the bathroom window to see if the new motion detector light he'd installed over the deck had come on. But the back of the house was dark and still. No heartbroken teenager busting up the new lights, no one throwing snowballs at the house or standing outside her bedroom window.

By the time Harry returned, Caliban had raised his head in curiosity, but wasn't alerting to any signs of an intruder. Muffy would certainly be going off if someone was trying to break in. Harry petted the Malinois and climbed back into bed. The house was locked up tight. His gun was in arm's reach and Daisy was tucked safely in his arms.

If the dogs weren't worried about one lone sound in the night, he wouldn't be, either.

EVEN IF DAISY was willing to risk a little PDA in front of the students hurrying through the front doors for a morning practice or the breakfast program, the dogs wedged between her and Harry in the front seat of his truck would have prevented it.

"You're spoiling them," she teased, pulling Muffy back to her lap to avoid the Shih Tzu's marauding tongue. She was pleased to see that Caliban had claimed his spot beside Harry on the bench seat. The older dog had perked up in both energy and personality since Harry had moved into the house. Patch stood with his front paws on the dashboard, wagging his little bob of a tail and watching the students and staff walk past the truck in the circular driveway. He just wanted to be a part of what everyone else was doing. "You've been to the dog park every morning this week."

Harry rubbed his hand around Caliban's ears. "It gives

me a little exercise, too. Plus, there aren't a lot of people there this time of year."

"Do you think you'll ever be able to tolerate crowds again?"

"Who knows? I'm a work in progress." He shifted his petting hand to Patch, who instantly crawled over Caliban to sit in Harry's lap. His stiff half smile faded as he turned his attention to the people walking past. "Look at all the blue coats and yellow caps going into Central Prep. Maybe you should invite me to speak to your classes."

"About what?"

"PTSD? My career in the military? How letter writing is a lost art and they should be glad you're teaching it to them?"

She understood what Harry's sudden willingness to spend the day with a bunch of hormonal teenagers was really about. "So you can keep an eye on me?"

"Too controlling?"

She reached across the seat to pull his gloved hand off Patch and squeeze it. "You aren't Brock Jantzen."

He squeezed back. "I'm just trying to be a better Harry Lockhart."

"You know I'll be waiting for you whenever you're ready, right?"

"What if I'm never ready?"

Daisy wondered if never being Harry's woman would be worse than being the woman he had loved and left behind because he decided he couldn't do relationships, after all. But that was too heart-breaking a topic to discuss on this sunny winter morning when Harry was fighting like everything to find his new normal. She smiled, instead, pulling her hand away to adjust Muffy's red sweater. "Fridays I don't have to stay late, so be here at three-thirty."

"Yes, ma'am. On the dot."

Daisy dumped Muffy off her lap and looped her pink bag over her shoulder. "Have a good day, Top."

"Be safe, Ms. G." When she turned to assure him she would, he was already leaning in. "Come here," he growled.

His firm lips scudded across hers in a searing kiss. His touch warmed her all the way down to the toes of her boots. Not that she'd ever complained, but he was growing more confident, less self-conscious with every kiss. Daisy touched her fingers to his jaw and would have encouraged him to explore his craft to his heart's content, but there were suddenly cold noses and warm tongues trying to join in.

"Blecch." Daisy flattened her hand between them to ward off the licks on her neck and chin while Harry retreated to his side of the truck, his deep chest bouncing with laughter. Daisy joined him. A genuine laugh from Harry was worth a hundred kisses.

She opened the truck door and climbed out. "Bye."

Daisy walked through a gauntlet of "woo-hoos" and whistles, and a couple of thumbs-ups from students and staff as she headed inside and crossed through the lobby. "You people need to go study," she admonished, hoping they'd mistake the blush on her cheeks as a sign of the cold morning air and not her happy embarrassment.

She ran into Mary Gamblin in the teachers' lounge and poured herself a mug of coffee before walking down the hallway to their rooms together. "Are you still feeling up to that party tomorrow?" Mary asked. "With everything that's going on, isn't it stressing you out?"

"No," Daisy answered honestly. "It gives me something fun and positive to focus on. You better come and help me eat all the cookies I've baked this week. If everybody doesn't bring the potluck dishes they signed up for, we're all going to be on a massive sugar high by the end of the evening."

"It's good to see you in a happy mood again. Does it have anything to do with that Marine you were kissing out front?"

There was no masking the blush on her cheeks this time. "Did everybody see that?"

"Enough people to start the rumor mill."

Daisy nudged her shoulder against her friend's, refusing to be the only fodder for gossip today. "What about you? Are you and Eddie coming to the party together?"

"I had to drop about every hint I could." Mary rolled her eyes and giggled. "But yeah. He asked me."

"Awesome." They reached their respective rooms across the hall from each other and inserted their keys into the locks. "Hey, I hung some mistletoe if you'd like to take advantage..."

"He's a slow mover."

"Maybe a Christmas kiss will help him move a little faster."

"Fingers crossed." They pushed open their doors. "Have a good day."

"You, too."

Once inside her room, Daisy turned on the lights and unhooked the lavender bow on her coat, unbuttoning the gift from Harry as she crossed to the front of the room to her desk. She set her coffee on the corner and pulled out her chair.

And froze.

No. Whatever she was feeling right now went beyond freezing. She couldn't think. Couldn't move. Couldn't feel.

Her bag dropped to the floor beside her. She stared at the neatly-wrapped oblong box lying on the seat of her chair. Decorated with an all too familiar card emblazoned with a sparkly green tree, the present taunted her with its ominous promise.

As the feeling returned to her limbs, she leaned over to read the words typed across the face of the card.

Get rid of him! Or I will.
You belong to me.
Merry Christmas from your Secret Santa.

"Oh, my God." A righteous anger suddenly flowed through her body, giving her the strength to move. Leaving her gloves on in case her tormentor had slipped up this time and left fingerprints, she picked up the box, finding it surprisingly heavy for its size. She dropped it onto the middle of her blotter and stooped down to dig her phone out of her purse.

Her first instinct was to call Harry. She needed him here with her. Now. Nobody else understood, nobody else cared as much, about how terrified she was of her stalker. She needed his arms. His growly comforts and complaints. His do-the-job-or-die attitude to make the terror go away.

Her hands were shaking as she pulled up the call screen. But it was pointless to pull up her list of contacts as she remembered they were more about touching and talking in person, and had been together so much of the past week that she hadn't needed to call him. Until she needed to call him. Like now. Daisy pushed to her feet. "Even if you can never say you love me, you are going to give me your phone number, damn it."

But the flare of anger, aimed mostly at herself, quickly abated. Red liquid was seeping through the wrapping paper from a corner of the box she must have bent when she'd dropped it. The liquid, viscous and thick, spread across the white blotter, creating a crimson puddle in the middle of her desk.

"Please don't be..." She untied the bow and lifted the lid. She squeezed her hand over her mouth, fighting back the urge to scream. The box held a soldier action figure, his face blacked out with ink. The whole thing was sitting in a pool of red liquid that could only be one thing. Blood.

Animal blood. Fake blood. A grotesque pint from her stalker, it didn't matter. Daisy turned away from the gruesome gift and swiped her hand across her phone, dialing 9-1-1. She needed to notify Mr. Hague, too. And more than anything, she needed to get a hold of Harry.

"9-1-1. What is the nature of your emergency?"

"My name is Daisy Gunderson. I'm a teacher at Central Prep Academy."

The bell rang and the hallway filled with noise as students came up the stairs and went to their lockers.

Daisy plugged her finger over her free ear and raised her voice. "Can you connect me directly to Detective Nick Fensom? Or take a report that will get to him? He's investigating a case for me and there's been another incident."

"It looks like Detective Fensom is attached to the Fourth Precinct. If this isn't an emergency, let me...."

Locker doors slammed and chatting students filtered into the classroom. "I'm sorry. Could you repeat that?"

"Yo, Ms. G."

"Do we have to take that test today?"

"How much of it is essay?"

She turned away from the friendly greetings and typical questions as the students came in, some automatically stuffing their phones into the shoe bag by the door, others gawking at the crude gift sitting in a puddle of blood on her desk.

"Ms. G., you can't have your cell phone in class."

"What is that?"

"Gross!"

She shushed the teasing and cringing so she could make her report.

And that's when the intercom over the door crackled to life and Mr. Hague made an announcement. "Attention, staff. Mr. Brown is in the building. I repeat, Mr. Brown is in the building. This is not a drill."

The students looked at each other. Some of the young faces were grave, others panicked a bit. A few were blessedly oblivious to the significance of the announcement.

"Everybody line up," Daisy ordered, pulling her phone from her ear. She picked up her attendance sheet, counted heads and quickly took roll. "Twenty. Twenty-one." All but one student accounted for. "Have any of you seen Angelo?"

There was a flurry of "nos" and "I-thought-I-saws" that were no help at all. "Somebody text him or call."

She opened her desk drawer to pull out her walkie-talkie for school emergencies, but it, too, was missing.

"He's not answering, Ms. G."

"He may not have his phone turned on. He knows you're not supposed to at school."

"Shouldn't we be going? Ms. Gamblin's class is leaving."

Daisy nodded. "If we pass your locker on the way out the door, you can grab your coat. Otherwise, keep moving." She searched two more drawers, knowing this was no drill, knowing they were all in serious trouble.

"Are you coming, Ms. G.?"

"I'm right behind you." She waved her class out the door. "Go."

She rummaged through the last two drawers. Secret Santa hadn't just left her the gift. He'd taken her walkie-talkie, isolating her from instant contact with the rest of the staff.

As per every evacuation, the fire alarm went off in a loud, continuous ringing, and Daisy's blood ran cold with fear. This was it. She felt it in her bones. Her fate was sealed.

"Ma'am, are you still there?" The dispatcher was prompting her to respond. She grabbed the clipboard with everyone's name and put the phone back to her ear. "My screen shows that we've already received a call from a Ryan Hague at that same location. Is this in relation to that call?"

Daisy mentally checked off the names on her list as each student filed past. But there was still one missing. It was too early in the day to have received the absentee list. She had to account for Angelo's location. "Down the stairs and out the door. Don't stop until you get to the church across the street."

"Ma'am? Are you there?"

Mr. Brown meant only one thing.

"Yes. There may be a bomb in the building."

Chapter Eleven

"Gunderson."

Daisy stopped her march toward the stairs and turned toward the summons. "Coach? What are you doing up here on the second floor?"

"Health class. Borrowing Musil's room since it's her free period. Showing a video—the kind you want a little more privacy for than in the gym." She scooted a group of students on past her and waited for Bernie to catch up before continuing toward the exit beside him. "Kind of sucky that I picked today of all days to borrow a room that's on the top floor." He snapped his fingers and pointed a young woman away from her locker. "Keep moving."

The frightened young woman linked arms with a friend and hurried to catch up with their classmates. "Slow down," Daisy reminded them, ducking away from the flashing light and deafening noise of the alarm as they walked past. "We want everyone to get there in one piece."

"Are we really taking all these kids outside in this weather?" Bernie asked.

"It's not a drill." Daisy lowered her voice so the students wouldn't overhear. "I just got off the phone with the 9-1-1 operator. Mr. Hague called them about a bomb threat."

Bernie let out a low whistle. "Somebody wanted Christmas vacation early, huh?"

More likely *somebody* didn't think she was frightened enough by threatening just her. Harry had been right about the violence escalating. Now her Secret Santa was threatening the people around her—the people she cared about—her students, friends and coworkers, Harry himself. And she had accused Harry of trying to control her. What an idiot. At least he had a legitimate reason for the pronouncements and territorial behavior—he was trying to protect her. Even Brock's obsession had never extended to hurting anyone beyond her.

Secret Santa had taken her life to a whole new level of scary this morning.

"My walkie-talkie is missing," she told Bernie. It was far easier to focus on her responsibilities as a teacher than to let one man's obsession get into her head and paralyze her with fear. "Will you call the office and find out if Angelo is absent today?"

"Don't have to. He's here."

"He wasn't in my first period class."

Bernie stopped in his tracks, muttering a curse that left a couple of students near the back of the line tittering at the grownup breaking a school rule. "They're cutting class now? That's the last thing Albert needs to do."

"But you saw them," Daisy clarified.

"Yeah. I had both brothers in my office before school to talk about putting Albert back on the team after the holidays. Part of Angelo's penance for the vandalism at your place will be helping his brother keep his grades up."

"Where is Albert now? Could they still be together? Maybe they've already exited the building with another group."

"I can find out."

"Mary? Ms. Gamblin?" Daisy dashed ahead to catch her friend at the top of the stairs and hand over her student roster. "Will you take my class with yours to the church? We have two missing students. The Logan twins."

"Of course." Mary herded both classes down the steps ahead of her. "Need any help?"

"We've got it covered. Just keep my kids safe." Daisy hurried back to Bernie, who was putting out an all call on the walkie-talkie on the missing student. "Who's got Albert Logan first hour?"

"I do," the answer crackled over the radio.

Recognizing the voice, Daisy pulled Bernie's device down to her level. "Eddie? Was Albert in class? Did you see Angelo with him?"

"No and no." Eddie Bosch sounded slightly breathless. "My chemistry class is already across the street. I'm running back in to look for him. I'll have to do a room-by-room search, including bathrooms and closets."

What were those boys up to? "I'm responsible for Angelo. I can help. What floor are you on?"

"I'll start in the basement and work my way up."

"I'll start on the second floor. I've got Bernie Riley with me."

The tall man nodded and put the radio back up to his mouth. "I'll check the first floor. Riley out."

"Bosch out."

Bernie caught Daisy by the shoulder and squeezed. "Will you be okay up here? You don't have a walkie-talkie."

She held up her phone. "I've got 9-1-1. As soon as you've cleared your floor, get out of here. I plan to do the same."

"All right." Bernie squeezed her arm again before releasing her. "Hague will be on the first floor, waiting for the first responders. I'll tell him that you, Bosch and I are still inside looking for the Logans. Meet me in the faculty parking lot when you're done so I know you're out of the building. Be careful."

"You, too."

He jogged down the stairs after the last of the students and disappeared around the corner of the landing.

Other than the jarring noise of the fire alarm, everything was a lot quieter now that the second floor had been evacuated and the main floor was emptying out. "Angelo? Albert?" Just like in their summer emergency training workshop, Daisy moved methodically down one side of the hallway, opening every door. "It's Ms. G. This isn't a drill. We need to evacuate the building."

When she reached the end of one row of classrooms, she crossed the hall and repeated the same search. "Is anyone up here?"

She reentered her own classroom, avoiding even an accidental glance at the bloody mess on her desk, and walked straight to her closet. Empty. There were only two classrooms left to search up here. There was probably a perfectly reasonable explanation for the missing twins. Maybe they'd never reached their first period classes and had been ushered outside by the first teacher who'd spotted them. But that teacher should have reported that they had them by now. Of course, without a radio, she wouldn't know if they'd been found. Best to keep moving, clear her floor and get outside.

She kept her focus out the bank of windows as she headed back toward the front of the room. From this vantage point, she could see the white steeple rising above the red brick church, and a sea of blue and gold Central Prep colors flowing slowly but steadily through the church's front doors. Maybe she'd be able to find the Logans once she was at the church with the rest of the evacuees, and they'd separated into their classes again in the various Sunday School rooms.

A latent image sharpened into focus and Daisy rushed back to the windows, wiping the condensation from the glass and peering closer. She recognized a loose-limbed stride and dark brown head. "Angelo? Albert?" She knocked against the window, knowing the church was too far away for anyone there to hear her. She could barely hear herself over the incessant ring of the fire alarm. Which one of the boys was that? With similar faces and matching uniforms, it was impossible to tell at this distance.

But she was certain she'd just spotted one of them. She pulled her cell phone from the pocket of her coat. Who should she call? She didn't keep student numbers in her phone. 9-1-1 would take too long. She needed an instant response. She could call one of the other teachers to track down the Logan she'd seen. But which one?

Daisy finally punched in her boss's number and hurried out the door. As the man coordinating the evacuation with KCFD and the police, he would definitely have his cell on him. When the principal answered, she quickly updated him. "I'm the last person on the second floor and I'm on my way down to the rear parking lot exit. I swear I just saw one of the Logan boys crossing the street to the church. Could you get someone down there to verify that for me?"

"Why aren't you on your radio?" Mr. Hague asked.

"*He* took it. I'm certain of it."

"He? The man sending you those messages?"

She entered the last room and checked the closet. "There was another gift on my desk this morning. Maybe the sickest one yet. I'm sorry, sir. I think this bomb threat is all about me. I never thought he'd endanger anyone else."

"I'll notify the police about your suspicions. Just get out

of the building. I'll call as soon as I hear anything about the Logan boys."

"Thank you, sir."

After disconnecting the call, Daisy hurried down the steps and walked as quickly as she dared without breaking into a run like the girls she'd chastised earlier.

But someone *was* running through the hallway.

"Daisy? Thank God, I caught you." She stopped and turned as Eddie Bosch jogged up to her. He grabbed her by both shoulders and gently shook her. "Why aren't you answering your radio? I thought something had happened to you."

Reaching up, she gave his wrist a squeeze of gratitude for his concern. "That sick Secret Santa of mine took it. He left me another present this morning."

"How bad?"

"Bad enough." She turned toward the exit, expecting him to walk with her. "Let's talk outside. I want to get to the church. I spotted one of the Logan boys there. Get on your radio and ask which Logan it is."

"It's Angelo."

She stopped again, frowning to see that he hadn't followed her. "How do you know?"

"Because I found Albert."

"That's wonderful news. Did you send him across the street?" When Eddie didn't immediately answer, she closed the distance between them. "What's wrong?"

"Albert is in the basement. He won't leave until he talks to you. Something about apologizing and doing right by you."

"That's ridiculous. Tell him to get his butt up here. I'll talk to him about anything—" she thumbed over her shoulder "—at the church."

"You don't understand."

"No, I don't." Why wasn't he moving?

"The bomb is real. I saw it with my own eyes."

Daisy shrank back at his grim declaration, hugging herself as an invisible chill washed over her. She'd known in her heart that this was no drill. But a real bomb? "I'd hoped it was just a threat."

Eddie shook his head. "I reported the location to Mr. Hague."

"Then we need to get Albert and go." She darted past him, moving toward the basement stairs.

But Eddie grabbed her arm and stopped her. "Maybe we should just let the police handle it."

Bernie Riley's voice cut through the static on Eddie's radio. "First floor is clear. If anyone has eyes on Ms. G., tell her I'm on my way out to meet her."

Eddie held up his radio. "Why are you meeting him?"

Daisy tugged her arm free. "He knows I don't have a walkie-talkie. We made a plan so that someone could confirm I was out of the building and the evacuation was complete."

"A plan? When did you talk to him? Where did you see him? His office and the gym are on the opposite side of the building from your classroom."

Daisy was backing away, needing to make sure one last student was safe. "A few minutes ago. Upstairs."

"You don't think that's suspicious? When did Coach Riley ever do something that benefitted anybody but himself?"

Bernie's explanation had been plausible. He'd had his class upstairs with him. But she supposed that could have been a cover. It would have certainly put him a lot closer to her room to leave that gift and steal her radio without being seen.

"You think Bernie is…" Daisy clenched her fists, shaking off the distracting thoughts. "Eddie, please. Either leave or come help me convince Albert to evacuate. This is my fault. That creeper who's after me—he's responsible. He can threaten me all he wants, but I am not going to let him hurt one of my students."

"Daisy." Eddie grabbed her by the wrist again, and she groaned with frustration. "The reason I couldn't get Albert to come with me…"

"What?"

"He's the one with the bomb."

HARRY PULLED OVER and slowed his truck as a third fire engine sped past in the oncoming lane. He didn't need Muffy sitting in his lap, barking at every flashing light, for the hackles on the back of his neck to go up.

Emergency vehicles didn't necessarily mean Daisy was in danger. There were other businesses and residential neighborhoods in that direction. There could have been an unfortunate vehicle accident.

Muffy spotted another speeding car and threw his paws against the window to bark at it. The fire chief this time. There were more sirens and flashing lights farther down the road, speeding toward them as if that part of Kansas City was under attack.

Speeding toward Central Prep Academy.

Toward Daisy.

Toward the woman he loved.

"Anybody else got a bad feeling about this?"

Muffy gave a sharp yelp as if the little dingbat understood the urgency firing through his blood. The rest of the troops were in agreement.

He could be wrong. The fractured bits of his brains had messed with his perception of the truth lately. But neither a dog, nor his gut, had ever once given him bad intel. And if Daisy was in trouble, he couldn't run away from the fight.

Harry made a U-turn at the next intersection, pulled his Beretta from the glove compartment, and raced back to the school.

DAISY KNEW IT was a trap the moment her foot touched the basement's concrete floor. The stairs had been cordoned off with yellow crime scene tape from the fire, but some-one had torn through it and come down the steps.

"Hold up," Eddie warned her from the top of the stairs. He'd been trying to raise Bernie on his radio to tell him that she and Eddie were tracking down Albert. "Coach isn't answering. Daisy?"

"Tell whoever's listening that we need an ambulance."

The door to the storage room had been propped open with a concrete bucket, and the entire locking mechanism had been removed. The char marks had been painted over with more of that gloomy gray paint. But a fresh coat of paint couldn't hide the reminder of one man's obsession with her.

Mine.

She was frozen in place—her blood, her breathing, the sharpness of her senses locking up with fear. And while she desperately wanted to turn right around and run up those stairs and out the front door, she couldn't. She couldn't run away from the trap, because she was a teacher, a caring person, a human being—and one of her students was lying unconscious in the middle of the floor. A gash dented his curly dark hair, and his yellow ball cap lay on the floor, soaking up the blood dripping from his head wound.

"Albert?" She forced her feet to move forward, slowly approaching his unmoving body, scanning all around him for any sign of the bomb or Bernie Riley. Albert hadn't made that bomb. He was as much of a pawn in all this madness as she was. And no one wielded more control over this young man than the coach. She was vaguely aware of Eddie relaying the request for medical help. If Eddie had seen Albert with the bomb, it hadn't been by choice. No doubt the young man had been coerced into giving Eddie, and subsequently her, a message that would not only keep her in the building, but bring her down here. "It's Ms. G. I'm here."

Seeing nothing that looked like a pipe or briefcase, like the bombs she'd seen on television shows and movies, she knelt beside him. She pulled back the collar of his team jacket and pressed her fingers against his neck. Thank God. He had a strong pulse. But he certainly wasn't able to answer any questions for her.

"Albert?" She petted the back of the unconscious teen's head. "I'm so sorry you got hurt. I'm going to get you out of here, okay?"

The sirens of the vehicles she heard pulling up outside reminded her that she wasn't alone. The noises also reminded her that it was far too quiet down here.

"Eddie? I need your help to move…" There was no answer. No sound of footsteps following her down the stairs. Had her friend abandoned her? Oh, God. Had something happened to him, too? "Mr. Bosch, answer me!"

Silence.

Daisy got up. But when she turned toward the storage room, she instantly retreated. Now *that* looked like something she'd seen in a movie.

There it was, sitting in the middle of the floor beside one of the folding metal chairs. A bomb. It was wire-y and liquid-y in clear tubes bound together with duct tape attached to a doughy-looking brick and a cell phone. The screen was flashing a series of numbers—32:26, 32:25,

32:24. A countdown. She didn't need to know how the thing worked. She just believed that it would.

"Oh, my God." She needed to call Harry. She needed him here. To hold her. To take charge. To make the fear go away.

She imagined the words in his letters, offering solutions. Assuring her that her problems could be fixed. Telling her that she had the power to do anything.

32:13

The bad guys don't get to win.

"We have to get out of here." Daisy hurried back to the fallen student.

She knew that moving an injured person wasn't the recommended procedure, but with a bomb ticking down just a few feet away, she'd make an exception. She wrapped her hands around Albert's wrists and pulled. His head lolled between his arms and he groaned as she dragged him toward the stairs. Good grief, he was heavy. Not just tall, but solidly built. When the back of her boot hit the bottom step, she gently lowered him to the floor and rolled him onto his back.

"Come on, Albert, wake up." She slipped her hands beneath his arms. With a mighty push of her legs, she got his bottom onto the first step before she had to set him down and lean him against the wall. Unless he regained consciousness, there was no way she was going to get him up these stairs. "Eddie?" she shouted up the stairwell. "I need your help. Can anybody hear me?"

Maybe she shouldn't keep yelling. If something had happened to Eddie, then she was alone in the building with a man who equated rape and violence and fear with some sick kind of love. And she was only giving away her position to him.

"Ms. G.?" Albert slurred her name out on a moan of pain. "You gotta…"

"Albert?" She knelt beside him, capturing his face between her hands, willing his groggy brown eyes to stay open. "Can you stand if I help you?" His eyes drifted shut. "Albert!"

His eyes opened for one fierce warning. "Get out."

Something hard and unyielding whacked her in the back of the head. Fireworks exploded behind her eyes as she collapsed over Albert's body and everything went dark.

Chapter Twelve

Harry recognized a command center when he saw one. He could also identify the men in charge by the way everyone else scurried to do their bidding. He parked his truck behind the last police car in the circular driveway in front of Central Prep Academy and crossed the median to reach a group of men that included Daisy's principal, a black-haired cop in a SWAT uniform, John Murdock from the KCFD, Detective Nick Fensom and his brother-in-law, Pike.

SWAT? That explained the number of first responders.

His heart squeezed in his chest. Scenes like this were only supposed to happen in a war zone. He needed eyes on Daisy. Now.

Probably because he wore a gun like all the other cops here, and moved with an air of purpose and authority, no one stopped him until he reached the back of the SWAT van where the men in charge were going over building schematics and access points.

"Let him through." Nick Fensom waved him over. "He knows one of our hostages."

"Hostages?" He didn't bother asking if Daisy was safe. He knew she'd be in the thick of whatever was happening inside that building.

"We're not saying victims yet." John Murdock from

the fire department exchanged a nod of recognition with Harry. "But our guy won't talk to us. He's cut off all communication. We don't have many details other than most of the students and staff have been evacuated and are safe in the church on the other side of the school."

"All he wants is Daisy." Of that, Harry was certain. "If anyone else has been hurt, it's collateral damage."

"Agreed." Nick scrubbed his hand over the dark stubble on his jaw. "Our concern is that when a stalker reaches this level of violence, he's usually got an end game."

He'd seen friends brought down by sniper bullets and roadside bombs. He'd lost part of his face and half his soul over in Iraq. Whatever Nick was trying to find a delicate way to say wouldn't shock him. "Meaning?"

"Most of these situations end in a murder/suicide."

"Like a suicide bomber. Or an insurgent waiting to detonate an IED when it'll do the most damage." Harry weathered the emotional punch of knowing Daisy was in a similarly volatile situation right now. He waited for the flashback to take hold, but it never came. This was a mission briefing. All he needed were his orders, and he could take action. Daisy was too important for him to sit on the sidelines and nurse his mental wounds or second-guess himself. He was getting better. He needed to be a part of this. "You said hostages, plural. This guy's got someone else in there with him?"

"One of the students," Pike answered. "We believe our perp used him as a decoy to bring Daisy to him."

"You got an ID on this guy?"

Pike shook his head. "There are two faculty members besides Daisy who haven't checked in yet—Bernard Riley and Edward Bosch. The student is Albert Logan."

"Unless Logan's our bomber?" Nick suggested.

"He's a good kid." Harry had worked with the teen

enough this week to suspect Albert just needed the right thing to motivate him, and he'd turn his young life around. He'd had good instincts with the dogs, and had been interested enough to ask Harry where he'd gotten his training. "Rough around the edges. Makes some bad choices. But he wouldn't hurt Daisy. What about his brother?"

The principal piped in. "Angelo is fine. He and Albert were working with Coach Riley before school and were on their way to class when the bomb threat came in and I sounded the evacuation order. Angelo told one of the teachers at the church that Mr. Bosch asked Albert to help with a student who's wheelchair-bound. The handicapped student is accounted for. Angelo is pretty concerned that he hasn't seen his brother. I haven't told him about the hostage situation."

Harry had seen the pictures. He'd seen the fire. He'd seen the terror Daisy lived with every day because of that bastard. "You have to get her out of there. This guy's got a temper. He'll hurt her."

The nametag on the SWAT cop's uniform read *Delgado.* "We can't risk a full assault or he might blow everybody up."

Nick glanced around at all the swirling lights and imposing vehicles. "He already knows we're here. It's a little late for stealth mode."

"And, we don't know their exact location," John Murdock reminded them.

"They're in the basement," Harry said, knowing he was right on this. He was learning this enemy, and he wasn't all that unpredictable. "I don't know if the bomb is there, or if there's more than one. But that's where he'll be. With Daisy. I'm familiar with that area of the building, and one man won't be detected—especially if you're making some noise and talking at him out here. Let me go in." He turned to his brother-in-law. "You got some spare gear in your truck?"

"What are you thinking?"

"That I know how to find an insurgent and an IED."

In a matter of minutes, his credentials were approved and the plan was set. Harry went with Pike to his KCPD unit. They suited up in protective gear, while Pike's German shepherd, Hans, danced around inside his cage, sensing he was about to have a job to do. Donning the flak vest, gloves and helmet, Harry felt like he was slipping into a familiar uniform.

"Daisy means this much to you?" Pike asked.

"That woman saved me more than once. I owe it to her to do the same for her."

"You love her?"

Harry checked the radio unit on his vest and slipped a pair of protective goggles over his eyes, ignoring the question. He hadn't told Daisy how he felt yet, not in real words. Not out loud. It didn't feel right to say it to anybody else first.

Pike clapped him on the shoulder, forcing him to look at him. "You can't go in there if your head's not clear."

Harry pulled the extra K-9 ballistic vest from the back of Pike's truck. "Did you know you were in love with Hope before you rescued her from that jackass who kidnapped her?"

"Yes."

"Did it stop you from getting the job done?"

Pike grinned. "Hans and I will be ready to go in with SWAT as soon as you radio that you've secured the hostages. Just get them out. We'll clear the building, do a bomb sweep and neutralize the perp. Keep your com open so we know each other's twenty and don't have any surprises. You're okay to do this on your own?"

Harry went to his own pickup and opened the door, revealing Caliban in the passenger seat, eagerly sitting at attention. He slipped the vest over the dog's back and clipped it into place. "I won't be alone."

DAISY WOKE TO a hundred fireworks shooting off inside her head. Where was she? What had happened to her?

She mentally shook off the confusion and opened her eyes. She was surrounded by a sea of gray. And as she focused in on her outstretched arm, she saw spots of red on her new coat. Was that blood?

Wait. Blood?

The nightmare came flooding back. Albert. Bomb. *Mine.*

She pushed herself up to a sitting position. She was in the storage room, surrounded by windowless walls and stacked-up chairs.

"I've been waiting for you to come back to me."

Her groan was half headache, half heartache. She'd suspected a lot of people of stalking her over the last couple of weeks, but not this one. "Eddie?"

"Merry Christmas, my love."

He was sitting in a chair near her feet, holding two walkie-talkies in his lap, one which she suspected he'd stolen from her desk. He cradled a cell phone in his hands. Her cell phone. She raised her gaze above the blue school jacket and loosely knotted tie and saw a smear of pink lipstick across his mouth. Her color. She touched her fingers to her own mouth and cringed at the thought of him kissing her while she'd been unconscious—at the thought of him kissing her, period.

The bomb with the different colored liquids and ticking timer sat on the floor beside her. Instinctively, she scooted away from the deadly thing.

14:25 and counting. And Eddie sat between her and the metal door he'd pulled shut behind them. Had he found another way to lock it? She was surrounded by solid walls and a room full of potential shrapnel. This bomb wasn't about bringing down the school or hurting anyone else. This was all about her. Daisy thought she might be sick. It had always been about destroying her.

She flinched when she felt his hand on her hair. "Why don't you say Merry Christmas to me? I've seen your room and your house. I know how you love the holidays. You're the only gift I want. I love you."

Ignoring the swimming focus of her vision, she stood. "We need to get out of here."

"We're exactly where we need to be. Together." His tone was so patient, so sweet, so creepy.

"How long was I out?"

"A few minutes. Long enough for me to make sure we won't be bothered in these final, precious moments."

"Final?"

He stood and came toward her. "It's the only way we can be together."

She backed away from his outstretched hand until she ran into a rack of chairs. Everything around her rattled, giving her an idea. A heavy metal chair could be as effective as a baseball bat if she could get her hands on one. The knot on her head and the wound on Albert's scalp told her Eddie had probably already thought of that.

Albert. "Eddie, there's a student on the other side of that wall. You don't want to hurt him."

"I've done my calculations. Albert finally served a meaningful purpose." Bait to lure her down here was hardly something to brag about. "He and Bernie were wastes of time and space in your life."

"Bernie? You hurt him, too?"

Eddie touched the front of his coat. "Once I borrowed his jacket again, I didn't need him anymore."

"It was you the night of the fire."

"I was afraid your soldier boy saw me."

"He did. But he couldn't identify you. We suspected Coach Riley. His jacket..." she inhaled a sniff of the stale air around her "...*that* jacket smelled like smoke."

"Do you honestly think that blockhead knows anything other than sports?" Eddie snickered as he rested his hand on the rack beside her head and leaned in. "I've borrowed his hat and coat a couple of times since his wife kicked him out and he's been keeping an extra set of clothes at school. It's a smart way to divert suspicion off me, don't you think?"

Yeah, Eddie was smart. Crazy. But smart. She eyed the tubes of chemicals on the floor behind him. "Now you've built a bomb. Is there more than one?"

He grabbed her chin and forced her gaze back to his. "We just need the one."

She nearly gagged at the taste of his mouth sliding over hers. Although she suspected she needed to stay calm and try to talk her way out of this, she couldn't squash down her fight-or-flight response. She shoved him away, slipped to one side, grabbing a chair off the rack. Several more chairs crashed to the floor, forcing him another step back, giving her a chance to swing the chair in her hands. The blow caught him in the shoulder, knocking him to his knees.

Daisy scrambled toward the door. But the very chairs that had created a barrier between them now became a blockade she had to push aside and climb over. Before she could touch the metal latch, Eddie's arms closed around her from behind, lifting her off her feet before he slammed her into the wall beside the door. She screamed at the pain of her head knocking into another hard object. Her glasses got knocked sideways. But she pushed back. "Let go of me!"

Eddie threw his whole body against hers, crushing her against the wall. He spat against her ear. "You held me the night I told you about Jenny—how she left me."

"Your fiancée died." It was hard to talk with her face mashed against the wall.

But Eddie wasn't listening. "I was there for you after that Brock fiasco. I was at your father's funeral, holding your hand. We have a connection you can't deny."

"We were friends."

"I love you."

"I don't love you."

"Liar!" He whipped her around, roughly clasping his face between her hands. She obliquely wondered what had happened to the cell phone and if losing track of it meant the bomb was going to go off any sooner. But she had a more immediate problem with the hands sliding down around her throat and the crazed anger in Eddie's eyes. "You confided in me. It was only a matter of time before you turned to me for something more. I encouraged Angelo's little crush on you because I knew it would bother you and you'd come looking for a man. For me. But then Soldier Boy came to town."

"Ed...die," she gasped.

His hands tightened around her throat. She didn't think he was strangling her on purpose, but he was so angry. He was beyond listening to reason. He was impervious to the scratch of her fingernails on his hands, begging him to free her. "Suddenly he's doing everything for you I'm supposed to. I was outside your house last night. I saw you go up to his room. You slept with him, didn't you?" She didn't answer. She couldn't. Incensed, he threw her away from him. "I knew it. You're a traitor. But I forgive you."

For once, she relished the cold, hard concrete because it meant she was free. For the moment. Daisy coughed her bruised airways clear and scooted away from Eddie's advance. "How did I betray you? I've always loved you as a friend."

"But you're *in* love with him, aren't you?"

"Yes." Even if no one else ever heard it, she was going to state the truth. "I love Harry Lockhart."

"I've shown you real love."

Her fingers brushed against the bomb and she screeched and rolled away. "Do you think I want a man to treat me like all those pictures? They scared me to death."

"They're love scenes."

"That isn't love. That's…a sickness." The pile of fallen chairs blocked her escape.

The anger left his tone, but the crazy remained. "That's how I think about you—about us—every night. I've loved you from that first night we were together."

"Drinking coffee," she reminded him, scrabbling to get to her feet. "Having a conversation. We have never been *together*."

"Stop fighting me on this. We are meant to be together. Always." He glanced away to look at the numbers ticking away on the bomb. "In another eleven minutes, we will be."

She had eleven minutes left to live? She'd fought off Brock and his knife, how did she fight a bomb? "How does the bomb work? When it reaches zero, it'll explode?"

"A small charge will blow out the stopper between the tubes. Then the chemicals will mix. Very volatile." He pulled her phone from the pocket of the jacket. "Or I can dial the number and detonate it sooner. Would you like that? It will be quick and painless, I promise."

"You've blown people up before?"

He smiled. "Such a wonderful sense of humor."

"I don't feel like laughing. Please, Eddie. Let me go. Let me get you some help."

"You're not leaving me."

Daisy dreamed she heard scratching outside the door. Fate coming to get her this time, she supposed. "What if I promise to come back? After you shut off the bomb and I know everyone is safe, you and I will sit down and talk."

"Liar! You'll go back to him." He reached for her again. "You're mine!"

The door behind Eddie slid open with a mighty shove. "Caliban, *Fass!*"

Attack.

A blur of black and tan charged into the room and lunged at Eddie's outstretched hand. Caliban clamped down on Eddie's forearm and knocked him to the floor. His fist hit the concrete and the cell phone skittered out of his grip. Eddie screamed. "No!"

Barely a step behind the attacking dog, Harry filled up the doorway, following the aim of the gun he held between his hands. "Down on the ground! Hands where I can see them!"

There was no time to feel relief or love or even fear of the one-man attack force looming over Eddie and taking charge of the room.

"Get the phone!" Her cell skittered away beneath a rack of chairs as Eddie and the dog struggled. She dove for the floor and stuck her arm beneath the rack, groping for the phone. "Don't let him push any numbers!"

"Damn it, Daisy. Stay back!"

"He can set off the bomb if he calls the number."

Eddie shrieked at the fangs sinking into his forearm and shaking him. "She's mine. You can't have her. She loves me."

Her fingers closed around the phone. "I've got it."

"Get behind me!" Harry ordered, moving between her and the dog and man wrestling and growling and screaming on the floor. "I'm going to call off the dog and you stay down. Understand? Do you understand?"

"Yes. Call him off."

"Caliban, *Hier*!"

The three-legged dog released Eddie and trotted back to Harry's side. Bloodied and dazed, Eddie reached into his pocket and pulled out his own cell phone. "She's mine!"

Harry knocked that phone to the concrete, crushed it beneath his boot. He smashed the butt of his gun across Eddie's face and knocked him out.

His big chest heaved with deep breaths as he grabbed her arm and pulled her close. His eyes were focused squarely on the bomb. "Are you hurt?"

"Not much."

"Stay behind me. I want my armor between us and that explosive in case it goes off early. We're backing out of this room." Daisy willingly latched on to the back of his vest and moved away from Eddie and the bomb. Part of her wanted to ask Harry why he was here. How had he known she needed him? How had he found her? Was he okay? Was this whole scene triggering the worst of his nightmares again? But she didn't ask any of those questions. The aim of his gun at the man on the floor never wavered. "Caliban!" As the dog loped out into the hallway with them, Harry turned his mouth to the radio on the front of his vest. "This is Lockhart. Hostages are secure. Move in! Move in!"

"Albert!" Daisy hurried over to the young man who was sitting on the bottom step and hugged him in her arms. "Are you all right? I was so worried."

Harry was still talking into his radio, giving information. She heard an invasion of footfalls in the lobby above her, and suddenly two men in full battle gear were charging down the stairs. Another man and woman with rifles and SWAT armor came down the stairs at the opposite end of the hallway, converging on Harry's position.

"You've got just under eight minutes." Only when the four uniformed officers entered the storage room did Harry move. He holstered his gun and cupped her elbow, urging her onto her feet. "We gotta go, honey. Clock's ticking." He pulled Albert to his feet and bent to lift the young man over his shoulders in a fireman's carry. "Up the stairs and out the front door. Don't stop moving 'til I tell you."

She nodded and climbed the stairs, with Harry and Caliban following close on her heels. When they reached the lobby, she saw another officer helping Coach Riley out the door. There was blood matted in Bernie's hair. Apparently, Eddie had knocked him out, too. He'd probably been faking the radio conversation with Bernie that she'd overheard. "Is he okay?"

She felt Harry's hand at the small of her back. "Keep movin', honey. There's still a bomb and we aren't safe. Take a right."

As soon as she hit the cold air outside the door, another officer ran forward to guide her through a line of armed responders and emergency vehicles toward the group of ambulances that were waiting in the parking lot. Even carrying Albert on his shoulders, Harry stayed close enough that she could feel him blocking the winter wind at her back.

A few minutes later, she was sitting in the back of an ambulance again while an EMT checked her vitals and crushed up an ice pack for her to hold against the knot on her head. She gasped when the back doors opened. Harry. Before she could say anything, he patted the floor of the ambulance. *"Hopp!"*

Her startled frown turned into a delighted smile when Caliban jumped up into the ambulance.

"Sir, you can't—"

"Come here, good boy." Daisy dropped the ice pack and welcomed her three-legged dog onto the gurney beside her, scratching all around his ears and kissing the top of his head as he rested his graying muzzle on her thigh. "I'm so glad you were there for Mama today. What a good, good boy." Because of this dog, she was alive. She tilted her aching head up to Harry. Because of this man, she was alive. "Is it over?"

His gray eyes reflected the bright morning light. "All except for the cleanup. The bomb was easy to defuse. A matter of disconnecting wires." His battle-scarred face was lined with concern as he studied her. "A hazmat unit is going in now to deal with the chemicals. KCPD has taken Bosch into custody."

Tears stung the corners of her eyes. She hadn't cried once when Eddie had touched her, hurt her, threatened her life. But she was about to bawl just looking at the man she loved so much.

"Give us a minute, will you?" Harry asked.

The EMT nodded and climbed out of the ambulance as Harry climbed in.

Harry picked up the fallen ice pack and sat on the other side of Caliban, reaching over the dog to hold the pack in place at the crown of her head. "Are you really in one piece?"

"Nothing a hot shower won't cure." She slipped her hand over Caliban's back to grasp Harry's thigh. "Thank you. Eddie was…" She couldn't fathom how skewed that man's brain must be to think that he loved her and that killing her was his idea of the two of them being committed to each other. A hot tear spilled over and trailed down her cheek. "I really attract the crazies, don't I?"

Harry wiped the tear away with the pad of his thumb. "I'm not going to be one of them."

A tiny knife of guilt stabbed her in the heart. She reached up to cup the side of his jaw. "I didn't mean you."

"But you're worried that me suiting up and coming after you may have triggered another episode. It didn't."

"Are you really okay?"

He shrugged and her hand dropped away. "Okay enough."

"What does that mean?" She turned to face him. "Harry, you have to know that I have feelings for you. As relieved as I was to see you coming through that door, I would never want to do anything to set back your recovery."

"You didn't do a damn thing. Bosch and no one else is responsible for what happened to you and Albert and Coach Riley today."

"Albert!" She pushed Caliban's head off her leg and tried to stand. "I need to find out if he's okay."

Harry caught her as she tripped over his feet, and pulled her down onto his lap. "He's fine. A concussion and some stitches. He and Coach Riley are in another ambulance, getting treatment. Angelo is with him and their grandmother is on her way. Right now, the only person you have to save is you."

"But if I can help…"

Harry feathered his fingers into her hair and straightened her bent glasses. "Damn it, woman, if you won't think about yourself, then think about me. I just saved your life. And I didn't crack up doing it. You're safe. It's over. And I love you." His stiff, handsome mouth crooked into a smile. "Don't you want to hug me?"

Daisy threw her arms around his neck as he pulled her to his chest. His hands fisted in the back of her coat and his nose nestled into the hair at her temple. She held on tight with all the love in her heart and wept happy tears.

Epilogue

After the last of the guests had left the party and the dogs had curled up on the couch, Harry reached beneath the Christmas tree and pulled out the present he'd wrapped for Daisy. The narrow, rectangular shape told her it couldn't be anything other than his journal. "I want you to know exactly who this is from."

Tears stung her eyes as he pulled her into his lap on the recliner. "Are you sure you want me to read this?"

"I wouldn't share it with anybody else." His arms settled around her waist and she detected a faint trembling in them. "I do a lot better telling you what I feel when I write it down." He took the ribbon and paper from her and tossed them aside. His chest expanded with a deep, steadying breath, and she knew that Harry was the bravest man she'd ever known. "Start at the end."

She pressed a kiss to his mouth, thanking him for entrusting her with this gift before turning her attention to the spiral notebook, thumbing through the pages until she reached the last entry.

Dear Daisy,
I never thought I could be anything but a Marine.
Nothing useful, anyway. The Corps gave me purpose
and a home when I desperately needed those things.
I love my job more than anything I've ever done. If

they'll still have me—if I pass the psych tests—I want to go on being a Marine until I'm ready to retire in another two years.

These ten days I've spent with you, though, got me thinking about other things. I came to you with the idea that the Daisy from your letters could save me—that you were this magic angel who could reach inside my head, erase the nightmares and make me whole again. Turns out you weren't anything like that angel. You're bold and brave. You touch and you talk. You weren't as much of a lady as I thought you'd be, and you frustrated the hell out of me more than once. There wasn't any mystical glow about you. But you **were** are real. You're heart and color and acceptance and hope and life and love. I'm a better man for knowing you and being a part of your crazy life. I'm healthier. Happier. I'm home when I'm with you. You weren't the woman I imagined, but you turned out to be exactly the woman I needed.

I've got some ideas now on what I could do when I leave the Corps, whether it's in a month or two years. Training dogs. Working as a cop or search and rescue with the fire department. Maybe you can even help me get through college so I can be a teacher or social worker who works with kids like Albert and 'Lo.

One thing I'm certain of, now and forever, is that I love you. If you can put up with a Marine who's gone on and off for a couple of years, or with a washed-up master sergeant who isn't sure what he's going to do with the rest of his life, I want to marry you. I hope I can get my act together well enough that you would consider saying yes.

Love,
Harry

Daisy's heart swelled up and spilled over in a sob of hot, flowing tears. She threw her arms around his neck and hugged him tight.

His hands fisted in the back of her sweater, holding on to her just as tightly. "Is there anything I can write that won't make you cry?"

"A grocery list?"

He laughed, and she scrambled off his lap and ran to the kitchen, pulling a red pen from her purse. Harry followed her, winding his arms around her waist and resting his chin on her shoulder while she scrawled a message at the end of the letter. "You're going English teacher on me now? Checking my grammar?"

She signed the short missive and held it up to show it to him. "Here's my letter to you."

Dear Harry,
I love you. With all my heart. I know we can get through anything together.
When you ask, my answer is YES!
Love,
Daisy

* * * * *